THE ALLENDALE FOUR

COMPLETE SERIES BOOKS 1-4

ANGEL LAWSON

PROLOGUE

"So, the guys," he said, looking over at the group of knuckle-headed boys surrounding the bonfire, "think I'm a virgin."

I stared at him for a minute, trying to follow his logic.

"They do," he insisted. His tone was a little desperate. His dark brown eyes were really desperate.

"Justin," I said. "You *are* a virgin. Welcome to the club."

"Shhh!" he hushed me. "They could hear you."

"Dude, they know!" I yell-whispered back. "It's not a big deal. Losing your V-card takes time, you know."

At least, it had for me. I was picky. So sue me.

He moved off the log next to me and settled in the sand at my feet. His big hands wrapped around my calves as he rested his chin on my knees. "It's embarrassing. They talk about sex all the time and I'm just...I don't know. Not ready."

"That's fair. You shouldn't feel pressured to do something you don't want to."

"Right," he said, eyes darting to the ground. "It's just that this community isn't very open-minded and I haven't exactly figured out where I fall, identity-wise. I'd rather wait to make any major announcements."

Justin was my best friend. He lived in a small residential community near the beach. Traditional. Old. Kind of poor. Pretty religious. I felt bad for him because I knew how stifling it could be to live here. I barely survived it myself when my parents lived in Oceanside. I had the chance to get out when my parents divorced. The scrutiny by some of the locals was so bad after my dad bailed and left me and my mom on our own.

We tried staying in Oceanside. Like, really tried, but this was my dad's hometown, and when he left and the rumors started and I wasn't doing so well...

Yeah, we didn't last long before moving one town over, hoping for a fresh start.

Things weren't much better there. We were still kind of poor but at least people didn't talk about how we were sinners and what my mom did to run off my dad. It was better, even though I never quite fit in socially. Which is why, as soon as I got my license I started coming back to Oceanside to hang with my only real friend.

I sighed and stared at Justin, thinking life shouldn't be this hard. People should be free to be who they are, love who they want, experiment on their own terms. Right?

Justin always stuck by my side, and I wanted to pay him back. He helped me through my rough spot and never told anyone my secret. Shouldn't I help him keep his?

"Well, what are you going to do?" I asked.

He looked up with puppy dog eyes and pushed out his bottom lip. "Well, I had this idea..."

I narrowed my eyes and brushed a lock of hair off his forehead. "What kind of idea?"

He lifted his eyebrows suggestively, "I thought maybe you and me...we could, you know...fake it?"

I pulled back. "Fake *what*? Because look, Justin, I love you and all, but I draw the line at being your fake girlfriend. In fact, I drew the line years ago being your *real* girlfriend."

There was a while, around fifth grade, where I had a super big crush on Justin. Why not? He was cute, tall, and had the best smile. He wasn't a jerk like the other boys in class. But I never acted on it. He was my best friend and I thought he had a crush on me, too. Then he asked me to the fifth-grade dance and later if I wanted to be his girl-friend. Despite my crush, I said no. It felt wrong. The risk was too high.

He chuckled nervously and tightened his fingers around the denim covering my legs. "No, not that. What if you like, kissed me or something? In public. To get the guys off my back." He ducked his head. I wondered if he thought I was going to hit him.

"You want me to kiss you?" I'd kissed Justin before, when we were thirteen, and even then, only on a dare from Paul. I looked across the beach at Paul, who had his tongue shoved down the throat of some girl with dark hair pulled back in a ponytail. Fucking horndog. No one cared who he kissed, even if it was a different girl every week. His dad was an elder in the church. Everyone looked the other way.

"Or something," he mumbled into my knees, bringing my atten-tion back to him.

"What do you mean 'or something'?" I had a horrible feeling in my stomach, because if a fake kiss was all he wanted, he would have just asked. We could get this over with now.

Justin looked up and I knew. I knew I was making a deal with the devil, but he was my best friend. My oldest friend. He needed my help, and I knew that before this was all over, I was going to cave to whatever it was he wanted.

I was the world's biggest sucker.

My MOM and I moved to Allendale in the 6th grade. She thought a fresh start before middle school would be a good idea. Of course, it was a terrible idea and the next three years were the worst of my life. Why? Because middle school sucked. Hard.

During that time, things got rough. My anxiety, which had always been a problem, grew and grew and grew until some days it felt like there was nothing else in my life. Then things got dark. Scars on my legs and arms dark. I still only wear long-sleeved shirts.

The weekend passed and my conversation with Justin still weighed heavily on my mind. He wanted to have sex with me. Well, fake sex at least. He wanted Paul and Davis and the other guys to think he'd done it so they would leave him alone. I got it—I did—but I wasn't sure if I was the right girl for the job.

Justin was convinced this would work. We had always been very close, and for us to suddenly have a relationship wouldn't be questioned too much. It's not like I had a boyfriend that would care or that even the kids at my own school would find out. He just wanted to put on enough of a show to be convincing.

I was most skeptical about that.

First of all, I had little experience. Okay, I had no experience. I wasn't exactly a prude or naïve. Other than a few make-out sessions with Justin's friends (I had regrets) the reality was…I just hadn't gone *there* yet with anyone, and I wasn't sure how good I was going to be at convincing a bunch of sexually experienced, douchebag townies that I made Justin a man.

Second of all, because of the anxiety, I liked to keep a low profile. Tricking an entire school of people didn't seem low-profile. It seemed like the opposite of low-profile. High attention. People in my business. I didn't like people in my business.

I mulled all this over as I walked into Chemistry, slipping through the desks and dropping my books on the slick, black top of my lab table. Mostly I was thinking about how I, Heaven Reeves, could ever convince anyone I wasn't a virgin. Not that I had official data, but I was pretty sure non-virgins walked different. They moved differently.

Right?

I observed the girls entering the classroom. Mallory Keats walked through the door and I immediately honed in. She's my polar opposite.

Her: blonde, blue-eyed, tiny hips and feet.

Me: reddish-brown hair, greenish eyes, curvy hips and monster feet.

She told everyone in 9th grade that she slept with her cousin's best friend on their annual summer vacation. Her non-virgin status was basically school legend. Covertly, I studied her movements. Her demeanor, her stature. Her hips shifted a little with every step. Her chest was pushed out and her lips pouted just a touch.

Damn it—there was no way I could pull that off.

I sighed and rested my forehead on my desk, closing my eyes. Best friend or not, this seemed like a really bad idea.

The chair next to me scraped across the floor and I heard a thump next to my head. My lab partner had arrived. *Great.* Figuring out what to do about a possible fake lover while sitting next to my desired *nevergonnahappen* lover made my life more like a joke than ever.

I had a huge, real, unrequited crush on Anderson Thompson.

"Reeves," he greeted, easing into his seat.

I opened an eye, the one not pressed against the cool, hard table. Anderson was adorable in that totally-out-of-my-league-way. He had floppy dark brown hair and bright green eyes. His eyelashes and cheekbones could rival any CW actor, and once, I saw his competitive swimmer body shirtless at the pool and almost died.

Literally almost died.

"Thompson," I replied, playing it cool.

He tipped the chair back, balancing his knees on the table. "Something wrong?"

I sat up and stretched, pulling out my books and a pen, ignoring the stupid smirk on his face. Anderson and I were school friends. Lab partner friends. That's *all* friends. Not that I was complaining. It's just that he knew nothing about my life or my issues. I certainly had no plan to tell him now. "Nope, I'm good. What did you do this weekend?"

He shrugged. "Hung out with the guys. Graced the town with my awesomeness. You know, same old. You?"

"The guys" were Hayden Pierce, Jackson Hall, and Oliver Baldwin. The three hottest guys in school, other than Anderson. Best friends, almost brothers, and ridiculously intimidating. They were nicknamed the Allendale Four. Loyal. Impenetrable. And incredibly exclusive.

They weren't exactly popular—more like legendary.

Oliver and I were friendly, sort of like me and Anderson. School only. I think mostly because I was quiet, didn't flirt with them or make any efforts to break into their little circle.

So when he asked, I told him the (vague) truth about my weekend. "It was interesting."

He cocked his head and smiled in amusement. My heart twisted a little like it always did. "Interesting good, or interesting bad?"

"You know, I'm not sure yet."

Mr. Baker walked down the aisle, ending our conversation while he passed out lab sheets and began discussing our assignment. Anderson placed the paper between us and leaned over. "Well, let me know when you figure it out, okay?"

I nodded, inhaling his intoxicating scent. I knew there was no way Anderson would ever figure out what I was referring to and I sure as hell wasn't going to tell him. I may be a sucker, but I wasn't a fool. The only reason I was even considering it was the fact that Justin went to another school and had an entirely different set of friends. What happened at the beach stayed on the beach. That was the rule.

1

———

"Okay so, once we get inside, I'm going to kiss you."

I scrunched up my nose. "Really?"

"Oh my god, Heaven! Do I repulse you that much?" Justin actually threw his hands in the air. Fucking drama queen.

I groaned and pressed my face into my palms. "Of course not. But give me a chance to freak out a little. I'm only going to lose my fake virginity once."

Justin leaned his head back and smiled. "I love you."

"You better. Now, let's get inside and kiss. And then, you better get me a drink to go through with the rest of this."

Justin followed my directions, helping me from my side of the car, holding my hand on the way to the front porch and pushing me against the door, his lips firmly pressed against my own the minute we saw a couple of his friends. The good news is that Justin really was pretty hot. He was tall and worked out a lot. His muscles seemed to have muscles so yeah, not repulsive. Just weird.

I wrapped my hand around his arm, feeling the hard, tight muscles under his shirt. His dark hair and eyes made his teeth white and pretty. If I turned off my brain, it wouldn't be so bad. Right?

My thoughts were interrupted by Justin's tongue pushing between my teeth and I pinched his side. "Watch it, okay?"

"Just trying to keep it real."

I gave him my best bitchface. "Go get my drink." With a slap on my ass, he ran off.

"Heaven!" I turned and found myself face to face with Sarah and Emily, girls who went to school with Justin. Emily assessed me, obviously taking in my ratty jeans and Allendale High sweatshirt. Yeah, I got dressed up for the event. She asked, "Since when are you two a thing?"

"Oh, you know us," I laughed. "We just, you know, thought after all these years we would give it a shot."

"Really?" Sarah asked. She had the most beautiful cheekbones. "I kinda thought he was gay."

I laughed loudly. Too loudly. "Justin? Gay? Did you see that kiss? No way, girls. Boy has skills," I purred.

I. Purred.

"Heav?" Justin emerged, holding up my drink and gesturing to the stairs that led to the second floor.

"Oh! Better go see what my man needs. He can be a little demanding, if you know what I mean," I said, waving a hand at the two girls and giving them an exaggerated wink as Justin pulled me up the steps.

Emily's jaw dropped and Sarah leaned in to whisper in her ear. And that's how gossip works. One flirty kiss at a time. Familiar anxiety rose in my chest but it was met by something else. I kind of liked being noticed for once in my life. No one was ever jealous of Heaven Reeves.

No one.

But we weren't done. Not by a long shot. Justin didn't just want to prove he kissed a girl, no, he wanted to prove much more, so we wove through the throng of students, stopping only to take a swig of our drinks and for me to get my neck mauled by his hot mouth.

Playfully, I pushed him away. "Don't make me explain a hickey to my mom, got it?"

His eyes widened. Yeah. Neither of us wanted that.

At the top, we stood outside his friend's room. "Are you sure?" he asked, low and quiet. He was giving me an out. I nodded and fisted his shirt, pulling him closer.

"Yeah, I'm sure. Let do this, okay?"

He smiled, grateful and sweet. "I'm gonna rock your world, baby." I rolled my eyes and let him lead me in the room, shutting the door on the handful of people on the other side, and gave them the show of a lifetime.

2

——————

THE WEIRD THING ABOUT BEING THE SUBJECT TO GOSSIP AND RUMOR IS that when you're the actual subject, you always seem to be the last to know.

Justin and I had fake, raunchy, party sex, saved his reputation, and all was right in his world. I left him safe and secure, in Oceanside with a new lease on life and no one in my life even aware it happened.

Whatever worked for him. I planned on business as usual at my own school—thirty miles away and a lifetime away from Oceanside drama. In Allendale I was firmly entrenched in the fairly-unseen part of the student body. Not popular, but not unpopular. I didn't really like people (okay, my anxiety didn't like people) and it seemed the feeling was mutual; people didn't really like me. I was okay with this. No one seemed to notice me much one way or the other.

What I didn't realize that night when Justin and I emerged sweaty and laughing from the bedroom was that there were some people taking photos at the party. What I also didn't know at the time was these party-goers went home and immediately sent images out on social media describing our tryst in detail. Not just to Oceanside kids, but to pretty much every student at our school, too.

Oh, and to top it off? The photo with the most likes and shares was a picture of me and my overly (Justin-styled) sexed-up hair emerging from the bedroom.

That was what I didn't know when I walked down the hallway with a creepy, eerie hush following me.

Maybe, I thought, tugging my bulky sweater down over my wrists, hyperaware of the scars underneath, I was wrong about being able to pull off a post-fake-sex walk. Could they tell what didn't happen over the weekend?

My first hint was before English when a hand wrapped around my waist. "Hey, Heaven. It's been a while."

I spun and looked into the pimpled face of Mark Amerson.

I shifted, moving the unwelcomed hand off my hip. "Been a while since what?"

"Since you know, me and you...you wanna go out?"

Curious. We've barely ever spoken. "Sorry but...no?"

Where was this coming from?

"Think about it," he winked. Ew.

I turned and left.

Craig Dickerson found his way next to me in the lunch line. "Hey girl, I've been thinking about you a lot lately."

I picked up a bottle of juice. "Excuse me?"

"You. I've been thinking about you and, well, me."

"You have?" I was no longer curious but downright suspicious.

I paid and moved out of the line. Craig shouted after me, "Can I call you later?"

No.

Alex stopped to talk to me on the way to Spanish. Spencer, with his skeevy long hair and too-thin goatee, waited outside the bathroom. Even Jackson Hall (Jackson. Hall. Best friend of Anderson and one of the Allendale Four) gave me a slight nod and skimmed my body with smoldering eyes while Hayden Pierce raised a smirky eyebrow in my direction before I slipped into Chemistry.

That was hands-down the most acknowledgement either had given me. Ever.

To be honest, a little attention from those two didn't bother me so much, but it was still bizarre.

But that wasn't all. If the boys were being suspicious, the girls were just being out-right bitchy. In the hallway Jennifer elbowed me in the ribs, offering a fake, "sorry," as she stomped away. Mallory muttered "slut" under her breath, which seemed a little pot-meets-kettle but whatever.

By the time I sat down at my desk, I was red-cheeked, flustered, and at a complete loss. Paranoia washed over me. Somehow, some way, they knew.

A familiar body eased into the seat next to me and I flinched. Did he know? Had he heard? Holy crap. Of course he'd heard. His best friend just gave me a once over in the hallway. The question was how.

Anderson and I had always been friendly, but our relationship was based on snarky jabs and constant put-downs. We're both good students, although his seems to be more about genetic superiority and mine hard work and a lack of a social life.

His circle of friends, *guy friends*, was tight and pretty popular but they mostly keep to themselves. Jackson Hall. Hayden Pierce. Oliver Baldwin and then Anderson Thompson. They were close. Super close, and no girl had ever broken into their ranks. Many tried. All failed. They seemed more interested in each other than in the opposite sex.

The boys and I had shared classes since grade school and I had harbored a crush on all of them, Anderson in particular, for a long time. Fine. *Years.* I knew it was useless. They didn't seem to date. The Allendale Four went to dances and stuff, but increasingly I suspected none of the girls were up to their standards. Smart.

If I were them, I would wait until college and not tie myself down to one of the Stage Five Clingers looking for a way out of this place.

Class started and much to my relief, Mr. Baker turned on a film. I took the opportunity to pull out my pen and write a note.

Jackson Hall just checked me out.

I pushed the paper in Anderson's direction. He looked at the paper. Then at the movie. Then at me and blinked. When he got back to the paper, he wrote quickly.

What?

Was that unclear? *He ogled me.*

Anderson smirked at that one and scribbled on the paper.

Jackson's a pervert. He's always staring at pretty girls.

Wait, what? Pretty? Nope. No. I ignored that jab. I sighed and tapped my pen on the table before replying.

Everyone is treating me weird. What's going on? Be honest.

Anderson placed his pen on the table and slipped his hand in his back pocket. I felt my forehead crease as I tried to figure out what he was doing. After a second, he pulled out his iPhone.

"What are you doing?" I whispered, looking around to make sure no one could see us. Phones were not allowed out at school.

He ignored me. I watched as his long, graceful fingers moved quickly over the screen. His silly hair was all in his eyes and from this angle his jaw was sharp and strong and—

He handed me the phone under the table. It was open to his social media page, to a photo of me. In the image, my fingers were gripping Justin's shirt and I was smiling up at him. We looked happy. Even in love, to the outside viewer. It was sweet but didn't show anything. What was the big deal? But I knew. They heard the rumors.

"So," I mouthed. I could feel the heat burn into my cheeks.

He motioned for me to scroll through the photos. I did and felt the heat burn into my cheeks and my stomach dropped. The images had taken a life of their own. Before and after photos tagged with my virginity status. Little graphics of hearts and stars. Questions about me in bed. What Justin liked.

What *I* liked.

Oh god.

The whole thing had gone wrong and according to the ticker at the bottom, *viral.* My chest constricted and my lungs froze. I wasn't sure if I could breathe. I pushed the phone back to Anderson and tried desperately to pull air into my lungs.

He shrugged, unaware of my panic, and took his phone back. He slipped it in his pocket. I focused back on the front of the room. On the desk. On anything, trying to keep calm.

I mean, the plan worked. Justin and I tricked everyone. Just not only the kids at his school, but mine too. Mission accomplished. Why was I freaking out? Did it matter? Do I even matter?

History said no.

The movie ended and right before Mr. Baker turned on the lights, Anderson leaned over and said, "If people are noticing you, I guess that's why. They look at you differently now."

I didn't care about people. Not most of them. The one that really mattered was sitting next to me. The other was down in Oceanside *not* getting harassed in the locker room. I found the paper we had written on before, scribbled a note and slid it across the smooth tabletop.

Do you?

Just then the bell rang and Anderson stood, taking the paper and balling it into his fist and shoving it into his pocket. I realized he wasn't going to answer and I said, "Anderson, do you think differently about me?"

He slung his backpack over his shoulder and frowned. "It doesn't matter what I think, but you need to be careful," he said before walking out of the room.

~

"HEAVEN, I HAD NO IDEA."

Justin was at my house after school when I pulled up. He leaned against his rusty Honda, all legs and long body. I'd been on the verge of a panic attack all afternoon and when he showed up, I lost it.

"I know. How did you find out?"

"Emily took the photos, but she swears it's not her account."

I twist my hands. Of course. Stupid Emily. She probably thought this was hilarious. Her family had been big on the "run the Reeves out of town train" back in the day.

"It seems a little detailed for Emily. I'm not sure she has the attention span to go full mean girl, you know." He nodded in agreement. "I did a little research. The whole account is brand new. It's some kind of Fakestagram. Apparently, it exists just to announce my exploits."

Justin reached for me and pulled me into a hug. "What do you want to do?"

"Nothing."

"What do you mean, 'nothing'?" The anger was clear in his voice. He pushed me back to look me in the eye.

"I don't want to change anything. We accomplished what we wanted. Right?"

Justin ran his hand over his head. "Not like this. Not with your reputation on the line. I don't want this to trigger anything for you—you've been doing a lot better lately."

I laughed. The idea of me having a "reputation" was still a foreign idea and he was right, I had been doing better lately. I should be able to handle this. "It's no big deal. Gossip for the week. I'm sure it will pass. I'd rather you be happy."

He eyed me warily. He knew about the anxiety and where it had led in the past. I'd worked hard to get better. Would the scrutiny make it flare up again? I shook it off and promised it would be fine.

"Are you sure? Because we can totally fake-couple it for a while. Make it real and they'll get bored faster."

I scrunched up my nose. "Eh, if this means more kissing, then no thanks."

"You really know how to make a guy feel special."

"It's a gift," I deadpanned. "I'm sure if we ignore it, everything will be fine."

A girl could dream, right?

~

"Heaven, do you have a minute?"

I was at my locker when Eric Oswald came up behind me. His question set me on edge...I'd heard it over and over this week. It wasn't the first time the joke had been made, but post-Fakestagram the ribbing increased, and two minutes didn't pass without some jackass making a hilarious play on my name and their desire for Seven Minutes With Heaven.

Seriously, what was my mother thinking naming me after a psychological horror novel from her teens? Honestly, it explained so much about her.

It just didn't say much about me.

I turned to the smallish boy with his thick mop of overly-styled hair and impeccable clothing standing next to me and prayed, *please-dontaskmeout*. I didn't feel like I had Jesus on my side, but it was worth a shot.

"Sure. What's up?"

He cast a glance around the hall. "In private?"

I eyed him skeptically, but Eric hadn't approached me all week and was notoriously well-liked and not a jerk. I nodded and followed him to the Student Government office. His name was listed under "President" on the small sign by the door. He closed the door behind me with a soft click.

I sighed. "What's going on, Eric?"

He moved and sat behind the desk and tented his fingers. "I know about you and Justin Blackwood."

"Yeah? So? The rest of the school seems to know, too." I folded my arms defensively across my chest and waited.

He shook his head and said, "No. I *know* about you and Justin. What really happened."

Well, that was a surprise. "What really happened?"

Eric cleared his throat. "Justin and I are friends."

I stared at him.

"You know," he moved his fingers in air quotes and lowered his voice, "'*friends*'?"

My eyes popped wide. "Wait...what? Really?" I thought of Justin. Tall, muscular, handsome Justin. And then I thought of Eric, not so tall or muscular. A little handsome. *Interesting.* I knew Justin had been questioning himself...things were starting to make more sense.

"Yes."

"So what did you want to ask me?" I asked, not sure where this was going. Was he trying to blackmail me? 'Cause I didn't think that would work.

Eric leaned forward. "I want you to pretend you made out with me, too."

I snorted. Out loud. "That's not what we pretended to do, Eric."

"Whatever," he waved his hands. "David Nash has been calling me a flamer since the third grade. Not only am I gay, but they know

I'm a virgin. I have six months before I get out of here. I have a scholarship to UCLA and I'm gone. Just help make the next six months a little easier on me, please?"

"Eric, no one cares if you're gay."

He stared at the papers on his desk. "I care."

The identity crises were strong in this school.

"If I helped you, what's in it for me?"

"My undying gratitude? A bump in the social structure? Good weed, invites to parties, a date to the prom? Maybe you can lose the label of being a frigid bitch for good."

The last one was a slap in the face. I knew what people thought. They mistook my lack of social skills for being a bitch. Normally I didn't care, but this last week made me look at things differently. I considered the offer and what it could do to change all this. Eric was extremely popular despite the issues he just brought up. Maybe if I got an invite to one of those parties, Anderson would be there...

Eric stood. "Just consider it. Meet me tomorrow morning at my car and we can discuss, okay?"

I studied the strange boy in front of me. "Okay."

Again, I had a bad feeling about this.

3

———

I LEFT SCHOOL FEELING LIKE CRAP. WORSE THAN CRAP. IF I SAID NO TO Eric, what would he do? Tell everyone Justin and I faked the whole thing? That would be social suicide for both of us. Things were awkward already. I can't imagine what would happen if they knew we lied.

I mulled over Eric's offer. If I said yes, what did that make me? I really didn't know. Stupid was the only word that came to mind.

I started home, walking down the sidewalk that led from the school to my neighborhood. Mom and I lived in a small house, the only thing she could afford after my dad left. She worked long hours at the police station as a secretary with an erratic schedule, but at least the benefits were good. Her shifts alternated every few weeks. Sometimes day, others night. Currently she was on the day shift, which meant I had a few hours before she got home.

I loved and hated that time alone. I liked the quiet, but it also gave me too much time to think. That was when I'd go down the rabbit hole, allowing my anxiety to take over. Anxiety was stupid like that... you know it's bad and it makes you feel bad, but it also has a strange sense of comfort. Comfortable pain.

I turned and took the long way home, walking past the Quick-Zip where all the kids with cars stopped to get drinks.

18

Fuck. Bad idea.

A red sports car pulled up next to me and rolled down the driver's side window. Spencer propped his arm in the open window and leaned his head out. "Heaven, hey, you need a ride, sweetheart?"

"No thanks," I said. It was hard to hear my voice over my thundering heartbeat. "I'm fine."

"You sure? I've got a few minutes to spare. I'm sure we can find a way to fill it."

Another car rolled up behind me and a shadow fell over Spencer's face. His creepy smile dropped and his eyes darted over my shoulder. My throat constricted, feeling the fear of being enclosed. What now? Who wanted a piece of me now?

I turned and saw Oliver sitting in his forest green Mustang, the engine idling loud. "Heaven, I've been looking all over for you. Did you forget we have that test in calculus tomorrow?" He raised his eyebrow and leaned casually across the black leather seats. I stared into his blue eyes and knew that he was offering a lifeline—a rope to pull me back to safety. How did I know? No idea, but behind me was a shark and I needed out of the dangerous waters.

"I totally forgot."

Oliver smiled and it was like a blessing from the gods. "I figured. Hop in."

"Hey," Spencer said, aggravated hurt clear on his face. "We were going to hang."

"Sorry," I apologized, which was dumb. Why was I apologizing to a jerk like that?

He frowned, stroking his nasty goatee, and muttered, "Whore," under his breath and sped off.

Once he was gone I leaned into Oliver's window. His eyes followed Spencer and his jaw tensed with controlled anger. "Thanks for saving me from that idiot. I can walk from here."

He set his eyes on me. "You're not walking anywhere. Not after that. Come on. I'll give you a ride for real."

I hesitated. Not because I didn't trust Oliver. I didn't think he was a jerk, but any other day would he have stopped to give me a ride? Or was it just because of my new reputation? It didn't help that a group of students from school, including Mallory and Jennifer, were watching from the doorway of the Quick-Zip.

He frowned when he saw my expression. "Heaven, I promise. I don't want anything but to get you home safely. Okay?"

I exhaled, feeling the tightening in my chest loosen a little. "Okay. Thank you."

I opened the door and it groaned and creaked. Inside, I inhaled the old leather and oil permeating from the classic car. I couldn't help but smile.

"What?"

"My dad had an old car like this. I forgot how much I missed it."

"Oh yeah? Well buckle up and we'll go for a ride."

"I'd like that." I clicked the metal belt into place.

He revved the engine and glanced over at me, floppy blonde hair falling into his eyes. It took every ounce of willpower not to push it aside. "When you're ready, you can tell me exactly what the hell is going on. Because that look on your face? It's not one I ever want to see again."

I nodded and looked out the window. The kids were watching me —us. Mallory's jaw was slack with disbelief, and jealousy was written all over Jennifer's face. I was in the car with Oliver Baldwin. One of the Allendale Four. Sure, they may all think I'm there because I'm nothing but a trashy whore, but looking over at the handsome, sweet boy next to me, I realized I didn't care.

I knew the truth and that was all that mattered. Oliver peeled out of the parking lot, taking me away from the stares and scrutiny. I knew the truth...at least that's what I told myself.

I DON'T KNOW WHY, but I told Oliver the truth too, and now he sat next to me with a completely dumbfounded look on his face.

"So what you're telling me is you pretended to have sex with Justin Blackwood, who was worried about his status as a virgin."

"Yes."

"And this could be because he may or may not be gay, but mostly because the other guys in Oceanside were harassing him."

"Right."

"Some snotty girls shared the photo all over social media, a Fakestagram was born and now you're the one with a bad reputation."

I pulled the lollypop out of my mouth. "Yep, pretty much."

Oliver's eyes flicked to the lollypop and back up to my eyes. "Well, that just...sucks."

And the worst part was, I hadn't even told Oliver what happened today with Eric because what if he thought I deserved it for getting involved with such a stupid idea in the first place?

We're sitting on the back porch of my house. My mom isn't home yet and I didn't feel comfortable asking Oliver in. No, that's not true. I did feel comfortable. I just didn't want him to think I was offering up a piece of Heaven.

Ugh. Everything was really confusing now. Including the fact Oliver Baldwin is sitting next to me on the porch swing.

How crazy was that?

Avoiding the Eric situation for now, I decided to bring up Anderson, who was a touchy subject, being his best friend. I thought maybe he could provide some clarity. "We always get along okay. Even flirting a little here and there, but once he showed me the photos, everything changed. He seems pretty judgey about the whole thing."

"Like he thinks you're a slut?"

"Did he say that? Do you think that? What about the other guys? I don't really know them, but Jackson spoke to me and Hayden..."

Oliver's jaw tenses. "Hayden did what?"

"Acknowledged me."

He laughed. Even he knew how difficult it was to get Hayden's attention.

"Look, I don't think you're a slut, and Anderson can be a little... reserved. He's probably just shocked. I mean, screwing a guy at a party and everyone knowing about it? That doesn't compute with the image we all have of you."

"What image is that?"

He rubbed his hands on his thighs for minute before saying, "You're quiet. Reserved. You wear huge sweatshirts that barely reveal you have curves. You never date. You skank-eye the more popular girls."

"You think I'm a bitch."

"No," he said, holding my eye. "But I do think that's your image and this whole thing with Justin and the photos? You just blew that wide open."

I groaned and leaned into the cushion on the porch swing, toying with the fringe on the edge. "No one up here was supposed to know! Mallory has sex. Tiffany North has sex. Why is it such a big deal for me?"

"It's a big deal because you've never done anything like this. Not just the sex part but the party and the gossip. You keep to yourself. Believe it or not, that kind of behavior intrigues people. You're an enigma."

"People are not interested in me." He rolled his eyes. "They just want to see me fail. They think I'm a goody-two-shoes. A prude."

"Well, there's that, too."

I looked up at the slats on the ceiling and thought about it. People noticed me. They thought about me. And one move outside my box threw the whole school for a loop. As awkward and surreal as it all was, it was nice to not be invisible for once. "You know, maybe I should embrace this. Have some fun for once in my life."

"Uh...what?"

"Maybe I should, Oliver. Who's it going to hurt?"

"Um...you? Your family? Your friends?" he said. But we both knew I didn't really have any friends, and that's when I told him what happened earlier that day.

"Eric asked me to fake make out with him!"

"He what?" His eyes narrowed and a thin vein appeared on his forehead.

I covered my eyes with my hand. "I think I'm going to do it."

"No way. This is a bad idea."

"I just want to shake things up a bit. I'm sick of the girls at school looking at me like I'm a pathetic loser and the boys like I'm invisible. It was nice having a little attention today."

"Even from Spencer?" His voice came out in a growl.

"Spencer's a dick. But maybe I can help Eric the same way I helped Justin. That has to count for something, right?"

"I'm not sure it works that way," he said, trying to be the voice of reason.

I didn't say anything else, trying to sort out my feelings. Oliver wasn't done.

"I think you'll regret it."

"They think I'm a whore anyway. What difference does it make?"

"Heaven...you don't see yourself clearly."

"Maybe I don't," I said. "Maybe it's time I defined myself clearly, for me and everyone else."

I wasn't sure what I was going to do, even after Oliver left and my mom came home. I had one night to decide if I wanted to alter my reputation forever. What did I have to lose?

~

THE RAIN WAS COMING down in sheets the next morning as I pulled into the parking lot at school. I spotted Eric's beat-up Toyota in its usual spot and pulled my mom's truck in next to it. Loud music shook his windows and I jumped in the passenger seat to get out of the rain.

"Hey," I said, tugging off the hood to my raincoat. "Sucky weather."

"Totally." His fingers adjusted the volume, making it lower. When he looked up at me, his forehead narrowed. "Did you straighten your hair?"

I rolled my eyes. I didn't even want to know why he noticed. "Yes. I do that sometimes even though it's ridiculous in this stupid weather." I lifted up my hair. "I even burned my neck trying to get underneath."

Eric didn't seem impressed or concerned over my injury so I dropped my hair and sighed. "Look, I want to help you, but I really think this is the wrong way to go about it.

"What?" he asked, devastation crossing his face. "Come on, Heaven..."

"I thought about it a lot last night and this really isn't the solution to either of our problems, you know? It's six months and you'll be gone. No biggie." I smiled weakly, knowing my argument wasn't what he wanted to hear. Oliver had been right though, the sacrifice was too much. He didn't even know how much.

The rain slackened and I attempted a look out the window but they had fogged since I got in. I could hear the other students' cars pulling into the lot—the bell would ring soon.

"No hard feelings, okay?"

He casted me a disgruntled glare but I could tell he wasn't mad—more resigned. All in all, he was pretty good kid. I flipped my hood over my head and opened my door. When I stood up, I came face to face with Jennifer Stevens.

"Oh. Hi," I said, slamming the door behind me.

"Heaven." She peered over my shoulder. She narrowed her eyes. "What's going on?"

"Um... none of your business." And it wasn't. She was the last person who needed to know anything, about anything.

A door slammed behind me.

"Hi, Eric," she said, glancing over at him. "So you gave Heaven a ride, huh?"

Oh, Jennifer. *Really?* I considered the places I could kick her. "No, my mom's truck is over there. We were just talking."

"Talking?"

"Yes, are you deaf? Talking."

"Like how you and Justin Blackwood were talking?"

My fists balled into the bottom of my sleeves. "Justin and I are friends. Since pre-school. You know that."

She nodded, her stupid frizzy hair bobbing along. "You and Eric were 'friends', too." Her eyes dropped and she reached over and pushed my hood back. "That looks fun."

My hand flew to the burn on my neck. I looked at the all-knowing smirk on Jennifer's face and shifted my gaze to Eric. I thought he would defend me but instead, he had his own all-knowing smirk on his own face.

I tilted my head and plead, "Eric..."

He shrugged, basically throwing me under the bus, and said, "It was fun, Heaven, see you around." He rounded the car and waved over Jennifer's shoulder. Frozen in my spot, I watched as the two of them walked into school.

4

Thankfully the school was abuzz with a different sort of energy that day. Every student was getting a school-issued laptop. We lined up alphabetically, shuffling through the library to sign the waivers agreeing to our end of the deal; any damage was our fault, any lost property was our fault, no porn, no games, nothing but homework and studying.

In theory, we couldn't watch porn or play games due to the controls set on the devices, but by lunch word had traveled around school about the way to circumvent this. Seriously, my generation was smart, but they needed to use their powers for good and not evil.

The Fakestagram account said this was a long-shot.

Oliver cornered me at my locker after lunch, new laptop tucked under his arm. He touched the burn on my neck. I sighed and glanced over his shoulder. Jackson Hall stood behind him, watching me intently.

"Who told you?"

"Hayden."

"Hayden? Why is Hayden talking about me?"

"He overheard Jennifer in Art. But that's not the point. The point is, less than twenty-four hours after I tell you *not* to pull this crazy stunt, I get word you were in Eric's shitty car and came out with a hickey."

"It's not a hickey." I sighed, grabbing my book and slamming the locker door. "It's a burn. I burned myself on my fucking hair straightener and for the record, I told him 'no', and that stupid skank Jennifer saw us together and blah, blah, blah, the rest is Allendale High history."

His eyes dimmed, realizing he'd yelled at me for no reason. "What happened to Eric?"

I groaned. "The last time I saw him, he was getting high-fives in the hallway from Mark and Alex."

"Assholes," Jackson says. I'd almost forgotten he was there. You know, other than the fact he's so handsome my hands had been sweating just knowing he was nearby.

Oliver nodded in agreement.

"I know." I felt like a fool. I turned the corner to where we could have a little privacy. "Everyone really will think I'm a whore after this. What am I going to do?"

"Who cares?" Jackson asked.

"Umm...everyone, apparently."

His gray eyes hold mine. "But do you?"

"No. I know I'm not a whore. Most virginal whore ever."

Both boys stared at my admission. Jackson ran his hand through his hair.

What Oliver said next took me by surprise. "I hoped it wouldn't come to this, but what you said yesterday gave me an idea. It's risky and it may totally fail, but really, at this point, it may be the best way to handle it."

I braced myself, already feeling the anxiety rising. "Okay, tell me...I'm ready."

But, I wasn't ready. Not at all.

〜

I SHOWED up the next day in an outfit that was a little tighter, a little shorter, and definitely a lot sluttier. My socks were tight, striped, and went up to my thighs. My skirt barely grazed the tops of them, and my shirt was from the children's department. Enough said.

I pulled my hair up, letting the red welt show on my neck.

That was Oliver's big plan, which was really *my* original plan, but now, for some crazy reason, it wasn't just me implementing it. I had allies. Two hot, popular allies.

Right. I was living in bizarro world.

I wasn't hiding anymore. They could think what they wanted, and for once, maybe I could change my reputation from nobody to somebody. I'd intentionally put myself out there. Maybe going from unnoticed to noticed wasn't the worst thing. Maybe it was time to take control of my life, do what I want and forget about everyone else.

Easier said than done, I thought, hiding with my head shoved in my locker. I pretended to rummage around for my books until I felt a tap on my shoulder.

"I think you dropped this?" I heard a deep, sexy voice say.

I turned and fought to keep the smile off my face. Jackson Hall was holding a pink Hello Kitty pencil in my direction. It wasn't mine, but whatever. "Clumsy me," I said, plucking the pencil from his hands. "Thanks."

Jackson wasn't Oliver or even Anderson. We weren't friends and if anyone was known as a player in the group, it was him. His gray eyes were glued to my legs and boobs and neck. Every time he shifted from one he got stuck on the other. I cleared my throat. "Bell's gonna ring."

His eyes snapped upward. "Yeah, um...okay."

My stomach was twisted in a pretzel. We were really doing this. Operation Heaven's A Slut was in action. Would I have liked Oliver to be the one doing this? Sure. Anderson? Definitely. Playing with Jackson was like playing with fire. I could get burned, but he was a means to an end, and I wasn't going to risk losing the opportunity because I was out of my comfort zone.

"Would you like to walk with me?" I said it teasingly. I'm pretty sure I sounded like an idiot. Man, flirting was hard.

A lazy smile crossed his lips. "Sure."

We took the short walk together, talking about classes and stuff. I tried not to appear as though my heart was about to bust out of my chest. I tried to ignore Eric as he winked at me from his locker when we passed. Jackson mentioned a party that weekend, although he didn't exactly extend an invite. When we reached the Chem lab, he abruptly stopped talking and looked away.

Anderson was waiting at the door. He gave me the same cocky smirk as he always did, but his eyes were stuck on his friend. Every other boy in the school had given me the once-over that day. Apparently, Anderson was immune.

"See you around, Jackson," I said, leaving the boys in the hall.

I walked to my seat and sat on the stool, dropping my books on the table. My eyes flew to the door when I heard a raised voice. It was Anderson. He and Jackson were arguing about something, and although I tried to use my supersonic hearing, they kept it low enough for me to not hear. Damn it. I needed a better superpower than being the good girl turned bad, especially since Anderson didn't seem interested in either. The last thing I saw between the two was some kind of staring contest, and then Anderson punched Jackson in the arm. It was hard enough that he winced and rubbed it as he walked away from the door toward his own class.

Anderson marched to our desk, head down, hair dipping over his eyes. He sat without a word.

"Fighting with your boyfriend?" I jabbed.

He brushed his hair back with perfect, long fingers and rolled his eyes. "Yeah something like that."

"I'm sure you'll make up." I tapped my pen on the desk, pretending to think. "You could write him a poem or something, expressing your feelings."

"Reeves," Anderson breathed, his voice thick with warning. "Not today."

I backed off, never having heard him annoyed like this. Whatever. Mr. Baker started the lesson and my attention was diverted, thankfully, until halfway through when he issued an assignment that required me to work with Anderson. We pulled out our books and began answering the questions.

"So what's with all this anyway?" he asked, focused on the paper on the table.

"All what?"

He looked up and his eyes roamed over my body. "This costume. That shit on your neck."

I faked being affronted, but my hand slipped over the burn mark anyway. "*This* is not a costume. I just decided to mix it up a little. Shed the hoodie. Lose the Converse. Why look like every other girl in the world?"

"*Okay.*" I wish I could say sarcasm didn't suit Anderson, but it would be a lie.

"Do problem eight," I directed, not wanting to discuss my choice in clothing any further.

Anderson scribbled down his answer and then shifted the paper toward me. "You don't, you know?"

"Know what?" I asked, confused and checking over his work.

He scrunched his nose like it hurt to say it. "You don't look like every other girl in the world."

I sighed. "I know, Thompson. I look stupid like this and boring like that, but this isn't really any of your business."

His eyes widened; his beautiful, green eyes. "No, that's not..." the bell rang and cut him off.

I stood and gathered my books. "Not what?"

But he only shook his head and tightened his jaw before he replied, "Never mind," and stalked out of the room.

"How'd it go?"

I slid my new laptop on the desk and then flopped on my bed, my tiny skirt flipping up and revealing everything. I flicked it back down. "Super."

"Really?" His eyes were glued to my legs.

"No, Oliver, Not really."

"Tell me exactly what happened." I hadn't seen him that day, other than from a distance in the hall. He'd left early for a doctor's appointment.

So I told him everything. About how all the boys in school were drooling over my new clothing choices. They loved the new me. They had visions of me in their bed. Or the backseat of their car. Or wherever they could think. Who knew the school needed fresh meat? I shuddered at the thought.

He was sitting in my desk chair, eyes glued to my legs, growing more and more tense with my description. If I didn't know better, I'd think he was angry. But why? This was his idea in the first place.

I tugged down the skirt but there was only so far it would go. "Jackson did a good job playing the part. So good I think he and Anderson got in a fight."

Oliver's eyebrows shot to his forehead. "Seriously?"

"Apparently, I repulse Anderson no matter how I dress. Nerdy. Hot. Whatever, I suppose my only value is as a lab partner. Nothing more, nothing less."

"You don't repulse him...he's just..."

"Just what? A hater?"

"No." Oliver ran his hand through his hair anxiously. He moved from the chair next to me on the bed. Having him so close excited me. And he was on my bed. Oliver Baldwin on my bed.

I tried futilely to control my breathing.

"Don't stress over Anderson. He's uptight and has a hard time knowing how to get what he wants, you know?"

"And you? Do you know what you want?"

Because I'd never been so confused in my life.

He nudged his shoulder into mine. "There's a reason I haven't filled Anderson in on our little plan, but in the end, I think we'll all get what we want."

Again, I wasn't sure what that was but I'm glad Oliver has a vision. "You think Anderson will come around?"

"I think we're going to have to drag him kicking and screaming. It's going to be fun to break him."

The heat from his arm warmed me and my brain tried to process the fact that Oliver was on my bed. We're sitting, just sitting, but it gives me an idea. I take out my phone and hold it over us and snap a photo. I run it through a filter, making sure everyone can see just where it was taken, and send it into the universe.

"Nice," Oliver says, once it appears on his phone. "That's going to drive everyone crazy."

I nodded but didn't admit it was driving me a little crazy too.

∾

NEEDING TO BOOST MY WARDROBE, I took my birthday money and hit the thrift store. My selection of sexy clothing was limited and to get this right I was going to have to suck up my fear of fashion and go with it.

The shop was fairly empty, the racks full of unappealing clothes, but I'd looked online for a few ideas and managed to luck out.

The following day, I knew I'd hit my mark when Hayden stopped dead in his tracks in the parking lot, nudging Jackson in the arm.

I fought a smile at my success.

After my research I figured I could stay within the dress code while pulling off a sexy look. Today was a ruffled shoulder-revealing shirt matched with a denim skirt with a frayed hem. Black booties covered my feet. I found a pair of big hoop earrings in my mother's jewelry box.

The minute the soles hit the pavement, a pair of hands pulled me from the car and slung my bag over his shoulder. My stomach dipped, wondering if Oliver had found me. When I turned, I plastered a smile on my face the minute I saw it wasn't any of the boys I'd hoped to see.

"Oh, hi, Garrett."

Garrett was tall and had light brown hair. I could see broad shoulders hidden under his flannel shirt. He wore thick-rimmed glasses and had a scruffy beard that made him cute in that hipster kind of way.

"Hi, Heaven." He was shy and artsy. Everyone knew it. We had all been to school together forever. Garrett and I were not friends, but we weren't *not* friends either. He opened and closed his mouth like he was preparing to say something, but no words came out.

"So, what's going on?" I asked, walking toward the building.

"I, uh..."

I stopped in the walkway, other students jostling me out of the way. "What's going on, Garrett? I'm going to be late."

"Can I talk to you—in private?

Oh, god. Not again.

My eyes bugged. I knew they did. I could feel it but this was my goal, to stir the pot and get people talking. I sighed and grabbed his arm, pulling him over to a picnic table in the school lawn. "I'll talk to you, away from everyone else, but not alone." Stupid Eric. Learned my lesson with that one. "What do you want?"

"Yeah, okay," he said, rubbing his hand on the back of his neck.

"Spit it out," I said. "Fine, look, are you gay? Because *that* I was not expecting."

His brown eyes snapped to my own, "What? No. No. I am *not* gay."

"Okay then what?"

"I thought maybe, um..."

"Tick tock, Garrett."

"Will you go out with me?"

"And by 'go out' you mean..." I prompted. It was pathetic that I had to ask.

"Out. Like for coffee or something."

I eyed him for a minute. "And by coffee do you mean have sex? Because I am not having sex with you."

"What? Oh my god, Heaven!" He looked around to see if anyone was listening. Surprisingly, no one was.

"Well, you can't blame me. You've heard the rumors."

It was his turn to look suspicious. "Yeah, rumors."

"Okay then. That's gonna be a 'no'." I knew I was being irrational. I looked like a slut, had been acting like a slut, but when called one I was getting pissy. I started off toward the building again.

"Wait," Garrett stopped me with a large, warm hand. "Look, just come with me. This afternoon to the coffee shop. I'll drive and pay. Just a date—nothing, uh, sexual."

"A date?"

He smiled. "A date."

5

———————

GARRETT WAS SWEET. AND FUNNY. AND COMPLETELY NOT INTERESTED in me. The minute we walked into the coffee shop, he flung a wiry arm around my shoulders and planted a gentle kiss on my cheek. It was sweet, but a little fast. I know people assumed I was easy, but come on, buy me a coffee first.

"What was that?" I hissed in his ear.

"What?"

"Garrett, don't make me walk out of here." Because I really didn't want to walk home. These booties were cute as hell but not made for a three-mile walk home.

He sighed. "Fine, look, do you see Sarina over there?"

I nodded; Sarina was a cute sophomore at school with us. She was busy helping a customer. More than once, she glanced in our direction.

"I wanted to make her jealous by showing up with you," he confessed.

"Garrett!"

"See, I knew you would be mad. This is why I didn't tell you."

"Really? Because I'm pretty sure I'm mad now because you *didn't* tell me, dumbass." I wanted to be indignant, but since I had my own plan to make one boy jealous by using another boy, it

34

seemed a little hypocritical. Although, I was a little bummed. Garrett was cute and nice.

Did these guys only want to use me to get something else?

Seemed like it.

"I'm sorry," he said. I gave him the stink eye. "No, really. It's just...Sarina is awesome, and way out of my league. I heard her talking about how she thought you were kind of badass the other day. So I thought if you would go out with me, then maybe she would, too."

I had to wonder what kind of morals Sarina had if she thought I was cool, in light of recent events. Whatever. The plan was to get people talking and for people to notice me. It seemed to be working.

"Why can you ask me out and not her?" I asked. "If I'm such a badass, you should be terrified of me."

He shrugged. We were in line now, moving closer to the counter. "I've known you forever. I'm not sure what happened down at the beach, but I figured you could say yes, or no. You said yes."

"Great. Well, now what?"

He adjusted his glasses. "I'm not sure."

Time was up and we were at the front of the line. Sarina smiled when she saw Garrett and her eyes widened just a bit when she saw me next to him. Motivated by his sad story and news of my badassery, I leaned into his side and wrapped my arm around his stomach, anchoring myself to him.

"What would you like, Heaven?" he asked. He was being all smooth and gentlemanly. Crap. Now I was bummed again.

"Just a hot chocolate, actually." I smiled warmly. Sarina watched our every move.

Garrett placed his order, chatting quickly with her. Minutes later, she slid the two paper cups across the counter. I decided to take the opportunity to do what Garrett was obviously too weak to do on his own.

"Thanks for the drink and the fantastic afternoon. See you soon, okay?" I kissed him on the cheek.

"Um...okay..." he stammered. His eyes flashed between me and Sarina. I threw him for a loop but I knew what I was doing. With a quick smile at her and a lingering hand on Garrett's hip before I walked away, I set it all in motion. She smiled back. She was no dummy. If she thought I was a badass, then stealing my recent conquest would pique her interest even more. Sure enough, before I even walked three steps, she saw the break I was giving her and began flirting with a confused but blissfully happy Garrett.

Feeling powerful, I pushed open the door and was hit by a gust of damp, cold air. Great. So much for an awesome exit. I had no car and no ride back to school. I wrapped my coat tightly around my waist and started walking. I considered stopping by the police station to get a lift from my mom, but she would wonder why I was stranded without a car in the first place, so that was out.

Now would be a nice time for Oliver to show up again.

As if a fairy godmother heard my plea, a sleek, black car drove up next to me. The passenger window rolled down and out popped the head of my Prince Charming. Jackson Hall.

"Hey, Heaven."

I stopped and peered into the open window. Anderson was driving. His eyes were forward, fingers tapping impatiently on the steering wheel. "Hey."

"You need a ride?"

I wanted to say no if Anderson was going to be a jerk, but there was a bigger plan, and my freezing hands and pinched toes begged otherwise. They wanted in that car badly. "If it's not a bother."

"Nah," Jackson said, that delicious grin widening across his face. He opened the door and hopped out of the seat, pushing it forward so he could cram his long legs into the back. He was giving me the front seat. Maybe Garrett wasn't the only one with manners around town.

"Thanks," I said, climbing in. I looked to the left. "Hey, Anderson."

"Hi." His fingers tightened on the leather wheel—the whites of his knuckles showing.

"Okay. Well, my car is at the school."

"Why'd you leave it there?" Jackson asked.

Our eyes met and I got the distinct feeling he already knew.

"If you must know, I had a date."

"And what? He ditched you?"

Anderson's knuckles turned white.

"No. Nothing like that. I was just ready to go."

He exhaled. Jackson began rambling on about the party this weekend. It was at Peter's house. Apparently, everyone was going. *Everyone.* Anderson said little, and I said less. In the past, no one discussed parties or weekend plans with me. Of course, in the past, no one thought I was an easy lay, either. Normally I was on my own or maybe with Justin. The entire topic made me uncomfortable.

Thankfully, the school was close, and Anderson slowed the car before he pulled into the parking lot. It was empty other than a couple teachers' cars and my mom's rusty truck. He swung into the space next to mine and I unlatched my seat belt.

"Thanks."

"No problem." I turned to smile before I got out of the car, but saw Anderson wasn't looking at me. His eyes were on the rearview mirror, locked with Jackson's.

These two. I seriously had no idea what was going on with them. "Yeah, well thanks again, and I'll see you later, I guess." I got out, leaving the door open so Jackson could move to the front. I heard the door behind me close as I dug around in my bag, looking for my keys.

"Heaven?"

I spun; Jackson was standing behind me. "Um, yeah?"

"So, Saturday...can I pick you up?"

I frowned. "Saturday?"

He raised an eyebrow and smiled. "The party? At Peter's. Can I pick you up?"

My heart almost lurched out of my chest. Jackson was asking me to go with him. I wavered. Was he for real asking? Not to make someone else jealous or because he was gay, (although he and Anderson...) but because he wanted me to? Or did Oliver put him up to it?

See? Things were super confusing.

"Can I call you later? And tell you then?"

His face fell a bit, but he recovered, tapping his fist on the side of my car. "Sure, call me. Tonight."

"I will. I promise."

"Great." He turned and swung the car door open. I saw Anderson inside. Not looking forward, not looking at Jackson. This time, staring straight at me. His jaw clenched tight. Anger rolled off him in waves as the door slammed between us. Moments later, the squeal of his tires confirmed that something was definitely not okay between us.

～

THAT NIGHT while sitting on my bed and doing my homework, there was a direct message from Eric. He was inviting me to the party at Peter's house. Payment, I suppose, for my services earlier in the week. I deleted it, but the invite was a reminder that I should call Jackson and give him my answer. I wanted to go, but at the same time, things were moving fast. I couldn't tell what was real and not real any longer.

Still wavering, I got his number from Oliver and called.

"Heaven?"

"Yeah. How did you know it was me?" I asked.

He laughed. "Lucky guess. I didn't recognize the number."

"Oh."

"So, is this about Saturday?" he prompted.

"Yeah."

"I can pick you up around seven..." He wasn't giving me much of an out. We had a plan. This was what I wanted. I repeated that mantra over in my head.

"Awesome."

"Yeah?"

"Yes. Definitely, I'll get you at seven, okay?"

I agreed and hung up the phone, unable to stop thinking about the last party I'd gone to and the fallout that ensued.

～

FIVE MESSAGES WERE WAITING on me when I stepped out of the shower. All from Oliver.

Wake up.

Wake up.

Wake up.

OMG WAKE UP.

Fine. Check your Facebook.

With only a towel wrapped around my body, I sat at the desk chair and opened my account. I had been tagged in two new photos from the anonymous account. One was of me getting into Eric's car. The other was of me and Garrett at the coffee shop. The picture was taken exactly when I kissed him on the cheek.

I texted Oliver back.

Do you know who posted these?

Nope.

A chill ran down my spine and I looked around my room. It was silly. No one was in here but I still had the feeling of being watched.

It was none of us. You okay?

Not exactly. I'm home alone tonight. Mom's working the night shift.

Lock the doors.

I'll be okay.

I put down the phone and wrapped my towel closer around my body and willed the fear to go away.

I'D FINALLY COAXED myself into a pair of soft cotton pajama pants and a heavy Oceanside sweatshirt when I heard the knock on the front door. I froze in the hallway, back pressed to a wall.

"Heaven!"

Stalkers didn't usually announce themselves, I considered, and I went to the window to take a peek. Oliver stood on the porch.

The look of relief on his face said everything when I opened the door.

"What are you—" I started but he stepped forward and scooped me into a hug. His arms were huge and he lifted me like a feather. He smelled amazing and I inhaled, feeling safe for the first time since I saw the photos.

"I could tell you were freaked out," he said, lowering me back to the floor. He brushed a strand of hair out of my face. "We wanted to check on you."

"We?" I glanced over his shoulder. I was shocked to see Hayden standing behind him. The boy—well, he was eighteen and looked more man than boy—stood on the edge of my porch. His longish, black hair was tucked behind his ears and his brown eyes watched my every move. Hayden was elusive, quiet. Sexy—there was no doubt about that one.

And he was on my porch.

I gave him a small wave and he nodded back before I shifted my gaze back to Oliver. "Thank you for coming. Really, I'm okay."

"You're alone, Heaven. With everything going on, there's no way we're letting you stay by yourself tonight. Oh and we brought food." He glanced down at the small table next to the door and I saw the pizza box.

It was obvious they had no intention of leaving, so despite the fact my mom had a pretty strict, "no visitors" rule, I opened the door and let them inside.

The two of them were huge in my small house; all broad shoulders and long legs. We lived in a small bungalow on the older side of town, perfect for me and my mom—walking distance to her job so we could share her little gray truck.

I couldn't help but gape at their size and the general idea that they'd come to my house, so I just stood awkwardly staring at them until it dawned on me to get plates. "You want something to drink? Soda? Water?"

"Water is fine," Oliver replied, looking over the house. He stopped at a photo of me around the age of three standing on the edge of the ocean in a mermaid bikini with same-aged Justin, his skin dark with a tan. "Is that your friend? The one that got you into all of this?"

I could hear the judgement in his voice. I filled two glasses with ice and water. "Justin didn't make me do anything. I volunteered."

Hayden peered at the photo and said, "I know him. We played football together when we were kids."

"I thought you played soccer?"

"I play both."

"Well, despite everything going on now, he's a good friend." My only friend, I wanted to tell them, but seeing them in my house like this made that seem less true. "Come on, we can eat in here."

The box was barely open before they both dove in, grabbing two pieces each. I watched in fascination as they inhaled their food, only stopping once to push the box in my direction. I took a piece before they got it all and bit into the gooey cheese, groaning when I realized I was starving. Both guys stopped eating and stared at me.

"What?" I asked, tugging at a piece of cheese and dropping it in my mouth.

They glanced uneasily at one another. "Nothing," Oliver said. "You're just funny."

"And hot," Hayden admitted. Oliver shot him a look but he just shrugged. "She is. You are. Hot. And groaning like that over a piece of pizza? Only made you hotter."

"Seriously?" I kept thinking I was being pranked. Was someone recording this right now? Anderson? But there was a glint in Hayden's eyes—something I could only describe as hunger, and I knew his belly was full.

Oliver sighed. "Heaven, you know we're not the kind of guys that really date around. The girls are school are a little..."

"Clingy," Hayden added, shoving more pizza in his mouth. "So freaking clingy."

"We're a tight group. Me, Hayden, Jackson, and Anderson. And our friendship has always come before any other kind of relationship. We support one another. We have fun together. It's just who we are."

My stomach twisted in apprehension, but I had to ask. "Where does that leave me? Why are you really here?"

"Because you need us and frankly, we need you." He moved to the couch and sat next to me, taking my hand in his. His hand was warm and his skin tingled against mine. "You don't know our history, do you?"

I shook my head. "I moved here in the sixth grade. Everyone already called you The Allendale Four."

Oliver looked at Hayden, who nodded his head, giving him the go-ahead. "Hayden, Jackson, and I were like everyone else in elementary school. Had a lot of friends. Played with the other kids. Everything was fine until Anderson's family moved here in the second grade."

"His family didn't live here all along?" New kids were rare in Allendale. It was one of the reasons my arrival had been so rocky. Cliques and friend groups were set in pre-school.

"Nope. He showed up with that silly hair, sticking up in a million directions, and even then he was a handsome kid. But he was also shy and that translated into him seeming stuck up. He was scrawny and a few of the kids at school decided he was fair game."

"They bullied him?" The thought made my heart hurt. Poor Anderson.

"Mercilessly. He was too smart, too wealthy. His parents are both doctors and lived in the biggest house in the district. And Mark Amerson and Spencer Harrison decided to make his life miserable."

"Ugh, Mark. I hate that guy." Spencer was just skeevy. "He tries to pretend like he's nice but he's awful."

Hayden busted out laughing. "Right? What a dick."

"Total dick," I agreed. "So what happened to Anderson? Seems like he survived."

"We didn't like the dynamics on the playground and decided to stick up for Anderson. It wasn't hard. After we scared the pants off of Mark and Spencer, we made a pact to always take care of one another and that's how we became the Allendale Four." He and Hayden reached out and performed a complicated handshake. It was totally bro-ish and adorable.

"That was really nice of you."

Oliver's fingers tighten in mine. "When we saw the whole school turn on you over the thing with Justin, we agreed to help you the way we helped Anderson."

"That's really sweet of you." I wrinkled my nose. "But what about the fact Anderson isn't into it—or anything to do with me?"

Hayden shook his head. "Anderson is an idiot. We love him, but he's an idiot. He's down with supporting you, Heaven. It's just going to take him a little while to warm up. After being picked on, he doesn't trust people easily."

That made sense and explained a lot about how some days he was friendly in class but never let it go any further.

"Give him time," Oliver said.

"We'll find out who's taking and posting the photos," Hayden added. "Until then, stick close to us. Always."

"And no more fake dates," Oliver said. "There's no way to know you're safe. The owner of the Fakestagram account could be anyone at school. If you want to prove something to the school, go for it. Dress how you want. Slut shaming is wrong. But if you want to push it further or fool around with a guy? You use one of us. Got it?"

"Is that why Jackson asked me to the party this weekend?"

Hayden laughed and picked up another piece of pizza. "Jackson asked you to the party because he thinks you're hot."

My cheeks flamed, but in reality, I felt warm all over. I'd never had people before. Just Justin. But this? Oliver was telling me I finally had a group I belonged to—The Allendale Four.

6

———

Knowing I had the support of the guys, I made a decision and refused to back down to whoever was bullying me. He or she apparently wanted to prove me a slut. Oliver was right. Slut shaming was wrong, so, fine. Whatever.

I dressed for the day: short, plaid skirt. Check. Tight, white blouse. Check. So what? I was channeling early '90s Britney Spears. No need to reinvent the wheel.

Jackson met me at my locker again before Chemistry. Apparently, this was going to be a thing. One of the guys would be around all the time. I didn't hate it.

Anderson watched us walk down the hall together. I pretended that Jackson's warm fingertips on my back didn't send a rush of butterflies to my belly, and that I didn't see the look of disapproval in his best friend's eyes. Typically, they had their weird stand-off in the hallway. I understood it a little better knowing Anderson's past, but it still hurt.

"Bye, boys," I said, leaving them to their drama.

Jackson's fingers slipped off my back. "Later."

During class, Anderson ignored me. Well, maybe not ignored. He was watching me when he thought I didn't notice. I *felt* more than

44

saw his eyes on me. Perhaps Anderson wasn't totally immune to me after all.

The rest of the week was pretty much the same. Boys swirling around me. Girls giving me the stink eye. Even though things were different from a couple weeks ago, at the same time, I still felt the hovering anxiety from so many people watching me. Even though Jackson had publicly staked his claim, I was curious when Benjamin walked up to our table in Chemistry on Thursday before Anderson came into class.

"Hi, Heaven."

I eyed him warily. Things had calmed down a little bit since Jackson had been hovering around. Benjamin was nice but a little dorky. I had a hard time seeing him attempting to pull something over on me. His eyes were glued to my chest of course, but I couldn't blame him. I had a pretty rocking rack.

"What's up Benjamin?"

"I just wanted to know if I could borrow your notes from English. I had a dentist appointment."

I breathed a sigh of internal relief. I really didn't want to have to say no to another fake sex/fake make-out/fake coffee date. "Sure, stop by my locker after school and I'll give them to you, okay?"

A loud scraping noise interrupted us and Anderson made his presence known. Benjamin glanced in his direction and offered a smile. Anderson gave a weak one in return.

"Great, after school?"

I nodded. "I'll see you then."

He walked away and the silence from our little table was deafening. The one person I'd hoped to gain attention from was still ignoring me, that was, until that moment.

That was the day Anderson decided to break his wall of silence.

"You know, he's a dick."

That was what he said after almost a week. Regardless, my heart stuttered at the sound of his voice. His words were quiet, low so Mr. Baker wouldn't hear. In return, I never looked up from my paper.

"What was that? You're a dick?"

I did look up for the reaction. I was rewarded with a grimace and then the hint of a smile. The only one I'd seen on him in a week.

"Are you talking about Benjamin, because he only—"

"I was talking about Jackson."

I pretended to mull this information over, tapping my finger on my lips. His eyes darted away from mine. Yeah, he was watching. "This may work for me, then."

"What?"

"Jackson being a dick. I'm a bitch and apparently a whore, so, yeah, we may be a good match."

I expected another laugh but instead Anderson's expression closed. I watched the bone in his jaw flex and retract. This simple motion was completely mesmerizing. *Mesmerizing.* I considered rubbing my thumb on the sharp angle of the bone jutting out. My fingers twitched and he moved, snapping me out of my trance. I realized that although that bony jaw was hot, it was also a little scary. He was pissed. In all our years of being classmates, we had always had an easy friendship. This? This was so different.

"You're not."

I flicker of hope spread through my chest. "I'm not what?"

"A bitch."

His jaw was still set and his green eyes held mine. I could hardly breathe. He said I wasn't a bitch. Which was nice. Awesome. What he didn't say was, "*I don't think you're a whore.*"

"And?"

He didn't respond.

"Fuck you." I stood up, grabbed my books and walked out of class.

7

<hr>

Since I left during the middle of class, the hallway was quiet. I couldn't actually leave school—the last thing I wanted was to get in real trouble. I pushed open the door to the girl's room. Refuge.

"Heaven Reeves." I heard my name called the minute I walked into the tiny, cold, cinderblock room. Amber Wasserman was standing with her back to the row of sinks along the wall.

"Hey, Amber."

"Whatever Heaven, don't 'hey' me."

I looked at the girl in front of me. Amber had a reputation for advocacy and activism. She led the environmental club, the National Organization of Women chapter, and she always wore some kind of feminist shirt to school. The one today was gray with just "girl power" across the front. She was definitely a little on edge. She was also apparently very angry with me.

I sighed dramatically, over her drama already. I was furious with Anderson and more than a little hurt. The last thing I wanted to deal with was her issues. I walked over to the mirrors and I smoothed the collar of my shirt. "What's the problem?'

"You."

I rolled my eyes. I *really* didn't feel like delving into her drama right now. "Spit it out, Amber."

"Leave Ben alone."

Ben? I almost laughed. He was so not of interest to me. Had she not heard? I had the Allendale Four following me around. Sure, they only wanted to be friends—sweet protectors of the innocent and weak, but still. I didn't laugh, though. Amber's fists were balled by her sides and I didn't want to get punched in the face.

Instead I smiled and said, "Sure. No problem."

"I'm serious. I saw you two talking earlier."

"Yeah, Amber," I shook my head. "He asked if I would let him borrow my homework. Is that a crime? What's it to you, anyway? You dump him every other week. Everyone knows you treat him like shit." I turned to face the mirror, fixing my hair. "Seems to me if you don't want anyone else to have a shot with him, then you better lock that shit up."

That shut her up, because other than staring at me with her jaw hung open, she simply grabbed her bag and ran out of the room in a huff.

"Psycho," I muttered, giving her a little space before I walked out the door. To my surprise Oliver was standing in the hall, eyebrows raised.

"Everything okay?"

"Yeah, I'm just doing what I do best—making enemies." I told him, feeling tears burn at the corner of my eyes. He slipped his arm around my waist and pulled me tight. He smelled good and his body felt perfect next to mine. So perfect that I didn't even care when we rounded the corner and the whispers started.

Let them whisper.

I had The Four at my back.

~

"What are you doing out here?"

I turned and stared at Hayden. We were on friendlier terms since the impromptu pizza night at my house, but otherwise I'd never been alone with him. Not until now.

"What are *you* doing out here?" I shot back, before I thought about it. Of all the boys, Hayden intimidated me the most.

Oliver was a teddy bear.

Jackson was genuinely nice, even if he couldn't take his eyes off my chest.

Anderson...he was Anderson. Less scary, more annoying. I was slowly figuring him out. Maybe.

But Hayden? He was a god. Like how did a man-boy like him even go to high school? He should be on a reality TV show or a model in New York. Possibly a superhero hiding out? I always figured he didn't date because he was better than the girls in Allendale. Now I know why he's part of the Allendale Four and what that means.

'Here' was the small area between buildings that held some kind of garden of sorts from the agriculture club. It was quiet and out of sight. I was waiting here until I could easily make my escape from school.

"Testy today?" he shot back, shoving his hands in his pockets. "I'm hiding from Mrs. Cooper. She's after my ass for detention for skipping class."

"I just needed a break."

"Someone bothering you?" A dark shadow fell over his eyes.

"No. I know you guys agreed to back me and I appreciate it, but I can't take much more."

He narrowed his eyes and tucked his long hair behind his ear. "What do you mean?"

"Oliver and Jackson are so nice—both laying their reputations on the line to hang out with me. Anderson is...well, you know..."

He blew a puff of smoke into the air and chuckled. "Yeah, I know."

"It's just coming from all sides. The girls still hate me. Amber Wasserman just accused me of trying to steal Benjamin from her." I rolled my eyes. "As if."

Hayden howled with laughter at that one.

"What?"

"Benjamin would have no fucking clue to do with a girl like you."

I'm not sure if I should be offended, but I kind of had the same thought. "Seriously. He just wanted to borrow my notes."

He smiled. It was glorious. "Figures."

I leaned against the building. "I'm just tired, I guess."

"You didn't mention me on that list..."

I raised an eyebrow. "No. I didn't."

"Why's that?"

I shrugged. "Not sure I know you well enough to say."

"We can easily fix that, you know." He walked over and leaned against the building, inches away. He smelled like a mixture of after-shave and rain. I couldn't keep my eyes off his face, and then he inexplicably reached out and touched my chin. "I'm shocked it took everyone so long to take notice. I've had my eye on you since the first day you moved here. All arms and legs. Thick braids. Scared of your shadow. I knew there was more and so did the others. Why do you think the guys befriended you?"

"Because I make a good lab partner?"

He laughed. "Well, obviously."

I eyed him skeptically. "If you could see all that about me, then how come no one else did?"

"The kids at school? The dickwads like Mark Amerson or Spencer? Oh, they noticed. They're all terrified of you."

"Yeah right," I scoffed.

Hayden placed his palm on the building and leaned close. I saw the dark ink of a tattoo on his bicep. "Totally. You're untouchable."

Untouchable. The high school equivalent of a disease.

"That's ridiculous. I've spent the last three years here fairly invisible."

"By choice," he pointed out.

"Maybe."

"Well, maybe that just drives them all a little crazy. Guys always want what they can't have. It's biology." I wasn't sure about that but he seemed convinced. "You've been off limits. They thought you were better than them."

"Sure, okay, say all this is true. Why now?"

"Justin Blackwood broke you. They all feel like they could have a shot now."

"Gross. Broke me?" This conversation was equally fascinating and repulsive at the same time.

"Justin is good-looking and popular. If you didn't shoot him down then they think *they* may have a chance. Like Jackson and the party."

"If he thinks something is happening between us there, he's wrong. I already made that party foul once."

He smiled and it took my breath away. "Jackson's no fool. He's probably had his eye on you for a while. I mean, he did ask you before Oliver stepped in."

"Huh." I found this hard to believe.

"Yeah. Look, I'm not trying to sell out my brothers or anything, but you know Jackson and Anderson don't date much. He was probably trying to get up the nerve to ask when shit hit the fan and he got his opportunity."

The thought of Jackson or Anderson being nervous to ask someone out seemed ridiculous. Who wouldn't say yes?

"Whatever," I deflected. "I'm pretty sure he's just trying to get in my pants."

He nodded. "Oh, definitely."

I stared at him for a minute, mesmerized by his dark eyes and wanting to run my fingers across the ink of his tattoo. These boys... they're too much, and frankly just enough. They're perfect. Funny. Strong, and well...if everything they're telling me is true, quite possibly mine.

"What about you, Hayden?" I asked, well aware of the way his eyes kept dropping to the visible cleavage pushing out of my shirt. "Were you too intimidated to ask me out?"

He swallowed and leaned in close to my ear. "You and I? We're not ready for each other yet. Once you've had some fun with my friends come and find me. Then we'll do it our own way."

He straightened and to my shock, brushed his lips across my forehead. I gripped the wall, willing my knees to hold me up right. His words came out less like a threat and more like a promise.

A promise, I realized as I watched him walk back into the school, I was determined to make him keep.

8

I was lying on my bed when the photo came through my feed.

Hayden and I in the school garden in the exact moment he leaned in to kiss my forehead. You couldn't see that though, the chasteness of it all. No, it looked like we were full on kissing. Plus, his hand is down by the hem of my skirt and it looked like he was feeling me up. The photo had been tagged with, "Heaven Bags One Of The Four. Who's Next?"

It only takes a moment for the comments to start. They fill up the screen of my laptop, flooding the page.

Fucking whore

Stupid skank

In public? Gross

Shady as hell.

Hayden Pierce? I'd do him.

Heaven Reeves? I'd do her.

Hope he gets tested.

Who does she think he is?

And on

And on

And on

I knew I should turn it off, but like any trainwreck it was impossible to step away. It felt like watching someone else's life unfold, but then I looked at the photo and remembered standing there, feeling Hayden's lips on my forehead, wanting him to do more.

Maybe I was a whore?

Maybe I deserved this?

Anxiety wracked through my chest and it's all just too much. Hayden made me feel better but now that had been exploited too. Was any of it real?

I pinched myself and felt the sting.

I did it again.

The house was quiet. My mom was gone again. I stared and stared at the photo, feeling like a worthless piece of trash. If I didn't do something, the panic would set in. I needed a way to release the anxiousness—the pain of being a loser no matter what I did.

I went to my desk and pulled out my pencil bag. There was a small sharpener inside and I knew I could break it open. Get to the blade inside. I'd done it before.

Dropping the phone into the docking station, I flipped on some music and stripped off my shirt so that I was down to a white tank. I saw the scars from before—back when things were darkest for me. They're all over my upper arms, pale and pink, where people couldn't see. I never tried to kill myself. That's not what it was about. The cuts...they were to release the pain. The stress and anger I carried day in and day out. Things had been better but all of this—I'd ventured too outside my box. How dare I try to make friends. How dare someone like me for me.

I fought to catch my breath, focusing on the music and staring at my face in the bathroom mirror. Mascara smeared down my cheek. My nose was red and splotchy. I'd promised my mom I wouldn't do this anymore, but it hurt so bad.

I smashed the pencil sharpener on the bathroom sink and eyed the sharp metal inside.

"What the hell are you doing?"

I screamed. I screamed loud, so loud, and spun around.

"Oliver! Holy shit!"

Oliver stood in the doorway, eyes wide with fear. He reached for me and snatched the blade from my hand. "What is this?" His eyes skimmed down my arm, taking in the scars. "Heaven, what are you doing?"

We stared at one another and finally I broke. I just broke, collapsing into a heap. A wail rose from the back of my throat but I didn't hit the ground. Strong arms caught me, lifted me, carried me out of the bathroom.

Oliver cradled me against his chest and lowered me to the bed, engulfing me in his arms. I cried against him, using his body for support. I cried as he stroked my shoulders and arms, kissing the old scars one by one. I sobbed, feeling the pain in my chest crack, finally having someone there to take care of me. I did this until there was nothing left. No pain. No despair. Only an empty shell.

I did all of this, felt all of this until, bound tight in his unwavering arms, he rocked me to sleep.

∼

I woke wrapped in warmth surrounded by the most fantastic smell. I didn't want to wake up, not yet, a cloud lingered in the distance but here I was safe. I wanted to stay bundled in the cocoon.

Eventually I realized the cocoon moved and was not a blanket but the warm heat of a body, a male body, and I blinked my sore, exhausted eyes and looked into the most handsome face.

"Hey," Oliver said, smiling down at me.

"Hi."

Slowly the events of the night came back to me. The photo. My breakdown. The blade. Oliver—god, Oliver. How did he even know I needed help?

"I'm," I started, feeling awkward and embarrassed. "I'm sorry about before. That was, uh…"

His hand stroked my cheek, blue eyes piercing into mine. "That was rough. Scary."

"Thank you for stepping in, I don't know what would have happened. I just broke. I don't know. The photo…shit, did you see it?"

"Yeah, that's why I came over. I was driving home and saw it.

Turned my car around. You didn't answer but I could hear the music blasting." He tilted my face to his. "I've never been so absolutely fucking terrified before."

"I'm sorry."

"Do. Not. Apologize." His voice was firm. "You've been through a lot, Heaven. So much. You're brave, dealing with those bastards every day. The bravest person I know."

I wrapped my arms tight around him. "I just felt so alone."

"Always call me," he said. "Me or any of the others. We're just a phone call away, got it?"

That was the strange thing. For the first time after a major panic attack, I felt different. Like a miracle had happened the night before. My chest was clear. The anxiety lifted. Oliver did it. Just by being here. By taking care of me.

I nodded and burrowed my face into his chest. It was so broad and muscular, the type of thing you see on TV. Not in real life. Not in my bed.

His hand ran down my arm, tracing the pattern of my scars. I wanted to hide them but he held me tight and kissed me behind the ear, whispering, "You're the most beautiful creature I've ever seen."

"It's embarrassing." I said back, a shiver tickling my spine.

"No." He kissed my shoulder. My neck. "They're a symbol of your strength, Heaven. You're a survivor. You survived then and you'll survive now."

My heart swelled and like him, I wanted to explore his body. I wanted to feel him. He watched me, allowed me the freedom to touch him all over. He laid still, allowing me to take my time and it was only when he grimaced, wrinkling his nose, that I realized the effect my hands on him had.

"Oh," I said, glancing at the small space between our hips. The distance shrunk as he grew. "Sorry."

"I told you," he said, closing the gap between us. "Never apologize."

His lips were only a breath away, pink and inviting. I held his eyes and he cupped my face with his hand. I licked my lips and he unconsciously mimicked the move. He was going to kiss me. I knew he wanted to, but something held him back.

"What?" I asked as his eyes searched mine.

"I don't want to take advantage. Not after everything you've gone through—not after tonight."

I laughed. The first time since yesterday and it felt good. So good. "You're not taking advantage, Oliver. Just fucking kiss me."

It was all the invitation he needed, and when his lips met mine it was like a chorus of angels singing. He tasted like mint, his lips soft while his mouth claimed me hard. Electricity ran through my arms and legs, building in the most forbidden places. This wasn't my first kiss but god, none had ever felt quite like this.

This was what it felt like to kiss someone that cared for you.

This was what it felt like to be with someone that gets you.

This was what it felt like to have your needs met and to want to meet the needs of others.

Late that night Oliver gave me the kiss that would give me back my will to live and the courage to handle the future. If one boy kissing me felt like this, what would happen if I kissed the others?

9

———

We slept until dawn, the sun breaking through my bedroom window. Oliver and I were smushed on my too-small-for-two-people bed. Especially since he was twice my size. I woke with my face in the crook of his neck.

"Sorry," I mumbled, trying to wake up.

"There are worse ways to wake up." He rubbed his face. "Damn I had some crazy dreams."

"Tell me about it. I dreamed I was being chased by all the guys at school. Justin and Eric were begging me for dates, but when I finally agreed, they just started kissing each other. Garrett lured me with roses and candy and then gave them to another girl. Jackson led me to Anderson's house where I thought I was safe, which I was until they surrounded me with white tigers and forced me into a hanging cage where I had to dance for them. I even had on thigh-high, white, go-go boots."

Oliver's eyebrows were knitted together in deep concentration.

"What?" I asked.

"Just imaging you in the thigh-highs, babe."

I pushed him playfully on the chest. "Don't be a perv."

"Can't help it." He stood and stretched, revealing the pale sliver of skin just above his waistband. His ab game was strong, as well as the

57

deep-cut V on each side, leading like an arrow. My mom would be home soon and as much as I hated it, he had to go.

She definitely wouldn't understand a boy, especially one that looked like Oliver, spending the night.

He stood at the door, giving me one last kiss goodbye. "I'll will say this though, you wear boots like that and you'll drive Jackson and Anderson crazy."

～

JACKSON WAS ONLY five minutes late. For that, I was grateful. I stood in front of the mirror, fussing with my outfit. I'd gotten the whole thing for eight dollars at the thrift store. With the help of the internet and the google words "Sexy casual party outfit," upcycling clothes may be my superpower. My mother said nothing about my outfit when I came down the stairs, but I knew what she was thinking: *When did my daughter start dressing like a tramp?*

My jeans were skin-tight, leaving little to the imagination, and lined with strategic rips and tears. I'd found a fantastic black V-neck tank top that I accentuated with a lacy, teal bra. It pushed my cleavage upward while flowing near my waist. My boobs looked pretty freaking fantastic, which was something I never thought I'd say, but since coming out of my shell, that was the first thing I realized. I have a good body. A rockin' body. Sure, I was covered in scars, but Oliver taught me they weren't something to be embarrassed about.

I was tired of hiding.

I didn't have the go-go boots from my dream but my black booties went perfectly with the outfit.

Unfortunately, my mother didn't agree with my outfit choice.

"You're not seriously going in that, are you?"

"What?" I said, finger-combing my hair. "It's not a big deal."

"Not a big deal? If you have one slip your nipples will fall out!"

"Mom!" I rolled my eyes. "I'm not showing my nipples."

"Yet."

So here was the problem with my mom. For my mom. She wasn't a bad parent...just not around. She was flighty and busy and the bad shit that went down between her and my dad exhausted her. And other than my dark moments I was a pretty good kid. I was easy to ignore. So her sudden interest didn't mean that much to me.

I had no interest in her approval.

Jackson drove up, his car loud on the wet street. I ran to the door, hoping to catch him before he came inside.

"Heaven Reeves, you let the boy come to the door," my mother said, appearing next to me. I cringed as she peeked out the window. "Boys, that is. You let them come to you, not the other way around."

I felt my eyes widen. "Boys?"

I pushed my mother out of the way and stole a look. Sure enough, Jackson was walking up to the front door and there was another person behind him. A person with messy hair and a determined sour disposition.

I dropped the curtain. "Holy shit."

"Heaven! Language." My mother was still standing there. Why was she still standing there?

"Sorry, Mom. I just didn't expect them both to come."

There was no time for me to prepare for this situation. The heavy tread of their shoes announced their arrival on the front porch. They were here, and apparently my date had turned into a double.

"Mom, go, now." I urged. She sighed, but reluctantly left anyway, giving us some space.

They knocked. I answered. Jackson smiled. Anderson frowned. I tried to look anywhere but their eyes. It was awkward. The two boys hulked in the doorway, Anderson a step behind Jackson. Jackson was taller, although you couldn't tell since Anderson had that crazy big hair and wide, broad shoulders. He was adorable. They were both adorable. Shit. I was staring and things were getting so, so uncomfortable.

"I thought Anderson may want to ride with us?" Jackson said breaking up the horribleness. "You know, conserve energy and all that."

I doubted that. "Yeah, sounds great."

Jackson's slate gray eyes took me in, starting with the boots, ending with my boobs. My cheeks burned from the obvious attention. "You look fantastic, Heaven."

"Thank you." I took in his fitted jeans and untucked button-down. His gray shirt that matched his eyes. Anderson's was white, which brought out the pure green in his eyes. They both looked so incredibly good, and a waft of their incredible scent struck me and my knees wobbled. "You look handsome too." I peeked around Jackson, "You too, Anderson."

Anderson looked surprised at my compliment and Jackson elbowed him in the ribs, hissing in his direction. His green eyes snapped to mine and a small, lopsided grin appeared on his face. "Thanks."

All it took was one genuine smile and I was a goner.

I grabbed my coat and walked to the car. Anderson drove, of course, the little control freak I suspected him to be. His driving made things weird. Are we going with the assumption that I'm still on a date with Jackson? Or that this was no longer a date of any kind? Should I sit in the back? What if Jackson offers me the front? If I could have bitch-slapped myself, I would've. My nerves were getting the best of me.

Thank goodness for Jackson, cool as always, he made the decision for us. He opened the door and directed me to the back, next to him. Anderson rode solo in the front—probably exactly how he wanted it.

Peter's house wasn't far (was anything in this podunk town?), but Jackson talked the whole way. To my relief he didn't bring up the stuff that happened with Oliver and the way he found me the night before. Maybe he didn't know. Did these boys keep secrets from one another?

Do they even know we kissed?

I tried to focus my attention anywhere but Anderson, but it was hard when I kept meeting his eyes in the rearview mirror. I was still hurt and pissed about the whore comment from before and it seemed pretty clear he wasn't offering an apology. For all the negative energy coming from the front of the car, Jackson did his best to make things easy. Our knees were forced into contact by the tight fit in the back of the car, and more than once he covered my hand with his own. It was warm and weird and nice, and I had no idea what I was doing.

The party was in full swing by the time we arrived. A tinge of anxiety filled my chest and I stuck to Jackson's side. We were in unfamiliar territory. The only parties I went to were down at the beach with Justin and the boys. They usually had bonfires and beer. I imagined this wouldn't be much different. Except it was with people I hated and maybe one that was stalking me. Was my stalker here?

"Look," Jackson said, pulling me aside. "You look fucking amazing in that outfit. Like so, so hot. The flies? They're going to be on you like honey. Don't stray from one of us, got it?"

I nodded, loving his protective side.

"Wait here," Jackson said once we entered the crowded, noisy house. He left me and Anderson as he disappeared into the crowd. My anxiety creeped. There was only one person that could offer support but Anderson looked as uncomfortable as I felt. Not just uncomfortable, that uneasy, hostile expression he wore so often shadowed his pretty face.

"You guys do this often?" I asked, trying to break the freeze. "Come to parties?"

I wasn't sure he was going to reply but he crammed his hands in his pockets and leaned back on his heels and said, "Jackson and Oliver like to come. Hayden will chill—if he's in the mood. They usually drag me along." He raised his eyebrows. "It's good to have a designated driver, right?"

Jackson pushed through the crowd and returned with three cups, and a tower of tiny paper cups.

"Here," Jackson said, handing me a full red cup of beer. "I snagged these, too." Placing several cups of what I now realized was a Jell-O shot in my hand. Oh, boy.

"To new friends," Jackson said cheesily, his slim fingers wrapped around the tiny cup, while his other snaked around my waist. "Super sexy, fantastic friends."

My cheeks burned and I slurped down my shot.

"Thought you didn't drink?" I said to Anderson.

"Yeah, sometimes you gotta do what you gotta do to get through the night, you know?" I watched Anderson take a long drink of beer and my eyes landed on the foam he quickly licked off the top of his lip. I think my own tongue copied his. The burning stare he gave me made me think he saw me do it.

Damnshitfuck.

"Yeah," I said. "I know the feeling." I gulped the second shot Jackson gave me and chugged the beer.

∼

THE THING about Jackson is that he is absolutely adorable. Dimples and a wide, easy smile made him impossible not to love. He charmed the room, but never left my side. No one said a word about me or the rumors flying around when I was with him, although there was no doubt every person in the room wondered how the heck I won the prize of sitting on his lap.

Oh right. I was easy.

"I'm going to get a drink," I said, easing away from the heat of his body. "Anyone want one?"

"I'm good," Oliver said. He'd shown up about an hour after we arrived with Hayden in tow. The Allendale Four commandeered the game table. Anderson held up his almost full cup and shook his head.

Jackson hopped out of his seat. "I'll come."

We walked through the kitchen to the back deck. Jackson filled our cups and he leaned against the wooden railing and took a long swallow, his Adam's apple bobbing beneath his perfect chin. I watched as he placed his cup on top of the rail and lit a cigarette. He watched me back.

"What?" I asked with a smile. My tongue was loosened enough from the beer to talk to him without feeling so nervous. Even though it was cold outside, I felt warm.

"You're alright, Reeves."

"I don't even know what that means?" I said, shaking my head.

"It means I like you and I'm not sure why we weren't friends before."

I choked on my drink. "Because you didn't notice me. Or, or according to your pal Hayden, because everyone thinks I'm a frigid, untouchable bitch." I eyed him warily. "Or because now that things have changed, you think you can get in my pants."

I don't know what reaction I expected, but all Jackson had for me was a smile. "That's where you're wrong. I've noticed you for a long time."

"Oh, really?"

"Yes, really. Pretty girls are usually on my radar and our school is in short supply."

The tips of my ears burned. He called me pretty. I was still sure he was trying to get in my pants, but I had to admit, his methods were pretty solid. "You don't seem like the type to hold back from asking a girl out."

"True," he said, pressing the cigarette between his lips and inhaling. "But, I had my reasons."

"Care to share?"

"Nope." He shrugged. "But for the record, I never thought you were a bitch," he smiled. "Well, not really. I kind of like bitchy girls."

"That's what I told Anderson!"

"Told him what?"

"That you and I would make a good pair since you're a dick and I'm a bitch."

His eyes were wide and he laughed. "You think I'm a dick."

Shit.

"I didn't say it." *Shit, shit.* He tilted his head in question. "Your boyfriend called you a dick."

"Oh, I see," he just shook his head and took a final, long drag.

We stood there together with new understanding. We're both attracted to one another. We both liked each other much more than expected.

"Thanks for sticking up for me at school all week. Things were getting rough."

He grunts. "That place is a cesspool run on hormones, gossip, and pain. When Oliver told me what was going on...it made me so angry. Then I saw for myself how they were treating you and it make me sick." He slid down the deck railing until we were only a hair apart. "I won't deny that I've always been attracted to you, Heaven, so yeah, when you walked in with your new look I appreciated it. We all did. But that slut-shaming shit? Fuck no. Unacceptable."

I shivered, partially from the cold but also just being this close to him. Jackson was so handsome; his face had the chiseled features of a Norse god. His hand gripped my hip and he pulled me against his body, sharing his warmth.

"Half of those kids will regretfully screw one another before the night is over. It'll be one giant nightmare of sloppy hand-jobs, sticky blow-jobs, and drunken, one-and-done, unsatisfactory fucks." His description makes me laugh because it's so freaking true. I could see Mallory rubbing her butt all over Mark on the makeshift dance floor from the deck. "What we have, babe, is a whole different level. It's not about sex. It's about understanding one another. Sure, they'll talk about the fact you walked in with two of the Allendale Four. They'll make up lies about me and you out here right now, but we know the truth about our commitment to one another."

His words slammed into my chest. Like Oliver, he seemed fully in on this relationship with me. And the crazy thing was that it had nothing to do with sex. They'd barely laid a hand on me. Oliver acted a gentleman in my bed, never taking it further than a kiss and cuddling. Had he wanted to go further? His hammering heartbeat and the noticeable tent in his pants told me yes. Same with the way Jackson's eyes swept over me. He made my skin itch. Burn. Like the only thing that would cool it off was his touch.

But that was what made these guys different. They were respect-ful. Of me and my situation. They cared. And every time they revealed themselves a little bit more to me, I fell harder.

A group of kids stumbled out to the deck, talking in loud voices and filling their plastic cups. The second they came into view, Jackson threw his arm around me protectively.

"You cold?"

"Not too much. The beer helps," I said. The warmth of his arm felt nice and I snuggled into the hard but inviting muscles of his body.

We watched the group struggle with the tap. Spencer was hanging around the edges. I couldn't help but notice him looking at me. He'd come up to me once or twice at school since the day he'd approached me in the parking lot. What a tool. He couldn't even keep the leer out of his eyes and I heard the low rumble of protection in Jackson's chest. Spencer turned away and eventually, they figured out the tap and filled their cups.

Once they were gone, Jackson moved back a little and said, "So what made you decide to go this route anyway? Not that I'm complaining. But is this really how you want to go down in high school history? As the easy chick? Because we can do this differently, you know."

Of course that's not what I wanted, but at the time what I wanted seemed out of reach. "It's hard being invisible, Jackson. It's something you wouldn't understand."

"Try me."

I took a deep breath, "I didn't start this for attention, mostly I was just angry and lashing out. But then people did start to pay attention to me in a new way. Sure, some of it was gross or even mean, but after a lifetime of solitude it was at least different. What's wrong with wanting someone to notice you?"

Jackson frowned and flicked his burnt cigarette off the deck. I looked away, trying to keep my emotions in check. I felt his cold fingers graze my chin and turn my face toward him. "People have always noticed you. The right ones. Don't ever think differently." He slid over and pulled me into a tight hug. It was nice, safe, and that ball of anxiety that I carried with me each and every day unraveled just a little bit.

I pulled back, just enough so that I could see his face. He looked down at me, eyes glued to mine. Jackson was so close I could feel the warmth of his breath on my lips. His tongue darted out and I couldn't help but stare at it. Him.

Everything around us fell away. The party. The music. The prying eyes. Jackson's hand pressed urgently against my back. I pushed up on my toes, not wanting to wait a moment longer.

"Are you sure?" he said, eyes darting behind me.

"They want a show, let's give it to them." But I knew he was aware this wasn't about them. It was about us.

"I thought you'd never say that." He smiled with a lazy, sexy grin.

He planted his mouth on mine and a jolt ran between us. Pure chemistry. I slammed into him, pinning him against the porch rail, and his cold fingers slipped beneath my coat to the warmth of my belly. I jerked, laughing at the sensation, but he didn't let my lips leave his. His tongue tasted like beer. His body felt like paradise and the longer we went and the more intense it became, I truly have no freaking clue why I waited so long.

10

———

Things I remember from that night:

- Lime green Jell-O shots made with vodka.
- Sitting close to Jackson on the back porch in a big, cushioned swing the size of a couch.
- Jackson's arm around my shoulder.
- Noticing he smelled like laundry detergent and that special boy scent. I may have sniffed him.
- Anderson's smile.
- Oliver re-enacting a scene from some play from the third grade where he played a carp.
- Feeling dizzy and needing to use the bathroom.

I wobbled when I stood, swaying just a bit. I felt Jackson's hand steady on my back. Ever since we kissed he hadn't stopped touching me. I kinda hoped he never would.

Anderson, who came outside a few minutes before, seemed intent to burn a hole in our flesh with his intense, disapproving glare.

"You okay?" Jackson asked.

I smiled. It felt funny and real but not real, since I was drunk. "Yeah, I'll be back in a minute."

"I can go with you," he said.

"I think I can handle a trip to the girls' room on my own, but thanks." I leaned over. "Anyway, I think your boyfriend wants a little time alone with you."

He glanced at Anderson and grimaced but gave me an understanding nod. Oliver was good with the situation. So good that when he spotted us from the game table kissing he gave us a double thumbs-up. Hayden? I hadn't seen him in over an hour. He was most likely camped out in front of the huge TV watching the football game. Who knew? But Anderson? He didn't like what was going on with me and the others. He hadn't said so, but his death glares made his feelings clear.

I stood and tried to ignore the way the porch swam around me. Just like I ignored the way everyone at the party kept looking at us. I hated the eyes on me but I loved the way it felt being so public with Jackson. In some ways it was like we'd transcended these people.

I had already been to the bathroom a couple of times so I knew it was in the back of the house. I just had to navigate through the dining room (beer pong), the kitchen (Quarters), down the hallway (groping couples) to the bathroom next to the laundry room. The door was locked when I finally made it there, so I leaned against the wall to wait. Leaned may be an exaggeration. Slid to the floor into a pile may be more appropriate.

The bathroom door opened and I considered going in, but I wasn't exactly sure how to get off the floor. Moving seemed really hard.

"You need some help?"

I looked up and saw Spencer standing over me. Gross. "No."

He quirked an eyebrow and watched me try to manipulate my legs bound in repressively tight pants into a standing position. The heels didn't help.

I sighed and reconsidered.

"Dammit. Yes, can I get some help, please?" I stretched an arm out and he tugged me up.

"You're wasted."

"No shit."

He looked around. He looked a little drunk, too. His hazel eyes were a little unfocused and his normally pale cheeks were red. "Where's Hall?"

"Outside. With his boyfriend."

He laughed, tossing his head back. "Those two. One day they'll come out."

"Tell me about it," I said, loving how close those guys were. "Okay, I gotta use the bathroom so..." I walked into the tiny room, closing the door behind me. Spencer was okay. A little dumb, definitely pretty. He used to have long, stringy hair that he cut off over the summer. That simple move increased his looks exponentially.

I took a minute in the bathroom, smoothing my hair, adjusting the neck of my shirt to maximum reveal. May as well give Jackson a good view since he was being such the doting boyfriend tonight. When I opened the door, I jumped in surprised to find Spencer waiting for me when I walked out.

He smiled and I ignored him and moved past.

"Hey wait," he said and pulled me to the side. His hand felt weird and clammy. I stumbled behind him, still a little wobbly on my feet. He led us further down the dark hall. "So how long is this thing with Jackson gonna go on?"

Of course. He still believed the rumors. I shook my head. "However long is none of your business, that's for sure."

"Don't be like that." He pressed a hand against the wall next to my head and leaned in. Hayden pulled the same move a few days before in the garden. The way he did it was sexy. Spencer, on the other hand...I felt the prickle of anxiety travel up my spine. "Maybe when you're done with him you can spend some time with me."

Oh god. Just. No. "I really don't think so, Spencer, but thanks for the offer."

"Whatever, Heaven, it's not like you have standards. You've got quite the trail of discards already. Blackwood melted the ice queen. I'd just be happy to be next on the list. You won't regret it."

Prick. "Are you kidding?"

He smirked. "Do I look like I'm kidding?" He moved his other hand to my hip and dragged me close. I felt his erection in his pants. Bile rose in my throat and panic stole my voice. "You're really pretty hot. Peel away the hoodie and wow, smokin' hot body. I never knew you were packin' all that and now I want to see the rest of it."

I forced my vocal cords to comply. "Shut up."

Did he really think those were compliments? That girls wanted to hear his skeevy lines? Feel his disgusting boner? I cringed while his eyes roamed over my body. I gather the courage to knee him in the junk when someone came and pushed him aside. Thank god. I really didn't want to see him cry over his broken balls.

"Beat it." The voice came from the shadows.

Spencer hesitated, his jaw tensing. "Dude, mind your own fucking business."

For the briefest of moments, I thought maybe the guy would listen. He would walk and I'd be left alone with this pervert. But a pale hand came down on Spencer's shoulder and I blinked, recognizing those hands from countless days of passing notes and sharing assignments.

"Heaven is my fucking business."

Spencer turned around, ready to fight, but he flinched, jerking his shoulder free. He'd just been caught hitting on a girl that came to the party with another guy, by that guy's angry but completely loyal best friend. That's who saved me.

Anderson Thompson.

"She's not worth it anyway," he muttered, pushing past Anderson. His words hit me like a slap and I watched dumbly as Anderson shoved him down the hall.

"Touch her again and I'll break your fucking hands."

Spencer flipped him off and vanished into the party.

The panic attack which had been rising since Spencer cornered me consumed me like a wave. Tears sprang to my eyes. Stupid. Fucking. Anxiety-driven tears. I wiped them with my sleeve and glanced away, unable to face Anderson, who had just done something incredibly brave and charming and made me feel mushy inside, but then I remembered something. He called me a whore. He'd been a dick all night. How dare he play the knight in shining armor?

"I didn't really need your help, Thompson." Which maybe would have been a convincing statement if I had not slurred my words in the process.

He snorted. "Of course not. I can't image you would ever get in a situation you couldn't get out of."

"Shut up."

"No," he replied quietly. "I won't."

I quirked an eyebrow, or I tried to, anyway. My face was suddenly feeling numb. I hated him for being so right and so wrong at the same time. "You think you know me," I said, "but you don't."

We stared at one another. Dangerous words hung on the tip of my loosened tongue, daring to spill out. I wanted to ask him why he was angry with me all the time. Why he couldn't just accept me like the others. Why so hot and cold?

Before I could speak he said, "I think you're better than all this."

"You think I'm a whore. You think I'm trash."

"No." He shook his head and stepped away from his side of the hallway, closer to where I stood. "I don't."

"You don't think I'm good enough for your friends, especially Jackson. You think I'm cheap and slutty and dress like a hooker." I couldn't stop. The verbal filter I'd tried so hard to keep on had loosened with eight shots of vodka-infused Jell-O.

"You have no idea what I think." His words were quiet. Daring. And because I was drunk, I was willing to push this a little more.

"You never tell me," I challenged, strong and forceful, but a wave of nausea passed over me and I tried to steady myself against the wall.

Anderson moved his arms to stabilize me because my legs were no longer working. "You okay?"

"I'm tired."

He laughed. "I know. I think it's time to go home." He was using his body to keep me upright, pressing me against the wall. It felt really good to be so close to him.

I reached out and brushed my fingers through his hair. Jesus, I've wanted to do that forever. I pushed the long strands to the side and caught a glimpse of his apple-green eyes. My hand moved on its own, touching the scratchy stubble of his cheek. "Why do you hate me?"

"I don't hate you, Reeves."

"Yes, you do."

We stared at one another for a long moment.

"Come on, let's go find Jackson." He moved his arm around my waist. I sunk into him for support and pressed my cheek in his chest. His T-shirt was so soft. I wanted to crawl into it and just sleep.

"I drank too much."

"I think you did."

"You smell good."

His chest vibrated with laughter. "Thanks."

Anderson dragged me down the hallway. I could hear Jackson's booming laugh in the kitchen, followed by Oliver's. I saw Jennifer whispering to Spencer and Spencer watching us. Amber and Benjamin were making out on a chair in the living room, oblivious to everything around them. Eric ran by with a towel on his back pinned like a cape and the music was so, so loud. Everything was loud and fuzzy and...

Anderson stopped and looked down at me with eyes as green and wobbly as lime Jell-O and lips way too pretty for a boy.

"Heaven?" His voice was a million miles away. Were we under water? "I really don't hate you."

The way he said it was sweet. And earnest. And totally genuine. Which was perfect. There was really only one thing I could do in a situation like this.

I was going to do it. I was going to tell him how I felt, except the instant I opened my mouth all the nerves and alcohol and drama came up in one swift wave.

I puked.

All over Anderson Thompson's feet.

11

THINGS I DON'T REMEMBER FROM THAT NIGHT (BUT WERE RELAYED TO me the next morning by Oliver):

- Puking all over the front porch of the house.
- Threatening to punch Spencer in the face (and taking a swing and missing)
- Jackson carrying me to the car.
- Anderson washing his shoes off with a hose.
- Anderson pulling the car over so I could puke again and falling out of the still-moving car on my face.
- Asking Anderson if he knew his eyes were the same color as lime Jell-O. (No, apparently he did not know this.)
- Oliver and Jackson sneaking me up to my room so my mom didn't catch me.

"I did not fall out of the car."

"Yes, you did."

"No."

"Yes." Oliver came back over around noon to check on me after my mom left for work. He found me moaning on the bed, eyes closed, willing myself not to get sick again. I watched as he got off the bed, closed my open laptop and plucked a hand mirror off my dresser. I grimaced when he held it up. Ouch. Road rash.

I gently touched the side of my face, feeling the scrape. "Why did you let me do that?"

He rolled his eyes. "Take this." He handed me a bottle of water and some pills. I swallowed both and prayed that neither came back up.

"Well, that was embarrassing." I looked for Oliver to agree but he had a weird expression on his face. "What?'

"Anything else?"

"Not that I saw, but really once you started hurling I tried to get out of the way."

"Are you sure?" Oliver looked wary. I thought about my night. Talking to Jackson, swinging on the porch, going to the bathroom, Spencer, Anderson, puke. It was all there; fuzzy, but there.

"Yeah, babe, I promise."

I raised an eyebrow. I liked it when he called me babe.

I leaned against the headboard. "Tell me what else I missed after I puked on Anderson's shoes. Exactly how mad was he?"

"He wasn't that mad. Promise."

That didn't seem right. "You sure?"

"Nope. Not even when you puked on his car."

"I didn't." Oh my god. Horrified.

"You did. All over the side."

I started laughing because, blech, how gross. "Good thing he already hates me."

"Babe, no one hates you. Not even Anderson. Actually, he felt pretty awful. He had no idea how sick you were." He watched me carefully. "He told me about Spencer. In the hallway."

The overall memory was pretty fuzzy but the fear I felt with Spencer and Anderson's protective nature wasn't something I'd forgotten. "He defended me. I was pretty surprised, considering how he feels about me."

"That's not all he did," he muttered.

"What?"

"Nothing. You need to take it easy."

"I got drunk, Oliver, I'm not sick." I sat up and grabbed his hand, threading my fingers through his. "What did you mean?"

"Well," he said, watching me carefully, "after cleaning off his shoes and dropping you off, Anderson went back to the party to pick up Hayden, who got left in the shuffle. Spencer was on the porch, bragging about kissing you outside the hallway."

My hand moved to my mouth. "He didn't."

He shook his head. "He did, because he's a grade-A douchebag, but don't worry. He won't bother you again."

"Okay," I said, feeling something was missing. "Why won't he bother me again?"

Oliver's blue eyes hold mine and his jaw tics. "Because Anderson and Hayden kicked his ass."

"What? Are they okay?"

He snorted. "Of course they're okay. Spencer is the one in pain this morning. Well, other than you, obviously."

"Oliver! You guys can't go around beating up guys who flirt with me."

He stopped cold. "That wasn't flirting, Heaven. He was harassing you. Don't mix the two up."

I knew he was right but I still felt weird about it. I was knowingly using my body to get attention but then got upset when someone I hated noticed? Wasn't that hypocritical? My head was so confused, not to mention pounding from the hangover. I leaned into his shoulder and he wrapped his strong arms around me.

"Thanks for having my back all the time. I don't mean to be so high maintenance."

He lifted my chin and kissed me on the lips, soft and sweet. It made me think of the passionate kiss I shared with Jackson the night before. These boys are so close yet so different and I'm lucky they opened their circle for me to join.

"You feeling up to going out later?"

I groaned. "Will it require me doing much more than sitting around, eating French fries, and drinking a diet Coke?"

He laughed and shook his head. "Interestingly enough, those are the only three things it does require."

"Good, then I'm free." I smiled, wondering what he had in store.

THREE HOURS LATER, I'm bundled in a warm winter coat, fur-lined boots, and sitting on the cold metal bleachers at the school soccer field. A red and black plaid blanket is spread over me, Jackson, and Oliver. My empty bag of fries and the remains of my large Coke sat a few feet away. I felt better. Well, enough not to barf all over the place anymore.

Hayden had a game and it was tradition for the guys to go support him. This was reciprocated across all their activities and now that they'd welcomed me into the group, I had to add cheerleader to my new life.

To make things more interesting, Allendale was playing their biggest rival, Oceanside. I recognized more than a few faces on the field. Just after halftime, Allendale was down by one and the energy of the crowd grew more antsy by the minute. A few spectators near the field shouted at the referee.

"What are they so mad about?" I asked.

"Oceanside should be winning by a much bigger score," Jackson said from my left. His leg was pressed against mine, his hand on my thigh. Oliver sat on the other side but held my freezing hand beneath the blanket. It was nearly impossible to get cold near these two. "But Hayden is killing it out there. Go Hayden! Keep it up!"

I'd never been a huge soccer fan, but up in those bleachers there was no way to keep my eyes off of Hayden. He played goalie; something I only vaguely understood meant keeping the ball out of the goal. He occupied the goal with physical dominance; his body the perfect mixture of height, size, and agility. Oceanside's forwards pummeled him with shots, over and over, and he stopped each and every one.

"He's really good, isn't he?" I asked, watching him fly through the air, catch a fast-moving ball and land hard on the ground.

"Amazing," Oliver said. "Everyone thought he was going to stick with football but he's just too good. Scouts have been coming to games for a while."

Hayden shouted to his teammates, taking command of the field.

He pulled his arm back and hurled the ball down the sideline, channeling it directly to our forward, Garrett, who made a break toward the opposite end of the field. Garret expertly handled the ball, crossing it over to the other forward, Parker Haynes, who tapped it in the goal like it was the easiest thing ever.

"Goooooooooaaaaaaalllllllll!" Both Oliver and Jackson stood up, yanking me with them to cheer for the team. I'm embraced in celebratory hugs, wondering why I never came to these games before. Oh wait, I didn't have two amazing guys to keep me warm, that's why.

"I can't believe Anderson is missing this," Oliver said.

"Where is he?" I asked without thinking. Jackson's annoyed look was all I needed to know. He wasn't here because of me. "Oh right."

"Babe, please understand this is not about you. It's about him and his stubborn, pain-in-the-ass self. He's being an idiot."

"But he should be here for his friend."

Oliver shook his head. "Trust me, Hayden would much rather you be here than Anderson." I doubted that but I asked why anyway. "Look, Hayden is an amazing player. Like I said, scouts have been following him around for months, but this?" he said pointing to the field. "He's not performing like an Olympic gold medalist for the scouts. That's all for you."

My eyes darted to the field where Hayden stood at the end of the field, completely in control. "Me?"

"He's a fucking show-off," Jackson laughed, squeezing my leg under the blanket.

"And you're definitely good luck," Oliver agreed. They both have an eye on the field and forget me once the ball is back in play. Oceanside gets a breakaway; one forward barreling down on the field with the ball. There's nothing between him and Hayden, all of the defenders chasing him down but there's no way, not a chance they'll catch him.

Hayden shifted, bending his knees to get in position, eyes narrowed in full concentration. If he heard the crowd screaming, cheering, panicking, I'd never know it. He waited...knee bouncing, hands raised until the forward shot the ball with lightning speed at the net. Hayden moved in time, diving to the ball. I covered my mouth, there was no way he could stop it. Too low, too fast, too accurate. Jackson gripped my leg so hard I thought it would bruise and I watched, fascinated when Hayden twisted his body an inch and elongated his fingers, making contact with the bare edge of the ball.

That was all he needed—all it took—to nudge the ball off course. It spun, careening off the field and Hayden slid across the field, through the mud and crashing into the goal post.

"Oh my god," I shouted, unable to keep my eyes off of him. He didn't move. Oliver and Jackson stopped breathing. His teammates ran over, falling to their knees. It took everything I had in me not to run over, too.

A second passed. Then another, and just when I thought I'd crawl out of my skin, Hayden sat up, face covered in dirt, and smiled in our direction, both thumbs up. The crowd reacted like animals, screaming and stomping on the bleachers.

"That was amazing," I said, my voice dwarfed by the crowd.

"That," Oliver said, tugging me into a hug, "was Hayden Perkins. And the only thing you ever need to know is to never, ever underestimate him."

As an introvert, I never dreamed my life could change this much. I took one risk, helping a friend with a stupid favor, and although it turned my life upside down in some shitty ways, it also opened me up to so much more. I no longer sat alone at lunch. I had people to talk to in the hall. A ride to school. Invited to parties, and now I stood on the bleachers cheering on the school's best athlete surrounded by two amazing guys.

After his amazing save and terrifying fall, Hayden got back up and the team managed to pull a devastating upset, scoring in the last minute to win the game. My eyes bulged watching him run down the field, stripping off his shirt and piling on his teammates to celebrate their victory. The lines of his body were god-like; muscular and lean. My heart skipped a beat when he turned and looked up at us, taking off at a run up the stadium steps before attacking his best friends. I stood awkwardly on the side, hands shoved in my big coat, watching with a smile. They were adorable.

And Hayden? Absolutely gorgeous.

If I thought I'd be left out of the excitement I was wrong, because a moment later, Hayden released Jackson and lunged for me.

"Congratulations," I told him, feeling the pounding of his bare chest. His skin was still overheated and he smelled like sweat, dirt, and victory. I inhaled, intoxicated.

"Thanks for coming," he said with a quiet smile. "It means a lot."

The statement was surreal. There was a full stadium of fans there just to watch Hayden. A dozen girls hovering around to congratulate him. Scouts. Coaches. The other team.

But he didn't notice them. His eyes were glued to mine and his hands clung to my back and the same sort of shift that had taken place between me and Oliver in my bedroom and me and Jackson at the party took place on the metal bleachers.

After a shower and change, Oliver drove us in his Mustang across town to Dad's Diner because they were "starving," and needed fuel. With Hayden's fingers linked with mine, he led me to their favorite booth, the circular one in the corner, and we piled in.

Anderson's absence was noted. He was texted. He was cursed. Then it was decided he was a loser for not coming and the food arrived at the table and he was forgotten, at least for the moment.

Already full on fries and coke, I only got a piece of pie, but the boys? They made up for my lack of eating with massive plates of hamburgers, fries, pies, and ice cream. They laughed and joked with one another, threw fries, guzzled drinks, and celebrated Hayden's win.

Despite my pleasure of simply being with them, I couldn't help but feel hyper-aware that from the outside it looked like the price for my inclusion in this group was my body. The only consolation was that I knew the truth. They'd asked me for nothing. And that was sexier than any pick-up line tossed at me over the past few weeks.

"There's no way you can beat me," Oliver said, rolling his eyes.

Jackson scoffed. "Dude, classic Ms. Pac-Man is my jam."

"Your jam?"

"Yeah, my jam. Don't mock my choice of lingo—or my favorite game."

Oliver eyed him. "I'll bet you a milkshake I can beat your high score."

Jackson shook his head. "Foolish bet, my friend."

I stared at the two of them in disbelief. I finally got a seat at the exclusive table of the Allendale Four and this was the topic of conversation. Ms. Pac-Man? I glanced at Hayden and he smiled at their nonsense and shrugged.

Oliver stood, stretching and flexing his fingers. "Excuse me, Heaven, I've got a bet to settle."

"Don't worry, babe," Jackson said, kissing me on the cheek and then standing himself. "This won't take long."

The two moved to the back of the diner, toward the video games, roughhousing along the way. At this point the diner was basically empty, just the cook and waitress working behind the counter.

I watched the boys go and raised an eyebrow. "This happen often?"

Hayden rubbed his face. "Every freaking time."

He took the opportunity to slide a little closer and threw an arm over my shoulder. He looked at my plate. "How's the pie?"

"Good." I licked my fork. "Want to try a bite?"

"I've been waiting for you to ask."

The implication in his voice was heavy, flirty, and having the full weight of Hayden's attention was a lot to handle. With the others there was something light—even the years-long jabs between Anderson and I—but Hayden, he was different. I felt it in my soul.

I scooped up a heaping forkful of cherry and crust and lifted it to his mouth. It hovered near his pink lips, which were twisted in a sexy smirk until he opened up.

I always, *always*, thought the whole feeding someone thing was lame. In movies, commercials, books...but holy shit, watching Hayden slowly chew while a small piece of flakey crust stuck to his bottom lip, did. Things. To. Me.

"Uh..." I started, at a complete loss for real words. I swallowed and pointed to his mouth. "You, uh..."

He touched his lip, then flicks his tongue out, swiping at the crust. It didn't budge, stuck with the gooey sugar of the filling. "Got it?" he asked, his eyes twinkling.

"Well..." I leaned forward and his hand slid down around my waist. My eyes were zeroed in on his mouth, the sugar, the soft pink of his lips. The world fell away from us; the diner, the waiter, the sound of the video games in the back, and I fell into him, kissing the crust off his lip.

He reacted instantly, moving his hands to my face. I tasted the sugar on his mouth, the hunger of more basic, primal desires. My heart pounded with excitement—exhilaration—I was kissing Hayden Perkins and damn, he was kissing me back.

There was no doubt he liked it. That he liked me and with the pie, and the game, and the others forgotten, Hayden and I slowly, seductively, got to know one another a little better.

12

Monday started with a burst of Fakestagram notifications followed by a flurry of new photos. This time they had a theme. Heaven dresses like a tramp.

The first photo had Ben and me by my locker, talking, and it would have looked normal except for my impressive cleavage, accentuated by the angle of the camera. Across the bottom was the hashtag, #desperate and #tramp.

More followed; close-ups of my legs, my ass, my lips.

The intimacy gave me the chills, but it didn't make me back off my resolve. This attitude was their problem, not mine, and I wouldn't let them push me into hiding.

Not again.

I could admit it. Even though I'd moved past the need to prove something to the school, I liked this new look. I liked the way my boys' eyes lit up when I walked down the hall. They liked me with puke in my hair or hungover at a soccer game wrapped in a heavy coat. They definitely approved when I was dressed to the nines.

Poor Ben though, his eyes were glued to the swell of my breasts like a deer in headlights. These things were getting me into all kinds of trouble.

It was old news between me and Amber but that didn't stop her from giving me the stink eye on my way into school, or Jennifer from calling me names in the hall. I could tell Jackson was getting pissed but I told him to roll with it. I did. I had bigger issues to deal with than jealous girls—the online bullying. It scared me. He threw a stiff arm around my shoulder and a possessive glare set in his eyes. It was enough to make people keep their distance.

"Who do you think is taking and posting these pictures?" he asked, steering me toward class.

I shook my head. "I don't know. It could be anyone around here. I'm not really sure what the point is. It's not like I'm hiding anything."

In Chemistry, seeing Anderson for the first time since the party prompted me to slide a piece of paper across our work table to him.

He held the paper between two very pretty fingers without opening it. "What's this?"

"Just read it."

"Why?"

"Oh my god. Just. Read. It." He didn't look convinced. Maybe he thought there was puke on it. I ground my teeth and said, "Please."

He opened it and laid it flat on the table. I closed my eyes and dropped my head into my arms.

Dear Anderson,

I apologize for puking on your shoes.

And your car.

And anywhere else you may have had the unfortunate opportunity to see.

Heaven

I heard the crinkle of the paper as he refolded it and waited, scared to look up.

"Reeves."

"What?" My words were muffled because I was still face down on the table.

"I accept your apology."

I opened an eye and looked at him. His expression was clear. He even had a bit of a smile on his pretty little mouth. "Really?"

"Yes."

I sighed in relief. "Good."

He seemed awfully amused by my humiliation, but I let it slide due to the circumstances.

"I'm sorry you got so sick."

"Ugh, me too."

Then he reached a finger out to touch my cheek. "Ouch."

I rolled my eyes. At myself, of course, because of the flutter rolling around in my stomach from his finger on my skin was enough to rock me like an earthquake. "Apparently, I fell out of the car."

"I tried to stop. You opened the door before I pulled all the way over."

"I heard. I don't really remember much."

A tiny smile tugged at his lips. "For what it's worth, I'm kind of happy you puked all over my feet."

I sat up and stared at him. "Umm...what?"

He ran a hand through his hair and grimaced. "Before I found you back by the bathroom with Spencer, Jennifer had been trying to get me to give her a ride home. You scared her off."

"Vomit shoes or Jennifer Stevens." I made a motion between my hands like I was weighing the options. "Vomit shoes every time."

"No other option, really," he laughed and opened his book as Mr. Baker started class. And like that, Anderson and I were back on solid(ish) ground. I wanted to thank him for more than just the apology. For defending me with Spencer. For going back and beating him up, but I didn't want to blow the small amount of progress we'd made. Who knew puking on the guy you liked could bring you closer? I suspected it would only work with one guy. A freak like Anderson Thompson.

∽

After my note of apology and Anderson's acceptance, things were generally less tense. I couldn't deny, though, that there was a block of sorts between us, and as time passed I realized exactly what was causing the awkwardness.

The Allendale Four. Or three.

Post-vomitous-party, my life changed. My social life, that is. Jackson, Oliver, and Hayden stuck close to me at school, meeting me at my car, hovering at my locker, sitting next to me at lunch. It was like we were dating...but not. Not that I had a lot of experience, but our relationship seemed to be crossing over into some kind of unknown territory. Can one girl date three guys? A month ago, I would have said no. But now? Things were getting interesting, even if one of the members of the circle had an attitude problem.

The rest of the school watched us closely but kept their mouths shut. Everyone knew what happened to Spencer at the party. They saw his busted lip and the way he kept his eyes diverted anytime any of us were around. But that didn't stop the rumors from flying or the anonymous Fakestagram page from posting photos of me non-stop. I pretended like I didn't care about the harassment but the boys knew. They saw the dark rings under my eyes and more than once Oliver checked my arms for new cuts. It made me feel stupid. And incredibly, overwhelmingly, loved.

Anxiety could be so conflicting and complicated.

"Can I ask you two something?" Oliver and Jackson are sitting with me one day at lunch. We were sitting in a tight cluster, alone for a minute. Hayden was in study hall and Anderson was buying a Coke out of the machine across the cafeteria. He'd slung his leather jacket on the chair across from us, holding his spot. Jackson had piles of food in front of him and I watched with fascination as he crammed four Oreos in his mouth at once.

"Sure?" He mumbled around all the chocolate.

Oliver nodded through a bite of sandwich.

"This," I said, gesturing between us. "What exactly does this mean to you? I've kissed you both and Hayden. You all seem okay with it, well most of you, at least." I glanced over my shoulder at Anderson, who was fighting with the machine. "Swallow before you answer, please."

Jackson chewed for a minute, swallowed, and took a giant gulp of his drink. His Adam's apple bobbed in response. I couldn't decide if I should be disturbed or turned on by his behavior. His eyes darted quickly to Oliver's but his following question was to me, "Do you really not know?"

"No." I shook my head. "I really don't. Is this something you've done before?"

"You know we don't let people into the group, Heaven. You're the first."

I scoffed. "Don't pretend like *I'm* your first. You know your first…"

Jackson reached over and takes my hand under the table. "You're the first where it matters, babe."

"But the sharing. Is it weird?"

"We've always shared everything, which is why we've never dated much. Girls got in the way of our friendship, but you…you're the perfect fit," Oliver explains.

My eyes flicked to Anderson, who was still in some sort of struggle with the soda machine. He was jabbing the buttons to no avail, running one hand through his hair, making it more and more feral with agitation. He was so pretty. "But what about…"

"He'll come around. I told you that."

"And Hayden?" They'd walked in on us after declaring their Ms. Pac-Man tournament a tie. Neither seemed phased by our red lips and flushed faces.

Now, they shared another look and laughed. Jackson shook his head and took another bite of cookie. "Don't worry about Hayden. He's all in. Honestly, this was all his idea."

I frowned. "Really?"

"There was a universal attraction to you, Heaven, but nothing splits us apart. Nothing. So coming to an agreement was the only solution," Jackson said.

"I'm telling you, we're in this together. Despite one of us being a bit of a baby." Oliver's eyes darted over my shoulder and he popped one of Jackson's cookies into his mouth. His big hand squeezed my knee under the table, sending a jolt of electricity up my leg.

When Anderson reached the table, he pulled his chair out with a loud scrape across the linoleum floor. He placed his bottle of Coke on the table and then a second one in front of me. "The machine gave me two."

"Umm, thanks."

"No big." He took out his own lunch, dumping it out of his bag and on the table in the same fashion Jackson had. He fished out a sandwich and ate half of it in one bite. "We need to figure out when to meet for our project."

Mr. Baker had announced a joint project due in two weeks during our last class. The kind of project that required meeting outside of school with your partner. There was definitely an awkward moment between the two of us during class when we realized we'd have to actually spend time together—alone.

"We can meet at my house," I offered.

His eyes flashed around the table. "Maybe the library?"

"The library."

He wasn't looking at me. His eyes were focused on opening a package of chips. "It's...easier."

Right. Because I was a skank who he didn't want to be left alone with. I may sully his reputation. I'd probably jump him the minute he came to my house, even though I was involved with his best friends. Okay, maybe not the best use of mental sarcasm.

I tried to swallow my anger, but I knew my expression betrayed me. Jackson must have seen it, too, because his protective hand was on my back immediately. "I've got some studying to do also. We can meet Anderson at the library together."

Anderson nodded and I agreed, but I felt sick. I thought we had made progress. I thought we were friends. He told me he didn't think of me that way—like a whore—but he obviously didn't trust me. Appropriately, his head was still down, refusing to meet my eye. He knew he was an ass. Jackson and Oliver knew it, too, and without offering an excuse, I gathered my things and left the table.

13

EVEN WITH ANDERSON ACTING LIKE A WEIRDO, I DECIDED I WASN'T going to make a big deal about doing this assignment. I'd take the high road. Of course, this attitude was within reason, my reason, and I had definite plans to make him squirm.

My version of the high road included my signature outfits that, despite his protests, I knew he liked. Over the course of a week during our after-school library meetings, I managed to flash more of my legs, ass, and chest than anyone would possibly want to see. My methods were fair, though, because every day Jackson and Anderson arrived freshly showered, smelling like soap and whatever delicious-smelling cologne they slathered on their bodies that made me insane. Have you ever smelled a squeaky-clean boy? It was all I could do not to shove my face in both of their chests and huff the two of them in the middle of the public library.

So right. Fair play.

Each day, Jackson left for his own corner to "study". I was pretty sure he was just watching videos on his phone. I thought Anderson would relax with Jackson around to chaperone our study dates, but he didn't. Our meetings were filled with a heightened tension. At first, I thought it was just his general dumbassery and hostile demeanor, but as the days progressed I realized it was something else.

There was an internal struggle going on with him, and as much as he hated it, the reason became perfectly clear: Anderson Thompson wanted me.

This whole time I thought he hated me. I thought I repulsed him. I was totally fucking wrong.

I knew this because of the way he stared at me when I wasn't looking. I knew because of the way he glanced at the ignorant figure of his best friend with guilt in his eyes. I knew because he came up with fake reasons to touch me, or get close to me, or move near me. I knew because every time he did one of these things he grimaced and frowned and refused to look at me for the next ten minutes—until he caved again. I knew, because if I learned one thing in this stupid game I was playing, it was that boys were weak at the sight of a nice set of tits and mine were spectacular.

What I didn't know was *how* he wanted me. Did he think I was a cheap and easy conquest? Could he just not keep his eyes off my rack? I wanted to ask, but I was caught in such a complicated situation with three other guys—his three best friends—that I didn't see an easy way out. So instead, I continued, pushing and pushing until one of us was forced to break.

Even though it was the weekend, we agreed to meet Sunday afternoon for the final review of our project. Jackson picked me up and I was barely in the car when I felt him surveying my outfit. I couldn't blame him. I was wearing a low-cut, black, sheer shirt that —with the assistance of a push-up bra—left either too little to the imagination or too much. The lace edge of my bra was visible at the top of my shirt. Extra revealing. Extra effect. Make no mistake, after a week of playing cat and mouse, I was going for the kill. The entire outfit was inappropriate for the library, but I had a goal to make Anderson melt into a puddle when he saw me, and if Jackson's response was any indication, this would be easy to accomplish.

"Why do I have the feeling you're not wearing that for me?" he asked after I buckled my seat belt. I tried to ignore his blue eyes bulging out at my chest. His jaw dropped too.

I leaned over and kissed him, feeling the quick sweep of his tongue. His hand grazed the underside of my breast and I felt the shock of arousal throughout my entire body. He smiled lazily when we parted.

"It's not that I didn't wear it for you. I mean, not when you kiss me like that, but yeah, I'm still trying to get a rise out of Anderson."

Jackson's blonde eyebrows shot up. "Oh, trust me, he'll get a rise alright. He probably already jerked off three times before leaving for the library just to get through it."

"Jax!" I slapped him on the arm. I didn't want to think about Anderson doing that...well, until I *did* think about him doing that and the image was a little more enticing than I thought. "You guys really do it that much?"

He stared at me and slowly nodded his head. "You have no idea. And with you walking around like that all the time? It's increased ten-fold."

"Ohmygod."

My face burned like a bonfire but at the same time the information was flattering. These guys thought about me all the time. Even Anderson. Truth be told, I thought about them a lot more when I was alone too.

My cheeks burned hotter and I shifted in my seat, busying myself with searching in my bag for my project outline. When I looked up, he was staring at my boobs again.

"Jackson!"

"I'm serious, Heaven. Those things are lethal. You're lethal." He turned into the parking lot of the library and found a spot easily. "You're gonna kill him, you know."

I unlatched my seat belt and adjusted my shirt. We were acknowl-edging this. Good. "I know. He has it coming."

"I don't know..."

"He does. He thinks I'm trashy and obviously nothing will change his mind. I may as well make him sweat." I was being petty. Stupid. I knew it, but at the same time, so was Anderson. He was either my friend or not, and this thing between me and the guys...well they were all in or it didn't work. The judgments needed to go. "I don't expect you to side with me over him, but his little game of hot and cold is growing thin." I opened the door, stood up, and straightened my coat. I pointed to my chest. "This is payback."

Jackson closed his door and slung his backpack over his shoulder. We walked together into the building, where the instant we were inside he said, "I'll be over there," pointing to a group of comfortable chairs. "Be gentle with him, okay?"

I rolled my eyes and looked around the massive room. Finally, I spotted Anderson, busily writing into our lab journal at a table on the opposite side of the building. Turning my attention away from Jackson and onto Anderson, I took in his tight, black t-shirt, and the way it strained against the wide expanse of his shoulders. I gathered my resolve and walked over.

"Hi," I said, dropping my book bag and pulling out a chair across from him.

"Hey," he said looking around. "Where's Jackson?"

"Over there." We both looked over at him sitting with his legs propped on a coffee table, feet tapping in rhythm to whatever music played on his iPod. I glanced back at Anderson, noting the obvious frown on his face when he realized he was left alone with me. Yep. I was so making him pay.

Anderson went back to his work, absently sliding the lab report over to me. "I completed the first three questions."

"Great." I unbuttoned my coat before turning to hang it on the back of my chair. "Do you want me to work on the next three?"

"I, um, yeah, um..." I heard his pencil drop on the tabletop.

I steeled myself. I had gotten pretty comfortable with revealing my body over the last several weeks, but the look on Anderson's face was enough to make me second-guess myself. Had I actually gone too far? He was completely flummoxed. I leaned over. "Questions four through seven?"

"Um," His eyes darted from my chest back to his paper. "Yes."

"Okay," I said, arranging my books and paperwork. I made an exaggerated effort to lean on one elbow. We worked quietly for a while, only talking when we needed something from one another. Anderson was blatantly avoiding eye contact and struggling to focus on his paper—that was, until I caught him, jaw slack and staring.

"Is something wrong?" I asked innocently, twirling a piece of hair around my finger. Maybe.

He blinked. "Um...I think you may have the wrong formula for number five."

"Really?" I asked. Because I was certain I didn't.

He snatched the paper and busied himself reviewing it. "Oh, no. I guess not."

"Sure?"

He glanced over at Jackson, who was still ignoring us, like he could save Anderson from being a bumbling idiot. "Yes, I'm sure."

"Good," I said. "I'll be over in the reference section. I'm missing something for question seven." I stood and adjusted my boot on the seat. He didn't even try to not look. Anderson had reached a point of no return. He couldn't keep his eyes off my chest or ass or anything else. Too bad for him that he thought he was too good for me.

I walked away, stealing a glance before I slipped around the corner of the bookshelves and saw him drop his head to the table, taking a few deep breaths. Sucker. If he was going to make me feel like shit, then I was happy to make him feel shittier.

Ten minutes later, I found the book I wanted. I had just pulled it from the shelf when I felt him behind me. Close behind me. I froze, trying to think of my next move. Should I get on my tip-toes and reach for a high book, exposing the skin around my waist? Should I pout and act confused—damsel in distress-y?

Before I could decide, he went on the attack.

"Why are you doing this? Dressing like this?"

"Why are *you* being such a dick?" I countered, feigning nonchalance. And then I felt it. His hand was on my hip and his chest was on my back. And it was just...whatthefuck?

"What are you doing?" I asked, pulling forward, only to feel his grip tighten.

"It's not fair." He said in a low voice. He sounded angry—no, distressed. "You doing this all the time and me...just resisting."

I struggled and turned around. My face basically pressed against his chest, he was so close. When I looked up I could see a manic expression on his face. "What do you mean resisting?"

"I mean..." He looked around and his tongue darted out between his lips. "I just want..." And then he pushed my back against the hard shelf of books and kissed me. Hard. On the mouth. And because I'm a fool and have wanted him forever, I kissed him back, lacing my fingers through the short, soft hair on his neck. The kiss was desperate, needy, everything from weeks, months...no, years of pent up frustration. His hips slammed into mine and I held him there, feeling him—breathing hard, until the wave crashed and he slowed to a gentler pace. I felt his tongue touch against my own and it made my stomach burst into a million pieces. He tasted good and felt good and it was Anderson, the one just out of my reach.

When he stopped and pulled away, I kept my eyes closed because I wasn't ready for it to be over. His forehead was pressed to mine and he spoke, weird and choked. "I'm sorry. That was...wrong."

My eyes flew open and my fingers slid down his shoulders and clenched the front of his shirt. "No, it wasn't."

"I shouldn't treat you like the others do."

"The others?" I rambled, pushing closer. The look on his face said it all. "They said you were okay with it. You'd come around." And his face dropped and too late, I slapped my hand over my mouth. It was the wrong thing to say. The worst thing to say.

"I can't do this," he said, pushing me away, leaving me breathing heavy in the stacks. I watched, horrified as he turned and walked down the aisle, hands balled into tight fists. His words hit like a load of bricks, because in his eyes told the truth. He wasn't into this—into this thing we were doing. He wasn't coming around and like always, I just made things worse.

A loud bang brought me out of the stacks and I saw Anderson running out the door. Jackson's eyes met with mine and he shook his head, chasing after his friend. I wasn't sure what happened just now but every fiber in my body was convinced I'd screwed up good. Familiar dread built in my chest, leading the way for the rush of anxiety to race through my limbs, shooting into my heart. Sweat beaded on my forehead and I reached futilely for something nearby to steady myself. Something to prop me up.

There was nothing.

No one.

I'd scared them all away.

My fingers slipped, knocking over books, but I kept grabbing, searching for whatever I could to stay upright but the fear was too much. My heart hurt—it cracked with one final glance at the door and I fell, succumbing to the painful, inevitable dark.

14

—————

THE LIGHTING OF THE ROOM WAS THE FIRST GIVEAWAY THAT I WASN'T IN my own bed. The smell—antiseptic combined with bleach—was the second. I turned my head and found my mom asleep in the hard chair crammed in the tight space between the window and the bed.

I looked down and saw the gown with tiny blue dots and the monitor strapped to my wrist. How did I get here? What happened?

"Heaven?" my mom called, and I turned back to face her.

"Hey Mom." I touched the monitor. "What happened?"

"You tell me, sweetie." She'd hopped out of her seat and was leaning over my body, brushing my hair out of my eyes. "You were at the library and passed out. The doctors think it was another anxiety attack."

It wasn't the first major one I'd had. There were a few right after Dad left. The fear of never seeing him again and moving to a new school was just too much. I dropped into the darkness of cutting. But that was a long time ago. I was better.

I glanced around the room, the sure sign that I was *not* better.

"I just got overwhelmed." I remembered Anderson leaving—storming out of the library with Jackson hot on his heels. Of course, Jackson picked Anderson. And of course, Anderson wasn't into this whole thing. Who would be? Dating four guys wasn't possible even if we were a perfect match. It was disgusting. Gross. Deviant.

It was crazy. I *was* crazy, and when they'd left me, the idea of being alone almost killed me.

I picked at the tape on my wrist and swallowed my tears. I'd been a pro at hiding my emotions for so long, but then he boys had lulled me into a sense of comfort. I wouldn't make that mistake again.

"I'll call the school and make an appointment with your counselor. Lighten your load." Mom smiled at me. She was always a fixer.

"Chem. With Mr. Baker, that's the class I'd like to be removed from."

Lines crossed her forehead. "Chemistry? That's always been one of your best subjects."

"Mom..."

"Right, sweetie. I understand." A shadow crossed the window in the door and my mom glanced up. "Oh, you have a visitor. A few, actually. Jackson is here and that other boy that drove you to the party that night. You didn't tell me you'd made other new friends."

New friends. The word tasted bitter on my tongue.

"They're just some boys from school—Jackson's friends, really. It's not a big deal."

She gave me a weird look. "They've been out there since the ambulance got here. Prowling around out there like cats in a cage. I think you mean more to them than you realize."

I looked at the ceiling, willing the tears not to fall.

"Tell them I'm fine."

"Heaven...you know it's okay to let people in."

No. It wasn't. It hurt too much.

"Tell them to go. I'm fine. They don't need to worry about me."

My mother, who was notorious for not always being around, who is flighty at times and a little clueless, knows me better than anyone. I waited while she chewed on her bottom lip, a sure sign she was worried. She started to walk but turned back around, placing her hands on her hips. "We've been through this before, Heaven. Isolating yourself isn't the way to handle your anxiety. It makes it worse, making you lonely and depressed. Those boys out there? They care for you. I can see it on their faces, in the very fact they've asked me a million times for an update on your health. You can push them away if you want, but I'm not doing it for you."

She squeezed my hand and walked out the door, leaving me alone with my thoughts. It wasn't three minutes later that I heard a scuffle outside the door and a brief argument that ended with the door swinging open, slamming into the wall. As much as I believed what I said to my mom, all of it fell apart when I saw Oliver standing in the doorway, eyes red with distress. He charged into the room, followed by Jackson and Hayden, all three surrounding me like an emotional blanket.

"Don't do that again," Oliver said, over and over, gripping my hand in his. He kissed my knuckles, my hand, my palm. "I almost lost my shit when I got the call. Absolutely terrified me."

A gentle hand ran down my cheek and I looked up to find Jackson staring at me. He had a black eye and his knuckles were raw and split.

"What happened to you?"

"I fell face first into someone's fist." He pressed his fingers to my lips. "I went outside to deal with Anderson and when I came back you'd passed out. I called the ambulance and rode over with you. You scared me so bad."

"I don't remember the ambulance at all." I searched my foggy memory. "You were there?"

"The whole time."

Hayden squeezed past Jackson and bent over, kissing me on the forehead. The look in his eye said he had more to say but not now. Later. In private.

Even with their size and presence, Anderson's absence was a massive, unspoken elephant in the room.

I exhaled. "Where is he."

"In the lobby."

I looked at Jackson. "Did you talk to him?"

He glanced at his knuckles. "Or something."

I sat up. "You beat him up?"

He pointed to his bruised eye. "Who did you think gave me this?"

I dropped my head into my hands. "God, everything is such a mess. It's too hard. All of us. Way too fucking hard."

Oliver laced his fingers through mine. "Don't you dare say that, Heaven. None of us think it. What we have? It's good. It's good for you and all of us. Don't doubt it."

"What about Anderson? He's your best friend. There's no way you'd choose me over him. I won't make you."

The door swung open. We all looked over and my breath caught when I saw him in the doorway. His hair was highlighted by the fluorescent lights. It looked like he'd tugged and pulled at it for hours, making it stick up in a million directions. His green eyes connected with mine and after a long pause of heavy tension, I asked the others, "Can we have a minute alone?"

Anderson, never taking his eyes off mine, shook his head. "No, they stay."

My heart ricocheted around my chest like a pinball in a machine, knowing what came next couldn't be good. Only an executioner needed an audience.

Oliver's hand tightened in my left hand, Jackson in my right. Hayden watched Anderson with narrowed, wary eyes. I knew for certain my heart couldn't handle being broken again.

Anderson stood at the end of the bed, the shadowy light accentuating the dark rings under his eyes and the split, puffy lip.

"I'm so sorry, Heaven." He ran his hand through his hair. "I've been such a dick. These guys saved me when I got here and they mean everything to me. Adding in someone new? Someone like you? It scared the hell out of me."

"What do you mean, someone like me?"

He shifted around the bed, like he wanted to get closer. Oliver released my hand and gave him room. I tilted my head to see him closer, only to have the urge to touch his lip and make it feel better.

"Dammit. It never comes out right. You're smart, Heaven. Funny. Kind. Absolutely fucking beautiful. Why do you think I sit next to you every year in our one shared class? It was my only place to get close to you."

"I don't understand what you're saying, Anderson."

He looked down, the tips of his ears turning red. "I've had a crush on you for a long time—longer than these fools know."

"Oh, we knew," Hayden said dryly. "She had your approval long before all this started. It's why we knew she was the one."

Anderson looked up in surprise. Jackson and Oliver nodded in agreement. "You knew."

"Dude, everyone knew, you were the only one that wouldn't take a chance so we took it for you and even then, you managed to fuck it up."

The guys laughed, shaking their heads at their friend. I watched, incredulous as the whole thing fell into place.

"Jealousy almost ruined this for me--for us." His hands clenched the railing on the bed. "I've been petty. Immature. I was afraid of losing them and the special relationship I had with you. It was so fucking hard seeing the guys at school look at you in those outfits. Seeing you exploited on that fake account ate me up. It made me so angry and insanely jealous. That was *my* skin they were looking at." My stomach flip-flopped at his admission. "And then...when I saw the photos of you with Hayden and then Jackson—the closeness you had —the stubbornness keeping me from having it, too... I just lost my mind and took it out on you."

"I don't want to come between you guys. Ever."

Anderson's hand reached out and touched my chin, turning my skin to flames. "That's the thing. You're not. It's the complete opposite. You're bringing us together. You're the bond we've been waiting for. They knew it all along, I was just too stupid to realize it.

His eyes burned into mine. "If you'll forgive me, I promise things will be different. I'll never act like a dick again."

Jackson coughed and muttered "bullshit" under his breath.

Everyone stopped and stared at him. He shrugged and gave his heart-breaker smile.

Anderson rolled his eyes. "Fine, I promise to try my hardest not to act like a dick again, to you, especially."

I inhaled, trying to process everything he just said. The crux of it all was that Anderson liked me—always had, and he is a jealous bastard—which was way hotter than I ever imagined. All that broody angst? That was jealousy. I lifted my hand and he took it in his. His skin was soft, except for similarly scraped knuckles to Jackson. I kissed the red welts. "I forgive you."

"Yes!" Oliver fist pumped. Jackson smiled. Hayden gave me a wink.

"I'll keep my promise if you'll take care of yourself—stay healthy —deal?"

I nodded, feeling a little foolish I ever thought they'd leave me. Their presence is like a cloak, warm and secure. "Deal."

A knock on the door interrupts us and the boys reluctantly drop my hands, taking a few steps back. Now isn't the time to drop my relationship status on my mom, even if she had encouraged me to talk to them. In her eyes, they were friends and that was okay.

"We should go," Oliver said. He took the risk to squeeze my foot as he passed the bed. Even in these circumstances, a shiver ran up my body at his touch.

"Thanks for coming to see Heaven," my mother said, looking up at the tall boys. She was even shorter than I was, and seeing her dwarfed by their size was adorable. "Come by the house when we get home, okay?"

"Yes, ma'am," Jackson drawled, winning her over for life.

The door shut behind them and a little bit of the light I'd felt left with them, but I felt different now. I knew where we all stood. Anderson, too. We could make this work.

"They really are sweet boys," Mom declared, walking over to the bed and fussing with my blankets.

"Yeah," I said, in full agreement. "They really are."

15

THE DOCTOR RELEASED ME WITH DIRECTIONS TO GET SOME SLEEP AND take a few days off school. There were signs of a slight concussion from hitting my head on the way to the floor. It didn't seem like a bad idea, because even though my mind and heart felt better, my body wanted rest and sleep.

Anxiety does that to a person, the build-up of stress and emotions, the physical pain and mental anguish. I was learning how to deal with it—the Allendale Four helped. Reclaiming my voice did, too. I liked the new me; the bold clothing and more socially active side. I just wished whoever had it out for me would back off. It wasn't funny anymore.

I was propped on the couch obsessing over it, scrolling through the fake-account's feed looking at a slew of new photos. The old ones were still up; me and Justin leaving the bedroom at the party. The day with Eric in the school parking lot—and later that week with Garrett in the coffee shop. Benjamin at my locker. After that it shifts to real moments, intimate ones between me and the boys. Me and Hayden in the smoking garden behind school. Jackson kissing me on the deck at the house party. Oliver holding my hand in the parking lot at school.

Whoever was doing this spent a lot of time documenting my life.

Way too much time, and more and more it seemed less like an asshole getting his kicks but someone with serious problems.

The refrigerator door slammed and I jumped, having given myself a case of the willies. It was just my mom.

She walked in carrying a bowl of mint ice cream and handed it over. I shut off the photo app and tucked my phone under the cushion. "Thanks," I said, taking the bowl and spoon. "So, when do you go in to work."

"I asked Captain O'Neal for a few days off, he and Deputy Atkinson have things under control."

I frowned. "What? No, Mom, we can't afford that."

She smoothed the blanket over my legs. "It's fine. This is more important and I'm not leaving you alone right now."

Guilt wracked me. There was no way we could afford for Mom to take a few days off work. She'd already taken one, and then the hospital bills. I inhaled and said, "What if someone else came over to hang out with me." Truthfully, I didn't want to be alone either.

"You mean one of those boys?" She laughed. "I'm not sure which of them has a crush on you or if it's all of them, so no way."

"You said they were sweet."

"I don't doubt they're nice boys, Heaven, but they're boys all the same. Now if you wanted to invite Justin over, that could maybe work."

"Mom, Justin is also a boy."

She rolled her eyes. "I know that, but he's also Justin. You've known him since diapers."

Mothers: not the sharpest tools in the box. She had no clue that Justin was why I was in such a mess these days, or ultimately the reason I had four new "sweet" boys following me around. But if it got her back to work, then I'd call him.

"Fine, let me contact him." I pulled back out my phone, making sure she couldn't see any photos. "It's been a while since I've seen him."

"You've been friends for a long time. It will be good to catch up."

And awkward, I thought, sending a text instead. I didn't go into detail, but Justin quickly agreed to come over and offered to spend the night. He knew the situation with my mom.

"He'll be here in an hour."

"Great," her former tense expression broke into relief. "I'll call Captain O'Neal." She dropped a kiss on my forehead and left the room.

She was right. Justin and I needed to catch up. I just had to figure out exactly how much I was going to tell him.

THE ALL-CONSUMING bear hug Justin gave me when I answered the door a little while later felt good. Right. It had been way too long since we'd seen one another.

"Make her rest," my mom said on her way out the door, after receiving her own hug. Justin frowned at the directive but simply nodded. "There's lasagna in the fridge. I expect it to be gone when I get back home."

"You got it, Ms. R." His eyes brightened at the idea of food.

The door shut behind her and her truck sputtered to a start on the third crank. Justin studied me from the doorway. "What was that all about?"

"Thanks for coming over," I said, heading back to the couch. I definitely felt a little woozy and my head hurt. "I had a little episode and Mom didn't want to leave me alone."

He sprang to life, following me to the couch and offering me his arm to ease down. "What kind of episode?"

I took a deep breath. "I had a pretty bad panic attack. I was at the library and just felt overwhelmed. I passed out—hit my head."

His eyes widen and the line that appeared between his eyes when he was worried shows up. "Holy shit. Are you okay?"

"I'm fine. It was just the accumulation of some stuff. A big project, new friends, constant online bullying..."

He sat on the couch and dragged my legs over his. "I've seen the photos. I'm so sorry I got you into all this. I thought they would stop but...Heaven, who are all those guys?"

I pulled out my phone and opened the app. With my index finger I flipped through each one. "You—fake. Eric—fake, which you already knew because oh my god you never told me he was gay!"

"Sorry. Not my place."

I huffed, knowing he was right. "Garrett fake. Ben fake." My finger hovered over the next one. Hayden and I in the garden. I could still smell him; the sexy mixture of cologne and rain. I recalled the way his lips felt on my forehead.

"And this guy?" he asked, narrowing his eyes. "That's Hayden Perkins, right? I played football against him. Big soccer star now?"

"Yeah, that's Hayden."

"You caught the attention of one of the Allendale Four. Impressive." He peers at the photo. "Although in that outfit...damn, you look hot."

I blushed at the compliment, even if it did come from Justin, and flipped through the others, my finger moving fast. I didn't add any commentary. "You've kept up this charade for a long time. No wonder you're exhausted. I never should have gotten you into this. It wasn't worth it."

I shifted uncomfortably. Justin's request started all of this. Some of it was bad, but other parts? It changed me into a different—better —person. I wanted him to know that.

"Not all of those were fake," I confessed.

His eyebrows shot up. "No?"

"No. I've met some really amazing guys. They mean a lot to me. That never would have happened if we didn't fake having sex that night."

His jaw ticked and his shoulders visibly tightened. "You're saying they like you because of what they think happened to us?"

I shook my head. "No. No, absolutely not. There are some guys that did act that way and I've learned a lot about everyone at school. But not everyone is awful. These guys, they defended me. They've protected me from the slimeballs at school. The disgusting perverts like Spencer and Mark. They're my...friends."

"Are you sure? Because if they're using you—or messing with you in any way, Heaven, I will tear them apart limb by limb."

I touched his shoulder. "They're not. I promise."

He exhaled, calming a little. "Any idea who's taking the photos?"

"No. It's creepy as hell, too. They seem to be everywhere." I'd been hesitant to use the word. "It's like they're stalking me."

"Have you told your mom?"

"What? No. I can't get her involved in this."

Justin ran his hand through his black hair. "Sure you can. She works for the police. They'll believe you."

The thought of humiliating myself more didn't sit well. I wanted my boys and some peace of mind. The look on Justin's face was clear how he thought about it and to get him to chill I said, "I'll think about it. For real."

He relented and stood up. "I'm going to heat up the lasagna. You pick out a movie, okay?"

"Yep," I said and he mussed my hair. Just like that, things were back to normal. I had my friend. I had the Allendale Four. Things were finally looking up.

16

———

"Awkward" was the best word I could use to describe my return to school a few days later. Even after his declaration at the hospital, I dreaded seeing Anderson. In fact, I would have skipped the entire day if that stupid project wasn't due. Which, by the way, was the only reason I was able to talk my mom out of changing my schedule. No reason to blow my grade now that things were under control, or at least that was my excuse.

There was a subtle shift after the hospital though. Jackson and Hayden arrived at my house, arranged by my mother, to pick me up for school. In the hallway Jax remained close, if not closer, asking me too many times about my head and if it hurt.

"I'm fine."

"Just checking, babe." He touched my head gently and kissed me on the temple. Okay, I didn't mind a little extra TLC.

After stopping at my locker and ignoring the glares of Mallory and the other girls (get over it already?) I braced myself to see Anderson waiting, like always, in the hallway.

He wasn't there.

"Where is he?" I asked as we neared their usual spot.

"Not sure, he was in Spanish."

"Hm."

"Your project is due today, right?" he said. He looked a little concerned. Anderson had become unpredictably predictable. Jackson stopped walking and narrowed his eyes. "I'm going to kill him if he bailed."

"He's still okay with everything, right?" The swelling on Jackson's eye had gone down a little but the bruise was still dark purple.

"Yeah." His eyes darted down the hallway. "I better run. You let me know if he doesn't show."

"I will."

He kissed me on the lips, much to Mr. Baxter's disapproving frown in the doorway, and disappeared down the hall.

"Yeah, well, I'm sure he's just late or something," I muttered under my breath, as I walked into the room. He wasn't late, though. He was already at our lab table. I eyed him from the doorway. White t-shirt, navy blue hoodie and hair that looked like it just came out from under a cap of some kind. The corner of his mouth was still red from the fight with Jackson.

I took a deep breath and walked to my seat. I sat down and opened my bag, rummaging for my papers.

"Hey."

"Hi."

I'd never been so nervous.

I handed my papers to him and we waited as Mr. Baker walked up and down the aisle, collecting the projects from each table. Once he retrieved ours and moved down the row, Anderson turned to face me. "How are you feeling?"

"Better. Just a slight headache."

He grimaced. "You sure you're ready to be back at school."

"I'm ready to not be trapped at home anymore."

"Gotcha, well if you feel sick or woozy or anything, let me know."

"Thanks, Anderson." He flashed me a lopsided grin.

Wow. Okay, had things really changed? Anderson Thompson hands down was the most confusing boy I knew. Nothing he did made sense. Of course, not much I did made much sense either, so who was I to judge?

Mr. Baxter droned on and on and my eyes were glued to the

minute hand on the clock above the door. Anderson sat still as a statue the entire class. Hands clenched on the table. He didn't seem angry. Stressed? Tense? Maybe he just felt bad about what happened? I couldn't deny part of me worried he wanted out of this relationship before it started. And if he left...

Stop.

Stop.

Stop.

Oliver and the others made it clear they weren't leaving me. I was ruminating all of this when the bell rang. When I stood, I swayed, feeling lightheaded.

"Hey," he said, easing me back in my seat. "You okay?"

"Just dizzy."

"Heaven, concussions are no joke. Hayden had one last year. Took him weeks to get cleared to play again."

I placed my hands on the table and stood. "No, I'm fine. Just a headrush."

In the hall he said, "Do you want to go to the nurse?"

"Nope."

A line of worry creased his forehead. "Can we at least go get some fresh air? I'm not comfortable leaving you."

His tone. His body language. His everything told me he was serious about that and I didn't want to leave him either. "Yeah, okay." I agreed, following him down the hall.

Anderson led the way, and the cold, fresh air slapped my cheeks. When he turned I knew he didn't get me out here because I felt sick. That was an excuse. One I could admit too, that I just wanted to be around him longer. That same look of worry he'd carried all morning still marred his pretty face and when he opened his mouth to speak, before he could say anything I blurted, "Look, I know this is weird... just if you're going to get out of this just tell me straight up. I can handle it."

I totally could *not* handle it.

Anderson stared at me for a moment, finally he said, "I shouldn't have kissed you in the library like that."

"What?" The memory of him kissing me was intense. Burned into my brain forever. His soft lips. His demanding tongue. The way his hand felt on my hip.

"You deserve better than that, Heaven. Not some clumsy grope between the stacks."

Damn he was adorable.

"Anderson, don't apologize for that. I wanted you to do it."

"You did?"

"Anderson, I'd been throwing myself at you all week. Like, literally throwing myself at you. Did you see what I was wearing?"

He nodded slowly at the memory. It was a memorable outfit.

"I wore that for you. To get your attention."

He swallowed, Adam's apple bobbing and he licked the split in this lip. "You definitely had my attention. Long before that."

I stepped closer, partially because of the cold but mostly because I wanted to be near him. He watched me carefully.

"We went over all of this at the library. You like me. I like you and yeah, I also like your friends. We fit. We can do this, but only if you want to."

His voice is husky. "I want to."

"Then take it from someone who excels in overthinking: stop overthinking."

He grabbed my fingertips with his own. His skin was cold and rough, but flares of heat ran through my body anyway. I wasn't prepared for what he said next. "I just want to kiss you again."

Oh, man. My heart dropped to my feet. I wanted to kiss him, too. On his pretty, pink, chapped lips. I forced myself to speak. "Are you going to run away this time?"

He shook his head, slowly. Then he took another step forward so that I could feel his body next to mine. My hand was still wrapped in his, hanging between our bodies.

I tilted my head. "Promise?"

He answered with his lips, a kiss so deep, so intense I felt it in my very core. He grunted when I bit down on his wound, but he didn't pull away. No, he yanked me closer and damn, it took forever to get Anderson to kiss me, but it was worth it.

Definitely worth it.

THAT NIGHT we agreed to meet as a group to make some decisions about how we wanted to proceed publicly with our relationship. Not just because of what people would think but because I had a stalker that just wouldn't let it go and he was circling like a shark.

"I'm okay with whatever you want to do," I told the boys. We'd gone straight from school over to Oliver's house. It was the first time I'd been there but from the sound of things it was the typical hang-out for the guys. I was pretty excited to see it, but when Anderson finally pulled into the curved driveway I couldn't stop staring.

The house was ridiculous. Massive and historic. The creeping sense of not belonging tickled my neck. I knew the Allendale Four lived in the nicer part of town. That Anderson's parents were doctors. Oliver's a professor at the small university nearby. Jackson and Hayden's parents had jobs at the college as well and that was gener-ally the line around here between the haves and have nots.

I stared at the house with massive white columns and a wide front porch. We definitely lived on different sides of the line and had I known, like really known, I would have been so horrified to have them in my tiny place.

"Oliver really lives here?" I asked Anderson once he'd opened the door and helped me out of the car.

"Technically," he said, "he lives out back. Above the garage in an apartment."

He took my hand and I followed him around the side of the house to a not-so-small building that looked like a smaller version of the house out front. He led me up the steps where Jackson stood, smiling down at me. Oliver waited in the doorway.

"Seriously," I asked. "You parents let you stay out here alone?"

"Let?" Jackson said with a snort. "When his dad got remarried it was heavily suggested Oliver move out here."

"How heavily?" I asked.

"I came home from school and all my stuff was on the steps."

"Your dad tossed you out?" I was horrified. Things had been hard for me and my mom since Dad left, but I couldn't imagine her abandoning me for another guy.

Oliver shrugged and pushed his hair out of his eyes. "My stepmom is a bitch. I like it up here." He stepped aside, welcoming me inside. "Since my dad felt guilty about it he loaded it up with all the perks. Cable, wifi, stocked fridge..."

"He even has a cleaning lady," Anderson said.

Hayden stood just inside, offering me a stomach-clenching wink. How does he do that? I step inside. "Wow."

It was the most impressive apartment I'd ever seen. The main room was filled with giant couches and two leather recliners. A huge flat screen was mounted to the wall. A gaming system sat on the floor. At the back of the room I could see the small kitchen and two doors against the wall.

"Bathroom. Bedroom." Oliver said, pointing to the doors. Jackson and Hayden made a beeline straight for the kitchen, pulling drinks out of the refrigerator and snacks from the cabinets.

I stood near one of the recliners, unsure what to do. They were all so comfortable here. I couldn't even remember the last time I went to a friend's house other than Justin. He'd freak if he saw how amazing this place was.

"Come on," Anderson said, maybe sensing my self-consciousness. He touched my lower back and directed me to one of the comfy-looking couches. "Hey, let me get you a drink. Coke?"

"Yeah, thanks." Again, I was alone even though the guys were bustling around the kitchen, talking smack about the day and just doing whatever it is they do. Again, I felt awkward on the couch but a moment later I'm surrounded, Hayden on one side and Anderson on the other. They sat close; their hips pressed against mine.

Bags of chips were opened. A Coke was pressed into my hand. Jackson reached for the game controller but Oliver shot him a look. "Business first."

He groaned and dropped the controller on the ground. "Fine."

"Dude!" Oliver said, staring at the ground. "You break it, you buy it."

Jackson rolled his eyes. Cranky much? "Okay let's do this."

I'd never had a relationship meeting before. Okay well, Justin and I had a meeting of sorts about our fake-hookup and I guess Eric tried as well. Was that how all relationships are? Business arrangements?

My feet bounced with nerves and I couldn't help but feel the heat coming off Hayden's leg. He was always so laid back and when he ran his hand down my thigh, helping me settle, I leaned into his chest and exhaled.

Oliver cleared his throat. "Although Heaven has made it clear that she doesn't care how we act with one another in public, with the stalker pics on Fakestagram and some of the other harassment at school, I think it may be best to downplay things some."

"When we're at school," Anderson clarified. Unlike Hayden, his hands were in his lap.

"Right."

"Why?" I asked. "It's not going to make a difference. Whoever is doing this is intent on making me look bad. I don't care anymore."

The guys all shared a look—one I couldn't quite place until Oliver spoke again. "After your trip to the hospital we made a decision. You're our biggest priority. We can take a back seat publicly until you're better and until we flush this bastard out. No one wants to give you added stress." His eyes held mine. "None of us want to go through that again."

"I'm fine."

Hayden's hand clenched mine. "You *are* fine, babe, we just want to keep you that way."

It was one thing to have someone sacrifice for you. It was another to have four. My heart pounded, but not with anxiety. No, this felt different. Alive. Hopeful.

"Then how do you want to do this?" I asked.

Anderson shifted next to me. "You've been seen most with Jackson. At school, the party, and the library. It makes the most sense for you to date him."

Jackson gave me a quick wink and a sly grin.

"How about I just not have any boyfriend publicly." Again, they looked at one another, this time bursting out in laughter. Hayden kissed my temple. "What? Why is that so funny?"

"There is no fucking way we're letting you walk around town without at least one of us having a claim on you," Jackson replied. My stomach turned into a wave of butterflies. "If you're with me, it makes more sense for the others to hang around with you too."

"People need to know you're not available," Anderson. "And less vulnerable."

I nodded in understanding. They were right. I didn't need to fight off the perverts anymore. "And the rest of the time?"

"We do we," Hayden says, nose grazing my ear. It was a play off the popular saying "You do you." It fit us perfectly.

"Okay," I said. "As long as everyone is okay with it." That statement is directed at Anderson. He's the one prone to jealousy.

He nodded his agreement and even added, "I think it's a good idea, Heaven. For you, the rest of us will cope."

Jackson leaned down picked up the controller, this time getting a pass from Oliver, who'd moved to turn on the television. Anderson reached for his drink on the table and a bag of chips, leaning into the end of the couch. His leg was still pressed against mine.

The video game had half of Hayden's attention while I had the rest, his hand running absently up and down my leg. I waited for something else—something to change, but it didn't. Anderson offered me the bag of chips. I drank from my Coke. When Jackson kicked Oliver's ass in whatever space exploration game they were playing, he hopped up, ran over and kissed me in victory with salty lips.

And like that we eased into a group. A unique but tight group. They were no longer the Allendale Four.

We were now the Allendale Five.

~

TURNS OUT, all three of my new secret boyfriends really liked me being their dirty little secret. There was something about fooling the whole school into thinking one thing about me and Jackson when three entirely different relationships were going on right under their noses. The hardest was Anderson, who I spent an excruciating hour with every day, but couldn't touch. The tension just built and built. Holycrap, it built.

The simple concept of his proximity made me simmer and burn, but I soon realized it was a straight boil for Anderson. That boy was hot for me and I liked it.

Which is why, right now, I wasn't fighting off the advances of Anderson's mouth and hands. Spending lunch with him, but not *with* him, was hard. Sitting through Chemistry where I could feel the heat roll off his body was harder. Randomly running into him at the coffee shop after school? Impossible to resist. So here we were, in the back hallway, going at it.

"Jackson's waiting," I breathed between kisses. The front of the shop was packed with students. Any one of them could walk back here without notice. It was unbelievably hot.

He licked my bottom lip. "He can wait."

I smirked at his inconsiderate behavior. "I suppose he can."

Anderson wove his fingers into my hair and kissed me again, this time pushing his tongue into my mouth. My back pressed against the wall. Good Lord. I always knew kissing Anderson Thompson would do me in, but I had no idea. Too many of my thoughts and actions became about him, being with him, and finding ways for his mouth to be attached to mine.

I'd learned a few things about my boys since we started hanging out more. Hayden was sweeter than anyone would ever know, his true personality hidden behind the size and strength of an impressive athlete. A beast on the field, commanding and sure, he changed when we were alone into something else.

Two nights ago, he showed up with a fresh slice of pie, this time feeding it to me. It quickly devolved from a snack into sticky kisses but they were the most sugary, delicious kisses I'd ever had.

Oliver was dependable. Genuine. He watched out for me and slid into the role of my bestie to make my mother comfortable. He made everyone comfortable and I'd learned to wear him like a soft blanket. A handsy-horny soft blanket. but he was so good for my anxiety. He got it, and me, like no one else had other than Justin.

Jackson? What you saw is what you got. Hot. Cocky. Incredibly skilled with his mouth and hands. Just seeing him made my skin itch. We were the "real" couple out and about and I got so used to him being there—being around—that it was easy to fall into the boyfriend-girlfriend thing with him. The two of us had it easier. We let a little of our tension out during the day. Played it up a little for the crowd and my stalker. It was delicious payback seeing Mallory and Jennifer's faces turn green with envy when they caught us kissing in the small alcove outside the gym. And then, well, Jackson himself was icing on the cake. Getting a taste of him whenever I wanted? Perfection.

And then there was the guy whose mouth I was assaulting in the coffee shop hallway. Anderson. God. I'd waited years for this one and my patience was rewarded. His hips pressed into mine, his crotch hard. He was always hard when we were around one another. He barely hid it and the groans when we made out were a sign *his* patience was running thin.

That only made him hotter.

There was movement down the hall and Anderson gently pushed me away. Flushed, I heard the men's room door swing open behind me as he made himself scarce. I nodded at the woman dragging her toddler to the ladies' room, judgment for our PDA clear on her face, and made my way back to the table where Jackson thumbed his phone.

"What's up?" I asked, reaching for my lukewarm cup of coffee I'd abandoned earlier.

He finished his text and placed the phone on the table. He took one look at my hair and face and rolled his eyes. He knew exactly what we'd been up to. "Making plans for us."

I raised an eyebrow and felt my phone vibrate in my pocket. We had a group text.

"We're going out next Saturday."

I reached for the phone to find out what he was talking about. The coy, teasing grin playing on his lips made me nervous. "What are we going to do?"

He paused and looked over my shoulder. I turned and saw Ben smiling down at me.

"I just wanted to thank you," he said, to my surprise.

"Oh, good. For..." I prodded. I had no idea what he was talking about.

"Amber got so pissed about me talking to you that day—about homework," he rolled his eyes, "that she agreed to work things out and stop being so wishy-washy."

I smiled. "That's good news, Ben. I think she really cares for you."

He beamed. "We'll see you guys at the dance then, right?"

Huh? "Um, no, I don't think so." I glanced at Jackson but he was suddenly busy doing...well, nothing, but he wasn't making eye contact with me.

"Too bad. Oh well, thanks again," he said, and walked off.

I turned to face my him. "Dance?"

"Winter formal. Bad music? Stinky gym? Crepe paper from the ceiling? Girls in slutty dresses?" He said all of this in his casual sexy way. I stared at him blankly. "Heaven, there are posters all over the school."

"So? I've been a little distracted, you know."

He smirked, knowing he was one of the reasons for that.

Anderson chose this moment to return from the bathroom. I could see a faint pink mark on his neck. I felt a surge of power rush through me. I thought marking territory was a male thing. Seeing that mark made me want to make more. Anderson looked at me quizzically and sat down repeating, "So what?"

Jackson leaned closer to both of us. "So, I was just telling Heaven about how we're going to the dance next week. Winter formal."

Anderson leaned back in his seat and drank from his coffee cup. "Oh, that's right."

I looked between the two of them. "What? You're okay with this?"

A hand squeezed my leg under the table. I had no idea who was doing the squeezing. "Sure. Who wouldn't want to see you dressed up?"

I blushed. Charming bastard. "I don't want to go with just one of you."

"I don't mind going stag." Anderson nodded toward Jackson. "I've never taken a date before. We usually just go alone, hang out, party afterward. This year you can go with Jackson for appearances, but otherwise it's no big deal. We'll all be there."

"Fine," I said. "If this is what you guys want."

I stood, going to the line to get a refill. A moment later, Anderson bumped my elbow. He leaned over and whispered, "Are you upset?"

The line moved and I moved with it, pushing my cup to the server. "Refill please." I made sure no one from school was watching. "No. I'm just not big on dances, and I think it's going to be hard with you all there and not being able to be myself all night."

He looked over his shoulder at Jackson. "Welcome to my world."

True. I picked my drink up off the counter.

"Don't worry, though," he said, low and a little threatening. In the best possible way. "I suspect we'll all find ways to make the night special for you."

My stomach turned inside out, not from his words but the look on his face. He looked hungry and horny and I felt like a lamb on the way to slaughter. I squelched my inner virgin and summoned my best, most confident, fake-experienced woman. "Promise?"

I was rewarded with a smirk. "Promise."

17

———

"Remember when you had that ripped Clemson T-shirt?"

I was lying on the floor of Thompson's living room, on my stomach. Our homework was spread between us. We used another joint assignment as an excuse to spend time together after school. This question took me by surprise. "Um...yeah? My cousin gave it to me."

"You wore it all the time. It was so threadbare. I sat one row over and two seats back from you in Mrs. Case's class. I could see your bra strap through the rip near your collar. I had dreams about that white cotton bra strap for months."

I looked at this boy-man lying across from me. Gorgeous and confident. He was always so smug. Right now, his green eyes sparkled every time he looked between the paper he was writing on and my face. Anderson just revealed he had been fantasizing about me for a really, really, *really* long time. "That was in the eighth grade."

"Yeah."

"You were thinking about my bra in the eighth grade?"

The tips of his ears tinged red. "Yeah."

"I, um..." I was speechless. Anderson pushed the books out of the way and tugged me to an upright position. He beckoned me with a finger and after I moved to him, he arranged me in between his legs. My back was to his chest and his was flush against the couch. His fingers pulled back the collar of my shirt and he ran a finger over the satin strap.

"Still hot."

"Really?" Genuine question. Boys are so weird. Walking around in sexy clothes I got. Bra straps and ratty shirts? Nope.

"Absolutely," he admitted. He was so honest. Always. I was nothing but. Having such intense anxiety made it hard to be truthful. I didn't want to lie. It just seemed easier. He wasn't done. "Although, I never knew your packaging would change so much."

I looked down at my tank top and short skirt. On the floor like this, the hem barely covered my ass. His lips were on my neck and my insides turned to mush. Burning, twisting, overwhelming mush. We rarely had time alone like this--most of our kisses and touches were on the sly. But Anderson's parents weren't home. Like *that*, unease mixed in with the hormones. I was still a virgin. Did he know that? Did he care? I eyed his mother's living room floor, wondering if this would be where I lost it. Surrounded by antiques on a soft gray carpet.

"Anderson," I started, "I, uh, oh, oh..." God, his mouth was amazing.

My heart was pounding so hard and I was pretty sure I could hear his, as well—feel it, rather—vibrating from his chest and then across my back. I felt Anderson move my hair and he placed another kiss on my neck, then nibbled and a lick.

"You taste so good." His forehead fell against my back and he took the deep breath I knew meant he was trying to control himself.

Let go, I wanted to tell him. *I'm ready.*

"I thought seeing you with the others would make me mad," he confessed. "Jealous, but watching you all week with Jackson? Knowing you were riding to school with Oliver—him seeing you first thing in the morning? Sneaking around for a brief moment with you? Goddamn it only made me want you more."

We weren't facing each other, and in some ways, it made conversation easier. In other ways, I couldn't see his face, which made it hard to judge what he was saying. I had to trust his words. I stared at the soft, grayish carpet on the floor. Tidy and neat. I could see the lines from the vacuum cleaner around the edges of the room.

"Sounds to me like you're a masochist. You could have had me a lot sooner, you know."

"You're a pretty scary chick, Reeves. I never would've kissed you if Jackson hadn't made a move." His fingers trailed softly down my arms. "And like I said in the library, you were getting a little hard to resist."

"I was trying to make you crazy," I admitted.

"Mission accomplished."

I twisted around and climbed in his lap. Bad move. Now his super hard, very erect cock was pressed right against the thin material of my underpants. Right *there*. Holyfreakingboner. I thought kissing felt good. This was some kind of crazy mixture of pleasure/torture. "Oh," I said, shifting against him. "Wow."

His jaw tensed.

"Is this okay?" he asked quietly.

"More than okay."

He slid a finger under the strap of my tank. "I'm not gonna lie. I want you."

I swallowed and said, "I won't lie and say I'm not worried it's all you guys want from me."

The worried line crossed his forehead. "You know that's not true."

I wanted to know it. So badly. I tried to lighten the mood. "Are you sure? This isn't just a way for you to fulfill some kind of perverted thirteen-year-old's fantasy?" I pushed him back playfully. I was joking, but the fear they wanted me only for sex lingered in the back of my anxiety-filled mind. My stalker pushed that narrative every day with a slew of manipulated photos.

His eyes narrowed. "You know that's not how it is."

I nodded. "It's my brain. It just won't stop sometimes."

"Your brain is a bully." He kissed my forehead, my nose and chin. "We agreed not to listen to bullies, didn't we?"

"Yes"

"But if you're worried, we take this slow, okay?"

I nodded, feeling a tinge of relief. Not because I didn't trust him. I think...this stuff with Anderson, it was new. It took him so long to come around. I needed to be sure.

He ran his fingers down my neck. "Anyway, I'm holding out for the day you come back in that T-shirt. You still have it?"

"Yeah." My answer came out breathy. Taking it slow may be harder than I thought.

"That'll be our signal. You wear that and I'll know you're ready. Until then, we just get to know one another."

"Deal," I agreed, claiming his mouth with my own.

Twenty minutes later, I was still straddling him on the floor. My skirt was bunched to the top of my thighs and his fingers were pushed underneath. They never wandered too far but I wanted them to. So much. We were tongue-deep, kissing and sucking—licking mouths, necks, and any other available flesh. We were alone for the first time and Anderson's kisses were different, less frantic than when people could discover us at any moment. I liked both kinds. I liked the eager, hungry Anderson who pulled me into quiet alcoves for fast and furious make-out sessions, and this one as well. The one that took his time and made my blood simmer to a boil.

"Dude, have you seen..." I heard a voice declare from the doorway. "Holy...oops." This was followed by a giggle and Anderson's hands flew out from under my skirt and quickly pulled it down to cover my ass. I peeked over my shoulder and saw Oliver, keys dangling from a finger. His hair was damp from just getting out of the shower and I could smell the clean soapy smell from my spot on the floor.

My face burned, being caught so intimately. "Hey Oliver."

He looked at his watch. "It's uh, after five and I told you I'd pick you up but if you're not ready..."

I slid off Anderson's lap and he helped me up to the couch.

"No, I think we're done here." The hungry, pained look in Anderson's eyes said otherwise. "Done with homework."

"Right," Oliver said. "I can come back?"

"Nah," Anderson said, stacking our books and dividing out the papers that'd been spread all over the floor. "Swim practice starts in an hour, you know…"

"Yeah, gotcha." Oliver winked.

Something passed between them I didn't quite catch.

Grabbing my books from Anderson, I smiled and placed a kiss on his cheek. "See you tomorrow?"

He shoved his hands in his pockets and rocked back on his heels. " Yep."

We left Anderson and his "problem" and headed to the driveway. The hunter green Mustang sat in the circular drive and Oliver held open the door for me. I hopped inside, taking the chance to look at myself in the mirror while he walked around. My hair was a mess, my lips red and swollen and my cheeks flushed. None of that had anything on the way my body ached at the moment. It was obvious that I left Anderson revved up and ready to go, but I felt the same. So much that it hurt.

I took a few breaths and smoothed out my hair, trying to get control of myself before Oliver got in the front seat.

"How was your practice?" I asked him.

"Hard. Cardio day. Coach was pissed after our last game so he took it out on everyone." He and Jackson had baseball right after school. Anderson was in a competitive swim league over at the University. It started later in the day. Hayden spent his life working out, either on the soccer field or in the gym. I liked how athletic they were, but it took up a lot of their time. Luckily that just meant I got to have a little alone time with each of them while they were busy.

He started the car and linked his right hand with mine. I wondered if he could feel the heat on my skin. At the end of the driveway I asked, "What was that look between you and Anderson just now?"

He turned onto the main road and glanced over, confused. "What look?"

"Right before we left. You winked at him."

He thought for a moment and then snorted with laughter. "Oh that." He shook his head. "No big."

"Then what? Was it about me?" I was genuinely curious.

Oliver fidgeted with the radio, settling on the classic rock station. "Uh, sort of, but really just a guy thing." I pouted and pulled my hand away from his. "What? You're gonna hold out on me because I won't say?"

"You guys have so many inside jokes and little secrets. I just want to be part of it all."

He rubbed his chin and then claimed my hand again.

"You really want to know?"

"Yeah."

He stops the car at a red light and looked over at me. There's a hint of amusement in his eyes. "Anderson needed a little extra time before swim to take care of some business."

I frowned. "What kind of business?"

He glanced down, pointedly.

I stared at him blankly.

The light turned red and the car behind us honked twice.

"I'm going," he muttered, eyes flicking to the rearview mirror. "Heaven, do you really not get where I'm going with this?" When I didn't reply, he sighed and ran his hand over his face. "Anderson's going to jerk off before swim. He couldn't put on that little banana hammock he wears with the raging boner going on his pants."

I sat back in the seat, both horrified and amazed. "He was going to masturbate?"

He smiled. "Yeah, babe."

"Because of me?"

Oliver howled with laughter. "Fuck yeah, because of you." His eyes skimmed my legs up to the high hem of my skirt. He rubbed my knuckles with his thumb. "Is that really so crazy?"

"It's uh..." the flush that lingered from Anderson's house intensifies. It's a strange sensation...not embarrassment. Something else. Powerful. I felt powerful. "I never thought someone would feel that way about me."

One-handed, Oliver jerked the car to the right, swinging into the parking lot of a park. The lot was empty, mostly there for people using the jogging trail. I held on to the door handle with my free hand and clasped Oliver's with the other.

"What the heck?" I asked, feeling dizzy.

He shut off the ignition, the loud engine petering out. Music pounded in the speakers and when he looked at me, my breath caught. "Babe, you need to understand something. We *all* feel that way about you. It doesn't matter if you're in one of those tiny skirts or if your tits are pushed out. Flannel pajamas, ratty T-shirts, bed-head, hospital gowns...whatever the hell you've got on, you're the fucking hottest, most beautiful, sexy woman any of us has ever encountered." He lifted my hand and raised his eyebrow for permission. I nodded. With a gentleness I'd never experienced, he rested my hand between his legs. My fingers trembled at the size of the hard bulge. "That is what I struggle with all day. What Anderson is dealing with right now."

That thought made my brain melt. Thinking about him doing *that* because of me. Feeling like *that* because of me.

"I'm eighteen. I can't lie to you and say I don't want you for your body, because I dream of the day we make love. I think about it all the damn time, but it's not just sex," he says, removing my hand and encasing it in both of his. "You're fun. Sweet. Sarcastic. You've got a wicked sense of humor and are ridiculously smart. You turned our entire school on its head. That was epic. You're epic."

We stared at one another or a long moment, so much truth laid on the table. I felt like I needed to confess. "I struggle, too."

"Excuse me?" I faced the window, feeling a wave of embarrassment. Did I just say that? He clamped his hand on my neck and turned me to face him. "What was that?"

"I struggle with all those feelings, too. You guys are ridiculously hot. You smell so good, like crack wrapped in a chocolate bar. You're so sweet to me and have stuck by me through all this bullshit." I reached for his shirt and lifted it, revealing his lean body and ladder of abs. "See? What is that, even? How does it happen."

"Hard work and a lot of focus," he laughed. "That's what happens when you don't have a girlfriend until you're a senior in high school."

I exhaled. "I appreciate you taking it slow and giving me space to get used to this and heal, but..."

"But what?"

"A girl has needs too."

He bit his bottom lip, eyes growing a shade darker. "Tell me what you need, Heaven."

I don't say the words, but I do lean over the center of the car and kiss him, channeling everything that had built up over the last few weeks into an explosive moment. The car was cramped but it didn't keep him from responding with his mouth and hands, fingers dipping gently under the short hem of my skirt.

I sucked on his tongue and spread my thighs. I didn't know what to expect but it wasn't the slow, laborious pace that he took. He moved with intent, dragging his fingers up and down the thin layer of cotton of my panties, sending jolting shocks of electricity through my body.

"Oh my god," I breathed, wrapping my hands around his neck. Oliver's moves were deliberate, controlled, and it drove me absolutely wild. I slid down the seat, skirt hiking up. I prayed no one drove by or came in to park. If he stopped, I thought I may die. Absolutely die.

His kisses slowed, moving at the same luxurious pace as his fingers. Every inch of my skin blazed with fire, an exposed nerve. Every pass of his fingers stoked the flame. I tried to hold myself upright, tried to maintain composure but I was consumed and melted into the seat, watching him as he lured me over the edge.

I thought he'd slip his fingers beneath my panties, I wanted him to, but he didn't, just using the friction building between us. My skin prickled, my mind disconnected and my breathing, oh my god my breathing...it grew heavy and embarrassing, uncontrolled and real. I couldn't stop myself now if I wanted to. I gripped the leather seats with both hands and fought against the relief I'd been craving for hours, days.

"Come for me, babe," Oliver said with a soft kiss. "Let go."

I blinked and looked into his blue eyes, his face shadowed by the lowering sun. He dropped his head, licking my lips, stealing my breath while breathing hard on his own, and finally...finally, I couldn't hold back any longer, allowing the sweet release to wash over me in a shuddering, all-consuming wave.

I bucked against his fingers and grabbed his wrist as my body spasmed with ecstasy. I cried against his mouth and panted...damn I panted, riding the crest of the wave until I heard him groan next to me. Foggy-brained, I laid spent, washed out on the shore of my own epic orgasm.

Minutes passed as I regained my senses, and Oliver gently spread my skirt down, covering my wet, destroyed panties.

"Uh," I said, smoothing the fabric. "Wow."

"Tell me about it."

I glanced at his crotch. "You okay? Like...I can...you know."

He shook his head. "Too late for that, babe. Nature took its course."

My eyes bulged when I comprehended what he was saying. "Oh. Gah. Sorry."

"No need to be sorry," he said, kissing me one more time. "That was about you, not me."

I leaned my forehead into his, feeling my heart racing in my chest. The good kind of racing, the natural kind. Just like his hands, his mouth, it felt amazing.

Later, after we pulled into my driveway and I felt less frenzied, I leaned into the open car window. "Next time it'll be about you," I promised.

He smiled, wide and full of love. "Oh, don't worry, I plan on getting my piece of Heaven soon."

He reversed and shot down the street, the loud engine of the car echoing long after the tail lights disappeared.

18

———

Despite all outward appearances of only having one boyfriend, my stalker didn't stop. In fact, once me and the boys got in a good, easy rhythm with one another the photos escalated.

"I don't get it," Jackson said. It was 11 p.m. on a school night and we're talking over a private chat group on the school-issued laptop. This had become a routine for us since everyone was busy and my mother was a little more hover-y than usual, post-panic attack. It was a nice way to say goodnight. It also didn't hurt that half the time the boys were ready for bed, fresh from the shower and often shirtless.

As soon as the notifications started, Hayden linked us all up.

Jackson studied his phone, his jaw clenched, ticking with anger. "How come we never see this guy? He's fucking everywhere."

"Or girl," Anderson adds.

"It's a guy," I said, having zero doubt about that.

"Maybe it's a ghost." Hayden shoved a piece of pizza in his mouth. "The kind on that show Heaven likes...the one with the hot dudes and the car."

"It's called Supernatural and it's a classic. And if I've learned anything from that show, it's that there has to be cold air and flickering lights for it to be a ghost."

Everyone stared blankly into their screens, obviously at me and

Hayden. What? I'd shared my love of Dean, Sam, and Cas with him. I had no shame.

"*Anyway*," Jackson said, "in the event it's not a ghost, I can't wait to get my hands on whoever it is and kick their ass."

Anderson frowned at his phone. "Where were you guys when this was taken?"

He held the phone up. The photo was of me and Oliver, kissing in the front seat of his Mustang earlier that week. The image doesn't tell the whole story, thank goodness. No one can tell his hand was up my skirt. Can they?

"Three days ago. I was giving Heaven a ride home from Anderson's."

"So a spontaneous stop?" Jackson asked.

"Totally spontaneous." He winked at me and my whole body tingled at the memory.

"It's fucking weird," Oliver said.

"And creepy." They all looked at me worriedly. I held up my hands. "I'm fine, but it is. Whoever is doing this has a problem. A big one."

Jackson put down the phone and looked into the webcam. "I think we need to stop it once and for all."

"How are we going to do that?" Anderson said. "Like Hayden said, he's pretty much a ghost. A corporeal ghost, but...well, you know what I mean."

Jackson's response surprised me. "I've been working on a plan. It'll take all of us but if everything goes right, we'll catch the fucking bastard."

"And then what?" It'd been going on for so long, I didn't think catching whoever was behind it would matter. I also wasn't sure about provoking whoever was doing it.

"Then he deals with the Allendale Four," Hayden replied. "And he'll regret the day he ever messed with our fifth."

19

"Honey, we're leaving in one minute!" my mother called from downstairs.

"Okay, one second!" I turned back to the phone where Jackson waited impatiently. Apparently, there was a massive video game tournament going on at Oliver's and I was missing it. "Sorry I can't come hang tonight."

"That's okay, your mom wants you to be safe. We do too."

Mom had a Civil Service banquet tonight. She was going with Chief O'Neal and a few other people from the station. I tried to tell her I could hang with the guys but the look she gave me said, hell no. She knew my social life had started revolving around them, and she liked them, but she was always worried about me isolating myself in one way or the other. In other words, I needed to branch out.

"Being agreeable seems to be the best route. Especially if I'm pushing for a late curfew the night of the dance."

"Wise woman," he said, raising his voice over the shouts of activity.

"I'll miss you," I said quietly.

"We'll miss you too," he replied. I heard the smile in his voice. "We're all actually in one place tonight. It's a miracle."

"Have a guy's night. Play video games. Inhale pizza. Don't," I said in a stern voice, "watch porn."

"You're the only porn we need, babe."

I rolled my eyes and grabbed my bag off the bed. "I don't know if that's the compliment you think it is."

"Hey! You knew it was a compliment, that's all that matters."

"Heaven!" my mom shouted from downstairs.

"Gotta go."

"Bye." He held out the phone and a chorus of 'goodbyes' sounded through the speaker.

I zipped up my sweatshirt on the way down the stairs. Mom had already gone to the car and honked the car horn as I was tying my hair up in a ponytail. Although I'd gotten used to my new style, the good about seeing Justin and going to the beach was I could ditch the heels and go for comfort.

"Sorry," I said, sliding in the passenger seat. Oceanside was on the way to the civic center where the banquet was being held.

My mother turned and looked at me. "You look nice."

I didn't, but the message was conveyed. Nice = not slutty. Thanks, Mom.

We drove out of Allendale and down the highway to the island. Halfway there, my phone buzzed silently in my pocket.

A photo appeared of all four guys blowing me a kiss. I couldn't help but laugh.

When I looked up, my mother was smiling.

"What?" I asked.

"You—smiling at that phone. Jackson?" she asked. Of course, she thought it was my "only" boyfriend. I felt guilty for lying over something so big, yet so trivial.

"Yeah—just a silly picture of him and the guys."

She nodded. "Are you two excited about the dance? I saw the cutest dress the other day..."

I stopped her before she went too far. "I have one."

"You do?" She pursed her lips. I wasn't sure if she was disappointed I found one already, or something else.

"What, Mom?" I pressed.

"Nothing. I can't wait to see it."

There was an edge to her voice...something I couldn't quite place until she followed up with, "I was just, um, hoping that it's appropriate. You know, for a formal occasion."

Ahhh. There.

"It is." I looked at my mother and said, "You'll love it. I promise."

"I just want to make sure you know that you don't have to dress a certain way to get a boy's attention. You know that, right?"

Boy did I know about that. I could write a book on how one little thing like a prank with your friend and changing your wardrobe could change your life. For the worse and better.

"Mom, I'm confident in my relationship with Jackson." And the others, I silently said. "I just decided to change things up this year. You're the one that always wants me to put myself out there a little more." She shot me a look. "Okay, bad choice of words. But it's true, and look at me now. I'm in a hoodie and jeans. Doesn't get more basic than that."

The last thing I needed was my mom suddenly paying more attention to me and my love life. I'd defend the guys to the end of time, but if she's worried about one guy...I could only guess how she'd react to four. Fortunately, my answer seemed to satisfy her and we rode the rest of the way to Oceanside in a strange, uneasy silence, but thankfully without bringing it up again.

AFTER A STOP for greasy food and milkshakes, Justin and I took a walk down to the beach. The path was rocky and dark but he carried a flashlight with a wide, bright beam. Tiny crabs scurried on the edge of the light, freaking me out a little.

"They won't hurt you," he laughed.

"I know, it's just all those legs and feet and pinchers." I shivered dramatically.

"They're more afraid of you than you are of them."

"I doubt that," I mumbled, grabbing on to his arm for support.

Down the beach, we could see the soft glow of a fire. "Who's that?" I asked.

"Probably the guys. Wanna go down there?"

"Sure," I said, feeling a little nervous. I hadn't seen most of them in a while. My new social life kept me busy. "Things still okay? Post-post-deflowering?"

"Yeah. I still owe you one." In the semi-dark I could see him shove his hands in his pockets. "It got everyone off my back and..." he rubbed the back of his neck, "It helped take the pressure off and cleared things up for me a little."

"Oh yeah?"

"I've been dating."

"Oh *really*? Names. I need names."

"Yeah, uh, Eric actually, but it's a small, small, small place and neither of us are ready to go public. I just don't want the judgments."

Oh my god. My first thought was that I got it. I wasn't ready to go public with my relationship(s) either.

My second; great, now my reputation would be the girl who turned Justin Blackwood gay.

I couldn't win.

"I get it. Living under the scrutiny of judgmental people sucks."

He shoved his hands in his jean pockets. "The photos?"

For one thing. "Yeah, they keep coming."

"Are you sure everything's okay? I mean..." he looked off at the crashing waves coming from the ocean. "Some of the photos are pretty explicit and there are a lot of different guys."

I stopped, feet squeaking on the sand. "You know the photos don't represent everything going on. There are ones of me and Eric. You know nothing happened there."

He nodded. "I just don't want people taking advantage of you. Getting the attention of popular, good-looking guys has to feel good."

I couldn't get mad at his suspicion. It'd taken me weeks to shake my own. I laced my fingers with his, hoping to assure him. "I have to try to trust them. Don't we all have to make this decision at one point or another?"

"I guess." He still didn't sound convinced,, and because I'd carried the knowledge of the Allendale Four all to myself for so long it spilled out.

"I'm dating them."

"Them?" He frowned. "Who?"

"The Allendale Four."

"All of them?" The wheels turned in his head. "You're dating them all...as in, dating around? Seeing different people? Not settling?"

"No," I confessed. "I'm dating them all. Like at the same time. We're in a relationship. The photos of me, Oliver, Jackson, Hayden, and Anderson are all legit. Anything else is a manipulation."

Justin stared at his feet, not speaking. I kept going. "I care about them and they care about me. What we have is really special." But as I said it out loud I knew I'd made a mistake. A big one. The look on his face shifted from confused to scared to angry. I couldn't stop. Like I said, I'd defend them to the end of time. "We have fun together. They protect me. They get my anxiety...showing up every. Fucking. Day to take care of me." Hot tears welled in my eyes and the feelings I had for them are so real. So very, very real. No one would ever get this. No one but them.

"Don't cry," he said. "I'm just worried. That's all."

I blinked back the tears. "You don't have to worry about me. I'm fine. For real. This is good for me. They're good for me."

We reached the bonfire and I saw all Justin's friends, most paired off with girls. A voice from the huddle around the fire shouted my name.

"Look who graced us with another visit. Heaven!" Davis shouted. "Justin finally brought back his girlfriend."

When he stood he had a shadow. One I didn't expect to see.

Spencer.

"What's he doing here?"

"He started dating one of the girls down here a few weeks ago. He keeps hanging around—like a bad rash."

At least that was something we could agree on. Spencer tried to put on a front but it was obvious he wouldn't meet me in the eye.

Justin noticed. "What's that about?"

"Oh, one of the guys kicked his ass at a party a while ago." Justin looked surprised. "Defending me."

He raised an eyebrow but the smile on his mouth didn't travel to his eye. "Oh yeah, maybe they are good enough for you."

"I told you. They're not bad guys."

Doubt still shadowed his features. He'd come around. Eventually. And if he didn't? It wasn't my problem.

❦

"You smell like the beach," Jackson said, running his lips over my neck. "And taste like a campfire." More lips, more tasting. "Not that I mind, or anything."

My mom texted, saying she was going to be late, and Justin gave me a ride home in his ancient, rusty Honda. There was an awkward moment when he pulled into the driveway and Jackson was waiting on my front step.

"Justin," I nodded. "Jackson..." That was painful.

"Good to meet you," Justin said and they shook hands and Jackson did some trick where his shoulders became as wide as the car.

"Thanks for bringing Heaven home," Jackson said. His body language made it clear he'd take over from here.

Justin eyed me warily. "I told your mom I'd stay."

"It's fine. I'll let her know I wasn't alone."

"You sure?"

"Yep. Thanks for hanging out tonight." I gave him a quick hug and he hopped in his car, driving away without another look back.

"Lost the straw draw?" I asked, after he drove off, car rattling down the road.

Jackson gave me a quizzical look.

"Checking up on me? Don't think I don't know what you're doing." My attitude was salty and he got the brunt of it.

"I certainly didn't lose," he replied dryly. "But yeah, we agreed someone should make sure you got home okay after hanging out with the guy that got you into a heap of trouble. Is that wrong?"

I sighed and re-explained that our families were friends. That we had known one another since we were kids. That Justin and I were also just friends.

"Babe, I know the story. We're not mad or jealous about any of that." Doubt flickered in his eyes.

I tilted my head. "Then what?"

"We don't like that he got you in such a mess."

"Without that mess, you guys never would have spoken to me."

He grunted, still not convincing me he wasn't just jealous, but he pulled me down on the step, lowering me into his lap, and kissed me. He needed my reassurance. I got that. And in turn, I gave it.

"We had a bonfire on the beach," I said, about the smoke, between kisses. "You smell a little smoky yourself." But not the same kind. His mouth had the faint tinge of beer. His eyes were lazy and a little red. He had probably smoked with the boys hours before. His fingers dug into my hips, pulling me closer, dragging me right over the hard ridge in his pants. Holyhardness.

"Does that hurt?" I blurted. Really, Heaven? *Really?* Thank god it was dark. Jackson stopped kissing me and stared at me with the funniest face. "Sorry. Inappropriate," I said. "Ignore me. More kissing, please."

"It's okay. Nah, it doesn't hurt. It feels pretty awesome. You feel pretty awesome." He grabbed my hips again and slid me over that rod of steel. This time though, I was distracted by the feelings in my own pants and not just his.

"Oh," I breathed. And then some form of jumbled, "Yessss," choked out from under the emotions I was trying to control. Because this is the exact moment my brain broke down. Between my crotch and his crotch and his fingers slipping under my shirt, and his cock getting harder and my pants getting wetter and it was too much. Too. Fucking. Much.

I bit down on his shoulder and groaned.

"Shhh...," Jackson warned about my volume. I didn't care, maybe since I had been faking slut for so long my body and mind went a little porn star on instinct. I tugged the zipper on my hoodie, shrugging it off my shoulders.

"Umm..." he mumbled, eyes glued to my chest. Tight, white 'beater, black lace bra. He licked his lips. I licked mine. He licked *my* lips and ran his hands down my now-bare arms, skimming down my scars, toying with my fingers. Nope. Not enough.

"Put your hands on me." The words flew from my mind to my mouth but it worked. Two massive boy hands were suddenly cupping my breasts in the most pleasurable way. His thumbs rubbed across the material like he'd done this a million times before, like he'd planned this out. But they hadn't been *here* before, and I felt like my boobs were connected to the spot between my legs and that moment I'd been dying to recreate since being in the car with Oliver was close, so close. He pulled the straps of my tank so they fell down my arms, but he didn't go further. Just enough so the tops of my breasts threatened to spill over but they were held back by the magic of cotton and lace. And Jackson, *holyshit* Jackson, with his reddened cheeks and nimble fingers that were dragging over my nipples and stroking my skin, now looked at me with glazed-over eyes. With adoration, and dammit all, if I didn't adore him back.

Abruptly, he changed tactics and his hands moved to my hips again, pushing and dragging. I watched as his eyes flicked from my heaving (yes--heaving) chest to my lips, to my eyes until I closed my own and just sank into the feelings. Who knew that rubbing and skin and jeans and seams, combined with the sound of his labored breathing, low, next to my ear, would cause my insides to wind and twist and wind and clench and wind and wind until everything became so tight there was no space left, nowhere to go but break into a million splintered pieces?

Not me. Holy-mother-of-All Things, that wire shattered, causing my body to experience the grandest of all things. And then apparently he did as well, because he froze and grunted twice, in a deep weird, cracking voice before dropping his sweaty head onto my shoulder and muttering, "Fuck," next to my ear.

Fuck, indeed.

20

───────

I woke up feeling good.

Like, really good for the first time in a long while. I told Justin the truth about the Allendale Four and the world hadn't imploded. I saw Spencer out in public and didn't scratch his eyes out. I dry-humped Jackson on my front porch and damn, I wanted to do that again.

The dance was in a week. Like I told my mother, I had found a dress—online. It was two pieces; the top was a beaded halter—the bottom, black tulle. A thin strip of belly showed between the two. It was fun. Sexy. The guys were going to love it.

I did need shoes and I'd planned to ask my mom to take me shopping that afternoon. Playing it safe and putting on my best daughter expression, I dressed in jeans and a sweater before running down the stairs. I hoped to catch her before she got busy with her day.

I found her in the kitchen, still in her pajamas, which was odd for this time of morning. She sat at the table, her iPhone in her hand. She scrolled down the screen, a line of worry across her forehead. I passed by to get a cup of coffee.

"Morning," I said. "Everything okay?

"No," she said in a quiet voice. "I don't think it is."

"What's wrong?" She'd come home late last night, after Jackson left and I'd locked up the house. "Did something happen at the banquet?"

She swallowed and glanced away from the phone. "I had a long talk with Justin last night—after he dropped you off. He said Jackson was here."

I felt the blood drain from my face.

I took a sip of coffee and calmed myself, prepping for damage control. "Yeah, he just came over to check on me. Make sure I got home safe."

"I thought that's what Justin was here for."

"Mom." I exhaled. "I wanted to spend a little time with my boyfriend. Not a big deal."

She slid the phone across the table. "That's what I said, until he showed me this."

Dread pooled in my stomach, turning to a heavy cement. There was no doubt about what she was looking at. The Fakestagram page. My page. A Piece of Heaven.

"Did he tell you someone is messing with me? I didn't post those photos."

"He did say that and that he'd tried to get you to tell me about this weeks ago."

"I was handling it and didn't want to bother you. It's just stupid high school stuff."

Her eyes flicked to the screen. Which picture was she looking at? Garrett? Eric? Anderson? The list was long and I felt my mouth go dry.

"I need you to explain what I'm looking at, Heaven."

I sat down at the table, feeling the disappointment rolling off my mother. I could argue all day that someone was setting me up, that I was being stalked, but the photos told another story. My clothing and change of behavior revealed a different, un-defendable position.

"I'm waiting," she prompted.

"It started out as just a prank by me and Justin." The rat bastard traitor, I didn't add. "And people took it the wrong way. I got mad and decided to push some buttons."

"I don't know what that means," she said. "I know you started with the more-revealing outfits. I tried not to judge. It's your life, but I also didn't want to set off another anxiety attack—not after the last one was so bad. But I had no idea you'd gotten so out of control."

"I'm not out of control."

She snatched the phone off the table and held up a photo. It's the most recent one—one I hadn't even seen. I stare at the photo, feeling the familiar twist of anxiety in my chest. It was of me and Jackson on the front step last night. There was only one way to describe Jax's expression.

Orgasmic.

I dropped the phone, feeling sick to my stomach at the invasion of privacy.

"As much as I don't want to see that, at least he's your boyfriend. I'm not naïve, Heaven. It's the other photos that are a problem. The other young men...men I trusted you were safe with."

A fat tear ran down my cheek. I brushed it away. "I am safe with them."

"No, honey...they're not. They're using you and taking advantage of a girl with a lot of problems who's desperate for some affection and attention."

"Stop. That's not true. You don't understand."

"You've been lonely. I'm not around as much as I should have been—your dad is gone. It's not unusual to want to find comfort with someone—anyone."

"Mom," I said, teeth grinding together. "Stop."

"I blame myself...I saw all the signs that something was really wrong. I should have known when you had that major attack that you were spiraling. It's not the first time and we'll get through this." She tried to reach for my hand across the table. I snatched it away. She sighed. "I know you're mad, but one day you'll see that I'm just trying to help you."

"What are you going to do?" I asked, knowing something big was coming. A punishment. Therapy. The spiral in my chest coiled, tighter and tighter.

"First, I'm reporting this bullying to the school and to Chief O'Neal. Whoever is doing it needs to be stopped. Then, things are changing around here. You're my number one priority from here on out. I'm taking your phone, no more social media, no more attention-seeking."

I couldn't breathe. "What about my friends?"

"Heaven," she said, her voice laced with pity. "You don't have friends. You have abusers. Users. It's unhealthy and it's stopping today."

Her words hit me like a wrecking ball, destroying everything in my life in one fell swoop. The walls closed in and the anxiety, which had been so much better lately, started to slip away.

"Can I at least tell them." If I didn't contact the Allendale Four, they would freak. Hell would rain down on the whole town while they tried to find me.

She looked at me skeptically. "One phone call. That's all you get. Then I want the phone."

She pushed the phone across the table. "Ten minutes. Then I'm disconnecting it."

My hand shook as I picked up the phone and stood. The chair scraped against the kitchen tile and I left the room. One phone call. I could keep it together that long.

In my bedroom with my door shut, I pressed the first number I saw, Face-timing him. There was no way I couldn't do this face to face.

"Hey," Anderson said, answering on the first ring. My heart kick-started when I saw his gorgeous face. Unsurprisingly, the others crowded around, smiling and waving. They were all in Oliver's apartment. Anderson's smile vanished. "What's wrong? Did something happen?"

How could I tell them?

"Heaven?" Jackson asked. "What's going on."

Four handsome faces, grave with concern, waited for me to speak. I swallowed the lump in my throat.

"My mom saw the Fakestagram page. She's going to the school and to the police."

Concern shifted to surprise.

"Okay, we can deal with that. You're being bullied. We can tell Principal Morrison that," Oliver said.

"Maybe the police can stop it once and for all," Hayden added.

I nodded, knowing there was truth in their words, but I hadn't told them the rest. My chest hurt. I'd never felt this level of heartbreak before. Not with Anderson in the library. Not when my dad left.

Jackson took the phone from Anderson. "What's going on, Heaven? What aren't you telling us?"

I inhaled, trying to steady myself. They'd made me strong and I needed to carry on for them right now. Until we could figure this out. I exhaled slowly and said, "My mom is putting me on lock-down. No phone. No social media." I swallowed. "No friends. Including you."

Jackson's jaw dropped and Hayden shouted, "What the fuck?"

The four fell into a variety of emotions, each playing out on the screen. Sad. Angry. Furious. Shocked. It hurt so badly not to be able to comfort them. All I wanted was to touch them. Feel their arms around me. And all of that was gone.

"How long?" Anderson asked. "How long will this last."

I shook my head. "I have no idea. I've never seen her so serious."

"We'll talk to her," Oliver reasoned.

"No!" I shouted. "It will make it worse. Let her calm down. Maybe in a few weeks she'll be ready to listen."

"Will you be at school?" Hayden asked.

"Yeah but I still don't think I can talk to you. I don't know."

There were so many unknowns. Would they wait for me? Or is this the end of the Allendale Five?

"One minute!" my mom shouted from the hallway. The weight of it all fell on my shoulders and it took everything I had not to burst into tears.

"I have to go," I told them.

"We'll figure this out," Oliver said. Hayden nodded next to him.

I smiled weakly, knowing it was impossible. "I'll see you at school, okay?"

"Love you, babe," Jackson said. The other three said it too. My heart cracked, deeper and deeper.

"I love you, too," I said, blowing them a kiss as footsteps sounded in the hall. I disconnected and threw my phone at the door, shattering the screen.

Pulling the pillow over my head, I cried. I cried for the loss of my boys. The loss of the life I'd recently built and for my freedom.

I cried because there was nothing else left to do.

21

———————

THINGS WENT FROM BAD TO WORSE ON MONDAY. FIRST, MY MOM DROVE me to school. Then, we went straight to the counselor's office.

Stepping through the front doors, there was no doubt to my classmates this was a "walk of shame," even though I was dressed in jeans and a baggy sweatshirt and not my more-recent sexy clothing. Every eye in the school followed me through the doors of the office.

For once, I didn't care. I didn't care about anything.

That was the irony in all this, my mother wanted me more involved. More engaged, and to do that she took everything I loved away from me. There was nothing left but for me to disconnect, so when the counselor and my mother started discussing my schedule and removing me from classes with any "unhealthy distractions," I didn't fight.

"Heaven, you'll move to sixth period Chemistry," Ms. Hemmingway pushed my new schedule across the table. "And Mrs. Rockingham, the librarian, said you can eat lunch in there. Less stress."

I couldn't be trusted to even eat lunch unsupervised.

"I've filed a report with the police," my mother announced. "And the school district is aware of the bullying. The Fakestagram has been removed but it's likely photos are still being passed around and a new account will be made." Mom's voice grew hard. "Whoever is behind the account goes to this school. I hope you're doing what you can to resolve it."

"I just wish Heaven had come to us sooner. We could have done something earlier." She looked at me with such sympathy. "I've made your teachers aware of the students that have been bothering you the most. They won't come near you."

"Who are you talking about."

"Heaven, you know who. The boys."

I couldn't form the words to tell her that I didn't want or need them kept from me. It was the opposite. Keeping them away from me wouldn't make anything better, it would leave me vulnerable to whoever was bullying me and make it worse.

The bell rang and I spoke while staring at my hands. "Can I go to class now?"

"Yes, sweetie," my mom says, reaching to squeeze my hand. I moved aside before she could touch me and left the room for the start of my new, lonely, miserable life.

~

Ignore them.

Ignore them.

Ignore them.

That was what I told myself as I walked down the hall and sat through classes. It hurt treating them like this. None of this was their fault. They opened their circle to me. Let me in—added me as Number Five, and look what happened.

Twice that first morning I caught sight of one of the Allendale Four. Oliver near his locker after second period and Hayden headed to the art room before lunch. Both looked as shitty as I felt, with deep circles under their eyes. I had no doubt they were losing sleep over me—for now. But soon, they'd move on. No one wanted to wait for a damaged, imprisoned girl.

Oliver made a move toward me but I shook my head. He stared at me like he'd been slapped.

I'm sorry, I wanted to tell him. But I had no doubt he was on the list of "undesirables" given to the school by my mom. Any communication and he'd be punished.

Hayden didn't stop when I brushed him off. He pushed me around the corner toward the gym and said, "Heaven, what the hell is going on?"

"I can't—we can't...you'll get in trouble."

"For what?" His gray eyes clouded.

"Talking to me." I peered over his shoulder and Mrs. Glass, the Art teacher, glanced our way. "I'm serious, Hayden."

"I don't give a fuck what these people want. I want you. You're one of us and we take care of our own."

I clung to his words like a life-preserver, but Mrs. Glass was on her way over. "Stay away from me, okay? It's not worth it."

His jaw clenched, revealing the sharp line my hands loved to caress. "Never say that again. You hear me?"

"Hayden?" Our teacher said. "Move along."

He didn't acknowledge the teacher and simply said, "We take care of our own, Heaven. Don't forget that."

Nerves frayed, I ducked into the bathroom before I went to the library for my solitary lunch. It was empty, other than Amber Wasserman. She stood over the sink, with a streak of blue in her hair, reapplying lipstick. Her T-shirt had a silk screen of Rosie the Riveter.

"Hey," she said, screwing the cap on the lipstick.

"Hi." I stood over the sink, refusing to look at myself in the mirror.

"You look different." She narrowed her eyes. "What's that all about?"

I shrugged. Amber wasn't awful to me. She'd been pissed when she thought I wanted Benjamin but cooled pretty quickly. I rubbed my forehead. "I don't know how to even go into how much shit has hit the fan in my life over the last three days."

"I saw the Fakestagram was pulled."

"Yeah."

"Another one went up this morning."

I shook my head. "Of course it did."

She took out her phone and before I could tell her I didn't want to see she shoved it in my face. Photos of me and the boys, each in a compromised situation, had a large X through the photo. So my stalker knew my mom wasn't letting me see them anymore. How?

I didn't have the energy to care.

Amber put away her phone and slung her bag over her shoulder. She paused before walking away. "For the record, I don't care how you dress or who you date, you know, as long as it's not my boyfriend. And to be honest, I apologize for that. It was hypocritical and I'm not a fan of slut-shaming."

"Thanks," I said, a little stunned.

"There's too much scrutiny in this school, as far as I'm concerned. They preach feminism and equal rights but there's a million dress code rules that basically turn us into sexualized objects instead of teenagers wanting an education. If I hear one more time that a boy can't focus on his studies because I'm wearing a spaghetti strap tank, I'm going to punch someone. Are they that weak? Do they have no self-control?" Her hands balled into fists and the tips of her ears turned pink. I was surprised to see how fired up she was about the subject. "You should be able to wear what you want. Date who you want. Who said you have to be monogamous at eighteen? What about poly relationships? What if a woman wants more than the traditional rules of a patriarchal society?"

I sighed and clutched my backpack. "I don't know, Amber, but let me know if you figure it out."

She touched my arm. "Don't let those bastards change who you are, got it?"

I eyed her warily—my trust issues ran deep—but branching out, having the guys in my life taught me I couldn't be so isolated anymore. "I won't. Thanks."

She crossed her arms and nodded. "Anything for a sister."

~

Coming out of the library, I ran straight into Jackson. Plowed into him was the better term. My stack of books slammed into Jackson's solid wall of a chest and his hands steadied my elbows.

Our eyes met and I silently willed him to let me go. He'd opened his mouth to speak when the squeal of the school intercom echoed through the hallway and the principal's voice bounced off the walls.

"I need the following students to come to the main office: Oliver Baldwin, Jackson Hall, Anderson Thompson, and Hayden Perkins."

Our eyes remained glued and his hands clenched my elbows. I swallowed and said, "I'm so sorry," before breaking away and going the other direction.

I didn't look back and spent the rest of the day with the cold dread knowing the guys were in trouble because of me. I sat on my bed that night, books open, but staring at the ceiling. My mother watched TV downstairs. She begged me to sit with her but I didn't. I couldn't.

Breathing, that was the best I could manage.

The following day, rumors swirled around school again. That the boys had been arrested. That they started the Fakestagram. That I had a restraining order out on them. That I was pregnant, had no idea who the father of the baby was, and leaving the school for the Sisters of Quiet Mercy over Christmas break.

I let them bounce off of me, like hail raining down on the rooftop; dinging me and damaging me one tiny hit at a time. I ducked into my new refuge, the seldom-used bathroom next to the library, wanting away from the constant whispering. I was surprised to find Amber at the sink again. This time she wore a shirt with "The Notorious RBG" and a profile of Ruth Bader Ginsberg.

She coated her eyelashes with mascara and said suddenly, "I feel like it's my obligation to ask...did you consent to this relationship with them?"

"Yeah, definitely." My cheeks flushed. "They're really great guys."

"I believe you. I just wanted to make sure you were in charge." I never thought of it that way, but I was in charge. They let me take the lead on almost everything in our relationship. It didn't matter if Amber believed me or not, but it was nice to know someone had my back. "Any idea who's behind this Fakestagram?"

I shook my head but that wasn't entirely the truth. A pattern had started to emerge and a few clues. A few possible suspects but I had no proof. Did it matter anyway? The guys had already taken the fall. If I said something, would it make it worse? The last thing any of us needed was another target on our back.

"Can you meet me back here after 4th period?" she asked.

I frowned. "I guess."

She gave me a swift nod. "Good. See you then."

I watched her leave the room, the heavy brown door swinging shut. By accident, I caught my reflection in the mirror and flinched. Holy shit, I looked bad. Hair messy. Dark circles under my eyes. My clothes sloppy and depressing.

I looked like I felt. Something to cast away and ignore.

EVEN THOUGH IT was an unspoken punishment, the library did turn into a sort of sanctuary. The assholes that harassed me all day didn't cross the threshold, probably worried they'd burst into flames if they gained a little knowledge. I'd always been a reader—a coping skill I'd learned while struggling with my dark days—so after I finished my lunch, I combed the aisles looking for something to pass the time.

I picked through the books, eyeing some of the more popular series that'd come out lately, avoiding the romances that my heart couldn't bear. Not right now. I didn't hear the footsteps on the soft carpet or see the shadow until it fell over the white book pages.

"Heaven, fancy seeing you here."

Exhausted and worn out, I didn't even look up at Mark's greeting. He leaned against the bookshelf, taking up most of the aisle. I ignored him, hoping he'd leave, but after a few minutes it was obvious he had no intention of going away.

I snapped a book shut and shoved it back into place. "What do you want?"

He smiled, slow and toothy. "I heard you were single again. Thought maybe you'd be up for that date we kept trying to plan."

"Yeah, no thanks." I rolled my eyes and moved in the direction of the tables, away from the isolated stacks. My exhaustion overruled all other emotions until another shadow blocked my exit and familiar beady eyes held mine. Spencer stood with his hands on both shelves.

"Or maybe a double date," Mark added, nodding to his friend. "Since you're into more than one guy at a time."

Every piece of hair on my neck rose, spreading straight down my spine. "Fuck both of you," I said.

Mark's eyes lit up and he grabbed his crotch. "That's what I'm talking about. Name a time and place."

At the same time, both boys moved toward me, trapping me in the middle of the stacks. I saw the intent in their eyes—both furious I'd rejected them.

I tried one last thing. "You know whoever is stalking me records everything. My every move. When I go to the police, I'll have proof."

The two boys looked at one another, I assumed processing my threat, but instead of backing down, Mark smirked and Spencer actually laughed.

"The police?" Mark's voice was smug. "I don't think we'll have any trouble with them."

"Why?" I asked.

He nodded at his friend, who had moved so close I could feel his breath on my neck. "It's a small world, Heaven. Did you know my step-father and your mom work together?" His hand grazed my lower back. I fought the bile rising in my throat. "Well, it's more like she works for him. Chief O'Neal?"

"That's your step-dad?"

"Yep. He and my mom got married last summer. You didn't know?"

No. I didn't.

"Who do you think he's going to believe? You or the son of the woman he's fucking? And even if he does, do you want to risk your mother's job? What would it look like for a representative of the police station to have such a whore for a daughter?"

All my bravado vanished, instead swallowed by sheer panic and fear. I felt their breath, their bodies, and knew that it would only take a moment for them to violate me. They didn't want a moment, though. I saw the dark intent in their eyes. The entitlement they felt over my body. They wanted so much more.

Spencer pulled out his phone and said, "Cheese," snapping my photo.

Everything clicked.

I opened my mouth to shout, to call out for the librarian or any kind of help when another shadow appeared at the end of the row.

Please be one of my boys. Please be one of my boys, I prayed.

I looked up and their eyes followed and no, it wasn't one of my boys, but it was an ally. Amber stood with her jaw set and her arms crossed. "Get your filthy hands away from her."

"This is none of your business, Wasserman."

Thankfully Amber had balls made of brass and she barged toward us, grabbing my arm. I glanced back and saw the two assholes, still smirking, still knowing they had the upper hand as Amber dragged me away.

22

———

Anger, violent and rage-fueled, replaced my fear. By the time we hit the hallway, Amber was dragging me away from them.

"Calm down," she said, pushing me through the bathroom door. I heard the distinct click of the lock falling in place.

"Are you kidding me? Did you even hear what they said? They're the ones behind this. They threatened to—"

"To what?" A steel-cold voice said behind me. I spun and saw Hayden, fists clenched. "Who threatened to do what to you?"

It wasn't just Hayden. Standing in a row in the small girl's restroom was all of my boys; the Allendale Four. I choked back a sob when I saw them and before I could take a step they descended, wrapping their arms around me. They were like a group of hyper, lovable puppies; peppering my face, neck, and hands with kisses.

The feeling of security rushed over me like a warm blanket. The past few days had been unbearable.

"Wow," Amber said, breaking our reunion. "That was intense."

They released me—sort of. Each one still touched my body in some way, recharging me. Oliver spoke first. "So what's this about someone threatening you?"

I knew I was opening a box of trouble but I told them anyway, "It was Mark and Spencer."

"Mother fuckers!" Anderson slammed his fist into the metal bathroom door. It swung and hit the cement wall with a bang. "Did they hurt you?"

"No."

"They tried," Amber said. "They had her cornered."

Jackson stormed the door. Amber blocked it and I ran after him, catching his arm. "No. Do not go after them. Not now."

He tugged at his floppy blonde hair. "Why not?"

I swallowed. "I found out some other stuff, okay? They've got leverage over me, you, and my family. I can't risk losing anything else. Not until we have proof."

Amber's phone beeped, alerting her to a notification. She checked the screen and sighed. "He posted."

"Who posted?" Hayden asked, walking over and grabbing the phone out of Amber's hand. I had no doubt what it depicted. Me in the library with Mark.

"Spencer is taking the photos and running the Fakestagram account."

"Why?" Anderson asked. "What's the point."

I couldn't tell them the truth and the expression on Amber's face said she knew it too. These boys would *murder* them if they found out what they wanted from me. How they planned to take it.

"They're dicks," Amber said. "Bullies that like to take advantage of a situation. But there are a few complications, like Heaven said, they've got leverage and as stupid as they look, they're not dumb. We need to be smart about this."

I raised my eyebrow, feeling brave with the Allendale Four standing behind me. "We?"

"I told you, I'm sick of the sexist bullshit in this community." I saw the fire in her eye. "You turned this whole school upside down for a few months, Heaven. You fought back and we still have one more round to go."

"I like this girl," Oliver whispered. "She's feisty as hell."

"What can we do? He has all the leverage," I said.

Jackson walked around me and leaned against the sink. "I told you guys I was working on a plan. With Amber's help and knowing exactly who's stalking Heaven, maybe we can pull it off."

"I'm in," Amber said.

I looked at my guys, all of them ready to fight for our relationship. They were waiting for me to make the final decision. I crossed my arms over my chest and nodded. "Let's do this."

WHEN AMBER HANDED me a T-shirt after school with "Smash the Patriarchy" on the front, I couldn't help but smile.

"I got two at a rally I went to last month. It's the perfect size for you. Extra small."

That made me laugh. It felt really, really good. It'd been too long.

The positive mood lingered through the rest of the day until I got a call from my mom.

"Hey sweetie, I've got to go into work this afternoon."

"Night shift?"

"Yeah, Debbie has the flu and I just can't say no after taking off so much time lately. I hate to do it but do you think you'll be okay alone?"

Guilt. She took that time off for me because of me being in the hospital and all the drama. I tried to sound confident when I said, "Sure."

"I know you're still angry with Justin, but..."

I didn't know what to do. Justin was out of the question but so was staying home alone. The guys would lose their mind if they found out and then we'd all risk getting in more trouble and the plan. If Spencer got his intel about my whereabouts from his dad and the police station, he would easily know I was home alone. The tickle of fear built in my chest.

"Heaven?"

"Look, Mom, can I go to a friend's instead? I just...I don't want to be alone."

She paused. "What friend?"

I held my phone up to Amber and she flashed me a peace sign. I took the picture and sent it to my mom. "Amber Wasserman, we're in Chem together now. She said I can come over. I really don't want to be alone."

"Amber? I think I remember her. You'll stay in the whole night?"

"Of course. We have a final coming up anyway."

Another hesitation.

"Mom, you were the one that wanted me to make new friends." Yeah, I learned how to guilt from the best.

"Okay." There was really no other choice. "Be safe."

"Thanks, Mom."

I disconnected, unable to keep the smile off my face. Amber crossed her arms over her chest. "Let me guess, we're having a sleep over?"

"Well..."

"Okay, you're telling your mom we're having a sleepover but you're really going to hang with the guys."

I wrinkled my nose. "Is that okay?"

"Fine by me. I have plans with Benjamin tonight, but I do think we need to be smart about it just in case your stalkers are watching."

I nodded, wondering when my life turned into a complicated episode of Mission: Impossible.

Amber looked across the parking lot, her eyes meeting with Ben's. A slow smile formed on her lips. I was really starting to like this girl.

23

Never underestimate an eighteen-year-old girl determined to see her boyfriends.

Benjamin happily agreed to divert Spencer and Mark's attention off of me and Amber after school. I had no idea what he told them, but for once I felt secure knowing no one was watching me.

Amber drove the long way to Oliver's fancy neighborhood and dropped me around back. I didn't knock on Oliver's apartment door. I knew he wasn't home. All of the guys had sports practice in the afternoon but I was perfectly content waiting for them.

I found the spare key under the zombie gnome at the top of the stairs just like Oliver told me it would be. The door opened easily and I exhaled when it was securely relocked.

The apartment smelled like the boys. A mixture of their heady musk, cologne, and soap. A wave of happiness rolled over me just to be back in this place—their place.

Empty bags of chips sat on the coffee table. The video game controllers were left on the floor. A full set of weights sat on a rack near the back wall. No surprise that they worked out in here. Their bodies were beyond fit. I noticed a half-full bottle of water by the rack. They were adorable but messy as hell.

One difference was the open door to Oliver's bedroom. Every time

I'd been here it had been closed and I hadn't been invited inside—not yet. Curious, I walked over and stood in the doorway. This room was neat, a sharp contrast to the living area. His bed was big—king-sized to fit his large frame. A few books sat in a stack on the bedside table, including the one we're assigned for English. His favorite hoodie was flung over his desk chair. On the desk sat his school laptop. Oliver was notorious for leaving it at home. I ran a finger over the screen, wiping away the thin layer of dust. I had a feeling he used that computer mostly for late night chats and YouTube marathons. I turned around and saw my reflection in the large mirror hung over his dresser and I approached, noting the tidy line of bottles on the top. I picked up a bottle of aftershave and inhaled. Damn. It made my knees weak.

Pictures, ticket stubs, and notes were tucked into the edges of the mirror. Most were of him and the boys at various events over the years, showing Oliver and Jackson in dusty baseball pants or Anderson smiling at a swim meet. There was a fantastic shot of Hayden flying through the air catching a soccer ball before it hit the net.

A different photo caught my eye, not a photo but a drawing, so real and life-like that I couldn't help but pull it from the mirror. Bright eyes look back at me filled with the sparkle of laughter. Full lips, wavy hair. Hayden's name is scribbled in the corner next to the title, "Number 5."

"Impressive, right?" A voice shattered the silence.

I didn't just jump at the sound of the voice, I screamed. I grabbed a bottle off the dresser and threw it at the door. Anderson's eyes widened and he jumped out of the way. The bottle slammed against the door and hit the carpet.

"Anderson!" I shouted, my heart racing a million miles an hour. "What. The. Hell."

It was a testimony of the panic I felt that I didn't notice what he was wearing. Or rather, not wearing.

The scent of soap wafted my way, coming off of his freshly scrubbed skin. His hair was damp, with tiny droplets of water easing down his neck and shoulders. He was shirtless with nothing but a pair of red flannel pajama pants with his team logo, slung low on his hips. His swimmer's body was a sight; broad shoulders, magnificent wing-span, lean, tapered torso. I swallowed thickly, trying to regain my senses.

"What are you doing here?" he asked. "Does your mom know?"

I shook my head. "She thinks I'm with Amber. She had to go to work tonight and I was scared to stay home alone." He opened his arms and I stepped into them, feeling the warmth radiating off his skin. "Why are you here?" I asked. "Thought you had swim?"

"The pump broke at the pool," he replied. "I used Oliver's weights for a quick workout and showered."

I sunk into his chest, deliriously happy for the twist of fate that led us to be here at the same time. His arms wrapped tight around my back and I heard the rhythmic thrum of his heart.

"I've missed you," he said, stroking my hair. "Chem sucks now. Mr. Baker tried to make me work with another lab partner but I begged off. I'm just working alone."

"Poor baby." I leaned back to look at him. "And you've got a dissection coming up. I know you hate those."

He grimaced. "Ugh, don't remind me."

"I missed you, too," I told him, pressing a kiss onto his warm chest. His breath hitched and he tilted my chin upward.

He dropped his mouth to mine, starting slow and easing my lips apart. His hands dropped to my back, pushing at the fabric of my shirt. It felt so good to be with him. So good to feel him close to me. The eagerness in his thin pants pressed against my lower belly.

He lifted me off the ground and I wrapped my legs around his waist. The sensation between us was dizzying. My stomach clenched with anticipation. I'd waited so long to be with him, feel him, and for once we were alone and on the same page.

He must've thought the same because he carried me over to the bed. I held my breath and waited for whatever came next, hoping it would finally happen. The bed, his body, this touch, but he paused.

"What's wrong?"

"No one knows you're here?" he asked, tilting his forehead against mine.

"Just Amber."

"Not Mark or Spencer."

"No. I made sure. Why?"

"Because I don't want anyone sullying this for us. No photos. No creeping. Just me and you, okay?"

I nodded, feeling relief. That's all I wanted too.

Anderson laid me gently on the bed, standing over me like a Greek god. Slowly we undressed, my sweater falling to the floor. His eyes widened when he saw what I had on underneath and he leaned over, poking a finger in the threadbare shirt.

It was the shirt Anderson admitted drove him wild.

"Remember what I said that day?"

I nodded. He'd told me to wear it as a signal for when I was ready.

My body, my heart, and my soul were beyond ready.

He reached for his pajamas but I sat up, stilling his hands. I kissed both his hip bones, teeth grazing the soft skin just below his belly button. He hissed and it made me laugh. I liked seeing him vulnerable. I liked having control.

His erection surprised me. Hard and bobbing. I touched it carefully but he just grunted and said, "It won't break, babe."

That made two of us.

I blinked and he was gone—having moved to the bedside table, knocking over the stack of books in his haste. They fell with a clatter.

"Shit," he muttered but ignored the mess, reaching in the drawer instead. He fumbled, finally pulling out a square package that he tore with his teeth. I watched the whole thing in fascination. Watching the perfection of his body, the dimples on his lower back that eased over the hard curve of his ass. The fine, lean muscles that corded his swimmer's body.

He appeared over me again, rolling the condom on, kissing me for my patience. After what felt like forever, he finally eased on top of me, lifting the orange and purple shirt. He kissed my belly, smiling when I squirmed, feeling ticklish and silly. Soon my shirt was with the other clothing, tossed on the floor. He touched my body everywhere, sending chills across my skin, and when he pushed inside, he took it slow, moving inch by inch. I gritted my teeth and clamped down on his shoulder.

"You okay?" he asked, distracting me with a kiss.

I nodded, savoring the pain. It was a different sort than I was used to. This was what I wanted, he was what I wanted, and I exhaled when he was all the way inside.

We were all alone when Anderson claimed me. Alone when he pressed his lips to mine and whispered my name. It was just the two of us when he thrusted his hips hard against mine, linking our sweaty hands and mingling breaths.

Anderson groaned, nose wrinkled, jaw tight, and I watched him through his release. His chest heaved and he rolled to his side, pulling out. I felt the loss, but his fingers trailed down my hot skin, over the curve of my hip. He touched the inside of my thigh, nudging me to open and I did, allowing him to relieve the desperate ache between my legs.

Those long, skilled fingers moved the stars.

After, when he pulled me tight against his chest, still sticky with sweat, I finally felt the healing begin on one of the missing pieces of my broken heart.

24

———

AFTER MIRACULOUSLY NOT GETTING CAUGHT WITH ANDERSON, I DIDN'T push my luck. I did everything I could to gain my mother's trust. Engaged at dinner. Spoke about school. Never mentioned my boyfriends.

Amber and I came up with a solid plan. One that should flush out Mark and Spencer while redeeming the Allendale Four. Unfortunately, to get everything in motion I was going to have to swallow my pride and do something painful.

I had to call Justin.

"Fuck no," Hayden roared, when I told him the plan. The others didn't have the same intense reaction, they also didn't seem pleased.

"I'm not forgiving him," I said. We were once again huddled in the bathroom right after lunch. "But he's my only way into that dance. My mom trusts him."

"You mom has shitty tastes." Jackson looked guilty after he said it. "Sorry."

"Don't be. She's got this whole thing wrong."

Oliver slipped an arm around my waist. "To be fair, it's a complicated, stupid situation. Your mother wants to protect you. I can't fault her for that."

I lean into him. "We've got three days until the dance. If I talk to Justin tonight, I think we can set this plan in motion."

"And if he says no?" Anderson asked.

We locked eyes, the heat of our connection burning hard since the prior day. It was impossible to look at him without thinking about what we'd done. I swallowed back those feelings, crossed my arms over my chest and made a promise. "He won't say no."

∼

LIKE I SUSPECTED, my mother happily allowed me to take her truck to Oceanside and visit Justin. He eyed me warily when I pulled up and it took everything I had not to walk right up to him and slap him across the face.

Okay, it didn't take everything, because I walked right up to him and punched him in the jaw.

"Ow! Mother fu—" I shouted, doubling over and holding my hand. That was a bad idea.

"Heaven!" He rubbed his jaw. "What the hell?"

My hand throbbed. My fingers were surely broken.

"That was for ratting me out, asshole."

"And you thought busting up your hand was punishment?" He reached for my hand and I snatched it back. He made a face and I reluctantly held it out. It really hurt, but he checked it over and said he thought it was probably just bruised.

"Did you really come here to beat me up?"

"Actually, I didn't, but seeing your smug, traitorous face made me snap." I grimaced and we had a long staredown. Justin had dark, soulful eyes that when he felt bad made him look like a shamed puppy. Even though I did nothing wrong, it felt like a punch in the gut. "No. You don't get to make me feel bad."

"I'm sorry, Heaven. I thought I was doing the right thing."

His apology sounded genuine but it didn't change the raw, jagged wound he left on our friendship. "You hurt me, Justin. I never thought you'd betray me. Never, not after what I did for you. I protected you and took the abuse from everyone at school for you.

You. And I found something good in all of it and then you just went and epically fucked the whole thing up."

"You're right," he said, eyes cast down. "You did all of that for me."

I inhaled deeply, ignoring the throbbing pain in my hand. "And that's why you're going to do me a favor."

He looked up quickly, forehead creased. "What?"

"I need you to do something for me. Stop this once and for all and maybe redeem yourself in the process."

"I don't need redemption."

"Every story needs a redemption, Justin, and here's your chance to earn it."

He nodded, seeming to understand I was giving him a second chance. We wouldn't be friends anymore but he could at least clean up his mess. "What do you want me to do?"

I smiled, relieved and thankful I didn't have to push harder. We had a lot to go over to get this right. Every move we made had to be perfect, but before we could start I held up my swollen hand and asked, "Do you have any ice?"

25

I TWISTED, CHECKING MYSELF FROM ALL ANGLES IN THE MIRROR. Smoothing the full skirt from the waist, I couldn't hide my pleasure at the simple, beautiful dress. The style was retro—fifties, full taffeta skirt. Tight, strapless bodice. Charcoal, with layers of black and white crinoline underneath.

Amber loaned me this one, determining my other not dramatic enough for the night ahead. She was probably right. Heaven Reeves had proved one thing over the past few months. She isn't like other girls. No. She was bolder. Stronger. And my winter formal wear should reflect that.

As suspected, my mother not only approved of my dress but also my date. Justin stood in my shabby but tidy living room, in a tight, black suit and skinny black tie holding a bouquet of wildflowers. There was a distinct lack of interest in his eyes; why wouldn't there be? I wasn't his type, amazing dress or not.

Amber and Benjamin showed up looking amazing and after a few rounds of obligatory photos, we piled into Ben's car and drove to the dance.

"Heaven," Amber said, twisting in the front seat. "You look amazing."

"You look pretty outstanding yourself," I told her. Amber's fashion sense was bold, opting for a solid white halter-top pantsuit. The neckline plunged, but in a classy, sophisticated way. She looked like a 1940s starlet.

"I'm just hoping I don't spill something."

I laughed. "You may be testing the gods on that one."

The dance was at the school, of course. There was no other place to hold it in our tiny town. I'd never been to a dance before, which contributed to the nerves fluttering in my belly. Despite my excitement, everything felt off. Justin's hand on my elbow felt wrong. I wanted a different experience—a different night with different guys. I wanted to think of ways to gyrate against Oliver while we danced, or how to get Hayden beneath the back row of the folded-up bleachers. I wanted a silly picture with Jackson and a slow dance with Anderson.

Really? Was that too much for a girl to ask?

"Stop it," Amber said, while the boys exchanged our tickets at the table near the front door.

I frowned. "Stop what?"

"All this over-thinking."

"There's a lot riding on tonight, Amber. One slip and the whole plan crumbles."

"Ready?" Justin asked, linking an arm through mine. Once we walked through that door there was no going back.

"I'm ready to get this over with."

He bent down and whispered in my ear as we walked into the gym. "You know, you really do look beautiful, Heaven."

"Thank you." It meant more than it should. Things were still really tense between us. Things were really tense in general.

"Oh look! A disco ball!" I was momentarily surprised at how not-crappy the gym looked. The dance/decoration/Martha Stewart-wannabe committee made the place not smell and feel like Teen Spirit.

The room had been transformed into a winter wonderland. Icicles hung from the ceiling along with twinkling lights. Glittery snowflakes sprinkled across the stage, accented with blue light. I searched the room and slowly, everything clicked in place.

I found my boys.

Anderson tried not to stare in my direction. He failed miserably. Those candy-apple green eyes raked over every inch of my body. There was no escaping the intensity of the way he took in the way the dress hugged my curves, showing nothing and everything. I felt exposed yet powerful. We could learn a lot from our grandmothers about fashion.

Jackson, in an expertly fit navy blue suit, grabbed Oliver's arm to pull his attention to where I stood in the doorway. Oliver jabbed Hayden in the ribs. He jerked his head toward Oliver but stopped cold when he saw me. They whispered to one another—I couldn't hear it over the music and from the distance but my heart pounded anyway. They looked fantastic and even if I was here with another guy, there was no doubt in my heart who my real dates were.

"Did the temperature just rise in here?" Amber asked, watching the scene unfold. She fanned herself with her clutch. "How long until we set this plan in motion?"

I dragged my eyes from the boys, glancing at the clock over the basketball goal.

"Thirty minutes?"

To my surprise, Justin interrupted. "Go, I'll cover for you."

"Go where?"

"The locker room? Under the bleachers? Oh maybe on the football field—like a movie." He squeezed my shoulder. "I was wrong, Heaven. I can tell from here how much they care for you. Go."

"You think?"

He smiled, softening his features. "I know."

"Make it the car, okay? The locker room is just disgusting and I'm not getting busted under the bleachers." I'd learned that lesson.

I walked over to Amber and Ben. "I'm going to take my coat to the car. I'll be back," my eyes darted to Justin's, "in a minute."

Amber rewarded me with an approving grin.

The gym lobby was crowded when I passed through it, filled with stragglers. I wove through the crowd and noticed them noticing me. I pushed my shoulders back and held my chin high—they could stare all they wanted. I didn't care. Tonight was the night I stop playing games.

I slipped through the double doors to get outside, fresh air slapping me in the face. The door opened behind me, closing with a click. I didn't look back. I expected a shadow, more than one, and the thought made the coil in my chest loosen.

By the time I reached the parking lot, I heard footsteps behind me and smiled to myself. I began walking intentionally, slowing my gait, trailing my hand over the curves of the closest car. The heels of my shoes clicked against the pavement until I reached the trunk and paused. A warm hand wrapped around my waist and I melted into it.

"Seeing you all like that and not being with you? That was painful," I said, leaning against the car, pulling his weight with me.

"Oh, yeah?" asked a voice that was decidedly not one of my secret boyfriends. He smelled smoky, like stale cigarettes. I froze, everything except my heart that pounded in fear. "Seeing you like this just makes me want you that much more."

Self-preservation brought me to my senses and I wiggled against his weight and in the shadowy light saw exactly who'd followed me out here. It wasn't my boys. Or Justin or anyone else I called a friend.

26

"SPENCER!" I YELLED, USING BOTH HANDS TO PUSH HIM AWAY. "GET off me!"

"Why?" he asked, eyes narrowed in suspicion, and he approached me again. "Who are you out here meeting? Your date is inside."

Again, I pushed him away and glanced around, hoping someone —anyone was out there to witness it.

"Back. The. Fuck. Off! I'm not meeting anyone out here. And I don't have to justify myself to you. But I am about to head back to the dance where my friend is waiting for me. I really don't think you want to deal with him if he sees you fucking with me."

Spencer didn't seem deterred by the threat of Justin, which was weird. Justin was a big guy, much bigger than Spencer. But he stood before me, grinning all sly and smirky and not in that cute way Anderson does when he wanted to grope me next to the water fountain. Or the adorable lopsided one Oliver gave me when he picked me up in the morning.

No, his smile was filled with danger and disturbing thoughts. Fear ran down my spine.

He took a step toward me and moved so close I could smell the sour alcohol on his breath. "I'm not really the one who has to worry."

"W—what are you talking about?"

He reached in the inside pocket of his suit and pulled out his phone, sliding his thumb over the screen. "I know about you and your circle jerk of perverts, but do they know everything about you? Like you and Anderson sneaking off and fucking in Oliver's apartment? In his bed?"

He passed me the phone. Dread filled my belly like a sinking stone. It wasn't a photo but a video this time of me and Anderson in Oliver's room. It starts with us hugging, then kissing. I looked away when he picked me up and carried me to the bed.

"How...how did you get this?" I reached for the phone, but he snatched it back.

He shrugged. "Seems like you should be a little more careful about the electronics in your room." He nodded at his phone. "Or the ones we carry around. There're people out there that want to take advantage of girls like you."

"My electronics?"

He shook his head. "Don't be so naïve, Heaven. We've all heard the spiel about watching the programs and apps we use. Not making friends on the internet that we don't know. Never. Ever. Posting things you don't want out there..." He ran his finger down my arm. "What do you think the others will say when they find out you chose one guy over the rest? That Anderson was the first and not one of them? Was he your first?"

"They won't care." My voice wavered, almost betraying me. I held my chin high.

"Maybe they won't, but I think your mom will care and Ms. Hemmingway and the principal. I think my step-dad may care and the sex crimes department with the police. It would be a shame if he decided to make you and your boyfriends an example to the community about the dangers of social media, when you could fix this so very easily."

All I could do was bluff. "How do you know the guys don't know about me and Anderson already? We're in a relationship *together*. It's not a crime. It's consensual. The only criminal here is you."

"So you finally admit you're a whore."

"Is that all you wanted? Was for me to admit that? Fine. I'm in a relationship with the Allendale Four. We're happy. We love one another."

"Do they know you're still hooking up with Blackwood?"

I threw my hands in the air. "I'm not."

"No?" Swiping the phone out of my hand, he waved it in front of my face a second later. It was another video, this time of me and Justin on the beach the night of the bonfire. I kissed his cheek and his long, lanky arm was resting on my hip. A moment later the camera shifts and it's two people in the dark having sex.

"That's not me."

He frowned. "No? Looks like you." He turned up the volume. I heard the deep, guttural moan that was unmistakably mine. I assumed from my time with Anderson. "Sounds like you."

"You faked that."

He shrugged. "Do you think anyone will care?"

I jumped for the phone.

"Give me the fucking video, Spencer."

He held it above my head. "Now you're scared."

If I could have smacked the stupid, smug look off his face, I would have. "What do you want?"

"I told you before. You."

Panic washed through me again. I desperately looked around for help. Where was everyone? "You wish."

"I do. I've had my eye on you since Blackwood wore you down months ago. Before then, even. I've offered the nice way, but you got caught up with those four, but now it's my turn." His eyes turned dark. Soulless. I had no doubt he meant what he said.

"Spencer, this is too much even for you. The games are up. You won, but you need to let me go back to the dance. People are waiting for me."

He grabbed my arm and I yelped in pain. "I can't. The way you look in that dress..." he made a disturbing feral noise with his throat. "Damn girl, even the most restrained guy would have a problem keeping his hands to himself."

"Spencer, don't do this," I begged. But the feel of his clammy hands and the weight of his body wasn't the only thing tugging at me.

The panic that resided in my heart swelled, threatening to cloak me from the pain. I couldn't fight him *and* the anxiety any more than I could have rejected the happiness and the love of my boys. *What's the point,* my brain asked, *if he destroys me now?* I should have given up long ago, back in the dark days when using a razor took away the pain.

I didn't deserve them and I didn't deserve the life they could give me. I choked on the rank scent of Spencer's breath and knew that was what the future held for me.

He tugged me behind the car, shoved me against the cold metal and pulled at my skirts. "Don't fight, it'll all be over soon and you can have your video and all the photos."

I stared across the parking lot, listening to the loud beat of music inside, praying for this to end.

Spencer grunted behind me. His hands dropped away. I heard feet scuffle on the ground and the faraway sound of voices as they descended.

"Heaven!" I looked over the car and spotted Amber, fear etched in her face.

I couldn't speak. My hands shook and I turned and saw a different kind of fear, this time plastered across Spencer's face. Hayden, all muscles and height, held him back. Oliver unleashed, punching him in the gut. Anderson rushed to my side and Jackson paced like a tiger.

"Get his phone," I cried. "Get his phone!"

Jackson retrieved it from his pocket and I took it, afraid to let go. Then he pushed Oliver out of the way and punched Spencer hard across the jaw. I buried my face in Anderson's jacket.

"Babe," he said, holding me tight. "I'm so sorry it took so long. Fucking Mark staged an epic commotion inside, blocking all the doors. Tell me he didn't hurt you."

"He didn't...he didn't hurt me." Not physically, at least. Spencer fought against Hayden, struggling uselessly against his muscular frame. Rage consumed me. I stepped forward and spit on him.

"You're pathetic," I told him. "Weak. Disgusting. You think what we have is deviant, but you're the one preying on people's happiness all because you can't handle a little fucking rejection."

He opened his mouth to speak but a shadow stepped out from behind the nearest car. "Did you get it?" I asked, eyeing the camera.

"Yep. Every word."

Spencer's expression fell when Eric appeared holding his phone out, recording everything. It was my turn to be smug. "Guess what? The whole world is going to see a video—this video—and then they'll know what a freaking creep you are."

I lunged at him, but Hayden jerked him away and Anderson grabbed my arms. Good thing, I thought, as they carried him toward the school. He didn't deserve anything else from me. Not my anger or rage.

"You're amazing," Anderson told me, cupping my face.

"We did it," I said, leaning into him.

"No," he replied. "You did it."

27

That was not how the plan was supposed to go down, not with me almost getting assaulted in the parking lot. My dress—Amber's dress, was ripped. My hair was a ratty mess. I couldn't imagine what my makeup looked like. Probably similar to a raccoon.

"Are you sure?" Oliver asked, taking the camera from Eric. Yeah, Eric was the guy behind the car, filming Spencer's confession and downfall.

I nodded, pushing the phone into his hands. Jackson gave me a wary look. I glared back. "He has to be stopped."

"Yeah but not at the risk of you still losing everything."

"He threatened to send that to my mom, to the police, and everyone else that could do us harm. He's right. They should see it but under our terms. It's time we took back control."

Jackson nodded and kissed my forehead before walking toward the school to finish what Spencer started.

Three days ago, Oliver figured out what Spencer had been doing to stalk me for the last several months. The school-issued laptops. When we signed the form accepting responsibility for the technology, there was a small box at the bottom. One giving away our rights to information and data on the machine.

We all checked it without thinking of the ramifications, including how easily the webcams attached to each device could be compromised.

Spencer wasn't just a fucking pervert; he was smart too. He figured out how to hack into our accounts, manage the streaming and record the images. After Anderson and I were together in his room and he turned on the computer, Oliver got the surprise treat of watching me and Anderson together.

Was he mad?

"Are you kidding?" Oliver said during our bathroom meetup the next day. I'd almost melted on the spot from embarrassment.

"Watching you like that, with one of us?" The way he'd looked at me was enough to engulf my body in a different kind of flames, but there was something else, a tension in his shoulders. "It was incredibly hot, but it was also obvious neither of you knew the camera was on. There's no way Anderson would do something like that without your consent."

"So he called me," Jackson explained further, leaning against the bathroom wall. "And I called Eric and we started to piece it together."

Yep, Eric, one of the ones that'd gotten me into all of this in the first place, helped figure out Spencer's methods for the Fakestagram and blackmail.

Eric, who'd followed me to the parking lot in his powder blue suit looking pale. Now he stood among us, pushing his glasses up his nose and looking awkward and ashamed.

"Are you okay?" Eric asked me.

I nodded.

"I was terrified he was really going to hurt you."

None of what happened tonight had been part of our plan. No one thought Spencer would go that far but he did, and because Eric had strict instructions to follow me everywhere I went tonight, we had enough to stop him. For good.

Justin met us just inside the back door. When he saw me, my messed-up hair and torn dress, he pulled into a tight hug. "Holy shit. I couldn't find you and this was not the plan."

"We got him," I said, smiling at my friend. Yeah, Justin was my friend again—although on probation. He still had a lot to prove to me, but I knew deep down he wanted me to be healthy and happy. I wanted the same for him.

He and Eric glanced at one another, their building affection noticeable. When I told Justin I not only needed his help but Eric's too, he didn't fight—even offering to call and set it up.

Amber ran out of the gym and into the lobby.

"They're about to announce the winter formal Prince and Princess."

"Can't we just go home?" I asked.

Amber gave me a pleading look. "Ten more minutes?"

I couldn't say no, not after all she'd done for me. I nodded, hoping the boys got Spencer to the security officer.

"Sure, ten minutes sounds fine." Anderson wrapped his arm around me, no longer afraid to show his affection, and together we walked back in the gym.

∽

OUR MAJOR PLAN had been to hijack the stage after the announcement and expose Spencer and Mark for their crimes. Obviously, that wasn't necessary anymore, and for the first time in weeks I felt an easing of the tension in my shoulders.

The gym was dark, music soft, and everyone faced the front of the room. Ms. Hemmingway, sponsor of the dance, stood before a microphone. Glittery snowflakes hung from the ceiling and blue and white lights cast a frozen glow. It all seemed silly after the altercation in the parking lot.

I'd come for the dance and to celebrate being a high schooler. Amber was right, being here was right. Anderson didn't leave my side. Neither did Justin. I felt safe between them.

"Time for the moment you've all been waiting for," Ms. Hemmingway announced. Most of the gym groaned. The winter Prince and Princess was a silly tradition, boiled down to popular, beautiful seniors. I spied Mallory and Jennifer with panicked looks on their faces near the stage. They wanted it and wanted it bad.

"First, the Prince," she said, opening the envelope. She stared at it for a long moment before raising her eyebrow and declaring. "We have a four-way tie. Anderson Thompson, Jackson Hall, Oliver Baldwin, and Hayden Perkins."

Amber raised an eyebrow. *She knew and that's why she wanted us to stay.*

Really, was there any doubt? The Allendale Four were the most popular boys in school. The most handsome and athletic, the most elusive. Even Ms. Hemmingway didn't seem very surprised.

Every eye in the room searched for one of the Allendale Four. The only visible one was Anderson, who stood next to me. The grin on his face was wide.

"Go," I said, squeezing his hand and pushing him toward the stage. The others came from the wings with wide, ridiculous grins. Hayden lifted his hands over his head in victory. Jackson crossed the stage with an easy-going swagger, like he knew he'd win all along. And Oliver just looked like a happy puppy, running circles around the stage. They welcomed Anderson from the floor with a big group hug.

Ms. Hemmingway stood before them with the crown in her hands, not sure what to do. Oliver took the crown, Jackson the sash, and Anderson the scepter. Hayden flung his arms around their necks. The student body cheered. Everyone loved these guys. I got it. I loved them, too.

With a roll of her eyes, Ms. Hemmingway turned back to the microphone, another envelope in her hands. "And our Winter Princess is...Heaven Reeves."

The whole room fell silent—everyone except Mallory, who shouted, "Are you fucking kidding me?"

Same, Mallory. Same.

The awkward moment was broken by the four guys on the stage shouting and calling my name.

I shook my head, sure she called the wrong name. Sure this was a huge mistake and another joke on me. My hands shook and my heart pounded as every eye in the room fell on me.

Ms. Hemmingway peered into the crowd, unable to see through the glare of the lights. "Heaven? Are you here?"

Amber nudged me with her shoulder. "Go claim your crown."

"It's a prank. Spencer or Mark."

She shook her head. "Trust me. It's not. While shit was hitting the fan and your life was taking a spiral, Ben and I decided to throw a monkey wrench into the traditional system of the antiquated themes of the winter dance."

I couldn't help but laugh. Only Amber could turn a winter formal into a protest vote. I hugged her and she squeezed me tight. It was really nice to have a friend.

"Go. Claim your crown and your men."

A hand caught mine. Justin smiled. "Need an escort?"

"Sure."

Together, with my arm linked in his, we took a different walk than the one that kicked all this off months ago. The first time a dozen eyes watched as we exited the bedroom. Now? Hundreds followed us as Justin walked me to the stage.

I kept my eyes ahead, on the Allendale Four waiting for me with handsome faces and brilliant smiles.

"They really do care about you," Justin said.

My stomach twisted with delight.

"They really do."

At the edge of the stage Jackson and Hayden rushed over, each grabbing an arm and lifting me off the ground. I squealed, feeling the air escape as I'm crushed in a huge hug. Ms. Hemmingway looked at us skeptically; the rules about us not being together still in place. Soon she'd find out what really happened and by some kind of grace, she didn't say a word, just placed the sash over my neck and the crown on my head.

She stepped back in front of the microphone. "Introducing the new Princess and, uh, Princes of Allendale High."

Oliver grabbed the mic out of her hands and shouted, "You can just call us the Allendale Five."

Under the glare of the bright lights, Oliver's words echoed through the room and my eyes darted to Mallory's sour expression and Jennifer's absolutely shocked face. I skipped to Justin and Eric standing close to one another at the edge of the stage. They're smiling for me and for themselves. There'd been a shift. I felt it. The room felt it. And it's only confirmed when Amber shouted from the back of the room, "Allendale Five!" and gave us a double thumbs-up.

Ms. Hemmingway nodded at me in that 'get off the stage' kind of way, but with a glance at the boys behind me I stepped forward, toward the microphone.

It squealed, screeching against the silent room. After months of maintaining my silence, letting people speak for me, standing quiet while my classmates texted, liked, and shared my life, I had something to say.

"I'd introduce myself, but even if we've never spoken there's no doubt everyone in this room knows me. Most likely since I moved here in the 6th grade. I've always had the reputation of being a little aloof. Nerdy, maybe? Kept to myself. Some would say bitchy. I would say shy.

"Recently though, other words have been used to describe me: Whore. Slut. Trash. Cheater

"Why? You know why. Because I slept with Justin Blackwood, and for some reason this was reason to tear me down. Well guess what, I didn't sleep with Justin Blackwood. Why did I pretend? I never thought anyone at school would find out about our lie. Stupid me. From there, the lie took a life of its own and others found a chance to boost their own reputation at the expense of mine."

I looked down, making eye contact with Justin and then Eric. I didn't back down.

"Eric? Eric took advantage of a hair straightener incident and worked it in his favor. Garrett tricked me into a date to win another girl, and Ben, as well as almost every other boy in school, simply spoke to me and the rest became history. Or legend. Whatever.

"What most of you don't know is while you were watching this soap opera unfold, two things happened: first, the world opened up to me in the form of four amazing, handsome, outstanding men."

I glanced behind me and winked at my boys. They stood in a row, wrapped in Prince-like gear, stunned. When I turned to face the crowd, the back door opened and a blast of light shot into the room. Two figures entered. My mother and Chief O'Neal.

I swallowed back the nerves that rose at the sight of them and continued.

"Besides these amazing new friends, something else occurred. The online harassment went offline. The first time was at a party, where one of our classmates attempted to assault me in the hallway. Luckily, a guardian angel had my back."

I turned and blew Anderson a kiss. He caught it in his hand and the audience laughed nervously.

"More recently, this same person admitted to me he was behind the Fakestagram account. That he'd been watching and following me. He bragged about hacking the school-issued laptops to watch me when I was unaware."

That revelation brought a round of gasps and murmurs from the crowd. My mother held her hand over her mouth.

"This person has blackmailed me. Harassed me. Bullied me and," I pointed to my messy hair and ripped dress, "tried to violate me. He wanted to destroy me, my family, and my friends. He almost succeeded, but what he didn't realize was that the relationship I have with these guys and with my other friends is stronger than rumor and gossip. He tried to strip that from me. He failed, and I'll never allow someone to try to take what's important away from me again. And the rest of you," I added, giving Justin a nod, "don't hide who you are either. Don't let someone shame you into a box. Be with the people you love. Be comfortable in your skin. Because that's the diversity that makes the world so amazing."

I made eye contact with my mother and saw the sadness and shame on her face. She didn't trust me. She didn't support me. Like everyone else, she'd believed the rumors and lies. Hopefully that would change today.

"Enough of this bullshit," I said, waving the boys to move closer. "It's a party, and as your Princess, I demand you celebrate. We've got one rat bastard off the streets, and if anyone else messes with the Allendale Five, you'll meet your day of reckoning. No doubt about that."

I didn't know what to expect from my spontaneous speech, but it's not the roaring round of applause and cheers from the audience. The whole gym went crazy; Amber shouting and pumping a fist in the air. Justin wrapped his arms around Eric, and Eric? He fell into him, like he was coming home.

The band started playing; fast, upbeat music. I felt the arms of my boys surrounding me. I loved the weight, the support and just having them near me. I leaned my head on Jackson's shoulder and looked each guy in the eye. "No more hiding, got it?"

Each rewarded me with a smile. A perfect smile just for me, and I knew nothing would come between us again.

28

───────────

HAYDEN LEANED INTO MY GIANT DRESS, HIS HANDS GETTING LOST UNDER the layers of netting. "Fuck, I think I know why women used to wear these. I can't get to the good stuff. Instant cock blocker."

I laughed at his frustration as he crawled over the dress and gave me a kiss. His mouth was needy and demanding. I couldn't stop licking his lips. "You taste like sugar," I told him.

"You too." We both laugh again, feeling the weight off our shoulders. "That's what happens when you eat a stack of waffles after the dance."

"That and my dress is too tight." I groaned and leaned into the passenger seat. We'd gorged ourselves on waffles after the dance. The boys ate so much I thought they'd explode. After we piled into cars, Hayden offered to drive me back to Oliver's, where we're all spending the night.

"That's why I was trying to take it off."

I raised an eyebrow. "*That's* why?"

"One of the reasons," he replied. I tucked his hair behind his ear and he stared at me with intense gray eyes. "I was worried about you, babe. If Spencer had done something to you..."

I placed my fingers over his mouth, not wanting to hear the name.

"He didn't. He's done. We'll go down to the police station tomorrow and confirm our statements."

He nodded and straightened my tiara, stealing one more kiss before hopping out of the car. Hayden jogged around the front and opened the passenger door for me.

"Such a gentleman."

"I just hope you think the same thing about me later," he smirked and pulled me into his arms. His comment rattled me; the thought of being taken by Hayden, with his raw strength and masculinity, sent a thrill through my body. He lowered his mouth to mine, kissing me so hard it took my breath away. His fingers dug into my back and I relished the feeling.

"When?" I asked, wobbly-kneed.

His eyes darkened in understanding, but headlights flashing down the drive interrupted his thoughts. Instead he said, "Tonight is about all of us. Four princes and our princess."

Oliver's Mustang pulled up and all three guys jumped out. It was a relief to see them, to be back together like this, without stalkers and judgments and everything else.

"You sure your mom is okay with you coming over?" Jackson asked.

"I told her we'd talk tomorrow and she agreed to let me have my space tonight." There'd been a change in her after my speech. Hopefully in the whole school. I knew I'd walked into that dance as one person and left as another.

I frowned, noticing the boys all staring at me. I looked down, fussing with my dress, wondering if I spilled butter down the front. Nope. Nothing. "What?"

"With all the insanity tonight, I don't know if we properly told you how absolutely beautiful you look tonight," Jackson said.

"Gorgeous," Oliver added.

Anderson's eyes swept over my body. "Breathtaking."

"Well, you all look pretty handsome, too." The moon sat high overhead and I glanced up, seeing a million stars above. "And I'd love to stay out here, but I'm freezing my ass off."

Hayden laughed, kissed me, and jogged up the steps, followed by Anderson, who trailed his hand down my back. "I'll go find the blankets."

"Thank you."

Jackson stopped before me, took my hands in his and said, "They lied tonight when they called you princess, babe."

I frowned. "What?"

"You're a fucking queen." He kissed me gently and then whispered in my ear. "I can't wait to treat you like one; pamper you head to toe."

Okay, so I wasn't exactly cold anymore.

"Promise?" The words came out in a croak.

There was zero doubt in his eyes. "Promise."

He sealed that with a kiss, harder than the one before, and I had no doubt whatever Jackson had in store was worth waiting for. He ran up the steps and I turned to face Oliver. He stood with his hands in his pockets, giving me the strangest face.

Unlike the other boys, I didn't see the primal hunger that had built between us. I saw something else intermingled with the certain lust.

"Why are you looking at me like that?" I asked.

He took a step forward. "I'm so proud of you, Heaven. I had no idea where this would lead when I picked you up in the store parking lot that day. You were scared, pissed, and hot. So fucking hot. I didn't know we'd end up your protectors, defenders, and best friends." He closed the gap between us. "I didn't know you'd bring us closer and add so much pleasure and light to our lives."

"I didn't know that either," I said, watching him closely.

He slid one arm around my waist and another around my neck. I felt his breath, smelled the syrup from before. "I certainly had no idea we'd find love. True, unbiased, kick-us-in-the-ass love."

My heat stammered. "Thank you for letting me join the circle."

"Thank you for giving us a shot at heaven."

He kissed me on the lips then surprised me by lifting me in the air, carrying me bridal-style up the apartment stairs and through the front door. Inside, the others were waiting for us, and I'd never felt so grateful and happy in my life.

All of this started with a prank.

It ended with the best happily ever after.

PROLOGUE

IF DATING FOUR GUYS IN HIGH SCHOOL WAS ROUGH, I FIGURED COLLEGE would only get easier. At least, that was what movies taught me.

Along with the increase in freedom and the decrease of adult supervision, and the addition of a less judgmental environment for sexual experimentation, it had to be better, right?

Those were my thoughts before my graduation party. My only concerns were trying not to get an 8:30 a.m. class, figuring out my meal card, and how to make sure one of the boys didn't feel left out (oh yeah, that happened.) My biggest other worry involved a talk I wanted to have with the guys about our relationship. It wasn't like there was anything wrong. No. Things were great. I was just ready to take things to a different level, and talking to one guy about sex was awkward enough, not to mention four.

But then graduation happened and I didn't even get to have that talk before shit hit the fan. Of course, shit hit the fan. Should I have expected differently? Assumed life would be smooth sailing after the harassment and bullying in high school? Sure, I wanted the fairytale ending. The happily ever after. The riding off in the sunset. I deserved it. My guys deserved it, but none of us are stupid enough to expect it. So, in the end, despite all the progress I'd made, I still had a lot of trust issues. Friend issues. Self-advocation issues and apparently...family issues, cockblocking my way to a happily ever after.

Good thing I still had the Allendale Four.

29

THE MUSTANG RUMBLED DOWN THE ROAD, TOP DOWN. THE RUSH OF the wind felt similar to the rush I felt inside.

"We did it. I can't believe we did it." I said, glancing over at Oliver. His hair whipped in the air.

He rested his hand on my knee and squeezed, sending a familiar shock of electricity across my skin. "Can't believe we graduated?"

"Graduated. Survived. Whatever you want to call it." I eased out of the blue graduation gown and tossed it and the cap in the back.

The loud roar of an engine barreled next to us, the tall Jeep dwarfing the antique Mustang in its shadow. Hayden smiled down at me from the driver's seat. Jackson winked and blew me a kiss. Anderson's green eyes burned into mine and like always, I felt the heat from knowing these guys were mine.

"See you at the house!" Hayden shouted, passing us.

"I also can't believe my mom is throwing a party," I said, watching them go. I had no doubt they're up to something. A surprise? A gift? I'd been suspicious ever since they suggested we take separate cars.

The truth was that I'd been working up to talking to them about something, and every time I thought about it, nerves of apprehension flared in my belly. I'd hoped after a week of exams, graduation activities, parties and preparation, we could finally find some time alone to talk about it, but I had a feeling it would move to the back burner.

Again.

"Your mom has chilled out a lot in the past few months," Oliver replied. "I think she feels bad for everything getting so out of control in the fall."

"If her guilt means we get to be together judgment-free, then I'll deal with a stupid party."

My mother had been one of the ones to blame the Allendale Four for the bullying and harassment that happened to me earlier in the year. She freaked out and kept me from them, which led to some scary moments with my depression and anxiety. But between finding out the truth--that it had really been her boss's stepson--and getting to know the guys a little better, (and that they weren't just with me to get in my pants—okay maybe a little bit, but the feeling was mutual) she'd relaxed.

Oliver glanced over at me, eyebrow raised. We were a block over from my house and there was no mistaking the line of cars on the side of the road. My mom had invited a surprising number of people. After the scrutiny of the last year—the Fakestagram accounts and making new friends—other people didn't panic me so much anymore.

Or at least that was my thought, until Oliver turned in the driveway and his fingers linked with mine—more for support than anything else. An older model, but still shiny, black Mercedes sat next to my mother's beat-up truck.

I squeezed Oliver's hand. Tight.

"That's my..." I looked over at him; my heart beating irrationally. Excitement. Fear. Anxiety. Oliver nodded, but a line of stress furrowed between his eyebrows. He'd known.

"Surprise...your dad's here." He lifted my fingers to his mouth and kissed the back of my hand, fully aware of my shock. "Your mom made us promise and you know we've been working to get on her good side—you know, trying to ease her into the idea we're all going to school together."

Surely, dating one guy had its own set of issues. Dating four? Not only are there relationship challenges, time management, and regular drama, but navigating other people and their expectations was hard. I'd love to just say fuck it. Fuck them, but it wasn't entirely realistic. Especially when I was still living at home and depended upon my parents' money to pay for college.

I watched as Hayden, Jackson, and Anderson walked down the driveway. Hayden Pierce is tall and muscular—star goalie of the Allendale soccer team and recipient of a full scholarship to the University. Matching in height is Anderson Thompson—with his lean swimmer's body; all torso and broad shoulders. His reddish-brown hair glinted in the fading sunlight. Between them walked Jackson Hall, blonde with a swagger and smile that threatened to break the heart of any girl that crossed his path.

Normally, the three oozed an unstoppable confidence. They had each other. They had me. But today, there was an apprehension in their moves, and I followed their gaze to the front porch.

"It'll be fine," Oliver said, eyes glued to the man standing under the "Congratulations!" banner. My father stood there in an expensive suit, watching me—us. "At least he's not holding a shotgun."

"Don't count on it," I muttered, wavering between the desire to laugh or cry. The guys didn't know my dad, what he was capable of, and why he'd vanished from our lives in the first place.

Now I couldn't help but wonder why he was back.

JOHN REEVES WASN'T AN IMPOSING man, at least, not physically. The Allendale boys dwarfed him, but he carried a gravitas that exceeded size. In a word, he was charismatic. Something that had both helped and hurt him in life.

That charisma had mostly just hurt me and my mom, and seeing him in the yard was a shock.

"Heaven," he said, spreading his arms wide.

"Hi, Daddy." As much as I didn't want to fall into his embrace, I couldn't help myself. He was my dad and he'd been gone for seven years. Seven long years. Tears threatened to spill over, just from the emotion of it all. He squeezed me tight, the kind of bear-hug only a father could give. My mom stood quietly in the corner, happy, but apprehensive. This was big for her, too.

"Let me get a look at you," he said, pushing me back. I'm in a graduation dress—a hand-me down from Amber. It was a sundress with thin straps at the top, and a full floral skirt. The top was a sweetheart shape, slightly more revealing than I'd like him to see me in. He assessed me and suddenly I felt like a child, not an eighteen-year-old on my way to college. Not a woman with experiences of my own, but the little girl that watched as her father left and her life fell apart.

I spotted the disapproval in his eyes but he said nothing about it other than, "You've grown into a beautiful young woman, Heaven."

I eyed my father, his skin a warm tan. He looked relaxed, and his expensive car, clothing, and accessories were out of place on our shabby porch.

"You look good, too."

"God was good for me while I was gone." He cast Mom a glance and her cheeks flushed. I didn't like it. I also didn't like it when he looked over my shoulder at the boys. They'd been uncharacteristically quiet since they got out of the car. "And who are these young men?"

"Daddy, these are my friends." I introduced them individually, making sure not to linger on anyone too long. They showed no fear as they each shook his hand, bringing a swell of pride to my chest. Amber and Benjamin strolled up and I almost sighed in relief to be able to introduce them as well. Anything to take the focus off the boys. I stole a glance at my mother, but her stoic expression told me she hadn't revealed the truth of my relationship with them.

Not yet.

And he never would know, if I could help it.

My father stared at everyone, trying to place faces and who they were and what they meant to me. "It's wonderful to see that Heaven has found a family here in Allendale. My own community of Oceanside has always been important to me. A sense of belonging is important."

"Kids, there's a bunch of food and drinks in the back," my mom said, going full hostess. "I know you're starving after the ceremony."

"Thanks, Ms. Reeves," Amber said, pulling Benjamin behind her. The boys looked at me and I nodded, knowing I needed one more minute with my mom.

When we were alone, I stepped close. "What is he doing here?"

She wrung her hands. "I don't know, Heaven, but he's here and he's your father. He wanted to be here."

The hurt in her voice was evident. It should be. He's tanned and relaxed while she'd been working double shifts at the police station to help pay for food on the table and save for college.

"We'll get through this," I told her. "And get on with our lives."

She nodded but grabbed my arm. "No matter what, Heaven, do not let him know about what's really going on with those boys. I'm okay with your decision. I know you trust them and I do too, but your father? He won't see it that way. You know how he is."

I looked down at the man I hadn't seen in seven years as he spoke quietly to my mother's supervisor and knew she was right. We'll get through today, keep quiet about our lives, and hopefully he'll disappear for another seven years.

30

———

"So," Amber said, cornering me in the kitchen, "did you get a chance to talk to them?"

"No, not yet," I whispered back. "And with my dad here, I don't see it happening."

"Well, it can wait. I mean, it's important, but not like, life or death, or anything."

No, what I wanted to talk to the guys about wasn't life or death. Just, you know, relationship important. It could definitely wait. If I ever got up the courage.

"Why are you so worried about it? I'd think they'd be into you wanting to expand your, uh," she lowered her voice, "level of intimacy."

I looked around, making sure no one heard that, but we were alone. "It's weird. I mean, can you imagine talking to Benjamin about the fact he's holding back on you?"

She nodded sympathetically. "Yeah, that's not a problem."

"Of course, it's not," I whispered. "What are the odds I have four —count them—four boyfriends that all want to take it slow?"

"You and Anderson have sex, right?"

My stomach fluttered at the mention of it. "Yeah, but I can tell he's restraining himself." I leaned against the counter. My cheeks burned

192

before I got the next comment out of my mouth, but it was driving me crazy and I had to talk to someone about it. "They're big guys. Athletic. Strong. Is it wrong that I want them to use a little of that power on me?"

Amber shook her head. "Not at all. Maybe it's just an access thing—we all still live at home—even Oliver in that apartment of his. Once we leave for school, you'll have way more time together and the opportunity for privacy."

I smiled at Amber. We'd only become friends this year, after she stood up for me with the bullying and harassment, but she got me. We could talk about almost anything; school, guys, sex…we'd even agreed to room together at the University.

"Heaven," my dad said, walking into the room. Amber tensed in his presence. "I'd hoped we'd have time to spend together this summer, but I hear you're starting school in a few weeks."

"That would have been great," I lied, "but yeah, we got early admission. Amber and I both start the summer semester in mid-June. Gives us a leg up on the rest of the freshmen class."

Truthfully, I didn't want to stick around Allendale without the guys. They all had athletic obligations and had to arrive at school for conditioning and pre-season training. I won't deny that a summer of freedom in the co-ed dorms seemed like a great way to start.

Not that the guys would be living there. Just me and Amber. They all had to stay in athletic housing. It was good, though. I loved my boys, but a little space to experience college wasn't a bad idea. The past year taught me about being comfortable in my own skin—branching out and experiencing new things. I wanted that from college and from the boys I loved.

Living in the co-ed dorm would make things less noticeable, though. No curfews or rules on male visitors. I couldn't wait for the experience.

My dad leaned against the counter. He'd taken off his jacket and rolled the sleeves of his crisp white shirt up over his elbows, revealing an expensive gold watch. With his tie removed, I could see the cross around his neck, the one he's worn since he was a teenager and committed his life to Jesus at church camp. Just having my father so close by made me uncomfortable. In many ways he was a stranger, but I also knew about his expectations. His beliefs, and I had no doubt he could ferret out mine quickly.

❧

"Heaven can you grab that bag of ice in the laundry room?"

"Sure, Mom," I said, slipping through the kitchen to the adjoining laundry room. The ice was in the freezer and I opened the top door to find it.

I felt the presence of a body behind me and an arm slipped around my waist. My senses were overwhelmed with the warm scent of soap mingled with the slight tinge of chlorine.

"Need any help?" Anderson asked, kissing me on the neck.

My knees wobbled but my stomach twisted with nerves and I pulled away, looking toward the door. He glanced over his shoulder. "Something wrong?"

I felt the hard muscle of his abs beneath his dress shirt and the pressure of his fingers against my hips. All I wanted was to run away with these guys, feel their bodies, and wrap myself in the safety of their arms. But that wasn't realistic, and their sense of overprotectiveness was already a bit of an issue.

"Having my dad here freaks me out a little."

His green eyes held mine and I noticed the tic of irritation in his jaw. "Is there something you're not telling us? Because you know we've got your back."

I touched his cheek. "I know, babe, thank you. My dad is just complicated. Having him back in our lives is unexpected. I just need to get used to it."

"I can understand that. You and your mom have been alone for a long time." My mom. I couldn't believe she let him back in the house. But then again...was it really a surprise? She'd never had much self-control when he was around.

"I just like how things are, you know?"

"Change makes you nervous. I may have a little experience with that." He bent down and kissed me softly on the lips, slipping his tongue into my mouth.

I twisted his shirt in my hands. "Speaking of changes, I uh, kind of wanted to talk to you guys about something."

His eyebrow rose curiously. "Yeah?"

"Later, when we're alone."

My mom shouted from the other room. "Heaven!"

"Coming!"

Anderson grabbed the ice out of the freezer and lifted it over his shoulder. I didn't miss the way my father watched us as we walked back in the room. Or the way my mother tried to divert his attention. I also didn't miss how Anderson's hand brushed against my lower back, making my stomach fill with butterflies.

All it took was one night and my life got really, really complicated.

"Dude, so what was that all about?"

Amber and I were in the truck, headed back to her house for a sleepover. Well, not true. We were really both going to our boyfriend's houses—her, Benjamin and me, Oliver's.

"You mean the fit my dad just had about me leaving?"

"Uh, yeah. That and the fact he was here at all." She turned to face me. "There seemed to be some tension."

That was one way to put it. "My dad is...spoiled? I guess. I don't know. He just likes to control things and he's been gone so long he hasn't realized I'm an adult now."

He'd been angry that I wanted to leave after the party, but Mom had already given me permission to spend the night out. I was proud of her for sticking to her guns, before he left she never would have done that. But if he found out about me and the guys...

I didn't want to think about it.

"He was nice and he said he was going to get us a TV for the dorm room, which is totally unnecessary, but still."

I didn't want to tell her that things from my dad came with strings attached. You never knew when you'd have to pay up.

Amber reached for my hand and squeezed it. "Look, I know you're a worrier. That's what you do, but we've graduated, we've made it into a great school and things are going to be awesome."

I smiled, wanting to believe her, but I had a hard time ignoring the gnawing feeling in my gut, that everything I'd worked so hard for over the last year was about to implode.

I dropped her off at Benjamin's with an agreement to meet at the diner by nine the next morning to cover our bases. Allendale was a small town so it didn't take long for me to get to Oliver's house. His father and step-mother showed up for the actual graduation but were leaving for Europe in the morning. Every light in the main house was out, so I used my phone to light my way down the back driveway.

Sleepovers were rare, and despite popular gossip, I didn't fuck all the guys at once and we definitely didn't have orgies. For god's sake, we're eighteen and I'd just lost my virginity six months before. Sure, I was more comfortable with myself now, but four guys at once? Nope. Not happening. What people didn't get was that my relationship with all the guys was an individual one as well as a group. What happened in one bedroom wasn't discussed together. And the truth was that even though I was really close with each of them, I hadn't had sex with anyone but Anderson.

That was something I hoped to remedy soon.

Despite the raging hormones and increased tension, we made a rule that when we're all together it was nothing more than a hangout. With snuggling. And usually a shit-ton of food because my boys eat like the world may run out tomorrow.

Jackson met me at the door, taking my bag from my hand.

"Hey babe," he said, leaning in for a quick kiss. Behind him was the usual set up. Bags of snacks littered across the coffee table, despite the fact they just ate at my house. Hayden and Oliver were involved in an intense video game (I guess. Seriously, I couldn't keep up.), while Anderson lounged on the couch and scrolled through his phone. He looked up when I entered and winked.

It was a relief to be here with them like this, but also hard since I knew it was probably the last time before we all left for school.

Anderson was right. I didn't like change—not at all—and I felt the shadow of anxiety tickling at the back of my mind.

"You've got to see this," Jackson said, pulling me into the house. I followed him across the living room to Oliver's bedroom. The bed itself was gone.

"What is this?" I asked, processing the room. The whole floor was covered in pillows and blankets. Er, maybe I'd been wrong about that orgy thing.

Jackson dropped my bag on the floor and slipped his arms around my waist, pulling me close. "Oliver did it. He wanted a way for us to all be close before we head off to school. It's a big change for all of us. Hayden'll be in full training for his fall season once he gets there. Anderson's swim season never ends, and Oliver and I will be in the thick of it with the baseball team."

I looked over his shoulder and saw the others. Hayden dropped his controller and jumped on Anderson's back. Oliver shouted for them to stop being so rough, but he barreled toward them, knocking both guys to the ground. I couldn't help but laugh at their silly horseplay and I didn't miss the wistful glint in Jackson's eye.

Change sucked and an intense shudder of anxiety gripped me.

"Heaven," Anderson said, escaping Hayden's grip. "Are you okay? Is it what you wanted to talk to us about?"

Their eyes lit up and every one of them focused on me. Here was my chance to let them know I was ready for more with them. I wanted to step outside the box, but all of that seemed stupid in light of my father coming back and the change ahead.

I felt the noose tightening about my neck.

"Is it your dad?" Oliver asked.

They had to know the truth—or some of it. I walked into the middle of the bedding and sat down, gesturing for them to follow.

"I need to tell you something." My hands shook and Hayden took one in his own to settle me.

Jackson touched my back. "Babe, you can tell us anything."

No, I couldn't, but they had to know enough to stay safe. "So, here's the thing, my dad is...pretty charismatic."

"He's a preacher, right?"

"He is, an evangelist and also a crook. When I was ten he was busted for stealing money from the church in Oceanside. He had a drug addiction and a whole heap of bad habits."

"Holy shit," Jackson said.

"The church agreed not to press charges if he joined their prison mission team, which involved traveling around the country preaching in prisons and to the less fortunate."

Hayden's eyebrows shot up. "Prisons? Like Johnny Cash."

"Shut up, dude," Anderson said, smacking him on the arm.

"I wish. No, he's nothing more than a petty thief and a con-man. He grew up in the oppressively religious town of Oceanside, and since the church covered for him and it appeared as though he left me and my mom, the town assumed we were the sinners. That's why we moved to Allendale." I took a deep breath. "I had no idea he was back. I doubt my mom knew either, until he showed up."

"Wow, that's pretty intense," Oliver said. "Why didn't you tell us about any of this?"

I shook my head, fighting back tears. "Because it's embarrassing and weird. I grew up with a lot of rules and shame was a common punishment. You guys were so different. So accepting. I didn't want to drag my past into our relationship."

Jackson spoke up. "He seemed excited to see you and he's taken an interest with school and everything. That can't be bad."

"My father has a way of manipulating people—things—and situations. He's very controlling. He believes in one set of rules for the women in his life and a whole other for himself."

"You're afraid he'll find out about us?"

And what he'd do to me or them if he found out.

I nodded. "We can't let him find out. And you can't engage him, do you understand? If he shows up asking for a favor or offers you a job of any kind, say no."

Anderson's forehead creased. "Heaven, is he dangerous?"

Physically, no. Emotionally...

His green eyes held mine and I had no doubt he understood me. He grabbed my free hand and said, "If you want us to stay clear of him, that's fine. We can do that. And as much as none of us want to hide our relationship, we'd already decided to take things slow at school. None of us want you to go through the stuff that happened at Allendale."

"Yep," Oliver agreed. "We're just your amazing group of BFFs that, you know, can't keep our hands off of you."

"Thank you. I hate dragging you into anything involving him or my family."

"Babe, you are our family," Jackson replied.

Hayden leaned over and kissed my ear, sending a chill down my spine that replaced the anxiety with something different—better. We'd get through this like we've managed every other obstacle over the past year.

Together.

31

———————

"Is that what you're going to wear?" my mother asked as I came down the stairs.

I shot her a look, then one down at my dress. It was a summer sundress that hit just below my knees and had criss-cross straps over my back. Zero cleavage. "What's wrong with this?"

Her outfit didn't escape me. I had no idea what corner of her closet she pulled it from, but she should have left it there. It was navy blue. The skirt was long and down to her ankles. A heavy cardigan covered her plain top. The outfit was bland, boring, and shapeless.

I touched the railing, feeling the strongest sense of déjà vu I'd ever had.

"Mom. My dress is fine. What are *you* wearing?"

We stared hard at one another before she said, "I just don't want to cause any problems."

"Mom, we fought long and hard to get away from that church. If it were up to me we would not go back today, but I understand you want to go support Dad. I can do that, but I'm not changing who I am."

She nodded, straightening her top. I could see the panic in her eyes. She didn't want to go either but my father...damn him, he got under her skin. One week back and he'd wormed his way into our lives, showing up at the house, sitting at our table drinking coffee and reminiscing about old times. Then Friday he asked us to come to the church and support him on his first Sunday back.

I couldn't believe my mother said yes.

She said yes and it was like the last seven years came crashing down.

Except, I thought, swallowing back, I had a week before leaving Allendale for school. If I worked hard and stayed focused, maybe I'd never have to come back here again.

"Hold on," I said, running upstairs. I grabbed a light sweater out of the closet and came back down. My mother saw it and sighed in relief. "I'm not changing for him," I declared.

"I don't want you to." I believed her.

My only real concern was if my father would accept it.

ENTERING the church was like going back in time. The smell, the sounds, the people. Nothing had changed. The walls were the same wood paneling, and yellowing stained glass blocked out most of the sun. The sanctuary felt stuffy and I irrationally gulped for air before walking in. My father combed the aisles, greeting parishioners as they took their seats on the hard, wooden pews. These people filed in up the center row, dressed in the same dark, drab clothing as my mother. Straight hair. No makeup. Ankle-grazing skirts.

Now I understood my mother's reaction to my sundress better. I wasn't one of the sheep. I buttoned the cardigan and noticed the head minister, Preacher Billips, with his white hair and face with hard lines of judgement sitting in the ornate chair by the pulpit.

Daddy walked straight toward us, smile bright on his face. It didn't travel to his eyes; no, that part of him was assessing, our hair, our clothes, our expressions. Did we meet his standards? Did we represent him properly? I knew I had too much eyeliner under my eyes, too many rings in my ears.

I smoothed the front of my skirt and plastered a nervous smile on my face.

"Hi, Daddy," I said, wanting to please him. Why? Why did I do it? His judgment ceased and he smiled genuinely.

"Hey, baby girl, you look beautiful. Thank you for coming." He took my mother's hand and squeezed it. I felt the oppressive stare of every eye in the church on us.

And then he was gone—speaking to others walking in the door.

It was like nothing had changed. Like he'd never been sent away to repent for his sins. In my mind I'm transformed into a little girl, sitting on the same hard pew, listening as Preacher Billips droned on and on about hellfire and redemption. I didn't know what it meant then, but now...my skin itched thinking of all the eyes on me.

Did they know about Justin? About me? About the lies and rumors that followed?

I swallowed nervously as the music came to a halt and Preacher Billips came down from his throne and told the story of the prodigal son. He rested his hand on my father's shoulder and it was clear all was forgiven.

The church had taken him back. He bought his way in by saving souls, and god knows whatever shady scams he implemented along the way. I'd learned a lot in the last year about trusting my instincts, about looking past the exterior to the heart and soul of a person, and everything about my father set me on alert.

"Thank you for the warm welcome," he said, smiling the preacher and across the sanctuary. "I can't wait to share my experiences from outside this wonderful community with you all, but most of all I'm grateful to be back home with my family."

The family he left.

The family this congregation shunned.

I plastered on a brave face, because that was who I was. My father's eyes connected with my own, and I realized that I learned that skill from him.

~

"Heaven, it's wonderful to see you again," an older woman said as I stood outside the church in the sweltering heat. If only I could take off my sweater. Oh wait. I can. I did.

"Nice to see you, too," I said to the woman I didn't recognize. Her eyes skimmed over my bare arms and the faint scars that were still visible. I smiled tightly.

"I see you're still a spit-fire, like your mother."

My mother was standing with my father, falling right into the role of minister's wife. Nausea rolled through my stomach.

"I guess I am."

The gray-haired lady looked up as my parents approached. She raised her eyebrows at my dad. "Just saying hello to your daughter. I'm hoping things settle down for her now that you're back home."

He doesn't respond to that but his eyes set on me and I squirmed as he sent her on her way.

"I see everyone here is as judgmental as ever," I said, feeling no shame.

"They mean well," he replied. "Following God's will is a challenge, Heaven. Even for the most faithful."

He was so smug.

"Well, this was great and everything," I said, "but now that the dog and pony show is over, I really need to get back. Amber and I leave in a few days and I have a bunch of stuff to pack."

"I'll go get the car, sweetie," my mother says, making a break for it. I don't blame her.

My father grabbed me gently by the elbow. "I've been meaning to talk to you about your housing accommodations at the university."

"What about them?"

"I took the liberty of contacting the school and learned you'd signed up for co-ed housing?" he asked.

"Yes."

"Well, I changed it to the all-girls dormitory."

"You—you can't do that. Amber and I already got our dorm assignment."

"I'm aware of that," he said. "But since I'm paying for your education now, I feel like I have the right to some of the decisions being made—and co-ed housing is out."

"You're paying for my education?"

I almost laughed. He hadn't paid for anything since he was gone. Not a dime.

"Yes, since I've returned here as associate pastor, Oceanside has offered me a generous salary. I've also spoken to your mother. It will be a huge relief to her to have assistance on this."

I swallowed. My mother had been working hard to cover just the first semester of school and financial aid was taking care of the rest. I'd planned on getting a job for extra expenses. But if Mom didn't have to pay, then she could stop taking double-shifts. She could rest a little.

"Mom knows about this?" I asked.

"I ran it by her."

Which means he told her what was happening. This was how he always was. Bossy and controlling.

"I can't back out on Amber."

"I wouldn't expect you to. Your friend should stay in appropriate housing as well. If it makes it better, I secured you a suite in the new Stetson Hall. Comes with a bathroom and a kitchenette."

I blinked. "Those are impossible to get."

He shrugged. "Someone owed me a favor. I secured you two a room to share. How does that sound?"

"No extra cost?" I asked. Amber's parents aren't broke, but Stetson Hall is the most expensive dorm on campus.

"None." He smiled, knowing he'd snared me like a hare. "Like I said, someone on campus owed me a favor. It's all taken care of."

A favor? I didn't want to know what kind of business dealings my father had on campus. Just because he was religious didn't mean he was legit.

My mother drove up to the curb and waved.

"I'll do this," I said, "because Mom needs a break. But don't think you can walk back into my life and change whatever you want."

He glanced around, making sure no one was listening. "I know you're angry I've been gone."

"I'm not angry, Daddy. It just is what it is. We've moved on. I'm not the same girl you left all those years ago."

I kept my eyes on my father, knowing he'd just manipulated his way back in my life. I bit back the fear it gave me, the anxiety blossoming in my chest.

"A girl needs her father," he said, watching me walk to the car. I sat in the front seat and clarity hit me like a bolt of lightning.

My father wasn't here just for work, to build the church. No, he was back in our lives, and I had the feeling it would be harder than ever to escape him a second time.

32

———————

Two Months Later

After a relatively quiet summer and acclimating to college life, the campus changed drastically with the fall semester. The students returned in droves, the quiet halls turned into echo chambers of laughter, shouts, and roommate squabbles. So far though, college had given me the taste of personal freedom I'd been looking for. No curfew. No suddenly returning fathers. And no checkered past. Amber and I still got along well (other than a brief fight over who ate the last Oreo—it was Jackson) and our other suitemates seemed...okay.

"So, the guys are headed over to a party at Hayden's frat house after workouts," Jackson said, running his nose along the column of my neck. Chills ran down every inch of my body and it took everything in me not to drag him through the common area and back to my room.

The best I managed was fisting my hands in his shirt and croaking, "Yeah?"

"You and Amber are welcome to come."

I raised an eyebrow. "You know I'm not really a party-goer."

"You may not like parties, Heav, but parties definitely like you."

Two girls passed us in the hallway, their eyes skimming Jackson's lanky frame. My father may have signed me up for an all-female dorm, but men were allowed in before curfew.

I cut my eyes at them in warning and they both looked away.

He noticed and laughed against my neck. "I love it when you're possessive."

"Yeah? I've had to work quadruple time for the last two months. I'm about to tag you all with a tattoo."

"Property of Heaven Reeves." He licked his bottom lip. "I like it. But it seems like it goes against our 'no public declarations' agreement."

Fuck that agreement, I wanted to say, but I stepped back instead. I hated that we had to hide our relationship in an environment where hook-ups and sexual experimentation was the norm. None of them had John Reeves, Oceanside Community Church Associate Minister, as their dad.

My father had been fairly MIA since I'd arrived. Just a few phone calls and texts. He'd moved back down to Oceanside to start his job of saving souls and bilking his congregation. He seemed busy, which was good. Less time for him to keep track of me.

Jackson's phone chimed—most likely Oliver in warning about their training session that started in fifteen minutes.

"Meet you guys around nine?"

"I'll ask Amber if she wants to go."

He nodded and gave me a quick kiss. Jackson, out of the four, was the biggest fan of PDA. Everything about him dripped of sexy confidence and it definitely made him hard to resist despite our agreements otherwise.

"So how long have you two been dating?" Ruthie asked after I caught my breath and came back in the room. She's a short girl with curvy hips and fiery red hair. She had a way of carrying herself that made me feel immature and consistently underdressed. Her side of the suite is covered in fashion magazine photos and supermodels. Whereas mine was a montage of photos from back home, movie posters, and Hayden's artwork. Needless to say, we didn't have a lot in common.

Amber and I shared a look. I might be a chicken but I just wasn't ready to tell them about my relationship status. For the first time in a year, I felt the freedom of not having everyone know all of my business. "A while."

"He's hot." She looked up from her magazine. I couldn't help but stare at her acrylic nails and how she looked like an insect while flipping through the pages. "What about his friend? The one in the baseball shirt. I saw him with you guys in the coffee shop."

"That's Oliver. He's uh, got a girlfriend from back home," Amber said, covering for me. I smiled at her gratefully.

Samantha, tall and slim with amazing curly dark hair, walked out of their room and joined in the conversation. "Oh well, poor thing. The girls will line up for him. They'll probably break up by Thanksgiving."

"Doubtful," Amber replied. "He's super loyal and head-over-heels for this girl."

"Sure." She tossed the book aside. "Maybe. But lesser men have succumbed for a taste of college pussy."

Amber and I wrinkled our nose at the word, not because we're prudes but...well yeah, maybe we were.

Once Samantha and Ruthie left the room, I asked, "Jackson wants us to go to a party at Hayden's fraternity tonight, you in?"

She and Ben were trying their relationship long distance—and with the open agreement to date others. It'd been a hard adjustment but she'd been flirting with the idea of going out.

"Sure."

Samantha leaned her head out. "Did you say frat party?"

I picked at the fringe on my jean shorts. "Uh, well one of our friends is in the soccer frat and..."

"We're in," she said. Ruthie squealed from the other room. "What time?"

"Nine? He said nine." My eyes darted to Amber's but she just shrugged. It wasn't a big deal to her but letting these girls into my personal life? After last year it was hard. Really hard, but college was new and these weren't the judgmental jerks I grew up with. Maybe they wouldn't care.

If they found out. I had no plans at all of them finding out.

"Great, be ready at nine," I told them, and they squealed again before slamming their door.

I groaned and leaned back in my seat. "So, first frat party," Amber said. She looked more excited than I thought she would—being the major feminist. I can only imagine frat parties fall onto her patriarchal shit list.

"Any idea what you're going to wear?" she asked me and I groaned again, falling back on the couch. "Come on." She laughed and grabbed my hand. The weird thing about Amber was that, for a girl out to beat the patriarchal system, she sure loved to dress up for a party.

33

Surprisingly, Ruthie and Samantha were ready on time, overly dressed in glittery tops and skin-tight jeans. Not that I'd judge, because I wouldn't. Women had the right to dress however they want, and if they felt like donning sparkly tank tops and wedgie-inducing pants, then more power to them.

It was late summer and I wore a gray, cotton halter that tied behind my neck and high-waisted shorts, with little diagonal buttons down the hips. I pulled my brown hair into a messy bun and slipped wide silver hoops in my ears. Leaning into the bathroom mirror I applied a deep red lipstick—one that Anderson told me he liked— and glanced over my shoulder at Amber.

I laughed at her T-shirt. "Nice one."

"You're really wearing that?" Ruthie asked, when she caught sight of her.

Amber held it out so the words were more visible.

Feminism is My Second Favorite "F" Word

The white shirt was knotted at the waist and she wore it with cut-off jean shorts. Her black hair hung over her shoulders in two braids. She was fierce but adorable.

"Sure, why not?" Amber asked.

"It's just a little...political?"

Amber rolled her eyes. "If someone can't handle my politics, then he can't handle me."

Ruthie walked past me, grabbing her bag and stopping when she saw the scar on my upper arm. "Ouch. What happened?"

"Accident," I said, covering it self-consciously with my hand, although I hadn't cut myself in months. I still felt the shame of that weak moment.

Our dorm was in the middle of campus and fraternity row was about a half a mile away. After the third hill I'm glad that I wore my Converse instead of heels like Ruthie and Samantha. Truthfully, I'd made that mistake at a party before and I didn't plan on doing it again.

Music pulsed down the street, vibrating and loud before we even arrived. Groups of students walked up and down the street headed to different parties. The whole thing gave me flashes of PTSD and I kept looking for Spencer or Mark to stumble out of one of the massive homes, secretly recording all my moves. Spencer wasn't here, though. After doing a short stint in juvie, his probation required him to stay close to Allendale for the next year.

"Why did we come again?" I asked.

Amber linked her arm with mine. "Because Jackson talked you into it and you have a very hard time saying no to that boy."

I rolled my eyes—mostly at myself, because that was true. "Too bad he doesn't have the same problem."

"Still haven't talked to them?" she asked.

"No. Not yet."

As we approached the loud party it didn't seem like tonight would be the night, either. Hayden's frat wasn't exactly typical since it was made up of just the soccer players. He'd spent the last few weeks juggling his practice schedule, rushing, and initiations. I thought the other guys may get upset knowing he'd be with new friends and teammates, but their bond was stronger than that. I just hated how busy he was all the time.

"Hey," I said, sidling up to Anderson, who was waiting out front. He looked amazing. Tall and lean. If the other girls knew about the swimmer's body he had hidden under that light blue T-shirt, they'd lose their minds.

He wrapped his arms around me and gave me a hug. In my ear he whispered, "You look fantastic and a little nervous."

"You too." Parties weren't Anderson's thing any more than they were mine. But we supported one another and Hayden invited us. We couldn't say no.

He pulled back and said hello to Amber and the other girls. They eyed us suspiciously. Ruthie didn't hold back. "Another handsome boyfriend? You've got to teach me your methods."

Anderson had never been one to play it cool. He was incredibly literal. Loyal. And incapable of lying. Thankfully, Amber interrupted. "Hey Anderson, I didn't think they let you guys out past six. Don't you have to get up at dawn for training?"

"Oh, you swim, right?" Samantha asked. "Heaven mentioned she had a friend on the swim team."

"Olympic development," I added. "He doesn't drink. Or party. Or really do anything fun. Total nerd."

He feigned hurt, but it was enough to make my suitemates head up the path to the house. Amber winked and followed.

He grabbed my hand and pulled me into his chest. His voice was low and deadly. "I may not do anything fun, but I do you."

His jaw tensed, like he was seconds from breaking the deal for no public displays. Anderson was right. He did do me and it was amazing. Every time I looked at him, a small knot of want twisted in my belly.

"So," I said, easing away from him, because now was not the time nor place. "Since you'll be heading to bed soon, we probably should go find the others. Check out Hayden's new digs?"

His eyes held mine for a beat longer. "That's the plan—unless you had something else in mind?"

"Nope. This is perfect. And be nice," I said, then added, "And no flirting with other girls. And no drinking because you do have to get up early tomorrow."

His forehead furrowed and it was adorable. "Since when do I flirt with other girls?" I looked up on the porch of the house where a dozen college girls stood around. All beautiful. Many available. He sighed and rubbed his neck. The Allendale Four were well acquainted with female attention.

"You may not flirt with them, but I suspect you'll have the opportunity." I smiled mischievously. "It's not fair to lead them on."

"Don't worry, I suspect I'll spend most of my time keeping Jackson and Hayden from punching any guy that looks your way."

"College is going to be tough, isn't it?"

I knew he wouldn't cheat, but a guy like Anderson? He was drop-dead gorgeous. Chiseled jaw, brilliant eyes, killer body. Oh, and he was broody, which drove me absolutely fucking crazy all through high school—so I got the appeal. He'd have a million girls chasing him around by the end of the night, and the ones not chasing him would be eyeing the others. But we would deal with it. We'd all deal with it.

A hulking figure pushed through the crowd on the porch. "Excuse me. Sorry. Oops! That was your foot, sorry man." Hayden appeared, beaming down on us with a smile.

"Heaven!" he called, running down the stairs and giving me a massive hug. He lifted me in his strong arms. "You came."

"Of course I came," I said, rolling my eyes, well aware of the scene we were making. I tapped his shoulder. "Can you put me down?"

"I can, but I sure as hell don't want to."

Jackson appeared at the top of the steps, holding two cups. "Dude, put Heaven down." He did so reluctantly and Jackson gave me the drink. It was a fruity spiked punch. Anderson sighed. Drunk Heaven was trouble. We all knew it. Anderson's shoes knew it. The side of his car knew it. I held the cup in my hand.

"I promise I will not puke on you, okay?"

He shook his head. "God, don't remind me."

Jackson grabbed Anderson by the arm and winked. "Come on, Oliver's playing Amber in Jenga. Let's go watch her kick his ass."

Hayden stood over me, tall and massive.

"So this is your new house?" I asked, trying to see it past the people and garbage all over the yard.

"Yep," he shoved his hands in his jean pockets. "You want the grand tour?"

Our eyes connected, because yeah, I wanted the tour, and to see his room and to be alone with him. That's why I came. No one would miss us. Not in a crowd this size.

With his hands still in his pockets, Hayden led the way.

～

THE LAST TIME I went into a bedroom with a guy at a party, my whole life flipped upside down. Today that wasn't the case, because I didn't know anyone here, no one in college cared if I went off with a hot guy. It didn't hurt that I had a few well-placed friends in the crowd that had my back.

"I've missed you," he said the instant the door shut. The music and voices from outside sounded muffled through the door. One side of the room was a wreck—his roommate's—while his bed was wrinkled but made.

"I miss you too. Soccer sucks." I pushed him against the wall, craving the feel of his body.

"Hey, don't blame soccer."

I looked up and smiled. He loved his sport, but from the glint in his eye and the hard bulge in his pants, not as much as he loved me.

If anyone would go along with my plan to escalate our relationship it would be Hayden, I was sure. I pushed up on my toes and kissed him hard, tasting the beer on his tongue. His hands gripped my waist, fingers pressing against my skin. His breathing grew rapid, his movements rough. I thumbed the button on his pants and his breath caught. His fingers wove into my hair and I kissed him again and again and again. He swung me around, carrying me to the small bed and throwing me down, eliciting a squeal. God, I wanted him so bad.

Hayden was huge; tall and broad. He held his upper body up as his hips ground into me. Butterflies filled my belly and his lips were so desperately hungry. I wanted him so bad and there was zero doubt he felt the same.

I hooked my thumbs in my waistband and his eyes glazed over for a brief second and I thought I had him, really had him, but instead he groaned and turned away.

"What?" I said, over my pounding heart. He ran his hand over his face. I stood up and he took a step back.

"We should go back downstairs."

"You're kidding." He didn't answer. "No really, you're kidding, right?"

"I should go back downstairs." He didn't look me in the eye. Couldn't.

"What's going on here?" I looked down at my outfit—glanced in the mirror over the dresser. "Is it me? Is there something wrong."

He reached for me, fingers trembling and pressed his forehead to mine. "No, absolutely-fucking not. It's not you. But this is not happening here."

"Why not? I'm ready. You're ready." I pushed against his crotch. He was *definitely* ready.

He gave me a hard look; one filled with want and something else —a hesitation. I searched for the reason for all this. The small issue that'd been building between us all for some time. Even with Anderson.

He swallowed hard, rebuttoning his pants and shifting to a more comfortable position.

"Look, Heaven," he grimaced, "the guys and I made a deal. No one treats you like a piece of ass. No matter how tempting you are."

I stared blankly at him. "You did what?"

"We love and respect you." He touched my shoulder but I brushed his hand off. "You've been through so much and none of us wanted to hurt you again—pressure you in a way you weren't comfortable with. You're fragile, Heaven, and none of us want to risk that."

"Shut up, Hayden. You're making it worse."

A knock at the door interrupted us but Hayden didn't move. His big arms crossed over his chest and his eyes locked on mine.

"Heaven—"

"Get the door. I'm not staying here."

He still didn't move so I crossed the room instead, opening it and letting in a flood of music. One of Hayden's teammates stood in the hallway. His expression filled with an apology when he saw us.

"Sorry dude, Bertram was looking for you and I...I didn't know you were up here with..." His eyes darted to me and back to Hayden.

"Take him," I said, pushing past him. "He's not busy."

"Heaven!"

I used the interruption to disappear into the loud music and writhing bodies of the party-goers. I saw the sparkle of Ruthie's dress as I passed the living room. The bright smile of Amber as she kicked Oliver's ass in whatever drinking game they'd moved on to in the kitchen. A bright-faced girl stood by her side, rooting against Oliver, and it all just made me feel more lost and alone.

It wasn't until I hit the warm air outdoors that I was able to breathe. Which just pissed me off more. Maybe Hayden was right. I was too vulnerable to push our relationships harder. The slightest bump and I completely panicked.

I left the trash-strewn yard and headed across campus toward my dorm. It was a modern building—taller than the rest—and I could see the rooftop peeking over the other facilities.

The guys would be furious to know I left without telling them. A sinking feeling built in my stomach. This was not how I wanted the night to go. I brushed the tears out of my eyes with the back of my hand.

My phone buzzed, flashing light. The texts rolled in.

Where are you?

What's wrong?

What the fuck did Hayden do?

Stay where you are—we'll come get you.

Heaven...

Babe, pick up.

"They're not going to stop until you respond to them," a voice said right behind me.

I screamed in absolute terror and spun around, lashing out with my fists. Wild hair and bright eyes came into view.

"Goddamn it, Anderson." He caught my wrists with his hands,

probably hoping to save his pretty face from a pummeling. "You scared the shit out of me."

"Well you scared the fuck out of us." He pulled out his phone and typed a message. It beeped on our group text and I checked instinctively.

Found her—Safe. I'll walk her home.

Jackson responded first. *Thx Bro*

"What if I don't want you to walk me home?"

He shrugged. "Then you can walk by yourself. And I'll just follow a respectable amount of space behind you and make sure you get there safely."

I clenched my jaw. "Do you really not trust me to walk to my dorm alone and get there in one piece?"

He frowned. "I don't trust the assholes on campus, Heaven, not you. It's dangerous for any female to walk by herself at night—right outside the party district."

I rolled my eyes. "So this isn't about me being too 'fragile'?"

"What are you talking about?"

"Hayden told me everything. I know what you're all doing. Why you treat me with kid gloves. You think I'm going to lose it again. That I'm vulnerable and if you push me too hard—in life, in bed—I'll break."

His lack of response and the tight tic of his jaw was all I needed to know that Hayden hadn't spoken just for himself. Guilt shadowed Anderson's expression. "Perfect, so you think it, too."

He spoke carefully. "I know we care about you—desperately— and that some of the shit that went down last year was intense. You've needed time to heal, not a bunch of horndogs humping your leg all the time."

Tears welled in my eyes and I pushed them away with the back of my hand.

"You guys don't get to make that decision for me. We're either in this relationship together or not at all."

Anderson's face was devastatingly handsome even in the shadowy lamplight that brightened the walkways through campus. He reached for my arm and rubbed his finger along one of the scars I no longer hid. He bent down and kissed the puckered skin with warm lips and a tenderness impossible to describe.

Acts like that made it super hard to stay angry with him.

"I think we need to talk."

"Me and you?" he asked.

"All of us."

He nodded and ran his hand down my arm, linking his fingers with mine. "Tomorrow. My room. We can have some privacy and hopefully clear some of this up, okay?"

"Thank you."

He brought my hand to his lips and kissed the back. "There's room in our relationships for growth. I believe that, and it's possible we've been too protective, but you have to understand how we feel. You're the most precious thing in our lives. We'll guard you with our everything. All the time."

His words sent a chill down my spine. I knew I had something special with the Allendale Four, I just didn't fully realize the lengths they'd go to protect me. But they also had to give me agency in my own decisions. I should have a say in our relationship—not just be directed. If I wanted that, I'd go back home.

34

ANDERSON

A MILLION THOUGHTS ran through my mind as I kissed Heaven goodnight outside her dorm. I did have to get up early for practice. I had routine, but damn if this girl didn't constantly want me to break it and every other well-defined rule in my life.

"'Night," she said, for the third time, not wanting me to walk away. She'd been mad when I followed her across campus. Upset really, embarrassed, but we'd fix that. I swore to her we would.

I groaned into her shoulder, feeling the instant hard-on in my pants and the elevated heartbeat that happened every time she touched me. She'd had this effect on me since we were thirteen and it never got easier. Not after we'd had sex. God no, it only increased, knowing what it felt like to be with her—*in* her.

I kissed her quick, fast on the lips, then ripped myself away like a Band-Aid.

"Love you," I said, already walking away.

"Love you, too."

She was like a damned magnet, but thankfully she finally walked inside and shut the door.

My phone buzzed.

It was her.

Don't forget tomorrow

I won't.

I passed a group of students, all a little wobbly on their feet heading back to the dorms. I skirted out of the way, not wanting to be trampled or vomited on. Taking the path back to my building, I scrolled through the phone and found the A4 group chat.

She's home. Safe.

Jackson-*You with her?*

Dropped her off.

Hayden-*Is she pissed? I swear I didn't do anything.*

She's upset—wants to talk.

Oliver-*about wughat?*

Jackson-*wtf?*

Oliver—a*bout WHAT. SHUT UP. I'm DUNK.*

My room. Tomorrow. She'll be there and we'll talk

Hayden-*Ok*

Jackson-*Yep*

Oliver-*ahoairneugougha*

I shook my head and shoved my phone in my pocket.

There was no way I was tipping them off about what Heaven was upset about. No fucking way. They'd lose their minds and want to come up with a plan, which is what got us in the dog house in the first place.

Heaven was right, I thought, climbing the steps to my dorm. We'd made a decision without her. To protect her, because even though she was a strong, amazing woman, she had to work through some tough shit over the last year. Heaven tried to hide the darkness that bothered her, but I knew it lingered—so did the others. The only thing we had control over was how we treated her. How we protected her and kept her safe. None of us wanted her to ever—*ever*—feel like she was just a body to us, an outlet.

Not like Spencer. Or Mark, or those other douchebags in high school that thought they could use and take advantage of her.

I walked in my room, tossing my keys and phone on the desk with a clatter.

We loved her. Cherished her, and she always needed to know that, which was why there was a line we'd drawn—one we were hesitant to cross. After all we were guys, teenagers, filled with hormones and sex-fueled desires. God, in my fantasies I'd done nearly every imaginable thing possible to her body. But that wasn't how you treated the woman you loved.

Was it?

Was I holding back? I thought, glancing at myself in the mirror hung on my door. I stripped off my shirt and jeans, getting an eyeful of the hard-earned muscles that lined my body.

Hell yes, I was holding back. Because if I crossed that line, the one between love and lust, the one where you let your animal desires take over, where did it stop? How did you stop?

And that's why we made the line, to keep that basic instinct in check. And now Heaven wanted to cross it.

I got in the bed and turned off the light, staring at the blank, dark ceiling. I knew one thing for certain: Heaven would get her way with us. She always did.

I just hoped it didn't open a can of worms we couldn't shut.

35

My phone rang on the way to Anderson's dorm.

"Hi, Mom," I said, lifting the phone to my ear.

"Hey sweetie, how are you today?"

"Pretty good." I didn't think she wanted to hear about how nervous I was about talking to the guys in a few minutes.

"How are classes?"

"They don't fully start back until this week, but I got everything I wanted even though my Monday, Wednesday, Friday biology class is at eight-thirty in the morning."

"You'll survive."

"With coffee, I suppose I will."

She paused for a minute and I crossed the grassy area that split the campus. People were already lounging on blankets, studying or just hanging out. I eyed one couple kissing openly, feeling jealous of their freedom.

"Honey, I wanted to let you know your father and I have been... seeing each other again."

I froze in the middle of the sidewalk. "What?"

"I know this is a surprise. I'm surprised, but things are going really well."

"Mom."

"I know, I know. I thought all of that was part of my past too. It's just...I think he's changed this time. It's just a feeling I have. I think he learned a lot while he was gone."

"Mom, your gut instincts are notoriously wrong." I wanted to remind her of how she handled the bullying situation last winter but didn't. It was still a tense subject.

"Heaven, I've made some bad decisions in the past where your dad was concerned, but I think he's really trying to clean up this time. Go legit. Pastor Billips at Oceanside is really taking him under his wing."

"Billips is a sexist pig, mom. That place is oppressive and just...I don't like it, okay?"

"We're taking it slow, Heaven, but it's something I feel called to explore."

Called. The word sent chills down my spine.

My heart thundered while she spoke and I scanned the area, trying to find something to focus on. A mop of blonde hair caught my eye and I held it in my sights as it moved toward me. "Be careful, Mom. He's hurt you before."

"I know. He has a lot to prove; like keeping a job and paying for your school. I need him to understand I'm not quitting my job and becoming a housewife again. It's not like I'm moving in right away."

"Moving in?" I asked. "Right away?"

"He bought the old Jameson place by the river. We're going to fix it up together, see how it goes. Then maybe I'll think about moving back in with him."

"Mom," I whispered as Jackson got closer, "do you even know where the money is coming from? For my school and this house? His salary can't be that great."

"I know he received a stipend while he was gone and he saved a lot of it. He was able to build a nest egg."

A nest egg? While we were barely scraping by?

That hit me like a ton of bricks. He had money while we were gone but never gave any to us? Even when Mom was working double shifts to pay the bills? I knew I needed to hang up before I said something I'd regret. "Hey, Mom, look, I'm about to walk into the library. I should probably go."

"Sure, honey. I just wanted to keep you in the loop." There was a muffled sound behind her. That was when I knew she wasn't alone. My dad had been there the whole time. "Your father wants you to know he'll be in the city on Wednesday night. He'll pick you up for dinner at seven."

"What? Mom, I'm not sure I'm available then!"

"I'm sure you'll work it out." She rushed out a goodbye and I was left holding the phone. Jackson stood before me with a curious look on his face.

"Everything okay?"

I stashed my phone. "Just my mom. She said my dad is coming up on Wednesday night for dinner."

"We'll make sure we're out of the way so he doesn't see us."

I hated it. I hated the lies and hiding. I felt like nothing in my life for the last year had been anything but one charade after the other. I'd finally discovered my personality—my style. I enjoyed dressing sexy. I liked flirting with my boyfriends. With my dad around, none of that was an option. He'd never approve.

Jackson watched me with his soulful, beautiful, blue eyes and I forced a smile. "Thank you. Hopefully he'll be gone early."

He linked our hands and directed us toward Anderson's three-story, brick dormitory. It was small and reserved for students with elite status in academics or sports that needed a quiet space to live. It was Saturday, though, and the rules were more relaxed.

"Anderson said you called this meeting? Is it about last night?" he asked. "Because if I need to kick Hayden's ass, I will. I mean, Oliver and Anderson will have to hold him down, but I'll totally kick his ass."

"Hayden didn't do anything," I said. Which is the problem. "Anderson didn't tell you what this is about?"

We climbed the stairs and he pushed the door open. "No."

I sighed, bracing myself for what I'd gotten myself into. A sex talk. A real one with my very real boyfriends. It was a topic that went against every aspect of how I was raised. Submissiveness was what a woman should be—not demanding or vocal in the relationship. But I also knew that was wrong—that type of attitude destroyed my parents' marriage and our family. I didn't want to be like them. I knew what I wanted and I planned on declaring that today.

We reached Anderson's room and Jackson knocked before opening the door, revealing the other three Allendale boys inside. They looked at me expectantly and damn it, there was no way to run.

Jackson closed the door behind me and Oliver, who looked like hell, made space for me to sit next to him on the bed. He moved slowly and groaned like an old man.

"What the hell happened to you?" I asked.

He ran his hand over his face. "Amber. She kicked my ass in drunk Jenga."

"Lightweight," Jackson said, sitting next to a quiet Hayden on the couch. Anderson sat in his desk chair and shook his head at the whole thing.

I glanced at Hayden, who just stared at his feet.

"First, I want to apologize to Hayden for leaving like that. It wasn't cool and walking off like that on my own was stupid. I can't promise I won't do anything like that again, but I'll try to keep it to a minimum."

Hayden's eyes snapped to mine. "I handled it all wrong. I shouldn't have said any of that."

"Any of what?" Oliver asked, forcing alertness. "What am I missing?"

Jackson was equally clueless. Anderson ran his hand through his hair, still damp from his morning swim. His jaw was shadowed with stubble. I looked to him for help and he nodded.

"Heaven feels like we've been a little overprotective—not just with things like her storming off last night, but in other ways."

Jackson faced Hayden. "Seriously, man, what did you do?"

"Nothing!" He held out his hands. "I swear."

"That's the problem," I blurted. "Hayden didn't do anything— well, at least not what I wanted."

Oliver frowned. "What did you want him to do?"

"We were in his room alone, for the first time in a while and..." I gave him a hard, pointed look. "He just stopped."

Oliver looked between us. I swear he wasn't this dumb. "Stopped?" he asked. Then it connected, like a lightbulb turning on. "Oh, right. Damn. Right. Well maybe it wasn't the best time. I mean, Hayden's bedroom is pretty funky."

"There were ton of people around, too," Jackson added.

"In the heat of the moment, I'm not thinking about those things. Can you honestly tell me any of you really are?" Guilt crossed their pretty faces. I looked at Hayden. "Did you really want to stop?"

He shook his head. "No, of course not."

Now they all looked down at their feet. Hayden's ears were red. I inhaled and then exhaled loudly. "I know you guys worry about me. I know my anxiety scares you and all the bullshit I went through last year, including Spencer trying—and failing—to assault me, was rough. But I'm okay. Better than okay. And you don't have to treat me like a baby."

Oliver reached for my hand. "But you're our baby, Heaven. Our sweet, sexy, fierce baby and none of us want to hurt you."

Jackson nodded in agreement.

Dammit. Even hungover Oliver was adorable. It was really hard to stay focused when they were sweet and sexy all the time. Focus, Heaven.

"You aren't hurting me," I told him. "You're holding back. Which is sweet and comes from a good place, but I want more." I glanced around the room. "From all of you."

From the expression on their faces and the glint in their eyes, I found myself caught in the crosshairs; four hungry men who definitely loved me—and wanted me—who'd been holding back for far too long.

"Are you sure you're ready for more?" Anderson asked.

"Yes, I'm sure."

"It's hard," Anderson said slowly, "Because the line between love and lust is thin and I don't think any of us ever want to give the idea that we're taking advantage."

"What if I want you to take advantage?" I asked, adding a little laugh. "You know I get horny too, right? It's not just a guy thing."

Hayden swallowed thickly. "You know you can't just say things like that."

"But I can! That's what I'm saying. I want you. I want your bodies. But I also love the way you love me." I look at Anderson. "That line between love and lust needs to be blurred."

"I'm game." Jackson said. "We'll do it your way, or rather the way it feels natural between each of us."

"Right," Hayden agreed. "No more stopping."

"Or frustrated, cold showers," I muttered.

Shocked eyebrows shot to the sky and Oliver's hand squeezed mine. The room was so quiet I could've heard a pin drop. Jackson opened his mouth to speak, the corner of his lips quirked up, but my phone buzzed—breaking the silence.

I took a peek. "It's Amber. I promised I'd get coffee with her and then go shopping for some last-minute school supplies."

Hayden cleared his throat. "For the record, I tried to walk Amber home last night, but she brushed me off for someone else."

"A guy?" As much as I loved Benjamin, it was time for her to move on—play the field a little.

Oliver shook his head. "No, not a guy."

I remember the blonde standing at the game table between him and Amber the night before. I knew it was time for her to move on but I didn't expect...wow.

I smiled. "I'll definitely get details."

"And now that school has started I'm going to make a group calendar for us—so we can keep track of everyone's classes and activities," Anderson said, swiveling in the chair.

"Good," I said. "I don't want to miss anyone's games or events."

I stood to leave but Oliver tugged me back down to the bed. He engulfed me in his arms. "Thanks for coming to talk to us, H. Next time don't take so long, okay?"

With the weight of my issue off my chest, everything felt different, freer, and I kissed them each on the forehead and left to find Amber. I was excited and maybe a little bit scared. I saw the hunger in their eyes. I'd felt their need. It was possible I'd just opened a box that I couldn't seal back, but I suspected we'd have fun figuring it out.

36

———

THE FIRST THREE DAYS OF CLASSES WENT SMOOTHLY; IF YOU CONSIDERED getting lost twice, forgetting to turn off my cell phone during class and watching the girls of the university discover the Allendale Four, smooth.

"Three different girls came up to Anderson after our Intro to Biology class this week," I grumbled to Amber. "I was standing *right there*."

"I'm sure he didn't notice."

"Who knows with him. You know he has a stone-cold expression." It was nice having Bio with him. It was kind of like old times but in a much bigger setting. The chemistry between us was just as intense as it had been back in high school—only now we weren't sitting behind lab tables but in a large lecture hall. Just today his leg brushed against mine and I nearly jumped out of my skin. I shot him a death stare and passed him a note.

No touching in class.

Why not?

The smirk on his mouth told me he knew the answer but I scribbled it down anyway.

Because I don't think our classmates want an actual biology lesson on reproduction, that's why.

228

He stared at that note long and hard. I thought he was finished but he scratched out his own note in perfect script.

Meet me after class then? Maybe get a little of this out of our system?

God I wanted that. So bad.

My dad is coming to town. Taking me to dinner.

He sighed, and I folded the note, tucking it into my hoodie pocket.

"Who knew college would be so busy I'd never have time to hang out with my guys," I said hours later. Amber came down with me to wait on the front steps of our dorm for my dad to pick me up.

"Maybe you can meet up after dinner?"

"You know Anderson goes to bed early—his swim time is around 6 a.m." I had to admit that wasn't the only reason. "I'm also keeping away from the guys while my dad is in town. I don't want him anywhere near them."

She nodded and said, "I think Ginger and I are going out on Friday night."

Ginger was the girl from the party. "Is this like a date or just a friend thing?"

"I'm not sure. I mean, I've never limited myself sexually, but you know Allendale wasn't the biggest pool of options."

"You do you, Amber, that's what college is about. Where are you going?"

"She's an art major and wants to take me to this little gallery downtown for a show."

"I love it. When do I get to meet her?"

She smiled shyly. I'd never seen Amber like this. Normally she was bold and brash—but this thing with Ginger was new. I got it. "Let's give it a little longer, okay?"

"Definitely."

A sleek black car pulled up to the curb and the window rolled down. My dad leaned over the passenger seat and smiled.

"See you later," I said. She gave me a sympathetic smile.

"Hi Dad," I said, walking to the car. I opened the door and sat in the front. He leaned over and kissed my cheek.

"How are you? How's the first week of classes?"

"Busy," I said. "All the information is a little overwhelming."

He drove the car off campus and into town. There were dozens of restaurants in the area and I shouldn't be surprised he picked the fanciest one. He pulled into the parking area and the valet opened my door.

"Thank you," I said, feeling awkward. I wanted to know where my dad got the money to pay for things like this. If he even had it—but there was no way I was going to ask.

He walked around the car and I tried not to flinch when he placed his hand on my shoulder, directing me to the door. "I can't tell you how much I've missed you. We have a lot to catch up on—everything you've been doing. My new job. It's an exciting time for our family."

We did have a lot to catch up on, but there was no doubt we both were keeping our own secrets. My father didn't want to know the truth about my life and I had a feeling he didn't want to tell me the truth about his. I followed him across the hardwood floors and into the quaint bistro with the distinct feeling that by the time the night was over, I'd have more questions than answers.

I SPENT the evening fielding questions about college, roommates and classes, and my thoughts on professors. My father gave away enough to let me know he was fully aware of my schedule and had taken the time to check up on my professors.

"Have you picked a church to attend yet?"

The question stumped me. Other than the week before I left for school hadn't gone to church since he'd left us—mostly because my mother and I couldn't handle the judgmental glares.

"No, not yet." I picked at my dessert.

"I notice you don't wear the cross I sent to you for your birthday."

I touched my neck, knowing it wasn't there. "Sorry Daddy, I took it off and forgot to put it back on."

Seven years ago.

"And are you dating anyone?" he asked, digging into his chocolate cake. He'd always loved sweets.

"Not right now," I replied, keeping it vague.

"Your mother said you were interested in a few boys from back home. The ones I met at the party."

I didn't like that my mother told him this, but the fact she kept her mouth shut about the specifics of me and the Allendale Four said a lot. She was letting my father back in but she still had her secrets too—our secrets. I wondered how long she'd hold out.

"We're just really good friends. They stuck by me during some tough times last year at school."

"Anything I should be concerned about?"

I shook my head. "Just regular teen drama. Mean girls. Stupid guys. I'm sure you've dealt with cliques before."

It was a jab at the snobby church community but I smiled to show I was kidding. He gave me a weak grin in return. We weren't to discuss his checkered past. I knew that, but I was also bitter about his leaving and the circumstances he left us in.

"Cliques are complicated but it seems like you made a smart decision—surrounding yourself with strong males." He held up his glass of wine and took a sip.

"I didn't befriend the boys because of their strength, Daddy. I'm quite capable of taking care of myself."

He smiled patronizingly. "I know you are, sweetheart, but you've always been sensitive." His eyes wandered to the faint scars near my wrists. "Too concerned about what others thought of you and allowing your fears to take control. Establishing healthy relationships is a good way to feel secure. Aligning yourself with dominant males is commendable."

I eyed him warily, knowing this meeting wasn't purely social. He wanted something and he'd spent the evening exerting his dominance over me with tales of his success and the fine dinner to lower my guard. I waited for the shoe to drop. It didn't take long.

"It was unfortunate that you and your mother had such a rough time while I was away on my mission. At the time it seemed best to cut all ties—let you have a fresh start. Now that I'm back I want to reconnect our family. It's important to me and for my position at the church. Your mother is willing to give me a chance and I'm hoping you are, too." He leaned back in his seat, dark eyes watching me carefully. "You're a beautiful and smart young woman, Heaven, and I'm happy to have the chance to assist you with your college degree. Your mother said you were going to have to take out loans and get a job otherwise, correct?"

"That was the plan, yes."

"You know I value hard work, and although I don't want you to take on a traditional job that would interfere with your academics, there are a few small tasks you could perform for me while you're here that would be beneficial to both of us."

A small knot of dread built in my stomach. "What kind of task?"

"I'm responsible for the growth of Oceanside Church and bringing in prominent members of the community. There is one family in particular that we'd like to join. Their son attends the university and it's my understanding he's very shy and a little socially awkward."

"Daddy, what are you asking me to do?"

"I'd like you to reach out to him. Make him feel supported. Represent our family."

"You know I'm not very social myself," I told him. "Like, small talk and that sort of thing. I'm afraid I'd do more harm than good."

He picked up his phone and scrolled through. My heart stalled in my chest, terrified of what he would show me. Pictures of me making out with ten different guys? The gossip and bullying? He held it out and I saw a photo of me on stage in my Winter Princess dress, crown sparkling on my head. "Although I'm not sure I approve of the dress, or the fact you appear to have four dates, you're definitely more charming than you give yourself credit for, Heaven. I think this is something you can do. Something you can do for me."

There was a tone in his voice—a heavy implication. I didn't have a choice here. He was paying for my education and housing. Not only that, I had secrets I didn't want him digging into.

"I can probably fit a few social events into my schedule."

He smiled. "Good. And these boys, you say they're all here at school?"

"Yes. They're all athletes and keep busy."

He folded his hands on the table. "I suggest keeping them at arm's length. What worked in the little town of Allendale may not benefit you here. I'm sure they're fine young men but you have a reputation to uphold—the daughter of a preacher."

"There's nothing inappropriate going on," I lied.

"The truth doesn't always matter, Heaven. If things look questionable, if they seem immoral, then that's just as bad."

Ignoring the irony of him telling me I needed to play nice to a shy boy in order of saving my reputation, I nodded, pretending like I was on board with his ideas. There was no way I'd ever cut my guys loose. Not for my dad. Not for anyone. I could play his game and perform his little tasks if it would keep him off my back.

37

MY FATHER'S CAR WAS BARELY OUT OF SIGHT WHEN I PULLED OUT MY phone and dialed.

"Can you come get me?"

"Of course."

I heard the forest green Mustang before I saw it and hopped in the front seat before Jackson could get out and open the door for me. The car smelled like a mixture of old leather and soapy skin. He sat in the driver's seat in a three-quarter-length-sleeved baseball jersey with the word "Allendale" across his broad chest in faded letters. His tan legs stretched out of blue mesh shorts and I saw the dark purple bruise on his knee, most likely from practice that day. A stark contrast to my dress and heels.

"You look amazing." His gray eyes raked down my body. "What's going on?"

I shook my head. "Just spent the evening with my dad and I need a brain scrubbing."

"You've got it. Where do you want to go?"

"Anywhere quiet—I just can't handle my suitemates right now or having to talk to someone in the hall."

He laughed. "Dorm life is hectic, right? I think it's the hardest thing to get used to." He rested his hand on my thigh, pushing the hem of my skirt up a little. "I think I have an idea of where we can go."

Jackson drove Oliver's car like it was his own. His hand loose on the wheel as he drove away from campus, away from town. In a short time, we were away from the residential neighborhoods that surround the campus and he slowed before taking a sharp turn down a side road. "I was afraid I'd miss it."

The drive was long and winding, cloaked with heavy tree branches. "Where are we?"

A small lake came into view along with a few picnic tables. A baseball field sat to the right of the parking lot.

"My little league team used to come out here sometimes. I remember riding in the back of the van, with Oliver and the other guys. We'd play a game, have a cookout, and swim in the lake. There's a little dock."

Before he opened the door, Jackson leaned over and kissed me. His moves were gentle, his tongue licking at my lips. "Mmmhmm, you taste like chocolate."

He tasted like sin and the butterflies in my belly knew how much trouble I was in.

He pulled away abruptly and hopped out of the car, running around to open my door before I had a chance to blink. I kicked off my heels and stepped into the warm, late summer night. He went to the back of the car and opened the squeaky trunk, lifting out a red blanket. He came back over, linked his fingers with mine, and walked me toward the water.

"I got my first home run on that field," he told me. "I can still remember the way the bat felt in my hands and the sound of the crack as the ball hit the wood."

"Even then, you were a stud."

He ran his hand through his shaggy hair and kissed me by the ear.

Sand coated my feet, and when we reached the dock, I stood on the edge and dipped my toes in the water. He tossed the blanket in the middle of the platform and wrapped his arms around me, resting his chin on my shoulder. The lake wasn't big—just a small swimming hole, but it was quiet and the sky overhead revealed a million stars.

"This is great," I said. "Thanks for coming to get me."

"Anytime, babe," he replied, flattening his hands over my belly. I felt the warmth build below my navel. The tiny coil and twisted from having him so close.

"One sec," he said and I watched as Jackson stretched the blanket on the dock. He took my hand and we sat together, leaning against one another's shoulders.

"So, your dad really stresses you out."

"You have no idea. He's just...he's not a good person. He's selfish and manipulating—I can feel myself getting caught up in his games."

"Can't you just ignore him? Say you won't see him anymore?" Jackson's parents weren't as MIA as Oliver's parents or as rich and perfect as Anderson's, but they were supportive in a way that he couldn't understand our family dysfunction.

"I wish I could but, he's paying for my school and I know my mom wants things to get better between them again. The occasional dinner isn't a big deal." I don't tell him there was more to our bargain—not now. Maybe not ever.

"Family obligations suck. I get that."

Jackson stretched out his legs and leaned back on his hands. I moved quickly, climbing into his lap. My skirt was flouncy. There was little between us but the cotton of my panties and the fabric of his shorts. Running my hands over his broad, firm chest, I leaned in, kissing his neck. He squirmed, laughing and grabbing for my hands, but I fought back, nibbling my way to his collarbone. It was no surprise when I felt him grow beneath me, followed by darkening and intensifying of his gray eyes.

He pushed the sweater off my shoulders and ran his hands down my arms, then touched my chin. "You're so beautiful."

I kissed him again, this time on the mouth, darting my tongue against his. The spot between my legs grew warm, wet, and I pressed against him, wanting to feel the heat.

Jackson and I had done many things together, but we hadn't gone all the way. Not yet. But now that we cleared the air—that I wasn't some fragile piece of china ready to break—we could take the next step.

I pushed him on his back and tugged my dress over my head. I hadn't worn a bra and his eyes widened, drinking me in. His fingers reached out but stopped inches away from my skin. "Are you sure about this? Outdoors? Because I'll stop right now and take you to a fancy hotel with a soft mattress and cushy pillows and room service and all that shit if you want."

I took his hands—both of them—and placed them on my breasts. "You promised me. No more playing it safe. I don't want any of those things. I just want you."

He nodded and squeezed, sending a jolt through my body. I tipped my head back, loving the way his hands felt against my body.

"I know you've wanted to do things to me," I said, my voice clear in the quiet night. "Don't hold back, Jax. Not now."

He sat up with a jolt, mouth crushed against mine. His fingers pushed at the lacy strip of fabric at my hip, tugging until I stood, straddling his legs, to get them off.

"Don't let me fall," I laughed, steadying myself by touching his head.

"Never."

He took his time, peeling them off inch by inch, blazing a trail down my legs with his fingers and lips. I stepped out of each side and the panties dropped to the dock, and I jerked in surprise when his hands moved to my backside, stroking my ass.

"Hey," I said, pushing at his shoulders. "Not fair leaving me up here. With nothing to do."

He ignored me, kissing one hip bone before traveling to the other, his mouth lingering over the sensitive skin. His lips brushed over my belly and my face heated with how close he was—how intimate we were. I stood naked on the dock, fully exposed, inexplicably trusting, with a million stars overhead. My knees buckled when I felt his breath between my legs. Breathless and shaking, I wove my fingers into his thick hair. My wobbly legs were held up with the one hand exploring my back side, while his other spread my legs wider.

"Is it cheesy if I say that you taste like heaven?" he asked, laughing over his words. I grunted in reply, unable to speak coherently. His tongue was hot, wicked; igniting a burning deep inside of me that I never imagined. Jackson kissed and sucked, taking me to the edge of the edge.

I blinked and caught my breath, tugging hard at his hair and forcing him to look at me.

"I want you inside of me. I want you to *come* inside of me."

He licked his lips, surely tasting me on them, and he pulled off his shorts, revealing his erection. His cock bobbed with freedom and he didn't hesitate—I didn't hesitate, easing down on his length.

"Goddam," he muttered into my hair. He filled me up—different than Anderson—and I liked this position. I *really* liked it. Sitting on his lap, eye-to-eye, mouth-to-mouth. There was no escaping the intimacy; the little pants that came with every roll of my hips. Every groan he buried in my shoulder. The rhythm was different this way— I was most certainly in control, although he'd pushed me so close to the edge that it only took a moment and his strong hand palming my tit that I came in a writhing mess while he continued to thrust.

My body contracted around him and his movement turned erratic, desperate and messy. His hips thrust upward and his hands gripped me like a man holding on for dear life. The strong line of his jaw tensed, all while mumbling my name and when he came, *god how he came*, I was still quivering, shuddering—feeling the exhilaration over every inch of my hot, prickly skin.

Jackson wrapped his arms around me and whispered in my ear, "Who knew I'd score two home runs at this park."

I couldn't help but laugh because damn, he was a fool. But he was my fool. When we parted, sticky with the residue of our lovemaking and the heat between our bodies, I watched as he stood over me, naked, ripped, and proud.

"You know what would make this even better?" he asked.

I shook my head, because nothing would make this better. It was already the best.

He offered me a hand and before I got all the way off the ground I realized what was happening.

"A swim."

"Jackson, no!"

We were airborne in a heartbeat and he smiled as we crashed into the water.

He reached for me under the water. It cooled my overheated skin. "I love you, Heaven Reeves."

"I love you too, Jackson Hall. But if I get bitten by a snake, it's your fault."

He pulled me into a kiss and I realized that he was probably right.

A swim really did make it better.

38

Jackson

I THOUGHT I'd feel guilty.

I thought she'd want me to stop.

I thought that crossing that line between love and lust was definitive. Two different, unique things. Things that you didn't do with someone you respected and loved.

You didn't take them to the edge of a ball park and screw them on a floating dock, until you did, and that's when you realized, well, *I* realized that the line was blurry and dammit, freaking amazing.

I didn't enter my relationship with Heaven a virgin, but before her I'd never been in love. Not outside myself, my family, and my brothers. I was a player. Elusive. Handsome and charming. I knew it. The girls back home knew it and no one begrudged it.

All of that stopped the minute Heaven came into our lives. Stopped cold.

That girl...she'd been barreling down the tracks with me before she sat on my lap and dry-humped me into oblivion all those months ago. I came so. Fucking. Hard, and the craziest thing was that it was enough. It was. I didn't have to claim her body. I had her heart.

But then we had that talk—the laying it on the line talk—about her needs and wants and desires. Not treating her like a fragile child. She was right, but the stuff she went through...it wasn't okay. Oliver fucking cried the day he told us about walking in on her with those blades. How he barely made it there in time to stop her.

We swore then to treat her with kid gloves.

Well, I just took off the fucking gloves.

I walked across campus the next day trying to hold back my swagger—the I-just-made-love-to-a-beautiful-woman swagger. Buuuut, it was impossible and when Anderson saw me coming, he raised an eyebrow.

"What's going on?" he asked. We waited here for Heaven before their class and suddenly nerves shot through me. What if she had regrets? What if I read the situation wrong?

And like that, I deflated.

In a low voice I said, "I took Heaven for a ride last night—she needed a break after seeing her dad."

"How did that go? I know she was nervous."

I shrugged. "Not great? Not awful? I think she wanted to blow off some steam."

We didn't ask. That was the deal—part of the Don't Treat Heaven Like an Object arrangement. We didn't discuss our sex lives with one another.

Anderson and I stood in a moment of awkward silence.

I cleared my throat. "We made some progress...on her request."

He nodded. "And everything went okay."

"Yeah. Like, fantastic, but..."

His eyes narrowed. "But what?" There was a threat in his tone.

"But nothing, swear. Jesus, Anderson, I treated her right. You know that."

He relaxed and ran a hand through his hair. "Sorry. I know. You said 'but'."

"What if what seemed okay last night in the dark isn't okay today in the daylight?"

"Did you respect her?"

"Yes."

"Did you get consent?"

"Of course." I wasn't an animal.

"Did you give her a choice? A chance to you know…participate?"

I thought about her on my lap, sinking down on my cock. I cleared my throat and shifted. "Yes, without a doubt."

"Then you're fine." He said with relief. "It was probably exactly what she wanted."

I stared at my shoes, hoping he was right. If I ruined it—or hurt her—or made her second guess herself in any way, I'd never forgive myself.

Anderson grew quiet, eyes cast across the student center. I brushed my hair out of my face and turned, seeing her for the first time since last night. She was gorgeous, red-cheeked with a small smile playing on her lips.

"Yeah," Anderson said. "I think you're fine."

I watched her come our way, hips swaying, and corrected him in my mind; we're fine.

39

IN HIGH SCHOOL, I wondered if virgins walked differently than women who'd had sex. It was back when I was trying to figure out how to pretend I wasn't one. I was sure the more-experienced girls had a particular swagger. I don't think I had a swagger as much as a strut. And although I lost my virginity to Anderson some time ago, I definitely felt a different spring to my step when I saw Jackson the following day on campus.

I spotted him before he noticed me and I took a minute outside the crowded student center to check him and Anderson out. I'd had sex with both of them—and planned to do it again. There was no loss of one to gain of the other—that was one of the perks of our specific kind of relationship. Sure, there were a lot of stressors balancing (and hiding) four guys, but experiencing the intimacy with them all was definitely not one of them.

Anderson noticed me first, raising a hand to get my attention. Jackson turned a beat slower, hair flopping into his eyes, although that doesn't stop him from checking me out, head to toe.

My cheeks heated, thinking about his lips and what they'd done to me the night before—how he'd explored me more thoroughly than anyone had ever before.

He licked his lips in memory and yeah, my walk was different. No doubt about that. It was one part eager, two parts confidence. Yeah, I felt confident knowing what we'd done and how I'd pleased him. I swallowed back the pride of seeing the way his jaw tensed when he came, and the weight of his arm over my shoulder as he walked me back to the car.

Yep, people who experienced that walked, talked, and felt different.

"Hey," I said. It sucked keeping my distance in public like this.

"We were just talking about Anderson's swim meet later this week against State. Think you can come?"

"I wouldn't miss it." Watching Anderson swim was like a gift from the gods. I turned to Jackson. "Thanks for hanging out with me last night."

"Anytime." He looked at the time. "Shit, gotta run. My stupid English Lit class is on the other side of campus."

"Later," Anderson said, giving him some kind of bro fist bump.

"Bye," he said to us both, tugging on the back of my shirt as he jogged off.

"Y'all hung out last night?" Anderson asked as we moved in the direction of our biology class. "Everything okay?"

"Yeah, I just needed to blow off some steam after dinner with my dad."

He nodded. "How did that go?"

"About as good as expected." We walked into class and took our seats. The professor wasn't there yet. "Oh, check this out, he brought up you guys—he thought I made a smart move by bringing you in last year during all the harassment."

"A smart move?" He took out his laptop. "Who talks like that?"

I laughed. "My dad. I told you—he's in a world of his own."

"So he's okay with you hanging out with us, then?"

I grimaced. "Eh, not so much. He thinks I need to broaden my circle at college." Anderson frowned and tapped his fingers on the desk. I laid my hand on his knee. "Hey, you know that's not how I feel, right? My dad is an opportunist, and right now he's worried about how my reputation will affect his paycheck. He doesn't think in genuine relationships but in how things benefit him."

"I know," he replied. He looked up and I saw my suitemate, Ruthie, watching us from across the room. I gave her a friendly smile and tried to discretely remove my hand from his leg. "I think I'm just overwhelmed with everything you know? I hate not being able to see you all the time."

"Dude, we have class three times a week together. I'm coming to your swim meet this week." I lowered my voice. "I have a feeling we can snag some private time before then, too."

His pupils dilated at the suggestion and he coughed, covering his mouth with his fist. "Actually, I thought maybe you'd want to do me a favor and help me study for the quiz on Friday."

I raised an eyebrow. "You know favors are what got me into a heap of trouble last year, right?"

He laughed. "A heap of trouble that brought me a lot of personal pleasure." He looks at the door just as the professor walks in. I get out my own laptop.

Anderson shifted his attention to the podium but he took out a small piece of paper and scribbled on it and passed it to me.

My meet is Thursday night and I have an approved practice that means I'll miss this class that day. Can you come over before the meet and bring me the notes?

Sure.

He replied back with a smiley face and I rolled my eyes, tucking the paper in my laptop back with the others we'd written so far this semester. With so many things changing in my life, the little things, like notes from Anderson and study dates, made everything feel a little bit more normal.

Amber and I were sprawled across the couch in the living room of our suite, binge-watching TV, when Ruthie and Samantha walked in laughing. They cut it short when they saw us and Ruthie pulled a couple of packages with trendy shop names to her chest.

"Ooh," Amber said. "Did you go on a shopping spree?"

The Ruthie and Samantha exchanged a look before she replied, "They were having a sale downtown. You know, clearing out for fall."

"Let's see," I said, sitting up.

She flashed two sweaters, one made of the softest-looking material ever. "Those were on sale?" Amber asked.

"Yeah." Her eyes slid to Samantha's. "But I think I got the last one."

She shoved it back in the bag and the two girls disappeared into their room, shutting the door behind them.

"Was that weird?" I asked, reaching for the bag of chips on the table. "It seemed weird."

"Definitely weird," Amber agreed. "Maybe she's one of those girls that doesn't want other people wearing what she's wearing."

"You mean, petty."

She shrugged. "If the shoe fits."

"God, I hate mean girls. So pathetic."

"I know you do. Me too. And it gives me an idea." A wicked grin spread across her lips. "We should go buy the same sweaters and wear them around all the time just to make her mad."

I snort-laughed and covered my mouth with my hand. "Dude, you're a feminist—being mean to other women isn't cool."

She rolled her eyes. "You're the queen of tit-for-tat, Heaven. Turnabout is fair play and all that. I just think that sometimes women who want to take down other women should be taken down a notch."

"You're ridiculous." My phone rang and I glanced at the screen. "Ugh. It's my dad."

"Ignore it."

It continued to buzz. "He'll just keep calling."

"Hey, Dad." I walked into the bedroom and shut the door for privacy.

"Sweetheart, how are you today?"

"Good." I waited for a beat, not wanting to share anything else. "What's going on?"

"There's an event I need you to attend."

"What kind of event?"

"Just a college thing. A social at the University Community Church. The young man I told you about will be there."

Ugh, a church thing? I didn't know how to respond.

"Noah has extended an invite to you as a favor to me. I'd like you to go and meet him."

"You want me to go on a date?"

"No, honey." I could hear the irritation in his voice. "I want you to go to a party. Have a little fun and while you're there, do me a favor by being nice to the son of a prospective church member." He took a steadying breath. "I'd really appreciate it if you could take the time to do this for me. It would help me out a lot. You know I've just come back and any extra effort goes a long way."

I still didn't know what my father was doing—recruiting a church member so hard seemed weird. I had to suspect the family must be loaded. My father was paying my tuition and if his job depended on him—or me—playing nice with this guy, then I didn't have much choice.

"Okay, I can do that. What's his name?"

"Noah Hancock."

"Okay. And he knows I'm coming?"

"Yes. He's going to send you the details."

I glanced at myself in the mirror and at the way I held the phone, knuckles white. Socializing like this wasn't something I was used to— my dad didn't get that. He just saw the photos of me as Winter Princess and that I had friends at my graduation party. He didn't know I spent the prior six months as a pariah or the seven years before that as an invisible nerd.

"Heaven?"

"Yes, Daddy?"

"I know you're nervous, but whatever you did to get the attention of those boys back in Allendale is what you should remember. That's all it is—getting a little attention. I have no doubt you can do it."

I hung up the phone and walked over to the mirror. I pushed my hair behind my ear and kept my eyes away from the largest of the scars on my arm. He was right, if there was one thing I knew how to do, it was to get attention. The problem was dealing with the conse-quences.

40

THE NEXT DAY WAS BRIGHT AND WARM AND IT DIDN'T TAKE MUCH FOR Oliver and Jackson to lure me down to the baseball field to watch them practice. The field was adjacent to the athletic complex and it wasn't uncommon for people to run or walk around the track during warm-ups or find a spot in the bleachers to study.

That being said, spotting my suitemate Samantha on the warm, metal steps was a surprise.

"Heaven?" she called before I could make my escape.

"Oh, hi." I looked around. "What are you doing here?"

"Well, to be honest I came out to watch your friend Oliver practice." She blushed. "I hope that's cool."

Uh, no. Not cool, Samantha. Definitely not cool.

"Oliver?"

She wrinkled her nose and pushed her long hair over her shoulder. "I overheard you tell Jackson you would come watch and I figured Oliver would be here too." Her eyes skimmed the field. Both guys were on the green lawn. They had on their practice uniforms. Tight gray pants, fitted T-shirts with the University's mascot across the front. They both wore caps; Oliver's low over his eyes and Jackson's turned backwards. My stomach fluttered at the sight of them.

"He's super-hot," she said, never taking her eyes off of him. "And really nice. He helped me carry a box up from the post office the other day."

When he came to see me, I wanted to add.

I'd admitted to my suitemates that I was dating Jackson—casually. And that I'd gone out with Anderson a few times as well. They seemed to accept that. Hayden and Oliver were harder to explain. The guys were around one another all the time and just like back at home, incredibly visible and noticeable. Four hot-as-hell best friends was a little impossible not to notice, even on a large campus. And me as the girl that hung out with them wasn't really a big deal. But pushing it beyond that was something I wasn't comfortable with. I glanced down to the field and Oliver looked up, catching my eye. He winked before throwing the ball with incredible force. I had the distinct urge to mark my territory.

"Oh my god, he winked at you! You are so lucky to have him as a friend."

"He's pretty amazing," I agreed. She shifted next to me, stretching out her long, thin legs. My eyes traveled up her arms, to the smooth skin, unmarred by scars or physical damage. Her eyes bright, unencumbered with a dark past.

Maybe Oliver deserved someone like Samantha? Maybe they should all get a chance to sow their wild oats, experience other girls —*normal* girls.

"Tell me something about him," she said. "What does he like? What's he into?"

Me.

He was into me, I wanted to tell her. He liked having his earlobe nibbled and he was the best snuggler. He treated me like a queen and was a really good listener. His cock was huge—like seriously—it was one of the reasons I hadn't had sex with him yet. I saw it and panicked, but I know when the time comes he'd be gentle and we'd have amazing fun.

"Guys," I blurted. "He's into guys." I made a face. "Sorry."

"Oh, what? Really?" She narrowed her eyes and studied him as though this would clear things up. "I thought you said he had a girl-friend back home?"

"I lied. I'm a total asshole. Just...I don't think he's into dating right now. He's super into baseball." Again, he looked up in the stands. I waved, feeling only the slightest bit of guilt.

"Bummer," she said, gathering her things. "I guess I'll head back and see what Ruthie's doing for dinner."

"I'm sure I'll see you later." I try to keep the smugness down a little, because I'd totally just pulled a bitch move.

She looked down on the bleacher next to me. "You got a text."

I picked it up. "Thanks."

She walked off, probably licking her wounds at losing out on a truly fantastic guy. Too bad he was already taken. Once she left I read the text.

Heaven! It's Noah Hancock. My father gave me your number. It seems we've been set up by the FTB (Fathers that Be--you know, instead of PTB) for a casual hang out at my at the UCC on Thursday. Although it's an awkward set-up I would really like for you to come. It's a kick-off party for the big game on Saturday so wear your team colors—and bring a friend!

Party starts at nine!

P.S. Love your name

Thursday night? Shit. Anderson's swim meet was that night. Surely I'd be over by nine. I typed out a quick response.

Noah,

The FTB really want us to meet up, eh? I figured I could do this one little favor—how bad could a party be? I'll be there around 9 dressed in red.

Heaven

He sent back a series of emojis and I tried not to roll my eyes.

A party wouldn't be so bad, but a semi-date? That was a complica-tion. The logical thing was to let the boys know. I looked down at the field and watched Jackson swing the bat. His shoulders flexed and his biceps strained and I imagined him cracking Noah in the head with it. Okay, so maybe that *was* logical but also potentially dangerous. Then I imagined my father finding out what happened and why.

Nope. None of that would work.

There was no way I could tell them about Noah, and I would just make it clear to this guy that I wasn't interested and be done with the whole situation. Surely Noah would feel the same, right?

～

As predicted, Anderson didn't make it to class on Thursday. He'd always been a dedicated student and athlete but the obligations to his sport had tripled since arriving at the University. He swam for the school team, which won the National Championship last year, and he's also on the Olympic Development track, which means that his times and scores in each race are being monitored.

I'd noticed the strain it was taking—school, swim, training, friends, us. Finding time to do it all was increasingly challenging and I felt like at least I could help him with his test tomorrow. Ease a little of the stress.

After class, I got the extra study guide from the TA and turned to leave the auditorium. Ruthie blocked my path. A small frown marred her mouth. "What's that for?"

I held up the guide. "Oh, my friend Anderson had training today for a big competition starting tonight. I told him I'd get his copy."

"He's lucky to have a friend like you." She smirked. "Although I don't think he'd have a problem getting someone to bring him his school work, if you know what I mean." When I didn't reply she rolled her eyes. "He's freaking hot, Heaven. I swear you're so used to those guys you don't even realize how genetically superior they are."

"I notice," I said, casually. Damn. I noticed.

"Well, Samantha told me Oliver's gay so that takes one out of commission. What about Anderson? Would he be interested in a different study date?" She flipped her red hair over her shoulder and batted her eyelashes at me.

Wait what? Was she trying to boot me? Hell no.

I swallowed back my annoyance. "Anderson and I have been study partners in science since the 9th grade. We sort of have a system."

"A fresh set of eyes isn't a bad idea."

252

"He's also like, the biggest pain in the ass ever. Grumpy as hell." Not a lie. "And he's super particular—like totally anal about his work." I flashed her a semi-fake grimace. He really was OCD about it all. "Not that you're not meticulous, I'm just saying, studying with Anderson is a chore—not a pleasure."

"Yeah, but his shoulders..."

"Are as broad as the side of a barn, I hear you girl. I hear you."

"Well, if he's that bad, what do you get out of it?"

We stopped outside the building, where dozens of students milled around. I clutched my bag to my chest. "Loyalty. Laughter. Friendship." I held her eye in case she wanted to challenge me. "Anderson and I have been through a lot and we're really close. We'll always be close."

Her eyes narrowed and she placed a hand on her hip. "Seems like you're a little territorial over these boys. You're 'sort of' dating Jackson and occasionally see Hayden. Oliver is suddenly gay and off the market and now no one is allowed to study with Anderson? What's really going on here?"

I wasn't sure what her accusation was about. Did she just think I was a jealous friend? Or a loser that clung to these guys?

Anger rolled over me. "The relationship I have with these guys is none of your fucking business, Ruthie. If you want to make a play on one of them, be my guest. In fact, go after Anderson. You have my blessing."

"You don't have to be such a bitch."

"Well, you don't have to leave your hair products all over the bathroom counter, either."

She drew back and laughed. "Are you calling me a slob? Your pile of laundry is the size of a mountain."

I sighed, knowing this was a stupid argument—although the bathroom thing had been bothering me for a long time. I rubbed my temple. "I've got to get this to Anderson before he leaves for his swim meet."

She blinked at me and then stormed off, leaving me in the middle of the walkway alone. Okay, maybe I didn't handle that well and maybe I did have some territory issues with the Allendale Four that were being revealed now that we were in college.

I tucked the study guide into my bag and walked across campus. I knew juggling four boyfriends was going to be rough—I just didn't realize how much.

41

I walked through the quiet halls of Anderson's dormitory relishing a moment of peace after the argument with Ruthie. Knowing Anderson was already stressed about his upcoming meet and the test tomorrow, I didn't want to unload on him about something as trivial as two girls fighting over hair products and men. Anderson had lightened up a bit since high school, but he still had little patience for drama.

I knocked on the door. When he didn't answer, I pushed it open and found Anderson sitting at his desk with headphones clamped over his ears. His wide shoulders bounced a little with the beat and I heard the tap of his pencil following along.

Closing the door, I dropped my bag on the floor and walked over. He still didn't notice me, but I couldn't stop watching him in this unguarded moment. Standing behind him, I lightly placed my hands on his shoulders and he jumped, startled at my touch, and spun around in his seat, already removing the headphones.

"Jesus Christ," he breathed. "You scared the hell out of me."

"Sorry," I said, not really sorry at all. I pushed my fingers through his hair and he closed his eyes. I couldn't help but notice the tension in his jaw and shoulders, along with the slight strain tugging at the corners of his eyes. "You okay?"

"It's just this test and then the race tonight. I've got a lot on the line."

"You do and you're handling it really well."

He chuckled. "You think? Because I don't feel like I'm under control at all."

I ran my hands down his neck, feeling the tight cords of muscle. "Turn around," I told him. He raised an eyebrow but spun the chair with his feet. Starting with his head I massaged and rubbed his scalp, working my hands down to his neck. I felt the sharp line of his jaw, the hard muscles of his shoulders. It took a minute, but slowly, inch by inch, he began to relax.

"I read this article once about how the Olympians deal with pre-competition stress," I told him, taking a peek at his face.

His eyes were closed but he replied with a soft, "Yeah?"

"There were a lot of different theories. Some coaches were super strict—like no one was allowed out past midnight. No fraternization with the other sex. Complete and utter focus on the games until their event was over."

"Sounds reasonable. My coach is always giving us techniques for focus. He's big into meditation."

I had a feeling my massage was barely making a dent. My hands were small compared to Anderson's broad shoulders but I kept working anyway, kneading with my thumbs and knuckles. "Then there were the others that channeled their energy elsewhere, hoping to take off the edge. Like having sex before a big event."

He stilled and the tension returned, although not the bone-deep kind, this was more of an attentiveness. "Did that work?" he asked, slowly.

"I think it probably varies on a case-by-case basis," I replied, appealing to his nerdy side. "They cited lack of sleep and focus to be the biggest negatives."

Anderson spun, facing me and catching me by the waist to pull me between his long legs. His green eyes were hooded and intense. I bent over and kissed him, continuing my desire to ease the tension from him.

"You're awfully distracting," he said, brushing my hair over my shoulder. His eyes flicked down to the V of my shirt. "I don't feel like this was what we agreed on for a study date, Ms. Reeves."

I smirked. "I'm happy to get back to business, Mr. Thompson. Let me go get your study guide." I turned to go to my backpack but his fingers dipped under the waistband of my shorts and he tugged me back.

"Not so fast. You can't actually bring up pre-event sex and then walk away."

I raised an eyebrow. "I can't? You were the one worried about being distracted."

He pinned me with a hard, heated look. "You've been distracting me since middle school, Heaven. If you were going to be the downfall to my success, I'd be back in Allendale lifeguarding and going to the community college instead of here."

I dropped my hands to his shoulders and trailed them down his chest. I felt the hard muscles and the points of his erect nipples. I knew his body and exactly what he needed to settle down.

He stiffened again when my fingers lowered to his red and black sweat pants. His name was etched over the school symbol on his hip. "Hey," I told him. "Just relax."

His jaw tensed. "Easier said than done, with you teasing me like this."

I pushed at his waistband and kissed him long and leisurely. "Lift up."

"Heaven."

"What?"

"You really don't have to—" Guilt mixed with hunger flashed in his eyes.

"It's okay to let me do this for you. Remember? We talked about this." Old habits died hard with my guys. Protective to the bone. "You're not over-protecting me anymore. You're not babying me."

He touched my chin. "I don't ever want you to feel uncomfortable, to feel demeaned or something."

I licked my lips, refusing to cave to his ridiculous notions. "Anderson, it's empowering to know I have this kind of effect on you." I blushed admitting it, but I was also determined. "When you suggest that it's anything different, it takes away a little bit of my choice. If I want to suck your cock it's okay, got it?"

A weird noise came from his chest but he stopped stalling, lifting his ass of the seat. I moved quickly, scared he'd change his mind, and lowered his pants, pulling them off his bare, sexy feet. His manhood bobbed between us, bouncing with unbridled excitement. To know I did that to him made me proud and I licked my lips.

Every moment was a new one with these guys. Every encounter something bold and exciting. I knelt between his knees, feeling his hand weave in the hair at the base of my neck. His grip was a little tighter than I expected, rougher than I expected, and I fought back a smile. I reached for him and our eyes met, burning with the connection that had always been so strong between us.

"You tell me if it's too much," he whispered.

I shook my head. "Don't hold back. Don't you fucking dare, Anderson."

He nodded and hot want flickered in his eyes. I may regret that last request.

With the flick of my tongue I did what I could to help ease a little of his stress and prove to him that I could love him on my own terms, in my own way. I proved this and more when he leaned back in his seat and let me take control, allowing me to enjoy his body as much as he enjoyed mine.

42

Following our activity (AKA: "best blow job ever") Anderson crashed for a nap. I did rouse him long enough to get in a solid thirty minutes of studying before he had to head down to the gym.

"I hope I didn't screw up your night or the exam tomorrow."

It was a quiet moment outside his dorm and he took a chance and kissed my puffy lips against the wall by the front steps. "Not a chance. If anything, I think you may just be my good luck charm."

I laughed. "I doubt that. Hard work and a killer level of commitment don't need luck."

He kissed me once more before pulling away and brushing my hair out of my eyes. "See you later?"

"I'll be there," I said. Then flinched. "I may have to leave early, though. My dad asked me to run an errand for him."

"At night?"

I shrugged. "It's with the University Church group. Pretty tame crowd."

"Ah, right. Make one of the guys go with you, okay? You don't need to walk around campus at night, even if it's to church."

I nodded and pushed him in the direction of the gym. He was going to be late.

"Go. Kick some ass, or swim fast. Or whatever the hell the right cheer is."

He winked and finally left.

When I returned to my suite, loud music thumped behind Ruthie and Samantha's door. I wondered how pissed Ruthie was about our argument after class. I knew better than to let jealousy get to me, but sometimes it was hard. Those boys made me as territorial as I made them.

"Hey," I said to Amber, who was sitting on her bed, focused on her laptop. I hooked my bag over my desk chair and flopped on the bed.

"Any chance you'd be up for a church social tonight?"

"What? Is that code for fraternity party or something? Or is this like a cult thing? Because I am not sure I'd fit in," she said, pushing her glasses into her hair. She'd recently cut her bangs super short. I was envious of her ability to pull off such a dramatic look.

"Nah. My dad wants me to go to this thing and meet a guy named Noah. Dad has some connection with his father. I'm supposed to go meet him—play nice."

She tilted her head. "Just meet him?"

"Well, I don't think it's an arranged marriage introduction." God, I hoped not.

"I'd love to be your wing-woman but I'm meeting Ginger tonight."

I sat up. "Ooh. Again? Things are getting serious?"

Amber smiled. "I really like her."

"Have you told Ben?"

She nodded. "The only way an open relationship will work is if we're honest with one another. I think he's been on a few dates at his school."

"And you're good with that?" Her kind of open relationship was way different from my relationships with the boys. We didn't fool around with outsiders and we were totally committed.

"Yeah, I am. We're going to meet up when he comes into town for the game in a few weeks."

"Are you going to introduce him to Ginger?"

Another small smile ghosted over her lips. "If everything keeps progressing, then yep, definitely."

"And then?"

"We'll see, I guess. I've never been in a relationship like this. Juggling two people seems hard."

I rolled my eyes. "Tell me about it. Try four."

"Oh, about that. I heard the news about Oliver."

I furrowed my eyebrows. "What news?"

"About him switching to the other team?"

I stared at her for a minute. "Oh, crap. You talked to Samantha."

She threw her hands over her chest. "She was heartbroken."

"I panicked," I admitted. "Then to make it worse, I got super territorial over Anderson today with Ruthie."

"She made a move on Anderson? Girl is lucky to still have her hair."

We both burst into giggles. "I'm not really good at this 'down-low' stuff or you know, making new friends."

"Yes, you are, but you need to go about it a little different," she said. "Since I can't go tonight why don't you invite Samantha, as a consolation for bursting her dreams about Oliver. Maybe she'll meet someone new."

"I'll ask." I glanced at my closet and frowned. "Now I have to figure out what to wear to this party. Church social isn't really my style."

"Ha! Nope, that's not your bread and butter."

"My dad told me to get attention like I did to become Winter Princess. I didn't have the heart to tell him I had to fake sleep with the whole school to get that title."

"Stop. That's not why you won and you know it."

I sighed. "I know he'll check up on this, so I need to play the part. I knew there would be strings—this is one of them."

She didn't look happy. At all. "What's the theme?"

"Team spirit—for the game this weekend."

"That's not so bad. Jersey and jeans?"

I twisted my bedspread between my fingers. "I hate letting him win, you know? Hiding myself for my father's beliefs that I don't agree with."

"Something in the middle. Chaste but cute?"

"That may work. I don't want to lead this guy on, even if I have to play nice."

"And the guys? Do they know about this?"

I gave her a face—one that said, *hell fucking no, they don't know.*

Amber sighed and then stood, walking to the closet we shared. "Girl, you're playing with fire."

"What else is new?"

I was caught between my father and secret boyfriends—my funding and the integrity of my relationships. It was stupid, but I'd warned them. My father was nothing but trouble. The best thing to do was to play his game and then hope for the best.

"So you need to straddle the line."

"Yep."

Amber pulled a red school jersey out of the closet and tossed it on the bed. She moved to my top dresser drawer and rummaged through, pulling out a plain, white bra and threw it my way. I caught it with a raised eyebrow. "Go invite Samantha. We've got a lot of work to do to make you a convincing church girl with enough sex appeal to make this kid, Noah, feel good about himself. God, I can't believe I'm involved with this."

I'd played this game before—with disastrous results—but this was just once—one night and one party. When it was over, I'd tell the guys and apologize.

At least that was what I told myself as I walked across the suite. What could go wrong?

43

I KNEW MY OUTFIT FOR THE NIGHT WAS GOING TO HIT THE MARK THE second I walked into the aquatic center. Three sets of eyes shifted in my direction, taking in the tight-fitting football jersey and cut-off jean shorts. Hayden's eyes lingered on the two French braids hanging over my shoulders. Jackson's were glued to my legs, and Oliver, he scanned me head-to-toe, eyes lingering over his favorite spots.

It was a work of art—designed with my knowledge of slutty school-girl wear and Amber's sense of empowerment. It was equal parts flirty and chaste. The perfect combination to get Noah's "attention" while still blending in. Honestly, I worried I maybe nailed it too closely, because all three of the boys looked like they may climb out of their skin. I untied the swim hoodie I stole from Anderson from around my waist and tugged it on.

"Heaven!" Jackson called, scooting over to make room. Samantha followed me and said hi to all the guys. Hayden leaned over Jackson and gave me a hug. Oliver winked at me and I smiled back.

"Hey, Samantha," Oliver said. "Did I see you at the baseball field the other day?"

The tips of her ears turned red and she nodded.

"She just came to hang with me," I replied. "But then she realized watching baseball practice was boring as hell and she ran away while she had the chance."

"Boring?" Jackson snorted. "Baseball is the thinking man's game. It's not boring."

"You made it just in time," Hayden said. "Anderson's big event is next."

I glanced up at the digital chart on the wall. Anderson's name was on up there: Thompson: Lane 5 200 Butterfly.

Oh god, Anderson was swimming butterfly. Be still my heart.

I scanned the pool deck, looking for the familiar body, and found him sitting on a bench behind the starter blocks. Earphones covered his ears and he wore a hoodie that matched mine but about two sizes larger. He stared straight ahead, obviously in some kind of zone. This wasn't my first swim meet of his I'd attended, but this was race was definitely the most important.

"If he gets less than 1:56, he'll set the school record and move to the finals," I told Samantha.

"Wow, so he's really that good?"

"Olympic good," Oliver answered. I heard the nerves in his voice. We all knew how much Anderson wanted and deserved this. I sure as hell hoped my pre-meet stress reliever wasn't a bad idea.

The swimmers of the prior race hopped out of the pool and the announcer called the men to the starter blocks. Anderson removed his headphones and unzipped his hoodie, revealing his muscular, toned back, chest, and arms. His abs were breathtaking and Samantha made a small noise from beside me.

I couldn't even get jealous. His body was a work of art, like a statue carved from marble, and deserved every impressed ogle he got.

Adjusting his goggles and cap, he climbed the step to the top of the small, square platform. His name was written over his forehead: Thompson. He looked ridiculously huge up there, shoulders wider than the block. The judge made a few comments and Anderson spared a glance in our direction. The boys took that as an opportunity to shout their support.

"Go Thompson!"

"Kill it, dude!"

"Swim, man, swim!"

His eyes locked with mine. I mouthed, *good luck* and he turned away, refocused on the race.

My stomach twisted anxiously, and I grabbed onto Jackson's arm. He rubbed my hand with his.

"Oh my god," I muttered under my breath. I'd never been so nervous for someone before. "I think I'm going to puke."

"Divers, ready!" They folded over, fingertips on the edge of the block, magnificent backs exposed.

Bang!

The starter gun went off and all eight men dove into the pool. Anderson's dive was perfection, long and clean under the water. He emerged last but farthest down the lane. His shoulders heaved out of the water, hands arcing over and crashing into the crystal clear pool. He was a beast and I was utterly transfixed on his graceful yet competitive movements.

He wasn't alone, a solitary swimmer chased him through the water. His opponent's yellow cap bobbed milliseconds behind.

"Who is that?" Samantha asked.

"Bobby Lee from Virginia Tech," Oliver replied. "He's beaten Anderson before at the Junior Nationals Finals."

The cheering echoed in the aquatic center, bouncing off the high ceilings. I wasn't cheering, though—I was petrified, breathless, in awe.

Anderson's turn was perfection, easing back down the lane toward the finish. His legs moved in tandem, dolphin-kicking away from the wall. His stroke was steady. The rest of the swimmers faded away, lengths behind him, but Lee persevered, chasing after him. His lean body bobbed off the waves Anderson created with his massive force.

I hadn't dared look at the clock—I couldn't bring myself to. It was less about beating Lee than beating the clock, although both were important. Anderson inched closer to the finish and the boys hopped out of their seats, dragging me with them. The cheering reached epic levels and Jackson muttered words of encouragement under his breath.

"I can't look," I said, but that was a lie; I couldn't tear my eyes away as he reached the finish line, both hands crashing into the touch pad a millisecond before Lee. Anderson spun and looked at the clock, his coach bent and talking to him already. Our eyes followed his and his time blinked from the top slot on the chart.

1:52

He killed it.

"Oh my god!" I shouted, Jackson picked me up in giant bear hug, his strong arms crushing me. I squawked and he laughed, releasing me.

"Come on," Oliver said, heading down the bleachers. We raced after them and at the edge of the final one, I jumped down the final step and Hayden grabbed my hands and helped me down.

"You're shaking," he said.

"I was so nervous."

He brushed my hair out of my face. "We really don't deserve you, you know that?"

I frowned. "What are you talking about?"

"You're so good to us; supportive and always there. I know you're stretched thin with school and your own stuff, but you always make time for us." His gray eyes penetrated mine. "You're A++ girlfriend material."

I glanced behind me, happy to see that Samantha had already followed the others across the deck. Anderson pulled himself out of the pool, water running down his body like a river.

"I love you, too." I touched his hip and he responded to it with a mega-watt smile.

"Go see him."

I pushed through the crowd of teammates and coaches. Anderson's parents had come down for the event and his mom gave him a huge hug. I eased in to the side, catching his eye. His lips curved into a grin when he saw me, his eyes so intense that my skin prickled.

I felt the eyes of everyone on me—his coach, his parents...Samantha, but I pushed past the worries over them seeing me. I was here to support my friend. No one needed to know anything else. He broke away from the others, pulling his cap off his head, revealing his mop of coppery-brown hair.

When he got close enough I lunged for him, slamming into his soaking-wet body. "You did it!"

"I know," he said, pulling me to his chest. "I can't believe it."

"I knew you could," I said, lifting my chin. "I knew it."

"That's the best time I've ever had. I broke the school record. It's just a smidge higher than Phelps," he said, rambling in his excitement.

"You're only going to get better."

He bent down so his mouth was close to my ear. "That thing you did before the meet? I told you—you're my lucky charm."

I snorted. "You think so?"

He smirked. "Oh, I know so. You know how superstitious we are before meets. You're part of the routine now."

I remembered how he felt, the way he looked as I pleasured him. Yeah, I was down for being part of his ritual. "So what are you saying...I'm a habit?"

He slung a wet arm around me and whispered in my ear, "A bad habit—but one I never want to break, got it?"

My cheeks flushed at his comment but I knew how he felt. Every day I felt the bond with these guys more than the day before. I loved it. And loved them.

My phone vibrated just as his coach called him over. He had two more events before the night was over.

I checked the message.

You on the way? I'm here and wearing my Terrance Ackerman jersey. #14—Noah.

I glanced at Anderson. The last thing I wanted was to leave him. He saw my expression and said, "I know you need to go do some stuff for your dad. It's okay."

"I'm so sorry," I said. "Samantha's going with me, so the guys can stay."

He looked over at my suitemate and nodded. "Be careful."

"I will. And good luck on the rest of the meet. I'll have Oliver record it so we can watch later."

He glanced at Samantha once again and mumbled "fuck it" under his breath before closing the distance between us. He pulled me in for a kiss—for luck—and a shot of electricity that curled my toes, lingering long after we parted.

I refused to look at his mom or even any of the other guys. I just said, "Good luck," and walked over to Samantha. "You ready?"

"Uh," she peeked at Anderson, who was already walking back to the swimmer bullpen. "Wow. That was hot."

"It's just a little good luck thing. Nothing big."

She followed me out of the pool and into the much cooler and less humid night air. "You can say that wasn't anything big, Heaven, but that guy...wow. It may not have meant anything to you, but it sure as hell meant something to him."

I stopped abruptly, feeling defensive, but that wasn't fair. Samantha was a friend. Or could be if I let down a few walls. "The relationship I have with these guys is complicated. We're super close. We've dated. We're all really good friends. But it's also super private and something just between us."

"Is that why you didn't tell them you were going to meet a guy tonight?"

I blinked. "What?"

"You told them you're running an 'errand' and being super vague about the fact there's a guy waiting for you at the party."

"That guy *is* the errand—set up by my father." I rubbed my temples. "Do you have a problem or something? I invited you to be nice—not to get an interrogation."

"I appreciate it, but I don't know, there's something shady going on with you and those guys." She looked me up and down. "Ruthie told me how defensive you got over Anderson the other day. Now I understand why."

I took a deep breath. "Look, my dad is a piece of work. I can't—no, won't—even go into it for your sake. But he's asked me to jump and I've got no choice. So yeah, I'm hiding what I'm doing from the guys tonight because they would lose their shit if they found out, which ultimately would get them caught up in everything. It's not a big deal.

It's just my dad, who is shady as hell. You're right about that. But it's easiest if I just do what he asks and then move on."

"Okay," she said.

"Okay?"

"Yeah, my dad can be a dick, too. When he's even around."

I fought off the feeling of anxiety from the vulnerability of revealing all that information. "I hear that."

"Come on," she said, easing her tone. "Let's go run your errand and check out this party. Since you're obviously not sharing, maybe I can find a guy on my own."

We walked through campus, headed toward fraternity row. Samantha seemed calmer now that she knew the truth and maybe I didn't realize how difficult I made things by having so many secrets.

The problem was that I didn't trust anyone—high school taught me that—but I had a feeling that if I was going to be happy, I'd have to learn to depend on people outside Amber and the Allendale Four.

The bad thing for me was that idea was absolutely terrifying.

44

Now that Noah and I had a plan, I knew it was time to tell the guys what was going on. The last thing I needed was for them to come across the two of us talking on campus and get protective.

It was Friday night, the day after Anderson's record-breaking swim meet and the party with Noah, and I was stuffed into a corner booth with the guys at The Griddle, a twenty-four-seven breakfast place.

I sat in the middle, surrounded by my handsome, starving boyfriends as they inhaled plates of food. I had my own small stack of pancakes and a side of bacon, but seriously, these guys' stomachs were bottomless pits.

Oliver groaned, dropping his fork, leaning back to rub his belly. Jackson stabbed the last piece of sausage off his teammate's plate. Hayden shoved in eggs and bacon because he'd recently gone low carb, and Anderson just ate everything in sight.

"You want that?" he asked me, about the half of a pancake left on my plate.

"No."

He picked it up with fingers and licked the syrup off with his tongue.

Jesus.

Invoking the son of God's name reminded me of what I needed to tell them. "Okay, so I have something we need to talk about."

All eyes shifted to me and I squirmed a little in my seat.

"First of all, I need you to listen and not react. Let me explain everything before you freak out."

"Wait? I need to be prepared to freak out?" Jackson asked. "What am I freaking out about?"

"I swear on my mother's life, I didn't do anything," Hayden said.

"You're not freaking out," I said. "That's the whole point."

"Let Heaven talk," Oliver said, rolling his eyes. "Lay it on us."

I smiled at him gratefully and took a deep, steadying breath. "You know my dad is a bit...controlling."

"Shady as fuck," Hayden muttered under his breath.

"And shady as fuck," I agreed. "Last night he asked me to run an errand for him. It wasn't exactly an errand—he wanted me to go meet someone. At a party."

Anderson lowered his fork. "At the church thing?"

"Meet who?" Hayden added. His shoulders hunched.

"No freaking out," I reminded them.

Hayden blinked. Oliver sat up in his seat and Jackson rubbed his chin. Anderson? Well he worked his jaw so hard I thought it may snap.

"His name is Noah and he seems fine. Both of our dads are worried about our social standing and want us to hang out together."

"Hang out?" Hayden asked. "Is that code for sex?"

"Dammit," Oliver said, punching Hayden in the shoulder. "I can't believe you just asked her that! It was a church thing, for Christ's sake."

"I'm just trying to figure it out!"

I sighed and rubbed my head. "Stop it. Noah is kind of a nerd who isn't into all this religion stuff as much as his dad wants him to be. Like me. We're both in a bind and we agreed that we could help each other out by being friends."

Hayden snorted.

"Of course he wants to be friends. You're fucking hot," Jackson declared. "Who wouldn't want to be seen with you?"

My cheeks heated at his compliment. "I told him no social media, no kissing, and absolutely no sex. Of any kind."

"No touching at all," Oliver added. Then he looked guilty for bossing me. "Sorry. I got carried away. Heaven, I trust you. If you feel like this is something you need to do to keep things on good terms with your father, I get it."

"Thank you. I really think if I play along, maybe my dad will get the funding from Noah's father and he'll back off on some of the other stuff." I looked around the table. "It sounds like Noah's dad is even worse. He pays his roommates to spy on him."

Jackson's jaw dropped. "Wow. That's third-level psycho. Are you sure this is safe?"

"I think it will be fine but look, I'll give you or Amber my location all the time if I'm with him. Full transparency with you guys."

"Did you tell him about us?" Anderson asked.

"I haven't told anyone about you," I confessed. "Although Samantha has her suspicions. I just don't want my dad to mess up what we've got. He's holding all the strings right now."

I could tell that didn't go over well with the guys, but what else could I say. I was trying to be truthful and that was the truth. My father had his thumb on me.

Hayden slung his arm over my shoulder and pulled me in close. "You know we just want you to be safe, right? That more than anything else."

I nodded and kept on a brave face. "I'm fine. This guy...he's pretty harmless."

"Yeah, that's what we thought about Spencer," Oliver said quietly. Spencer did seem pretty benign until we found out he was the one stalking and harassing me my senior year. I didn't fully appreciate how dangerous he was until he tried to attack me at the winter formal. A rock settled in my stomach at the memory.

"He's not Spencer. And nothing is going to happen. We'll get through the next few weeks and then I'll tell my dad it's just not working and move on, okay?"

They all nodded, well, everyone but Anderson, who looked like he may stab the table with the fork he continued to grip like a weapon in his hand.

"A few weeks," he finally said. "But after that, we have to come up with something else. This is too hard on you and too hard on us. Deal?"

I held his eyes, green and unforgiving. He was right. This was only a short-term game—nothing longer. I nodded in agreement. "Deal."

~

"Yes, Daddy," I said, holding the phone between the crook of my neck and chin, "Noah was really nice. We hung out at the party and plan on spending some more time together."

"That's good to hear, Heaven. I know his father's been worried about him."

I had an overflowing laundry basket in my hands and I leaned against the wall to catch my breath. "I'm not sure why. Has lots of friends and seems pretty nice. What's there to be worried about?"

"Success is measured in different ways, Heaven. It's a man's world —don't worry about the little things."

I dropped the basket on the floor with a loud thump. "Excuse me?"

"I said it's a man's world—you just need to find your role in it. I knew the minute I saw how beautiful you'd become that you'd be a good asset to my mission at the church. God blesses us in many ways."

"Dad," I said, trying to keep my cool, "women aren't considered an asset and it most certainly isn't only a man's world. I know you've been," I swallow back my rage, "away and that you grew up in a pretty conservative environment, but women can do anything a man can do, you know that, right?"

"Sure, honey," he said unconvincingly. "Who knew you'd turn into such a spit-ball? When I left you were so quiet and meek. Your mother told me you struggled and I wasn't sure if you'd get out of that frame of mind, but I can see that you're different now. I like it. I bet Noah will like it, too."

I fought back a groan and picked up my basket, relieved Amber walked through the door so I could go through.

"Look Daddy, I'm going to do laundry. I should go."

"Okay sweetheart, you take care of yourself. I'll be in touch."

I hung up the phone and muttered a few choice words under my breath.

"Your dad?" she asked.

"How did you know?"

"You get this little wrinkle between your eyes when he calls."

I mounted the basket on my hip and rubbed the spot with my finger. "Great, now he'll give me wrinkles as well as a complex."

"A complex about what?"

Oh hell no would I tell Amber about my father's ideas about women, she'd lose her shit and confront him. We'd both have to drop out of school. See? Strings. "Never mind."

She frowned but let it go. "What's this? You've got a big night doing laundry, huh?"

"Actually, I have a date. A laundry date."

"Oh yeah? With who?"

I smiled. "Hayden."

"Hayden does laundry? I'd pay to see that."

"Right? I don't think he's actually bringing laundry. He asked me to pose for his drawing class and this is the only free time I have."

She smirked. "He wants to draw you? That's pretty sexy."

It was sexy. I'd seen Hayden's work before—even drawings of me—but watching him do it? A chill ran down my spine. "Yep. Sexy."

Amber opened the door to the community laundry facility in the basement of our building. "Have fun. Don't do anything I wouldn't do."

I frowned. "In the laundry room?"

She smiled wickedly. "You never know."

45

After the insanity of the week, finding a time to see Heaven and get my homework done seemed like a constant struggle. Every encounter with her was too brief. Our lives were all chaotic and with the addition of this Noah kid, he would only take up more time.

That was why, when Heaven said she had to do laundry, I took the opportunity to kill two birds with one stone. I packed up my art supplies and headed over to Stetson Hall.

The girls' dorm was a world apart from athletic housing. It smelled like perfume and shampoo instead of feet and old cheese.

"Can you direct me to the laundry room?" I asked a tiny girl with glasses. She pointed to a door down the hall. Her eyes were wide at my sheer size.

"Thanks," I said.

"Sure," she squeaked.

I pushed open the basement door and jogged down the stairs, stopping when I caught sight of my girl, bending over the washing machine.

Have mercy.

I watched her for a moment, eyeing her ass in a form-fitting pair of gray and black leggings. They fit tight over every inch of her hips and thighs, leaving zero question about the thong panties she wore underneath. She wore a red tank, with cut-outs and ties at the shoulders. Her hair was bound in a knot behind her head. She was damn sexy and I thought about her all the time. All. The. Fucking. Time. Not a day went by that I didn't kick my own ass for giving up the chance to make love to her in my room that night. A night I sorely regret. I'd only pissed her off and cockblocked myself, but even now I knew that wasn't the right time or place. We were still percolating. Building this relationship slowly.

The tightening in my jeans told me our dance was running out, though. I didn't know how much longer I could hold out. Not when she wanted it so badly, too.

"Hey," I said, taking the last few steps and walking across the room. We were alone and I didn't hesitate before closing the gap and pushing a hand into her silky hair.

"Hi."

I leaned over and kissed her softly—twice—taking my time. She sucked on my bottom lip, encouraging me, and I kissed her again, this time little harder. She pressed her hands into my chest, surely able to feel my hammering heart.

"Don't you have a drawing to get started on?" she asked in a breathy tone.

I licked my lips, tasting her. "Look at you, cracking the whip."

Her eyes carried a devilish glint and she ran her fingers through the shaggy hair hanging in my eyes and skimmed my jaw. "Get to work and maybe I'll reward you later."

"Yes, ma'am."

I moved to the table used for folding clothes and opened my kit, spreading my pencils, erasers, and charcoal in an orderly row. I took out a large sketchbook and laid it on the table, flipping to a fresh, blank sheet.

"Where do you want me?" she asked.

On this fucking table, I almost said. *On the floor. Bent over the washer* —Jesus. I cut the internal monologue. "Do you mind standing?"

"No, I can do that, although I can't guarantee it won't be awkward."

I laughed, because her awkwardness was what made her so endearing. She was small but full of a graceful passion. When I was around her I felt like a brute. Too big and powerful. Massive in a way the other guys weren't. All muscle where they were mostly lean. I needed the hard-packed bulk to dominate the soccer goal. But with her it just made me nervous. What if I hurt her? I was used to fending off six-foot forwards, not hundred-pound sexy girls I could crush with my hands.

I made her nervous, I always had. My presence was what kept me at a higher station from the rest of the school, from the members of my team. But Heaven? She knocked me to my knees.

"I'd like to do a full body pose," I said. "Here." I grabbed her shoulders and shuffled us over to the old, mustard yellow washing machine. "Like this, I think."

"You want me cleaning? You may be more like my father than I knew."

"Trust me, sweetheart," I said in a low voice. "I'm not your daddy."

I pushed her against the machine, manipulating her hands so they were flat on the top and then shifted her shoulders so they were slightly to the side. "Lift your chin."

She followed direction, catching my eyes. I used my finger to tilt her to the left then right, until Heaven was ultimately looking slightly over her shoulder. I reached for her hair, unraveling it and combing it into a long sheet down her back. "Tell me if you get tired."

"I will," she said. I couldn't help but stop and stare at her. "What? Do I need to move?"

"Nope. I'm just thinking about how fucking beautiful you are."

Her cheeks flamed red and I wanted to kiss her so badly.

Instead, I moved just out of her line of vision and hopped up on the work table. I crossed my legs and placed the sketchbook on my lap. Choosing a stick of charcoal, I sketched an outline of the scene; the wall, the machine, Heaven standing in the foreground. The machine vibrated under her hands, making her hair shiver, and the only sound in the room was the whirring of the washer and the stroke of the charcoal.

After a while, the rhythm of the machine seemed to lull Heaven into a quiet trance and the moment shifted, charging with intimacy. It was different than any other we'd had. The rest of the campus was out and about on a Saturday night like they should be, but here we were, alone in the laundry room.

"I remember the first time I saw you," I said suddenly.

"When was that?" Her neck craned but she forced herself to stay in position.

"Not as early as the others," I admitted. "I mean, I remember you transferring in middle school, but you weren't on my radar back then. I was mostly about food, sports, and video games back then. I don't think we had any classes together and you were just this girl Anderson wouldn't stop bitching about."

She laughed.

"Jackson had his eye on you for years. He always had his eye on the hot girls. Oliver knew you from class. But I was out of the loop. Self-absorbed and not paying attention, until one day I only vaguely knew who you were and then all of a sudden you were just there. Occupying way more mental real estate than I knew existed."

"What got your attention? The thigh-high boots or the school-girl plaid skirt?"

I laughed. She knew me well. I never paid her a bit of attention until she amped up her slutty clothing game. Not because I was into sluts, but there something about her—about her attitude, her style. I couldn't look away. Just like right now.

That was the thing about Heaven—the most normal moments became tense and filled with desire. The grasp of control I had when it came to her was wearing thin.

I wanted Heaven so badly. I wanted every part of her, but I wasn't a gentleman like Anderson. Or kind and careful like Oliver. I wasn't even a horny bastard like Jackson who could smile and make everyone feel special.

I was filled with testosterone, aggression, and pure passion. I worked, played, and loved hard, and I'd held back for so long that I didn't know what would happen if I allowed myself to cross the line.

I waited a beat—two, telling myself to keep away—maintaining my distance. This was not the time and definitely not the place. Heaven stood frozen against that machine, her tits bouncing slightly with the vibration of the machine. I could handle it. I *was* handling it until she tilted her head in my direction and licked those pink, puffy lips and there was no doubt in my mind it was an invitation.

And I was out of fucks to give.

Every. Damn. One.

46

———————

I heard him slide off the table and walk over. I didn't move an inch. "It was that fucking skirt," he said. "That day in the garden. I knew Oliver and the others had plans to protect you from those douchebags at school. I was down for that, but that day when you came out in the courtyard, red-cheeked and upset. Damnit. I knew right then what all the fuss was about."

He stood behind me, hand lightly grazing my back. I inhaled, consumed with his closeness, his towering height. He touched my hair, pushing it aside to expose my neck. His lips blazed hot on my neck, under my jaw. His fingers tugged at the back of my shirt, moving to my arms and lighting a fire across my skin. The pads of his fingers danced over the scars and my belly filled with desperate want.

"So you liked my skirt?" I asked, too aware we were in a semi-public place.

"Hell yes. It was all short and barely skimming your perfect, tantalizing ass." His hands wandered down to my leggings, cupping the curve of my butt. "And those pigtails and that tight, white shirt. School-boy fantasy, babe."

I swallowed. "What other kinds of fantasies do you have?"

He grew still, fingers still teasing my backside. He bent and kissed my shoulder, ignoring my question.

Touching the edge of the washer, I moved to turn, but he held me in position, his hips pressing into my backside. He was hard and the mere thought, *feeling*, of it created a flurry of excitement in my lower belly. I blinked, looking at the wall in front of me, at the poster explaining how to call maintenance if there was a problem, and remembered that day. If that day turned him on, it wasn't just the clothes, it was being outside—alone—but also in public. Like now.

I eased back, feeling him behind me, and his teeth scraped along my collar bone. "Is this what you want? How you want it?"

He grunted. "The guys would kill me."

They still had hang-ups. Each one of them were terrified they'd break me or offend me or treat me wrong. The reverse was true. I was having to break them down one at a time. "The guys aren't here. This is between you and me. Our relationship. Our rules."

He still wasn't convinced. I felt the hesitation tremble in his body. I lifted a hand back behind my head, touching his hair and neck. I leaned into him and he wrapped his strong arms around my stomach.

"I know you think it's easy," he said quietly, "But we promised one another we'd always treat you right, take care of you and respect you." He ran his nose down the column of my neck. "The things I want to do to you...they are definitely not how you treat someone you love."

The strain in his voice, the undeniable desire...it made me weak in the knees. I couldn't help but say, "Tell me what you want to do."

He swallowed thickly, his voice quiet in my ear. "I want to take you here—now, with the risk of someone catching us. I want to claim you, let the world know you're mine and most of all let you know that I'm in—all in. That I love and worship you. I want to hear you cry my name when you come. I want to have to hold you up because you're so overwhelmed you can't stand."

Holy. Shit.

"It's too much," he confessed.

"No," I breathed. "No, it's not. If anything, it's not enough. When you hold back it makes me feel...inadequate. Like you don't think I can take it. That I'm still the pathetic Heaven that had no friends and gets used by the people in my life. Not the person I've strived to become."

He spun me around, gray eyes searching mine. "Inadequate? You're fucking with me."

Tears burned in my eyes. I don't know why I had to have this conversation with them over and over but dammit, I wanted more.

His jaw ticked and he bent down and kissed me softly on the lips; a strange, gentle gesture. When we parted, the color of his eyes shifted, darkened, and he turned me back around.

"Let me explain something to you," he said, in a gruff voice. "I hold back because I'm terrified of myself." He placed our hands together. His dwarfed mine. "It's not your mind that I'm worried about, babe. It's your body. If I let go, like really, really let go, I could hurt you."

"I'm stronger than I look."

We stared at one another for a beat longer and with sudden force, his chest slammed into my back and I leaned into him. Hayden's hand crept up my shirt, palming my breast. His movements weren't gentle, but firm. He knew what he wanted and god, I wanted it, too.

His fingers dipped under my waistband, diving deep, touching me between my legs. His breath grew ragged and deep.

"Put your hands on the washer," he told me.

I did, and he rummaged through his pockets dropping coins, wadded up paper and a condom nearby. He picked up the condom and tore the wrapper with his teeth.

I heard the clink of his buckle and the rustle of his jeans as they fell to the ground. I felt the soft brush of his cock across my backside as it sprang to life. Then he rolled the condom on and I waited, petrified to move—scared he'd change his mind.

He reached for my leggings and yanked them down, the cool air from the basement hitting my thighs. He ran his hands over my ass, cupping my cheeks, then easing my panties over my hips.

I trembled at his touch and he said, "Heav, you okay?"

I nodded.

"Speak up, or we can't do this."

"Yes. I'm okay. I want this."

He tapped my hip. "Spread wider."

My stomach dropped, but I did as he directed. The weight of his hands dragged down my sides, landing at my hip.

His cock pressed into me, slipping between my legs, until he pushed in, catching me off guard. I gasped, adjusting for the briefest of moments but the feeling was so powerful, so intoxicating that I slammed back, taking him all the way in.

Hayden responded with a deep groan that shuddered from his chest through my own. At first, he moved slowly and I let him take the lead. I didn't know what I wanted—what he wanted—this was the first time I'd done something like this. Was I doing it wrong? Was there a reason he moved so slow? His fingers tightened at my hips and a feral moan fell from his lips and he just...let loose.

The tentativeness from earlier was gone and Hayden pounded into me from behind. I clung to the washer, watching the coins from his pocket bounce across the metal with every thrust until they found a pace, a rhythm that was uniquely ours.

A slow-moving wave rolled over me, separating my body from anything that wasn't connected directly back to my person. Anything that wasn't Hayden in this very defined moment. My elbows buckled and his arm snaked around me, holding me up just like he'd wanted. I felt him everywhere and the tight coil inside my belly wound and wound until I was sure it would snap, breaking me into a million pieces.

"Oh god," I cried, barely able to speak. Hayden held on tight, never stopping, never letting go. My name fell from his lips.

I fell forward, collapsing on my arms, my insides quivering with release, which only seemed to encourage him. Hayden pumped in me harder but more definitive, eventually groaning with deep satisfaction. He eased in and out, slowing, finishing, until his hand landed on my back and he pulled away.

I rested my face on the cool metal of the washer, overcome.

Breathing heavy behind me, he walked off for a second, tossing the condom in the trash. I watched him go, looking at the lean muscles of his thighs, the red heat of his cock. He glanced my way, worry marring his face. I lifted up to my elbows.

"Tell me you're okay."

"I love you."

He stopped cold. "Even after acting like a barbarian?"

"*Because* you acted like a barbarian."

He smiled and footsteps sounded on the stairs.

"Fuck," he whispered. With wide eyes and laughing we scrambled, tugging on clothes and covering ourselves before two girls from the second floor barged in with their laundry baskets.

I busied myself with changing out laundry and Hayden shoved the condom wrapper in his pocket. We carried a load over to the table, ignoring the girls and the heat of our cheeks for almost getting caught. I glanced down and saw his sketchpad and picked it up.

I shook my head and laughed. Sure, it was a drawing of me standing at the washer, looking to the side just as I'd posed. But instead of a tank and leggings, he drew me like he'd seen me that very first day. White shirt, plaid skirt, the edge of my ass hanging out.

We may have fulfilled one of Hayden's fantasies tonight, but one day I'd definitely have to dig out that skirt again.

47

———

On Monday, after class, I was surprised to find Noah in my suite.

"Hey," I said, walking through the door. He's sitting on the chair and Ruthie lounged on the couch. "What are you doing here?"

"I was looking for you," he said. "Your dad gave my dad your address, I hope that's okay."

"I told him he could wait," Ruthie said. "I knew your psych class was over at four."

My suitemate had on a workout outfit, her red hair pulled back in a high ponytail. Full makeup covered her face and I didn't know if she actually exercised that way or not. My eyes slid to the square Apple watch on her wrist. I hadn't seen it before.

I turned to Noah. "What's going on?"

His eyes darted uncomfortably to Ruthie and she took the hint, standing and making an excuse to leave. She programmed something in her watch, grabbed her headphones and walked out the door.

"My parents are coming up this weekend for the game. They have a standard tail-gate spot and I thought maybe you could join us."

I mentally scanned my weekend. I didn't have much planned. The guys were all involved in their own sporting activities—most off campus. "Yeah, I think I can do that."

He broke into a wide grin. "Great. I think this will be the perfect thing to get my dad off my back."

"Maybe it will work for both of us."

He relaxed into the chair, letting his legs take up most of the floor. "This dormitory is pretty nice. All girls?"

"Yeah. That was my dad's idea."

"I bet. So, yeah, I wanted to ask...are you dating anyone?"

Loaded question. I wrinkled my nose—surely a tell for lying. "Not seriously."

"Good," he said. "I wouldn't want to make some guy mad that we're hanging out."

Try four, I wanted to say.

"Eh, what we're doing is family obligation," I said, not liking how it felt. Sure, I'd been truthful about Noah to the guys and I'd tell them about this weekend, but Hayden made one thing clear Saturday night. He wanted the world to know I was his. Theirs. I was blurring lines and didn't like it.

"I've never tailgated before," I said. "Should I bring anything?"

He shook his head. "Nope. My mom and her friends put out a massive spread. Food, drinks, dessert. They bring all these games. It's a huge party."

"Okay. I can do that." I stood, giving the idea that he should probably go. He took the hint, hopping up.

"Can I pick you up? Around eleven? Game starts at four."

"Sure," I said. "Sounds fun."

He shoved his hands in his pockets and smiled shyly as he walked out of the suite. Noah was a good guy, I figured, just caught in a bad family situation like I was. Maybe together we could make it a little bit easier.

～

"Is it just me or is Ruthie watching us all the time?" Anderson asked after class on Friday. He made a concerted effort not to make eye contact with the red-head lingering by the door.

"It's not just you," I said. "I've been getting weird vibes off her all week. "Ever since Noah came over on Monday."

Anderson responded to Noah's name with a grunt. I'd told them all about tailgating and the game, promising to check in frequently. "Maybe she could go out with Noah," he suggested.

I rolled my eyes. If it was only that easy, but to be fair, I'd wondered the same. "I have a feeling Ruthie'd eat Noah alive." I eyed Anderson's fit body. "I think you're more her type."

His eyes flicked to mine. "You know I hate that I can't take you on the road with me."

"For luck?"

They walked down the stairs. "Luck, companionship, snarky jabs. Any would do. I hate being away from you."

I frowned. "I hate it, too. Maybe you should quit the team and hole up with me all weekend."

He groaned, but I noticed how his hand clenched around the strap of his backpack. He'd do it if he could—I had no doubt—but Anderson's passion and commitment was one of the things I loved about him—all of them. The Allendale Four played and loved hard.

"Hi, Heaven," Ruthie said. "Anderson."

"Hi," I said. Anderson nodded.

"All ready for your big date with Noah tomorrow?" Her eyes never left Anderson's. If she thought she was going to bust me in a lie with one of my boys ,she gravely misunderstood me.

"Heaven promised she'd bring me back one of those big foam fingers," Anderson said, giving me a wink.

Ruthie studied her cherry-red nails. "I've got tickets, maybe I'll see you there."

"Maybe," I said brightly, unwilling to let her get me. I wasn't sure what her problem was, but I needed her off my back.

She turned, flipping her red hair behind her shoulder, and Anderson watched her retreating form. He raised his eyebrows. "Any idea what that's about?"

"If I had to guess, I'd say she has a crush on you. She's been bugging me about you for weeks."

"Not interested." He didn't look but I did, noticing how Ruthie's hips swished as she walked. "You know I only have eyes for one incredibly sexy, super lucky girl."

"I know," I replied, feeling foolish. "Back in high school you guys made it clear there was no one in Allendale that caught your interest. But here...there's a lot to look at."

"I'm only interested in looking at one woman, Heaven Reeves. That was true then and it's true now."

I took a deep breath, pushing Ruthie out of my mind. "Good luck this weekend. You call me after every race, got it?"

"I will." He grazed my cheek with his thumb. "And you be careful. I'm serious. Don't take any chances—no matter how much you want to please your father."

I nodded. "I won't. I promise. Noah is harmless. Plus, his ultra-conservative parents will be there."

We walked across campus and Anderson pulled me behind a bush near the school chapel. He kissed me, muttering, "I hate keeping this quiet. I hate it."

I kissed him back, hoping he knew that I felt the same.

NOAH ARRIVED at eleven on the dot, standing at my door in a crisp, white, button-down shirt and plaid shorts. Sunglasses perched in his hair and a small gold cross hung around his neck from a chain.

I'd asked Samantha what to wear and she suggested a dress. I found a short-sleeved, red-and-white-striped cotton dress in Amber's closet and accessorized with white Converse and a row of chunky bracelets on my arm.

"You look great," Noah said, taking me in. The dress was modest; I didn't feel comfortable showing off too much skin with him or his parents. The last thing I needed was word getting back to my dad that I'd embarrassed him somehow.

"You look nice, too," I said closing the door behind me. Amber was still asleep and Ruthie and Samantha left earlier carrying red and black pom-poms for the game.

"My mom's a traditionalist. Dressing up for the games has always been a big deal for her."

I looked down at my shoes. "Too casual?"

"Nope." He smiled. "Perfect."

The whole campus transformed overnight, turning into one big party. Cars, campers, buses, and tents occupied every open space. Noah explained that his family had staked out the same location for the past thirty years, when his parents went to school at the University.

"I guess he wants you to follow his footsteps?" I asked.

"Yep. Business degree. Fraternity. Girlfriend. It's like he wants a clone."

"Can't you tell him you want to live your own life?" I asked, walking around a grill someone had set up in the middle of the parking lot.

He looked at me from the side. "Can you tell your father that?"

"Apparently not."

Noah introduced me to his parents, Mr. and Mrs. Hancock. They were clean-cut and professional-looking. Everything about them screamed vanilla with a side of wealth. What was my father, a small-town evangelical, doing with this man? Something didn't add up.

Mrs. Bennett was lovely, handing me a plate filled with barbeque, deviled eggs, and piping-hot cornbread. She asked me about my classes, my mother, and where I was from. I couldn't imagine my mother talking to this person for more than a few minutes. My skin itched from the anxiety of being around someone so genuine. I felt like I was in an alternate reality.

"We've been so worried about Noah since he started college. He's always been a little rebellious—pushing his father's buttons," she said in a quiet voice, touching her very blonde hair. A huge diamond glinted on her finger. "But when he started this year I prayed for a change in his heart. I had no concerns about him not having a steady girlfriend. I always knew he'd find the perfect girl, but Roger is definitely feeling a little relieved. Kids date around these days, don't you think? Everyone is less worried about settling down. It's smart, if you ask me."

Noah walked over with a plate filled with food and eased up next to me. Then he rested his hand on my back.

My lower back.

I tried not to jump out of my skin but instead cleared my throat and said, "Do you have a water?"

"Oh sure, honey," his mother said. "A whole cooler full, right over there."

I made my break and wasn't exactly surprised when Noah followed me over.

"What the hell was that?" I asked.

"Just playing it up for my dad. He's watching us closely, haven't you noticed?"

"Not really," I said, twisting off the bottle cap. "I've been talking to your mom."

He nodded. "She likes you. I can tell."

"Noah," I said, as evenly as possible. "It doesn't matter if she likes me. This isn't real."

"I know," he said, frowning. "But they need to think it is, or he'll never get off my back, and your dad..."

"My dad what?"

"Your dad wants my father's funding and it's my understanding there are some concerns."

"What kind of concerns?" We're surrounded by dozens of football fans. Most dressed in red and black. The air smells like food and smoked meat. Noah's parents stop every three seconds to greet someone they've known their whole lives. I definitely felt like a foreigner. My parents would never fit in here.

"Just some questions about his past have come up. My father asked me to do a little digging into his background. He's not the most technologically savvy. It looks like there's some questionable history with his taxes. Plus at least one charge of extortion filed about a decade ago." That was when I saw the sliver flask creep out of his pocket. He took a fast swig and the scent of whisky lingered after.

"You're drinking?"

"It's the only way I can get through these things."

"Do your parents know?" I didn't hide my shock.

"June and Ward? Fuck no. They're total teetotalers." He offered me the flask and when I shook my head he took another swig and then shoved the bottle back in his deep pockets.

I eyed him suspiciously, realizing I didn't know him at all. How could I? But it seemed he knew about my father, so I said, "Noah, I'm not going to lie and say my father has always been the most respectable person. He's had his share of troubles and if that scares your dad away, I get it. I don't blame him."

Noah gnawed on a piece of chicken and tossed the bone in a trashcan his mother set up. "That's the thing. I haven't told my dad about your father's history yet, because during my sleuthing I found something else." He cut me a look. "About you."

"What about me?" The familiar wave of anxiety rolled over my shoulders, daring to drown me.

"I know you told me you weren't as religious as your father, but I have a feeling he's not aware of your flamboyant lifestyle in high school. I imagine he'd be very disappointed to find out how promiscuous you were." He shrugged. "Are? Is it over? Because I've seen you on campus with a few of the guys in the photos."

I knew the photos would be out there somewhere. The internet lasts forever. I'd decided that I'd live with it, but that was before my dad came back with his demands and expectations.

No longer hungry, I tossed my plate in the trashcan. "What do you want, Noah?"

"I know we agreed to no kissing or physical intimacy, but if you want me to keep your father's sketchy background from my dad, I'm going to need a little bit more from you."

I crossed my arms, hoping it'd keep my heart from bursting out of my chest. I asked quietly, "Why are you doing this?"

"Because I'm sick of my father looking at me like I'm a failure, and you fit every qualification he has. Pretty, smart, sweet, polite. You're like Jackie O but without the Catholicism."

"Noah, I'm not going to be blackmailed by you."

"It's not blackmail if we're both getting something out of it. Your father will not only get his funding but he'll think you've got the perfect boyfriend." He smiled boyishly. "I'll get them off my back and have the chance to show you off."

"No."

"Don't be so quick. Think about it. I'll give you until tomorrow to decide."

"You want me to spend the rest of the day and pretend like this isn't happening?"

"If you leave now, the game will be ruined and my father will have a million questions. Not to mention my mother will be crushed." He looked over my shoulder and smiled at the woman I knew was behind me passing out pieces of pie. He shifted his gaze back to me. "There's no way it won't get back to your father that you vanished in the middle of the day."

This kid was good. He'd give my father a run for his money. He raised his eyebrows. "Are we good?"

It took everything I had not to strangle him, but I didn't. I gritted out the words, "Yes, we're good," before plastering a smile on my face. Noah's hand landed low on my back again and I fought off a tremor of repulsion. I'd been blackmailed before, harassed and victimized, but something about this, doing it with a smile on my face, was the worst it'd ever been. I had no idea why I thought my past could stay behind me, that the bad decisions I made would ever fade.

More than ever, I believed I was cursed to repeat the sins of the past over and over again.

48

———

MY FATHER WAS RIGHT, IF THERE WAS ONE THING I'D LEARNED IN HIGH school, it was how to make a scene and get attention. I knew the instant we walked through the door to the party and spotted Noah across the room. Noah was like Justin and Eric and half the other boys in my high school; a little nerdy, a little lost, and desperately in need of an ego boost.

Heaven to the rescue—saving one socially awkward boy at a time.

"Seriously, thanks for coming with me to this," I said. "I don't know anyone here."

She shrugged. "Maybe I can corrupt one of these guys. I like a challenge."

Yowza.

I unzipped my hoodie and hung it on the rack by the door. "So why did your dad send you here?" Samantha asked.

I shook my head. "See Noah over there?" I pointed to the guy in the number fourteen jersey, just like he'd told me he'd be. He was skinny and had a patchy beard that made him look more mature than he'd look without it. He stood with a couple of other guys.

"Yeah." She wrinkled her nose. Samantha had made it perfectly clear she was into big, athletic guys.

293

"I'm supposed to make him feel special. Stand by him and laugh at his jokes. Look pretty on his arm."

"You're kidding." She looked at the hint of cleavage popping out the V-neck of my jersey. "He wants you to…"

I shook my head. "Trust me, I've done it before. I can handle it."

Retrieving my phone, I typed out a message.

Hey, #14, I'm here!!

I pressed send.

I waited a heartbeat and he reacted to the vibration in his pocket. He looked up, made eye contact, and smiled. I smiled back.

He walked over and pulled me into a hug. Okay, then.

"Noah?" I asked.

"That's me. And wow, when they named you they sure had it right." He had a slight southern drawl. I had to admit it was pretty cute.

"This is my roommate, Samantha."

He smiled. "Glad you could come. You guys want a drink? We've got some Jesus Juice."

"Uh, Jesus Juice?" I asked.

"Well, the frats all have their special cocktails. Ours doesn't have liquor in it but it tastes pretty good."

"Sure, that sounds great."

"Come on, I'll show you around.

I followed him through the living room. The Christian Center was located in an historic home—just like the frats, and surprisingly it was one of the bigger houses; historic with large columns. He led us to the back door where it was obvious the party was in full swing. I heard a shout, followed by a splash.

"You have a pool?" Samantha asked.

"Yep. And a hot tub," he replied, smugly. When we both looked surprised, he said, "I know we're religious but we're not prudes. Showing a little skin isn't a sin."

My father would die if he heard that.

Samantha scanned the patio and her eyes brightened. "Oh, I see a friend from class. I'm going to say hi." She looked at me. "Is that okay?"

"Sure, have fun. We'll catch up soon."

Noah had curly black hair that was long on the top but short on the sides. He was cute enough—but not my type—and I needed to figure out what he wanted out of this meeting

"So your dad knows my dad," I said, taking a sip of the fruity Jesus Juice. It was pretty good.

"Yep, they set this whole thing up."

"Any idea why?"

His eyes raked over me. "Not specifically, but I'm glad they did." He took a sip of his drink. "My father believes in establishing contacts through the church—linking up with the right people."

I laughed. "Not sure how I'm going to help you. I'm new on campus, overwhelmed by classes. Not super social or anything or, frankly, very religious." I clamped my mouth shut. "Don't tell my dad that."

He smiled. "I won't, and for one thing, you're beautiful, you've got that going for you."

Wait...what happened to shy Noah? My dad may have had his information wrong.

I raised an eyebrow. "If I had to guess, this is really about my dad making a point about who he thinks I should make friends with at school—while developing those connections your dad is fond of."

"What? He doesn't like your friends?"

I hadn't given him the chance to get to know them.

"I try to keep my personal life away from my dad. He has a way of getting too involved." I smiled. "You know, like this entire situation."

"Maybe he's just protective." He slid a little closer. I really didn't know what my father had set up before I came here. Did he want me to date Noah? Flatter him? There was no doubt we'd gotten a little attention since we staked out this corner of the kitchen.

"I heard you were shy and needed a friend," I confessed. "That doesn't seem to be the case. What gives?"

Noah looked over my shoulder at a few girls walking through the kitchen. If we added a keg and a dose of machoism, we'd be at a standard party. "My dad financially supports this center with huge donations. He wants me to be a leader in the church and in his eyes, I can't do that without a nice girl on my arm. I think he's also embarrassed I don't have a steady girlfriend—he's accused me more than once of being gay."

"Are you? Because if you are, that's not a big deal for me."

"I'm not gay," he said. "But I'm also not a saint. Not the kind that my father wants me to be."

I sighed. "Totally get this. I'm not who my father wants me to be, either."

Things were starting to click. I'd been down this road before, but this time the arrangement was helping my dad, whereas last time it only benefitted Justin. There wasn't much I could get out of this other than getting him off my back.

"Basically, we both need a cover for our true selves. A steady friend of the opposite sex for them to feel comfortable with, and if your dad is happy..." I suggested.

"Then he'll donate to whatever project your dad has in mind at his church," he replied with a sly grin.

"What kind of proof do you think they'll want? What sort of evidence?"

"My dad has spies all over the place. He keeps tracks. Fuck, I even caught him paying my roommate to send him details on any women I'm seeing."

"You're joking."

He shook his head. "Nope."

"My dad is really up in my business, too. It sucks." Although I didn't think he'd gone so far as to pay off Amber for dirt on me. I planned on asking her though.

"So maybe if we do this, they'll back off?"

"Do what?"

"Hang out together. Post a few photos—"

"No!" I shouted, garnering a few looks. "Sorry, I just don't do social media. Ever."

"Maybe just a few sent to our fathers? Let them see we made friends? Maybe they'll ease up."

I eyed him skeptically. "What are your expectations? Because I'm not sleeping with you. Or kissing you."

He blinked. "Wow. Okay. That wasn't my intention, Heaven. I think hanging out a few times on campus, and if they come to town, we can have dinner or something."

"No social media."

He held up his hand. "None. I promise."

"Okay, we can do a few things, but not a lot. I'm busy and I'm sure you are too. Next time my dad comes up we can have dinner."

He smiled wide, relieved. "I think that's a great idea."

Noah held out his hand—offering it for me to shake. I've made deals like this before and they've gotten me nothing but trouble in return, yet I grasped it anyway, finding myself once again playing with fire.

49

———

I MADE IT THROUGH THE REMAINDER OF THE TAILGATE AND GAME without losing it completely. Oliver texted mid-afternoon. He and Jackson were at an exhibition game down at State.

Hey babe, how's it going?

I stared at my phone, trying to figure out what words to say. Come get me? Help? I've done it again?

Instead I type, **Good. We're winning by 3**

We're on the bus headed back. See you tonight

Noah's hand curled around my waist. With my left hand I pried his fingers off but he smiled at me, knowing and loving that he had the upper hand.

Too tired. Maybe tomorrow?

K-Text when you get to the dorm.

Love you.

Same

"Heaven, would you like to join us post-game? I brought dessert."

More? We'd already had pie and she doled out cake as well. How did this woman stay stick-thin?

"It's been a long day," I told her. "Thank you so much for having me, but I really think I should head back to the dorm. I've got a busy day tomorrow."

She smiled approvingly and gave me a hug. Mr. Hancock clasped my hand and told me how nice it was to meet me. I couldn't help but notice that his eyes lingered over my chest for a few seconds too long. Noah hovered nearby like a prison guard waiting for me to make a break for it. He wasn't wrong.

"I'll come back after I drop Heaven off," Noah said. He linked his sticky hand with mine and I forced myself not to fight it until we were out of sight. Then I shook him loose.

"Don't touch me." The rage from the day had built into something I could no longer contain. "This whole thing is insane, Noah. I don't think you're really a dick. You're just desperate to please your father."

"And you're not?"

I stopped outside Stetson Hall, having no intention of asking him in. He touched my chin and I shifted away.

"We made a deal," he said quietly.

"You reneged on our deal."

"This is business. Rules are renegotiated all the time." His eyes zeroed in on my lips and his hand reached for my hip.

"Don't," I whispered. Not wanting to make a scene.

He didn't stop, leaning in to brush his lips against mine. I twisted my head and he caught me on the cheek. With both hands I pushed him away and ran to the door.

"Night, Heaven," he said loudly. "I had a great time."

I didn't breathe until I was in my suite with the door shut and locked.

Thankfully no one was home, and I stripped down and got in the shower, desperate to wash the day away.

My phone rang before I was dry. I wrapped the towel around me and answered.

"Hello?"

"Heaven!"

"Hi, Mom." I sat on the bed in my room. It was only 9 p.m. but it felt way later.

"You okay? You sound funny."

"I'm fine. Just tired. It was a long day."

"How was the game?" she asked. My mother never seemed interested in my high school days, but now that I'm in college and a hundred miles away, she found time?

"It was fun. We won."

"And Noah? How was he?" She said his name in a flirty way.

"Noah was okay." I fight to add some enthusiasm but it was hard—if not impossible.

"You don't like him?" she asked and a light bulb went off in my brain. Maybe this was the universe intervening. I could tell my mom about Noah and she'd get it.

"Noah is—"

"Your father is so excited you two have linked up," she gushed, interrupting. "This fundraising deal at the church is huge and could really solidify him back in good graces with the head pastor. Your dad is really good at reaching out to people in the community and your involvement in connecting him with the Hancocks has really helped. He already spoke to Mr. Hancock today. He was impressed by you and said his son is smitten."

"Mom—" I tried to interject.

"Things are so different this time. Everything is above board. The job, the house...us. He's been really great to me, Heaven. So much more attentive and transparent about his work—his mission. I know he's pleased with the strides you two have made as well."

I swallowed over the lump forming in my throat. "So things are going well?"

Her excitement shifted to something else. Something hopeful. "Really well, Heaven. It's like it was before the trouble—back when you were little and we were all happy."

"Mom, that's great, but you've got to remember..."

"I remember," she snapped. "I remember working double shifts and coming home to find you spiraling out of control. I remember the medical bills and doing it all alone. Finding that garbage about you on the internet—learning how bad of a mother I'd been."

"That's not true. You're a great mom," I said, feeling the weight of the day crashing down. "I'm just scared he'll hurt you again."

"I need someone in my life, Heaven. I love your father and I'm willing to take a risk on him. I think you should, too."

I nodded even though my mother couldn't see me, but if I spoke I'd probably break down. My mom was right. I'd put her through hell and back and it was her time to be happy. She'd given me that when she backed off about the guys. I understood what needing support was like. I got it.

"I still haven't told your dad about the boys and what they mean to you, but he isn't wrong about finding a nice boy with a good family. One boy, Heaven. You needed them in school but you've grown so much since then. I think you're ready to live a functional, normal, Christian life. Don't you?"

I pushed the lie. "Yes."

"Noah seems like the perfect way to start."

I didn't reply and she didn't seem to care, heading into reminders about fall break coming up and my return home. It'd be the first time we'd spend as a family again and she couldn't wait.

I hung up the phone when she finished and texted Noah.

Fall break.

What?

I'll play this game until fall break. Your rules. But after that we come up with an amicable breakup and my father gets the funding.

There was a pause before he responded.

Ok. I can make that work. But you don't get to play that game like you did today. You're all in when we're in public.

Ok.

I tossed the phone on the desk and got into bed.

OVER THE NEXT few days I sunk into a familiar mode. Functional on the outside, crumbling on the inside.

Monday morning started with a text from Noah, informing me of where we'd meet that day and when, with an added note of clothing suggestions and how to wear my hair.

Oh and a little lipstick would be nice.

In biology, Anderson noticed the hair first, eyes lingering over the bouncy waves that took me an extra hour that morning. It was the typical, "long-hair-girl" style, one Amber and I often mocked for being the most safe and unoriginal by our peers.

"Hey," he said, reaching for my leg to squeeze. I shifted, keeping an eye on everyone around me. Ruthie sat in the front row, ignoring us for once, but with what Noah told me about his father's spies, I no longer could be sure. "You okay?"

I evaded the question. "How was your meet? I'm sorry I missed your text Saturday night. I crashed."

"Eh, I did okay. No records or anything," he said. "I think I missed my lucky charm." He glanced down at the twin-set sweater and jeans. Amber had the sweater set in her closet, part of her retro flair. "You look different."

"I was in a rush." Which was the biggest lie. It took me hours to get ready, feeling the added pressure of pleasing Noah's whims.

"Heaven." He frowned. "What's going on?"

The professor walked in and I opened my laptop, using it as an excuse to avoid Anderson. He knew me well—better than most—and I'd crack if he pushed me too hard. I flashed him what I hoped was a convincing grin. "I'm fine, babe. Just a busy weekend and this week looks like a monster. Hopefully it will calm down after mid-terms."

Fall break. That's what I had to get to. Fall break and everything would go back to normal.

50

ANDERSON

"SOMETHING'S WRONG WITH HER." I'd run into Oliver and Hayden outside the student center.

The change had been slow but distinct over the past few days. Each time I saw her, Heaven seemed different. At first it was her affect, the way she carried herself and the fact she'd stopped flirting all around. Heaven always flirted with me, even when she was busting my balls.

Then it shifted to her clothing. My girl was hot even just in a hoodie and baggy jeans. But when she'd shed that style and moved to the curve-revealing, cleavage-exposing outfits of the last year, she'd gained so much confidence. Heaven was like a caterpillar turned into a butterfly. Cute and fuzzy before, breathtaking after.

I didn't know how to explain what was going on this week or exactly what the difference was. She still looked gorgeous, but also tired. Her outfits lacked the spunk of her middle-fingered fuck you. Instead it was sweaters and conservative jeans. Sensible shoes and not a trace of the sexy boots she routinely wore to class to drive me wild.

Something was off and I was determined to figure out what.

Oliver frowned. "Do you think she's depressed again? I know the stuff with her dad has been bothering her."

The idea terrified me and had definitely crossed my mind. She'd worn long sleeves all week. "I don't know, but I think we should keep an eye on her."

"How long has it been going on?" Oliver asked.

"A week? Maybe two?"

"We went to the library last Tuesday. I helped her with Spanish. She seemed okay then."

That was good to know.

"What about you?" I asked Hayden. His eyes had darkened and I noticed his fist balled tight. "What?"

"Last Saturday she and I were together."

"Okay..." Oliver and I looked at one another. "Together how?"

His jaw clenched. "Together together. Things got a little intense."

I trusted Hayden with my life—he was my brother—but I'd kick his ass if he hurt her. I'd worked into a mid-level fume when Oliver jumped in, "Did something go wrong?

"No," he said. "I made sure but she wanted to push me and I let her. She was really into it, I swear."

I grimaced. "Maybe you read the signals wrong. I know she thinks she wants to get adventurous but maybe she's not as ready as she thinks she is."

Hayden nodded. "I'll talk to her."

"Maybe we can hang out this week? All together. Make sure we're all on the same page." Managing a relationship like this was hard. It took commitment from all of us.

"This week is slammed," Hayden confessed. "We've got a game Saturday and Coach is all over us with extra practice and training."

"Same with us," Oliver said. "Double-header this weekend."

"We'll figure something out," I said. "Text her or call. Drop by. Whatever it takes." I pinned Hayden with a stare. "And make sure you're good."

He nodded and looked up at the clocktower over the student center. "Shit, I gotta run."

"Me, too." Oliver said.

I watched them go and started back to my room. I had the next few hours free. We'd come a long way since the start of our relationship. I didn't want to lose it now.

<h1 style="text-align:center">51</h1>

Noah waited for me outside my Psych class with his backpack slung over his shoulder. He carried himself with a confidence I didn't recall from before and I wondered for a brief moment if he was a vampire, sucking away my energy and taking it for himself.

Maybe not a vampire—not cute enough, but he definitely was a parasite.

"Hey babe," he said, using the term her boys called her. It made her skin crawl but one thing she noticed about Noah was that the more she pushed back, the more he continued. He eyed her outfit. "You look amazing."

"I look like a Stepford Wife."

He reached for my hand and I let him take it.

"I knew your hair would look good like that."

I shook my head. "Why do you care what my hair looks like? Or my clothes?"

"Because we're trying to convey an image here, Heaven." He pulled me against his side and directed me down the path between buildings. "You're the sweet, virginal co-ed. I'm the dedicated, hard-working Christian."

I squirmed away but he held tight. "Gross, Noah. No one thinks that but you."

"You don't think so?" he asked, glancing around us. Sure enough, even though we were on a huge campus a few people seemed to be watching us.

"Why do they even care?" None of it made sense to me.

"People are nosy, but I'd think you'd know that from your past online exposure."

I stopped and this time moved away from his body. "Noah, what happened to me in high school is a long, complicated story. It involves a prank, more pranks, and a sexual predator going to jail. I don't think that's a game plan you want to emulate."

He stepped forward. "Kiss me."

I frowned. "What?"

"Kiss me. Or I call my dad."

His brown eyes carried a darkness I didn't want to test. I leaned into him and went for his cheek, planning a chaste peck. He caught me, pulling me close and slammed his mouth into mine. The kiss was too hard, his tongue demanding. I dropped my chin and turned my neck to get away. "Needs a little work," he said in my ear. "Meet me at the University Church tomorrow night at six. We're having a dinner."

At least it would be in public, I thought, feeling the need to wipe him off my mouth. He ran his hand down my arm.

"Heaven?"

I spun and found Amber and Ginger walking toward us.

"Hey guys," I said, using the interruption as an excuse to break away and hug my friend. When we pulled apart, I introduced them. "This is Noah. We met through our dads. Noah, this is my friend and roommate, Amber. And this is Ginger."

Noah nodded his head in greeting, eyes sweeping over the girls. There was obviously nothing about either girl that screamed "lesbian" or "I'm bisexual" but Noah was savvy and had a knack for ferreting out personal information for his own purpose. A deep sense of dread coiled in my stomach. I didn't want him near these girls. Not when Amber's housing depended on my father and he knew about her relationship...

"You've got class now, right?" I said to Noah. "I'll be at the dinner. Thank you for the invitation."

His eyes flirted between us. I gave Amber a pleading grin. The last thing I needed was for her to decide to push him. She gave him a fake smile. "Nice to meet you, Noah."

"You too, ladies." He touched my chin and walked off with a confident swagger.

Ginger stared. "Okay what the hell was that about?"

"Heaven, he's creepy as fuck."

"I know. I'm giving my dad two more weeks and then I'm calling it off."

Amber shook her head. "I don't know how you'll make it two weeks. And if the guys meet him? Prepare for an epic showdown."

"Which is exactly why they can't meet him." I faced the girls. "I need this to work out. My dad is all over me right now and my mom has a lot riding on his job."

"Babe, this is not your problem." She squeezes my hand. "We can figure this out. Move off campus. Squat in the nasty dorms by the railroad tracks. I don't like this."

Amber was a good friend. Too good for me and the situation I'd gotten myself into. "Give me a few more weeks to clear it up. If that doesn't work, we'll figure something out, okay?"

She and Ginger exchange worried looks but Amber nods in agreement. "Okay. As long you promise to be safe."

I smiled gratefully at my friend. "I promise."

WHEN I GOT BACK to the dorm, Amber and Ginger were holed up in our bedroom. I owed them for earlier that day so I camped out in the living room. Samantha sat on the couch next to me, streaming movies over her laptop with large headphones over her ears. I pretended to study but spent most the time fighting the creeping urge to hide in the bathroom. I knew I shouldn't, but the idea wiggled into my brain after seeing Noah that afternoon and wouldn't leave.

I knew if I got through the next two weeks, I'd be okay. I knew I could handle it. I'd been through worse, right?

Anxiety rose higher and higher, climbing up my throat.

I glanced at Samantha to see if she noticed anything different about me but she was focused on the screen. I felt like my pain was visible all over my skin. It prickled. It felt raw. I peeked at the bathroom again. It was so close and I knew there was a razor in the shower.

No. I promised myself. *No.*

Tacked to the back of the suite door was a poster of Jim Morrison that Amber bought at the head-shop downtown. It was the classic pose, bare-chested Jim with a beaded necklace hanging twisted off his neck. I stared at his face, hoping he'd give me a clue where to go next.

A knock on the door jerked me back to the now and my eyes widened at Jim, wondering if this was my sign.

"Can you get that?" Samantha asked, never taking her eyes off the screen.

"Yeah, sure."

I rose and crossed the room. Hayden stood on the other side.

"Hi," he said. "Can I come in?"

I glanced back at my closed bedroom door and my suitemate on the couch. She looked up and waved at Hayden. He smiled in return. "Let's talk out here."

His face fell, although I wasn't sure why. I'd rather have privacy.

Hayden did that thing, the move he pulled on me that very first day, leaning against the wall in the hallway. His long body took up most the space and girls from the hall skirted around him while eyeing his form.

"What's going on?" I asked, pushing the sleeves of my sweatshirt over my elbows.

"I just wanted to see how you were doing. Things have been hectic lately and the last time we were really together things got…"

"Intense," I said, completing his sentence. Hell yeah, they did. What I'd give to go back to that night—to the way things were before all this shit started.

"It was, and I don't know," he ran his hand through his hair, "was it okay? Any regrets? I hope I didn't cross a line."

I frowned and shook my head. "We went over this. It was great.

Exactly what I wanted." I scanned his face. "Are you having second thoughts?"

"Fuck no. No. You just...you seem stressed or something. I wanted to make sure it wasn't with me."

With everything going on, Hayden questioning what happened between us hit me like a slam in the gut. Couldn't he tell that I enjoyed it? Did he not believe my words? I'd asked him to do it—begged him, almost. With anyone else I would've been embarrassed, but maybe we weren't on the same page like I'd thought.

Or maybe he was here because of Noah. Had I been seen? Did he know?

My mind whirled with confusion.

"It was great," I told him, sucking up my emotions.

His face relaxed with relief. "Okay good. The guys were hoping to get together sometime this week. It's a crunch but let's figure it out, okay?"

I smiled. "That sounds like a really good idea."

His eyes searched mine and he reached for my hand. I pulled back, ignoring the confusion and hurt that followed.

"I should go, Hayden. I have a ton of homework."

"Yeah," he said. "Okay. Call me if you need anything."

"I will."

He looked like he wanted to say more, his jaw working overtime, but I used his hesitation to slip back into the room, shutting the door behind me.

I took a deep breath and leaned against the door, waiting for Samantha to say something. She didn't. I stared at my room, where Amber's voice could be heard through the door followed by Ginger's laughter. I waited, feeling my heart pounding in my chest, the dark wave of anxiety taking over. When it didn't subside, I took a shaky breath and succumbed to the pressure building inside and walked into the bathroom and shut the door behind me.

52

Since Noah was on the organizing committee he told me to meet him at the house for dinner instead of picking me up. Like the past few days, he instructed me on what to wear: casual dress, nice shoes.

He eyed me the moment I walked in, a small grin lingering over his cracked lips. I felt the heat of his gaze—he didn't want me. Not like the Allendale boys, no, there was something else, the glint of knowing he had me under his thumb. I'd seen it before in Spencer's eyes. I'd also seen it in my father's, too.

"Heaven," he said, calling out my name. I tugged at the sleeves of my dress. It looked like a T-shirt, giving my body a boxy shape. I liked it because the sleeves were long. Noah looked down at my shoes and a small frown tugged at his mouth. I had on black booties. It was the best I could do.

"Hi, Noah," I said, accepting his kiss on my cheek. At least here he won't try to push himself on me, which was a fear that grew by the minute. I'd known guys like Noah before. He wouldn't be happy until he owned me.

Two weeks. That was all I needed.

A full spread of food was on the table. Apparently, the church group met every week to share a meal. The idea was nice, but even in my dowdy dress I knew this wasn't my kind of group. Everyone seemed nice enough; clean-cut. Sweet. Not the type to fool an entire student body or cause a social media sex scandal. Not the kind to lie just to help their dad. I stared at Noah, who looked the picture of a perfect Christian. Then again, maybe they were my kind of group.

"I'd like to take a moment introduce you all to my girlfriend, Heaven," Noah said loudly over the group. "I was blessed when she entered my life a few weeks ago—love at first sight."

I smiled, forcing my lips to curve upward. "So blessed."

Then he stood in front of the group and said a blessing, thanking God for all our bounty, the whole time feeling more and more separated from the event. Everyone in the room closed their eyes but I watched them, wondering if they knew the truth about this man and his family, or for that matter, mine.

"Noah, help me bring in the extra chairs," someone said and he vanished from the room. The girl next to me, with hair identical to mine (long-haired-girl curls) pointed me to the start of the buffet.

"I'm Julie," she said. "How did you meet Noah?" Her question sounded genuine—curious.

"Our fathers are friends. Through some church connections."

She shook her head. "Ah, so you passed the Daddy test."

I frowned. "What do you mean?"

She gave me a startled look, her blue eyes apologetic. "Look, I'm not trying to start anything, but Noah's always been a little elusive. Lots of girls have tried to date him. He's never been one for a serious relationship and we all figured it's because he was looking for a specific kind of girl. The kind approved of by his father. You're the first one he's brought around."

The fact that every girl in the room looked like a Noah-specified clone, there was no way I fit any sort of physical standard. I gave him something no other girl could: leverage.

I scooped a mound of mac 'n cheese on my plate. "His mother said he's shy, but he doesn't seem that way to me."

Another girl stood across from me, adding salad to her plate. She snorted. "Noah's not shy. And no matter what he says, don't let him talk you into going to his room. He's not the gentleman he claims."

"Did you date him?" I asked.

Julie's cheeks reddened and she glanced toward the door where Noah and the other guy entered carrying a stack of metal folding chairs. "I wouldn't call it dating." Her nose wrinkled. "Just be careful."

I nodded. "Don't worry. I'm not as naïve as I look."

"Hey, babe," Noah said, cutting in line to stand next to me. "Didn't you get me a plate of food?"

I blinked. "Oh, sorry. I didn't think."

"No, you didn't, but it's no big deal. I'll just go to the back of the line."

He stared at me and I felt everyone watching. Julie had already walked away, casting an empathetic glance in my direction.

"Here, you take my plate. I'll go to the back of the line."

He smiled condescendingly. "Thanks, babe." He kissed me on my nose and squeezed my hip.

I walked past the rest of the line and stood in the back. The whole scene was weird and demeaning. Noah was the exact opposite of my boys. They'd move mountains for me.

To my astonishment, he did save me a seat, and when Julie asked me about my name, he spoke over me. "Her father is a minister."

"Actually," I said, "my mother named me. After her favorite character in a book."

The girl next to Julie who had short brown hair and big blue eyes said, "Wait. You mean V. C. Andrews? She named you after those books?"

I nodded, eating a carrot off my plate. "She was obsessed with those characters."

"Oh my god, me too. I read them all in seventh grade."

I laughed. Those books were insane but completely addictive. "Heaven was my mom's favorite."

Noah gave me a weird look. "Why didn't you ever tell me that?"

"You never asked."

Later, once the meal was over and the table cleared, Noah took me to the side and brushed my hair over my shoulder. "I forgot to tell you that you look nice tonight." His eyes skimmed down my legs, landing at my feet. "Those shoes are a little...risqué for the church group, but you feel free to wear them the next time we're alone."

"Noah, I have no plans on being alone with you. That's not part of the deal."

"How about you and your roommate?"

"What?"

"She's into chicks, right? I've always wanted to be with two girls. She looks like she's probably a howler."

"Noah, you need to shut the fuck up, right now."

He took out his phone and scrolled through. My stomach twisted into a familiar knot. He held up the screen. It was a photo of me and Hayden from two weeks ago, leaving the laundry room holding hands. A bizarre sense of déjà vu rolled over me.

"Where did you get that?"

"Heaven, I told you. God is always watching. I'd hate for this photo to get sent to the wrong person."

"Hayden's a friend. My father knows that."

"Does he?" He slipped the phone back in his pocket. "That website had some interesting information. Whoever concocted that plan was pretty smart."

"Spencer is a psychopath."

"Those two things are not mutually exclusive." He ran a finger down my cheek and I jerked away.

"Two weeks," I told him. "My father gets the funding and you get the hell away from me."

"Or what?" he said.

"You don't want to know the leverage I have on my side," I said, knowing that if the guys found out about Noah they would tear him to pieces. I didn't want that. It was too risky and they had too much on the line but the threat itself was solid.

He tilted his head at my statement, undeterred. "Study with me, tomorrow night."

"Where?"

"In my room."

The girl's warning from earlier rang in my head.

"Not a chance."

He lifted his chin, amused. "Library, then."

"Main floor. In the study area. Nowhere private." I gave him a smirk. "It wouldn't be appropriate for us to be alone like that. I'd hate to tell my father that you're pressuring me."

If I thought sticking up for myself would make Noah back off, I was wrong. If anything, I was learning he liked a challenge. Noah Hancock wanted to break me—I had no doubt about that now.

I took the chance when a few of the other girls I learned lived in my dorm were leaving and followed them out the door. I was quiet on the way back, trying to figure out a way out of this situation. My father was no help. My mother was caught up in his world. The guys...they'd kill him. The best thing I could do was wait it out and hope he stuck to his promise.

THE SUN BEAMED down the following day, bathing the University in one last day of warmth before fall entered winter. The leaves had all fallen and the mornings and evenings were cool, but for a few hours in the afternoon everything was perfect, sunny, and warm.

I walked toward the dorm and heard the loud, familiar rumble of an engine turning down the road outside Stetson Hall. Shading my eyes, I looked up and saw Oliver hanging out the window.

"What are you doing?" I asked, walking up to the car.

"I came to see if you wanted to go for a ride."

I looked at the stack of books in my hands and frowned at the idea of a study date tonight with Noah. "I've got a ton of work."

He smiled, drop-dead gorgeous and persuasive in a way that had always hit me in the knees. His hair tousled in the fall breeze and his still-tan-from-summer face lit up when he looked at me. "Just for a few hours. I'll get you back in plenty of time to shove your pretty little nose in those books."

Just being in his presence was like a hit of adrenaline. "Okay," I said, breaking into a grin. "Let's get out of here."

He crawled through the front seat to open the passenger side door and I tossed my books in the back. I'd worn a black skirt that went down to my knees and a soft gray sweater. The silver cross my daddy gave me hung around my neck and it glinted in the sunlight when I caught my reflection in the rearview mirror. I tried to ignore the dark circles under my eyes, flipping up the visor.

Oliver took my hand and revved the engine, announcing to the world we were leaving campus.

The leather seats were old and cracked but they had a worn softness. I sunk into them and played with Oliver's hand.

"I've missed you," I said.

He lifted my hand and kissed it. "I didn't know we'd been apart."

I felt like it though—I felt like I'd gone on a trip for weeks, barely coming up for air. The sanctity of our relationship had been tested by an outside force and I didn't know if I had the energy to keep it all up.

Oliver drove, hair blowing from the open windows. I felt my own hair, the perfectly spiraled curls twisting in the wind. I inhaled, smelling the scents of fall, and closed my eyes.

I must have dozed off because I didn't realize we'd stopped or that Oliver was no longer holding my hand. The sound of the engine rumbling to a stop, then cutting entirely jarred me awake. I looked out the front window and saw the green grass and trees of the botanical gardens sprawled in front of me. I felt the tickle of fingertips on my arm.

I turned, facing Oliver, but froze when I saw the expression on his face. Tears welled in the corners of his eyes. A deep-set frown clung to his lips. My eyes drew to where his were focused—the fresh wounds on my forearms. I yanked my arm back, but he held it, gentle but firm.

"Tell me what's going on."

"Nothing," I lied. "Just you know, the stress of school and everything."

"Heaven, don't lie to me. I can't take it." His voice trembled and it scared me. I scared me.

The cuts were thin, red dashes against my pale skin. Superficial would be the term, but each slash cut down to the depths of my soul. I hated him seeing them. I hated looking at them. My stomach seized.

"Baby," he said, reaching for me across the seat. "Tell me what I can do."

A sob caught in my chest. I didn't allow it to move. "There's nothing you can do," I said. "There's nothing anyone can do. It's just who I am. It's how I'm made."

He opened his mouth to say something but thought better. Oliver was smart—quick. He didn't work on emotion or rage like the others. He climbed over the seat, pulling me into his lap.

I wanted to fight him—to push him away like Hayden, but Oliver wrapped his arms around me and held me tight.

"We've been through this before, Heaven, and got through it, but I can't help you if you aren't honest with me."

I didn't want to talk about it. I just wanted to feel something other than pain, and I shifted around so that I was facing Oliver and touched his chest.

He touched my hair, wild from the wind, and his thumb rubbed against my bottom lip. I licked the pad of his finger.

He grew hard beneath me. I felt the heat and want between his legs. I snaked my hands around his neck and kissed him again. For some reason, Oliver and I always ended up in the car like this, the two of us frustrated and breathing heavy. I reached between us and fumbled with his buckle.

He sighed and stilled my hands, leaning back into the seat.

"What?" I asked, searching his face. "Why'd you stop?"

"Because this is wrong."

"Why? Because we're in a car? Because I'm upset? I told the others and I'll say the same to you—don't treat me like I'm a baby." I tried to catch his eye but he didn't let me.

Oliver scrubbed his face with his hands and looked out the window. He pressed his knuckle against the glass and tapped against it, looking into the distance. The sun was no longer shining—instead blocked by graying clouds. "There is nothing I want to do more than make you feel better, but the two of us..." he swallowed, "making love won't do it."

"You don't know that." All I wanted was to *feel*. That was all.

"I do know it, Heaven. Something is wrong, really wrong, and I can't just let my hormones take over and let your issues get pushed aside. Not again."

I crossed my arms and stared at him, hard, but he never looked my way. I threw my hands up and reached for the door, climbing off his body to get outside. He followed, scrambling after me, adjusting the front of his pants.

"What are you going to do? Tell the others? Call my mom?"

"I don't know. I'm in over my head here. So are you."

The black hole swirled around my feet, threatening to suck me in whole. I stared across the lake.

"Take me home," I said, walking back to the car and slamming the door.

He stood outside and gaped at me. "We're not done."

"Yes," I said through the open window. "We are."

He walked around the car and got inside. I refused to look at him. Not because I was angry, but because I was terrified I would cave and tell him everything. But what could Oliver do about my father? About Noah? A few weeks and it would all be over. I could repair the damage then.

It was dark when he pulled up to Stetson Hall. The wind had picked up and I spotted jagged lightning in the distance. My phone had a dozen messages from Noah trying to find me since I bailed on our study date. I ignored them all and before he could think of walking me in, I rested my hand over Oliver's on the gear shift. "I'm sorry about all of this. I think I just need some time to get my head on straight."

"Let me walk you up." Those were the first words he'd spoken since we left the botanical garden.

"Not tonight," I said. "I just need a little space, okay?"

He frowned. I'd asked these boys for many things but distance wasn't one of them.

"I'll call you."

"Any time. Day or night."

"I will."

"Be safe, Heaven."

I slammed the door and ran to the building.

53

OLIVER

I WATCHED her get out of the car, knowing I should go after her. She'd looked so sad. So rejected when she'd been on my lap but dammit, I knew the timing was off. Her shadow vanished, entering the building, and rain started to fall. I slammed my fist into the steering wheel.

"Fuck!" I shouted, less about the pain to my knuckles than her walking away like that. "Fucking fuck!"

I reached for my phone and called her but hung up just as fast. She wanted space and that was okay. Right? People needed space. They needed time.

I didn't like it. Not at all.

I texted the others.

Meet me at Hayden's. 911

Four thumbs ups followed.

We'd come up with a code months ago, after the first time I caught Heaven trying to cut herself. That night scared the hell out of me but I knew I had to be strong. Even so, we made a code—911 meant Heaven was struggling and we needed to figure out what to do. Hayden's house was in the middle of campus, by the time I found a parking spot and ran through the rain to the porch, the others were there.

Hayden stood in the door.

"What's going on?" Anderson said. He was breathing heavy, having run the farthest from his dorm. He shook his head, spraying rain on the rest of us. "Where is she?"

"At her dorm. She's...she hurt herself again. I saw the cuts."

"Fuck," Hayden growled, slamming his fist into the door. "I apologized, guys, and she just turned me away." He ran his hands through his hair. "I knew something was wrong even though she denied it."

"She keeps avoiding my calls. Super short in her text replies," Jackson said, quietly. All signs of his normally light-hearted demeanor were gone. He looked terrified. "I thought she was just busy—I had no fucking clue things were so bad."

Anderson's sharp jaw and angular cheekbones looked deadly in the shadowy light of the porch. "This has something to do with that Noah kid. No doubt about it."

"Dude, we don't know that," I said.

"Between him and her dad, they were getting in her head. I have no doubt."

"Who would know? Amber?" Hayden asked. "Have you talked to her?"

"She's got a new girlfriend—I haven't seen her for more than a minute in a few weeks."

"Shit." He replied. We all knew that was just one more support person that failed Heaven when she needed us.

"What about the other two girls?" I asked. "Samantha and the redhead."

"Ruthie," Anderson said. "She has bio with us and there's something going on there."

"Something how?" Jackson asked.

"She watches us a lot and it definitely unnerves Heaven. I think she gives her flashbacks to high school drama."

"What do you want to do? How do we handle this?" I asked, "Because she shut me out."

"Me too," added Hayden.

"Call her mom?" Jackson asked.

I shook my head. "She'd kill us and with everything going on with her dad...god knows how he'd handle it."

Anderson and Jackson exchanged looks. "How about we go over. See if we can get her to talk? Maybe she needed a minute to cool off."

I didn't think so, but it wasn't a bad idea. "You guys do that. We'll wait here with the car if you need us."

Anderson nodded and Jackson stuck out his fist for me to bump it. "Take care of her," I said.

"We will. We'll get her the help she needs."

Hayden and I watched as they hopped off the porch and into the rain.

"I'm worried about her," I admitted. "Really fucking worried."

Hayden threw his arm around my shoulder. "Me too, but it'll be okay. We've been down this road before."

I knew he was right, but as Anderson and Jackson ran toward her building I couldn't shake the feeling building up inside. Heaven was in trouble and I may have destroyed any chance I had to help her.

54

———

HEAVEN

"BE SAFE."

It was something I couldn't promise Oliver. Not when everything around me was falling apart. I rode the elevator to my floor and unlocked the door with my key. Samantha sat on the couch, headphones on and the distinct sound of a couple having sex floated through the room.

I connected eyes with Samantha and whispered, "Amber?"

But a man's grunt caught me off guard and I glanced toward the closed door of Ruthie's room. Wow.

I froze, listening to Ruthie and her partner reach their climax. They were loud and totally abandoned. Samantha wisely clamped her earphones back on her head. For some reason, my feet wouldn't move.

That was until the bedroom door opened and Ruthie stepped outside wrapped in a silk bathrobe, her long red hair hanging over her shoulder. My eyes flicked behind her and I saw her partner in the bed, hair wild and face sweaty. My heart jerked in my chest when I saw him; Noah, shirtless and well-fucked in Ruthie's bed.

"Sorry we made so much noise. I hope we didn't disturb you," Ruthie said, rummaging around the refrigerator.

My gaze shifted between the two and Noah just shrugged with a smirk on his face.

Rage took over.

"What the fuck?" I said, barging into Ruthie's room. I heard the refrigerator door shut in the other room. Spinning, I slammed the door right in her face and locked it. "What the hell are you doing?"

"You bailed on me tonight, Heaven, and an interesting opportunity presented itself." He frowned and whispered conspiratorially, "I don't think your roommate likes you very much."

"You're kidding?"

"About her disliking you? No. I think she really hates you. Why else would she fuck me like that knowing I came here to see you."

"No, you jackass. You just fucked some other girl because I wasn't here. What if I was in an accident? Or hurt?"

"I sent you a dozen texts. You ignored them. I had no choice but to believe you'd backed out." He held my gaze, daring me to lie. I didn't have the energy to do it. "Well, as far as I'm concerned, our deal is over. To be honest, I think if I get Ruthie to hang a cross around her neck, she'd pass Father's specifications."

"You're ending our deal? And replacing me with...her?"

He laughed. "She's sneaky, did you know that? She told me everything while we were in bed. How she's been spying on you for your dad and he's been paying her off." He made a face. "I wonder if my dad gave him that tip."

"She what?" I couldn't keep up. All of it was coming so fast, but little things flashed in my head. The expensive clothes, the new high-tech watch, the sleek nails and her constant presence. I turned around and flung open the door. She stood on the other side smiling wickedly. "You've been spying on me?"

She lifted her tiny shoulders. "Your daddy is very curious about your activities, Heaven. It's a little weird. He wanted all the details about you and those guys you're so possessive of."

Samantha sat on the couch watching the whole thing. I looked at her. "Were you in on this, too?"

"No." She held up her hands. "I promise."

"Basically," Ruthie said, "you're a lying whore and your father knew all along that you'd ruin his plans. He just wanted a heads up before shit hit the fan."

"That's not true."

"Yes, sweetie, it is. He knows about the guys, the games, the sneaking around. He knew before he contacted me but he wanted proof. Said we should go ahead and find a new roommate, that he'd have you back home by the end of the semester."

My heart thundered in my chest. The house of cards I'd built around me shuddered at my feet. My father knew who I really was. He knew about the sinful life I led. I'd let Noah kiss me, *touch* me, for no reason at all. I'd pushed Oliver and Hayden away. Anderson and Jackson were next. The life my mother banked on was going to crumble and it was my fault. *All my fault.*

"You're pathetic," I told her, then looked over her shoulder. "And you're a fucking creep."

Ruthie rolled her eyes. "You're nothing but trash—a filthy whore with a shady past trying to play off like you're a good girl." Her lips twisted into something evil and I didn't know if this was just her way of getting back at me for having the Allendale boys, but her words cut anyway. "Go home, Heaven. Beg for forgiveness. Because you're going to need it."

For the first time in ages, I had no one to turn to. Not my boys. Not my mom. Definitely not my father.

Ruthie was right, the only thing I could do was repent. Beg for forgiveness. I didn't know where to start, but I knew it wasn't here.

I left Ruthie and Noah in her room and walked across the suite, entering my room. Amber wasn't home—she never was anymore—having found the freedom she craved in college. I saw her car keys hanging over her desk and snatched them off the hook.

"Where are you going?" Samantha asked. "Are you sure you should driving like this? You're really upset. I don't blame you."

"I can't stay here." This wasn't my home. I didn't fit in. Would I ever?

"Do you want me to call Oliver? Or Jackson? I know they'd come."

"No." I walked back into the common area. "They can't know about this."

"Heaven," she said, "You didn't do anything wrong. They won't be mad."

I stopped and faced her. "I did so many things wrong. So many things. I let Noah use me. I lied to the guys. I pushed them away. My dad...he's going to be so disappointed. You don't know who I really am."

"I know you're kind. And funny. And a good friend."

"That's nice of you to say. Thank you."

I didn't wait for more. I didn't want to hear more. I just left, taking the stairs and walking out of the building I'd called home for the past few months for the last time.

55

Jackson

My sneakers slapped on the wet sidewalk as I chased Anderson across the campus. His fucking long legs had me beat by a mile and he was already in the front door before I got there.

"I'm going to have a stroke," I said, holding my chest. He pressed the buttons on the elevator. When it didn't come fast enough he eyed the stairs, but I held out my hand. "Seriously dude, I will die."

Bing!

Saved by the fucking bell.

The ride was quick up to Heaven's floor and Anderson pushed through a group of girls standing in the hallway.

"Excuse us," I said, following in his wake.

He pounded on her door with his fist unrelenting until it swung open and Samantha stood inside.

"Where's Heaven?" he asked.

"Can we come in?" I added.

She stepped back and said, "She's not here. She left a few minutes ago."

"Left where?" I asked. Anderson had barged through the living area and into her room, checking for himself. His jaw was clenched so tight I thought it may actually break.

"I don't know. She grabbed Amber's car keys and took off." She frowned. "She was a little upset."

"About Oliver?" Anderson blurted.

Her eyebrows furrowed in confusion. "Oliver? No. She and Ruthie..." she glanced backwards to the closed bedroom door. "There was a situation."

"What kind of situation?" I asked, but she wrinkled her nose. "We're worried about Heaven. It's not like her to take off like this, not without telling one of us, and she and Oliver had a fight. If something else happened we really should know."

Samantha rocked back on her heels and exhaled. "All I know is that Heaven was supposed to meet Noah tonight and when she didn't show up he came over. Ruthie, being Ruthie, took advantage of the situation."

"How?" Anderson asked.

"She and Noah had sex and then there was a really big blow up."

"Who and Noah had sex?" I asked, feeling my blood pressure rise.

"Ruthie," she clarified, hands in the air. "Ruthie and Noah had sex, but you know there was something going on with Heaven and Noah—I don't know what—but it was a bitch move for sure."

I glanced at Anderson. He was thinking it all over in that quiet way that always freaked me out. He waited for a beat, as if weighting his options, and then strode across the room toward Ruthie's door. He didn't knock and Samantha's eyes were wide as he barged in the room to find the two of them snuggled up, naked, in bed.

"What the fuck?" Ruthie cried, but she watched Anderson closely. She wasn't nearly as offended as she acted.

"What did you do to her?" Anderson asked quietly.

"To who?" she played dumb. I walked across the room and stood in the door behind him, crossing my arms over my chest. She rolled her eyes. "You mean Heaven? We didn't do anything to her. She just freaked out when she saw us together."

"Why would she freak out?" I asked. Because there was not one goddam reason seeing Noah with another girl should bother her...unless.

Nope. No. Fuck no.

Ruthie stroked Noah's arm. "I guess she was jealous."

"No," I said, curtly. "There's no way she was jealous. What the hell did you do?"

Anderson—who was always a ball of tension coiled way too tight —snapped. He lunged over the bed and dragged Noah off the mattress and onto the floor. Thank god he had on shorts.

"Oh," Samantha said, reaching for her phone. I gave her a warning look and she stopped.

"Look, dude," Noah said. He lifted himself off the floor. "I'm sorry Heaven didn't tell you what was going on with us. She's like that; a liar and a whore. She was all over me and I did what I could to let her down easy but—"

The sound of Anderson's fist shattering Noah's cheek ricocheted through the room. Ruthie screamed while holding the blanket up to her chest and Samantha gasped, and I jumped on Anderson before he could do it again.

"Stop," I told him. He pulled his elbow back, ready to go in again. I grabbed him by the crook of his arm. "Anderson!" He'd lose his scholarship. His spot on the team. His future. I shoved him back and moved in between them.

"Noah, dude, I don't know who the fuck you are, but I do know Heaven. She is not a liar and she's definitely not a whore. And yeah, she did tell us about why she was hanging out with you—something that had to do with your parents."

Noah cradled his cheek. "Her dad is a petty con-man preacher trying to get my father to fund his program. My father told me it was never going to happen but to play along for my mother's sake. She wanted me with a sweet little Christian girl—who better than a doe-eyed girl named Heaven?"

Anderson grunted behind me and I held out my hand.

"So what? She thought she was helping her dad?"

"She felt obligated and I played up to it. The girl is pretty naïve for growing up with a dad like that. But, yeah, I figured I could string her along for a while, get her to put out and then walk away." He winced. "Unfortunately, she was a pain in the ass so I had to use some leverage to keep her around."

"What kind of leverage?" I asked.

"I found the cache of photos of her from high school. You're in them—both of you. And a bunch of other guys, too."

"That was a set up. She was harassed all year," Anderson said. Noah glanced at him warily.

"Yeah, well she didn't want her dad to know about it. And she certainly didn't want him to know she was still seeing you guys, and was willing to do what it took to keep that information safe. Or at least I thought so, until she bailed on me tonight, effectively calling off our deal."

"And that's when you fucked Ruthie."

"Hey!" Ruthie said, feigning offense. "I was just trying to help a guy out. I didn't know he was playing so many games."

"What? Like you haven't been playing them yourself?" Samantha asked. We all turned in surprise.

"I don't know what you're talking about." Ruthie sniffed.

"Heaven's dad approached both of us about keeping tabs on her. He wanted any kind of evidence about her friends, her social life, her grades."

"And you gave it to him?" I asked her, feeling disgusted.

"Hell no. It was weird and he's a scary guy." She nodded at her roommate. "Ruthie took the money, though."

"Hell yeah I did." She shrugged, making her red hair tumble down her shoulders. "I tried to make friends with her. And you guys for that matter. She was possessive and spoiled and I got sick of it."

"That's your excuse for betraying someone's privacy?"

"That and the fact I like nice things."

"You sold your roommate out because you 'like nice things'? You've got to be fucking kidding me." My rage was barely contained. "And you want to call my girl a whore? You've got no clue what it's like to be someone like Heaven. She's smart and kind. She's kick-ass and sensitive. She struggles. Do you know that? She struggles every goddamn day of her life and the last thing she needs is a bitch like you dragging her down."

"How dare you—"

"No," Amber said, suddenly appearing in the door. "I'll take it from here, Jax." She stepped closer to Ruthie. "You don't get to defend yourself. You get to shut the hell up. Take your blood money and get the hell out of here, because if I ever see your face again I will scratch your eyes out."

Ruthi whimpered but shut her mouth, sinking back on the bed.

I looked away from the shitshow surrounding us and faced Anderson. "We need to find her."

He nodded. "I think I know how."

"Will you stay here in case she comes back?" I asked Amber.

"Yes, and I'll throw out the trash while I wait."

Noah called out as we walked toward the front door, "Don't think I won't press charges. My father will sue!"

It took enormous strength but Anderson walked out the door. I stopped and looked at Noah, restraining myself. We locked eyes and I said, "Don't think that I won't let him come back and finish the job. You better hope that Heaven's okay when we find her."

56

HEAVEN

THE RAIN STARTED while I was inside—while my world imploded. I jogged down to the student lot. My phone vibrated steadily in my hand and I shut it off, stashing it in my pocket until I reached Amber's car. I felt like a thief, but I slipped behind the wheel anyway and embraced the quiet.

"What have you done, Heaven Reeves," I muttered to myself. What had I done? So many lies upon lies. Why did I think I could live this life—have it all?

Part of me knew this was fixable...a small part, but the dark dread that lived in my chest—in my mind—all the time beat away at the logic, twisting it in my brain until it no longer mattered. I was doomed. Fated. Anything I touched turned bad and the look on Oliver's face earlier confirmed this. I couldn't put him through this again. I couldn't put any of them through it.

Especially myself.

I wiped off my face and suddenly knew where I should go. Where I had to go.

Home.

Pulling into the heavy rain, I drove and formulated a plan. A plan always helped and I'd been without one for too long, allowing my father and Noah to dictate my life. Letting fear take over. Things were out of control and I needed to take it back.

The roads were dark and slick—forcing me to drive slower than I liked. Finally, my lights flashed on the sign for Allendale and I pulled off, stopping in a closed gas station parking lot. My phone lit up with messages but I ignored them, hitting my mother's number instead. She'd talk me through this. We'd work it out.

It was late and I worried she'd not answer, but my heart leapt when I heard the click.

"Mom?" I blurted.

"Hello? Heaven?"

My heart sank.

"Hi, Daddy."

"It's late sweetheart, is something wrong?"

I stared out the window, watching the rain fall. "I screwed up your plan, Daddy. With Noah."

"What?" he asked, obviously confused. "I don't understand."

"Noah's a creep." My fingers clenched the steering wheel. "I couldn't do what he wanted. What you needed from me. I just couldn't."

He sighed. "Heaven, I have long prayed for your soul. Ever since I found out about the sinful ways you lead your life while I was gone. Leaving you like that—without a father to guide you—your path went astray."

His words hit me hard. "No, Daddy, that's not what happened. It wasn't like that."

"No? Are you telling me you didn't sin with those boys? That you didn't display your sexuality with inappropriate clothing? That you weren't fornicating outside of marriage? That you're not supportive of homosexuals and sinners?" he asked, listing my sins. "Did you really think you could keep it away from me?"

"I...I..." I chewed on my fingernail, tugging at the skin around it until it tore and bled. I wanted to deny his accusations, but they were all true. All of it. Except I knew in my heart it wasn't so simple. "It's not as bad as it seems. So much of it was lies. I was being stalked. Bullied."

"I saw what you were wearing. What you did. You asked for it."

"No. I didn't." *Didn't you?* my brain whispered. "Things got out of control and it was happening again with Noah."

"Baby girl, why do you think I sent you to Noah? He's a sinner just like you. I figured you'd be fine with doing what you needed to make the arrangement between his father and I work."

I blinked. "You what?"

"You had one job, Heaven, and that was to please Noah Hancock. Obviously, you've failed at that, just like you've failed at everything else in your life."

"You *wanted* me to have sex with him?"

"Why not? You spread your legs for every other male that crosses your path. What's one more? Oh wait, I know." His voice turned hard. "Noah was the one that held the key to the funding I needed to continue my work at the church. The one that would pave the way toward your mother's happiness and our future together. She's told me of your selfishness, Heaven. The dramatics and intentional harm you did to yourself. The hours lost. The money spent. She assured me you'd gotten better, but obviously you're still an entitled brat incapable of looking out for anyone else."

Tears ran down my face, hot and bitter. Every word he said was dipped in truth.

"I'm sorry, Daddy," I choked. Hardly able to see through my tears.

"It's too late for apologies, Heaven, but thank you for the call. I can at least try to attempt some damage control with Mr. Hancock in the morning."

He hung up and I sat in the silent car holding the phone, feeling the darkness spread until the flicker of an idea tugged at me and I started the car. I turned away from Allendale and got back on the two-lane highway.

I felt a pang of homesickness as I drove away; for the small house I'd shared with my mother, the bedroom the boys snuck into at different times, squeezing their large bodies into my small, single bed. That was where they'd learned the truth about my self-harm and when they built the protective wall around me. A wall I continued to jackhammer away with my bad decisions.

I sped away from the main road that passed the high school where I won Winter Princess and Spencer tried to rape me in the parking lot. Going further would take me to Oliver's massive home and his cozy apartment. The place Anderson took my virginity. The place where that precious, special moment was recorded and used against me.

Everything good in my life had an equal and resounding negative reaction.

They were the light. I was the dark and as long I was in their lives I would continue to taint them with pain.

My father made that clear.

With both hands on the wheel, I kept going, knowing now that Allendale wasn't the place for me to make my peace. I needed to go further down the road, past the tree line to the place where the ocean met the shore.

I got off at the final exit—the last one before the road took a sharp left up the coast. The sign read Oceanside, the letters rusty with age, like everything else about this town. Unchanging. Unrelenting. This was where I came from. The soil from my birth. If any place could wash away my sins, it would be this tiny edge of earth.

I drove down the quiet beach road. It was late. The locals were all asleep and it was long past any kind of tourist season. There was a small dirt road that led straight to the water. I'd been down it many times with Justin and when I found it, I took it. The rain drops lessened, and by the time I parked they'd stopped entirely. Rolling down my window, I caught the strong scent of salty air and the rumble of crashing waves, feeling a sense of peace that'd been missing for too long.

Kicking off my shoes, I stepped into the cool, wet sand. The wind blew hard, pushing the storm out to sea, and my ears filled with the roaring waves.

The clouds vanished, revealing a sky full of stars. For the first time in ages I felt whole. On the edge of the continent I was just me.

Heaven. Not the slut or the whore. Not the girl that could be manipulated and used. Not a body or a vessel to further someone else's agenda.

Out here, I couldn't hurt anyone else and no one could hurt me.

Taking a deep, solidifying breath, I waded in.

57

***

OLIVER SCREECHED the Mustang to a stop outside of Stetson Hall. I climbed in the back, leaving the seat up. Jackson scrambled in, wet from the rain, and Anderson sat in the front. His hand was bloody and swollen.

"What the hell happened to you?" I asked, reaching forward.

"He punched Noah," Jackson said. "Fucker had it coming."

Anderson let me inspect his hand—I'd busted mine up dozens of times in the goal. "I don't think you broke anything."

In his other hand he held up his phone. "I know how we can find Heaven."

"Remember a few months ago when we went on that trip to the amusement park? I put that tracker on everyone's phone so we could meet up."

Oliver nodded. "It's still on there?"

"Unless Heaven turned hers off. I've used it a few times since to check up on everyone." He looked at me. "You know, when you're running late."

"Stalker."

"Well, my stalker-ness may just save our asses tonight. Shit has officially hit the fan." He glanced at Oliver. "You were right. Things are bad. We've got to find her."

He pulled up the app and a red star popped up on the map. Anderson frowned. "She's headed down the highway." He looked back at us. "Toward home."

Jackson shook his head. "That's not good. She doesn't know about her dad."

"Know about what?" Oliver asked.

I sat in the back of the Mustang, my long legs cramped and antsy, listening as they explained what happened upstairs. The rumble of the engine made it hard to hear but it didn't stop the wave after wave of anger that rolled through me. Noah had no idea how lucky he was that Anderson was the one that punched him. He was too civilized for actual violence. But me? I would have torn him to pieces.

"He was blackmailing her?" Oliver asked.

"And her father was spying on her," Jackson said, adding, "and us."

"Shit," I muttered, looking out the window and into the dark. "So he knows everything."

"Seems like it," Anderson said.

"She'll be crushed."

Because that was what this was all about. What we'd spent months doing for this girl that we loved so much. Keeping her safe. Building her up. Making her feel sexy, wanted, and whole. There was a glitch in Heaven's brain that told her otherwise, which was why we reminded her constantly.

But these two bastards came in her life and in a matter of days tore her down again, and it was my biggest goddamn fear she wouldn't survive.

I tapped Oliver on the shoulder. "Drive faster."

He pressed down on the gas, kicking the engine into high gear.

The car grew quiet. Oliver focused on the road. Jackson dialed and redialed her number. Anderson held out his phone and we watched the red star, the distance closing between where we were and where she was headed.

Until her star stopped.

"Where is that?" I asked, leaning over the seat.

"Outside Allendale." Anderson zoomed in. "Looks like the gas station on Route 4?"

"It's two-fucking-a.m. What is she doing there?" Jackson growled.

We watched silently as our little star got closer to hers. My adrenaline surged, thinking we'd make it to her.

"What? Where are you going?" Anderson muttered as the star started moving, taking a sudden U-turn.

"Is she headed back?" I asked.

Jackson pulled out his phone and dialed her number again. He slammed it against the seat when she didn't answer.

"No. She's going toward the coast."

Oliver frowned. His eyes caught mine in the rearview mirror. "Is she going to see Justin?"

Not the best thing but certainly not the worst.

"Maybe, but I don't think they talk much anymore," Jackson said, leaning into the seat.

The Mustang ate up the miles, getting closer and closer. Anderson held up the phone. The star clung to the edge of the land —nothing but blue beyond. "She's at the beach."

"I don't like this," Oliver said.

The uneasy feeling in my chest blossomed into sheer panic. "I don't either."

Oliver turned off the highway toward Oceanside, rumbling down the deserted road. The rain ceased, making the windshield wipers scrape across the dry surface. Jackson barked for Oliver to turn them off. Tension—fear—ran high.

We kept our eyes peeled as Anderson barked out directions. We were close. So close.

But would we be there in time?

58

ICE-COLD WATER RUSHED over my toes, swallowing my ankles in white-foam. The moon appeared from behind the drifting clouds, giving me a path reflecting off the dark water to follow.

One more step.

Then another.

Then it would be over.

The pain.

The disappointment.

The shame.

The hollowness.

I touched the puckered skin from my most recent cut, hating it and craving it at the same time. No more of this. No more.

The boys—I pushed them out of my head. I couldn't think of them now. It was just more pain. Their lives were better off without the tangled web of darkness that followed me.

I took another step, thinking of my father's world. I'd cleanse myself. Make myself pure again. Maybe then I'd be worthy for the other side.

Another wave rolled over my knees, lapping at my skirt and at the cuffs of my sweater. The cold water chilled my skin, soothed the cuts. Took away the pain.

I took one last look at the stars above and plunged beneath.

59

AMBER'S little red car sat alone on the dirt road leading toward the ocean. I hopped out of the car before Oliver even stopped, running in the direction of crashing waves.

Something was so very, very wrong.

My shoes bogged in the wet sand and I kicked off my sneakers as I ran over the dunes down the path that led to the beach.

Moonlight lit my path, like a signal from the heavens, revealing fresh footprints in the sand. Voices called behind me—shouting her name. I didn't waste my breath. I knew. In my heart, I knew.

I shucked off my hoodie, tossing it in the sand, following the footsteps straight to the edge of the water, heading into the icy ocean.

"Anderson!" I heard my name shouted in the wind. Oliver stood on the shore behind me. Jackson and Hayden took off in opposite directions of the beach.

I ignored him, shouting her name instead. "Heaven! Heaven!"

It was so dark. So ridiculously dark, and the water was freezing. I didn't stop, knowing she was out there. Water seeped up my legs, pulling at my jeans. I waded in deeper. "Heaven!"

The tide tugged at me, sucking me under a cresting wave. I pushed off the bottom with my toes and on the other side, in the clear spot behind the cresting wave, I saw a splash of water.

"Heaven!" My voice was lost in the wind. "Heaven!"

I dove toward the wave, arms forward, using every ounce of skill, every hour of training, every moment of preparation to save my girl.

The cold water hit me hard, combining with the adrenaline pumping through my system. The denim of my jeans held me back but my arms are powerful and they searched through the water. I surfaced, shouting, "Heaven! Baby! Can you hear me?"

And got nothing back but the sounds of the ocean. I called again, my voice cracking, then smothered by a wave.

I swore I heard a cry.

It was so cold and my muscles trembled and I didn't know how much longer I could stay out here. I looked to the sky and whispered a prayer. For me. For the guys. For Heaven.

Something hard kicked my leg and I jumped, spinning around. Bubbles floated to the surface and pale white skin shimmered under the water.

A wave rolled toward us and I dove under it, eyes wide in the dark, vast ocean, but she was here and I was going to get her. I would not leave without her.

60

THE WATER SHOCKED MY SYSTEM, screaming at my lungs and piercing my skin...but then...numbness crept across my body and I curled into it like a blanket.

The peace I craved came rolling over me, draining away the pain —the heartbreak and loss. My ears filled with the roar of water. I was flung under, sucked down. Spit back out. I cried, feeling the cold air slap my cheeks.

Again, the ocean grabbed my feet and pulled me to the depths. My arms flailed and my lungs burned and flashes crossed my eyes. Anderson sitting next to me, pencil tucked behind his ear. Oliver smiling sweetly, caressing my marred skin. Jackson smirking cheekily and Hayden, his eyes holding mine, looking through my soul.

I reached for them, through the black, murky water, finding nothing. I panicked, flat, hollow screams—water searing my lungs. I flailed, hitting rock and succumbing finally.

Finally.

I bobbed under the waves, the blanket shifting, tugging, dragging me away. Life wasn't easy. Death would be worse. My father told me

I'd paved my way. The hands of the devil were strong and when I looked up, blinking away the salt and the water, he was handsome, too.

Not the devil but an angel, with sharp cheekbones and eyes as green as a field of grass.

"Help," he cried, and I opened my mouth to speak but my lungs were full, so very full.

He lifted me like a feather and the sound of waves crashed into the skies above. I had no doubt that this angel was here to take me home.

I WOKE, searching for stars and only finding florescent light.

My mother sat in the chair next to my bed, an old, wrinkled tissue twisted in her hands, staring at my feet.

I'd been here before. Or was it the same time? The beep of machines. The scent of antiseptic. The sound of voices in the hall.

I shifted my head, feeling pain wracked through my chest, like a hundred-pound weight held me down. My hands were tied down. My throat dry and raw.

"Mom?" I whispered, closing my eyes in pain.

A shadow crossed over me. A hand touched my forehead, my wrist. "Heaven?"

"Mom."

I didn't know what to say. *I'm sorry. How did you find me? Why did you save me?*

I felt the tears on my face.

Mine or hers?

A chair moved. Feet shuffled. I waited for the prick of a needle. The sting of alcohol. I felt warmth and weight.

"Babe," I heard whispered and I blinked, searching for the eyes of the angel.

I found four.

A sob wracked through me. "I'm so sorry." I meant it. Seeing their faces. How could I give that up?

"It's not your fault."

I shook my head.

"It's not your fault."

I bit my bottom lip.

"It's not your fault, Heaven."

I felt warm lips on my forehead and another on my cheek, followed by a press on the back of each of my hands.

"Rest. Sleep," a voice said.

I opened my eyes and they stood crowded around my bed. My mother, exhausted and drained, against the wall. "Don't leave me."

"Never again," Oliver said, dropping his forehead to mine. "Never again."

61

Eight Weeks Later

It felt a little like déjà vu when Oliver arrived at my house looking like a hundred and fifty million bucks in a dark blue suit and with a matching bowtie. He stood at my door holding a bouquet of silver roses that matched my glittery dress.

That I wasn't wearing because he was an hour early.

I opened the door in my ratty Clemson sweatshirt and a pair of shorts and one eye made up. "What are you doing here? Is something wrong?"

"No," he said with a lopsided grin. "I just couldn't wait to see you."

I raised an eyebrow. "Seriously?"

"Yep." He rocked back on his heels, squinting with brilliant eyes. "Love your makeup."

"Shut up."

I let him in and he followed me up the stairs to my bedroom. All the new stuff I got for my dorm room was spread around the room. The comforter that matched Amber's. The shower caddy. I didn't need these things here but I was living here now, so...right.

"I'm glad you came early, but something tells me you had an ulterior motive."

He stood in my doorway, looking too big and definitely overdressed. "What? I can't be excited to see you? Maybe snag a little time alone before the big event?"

I passed him and he grabbed my arm, giving me a kiss. It wasn't a gentle peck, but the toe-curling, heart-shattering kind.

I rubbed my lips when we parted and eyed him skeptically. A year had passed since the Winter Formal at Allendale High, and we'd been invited back to pass the crown down to the next generation of royalty. Oliver had been tasked with driving me and the other guys would meet us there.

"You came here to keep an eye on me," I said, walking to the bathroom to resume my makeup application. "You're babysitting."

He scoffed. "What? No."

I dug around for my mascara wand. "You know this is the first time I've been alone since I left the program."

The program. The hospital. Peaceful Harbor. Whatever you want to call it.

"Is it?" he asked nonchalantly. He knew it was, because he and the guys were all on the same page; the 'keep Heaven safe' page.

It was pretty sweet.

I ignored him and worked on my face. I'd gotten pretty good at cosmetics at Peaceful Harbor. My roommate was obsessed with hair and makeup—she had big dreams of working in the movie business one day. The program allowed us the essentials—it wasn't prison, but a therapeutic program with constant group, family, and individual therapy. We had art and yoga. During down time, Bianca begged me to be her model and then later I morphed into her student. I realized, after all that dressing up I'd done, I kind of liked fashion and creating costumes. After four weeks of intensive therapy and tutelage from Bianca, I could whip up a hell of a smoky eye.

Through the mirror I studied Oliver as he combed through my bookshelf, pulling out each one. He was assessing me, like I was assessing him—tip-toeing around the fact this wasn't new but it also wasn't the same.

Things had changed a lot over the last few months.

～

It was an odd place—a particular state of limbo—when you tried to take your life and failed.

Everyone around you is relieved but you—*I*—just feel lost. More confused than before. Embarrassed. Guilty. Raw.

I hated the concern in their eyes. The tense set of their jaws. The fear that lingered and their tentative touch. But the worst thing...the absolute worst thing was the fact that Anderson nearly drowned.

My memory of anything other than walking onto the beach was fuzzy at best, but they told me that Anderson saved my life, diving into the dark, frigid water to find me. Hayden performed CPR. Oliver called the ambulance and Jackson took care of Anderson.

I stayed in the Allendale hospital for a week before they found me an open bed at Peaceful Harbor. My father tried to see me, but I wouldn't. Couldn't. I wasn't ready. My mother and doctors agreed. It was my choice. It should have left me empowered, but I just felt hollow.

Despite all this, there was one person I wanted to speak to alone: Anderson.

"You shouldn't have risked yourself like that," I'd said. We were sitting across from one another in uncomfortable vinyl chairs. "You could've died."

"You almost did. I wasn't willing to risk that." I started to argue but he looked up at me with haunted, green eyes. The rings underneath were as dark and pervasive as my own. "You've never understood that we're in this as much as you are, have you? That you're not alone. If it wasn't me, it would have been Oliver. If not Oliver, Hayden. If not Hayden—"

"Jackson. I get it. But it's not fair for me to risk your life." I'd stared at my hands, not his face, because I loved his face so much and it hurt too much to see the worry etched all over his. "You have so much to live for; swimming, the Olympics, school. You're going to be an incredible man."

He took my hands in his. They were warm and rough. A scab grew over his knuckles. "I love you, Heaven. I can't help it, but if you can't see the value in your life, I don't know what to do anymore."

I didn't want him to leave. I loved him too, at least I thought I did. Right then I felt nothing but pain and despair. The feeling wasn't active but more passive. A constant pull against my mind and body.

That moment, looking into his beautiful face, knowing I almost risked that, it was when I realized I needed help.

I just needed time to get better. Healthy. For real this time, not just a Band-aid over the old wounds, but healing them for real.

So I started at Peaceful Harbor. And it sucked. They searched for contraband, which could be anything from mechanical pencils to earrings. They confiscated my phone, inspected my shoes. Took my jewelry, laces, and belt. It wasn't a prison, but at times it sure felt like it was.

I started with a psychiatrist and they fed me round, brown pills. Bianca sat next to me and I saw the gnarled scars on her wrists. For the first time in a long time I didn't feel so alone—so lost.

Family therapy? Well—it was worse than anything. The boys gave me their unconditional love. They'd always had, but my mother? She had to get her head out of her ass, and my father's, before we could work through it all.

Stuff came up; like how my dad was a really shitty guy. Emotionally abusive and manipulative as hell. With my therapist sitting next to me I told my mom I wasn't coming home if he was there. Ever.

To her credit, she kicked him out that day and found her own therapist. She had some shit to work through, too. People like my father spend their lives mind-fucking everyone they know. It makes you second guess yourself. Question your judgement. I understood that a little better now. I looked at my own reactions to things; why I was so reactive? Self-destructive? Why I pushed away the people I loved?

I did have choices. I had control. I had a support system. And frankly, something in my brain was a little out of whack. The meds helped getting the chemicals back in line. When all of that got stabilized and I felt less neurotic zombie and more like Heaven, I came home. The therapy wasn't over, but the healing had begun.

～

I COATED my eyelid in a final dusting of silver powder, still aware of Oliver as he made it around the room.

He fingered the photographs I'd pinned to a bulletin board. "I like this one," he said. I was about five years old, holding a giant sunflower as big as my head. Oliver turned to me to say something else but stopped cold.

"What?"

"You're just beautiful. I never get used to it."

I shook my head. "You know, if you say it too much it may lose its effect."

"I'll take that risk." He walked over, nearly killing me with the lines of that suit. It accentuated his everything and it stirred the spark of desire I'd only recently been feeling again. He stood before me and touched my neck. "You know Anderson used to talk about this sweatshirt all the fucking time. I think he went home and jacked off to the Clemson spiritwear catalogue the way the rest of us used Victoria's Secret."

I wrinkled my nose. "That's ridiculous and a little gross."

He laughed and shrugged. "Now I get it, because that is the sexiest damn thing I've ever seen."

I pressed my back into the bathroom door frame and looked into Oliver's eyes. What was going on here? I'd been certain he'd come over early because my mom had a shift at work and I needed watching. All the guys had kept their flirting pretty PG since I'd returned home—sliding right back into protective mode. We'd watched a lot of Netflix and shared a lot of hand-holding and kisses. It'd been nice.

But right now? Oliver wasn't giving me babysitter vibes.

"I really should probably change."

His eyes flicked over to me. "Are you sure about that?"

His hand connected with my hip and his eyes searched mine. I pushed up on my toes and touched his cheek before kissing him. It

350

started slow, his mouth and tongue exploring mine. His hand inched up my side, brushing underneath my bare breast.

Oliver swallowed and held my eye. "Before all this went down you told us not to hold back, that you weren't a fragile, vulnerable girl. You're the strongest person I know, Heaven. So incredibly strong." He cupped my face with his hands and his voice trembled as he spoke. "I'd never held out on you. Not once. I was waiting for the right time —the right moment. We could have fucked at any point. In the car, in my apartment, behind the dugout at the field, but that's not what I've ever wanted with you."

His words rushed over me, bold and honest. His hands slid down my shoulders and around my waist. He pulled me tight and whispered in my ear. "When you're ready—if you're ready—I want to make love to you, Heaven Reeves. I want to adore you, worship every inch of you."

Tingling warmth spread through my body and limbs. I loved the feel of his body close to mine; the weight, the want. He looked like a movie star in that tux but he held me in my ratty clothes like I was already in my fancy dress.

"Now," I told him. "Let's do it now."

He raised an eyebrow. "Now? I didn't mean now."

"I don't care."

"We have, like, forty-five minutes."

"We'll be late."

A slow grin appeared on his face combined with dark intensity in his eyes. He leaned forward, licking my bottom lip. I snaked my arms around his neck and he lifted me, carrying me over to the bed. After laying me on the bed he said, "I've got to get off this suit before I destroy it."

I nodded and watched him undress. Shrugging off his coat and tugging the bowtie out of his collar. He fumbled with the buttons, revealing his muscular chest. I fought a laugh as he draped it over my desk chair along with his pants. My smile froze when I saw him in his shorts, erection hard and pushing for freedom. I'd known Oliver was big—and not that I compared, but lord, he was bigger than the others. He climbed on the bed and kissed my ankles. He moved up my calves and I seized when he reached the soft spot behind my knees.

"That tickles," I said, squirming away.

"I know." He continued, slowly making his way up my inner thigh. "I like it when you get riled up and squirm."

He pushed at my shorts before reaching for the waist and tugging them down. Coming back, he kissed my hips, my belly, and reached for my breasts. I wanted him badly and god he was patient. I should have known this from how long it took us to get here. How he'd bided his time to do it the way he wanted. I sat up and reached for his neck, "I love you, do you know that?"

His eyes lit with fire. "Yeah, I think I do."

The remainder of our clothes fell and I tried not to gawk at his size when he finally kicked off his shorts. I was ready for him. So very much ready, and he took it slow, kissing me the whole time, loving me the whole time, whispering in my ear the whole time, until he filled me and I felt a special sense of completion.

"When I look to the stars you're all I see," he said, pushing inside and touching me the way I liked. "You're the sun and the moon and everything in between." I kissed him and he kissed me back. I rocked my hips and he rocked his, until there was no more talking, just the sound of two people in love, making love, being in love and all the ecstasy that came with it.

62

"I know this is a cliché, but damn it looks so small," Oliver said, just outside the door.

"No, you're right." I studied the gym entrance, one I'd taken a million times before. "It does look small."

"I guess it means something when you're bigger than the place you came from, right?"

Bigger. Stronger. Whatever the word, I'd take it.

Oliver moved to the door but I'm stuck in place.

"What?" he asked with a frown.

"You think they'll laugh when they see me? Do you think they know what happened?"

He pulled me against his chest. A group of younger girls in low-cut, pageant-style dresses walked by. They looked forty years old. They didn't giggle when they passed but I saw wide eyes and dropped jaws as they took Oliver in.

Oh, the Allendale Four. The stuff of legends.

"I think that you're beautiful and a survivor, but if you don't want to go in, then that's fine too. I'm ready to get out of this suit and go eat some waffles down at the diner."

I tugged at his lapels. "You literally just put this back on."

"For you? I'll take it off again."

God he was so cute.

"We have to go in," I said. "The guys are here."

He nodded. "They're definitely going to want to see you in that dress."

It was sparkly, covered with a million silver sequins. I carried my tiara in my hand, ready to hand it over to the new winner.

"Heaven!"

I spun in the direction of the voice. Amber and Ginger strolled up.

"What are you doing here?" I asked after giving them both a hug.

"Ginger wanted to see where we grew up."

Amber and Ginger...they were a real thing now. They'd moved into a suite with Samantha after I withdrew. Sam didn't have a roommate right now, saving a spot for my return next semester.

"How are you doing?" Amber asked. It took her a long time to believe me when I told her I didn't blame her for being MIA during a lot of my drama. She had a life and I was really good at keeping secrets.

"Better. I think every day is a little better."

"I can't wait until you get back." She squeezed my neck.

Oliver held up his phone. "We need to get inside. The guys are getting antsy."

I took a deep breath and with Oliver and Amber at my side, going through the door wasn't as difficult as I expected.

The inside of the school seemed smaller too, and we took the back hall to the side of the stage where the other Allendale boys were waiting. They each wore a suit, of various shades. Jackson looked deadly in black. Hayden like a dream in charcoal, and Anderson found a color of light gray that brought out the green in his eyes.

"Damn," Jackson muttered when he saw me. He gave Oliver a dirty look. "No wonder you're late."

Oliver grinned like the cat that caught the canary. It wasn't lost on anyone. If Oliver broke through the mental health sex embargo, then the others knew their chance would come soon.

Yeah, I was as excited as they were.

"You guys look pretty handsome, too," I said, walking by and running a hand over their chests. "Who knew when you took off those T-shirts and uniforms you'd clean up so well."

"I did," Ginger said. "I mean, I'm not surprised."

Amber beamed and kissed her on the cheek. Ginger turned and kissed her on the lips. The rest of us watched, eyes wide.

"Huh," Anderson said, watching them more closely than necessary.

I punched him in the gut and he shrugged sheepishly.

"College is about experimenting," Hayden said, then coughed. "You know, if you're not in a committed relationship."

Ms. Rivers, the vice principal, walked up the stage stairs and stood in front of the microphone. My life had come a long way in the last year but one thing remained the same...

"Welcome back, last year's princes and princess," she called, waving us on the stage. Amber pushed my back and Oliver took my hand.

Even if I felt like it at times, I wasn't alone. Even if my brain tried to fight me, I had these guys at my back. There was one thing for certain, we were The Allendale Five. Forever.

EPILOGUE

SUMMER

"ARE YOU SURE ABOUT THIS?" Anderson asked. We sat in his car while the others waited in the dusty parking lot.

"Hanging out with the four of you shirtless all afternoon? How could that be a bad idea?"

"Reeves..."

Uh oh, when he used my last name, it meant he was fed up. "Yes, I'm sure about this, but if you have a problem I respect that. I know this is hard for you, too."

He leaned his head back in the seat, his long hair flopping in his eyes. I brushed it away, letting my hand linger on his cheek. "There are bad memories out there, Heaven."

"My therapist says we should make new memories. Better ones."

He nodded and took a deep breath. After a moment he grabbed my hand, kissing my fingers. "Okay, let's go."

The sun was hot when I got out of the car; the air salty and humid. I heard the rumble of waves and yeah, it caught me off guard. I paused and four sets of eyes watched me carefully.

"I'm fine."

They nodded and continued their watch.

I loved them for it.

They were loaded down for the day, beach bags, coolers, blankets, and umbrellas. I wanted to make a day of it. Fun. Silly. Everything the last time we were here wasn't.

I kicked off my shoes and felt the sand burning into my flesh. It felt good. Alive and pushing past every ounce of anxiety I had started to run, leaving the boys behind for the edge of the world. What was almost my grave.

I peeled off my sundress and took the first tentative step—the water was still cold but July cold, not winter cold, and it was very different. Titling my head up, I felt the sun heat my nose.

Footsteps sounded behind me and a pair of strong arms wrapped around my waist. I leaned back into the solid chest with my eyes closed. "Thank you for saving my life," I said, feeling his heartbeat against my back. Shadows crossed and more footsteps came and soon we were a circle at the edge of the sea.

"You're the strongest of us all, Heaven Reeves."

I blinked, taking them all in. My friends. My lovers. My protectors. My saviors.

With a grin on my face I broke free, pushing past them for the water. They stilled, afraid, but that's why we were here. To fight our fears. To cleanse our souls. To make new memories.

I curved my finger, drawing them to me.

I wanted them to be in every last one of mine.

The End

(Except keep reading for one extra little scene. Rated R+)

63

THE TRAILER DOOR SLAMMED JUST AS I PULLED ON MY RUBBER GLOVES. I used my foot and spun the chair around, and the man slumping into the seat offered me a gruff, "Morning."

An assistant followed, shoving a paper coffee cup in his hands while scanning the daily schedule. *My* assistant, Lea, hovered nearby with tools in her hands. To the untrained eye, they looked a little like torture devices.

"Good morning, RJ," I said, looking down at the young actor. Despite the tired circles under his eyes, he was still strikingly handsome. "You're looking chipper today."

"These 5 a.m. wakeup calls are going to kill me." His eyes flickered shut, like he was trying to block me and everyone else out.

"You're twenty years old, lack of sleep won't kill you. Partying all night at the Paper Plane may do it, though."

He cracked an eye, giving me a peek of the brilliant blue that helped him land an agent in the first place. "How do you know I was at Paper Plane?"

I shook my head and prepped his face with toner. Paper Plane was a local bar--which RJ was too young to go to, but I supposed rules were bent for celebrities. "I learned a long time ago that it's best to check your social media first thing in the morning to make sure no

358

one is talking about you—or if they are, that it's not going to destroy your life."

He perked up a little and his assistant handed him one of the three phones he carried for various aspects of his job. His thumb quickly scrolled down the photos, pausing on one of him huddled in the corner with a faceless blonde. Our eyes met in the large mirror in front of us, in the narrow slot not piled high with makeup and supplies. "Shit."

"Sorry," I said, feeling a mixture of genuine empathy for him along with a heavy dose of the fact he should know better. I felt a million years older than this kid. Wiser. Yet he was the one making a hundred thousand dollars an episode, while I got paid to turn him into a monster every week.

RJ mumbled a few directions at his assistant—damage control—I got it. I'd been there, just on a much less-public level. I reached out to grab a tin of glue and a brush and started on my efforts to turn this handsome kid into a terrifying creature.

I'd slathered on the first coat when he eyed me and asked, "How could a woman with a name like Heaven know anything about social media scandal?"

I snorted. "Trust me, I know more than you'd think."

"Explain."

"A high school prank gone wrong," I tell him, glancing at my assistant, Lea. She knew the story. I told her everything one night over too many margaritas and a binge watch of Buffy The Vampire Slayer. "But that's a really long story and it happened a really long time ago. Trust me, everything about that period of my life is in the past." I caught my reflection in the mirror, looking for the girl I used to be. Other than faint scars on my arms and familiar blue eyes, I could barely find her.

"How long am I going to be in this chair?" RJ asked.

His assistant looked at the clock. "Two hours."

His bright eyes met mine again in the mirror. "I've got time, Heaven Reeves, I want to hear that story."

~

Two hours later, RJ no longer looked like a handsome TV star but like a creature from a demonic dimension. He was on a weekly TV show, Creature Feature, which was about a group of best friends that jumped from one alternate reality to the other, fighting demons and saving the world. Part X-Files, part Supernatural, it unsurprisingly became the breakout hit of the season. And by some crazy mixture of fate and luck, I'd secured the job of head makeup person.

I couldn't see RJ's actual expression under the gobs of liquid latex and paint, but his assistant stopped typing on her phone about fifteen minutes into my story. Lea, with her non-committal expression and purple-streaked hair, patiently handed me my supplies while I spilled the sordid details. Everything. Justin and the favor gone tragically, socially, wrong. Spencer and his harassment. The bullying. I left out the self-harm but I didn't forget the Allendale Four. How could I?

"This sounds like a TV show," RJ said. "Why haven't they made this into a TV show? One girl, four guys, all in love with one another. There's danger, social commentary, mental health issues, and an incredible romance."

"It's not a story anyone would ever want to put on TV," I said, fussing with a scale on RJ's forehead that wouldn't stay down the way I wanted. I reached for my superglue.

"Why? Because of the polyandry lifestyle?" Lea asked. "It's not so taboo anymore."

"There's that, although in my experience it's hard for people to understand the complexity of that relationship, but also—" I was interrupted by a bang on the door, announcing that it was time for RJ to get on set. I whipped off the apron covering his clothes and pushed down the scale one more time.

"Also, what?" he said, facing me. He looked terrifying and I couldn't help but smile.

"My story doesn't have a happy ending, and who wants to watch a show like that?"

64

"This is a bad idea."

"Heaven, how long has it actually been since you've gone on a date?" Lea asked as we walked down the street. We were in the trendy part of town—yes, Allendale had a trendy part of town now—something that had changed while I was away at school.

Allendale had always been a small but thriving city. We had a university and hospital and those both provided jobs for many people in the town. I went away for college and then for art school. While I was gone, Hollywood took notice of the quaint downtown area, the beach not too far away, and all the things they needed for TV shows and movies. They set up shop, which was perfect timing for my specialty in makeup/FX design. *Creature Feature* picked Allendale for the shooting location of the long-term series and the union has rules about hiring locals. I was literally in the right place at the right time with the right skills.

With the industry bustling, it was easier for me to start over than I'd thought. The historic part of town became trendy. I lived in an old high school that was converted to loft apartments. I avoided the places that hurt the most, the neighborhood where I grew up, the community where my father's now-defunct church stood abandoned and empty. His money schemes eventually ran him out of town and left the church in bankruptcy. My mother still worked at the police station, but even so, I didn't see her often. Years of therapy made me realize our relationship was better with a little distance.

I had goals of something bigger and better—New York or Hollywood--but something about Allendale still felt right to me. I was a small-town girl—woman—at heart.

"Heaven?"

I glanced at Lea. She looked at me expectantly with bright brown eyes. She was Korean and a whiz at makeup and FX, but still in school part-time. We'd become close when we both landed our dream jobs and scrambled to learn the ropes.

"What?"

"I asked how long it had been since you'd gone on a date?"

"Not long enough to know that I'm not a fan of dating, especially blind dates."

"Look, we're in the same boat. Double blind dates. Set up by RJ, who I'm hoping knows some attractive guys. Don't they have a club or something?"

"The hot guy club?" I'd laugh but I'd known a club like that…well, not really a club, but a group of ridiculously hot guys that all hung out together. But I also knew Lea had a point. Did you say no to a famous actor agreeing to set you up on a date with some friends? No. You didn't. Sure, it would probably end up a total disaster but would make for a good story and laugh at some point.

Plus, even I couldn't bear another night of reality TV at home alone. Seriously, I needed to do something other than work and binge Netflix all night.

We arrived at the sushi bar—one of the kinds where you ordered at the bar via computer and a conveyer belt carried out the food. It was new and trendy and I expected it to last about three months before something newer and trendier took its place. That was half the reason I agreed to come tonight. I want to see my shrimp tempura slide across the counter on tiny plates.

It was as much of a bar as a restaurant and the bouncer waved us in. RJ told Lea we'd meet the guys here, probably afraid I'd bail if they showed up at my loft. I scanned the room but I saw nothing but a bunch of young people looking like they were trying too hard to have fun. Faking a good time had never been easy for me—and when it was, it only got me in hot water.

"What do we know about these guys?" I asked, sliding into a bar stool.

"They're guys," was her only reply. When I make a face, begging for more,, she rolls her eyes. "If I knew anything it wouldn't matter. Anything I say will only get some kind of snarky reply."

"That's not true." I ordered a Japanese beer from the bartender. "Why would you say that?"

"Because you have a particular type—one I haven't figured out yet. It seems to be a vague mix of some kind of unattainable, imaginary guy that doesn't live up to your exes."

I sighed, thinking about the Allendale Four. "If you knew them, you'd understand why they're hard to surpass."

"I'd love to get to know them, but since you cut them out of your life it's not happening." She took a drink from the shot glass the waiter pushed toward her, and grimaced. "You don't use social media for anything other than work, so I can't stalk them there. You refuse to talk about them—all I know is that you had this epic romance, until you didn't."

"Epic may be an exaggeration."

Leigh gives me a hard look. "They were a big part of your life. It has to be weird not having them involved anymore."

"First of all, I didn't cut them out of my life. We, as a group, made a decision. And that decision was that everyone should be free to pursue their dreams. We all had different ones and continuing our relationship was only going to hinder that."

I took a long swallow of my beer, trying not to think of the day Anderson got his invite to train year-round with the US National team, and earned his first spot in the Olympic games. I didn't want to remember the mixed feelings when Hayden was recruited to play professionally across the country—only available a few weeks of the year. I refused to remember how Oliver and Jackson sat down with me, tears in their eyes, and told me it didn't feel right to go on. That there was a fracture in the group. I felt it. They felt it. We were incomplete and that led us to find different homes, different jobs, and different lives.

So, we cut ties. Completely, and other than seeing a few things in the news occasionally about Hayden or Anderson, I'd walked away completely.

"I get why you ended the relationship," she said, "but there is no way they wanted you to go on forever alone, creating monster faces and living a nun's life."

I fought back a grimace. I sure as hell hoped they were living a monk's life, even though I knew it was ridiculous. The idea of them with anyone else...

I took another gulp from my drink.

"Okay." I exhaled shakily. "Tonight is the night I move on. No snarky comments. No leaving before midnight. Tell me what you know about these guys."

"All RJ said was that he met them at the gym."

I made a face. "Seriously? Gym rats?"

"Stop, you promised!" I adjusted my face into something more pleasant and she continued. "He met them there but I think they train him or something? They're connected to the business somehow. A group that specifically works with the entertainment industry in town."

That was logical. All RJ did was work and exercise, training his body into a work of perfection. His physique, his face, and his eyes were what got him into this business. It was ironic that my job was to cover it up. To be honest, I was a little surprised he set Lea up on a blind date. The flirty vibes between them lately were intense.

"Okay, so they're athletes." I could handle athletes. Four of them, in fact. I scanned the room, trying to figure out if they were here yet. There were a few suspects and one guy across the room caught my eye. Handsome. Built. Definitely worked out. His dark eyes met mine and I raised an eyebrow; was this one of the dates?

I opened my mouth to point him out, but Lea's small hand wrapped around my forearm and squeezed. "I think that's them," she said in a low voice.

The hair prickled on the back of my neck long before I looked at the door, like a spidey-sense warning me of trouble. It was too late, though, because I ignored the feeling and locked eyes with the brightest of blues. My heart jumped to my throat and my knees threatened to buckle.

His reaction was nothing more than a blip, the quick rearranging of his face to disguise his shock but zero halt to his swagger. I braced for a second time when I spotted the man behind him, who wasn't as smooth. His jaw, leaner than before, tightened. There was no mistaking the shock and conflict in his eyes.

"Shit," I muttered.

"Hot, right?" Lea asked, taking in the curly, tousled locks on the first one and the broad chest on the second. When I didn't reply, she glanced at me and frowned. "What's wrong?"

They stopped before us and the guy with soulful brown eyes grabbed my drink out of my hand, gulping down the contents. Lea watched in shock, waiting for an explanation.

"Lea, this is Jackson and Oliver." I pointed to each one, my world spinning on its axis. "My exes."

~

"A BEER, PLEASE," Oliver said to the bartender. Jackson elbowed him. "Make that two."

"Three," I added before looking at them, terrified to do so. "What are you doing here?"

"What are you doing here?" Jackson asked back. "Since when do you hang out in bars?"

"We're waiting on a blind date," Lea replied. She smiled brightly and brushed a stripe of purple hair behind her ear. "Hi, I'm Lea."

Oliver's eyes darkened. "Was this date set up by someone you work with?"

I didn't say his name. That's part of the business, not spreading around celebrity contacts. "Yes."

"Is he famous?" Jackson asked, reaching for the green bottle off the bar top. He knew my profession, even if I didn't know theirs.

I stared at him, non-committal, as though I wasn't about to fall

365

apart. I wanted desperately to hug him, ask him a million questions, drag him back to my house, but that wasn't who we were anymore. I kept my mouth shut and watched him, noting how freaking good he looked. Both of them did, and I had to fight back on my gawking. They'd grown since I'd seen them last, matured, and it suited them better than I could have anticipated.

When I didn't answer, Jackson admitted quietly, "RJ set this up, okay? We had no idea."

"How do you know RJ? He told Lea something about trainers?"

Jackson grinned proudly. "We opened a gym. Specifically for the talent coming into town. We've got everything from weight lifting, Parkour, and sports training, like baseball and soccer."

Lea thought this over for a second, then her eyes lit up. "Oh, I've heard of you guys! A5 Training?"

He smiled wider. "That's it."

A5. Oliver glanced my way then averted his eyes again. He could barely look at me. My stomach tightened and twisted. I wanted nothing more than to just run and pretend none of this had happened.

"Did RJ know?" I asked suddenly. "Did he do this on purpose?"

Lea frowned. "No, Heaven, I don't think so. This is just a bizarre coincidence."

I shook my head. "There's no way. He must have done some digging after I told him about us."

Oliver's head jerked my way. "You told him about us?"

"Not your names or anything specific. We were just killing time during a long session in my makeup chair." I eyed them suspiciously. "Does he really train with you?"

"Yeah, three times a week," Jackson replied, his eyes and voice softening. "I agree, it's a weird coincidence, Heaven, but stranger things have happened."

I wasn't so sure about that. Sure, Allendale was growing, but it wasn't that big of a city. I knew the internet was forever. If he dug around, he could find what he wanted. I sighed. If RJ was playing games...it was the wrong subject. Even though it had been two years, everything still felt raw. There was no doubt they felt it, too.

"Well, I've been waiting forever to meet one or two of you guys; I want to hear everything about everything," Lea said, leaning eagerly toward Jackson.

I couldn't do it. Not a chance. I couldn't relive the stories, the good times or the bad. I'd worked too damn hard to get my shit together for these two to walk in and rip me apart again. My hand shook when I reached into my bag and found my wallet. I tossed cash on the bar. "With things going sideways like this, I'm calling it a night."

"You're leaving?" Lea asked, frowning.

"Same," Oliver agreed.

"Dude," Jackson said, but Oliver was already headed to the door without another word.

Jackson and I watched him go and it hurt. Fuck, fuck, fuck it hurt. He turned back to me and gave me a sad, lopsided grin. "It was good to see you, Heaven."

"You too, Jackson. You look good, both of you, and I'm proud of you for opening the gym and figuring things out."

He shoved his hands in his pocket. "I'm not sure any of us ever figured anything out but, thank you. Your approval means everything to us."

Lea watched us like a tennis match, but I felt the wounds being picked at like a scab. It was time to go, so I left. Again.

65

____

OLIVER

The warm city air hit me as I strode out of the bar. I ducked past the line of people trying to get in, a few women smiling in my direction. I only wanted one woman to grace me with a grin tonight, and she could barely muster eye contact.

I'd known going on a blind date was a bad idea, but Jackson assured me it was good for business and developing a relationship with someone as influential as RJ Malone. I saw his point, and it wasn't like we were finding a lot of dates on our own. The business took up most our time, and thankfully, it left us with a valid excuse for our monk-ish lives. Things had never shifted back for either of us after the group split. Anderson was laser-focused, like always. Training. Competing. Wash, rinse, repeat.

Hayden spent the first year traveling across Europe before winning a spot as the first-string goalie on the Atlanta United Team. Increasingly, his face was everywhere from endorsements to celebrity events.

And Heaven? She'd been down the road from us but we kept our distance. We made a deal and despite the proximity, stuck with it.

Until tonight.

368

We should've known it was only a matter of time before we ran into one another, but a blind date? You couldn't make that shit up.

It felt wrong going to meet another woman. It always did—had—since the day we forged our relationship with Heaven. We were just kids, but what we had? It was more. I'd known it then. I knew it now. Walking in that door felt like a betrayal, followed by a punch in the gut seeing her standing there; smiling, confident, and absolutely gorgeous.

It wasn't the body of a girl that stood by the bar. It was one of a woman; it was like I thought I knew what she looked like, thought I knew her body, but there was a subtle difference—just enough to stop me cold. Long legs, the slight curve of her hips, the leanness of her arms, and sharp cheekbones were the make-up of an enhanced Heaven Reeves. I'd absorbed everything in a matter of moments, the way she wore her hair was up, twisted at the back of her head exposing the long, swanlike column or her neck.

I'd known I'd missed her, but not exactly how much until that moment, and now, after a bit of fresh air, I felt like a complete dick taking off like that. I'd never walked away from Heaven before. Not during the dark days. Not during the hard shit. Never—but that didn't stop the wedge of time from separating us and changing everything.

We'd made a deal.

I reminded myself of this every damn day. I knew Jackson did as well. I know he floundered, brushing off the advances of our female clients, the accountant, the saleswoman that came once a month to demonstrate the new equipment. He'd had opportunities, we both had, and neither of us ever took the bait.

Except this one fucking time.

My phone buzzed in my pocket and I expect it to be Jackson, but it wasn't. Anderson's name flashing on the screen. Did he know? I refused to believe Jackson called him. Not a chance.

"Hey," I said into the phone, ducking into the alcove of a closed shop. I stood across the street from new, trendy lofts.

"Hey, man," Anderson said. "I had a break and thought I'd check in—see how you're doing."

Yeah no, he didn't know. Talk about coincidences.

"Everything's good here. Busy. The industry is strong here and we're picking up clients left and right."

"That's awesome."

"How's the training?"

"Same," he replied. Anderson had been committed to an Olympic swim career since he was eight years old. During the last Games, that dream came to fruition. The next one was only a summer away. "Qualifiers are coming up. You wouldn't believe the amount of food I'm eating right now just to keep my strength and energy up."

"God, I'm jealous," I laughed. "I've been on this low-carb, cutting diet. It sucks."

"Sounds awful. I'll eat some pasta for you."

"Do that." I spotted a figure walking down the street, the gait quick and familiar. I knew the swing of those hips. Fuck. I ducked deeper into the shadows. "Have you heard from Hayden?"

"Yeah, his tournament starts in two weeks. He said things look good for them to make a run at the championship this year."

"Awesome." Hayden's skills only amplified when he got out of college. If he was a beast then, he was more like a dragon now. "We'll catch the game this weekend."

"Good, I'll call then and we can watch together."

My eyes were still trained on the woman walking across the street. She stopped and climbed the stairs toward the lofts. Did she live there? The instant she hit the top step I found myself avoiding traffic and crossing the street, following her up the cement staircase. What the hell was I doing?

"Oliver?"

"Yeah?" I realized he'd still been talking about the game. "Sorry, I ran out for a bit and was just dodging cars."

"Huh, you have a date?" he asked, surprisingly.

Surprising that he asked and surprising that in theory, I did. "Uh, no. How about you? What's going on with Caitlin James?"

"Nothing's going on with Caitlin." His voice was hard. "We're just both repped by the same aquatic group. We have to travel a lot together."

"Okay, got it." The implication was clear. Anderson didn't date any more than me or Jackson. Heaven entered the front door of the building by pressing a code. Against all instincts of self-preservation, I dashed behind her and caught the door before it swung shut. "Yeah, uh," I said quietly, "I should probably go." I heard her footsteps a floor up. Maybe two. I'd lost my damn mind.

"Yeah, I need to go eat. Talk to you Saturday?"

"Yep."

"Love you, man."

"You too, bro," I replied softly and shut off my phone.

I was breaking a million rules right now, I thought, following Heaven up the stairs, arriving on the second floor just in time to see her apartment door close.

I had no idea how long I stood there; minutes? An hour?

But there was no way I was leaving without talking to her. Alone. Just this once. Heaven Reeves had always drawn me in, like a moth to a flame, and like a stupid, fucking moth, I was willing to get burned.

66

Heaven

Jackson and Oliver.

Oliver and Jackson.

Of all the guys in this town. Of all the guys to get set up on a date with…

What was the saying? Karma's a bitch.

I'd barely entered the loft and kicked off my shoes when I heard the knock. The last thing I wanted to do was hash all this out with Lea, so I braced myself for standing my ground. I opened the door, tugging my hair loose at the same time.

It wasn't Lea.

"What are you doing here?" I said, eyes glued to the man in front of me. Man. Oliver was a man. Not a boy. Not a boy-man. A man-man, with the shadows of a full beard and wiry chest-hair at the edge of his button-down shirt.

"I didn't follow you," he said. "I just…you walked past me and I just…"

He ran his hand into his hair, pushing through his short blond locks. We stared at one another for a long moment before I said flatly, "Do you want to come in?"

"I shouldn't."

I shook my head. "No, you shouldn't."

"I had no idea, Heaven. Blind dates aren't something we do, but Jackson didn't want to say no to RJ and it's, it's been a long time…"

I held up my hand. "I don't want to know."

"Right. I know. I know."

His expression was grim while I tried my hardest to keep a straight face. I tucked my emotions tight, refusing to let them be seen. I couldn't go down this road. Not even an inch. Not the slightest. I knew—he knew—*we* knew where it would lead.

"I'm willing to chalk this up to a crazy fluke if you are," I said, trying to diffuse the situation and get him to leave.

"The craziest."

We smiled at one another. I looked away first.

"It was good seeing you, Oliver," I said, swallowing back a million other words.

"You, too, Heaven." He turned to leave, knowing it was a dismissal, but he stopped, hand on the door frame.

"You look great, by the way." His eyes skimmed over me, but they weren't filled with heat. More like awe. "Can you tell me one thing?"

"I guess."

"Are you happy?"

"I am," I replied honestly.

"Good." He nodded, seeming relived. "Good. That's all that matters, you know?"

"I do." I offered him a tight smile. "Good luck. Tell Jackson the same."

He took a step back and I shut the door, closing it and twisting the lock. Not to keep him out but to hold me in. I leaned against the wood, controlling my breathing, my heartrate, all too aware that I wasn't ready to see him—them—again. I'd made the right choice. We all had, because I couldn't go through recovering from the Allendale Four a second time.

Once almost killed me.

67
———

I DIDN'T SLEEP WELL, and it showed when I rolled onto the lot the following morning. The security detail at the entrance gave me a once over and I scowled at him before finding a parking place behind the empty school. The production moved around, site-to-site for whatever the story called for. This week RJ and his friends landed in a school full of zombies. Zombies were one of my favorite monsters to create, so even though I was tired, I was excited about tackling the project.

My trailer was parked around back and I avoided Lea's eyes when I walked in, dropping my bag and coffee on the counter.

"Heaven..."

"I don't want to talk about it," I said, rubbing my eyes.

"I had no idea that was who RJ set us up with."

"Of course you didn't." I skimmed the schedule. Thankfully RJ looks like a normal high school kid, and that meant Lea could handle it. "It was a fluke. A stupid fluke that I'd rather not speak of again." Her mouth opened to respond but I quickly added, "Ever."

"Okay," she said, prepping her own work space. Lea was a small woman, her skin flawless—she was an amazing makeup artist but wore little herself. She didn't need it. She flitted around the trailer with an amount of energy I couldn't comprehend, but I liked her, and I knew she meant no harm.

And maybe I owed her a little bit more of an explanation.

"Seeing them again," I said suddenly, "was just...unexpected. We made some firm rules when we broke up. We've stayed completely out of one another's lives. No spying. No creeping. The only ones I have a vague sense on is Anderson and Hayden because of their recognition."

"It's hard not to notice, especially Hayden Pierce."

I rolled my eyes. Who knew Hayden would let fame go to his head? "It's been a challenge because we didn't end our relationship with each other because we didn't love each other anymore. We stopped seeing each other because there was no way it would work with everyone being split apart. Our relationship was a tight balance that worked. Until it couldn't anymore."

She glanced at me, our eyes meeting in the lit-up mirror. "That doesn't seem fair."

"No one said life was fair."

"Well if it makes you feel better, Jackson seemed kind of thrown off, too."

I snorted. "No, that doesn't make me feel better and yeah, I could tell."

"You could? Behind that lazy grin and easy talk?"

"Uh, yeah, that's Jax. Adorable and aloof. He knows how to work a room." I frowned. "Did you talk to him after I left?"

Guilt ran over her face. "For a little bit. You and Oliver took off. We ended up hanging out for a little while."

I wasn't sure what expression landed on my face. I tried to keep it civil but before I could even react, Lea held her hands up and said, "Nothing happened. Swear. I think he just needed someone to talk to that understood. I got the feeling he's a little lonely."

I had no doubt he felt lonely—that they all did, with the exception of Hayden. With an edge, I added, "Lea, let me make one thing clear—I will murder you in your sleep if you start something up with one of these guys—got it?"

"Absolutely."

"Sorry," I said. "That sounded possessive and crazy."

"No. We're friends and co-workers and I get this is super hard for you." She pulled jars and containers out of the cabinet. "And yeah, you do sound possessive, which means you're not over them and it's obvious from last night they still have feelings for you, and I am definitely not into guys that are into other women. Been there, done that, and it sucked."

I spun my makeup chair around and dropped in it. "It's such a fucking mess."

"Well if you want my opinion—"

"I don't."

"But if you did..." She gave me a sweet smile. It was hard to be mad at her. Even that one time she left all my brushes in the sink and ruined them. "I think Jackson is a little lost and overwhelmed. I think you should talk to him. Maybe both of them, and see if you can work past some of this. It's obvious you guys are struggling."

I thought about seeing Oliver the night before, the way he looked in my doorway. Handsome, sure, but there was something else...a sense of loss and utter lack of being able to speak to me. That wasn't how I wanted this to end between us all.

"I'll think about it."

"Yes!" She smiled right as the trailer door opened. Two guys that needed to be made into zombies rolled in, half-awake, with coffee in their hands.

"Don't push," I warned her.

"I won't." But the twinkle in her eye made me feel uneasy. What Lea didn't understand was that Jackson and Oliver weren't the hard part. Those two were a cakewalk as far as the Allendale Four went. Sweet. Fun.

The problem was that if I opened that door again, really opened it, there were two others I'd have to deal with. The two that had really moved on, and I wasn't sure my heart could take it.

~

DURING A QUIET MOMENT that day when everyone else had left for lunch, I sat in the makeup chair and opened my laptop. I'd never been comfortable spying—not after my high school experiences—but in my mind, I called this research.

In the search bar I typed in A5 Gym, and it only took a moment for links and photos to appear. The building wasn't that far away from my loft—just further into the industrial area. It was a large warehouse, with a basic sign out front. No one knew what that name meant—no one but the five of us—and it was a kick in the gut to see it in the photos. It meant that they were still carrying this with them. As much as I did.

Lea was right. We needed to talk.

I clicked the link to their Facebook page, which was surprisingly active. Videos of workouts and training sessions seemed the most popular. I clicked on one and watched RJ flip a tractor-trailer tire down the football-length mat; his defined muscles rippling with every turn. There were other tutorials; images of guys running through a Parkour course. Basic weight training. A few other notable celebrities that worked in our area. The client list was impressive. There were a few actual superheroes in the bunch.

I scanned down the page and stopped on a link, pressing play. It'd turned into a game; Guess the Celebrity. A broad, shirtless, back came into view, focused on the hard muscles. After a moment the man jumped, hanging from a pull up bar. Quickly he dipped up and down, the muscles in his back quaking, the lines of his sides tapering to a slim waist. Loose shorts hung from his hips, revealing lower muscles, ones that ran to the curve of his ass. The video played through and I watched like a woman dying of thirst. I couldn't get enough...until the very end when the man dropped from the bar and turned around, a bright smile on his face.

Oliver.

I pressed pause.

Oliver had always been in shape—all the boys had been. Athletic and fit...but Anderson dominated with his swimmer's physique; long

377

and lean with a wingspan to die for. Hayden was a monster of hard-packed muscle. Jackson and Oliver had a more basic fitness.

Not anymore.

My eyes grazed to the bottom of the screen, looking for a glimpse of what I knew hung between his legs, when footsteps sounded on the metal stairs of the trailer and I snapped the computer shut.

Too much. Too much. How was I ever going to establish a friendship-only with them if they kept getting hotter?

The conflict lingered in my mind all day as I applied and reapplied the makeup on the actors coming in and out of my trailer. I hadn't stopped thinking about them even after I got home and put on a cozy pair of pajamas. I opened the laptop again and found the page still open.

I didn't watch the video again—*that* was a test I'd likely not pass twice, but I did go to the box that let me make an appointment. It was shady as hell and it gave me an out if I wanted to bail. I signed up under a fake name, securing an appointment the next day right after work.

Lea was right, I thought, scrolling through the photos of the gym and seeing the testimonials from the clients. It was time for all of us to move on—to work through the breakup instead of lingering in the purgatory of the past few years. From the look of it, their business was successful. I was successful. We had lives. We could do this.

Maybe.

68
———

KEEPING AN EYE ON THE BALL, I waited as the pitch flew through the air, passing right over the plate. I swung, catching the rawhide with the edge of my bat, tipping it foul.

"Fuck," I mumbled, waiting for the next pitch.

Crack!

That one slammed hard into left field, catching in the mesh net hanging from the ceiling. I took a step back, letting the next one pass and shaking out my arm and elbow.

"Dude, you've been in there for an hour," Oliver said from outside the cage.

"I'm just getting warmed up."

"You're being ridiculous."

I stepped back to the plate and eased into position, the next ball flying toward me. Again, I nailed it, hitting the sweet spot and watching it sail into the outfield.

I waited but the machine spun endlessly, out of balls. I hit the stop button and the pitching machine came to a halt. I moved to

379

collect the balls scattered all over the batting cage, but Oliver shouted for Tony, one of our employees, to clean up.

"I'm not done," I said, hooking my bat into the rack near the door.

"Yeah, you are."

"Don't be a dick, Oliver. You know this helps me relax."

He held my eye and spoke quietly. "You're freaking out the staff and clients. You've been a caged animal all afternoon. Chill out. Take a break. In the office, away from the floor."

"I know you were here at five a.m. beating the shit out of a punching bag."

"Maybe I was," he said, arms crossed. "But by the time the floor got crowded, I was cleaned up and ready for the day."

We stared at one another for a moment, a blink of time as far as the history of our relationship went. I knew he was right. I'd been riled up since seeing Heaven the night before. Upset, depressed, sad, angry. The emotions ran through me but I ended in the same place time and time again: lost and lonely.

Oliver opened the cage gate and I reluctantly walked out.

Going on the blind date had been the first mistake. Not turning around the instant I saw her was the second. Not kissing her was the third.

I regretted all three. All fucking three.

Ignoring the looks of everyone else on the gym floor, I grabbed a clean towel from the bin and wiped my face as I headed into the office. I sat on the leather couch and Oliver shut the door behind me, sitting in the chair behind the desk. The office was an example of our success. Fine leather furniture. A sleek stainless-steel desk. A huge glass wall so we could look out over the gym. The warehouse was massive, big enough for almost any kind of training our elite clients needed.

Neither of us planned to attempt a pro career like Anderson and Hayden. We were good athletes but not major league material. We planned for it and Oliver got a combined degree in sports training and management. I focused on business and marketing. When everything fell apart with Heaven, we were lost—floundering—until we channeled everything into our other passion and built this place.

It was a rough first few months, but we had two heavy hitters in our back pocket. Two rising stars in their respective sports; Anderson Thompson and Hayden Pierce. They bought in financially and allowed us to use their faces to sell our program.

It worked.

It also kept us so busy I wasn't sure we had time to miss Heaven, other than the dull ache that lingered as a daily reminder.

Until last night.

I groaned and leaned back against the cushion, wanting to tell Oliver to fuck off with his worrying, but I saw the same haunted look reflected back at me. He felt like shit, too. Finally, I said, "Last night was unexpected."

"Totally."

I twisted the towel in my hands and stared at them. "She looked good."

"Healthy."

Her eyes had been bright. No trace of the dark shadows that lingered for so long. Her skin was clear. Her body looked strong. I tried not to be obvious as I looked for the signals of depression and self-harm, but there were no dark circles under her eyes. No new scars on her wrists. All of that felt like a wave of crashing relief. We'd been through so much pain together and I never knew if she'd falter again. Depression wasn't something you just beat. It was something you survived, and Heaven was a fucking survivor.

"She didn't look pleased to see us," I added.

"Well, we made rules, and in one night they were smashed."

"Stupid blind date." I glanced up at him. "I knew we shouldn't go."

"Dude, you were the one that convinced me!"

I tossed the towel in the bin by the door. "I know. I'm sorry. I just had no idea..."

"Of course you didn't." He sighed. "It's not the end of the world, Jackson. We exist in the same city, maybe it's time we tried to work through some of it. Get to a stable, functional place."

I studied him to see if he was being genuine, because opening that wound...it may go someplace we couldn't control. "I don't know," I told him. "With Hayden and Anderson gone, it feels wrong."

"To be friends?"

"Friends is a tricky concept. You know that."

His eyes flicked to the glass windows behind me and he stilled. "What?"

I sat up and twisted to get a look. Famous client? The superheroes were back in town filming the next installment of their series—seeing them never got old. Oliver's chair rolled back and he stood. Although I still didn't know what for, I did the same.

That was when I saw her; wandering in by the door. Her eyes cast up at the huge A5 Gym sign over the front desk and the two huge banners that flanked the sign. Our star athletes, Hayden and Anderson, greeting each client that walked in the door.

"She's here," Oliver said quietly.

We'd both known this day would come. At some point. Which was probably why the last twenty-four hours had been so terrifying. Heaven was here and there was no more avoiding it, the business, and our history.

69

A CUTE BLONDE at the front desk greeted me with a smile. Her collared shirt had her name stitched on it: Peyton.

"Welcome to A5, can I help you?"

I wanted to respond, but I couldn't stop staring at the massive banners hanging from the warehouse ceiling. On the right was an image of Anderson, just out of the pool from a race—Nationals, if I remembered correctly. Water ran down his genetically superior body and his smile, fresh from victory, was heart-stopping.

On the left was Hayden, protecting the goal. He'd been photographed airborne, arms extended to catch the ball. His muscular legs were caked in blood and dirt and the look on his face was deadly. I'd been on the other end of that predatory stare and a chill ran down my spine at the memory.

"Hello?"

My eyes snapped to meet Peyton's. "Right, hi. I have an appointment. Sheena Jacobson."

"Ah, I've got you." She smiled when she saw me check out the banners again. "Those photos are distracting, right?"

"Yeah. They really are."

She leaned forward and whispered, "The owners are good friends with them. I'm hoping they come in one day and I get a chance to meet them."

I forced a smile. "That would be exciting."

Movement across the room caught my attention; familiar yet different bodies, hair, and faces. I slid my eyes in their direction and my stupid, predictable heart kicked in gear just seeing them walk across the facility.

"Are you ready for your tour, Sheena?" Peyton said a little too loudly, well aware her bosses were walking over.

"Thank you, Peyton, we'll take care of, um, Sheena," Oliver said.

I pretended there wasn't a deeper meaning in his words. Shit. See? Why couldn't I keep my mind out of the gutter with these guys? Our relationship was definitely not just about sex. It took us a long time to work through that side of things and when we got there it was good—so good—but there was so much other stuff. Real stuff. Friendship and support. Laughter and fun.

I tried not to focus on Oliver's broad shoulders or Jackson's marble-like jaw.

Maybe I kept thinking about sex because I hadn't had sex in ages.

That could definitely be the reason.

I braced myself and said, "Peyton and I were just admiring your friends hanging up on the wall."

Jackson and Oliver both look over my head. Oliver raised an eyebrow. "You wouldn't believe how long it took Anderson to find a photo he approved of."

His comment caught me off guard. "Really?"

Jackson slid a hand in his pocket. "Oh yeah, he got super anal about it. We actually had three other banners made, but he refused to let us put those up."

I snorted. Anderson was always something of a diva. "What did you do with the ones he didn't approve of?"

"Sent them to his apartment. They're probably hanging over his bed."

That time I laughed out loud. "Stop. He's not that bad."

"He's worse and you know it." Jackson smiled.

I glanced back. "What about H?"

"His agent had final approval."

Ah.

"It's a good photo." Although, I was pretty sure Hayden didn't take bad photos.

Silence ebbed between us. It was the first normal conversation we'd had in years. Jackson glanced at Peyton, who was busily arranging something on the front desk while totally eavesdropping. "So, right, you want a tour?"

"If you have time."

"For the one and only Sheena Jacobson? Why not?"

I only half-listened as they led me through the gym. Dozens of employees oversaw different sections of the operation. They'd covered everything and had all the latest trends. "Full-body workouts are really important right now," Jackson said, leading me through the area I'd seen in the videos. Huge tires and basic weights lined the walls. "These actors want the lean cut to show off all their hard work. We handle the fitness part—their nutritionists, the rest."

"I'm really impressed, you guys have made something amazing here."

Oliver crossed his arms and leaned against a metal beam that reached the ceiling. "We needed to do something to distract ourselves. So we went all in."

I stepped forward and touched the logo on his chest. I felt the quiver of his muscle.

A5.

Wrinkling my nose, I said, "You didn't have to add me in."

"Don't be silly," Jackson said. "Everything we are today is because of the bond between the five of us. I can't imagine where we'd be if we hadn't joined forces long ago."

"You'd probably have a wife and three kids." It was a joke, but I meant it. Our relationship stunted any normal follow up.

"Sounds like a nightmare," Oliver replied. But he's not being truthful. He wanted to get married. And kids. The whole package.

A long moment stretched between us and I finally said, "Thanks for showing me around. Seriously, I'm proud of you."

Jackson glanced at Oliver and blurted, "Well, you got to see what we're doing...don't we get to do the same?"

"Yeah," Oliver frowned. "Monster makeup? Handsome actors? Sounds pretty exciting."

I smiled, proud of my work. "It's fun. I never expected life to lead me down this path, but so far, it's been great."

"Maybe we can get together some time and hear more about it," Jackson offered.

"Maybe we can."

It wasn't a guarantee, but it was the best I could give at the moment; from the looks on their faces, they seemed okay with it.

I thought I should make a break for it, but that was foolish. Oliver grabbed me with both arms and pulled me into a hug. One I'd suspected we'd both been craving for days now.

"I missed you," he said into my ear, his breath warm and familiar.

I stared at Jackson over his shoulder. Both his hands were crammed into his pockets like he was forcing himself to stay back.

Oliver released me and I took two fumbling steps back. He looked instantly regretful and opened his mouth, obviously to apologize. I shook my head and said quietly, "I missed you guys, too," and ran for the door.

70

———

THE FOLLOWING day I walked into my trailer and found a massive bouquet of flowers. Lea peeked her head around it, a wide smile on her face and the purple streaks in her hair matching some of the blooms.

"There's a note!" was all she said, grabbing it from the stems. "Who's it from?"

I had a feeling I knew who and grimaced as I took the small envelope. Obviously, they were from the guys. Who else would send me flowers? But flowers? That was a bold, too-fast move, and it knocked me off kilter.

Lea watched me closely as I tugged the card out of the envelope, my cheeks reddening at the idea of her seeing me—this—private moment.

Heaven

Sorry for the mix up the other night. Only I could pick the two guys off limits in this city!

Forgive me,

RJ

"So?" she asked, a bubble of energy.

I passed her the card. "From RJ. Apologizing."

Her jaw dropped. Look, we may work with famous people but we're in the peripheral—not *in* the circle but holding the circle together with paint brushes and film and everything else that creates a TV show or movie.

"RJ Malone sent you flowers."

"*Apology* flowers. He's probably hoping to smooth things over since he'll be back in my chair today."

"I guess, but come on, you know it's weird when the actors even notice."

I shrugged and took the card and put it away—also moving the bouquet out of the way so I could get to my chair. "He's young and he's probably terrified the guys are going to kick his ass in a training session."

"Guess that's why you don't set up people on a blind date without knowing all the details first."

I started setting up my workspace. "Honestly, I should be thanking him. That mix-up got us talking for the first time in years." I gave her a quick look. "I went to see their gym yesterday. It's really impressive."

"I snooped online and saw their client list. They're doing some-thing right," she agreed. "How did it go? Talking to them again?"

I got out my palette and started mixing zombie paint. "It was weird. Stressful, but also kind of nice."

"You plan on seeing them again?"

"We left it in the air."

A bang on the door thankfully brought in our first zombies of the day, and there wasn't time to talk about my love life or anything else on the set. Another reason why this was a good job. It kept me busy.

When I finally took a break and checked my phone I saw the text from Jackson.

J: Saturday 6:00 PM Parkside Tavern for H's game?

I didn't reply right away, diving back into my work. Eating lunch. Laughing with Lea. RJ came at the end of the day; I assured him I wasn't mad. Something told me he didn't come by to check on me, but on my assistant instead.

If Lea noticed, she wasn't giving anything away.

When I got in my car and pulled out my phone again, that message waited for me, and also another one.

J: No pressure

It was a soccer game—for once not being played at the crack of dawn since it was in the States and not overseas. I stared at the phone, thinking about what going would do to our fragile co-existence. What saying no would mean. What doors and wounds and history this would rip open.

"Fuck it," I muttered and typed in my answer.

See you then.

I HAD three days to panic, reconsider, and back out. I did the first two a dozen times, but I didn't back out, and that scared me more than anything else.

By the time the game rolled around I was in a state of denial, checking and rechecking that message. What if he sent it by accident? What if he was just being nice? What if it was a test and I was supposed to say no but said yes and in the end, I was the one that led us down the path to ruin.

Good god.

I picked up the phone and pressed the name at the top of the list.

"Hey babe," she said, picking up on the first ring. "What's going on?"

"I'm in trouble, Amber. Super big trouble."

"What did you do?" Worry entered her voice. "Are you okay?"

"Oh," I said, realizing she misunderstood my statement. Rightfully so. I sat on my bed and picked at a loose thread. "I'm fine, but I just...I said I'd meet Jackson and Oliver at a bar to watch Hayden's game."

There was a beat. A long one, and then, "You did what?"

"You heard me."

She sighed and I could see her sitting in her apartment in New York looking over the busy street below. Amber and Ginger bolted after college for the big-big city. "It was bound to happen at some point, right?"

"I guess. I should have said no."

"Why would you say no? I mean, it's a soccer game and your friend is playing. It's not an orgy." I coughed and she apologized. "Kidding. Just kidding. I know you guys never had orgies, although for the life of me I'm not sure why."

She had a point. If ever there was a slippery slope...

"These guys were never just my friends, Amber, you know that and that's what makes it so hard. How do I *just* be friends with them? I don't even know how to be an adult with them. Or just hang out at a bar eating nachos and drinking beer."

"You hate beer."

"See? I don't even drink beer like a normal person."

Amber grew quiet for a moment and I knew she was thinking. Just when I'm about to start hyper-ventilating she said, "You've faked it before. You can fake it now. For one night." I started to argue. "Heaven, you faked liking someone way more than once in your life. Turn that shit around and just fake be a normal girl with normal guy friends for one night. Hang with the guys like they're...just guys."

"What if I can't?" Again, she was quiet. It was different though. "Amber?"

"This isn't the way I wanted to tell you but, I have some news."

I perked up. "What kind of news?"

"Ginger and I are getting married."

"What? Oh my god! What?"

"Heaven!" her voice jolted me back down. "We want you at the wedding and we want the guys there, too. You've all been a big part of our lives and maybe this is the opportunity you need to get this together."

"You're getting married?"

"Yes!" I heard her smile through the phone. "Will you be my maid-of-honor?"

"Yes! Of course!"

"Awesome! I can't do this without you, you know that, right?"

"I know that I need every single detail!"

"No, you need to go to the bar and play nice so I don't have to have the most awkward wedding in the history of weddings, okay?"

I nodded. "I can do this. For you."

"Don't just do it for me, Heaven, do it for yourself so you can move on, okay?"

"Holy shit. I can't believe you're getting married."

"I know! But go! We'll talk later." I walked to the closet to dig for an appropriate outfit. A just-friends outfit. "Oh, and girl, do me a favor."

"Sure, what?"

"Don't tell them about the wedding yet. We're going to officially announce it, but...well, you caught me off guard."

I held up the jersey for Hayden's team to my chest. "I'm so excited for you, Amber. Both of you."

"Thanks. And I'm excited for you, too. Go to the game. Give them both a big kiss—wait no, don't do that. Tell them I said hi. Don't make a fool of yourself."

I rolled my eyes. "I can promise two of those things. Nothing more."

Her laughter sounded like a song, and I felt a million times better after hanging up. Amber was getting married and I was growing up—having guy friends. Or at least, that was what I told myself.

71

———————

Heaven

Parkside Tavern wasn't unfamiliar to me. I just hadn't been in a long time, knowing it was the boys' haunt for watching soccer games on the dozens of screens hanging from the ceiling. The bar specialized in major league games, showing every big event across the country and overseas, something almost impossible to find on regular TV. Hayden's team, Atlanta United, was one of the fastest-growing teams in the league.

The strong scent of beer and fried food hit me when I entered the bar and I cast my eyes toward the table in the back corner. They'd claimed it long ago, when we first graduated and moved here. Sure enough, I spotted the two with drinks and food in front of them, eyes glued to the pre-game commentary on the screen. As with many things about the Allendale Four, they were creatures of habit, and I found the familiarities both comforting and unnerving.

I tugged at the snug-fitting jersey Hayden had sent me when he made the team, his name and number, 05, emblazoned on the back. In the past it would have implied him marking his territory—now,

I'm just another fangirl in a world of fangirls—rooting for Hayden Pierce, the hottest goalie in the States.

"Heaven!" Jackson shouted, waving me over. I smiled and took a deep, steadying breath. I could do this.

"Nice shirt," Oliver said, eyes skimming the way it tapered over my hips. He pointed to his own, the male version of mine. "I assume you got that in the mail, too?"

"Priority," I laughed, sitting in the seat Jax offered me. His blond hair dipped in front of his eyes and I fought the urge to push it back. "He was so proud."

"He should be," Oliver said. "AU is killing it this season. I read the other night they had the biggest crowd for a soccer game, ever."

"All time," Jackson added. "There's no doubt Hayden's some of the appeal. His game has reached new levels." He pointed around the room and sure enough there were lots of number 05 jerseys. "And damn he's popular."

More than a fair share of the jerseys were on women and I had zero doubt why. Hayden was still heartbreakingly handsome and physically imposing—more so than before. Women watched as much for a peek at his rock-solid abs as they did for his gravity-defying saves.

"You know Hayden's always had that elusive, quiet thing going on," I said. The waitress came over to the table and asked for my order. I wanted nothing more than to say Diet Coke, but I remembered what Amber told me and played up the friend role and ordered beer.

I could do this.

If either Oliver or Jackson noted my actions they said nothing, and it dawned on me that maybe they'd already made this move— into the friend zone. Maybe I was the only one still hung up. The thought left me conflicted, but the game started and it was easy to focus on that instead of everything else; like the way Oliver's jaw tensed when the other team had the ball or how Jackson licked his fingertips after inhaling a plate of wings. I ignored the women that glanced at our table and gave a high five to the man at the table next to ours when AU scored. I kept my breathing steady when the ball careened toward Hayden and he made save after save, some alarmingly dangerous.

"One of these days he's going to hurt himself," I muttered into my second beer, watching him pick himself off the ground and walk with a cocky swagger to the goal line.

"He takes a lot of precautions in his training and equipment," Oliver said, "but I agree. He's getting risky."

Jackson shook his head. "Fucking show off."

More than once, after a particularly impressive save, the camera would pan to the sidelines to a pretty blonde. She paced the sidelines with a worried expression on her face. After the third time I asked, "Who is that?"

Oliver and Jackson exchanged a look. The former cleared his throat and said, "That's Sabine Rakestraw. His physical therapist."

"His what?"

"You know he had a concussion last fall, right?" Jackson asked.

No, I didn't. I shook my head, concerned I'd missed it.

"Well he did—it was at the end of the season, which is why it wasn't well known. He spent the winter in therapy and got the clear to play this season. Sabine has been working with him for months."

"Why..." I started to ask, why didn't anyone tell me, but why would they? We made rules and if I'd been paying attention to Hayden's career, I would have known. "So he's better?"

"Yes," Oliver said.

"And his therapist?" I asked, knowing already. Just a feeling. A tug at my chest.

"He hasn't told us anything, Heaven, but the newspapers say they're dating. They've kind of become a couple to watch or something."

I arranged my face into the calmest expression I could muster and ignored the weight of the two men watching me closely. I hoped my voice was steady when I said, "I get not telling me, I mean when would he? We haven't spoken in ages, but why hasn't he said anything to you?"

Jackson shrugged and took a sip of his beer. Oliver said, "Maybe it's not a big deal. You know the tabloids want to make everything into something bigger than it is."

Or maybe it's the exact opposite. Maybe it's real and he's scared to tell them—us.

The crowd around us started shouting at the TV screens; the opposing team's forward barreling down the field, Hayden crouched, ready to spring into action. The striker took the shot and Hayden jumped, but the ball hit the cross bar, bouncing back into the field. This time, instead of only one forward on a breakaway, three others were there, along with a handful of AU defenders. Play got messy, and Hayden desperately tried to keep his eye on the ball, to anticipate the next move of the other team. The shot took off, arcing off the foot of the forward at the same time another player slammed hard into Hayden, knocking *him* off kilter, head bouncing off the goal post.

"Oh my god," I mumbled into my fist, heart leaping up my throat. Jackson's hand slipped over my knee, squeezing. The entire tavern fell silent as the goal box cleared and AU players fell to their knees around the mass of body lying there. Unmoving.

"Shit," Oliver said. "Shit. Shit."

He stood, pushing his hand through his hair.

I glanced next to me, feeling the burning in my eyes. "Jax?"

He looked as worried as I felt. "He'll be okay," he said, but his tone felt wrong. I felt wrong. Like a part of my body fell limp.

Oliver grabbed his coat and my hand. "Let's get out of here."

"But," I looked at the screen. Medics ran on the field, including the blonde, Sabine, from the sidelines. My eyes trained on her as she knelt next to Hayden, touching his face.

"We can get better info at the gym. I promise." He pulled out his phone, scrolling the contacts.

My stomach lurched and Jackson wrapped his arm around my shoulder. I nodded. "You're right. Let's go."

They led me away from the table, but the screens mounted through the bar followed me out the door. I couldn't help but take one last look at the TV. To my relief, I saw Hayden's eyes opening, blinking, but that relief twisted into something different as he reached his hand to graze Sabine's cheek, as he looked into the eyes of a woman by his side—a woman that wasn't me.

72

"LEA, I NEED A FAVOR."

"Sure, what's up?" She had me on speakerphone. She must be driving.

I stuffed a sweater and then another short-sleeved shirt in the bag. I had no idea what the weather was like in Atlanta right now. It was early April and although it was cold here, it may be a lot warmer there. "I'm leaving town and I need you to cover for me at work."

"What? Leaving town? For where? For how long."

I glanced at my computer screen. Hayden's story was all over the sports pages; Atlanta United's star goalie was critically injured in the game the night before. He was stable but had serious injuries the team had not released to the press. The only thing I knew was that he was hurt and I needed to see him.

"Someone I know is in the hospital and I've got to go...I just have to go. And I don't know when I'll be back. Hopefully in a few days." God willing.

I went to the bathroom and collected my toiletries. Hairbrush, makeup bag, and the two pill bottles sitting on the counter. One of those pills kept me from spiraling into depression. The other kept my moods from shifting like a boomerang.

"Holy shit, Heaven, are you okay? Do you need someone with you?"

"No," I replied at the same time as a bang at the door. I checked my watch. Did Uber drivers walk to the door? "I'm okay. If you can cover for me for a few days, that would be great. I'll get in touch with Derek and let him know, okay?"

I'd already texted our boss, Derek, but it was early and he probably hadn't seen it yet. Whatever. The person at the door banged again.

"I'm coming!" I shouted and then said, "Gotta go, but I'll be in touch, okay?"

"Definitely call me."

"I will," I said, grabbing all my things. "And sorry this is such short notice..."

"No, honey, it's fine. Go do what you need to. We'll be here when you get back."

I flung open the door, expecting the Uber driver, but I stopped short. Jackson stood in the doorway. He frowned at the bags. "Where are you going?"

"Atlanta. Where do you think I'm going?"

"Heaven," he said, following me down the hall. "Listen, Oliver talked to Sabine this morning." I cut my eyes at him. Really? Sabine? He ignored the glare. "They're not talking because of the press, but she sounded hopeful. He's awake. Probably had another concussion and maybe some internal injuries."

"That's pretty vague, Jax."

"I know, but you can't just race out there."

I stopped at the front door and faced him. "Yes I can. I have to."

"Why?"

"Because he came for me every time I needed him. Just like you did. And Oliver. And Anderson. Every hospital trip. Every counseling session. Every breakdown. You guys were there and I'm going to be there for him."

Understanding spread across his features, his blue eyes flashing at the memories. "Things are different now."

I shook my head. "Not at times like this, they aren't."

"He has other people in his life. People that are there for this sort of thing."

Ouch.

I pushed him aside but he grabbed my arm, pulling me uncomfortably close. I smelled his familiar scent, the tang of his shaving cream. His eyes bore into mine. "Promise me one thing."

"What?"

"That if you go out there and things don't go as planned, you can't run away again." His hand was warm around my wrist. "We just got you back."

I nodded, unable to speak, and the words that floated to my mind weren't the right ones to speak anyway. It wasn't until I was in the car on the way to the airport that I allowed myself to think on that moment and what he meant.

Did Hayden really not want to see me?

And who was he to say I ran away? That wasn't how it happened. But is that how they think of me?

I HADN'T BEEN at the hospital since I was a patient myself. I don't even remember coming in the two times I was admitted. Once I'd had a panic attack at the library and Jackson brought me in. The other—I shook the memory from my head. I didn't want to think about it.

The woman at the desk pointed me in the right direction and I found myself searching the hallway for his room. Turns out, Hayden was in a small private section of the hospital with a doorway blocking the rooms. A small waiting room filled the outer space. I didn't recognize anyone in the room until the door opened and I saw the shock of blonde hair and the clothes from the sidelines on the TV the night before. A handsome man about a decade older than me spoke on a cell phone in the corner. He glanced at me absently and continued to talk.

"Hi," I said, approaching Sabine. "I'm looking for Hayden Pierce. You're friends with him, right?"

She looked me up and down and I had the distinct feeling she recognized me. "Hayden's not allowed to see visitors right now."

"You were just in there."

"I'm his physical therapist and..." I raised my eyebrows, daring her to say more. "And the doctors have insisted he needs rest right now."

"Can you tell me what's wrong?"

She frowned. "I'm sorry, who are you?"

"I'm a friend of Hayden's. An old friend. I came when I heard he was here."

She eyed my suitcase and my wrinkled travel clothes. She opened her mouth to speak but the man walked over and cut her off. "Did you say you were a friend of Hayden's?"

"Yes. I'm Heaven. A friend of his from back home."

He offered me his hand. "I'm Bryant Gibson, Hayden's agent."

"Oh, hi, nice to meet you," I said, taking in the expensive suit and watch. His hair was perfectly done, his face smooth without a single wrinkle or mar. I glanced at the door. "How is he? Any news?"

"I'm sorry you traveled all this way," Sabine said coldly, "but news about Hayden's condition is private and we can't share that with anyone outside his family or medical team."

"Okay," I said slowly, trying not to misinterpret the vibe.

Before I could add anything, she said, "And you definitely can't see him tonight."

I was about to argue when another voice interrupted us from the doorway leading to the private room.

"Let her in."

A voice that sounded like a salve to every frayed and exposed wound that I had. I swallowed and turned, knees quaking.

"I really don't think that's appropriate and I don't think you have the authority to make that decision—" Sabine argued.

I stared into those green eyes. Eyes I hadn't seen up close in so long that I thought maybe I'd imagined their intensity. Nope, real.

"She's family," Anderson declared, extending a long arm.

"Family?" Sabine swallowed back a cough and I walked forward, taking care not to touch him as I passed.

"Yes. Family." He looked at me expectantly.

"It's fine, Sabine," Bryant said, laying a hand on her shoulder.

"Thank you," I whispered, walking away from both of these people that seemed to know more about Hayden than I did. I dared a look back at the cold anger on Sabine's face. I had no doubt she knew exactly who I was.

73

———

Heaven

I wasn't ready.

For his voice.

For his emerald green eyes.

For his overwhelming presence.

I only glimpsed his face for a moment before he quickly turned away, placing his broad back between us. It wasn't before I saw ringed, dark shadows under his eyes. A million memories flashed through my mind. Anderson at eighteen, nervous the first time we'd made love. Later, older, lithe and sweaty as he hovered over my body. Then something darker; Anderson wet and cold, dragging me out of the water. Anderson the last time I saw him, jaw clenched tight. Tears threatening to spill, getting in a cab for the airport.

No, I wasn't ready for the wound in my heart to split back open, ripping out the sloppy stitches that barely held.

Now he stood before me in jeans and a hoodie, looking like he hadn't slept in days. His jaw was covered in heavy scruff, something I'd never seen before.

"Thank you," I forced out, following him down the hall.

His eyes were cast forward—as if he couldn't bear to look at me. Couldn't. Wouldn't. One of the two.

"Like I said, you're family. Hayden added you to the list."

I stopped. "When? Now?"

"No, when he signed with the team. He filled out medical forms, including next-of-kin." He placed his hand on the wooden door and glanced at me. God, it was like looking into the sun. "You made the cut."

The news startled me, but not enough to keep me from asking, "And Sabine?"

He shook his head. "No, but that guy Bryant is, and he talked the nurse into allowing her in as a representative of the team and as his therapist. I don't think either of them are happy we're here."

Was he happy I was here? I wanted to ask. I tried my hardest not to show any emotion, just in case he dared look at me for more than a second. But he didn't.

Before he could open the door, I moved to the gap between him and the door. "Tell me what's going on with Hayden. How is he?"

His eyes flicked to mine. Guarded. "He suffered a bad concussion —his second in three months. He has two broken ribs and a twisted ankle. They won't know how bad until they do more tests and X-rays."

I swallow. "Is he awake?"

"Yes. But sedated. The nurse just gave him a shot." A smile flitted over his lips. "He's high as a kite."

I nodded and moved so he could open the door. Anderson paused and I saw the tic in his jaw. I knew that tic. "What?"

"Jackson told me you were on the way."

"Ah, he prepared you." Hurricane Heaven was about to crash land.

"He told me why you felt obligated to come." His fist clenched on the doorframe. "You know you don't owe any of us anything, right?"

"Hayden's hurt. I'm not stepping aside if he needs help."

He unfurled his fingers and ran them through his hair. Something I'd seen him do a million times over. "Don't walk in that door if you're going to vanish again."

"Excuse me?"

"You heard me. If you go in there, you're opening old wounds and yeah, I think he'll want to see you, but there's enough broken in him right now that the last fucking thing he needs is to mend a broken heart."

I looked into Anderson's eyes. Green and flaring with pain. Pain I didn't cause. It was the second time the accusation had flung my way in the last day and anger boiled past my grief. In a low voice I said, "Don't you dare lecture me on broken hearts, Anderson Thompson. I'm not the one that got on that plane and flew across the country without another look back. Or took a job traveling around the globe playing a game. I didn't start a business and build an empire with my buddies. I didn't make the rules about our relationship and I certainly didn't get to keep my best friends once it fell apart."

Anderson held his breath as I continued.

"You're the one that said it; we're family. And if there's one thing I know it's that family is messy as hell, but I also know that we're stuck with one another. We have to forgive one another and we have to fight for one another when shit hits the fan."

He swallowed, his Adam's apple bobbed beneath the scruff of his unshaved face. Without another word he opened the door and I braced myself for what was on the other side.

To his credit, the minute we walked into the hospital room, Anderson's demeanor changed. Whatever anger and hostility he had for me vanished and he focused completely on his friend. Thank god, because I was a blubbering mess.

Hayden's gray eyes were droopy and glazed when they passed over me but the smallest hint of a smile tugged at his lips. His face was bruised, mostly around his eye, and a deep cut split his lip. His foot was elevated in a cast and although he was shirtless, his entire torso was wrapped in thick, white, bandages.

"Fuck, I must be realllllly hurt," his eyes jumped from me to Anderson, "if you two showed up at my deathbed."

"You're not dying, asshole," Anderson said, but I heard the way the words were forced out of his throat. He was freaking out, too. "I do think maybe you've lost your handsome looks for good, though."

Hayden shifted his attention to me. "What do you think? Are my modeling days over?"

I inhaled, trying to steady myself from wave after wave of emotions rolling through me. My hands clenched around the bed railing and I thought of myself on the other side, when they looked down on me like this, and I don't think I ever comprehended how much fear they had until this very moment.

"Heaven," he said. "I'm going to be fine. Promise."

"I just had to make sure you were okay. I saw the game—watched it—and when you went down, I don't know. We called and there was no information and no one would say anything and I just panicked." My hands shook so bad that I barely noticed when Anderson took one in his. "Don't ever do that to me again, okay?"

Hayden's eyes locked with mine. "Wait...you watched my game?"

I nodded and he smiled lazily, pleased.

Anderson walked over to the table and returned with a handful of tissues. I took them and wiped my face. "Tell me what I can do."

He glanced between the two of us and said, "Just sit with me? I'm pretty sure I'm going to crash in about five minutes, but sitting with me would be great. Just knowing you're here helps." His words were already slurred. I stepped forward and tentatively took his hand, linking his fingers with mine. A spark passed through me, one of familiarity. I squeezed tight and ran my hand over his short hair as he exhaled and his eyes fluttered shut.

74

Heaven

The alarm on my phone trilled and I quickly stopped it before it woke up the two sleeping beauties in the room. It was 10 p.m., and the alarm was for my medication, not sleep. Regardless, neither moved an inch. Hayden was helped by doses of painkillers and Anderson, in the uncomfortable chair, from sheer exhaustion. His long legs sprawled under the bed and his hands were crammed in his hoodie pockets. I knew he had the ability to sleep anywhere; partly from being male but also from so many long days at meets.

I quietly crept into the bathroom, rummaging through my purse for my medication. I'd been on it since freshman year, with a few alterations here and there. It definitely helped keep my depression in balance. That didn't mean every day was a good day. Depression didn't work that way, but the meds kept me a little more even and the demons at bay.

I popped two pills in my mouth and took a swig of water from the bottle by the sink. A glance in the mirror told me I looked like hell. My brown hair felt greasy and needed a wash. Red rimmed my eyes from exhaustion and tears. But inside it felt right to be here. I knew how much it meant to wake up in a hospital bed and find someone you care about waiting for you.

He'd done it for me and I'd do it back.

I opened the door and Anderson consumed the doorway, his eyes bleary with sleep, although not tired enough to not notice the two bottles of medication in my hand. I shoved them in my bag.

"Everything okay?"

"Yeah." I dragged my hand through my hair. "Just trying to wake up a little."

He grunted and we swapped places. When he appeared a few minutes later, Hayden was awake and the doctor had come in to check his progress.

"Mr. Pierce will be in testing most of tomorrow and they'll start early. The doctor wants to do an MRI for the concussion and X-rays on his knee," the assisting male nurse said, adjusting Hayden's bed. We'd been in the room for close to twenty-four hours. Every surface was covered in coffee cups and plastic wrappers from the vending machine food. "I suggest you go home for the night and rest."

"I'll stay," I said, glancing at Hayden. "I don't mind."

"Bab—" He stopped the endearment. "Heaven, seriously. Go take a nap."

"I'm fine."

"Thompson," he glared at Anderson, "get her the hell out of here. She's about to crash."

"You don't want me to stay?" I asked.

His eyes flicked over me. "I want you to rest. Take a nap. Eat some protein." He jerked his head at Anderson. "My boy needs a..." He grappled for the word, but finally adds, "shower."

Anderson rubbed his face and head, sending his reddish-brown hair into disheveled spikes. I had a feeling if I didn't go, Anderson wouldn't either, so I finally relented.

"Fine. I'll head out for a few hours and be back tonight, okay?"

"Tomorrow," Hayden said with a firm but tired look. "Sleep for real, okay? And then come back tomorrow so we can talk over some stuff."

Anderson frowned. "What kind of stuff?"

The doctor replied for him, "Mr. Pierce is going to need to work out a treatment plan for the next few months. It's best to have a loved one present to understand the details."

Treatment plan. Months. Loved one. Wow. The words swirled in my brain, like wicked sense of déjà vu from my own stays in the hospital. Recovery took time. Physical or mental.

I plastered on a smile and walked over to squeeze Hayden's hand. "We'll be back in the morning."

"Thank you."

"Of course. Take it easy today and call if you need anything."

"I will." He looked between me and Anderson. "And you two play nice."

"What does that mean?"

He rolled his eyes. "You know what I mean. Don't think I can't smell the tension. Be nice to each other. Rest and we'll figure out the rest later."

Anderson reached out and they bumped fists, a ripple of communication rolling between them. I grabbed my bag and Anderson picked up my suitcase and we walked out the door.

"Do you have a car?" I asked, suddenly feeling lost in a new city with no destination other than this hospital. "I need to find a hotel."

He shook his head. "You'll stay with me."

It wasn't a question. I raised an eyebrow. "You think that's a good idea?"

"I think we both need sleep and a shower. I can provide both."

I followed him out the door, wondering how in one week I'd fallen back into the world of the Allendale Four. My biggest concern wasn't how hard it was to be around my guys again—it was how easy —and how much it'd hurt when it was over.

ANDERSON'S APARTMENT was located near the aquatic center. The facility was built during the Olympics in 1996 and now was used for collegiate-level teams and beyond. Anderson's coach moved from our university down here and he followed, continuing his training. It was a weird but awesome coincidence that he and Hayden ended up in the same town.

I didn't pay much attention to my surroundings as we drove from the hospital back to his apartment. It was late. The streets were empty. Exhaustion set in quickly and he carried my suitcase into the house.

"Make yourself at home," he said as we entered the small space. The kitchen and living room butted up against one another. One bedroom sat off the main room. He pointed inside. "The bathroom's in there."

"You go first," I told him, setting my suitcase in the corner. My senses were overwhelmed by...everything. The place felt like Anderson. *Smelled* like him. I ran my hand over a throw pillow that must have come with the leather couch.

"I'm not going to fight you," he said, heading to his room. We looked awkwardly at one another as he shut the door, giving himself privacy. The click of the lock echoed in my ears.

I sat on the couch and took a deep, Anderson-scent-filling breath. I shouldn't be here. Not if I wanted to keep my sanity. Anderson of all the guys...our history was so tightly woven...more so than any other. Even if there was no Allendale Five, there probably still would have been an Anderson and Heaven.

Which was another reason all of this was so confusing and difficult.

I gathered my pajamas and wandered the small living room while the water ran in the other room. The décor was sparse—fitting for Anderson's all-work-no-fun attitude. A shelf of trophies sat over the television. These were all new. Awards and medals. The trophy he received at Nationals. I ran a finger over the engraving, feeling pride for his accomplishments. He worked so hard. They all had. *We* all had. There was nothing to regret.

A stack of news clippings sat on the shelf. Sports articles about Hayden. The press release about A5 opening in Allendale. I flipped through them and stopped short when I saw a small grouping at the bottom. It was a list of every TV show and movie I'd worked on over the last two years.

The bathroom door opened and I dropped the papers, stepping away from the shelf. Anderson walked out of the steamy bathroom, in a gray t-shirt and shorts, drying his wet hair with a towel.

"All done," he said, moving out of my way. "Listen, you take the bed. I'll crash on the couch."

"I'm not taking the bed."

He frowned. "Heaven, just take the bed. It's not a big deal."

I looked behind him at the mahogany headboard, and the quilt his grandmother sewed him as a baby. "Did you get a new mattress?"

A small smile tugged at his mouth. "No."

I groaned. "So you've still got that amazing one?"

His arms crossed. "I do."

"Dammit," I muttered. His mattress was amazing. Perfectly molded to fit his body and anyone else that laid down. But I suspected it smelled like Anderson and the last thing I needed was to be fully enveloped in his scent. "Take the bed, Thompson. I'll be fine on the couch."

A beat held between us and for the first time since arriving, I felt the old sense of comradery. I escaped to the bathroom before I suffocated on ancient history.

75

The couch wasn't just uncomfortable, it was basically a torture device.

I flopped on my back, then my side, then my stomach.

I stared across the room, toward Anderson's door where the most comfortable mattress in the world cradled him like a warm hug.

His room was also pitch dark with blackout curtains. He didn't have the glare of parking lot lights peering in the living room windows like a beacon. God, I was so tired.

I rolled over again. Then once more. I settled on my stomach.

I heard a creak, then the padding of footsteps, and closed my eyes.

"I know you're awake."

With my eyes still shut, I said, "I'm not awake."

"You've been tossing and turning for an hour." I peeked at his crossed arms and long body leaning against the doorframe. "The leather squeaks. Come on, let's switch."

"I'm fine, Anderson."

We stare at one another in the faint light, caught in an impasse. I saw the wariness in his eyes, the reluctance of having me in his home

—in his life. "The last thing I wanted was for you to hate me," I blurted.

"What?" He blanched. "I don't hate you, Heaven."

"You've barely spoken a full sentence since I got here. Not at the hospital. Not in the car. Not here."

His jaw tightened. "Maybe I don't know what to say."

"A lack of words has never been an issue for you, Anderson. You're mad. You hate me—I betrayed you somehow, I'm sure." He'd alluded to it in the hospital hallway when he threatened me about running again.

What he says next takes me by surprise. "I don't hate you, Heaven, I hate *this*."

"Hate what? If not me, then what?"

"The tension between us. The...distance...whatever it is." His eyes averted. "I don't think we should talk about this. Not now."

"Why not?" I glanced around the dark room. "We've got time."

He doesn't speak, but his eyes flicked to mine and I caught a glimpse of something I'd seen before. Worry. For me.

"You're afraid I'll get upset?" I asked.

"I think we're both under a lot of stress."

"But I'm the fragile one. You can take it, but I can't."

He shook his head. "I didn't say that."

"I'm better, you know. Taking my meds. I have a great job. Friends. All of that stuff is in the past."

"I'm glad. I really am."

"Then why the look? The frowny lines over your forehead?" He smoothed them with a hand subconsciously, before they delved into his hair.

"Seriously?" he asked. "I haven't seen you in two years, Heaven. We went through a lot of shit together. Don't forget I was the one—is it wrong for me to think maybe I need to take precautions?"

"I haven't forgotten," I said, well aware that he saved me that night in the ocean.

I wasn't being fair though, I knew that. How would he know about my mental stability? How would he know I was doing well?

"I'm sorry," I said. "You're right, we did go through a lot of shit together and I desperately try to leave that in the past. I'm better. For real, and if I never said it or never said it enough, I appreciated everything you did for me."

There was a beat of peace that flowed between us. Maybe that was why he'd been so angry. He was concerned? He'd never been one to handle his emotions appropriately.

He ran a hand through his hair. "I hate that it took Hayden getting hurt for me to see you again."

I sat up on the couch, pulling the blanket with me. I jerked my head, implying but not asking for him to sit next to me. If I asked and he said no, I might crumble entirely.

He moved slowly, like he had to consider it—consider the ramifications—but crossed the room and sank down in the leather. "I never wanted any of this to happen between the five of us," I said. "But you know as well as I do that things just weren't the same."

He didn't respond.

"What we had together—the five of us—was special, but also so unique it existed in a fragile bubble. Careers, travel, life...none of us, especially me, knew how to make that work," I confessed.

"And when that bubble burst, you ran."

I frowned and shot him a look. "I didn't run. Why do you keep saying that? We agreed to be apart. Completely apart."

"No, you agreed to that and we gave you space. I came out here. Hayden joined the team. The guys built their business and you just... vanished." His words cling to a hollow in my chest. "You know I still talk to them—almost every day. We text and call and all that shit you do when you're close to one another."

"But you were friends before me and it makes sense you'd be friends after. I didn't know where I fit in that once..."

"Once we stopped having sex?" His tired green eyes surveyed me from the other side of the couch.

"Yeah. Isn't that what all break-ups are about? Balancing the love of friendship and intimacy." God, what we wove was so complicated. So very fragile and complicated. "And when you still—"

"Still what?"

I swallowed back the word love. "When you still care for someone, it's impossible to see them without feeling the loss over and over again."

He nodded in understanding and the tears that had been welling in my eyes for days started to spill. Anderson looked panicked by my sudden burst of emotion but sitting here with him, seeing Hayden—all the bruises and his injuries. It was all too much and I broke.

"Heaven," he said, tears glistening in his own eyes. In a fuck-it-all move, he reached out for me and pulled me against his chest. It was wrong—so wrong, but it felt perfectly right. His firm chest, the weight of his arms, the thunderous pounding of his heart.

"I shouldn't have brought it up. Not now," he said, stroking my hair. "I'm just freaked out about Hayden. What he's going to do while he recovers and if he'll ever get to play again. They're getting more and more strict on the head injuries—as they should—but it's his whole life, especially since..."

"Since we broke up." I completed the statement for him. "He has Sabine. He was moving on."

Anderson grunted, arms tightening around me.

"We agree on one thing then," I said, my tears having dried on his shirt.

"What's that?"

"That Hayden is our number one priority."

He nodded. "Yes, he is."

Releasing that built-up dam of emotions pushed through my anxiety and I finally felt myself relax. Anderson didn't move his arms and I slowly felt myself sinking into his side, comfortable for the first time all night.

76

Anderson

I didn't dare move.

Not an inch.

I couldn't wake her—not just because she needed sleep, but because the feel of her, the weight of her against my chest, settled me in a way I thought I'd lost forever.

I had zero doubt that once she woke she'd take off...again.

I knew I'd been hard on her the day before. Two years of tension wound into a heightened moment that had been compounded by my fear for Hayden's health. But when I saw her in that waiting room my insides shattered, every emotion I'd held onto for so long splintering into a million pieces. Anger mixed with sadness, mixed with longing, mixed with desperation...the results weren't pretty.

Even under the strain of worrying about Hayden, she'd startled me with her beauty. She'd grown from a skinny girl to a curvy woman. Her face looked different; thinner and more defined. Her eyes didn't carry the tinge of sadness that had lurked there for so many years. She looked good—healthy—and that nearly broke my

415

heart again. She was doing well without us. Maybe better than with us.

And that was the crux of it all…maybe we were all better off separately. It didn't feel like it, especially not at first. I'd thrown myself into my competitions, channeling the pain into sweat and gold medals. Each win was hollow without her at the end of the pool, but I persevered because I had a dream, with or without her, and failing…that wouldn't bring her back. Instead I swam each race as a tribute to her strength, fighting every day for her health.

And here she was, healthy. Strong. Sad about our friend, but ultimately strong.

She shifted beneath me, forcing her shirt to rise up, revealing her lower back. Dark marks caught my eye and I strained to get a better look.

A tattoo.

I blinked, reconciling that Heaven had a tattoo, and carefully lifted her shirt a bit higher. I realized quickly that it was a scattering of stars, a constellation.

I grazed my fingers over each one, counting the number over and over again.

There were five.

She moved beneath me and I willed my body to behave. I glued my hands to the edge of the couch, away from her soft skin, and made myself relish in this one moment, fascinated by the fact I'd learned something new about her. What else did I not know? How much had she changed?

It broke my heart knowing she'd moved on without me—us—but it also made me proud.

77

THE HOSPITAL DOORS slid open and we entered the building with considerably less tension than when we left the day before.

We're both avoiding the way we woke up, groggy and intertwined on the couch. Anderson blinked at me, like he was surprised to see me there, and I pretended I didn't feel the natural presence of his hard length between us.

"Uh, sorry," I mumbled, scrambling off the couch and into the bathroom to change. In my mind, I prepared a dozen statements for when I reentered the room, but he just handed me a coffee and a bagel with peanut butter, exactly how I like them, and slipped into a silent agreement not to mention it again.

Times like this, I truly appreciated Anderson's stubbornness. It made denial so much easier.

"So, we'll meet with the doctor and then what?" I asked, entering the elevator.

"Hopefully get a plan together." He leaned against the wall. "I don't know if he'll want to stay here while he recovers or..."

"Or what?"

The elevator doors opened, and standing just outside are two familiar faces. My heart seized and I wipe my palms on my pants. This couldn't be happening.

Jackson greeted me with a lazy smile before pulling Anderson into a hug. Oliver watched me carefully while exchanging a bro-handshake with Anderson.

"What are you doing here?" I finally asked when I was able to find my voice. I hadn't been in the room with this many Allendale boys in a long time.

"These guys have some ideas about Hayden's treatment," Anderson said.

"You talked?" I asked him, feeling a bit betrayed. Anderson and I had spent most of the last two days together.

Jackson shrugged. "Anderson's been giving us updates. It gave us time to make arrangements at the gym and get out here."

We entered the small private waiting area outside Hayden's room and I felt like an observer in this surreal situation. What happened to our rules? The agreement for space? Did it all go out the window if one of us needed help?

I knew the answer to that and it left me unreasonably conflicted.

The door opened and all eyes shifted to Sabine walking through, ear to her phone. She passed us without much of a glance.

"Have you seen him yet?" Anderson asked Oliver and Jackson.

Oliver replied, "No, they were doing some tests and asked us to wait. How's he doing?"

I waited for the tears to well in my eyes again but to my surprise, there were none. It was likely I'd spent them all the night before during my breakdown. "He's okay," I said. "A little confused—I think it's from the concussion. His body is beat up pretty badly and he'll have to stay off his ankle, but I guess it could be worse."

I heard a snort from across the room. We all turned. Sabine rolled her eyes. "Worse? How could this be worse? He's missing the final games, including whatever shot they still have at the finals. Then every event we've had on our calendar will have to be cancelled. But the biggest thing is, if he doesn't make it to pre-season practice on June first, they will give his spot to someone else."

Jackson, adept at hiding his true feelings behind his handsome face, arranged his expression into something neutral. He stepped forward and said, "I'm Jackson Hall. This is Anderson, Oliver, and Heaven."

"Oh, I know who you are," she replied and cut Anderson a glance. "Friends—not family like you told the doctor."

"We're on the paperwork," Anderson replied calmly.

"Well, that was a mistake. I'm his girlfriend," Sabine said, "*and* physical therapist. There are protocols for a reason."

I tried to follow Jackson's lead with my expression but there's no doubt I made a sound. A squeak. A growl? Something, and a warm hand landed on my shoulder.

"Sabine, right?" Jackson asked, knowing her name already. He could be such a brat. I loved him for it. "I've seen you on the sidelines of the games and in the tabloids."

Her cheeks flushed at that little tidbit and she smiled again. "Therapist for the last eighteen months. Girlfriend for six. And yeah, Hayden's a very popular athlete, the media can't get enough of him, which means we also have a lot of obligations socially and for his endorsements. His injuries are going to cause a problem."

"A problem?" I blurted. "Because you can't go to a party or something? He's hurt and needs time to heal and hopefully get back on the field."

Sabine stiffened. "I know what he needs. I'm his physical therapist. I've helped him through dozens of injuries over the past year." Her eyebrows raised. "What have you been here for and do you have any idea, the slightest concept, of the sacrifices he's had to make because of his relationship with the four of you?"

It was a direct hit, with the implication she knew exactly who I was and the others and how much my absence, in particular, was noted. Before I could respond, Hayden's doctor appeared in the doorway, forcing us all to settle down for the moment.

"Doctor," Anderson said, walking over and shaking his hand. "How is he today?"

"He's making decent progress. His mind is a little clearer. He's still in a lot of pain from the injuries though, mostly the ribs." He glanced around the room. "Hayden has asked that you all attend the meeting about his treatment plan."

"Everyone?" Sabine asked. "Why would all of you need to be there?"

"Because," Oliver said, quietly, "he asked. Despite what you may think, Hayden is our family and we're here to take care of him in any way he needs."

"But..."

Jackson gave her a sympathetic grin and threw an arm around her shoulder. "Don't see it as a threat, Sabine. Understand it for what it is. You don't just date Hayden. You get all of us in the package, like it or not."

The doctor opened the door and Jackson led Sabine through. Anderson followed, leaving me and Oliver last. Rage at Sabine boiled under my skin. Possessive, violent, rage. Oliver looked me over. "Are you going to be able to do this?"

For Hayden? "Yes, that girl just gets under my skin."

"Mine, too," he said, reaching for my hand. Probably out of instinct. I didn't push him away. "But something tells me she didn't quite know what she was getting into when she started dating Hayden."

"You mean his baggage?"

He smiled grimly and led me through the door. "I mean *all* of our baggage."

Bryant, the agent, with his carefully constructed hair and smile, was already in the room. He greeted each of us, shaking hands and introducing himself to Oliver and Jackson.

The room felt tight with all of us in it, and my hyperawareness of being so close to all my boys again rocked me. I vaguely recalled greeting Hayden and taking his hand as Sabine took the spot across from me. Her eyes flicked at our hands. I knew I should let go, give her the role of devoted girlfriend, but he clung to me like a lifeline.

"Hayden wanted me to share the details of his injuries with the people he feels will be integral to his treatment," the doctor explained. He mentioned the concussion and swelling in the brain. The need for time and healing.

Hayden's fingers were the only thing that told me how panicked he was about the information. The slow stroke of his thumb as the doctor spoke. I stole a glance at his face, and underneath the stoic expression was a man terrified his career—his dream—was over.

I fought back on my own wave of emotions—the sadness and fear. How overwhelmed I was to be back in the room with them, and focused on the man that needed me—needed us.

"At the very least you're out the rest of the season, Mr. Pierce. At best...well, we need to see how your therapy goes. I'm hopeful that with enough care you can make a full recovery."

"And you think he can make that recovery by June?"

It was early April, so that only really gave him eight weeks. The doctor hesitated but said, "Hayden will have to follow the therapy closely. No pushing. No slacking."

Only the medication dulled the reaction on Hayden's face, his hand clenching mine at the news. Soccer was his life—his passion-- and the idea of giving up wouldn't be an easy one to swallow.

"Got it, Doc," he said. "I'm committed."

"And if he doesn't make a full recovery by then?" Sabine asked.

"We'll play that by ear," Bryant said quickly.

Oliver cleared his throat. "Since three of us still live in Allendale, we'd like to propose that Hayden return home with us as he recovers. He can use our facility for therapy. He can live with me and Jackson. Anderson's father is orchestrating a transfer to the university hospital right now."

"What?" Sabine blurted.

Bryant's calm demeanor shifted just a little. "I'm not sure taking him away from the doctors and trainers he's used to is a good idea, do you, Doctor?"

"Well, I do like the idea of Hayden having a strong support network and being in a familiar place. Getting away from the city could do you some good." The doctor looked up from his papers. "What do you think?"

At first Hayden didn't answer, his eyed shifting from Bryant to Oliver, struggling with the two options. I squeezed his hand, hoping to show support. It was his decision but I knew I could be more helpful if he was back home.

"Hayden..." Bryant said, clearly not wanting to discuss this in front of us. "Maybe we should take a minute to think it over. Go over all the options."

When Hayden replied, his words came out a bit slow but his intent was clear. "I think it would be for the best. I trust the hospital and I know I'll be in good hands with these guys."

"What? You want to move across the country?" Sabine asked, barely above a whisper.

Bryant rubbed his chin. "You are an owner in the A5 gym. Maybe it would be a good show for you to spend your recovery there. Boost the visibility of the facility."

Jackson rolled his eyes but said nothing.

Again, Hayden his thumb swiped against my palm and a shiver ran down my spine. I looked up and Anderson watched us closely, a thin line slashed across his forehead. Our eyes met for a brief moment and my neck flared with heat. Hayden and Sabine fell into a discussion. I felt caught in a battle I hadn't agreed to. Slowly I extracted my hand and moved to exit the room.

Oliver grabbed my arm. "Hey, everything okay?"

I nodded. "Yeah, I just need a little air."

"We don't expect you to help, only if you want, when you want."

And there it was.

"Of course. I'm happy to do anything it takes to get Hayden back to one hundred percent. You let me know where I fit into the plan."

It came out harsher than I wanted, but the emotion of it all crashed over me. Where did I fit into this? I'd woken up in Anderson's arms, but he'd barely spoken to me all day. I'd only just opened up a tentative relationship with Oliver and Jackson. I thought we may hang out occasionally. Grab a drink—move on from the past. I thought this would happen on my terms and on my time.

But now?

I took a last look at Hayden in the bed, his gray eyes sweeping the room for me and stopping when he spotted me at the door. Sabine still spoke into his ear, the doctor huddled with Anderson and Jackson.

Oliver watched me with pained, worried eyes.

It wasn't the first time the feeling had overtaken me and I was now certain it wouldn't be the last.

Entering the circle of the Allendale Four wasn't a temporary thing.

It was for life.

78

———————

"I think Hayden has had enough visitors for now," the nurse firmly announced shortly after the doctor left the room. "Let him have a little rest."

"Later, man," Jackson said, gripping my hand. "We'll be back tonight."

"Can you bring me some tacos?"

"Yep." He nodded at Oliver. "A whole bag."

"Thanks." My head pounded with every word. Not to mention the ache in my side and the throbbing of my ankle. "For coming and setting up everything back home. Not just the tacos."

"You got it. We'll get you back on the field. Challenge accepted," Oliver said and bumped my fist.

I nodded then shifted my eyes to Anderson. "Tell your dad thanks, too, okay?"

"I will." The others left the room and gave Anderson space by the bed. "I know it's been weird for you to come back home after your parents moved overseas and, you know," his eyes flicked at Bryant and Sabine, huddled in the corner talking, "everything else."

"My mom called today and tried to come over here. I was a hard no on that. She'll just stress me out."

"I hear that."

"Did you two get along last night? Everything go okay?" I didn't say her name. Not in front of Sabine or Bryant. I'd already seen the disapproval in their eyes.

"Okay. We had a heart-to-heart at 3 a.m. because she was being stubborn about sleeping on the couch." He shook his head in annoyance. "But I think we needed to clear the air. Maybe you two should talk. It may help with some of the unresolved feelings."

I simply nodded, not committing one way or the other. Anderson didn't push. Especially about this, but my relationship with Sabine was public enough, intentionally so, that they were aware of her. I used that relationship now to create a buffer between Heaven and myself—or I tried to. The medication and stress of the morning made me forget for a minute and I found myself holding her hand, feeling her soft skin.

Anderson leaned down and said, "Did you know she had a tattoo?"

"No." My heart skipped a beat. "Where?"

"Lower back. Five stars."

No. I did not know that and now I had a million questions.

Bryant caught my eye and cleared his voice, interrupting our conversation. Anderson caught the hint and said, "I'll come back with the guys later. Take a nap, you still look like shit."

"You like it when I look bad—makes you the handsome one for once."

We bumped fists and Sabine and Bryant watched him go out the door.

Bryant's non-committal gaze shifted in my direction the instant we were alone. "So that was the infamous Allendale crew."

"That's them."

"I knew from my research they were an impressive group, but in person they're pretty intimidating. I can see why you guys had quite the reputation in high school and college."

I shook my head. "We were just a group of friends—nothing

425

more. You know how petty high schoolers are with cliques and popularity."

"And then there's Heaven."

Sabine looked away, a deep scowl tugging at the corners of her mouth. It wasn't a good look on her.

"What about her?"

"She sure ran out here as fast as possible," Sabine remarked.

She had, and it'd surprised me, but it also stirred something in me that I'd long pushed aside. Sabine, no doubt, picked up on it. I ran my hand over my head. "She and the guys were watching the game when I got hurt. She panicked and came out here. She knows my family isn't in the States. If anything, it was just out of habit."

There was no part of me that thought Heaven came back here to reconcile. And the little post-visit meeting with Bryant and Sabine was to remind me there was no chance it could ever happen anyway.

"Hayden," Bryant said, in a voice that made my head throb even more than before, "when I first brought you on as my client I did thorough research on your past. I had to. You know it wasn't to invade your privacy. It's to make sure that when we sign contracts and establish business relationships with sponsors and endorsements that nothing is going to come back and bite us. Your history was a little tricky. No drugs, no arrests, no sorority girls claiming you'd assaulted them in the back of the frat house. But one thing kept coming up. It was this little scandal concerning your friend, Heaven Reeves. And the more I dug, the more I found out that Heaven wasn't just your girlfriend, but sort of this little pet kept by your group of friends. And then the more I dug past that, I found the gossip and the rumors and enough photographic evidence to cause me some worry."

"Don't," I said, with as much force as I could muster, "call her a pet. That's fucking demeaning."

He had no idea what Heaven meant to us—to me.

"I apologize," he said with perfect contrition. "But remember, I told you at the time you had to do two things for me to take you on as a client. One was stay away from Allendale, and two was getting a new girlfriend, so that if anyone found out about Heaven they'd realize you've moved on."

"And I've done both of those, haven't I?"

He nodded. "Until today, yes."

"So what's this about? Me going back to Allendale? You said it yourself, I'm a partner in the gym. It makes sense for me to be there."

"It does, but if the press follows you out there they may start digging around, and normally I'd say going back to your hometown would be no big deal, but Allendale has so much movie business now that the paparazzi has a reason to be there. We've talked about this before. Part of the reason we came up with this plan is not just to protect you but protect her."

And that was why I'd agreed to it. If Heaven thought high school mean girls and bullies were a problem, she had no idea what it was like to be associated with a celebrity. And that was what I was now. A celebrity. The media wanted a piece of me and they'd take a piece of her if they could. They'd pull up her medical records, her father's past, her depression—all of it.

I wouldn't allow it. Not a chance.

"I'll keep a low profile. I'm there to recover, Bryant. Nothing else. Trust me, I don't want the press digging around any more than you do."

"And Heaven?" Sabine asked. "What are you going to do about her if she pushes it?"

"I doubt there's much I'll have to do. Did you not see her leave? She's not comfortable with any of this. If I had to guess, she showed up here out of obligation—once the guys have me on a routine, I doubt I'll see her. She has a job in Allendale. A life. Friends of her own. None of them hang out anymore."

"Except they were together when you got hurt," Sabine said. When I gave her a questioning look, she glared back. "I overheard them talking about it."

I reached for Sabine's hand, knowing she needed a little reassurance. "I promise you—both of you—that nothing is going on with me and Heaven."

"And our relationship?" she asked. "How do we plan on keeping that up while you're gone."

"We'll figure something out. A few well-placed excuses should work."

I nodded but didn't admit a break from Sabine wasn't the worst part of this recuperation.

"Fine," Bryant said. "I'll get working on the press releases and letting your sponsors know what's going on. I'll talk to the team, too." He gave me a long look. "You have eight weeks to heal and recover. Focus on that, Hayden, and we'll take care of the rest."

"Sounds good." My eyelids were growing heavy, the last dose of medication kicking in.

Sabine gave me a hard look. "Don't embarrass me while you're there."

I frowned. "I wouldn't do that."

"Good." Her features softened and she gave me a quick kiss on the forehead. "You look like you're about to pass out. Take a nap, Hayden. The next eight weeks are going to be hell."

They left me alone, finally, taking their conniving and manipulations with them. They both meant well, but they were ruthless when it came to my brand and business dealings. A break from them both may be the best part of this disastrous situation.

That, I thought as I slipped into sleep, and going home.

79

Heaven

The line at my neighborhood coffee house was long but the service was quick. I spotted Lea already at a table, steaming cup in front of her, and waved. We had the day off from work and we needed to catch up before I started back the following day.

I gave her a hug before I slid into the green vinyl chair across from her. I swirled my cup, mixing the cream in my iced coffee.

"How did everything go at work while I was gone?"

Lea looked tired, but a light twinkled in her eye. Her dark hair was twisted in a bun on top of her head with little purple strands sticking out of the top. A thin row of silver hoops lined her earlobe and she smiled. "Smoothly. Well, other than the day we ran out of epoxy and I had to send Micah to the craft store to find some."

Micah was one of the runners on the show. Running out of something like epoxy could hold up production, which was a huge no-no in the business. Time is money and all of that. "Shit, did it turn out okay? Did they get behind?"

"No," she replied with a look of relief. "But it was a mixture of an action adventure and a buddy comedy as Micah and Rory sped off to get to the store before it closed. Rory tripped on the curb in the parking lot and showed back up covered in blood."

"Oh no!"

She waved her hand. "Just his lip. It bled way more than it was actually injured. Anyway, we got it all together and done on time."

"Sounds exciting. I miss all the fun."

She eyed me. "What? Hanging out with four ex-boyfriends wasn't fun?"

"Ugh." I leaned back in my seat. "It wasn't a vacation, that's for sure." I gave her a rundown of Hayden's injuries and the plan to move him back to Allendale to heal. I briefly explained that I stayed over at Anderson's that first night and then moved to a hotel for the second. I kept my interactions with the boys limited after that. It was too hard. Too complicated.

"I guess it would have been too easy for things to slip back into place, right?" she asked.

"That's part of the problem. The lure to slide back into our old roles is pretty alluring. But it's wrong. We can't do that. We're not the same people, but at the same time it's just like this thing is hanging over our heads, you know?"

Lea stirs her tea and I noticed her nose wrinkle.

"What? I asked.

"Nothing."

"No really, what's going on?"

Her eyes flicked to mine and I noticed the twinkle again. Finally, she admits, "I had a date last night."

"You did!? Why the hell are we talking about my tragic, yet incredibly boring life? Tell me!"

Her cheeks reddened and she shyly studied her cup before glancing around. In a hushed voice she said, "It was with RJ."

My eyes popped open and my jaw most certainly dropped. "RJ? RJ Malone? *The* RJ Malone?"

"Shhh!" She hushed me and glanced around the room. No one seemed to be paying us much attention. Why would they? They had no idea one of us just went on a date with RJ Malone.

"Tell me everything."

"Well, when you were out of town, I took over his makeup. And we just started talking more and he said he felt bad about the blind date going wrong and wanted to make it up to me. I thought he meant setting me up with someone else, but in the end, it was him."

"Like he just showed up?"

She nodded. "At my apartment. With flowers."

"Did you go somewhere?"

"After a few awkward moments where I tried to handle the reality of the moment, we decided to order in food from that new Greek place—you know, to keep any attention off of ourselves. I didn't want to be splashed all over Twitter like those other girls, and he agreed."

"Holy crap, Lea. RJ Malone." I took a sip of my drink, thinking it over. "He's young, but I guess so are you."

"Young but...uh, experienced." A wicked smile curved her lips.

No doubt about that—not with his face and body and the time he'd spent in the business. "And you had fun?"

"A lot. He was sweet. Romantic."

"Not a player?" You never knew.

She rolled her eyes. "What do you know about players?"

"Uh, you met Jackson, right? Biggest player out there." I thought about that lopsided, sexy grin. "It's one of the reasons I keep my distance. He definitely knows how to wear me down."

"I bet. He's a charmer, that's for sure."

"But not the others?"

I laughed. "Oh, they definitely have their strong points. Oliver is sweet—like he's the one that you want with you when shit hits the fan. He's strong and focused. He doesn't panic. And well..." I clamped my mouth shut and blushed.

Lea's eyes lit up. "What?"

I glanced around but still, no one paid us a bit of attention. "He's fucking huge."

Lea coughed in reaction, shocked, but I just nodded.

"And the other two?"

"Hayden Pierce is a force to be reckoned with, but a charmer? Not exactly. I mean, he's sexy, really sexy, in that totally-out-of-reach kind of way. Kind of like a god."

"He certainly has made a name for himself in professional soccer. I see his name everywhere. The press loves him."

"And his girlfriend," I interjected.

"Eh, I've been following it some since you told me you dated him. I'm not convinced on that one."

Lea was a known celebrity gossip follower. "Why not?"

She shrugged. "Just a feeling. It all comes across as a little too forced. It's like last night with RJ. If he wanted to be seen with me we would have gone to one of the popular restaurants or been seen over at the Market Street bars. There's a method to it. Hayden Pierce and his trainer are seen at all the trendy spots. They *want* to be seen."

I knew they were seen around—I didn't live in a cave—but I did keep my snooping to a minimum. I certainly didn't know the ins and outs of celebrity fame-whoring.

"She was at the hospital making sure she staked her claim."

Lea considered this. "We'll see how devoted she is once he's out of the spotlight for a while." She pushed her empty teacup away and leaned her elbows on the table. "And the final one? The one and only Anderson Thompson?"

"Well if you follow the news on that one, you'll know he's basically a recluse."

She snorted. "That's the truth. It's hard to find anything about him at all. A few rumors about him and that other swimmer, but he seems to do his best not to encourage it."

"Anderson is his own man, that's for sure. He'd never put a relationship in the spotlight, but I don't think he'd deny her, either. Even to spare my feelings." I thought about our late-night talk when I was out there. "He's struggling. Like the rest of us."

"It sounds like there are just a lot of unresolved issues."

"We ended abruptly. Like a Band-aid being torn off before the wound was fully healed. It was what we had to do for the circumstances. You can't linger with a five-person relationship. We made the decision and separated. So yeah, unresolved is probably accurate."

"So there was never any real closure."

I hadn't really thought it that way before but... "Nope."

"It's not that uncommon, but with four guys?" She shook her

head. "My last boyfriend and I broke up but it was while he was on a study abroad trip. When he got back, we hooked up one last time—it was like we both needed to do something so we could move on with our lives."

"Did it work?"

"Yeah, I think so. We shagged, like hard-core, and it was like all those feelings from before weren't there anymore. It was more physical than emotional. Kind of raw and dirty but once we were done I realized I *was* done. I guess it helped me realize it was really over."

"And you never did it again?"

"Nope." She smiled. "Which means I'm free to date whoever I want—like RJ Malone."

"You've been dying to get back to that the whole time, haven't you?"

Lea laughed and her face lit up. "I really have. I mean, RJ Malone."

"It's pretty exciting." I was happy for her. Really happy, and that made two of my friends moving on with their lives in productive ways while I continued to tread water. Except Lea had planted a seed in my mind, one that began to take root.

80

"You know you don't have to go," I said, helping Hayden into a gray sweater. We'd spent five minutes slipping on the clean white T-shirt just before. He wasn't an invalid, but even three weeks after the accident his ribs were still sore. The first two weeks had been in Atlanta, mostly still in the hospital, and Anderson and Sabine took care of things. During that time, Jackson and I got the house and gym ready. They transported him back to Allendale. The first few days were tense, mostly because of Sabine's general presence, but thankfully she'd been called back to work the day before.

Much to all of our relief. I couldn't imagine the fallout if she came to dinner with us all tonight.

"If I have to sit in this house for another night, I'll lose my mind."

I straightened his collar. The bruises on his face had begun to heal. No longer purple but a dark yellow. The swelling on his lip was down, although the thin crack was still visible.

"Sorry we've locked you in the dungeon, H."

He rolled his eyes. "Shut up. You know I appreciate everything you're doing. But dude, this sitting around and healing thing sucks."

I had no doubt this was the longest he'd gone without exercising in his entire life. Which was part of the problem. He hadn't allowed those past concussions to heal all the way. Now he was paying for it with extended time in bed before we could start his real physical therapy.

"Amber coming back in town gives us a reason to get you out of your boxer shorts and smelly t-shirts."

"What do you think this is about?" he asked. "It's not like Amber to call us all together. I mean, we talk occasionally, and I know you've kept in contact, but ever since..."

Our eyes met. Yeah, ever since we split from Heaven, our relationships with Amber had shifted. No longer a group thing.

I shrugged. "Maybe she has some kind of news. Maybe she just wants to see if you kept your good looks. The tabloids are going crazy trying to get an update."

He ignored my tabloid comment. "Heaven was vague when I asked her about it. I think she knows."

"Maybe Amber and Ginger will move back to Allendale, too, and the whole gang will be here again." I laughed.

"It's been weird being back," Hayden said quietly. "A lot of old feelings, I guess."

That time I didn't meet his eye. I knew about old feelings and how they screwed with a guy's head...and heart. Ever since the blind date with Heaven and then Hayden's injuries, our lives had been tossed back together again. It was nice. And incredibly hard. None of us really knew what to do or how to handle it. So far, it'd been mostly avoiding it and one another, if possible.

"We're meeting Anderson there?"

"Yeah he'll ride over from his parents' house."

"And Heaven?"

"She'll probably meet us at the restaurant."

"I know she's busy and has job that requires a lot of her time, but she's only been over once since I got back," he replied. "I'm getting a weird vibe from her."

"What?" I asked. "The 'your ex doesn't want to see you' vibe?

Welcome to the club, Hayden. And fuck no, she doesn't want to see you—especially not with Sabine around here."

He looked away at her name and said quietly, "Things are complicated with Sabine. When the endorsements started rolling in, Bryant felt like I needed more visibility. I wasn't up to it alone. Sabine...she was a good option."

I leaned against the dresser. "I'm not judging you for dating someone, Hayden. None of us are."

"I'm not—"

I held up my hand. "Seriously, it's better to own it and move on. It's what we've all been trying to do, and honestly it may be the first step toward that for the rest of us. If you can find someone else—be with someone else—then maybe there's a chance for the rest of us."

His gray eyes flicked to mine and his jaw tightened. "Do you really think that?"

No, I wanted to say. Fuck no. But I wasn't telling him that I lay awake at night pining over the girl I let get away—that *we* let get away.

"I do," I said, carefully helping him off the bed. He grunted and looked down at his feet. His left ankle was swollen and wrapped.

"I need some socks."

"Oh, right." I grimaced. "Jackson and I flipped for it. I had to help you with your pants. He's on sock duty. There's no way in hell I'm touching your feet."

Hayden cursed me under his breath and despite it all, it was really nice having him back home again.

81

———

"Before they get here, I need to know everything going on with you and the guys."

We were all meeting at the restaurant at six. Or so I was told. I showed up first and Amber's sly smile suggested something was off. It only took a little arm twisting for her to reveal that she'd told me to come early so she could talk to me about Hayden being home, us all being at the party together and how I felt about it.

I took a swallow of my drink before answering, feeling the warm burn down my throat. No chance in hell I'd get through the night sober.

"Nothing," I said. "Nothing is going on with me and the guys, other than, I guess, friendship."

"Friendship. You and the Allendale Four?" She eyed me skeptically.

"We're making it work—for Hayden."

"And everyone is cool with it?" She took a sip of her own drink.

"Sure, why wouldn't they be?" I didn't like this conversation. I didn't like lying to Amber. We'd always been honest—that's how our relationship started in that small high school bathroom years before. This was me telling her what needed to be said—the right things— not the mixed-up jumble of emotions that rolled over me each and every time I thought, heard, or saw the guys.

So I kept my expression neutral, regardless of the turmoil running beneath.

"Even Anderson?" she pressed. "Because he can be…"

"Difficult, yes, I know." I pushed my hair over my shoulder. "He and I hashed it out a little while Hayden was in the hospital. I think we both said some things we'd been holding onto for a while, and even though it didn't solve anything, and holy crap it hurt my feelings, it needed to be said."

Her eyebrows raised. "What did he say to you?"

I stared down at my glass. "That I ran away and bailed on them." She didn't say anything and I looked up. Her expression filled with conflict. "What? You think I ran, too?"

"I think you made a choice. One that was difficult to make under the circumstances."

"Do you think it was the right choice?" I asked.

"I think things got complicated, and sometimes going from a relationship when you're just a kid to an adult is hard. Ginger and I have made a thousand adjustments as adults. Paying bills, dealing with job stress, making decisions and the basics of settling into a long-term relationship. That rush from the early days is gone, but if you stick through it something else emerges. Something really good."

"You think I should have tried harder?"

"No, I didn't say that. I just think what you guys had was incredibly complex. There was probably no win, you know?"

"Well, for what it's worth, I'm really happy for you. I'm glad you and Ginger are win-win."

She grinned. "You were there for it all. My angsty youth. My awkward coming out. All my freak-outs and panics over Ben."

"I was just happy to have a friend that was as much of a mess as I was! And I'm the one that owes you thanks for being my best friend through all of this. I mean, it's not like you didn't know you were getting involved in a drama-fest the first day we met, but to stick through it all these years? I couldn't ask for anything more."

The door swung open and a rush of cool air tumbled into the room. All eyes shifted to the entrance and my stomach clenched at the sight of the four of them. Jackson strode in first, curly hair dipped in front of his eyes; his grin spread when he spotted us. Oliver, still a surprising sight with his more defined adult body, held the door for Hayden, who entered the restaurant on crutches, limping and grimacing the entire way. His gray eyes linked with mine and that familiar chill ran down my spine. Anderson came in last, handsome as always, jaw tense and his mind whirring with internal thoughts.

"Damn," Amber muttered. "The Allendale Four grew up."

"They sure as hell did."

"Heaven..."

"I know," I said, consuming the last of my drink. The burn of the liquid was replaced by something else entirely. "They're as dangerous now as they were then."

"That's not what I was going to say."

"What then?"

"That these guys may be more dangerous than before."

She gestured to the bartender and ordered me another drink.

"What's that for?"

"You're going to need that to get through the night."

THE BIG NEWS went over as expected; Ginger and Amber ridiculously adorable and the guys beyond happy for them. I kept the smile plastered on my face and desperately tried not to think about how their relationship was going in the right direction while my past ones were stuck in shark-infested water and there was nothing new in sight.

"Need another drink?" Jackson asked, sliding into the empty seat next to mine.

I shook my head. "I stopped after two. Amber and Ginger do not deserve having to deal with drunk Heaven at their engagement announcement."

"Drunk Heaven can be fun."

I shook my head. "Not for all of us. Ask Anderson's car and shoes."

He laughed, blue eyes twinkling at the memory. "He's still pissed about that."

"Bastard can hold a grudge."

The copper-headed man glanced in my direction like his ears were burning. After a beat, I averted my eyes.

"I shouldn't be surprised by the engagement," Jackson said, watching the beaming couple by the bar who'd been adorably happy all night, "but it still feels surreal."

"How so?"

"It feels grown up, and sometimes I still feel like a bumbling kid, unable to figure out my role in this world."

I frowned. "What are you talking about? You've never been bumbling, Jackson. You're the smoothest person I've ever met. Even as a teenager. You reeked of confidence. I remember those days back in school when I was really a mess; lost and trying to make a statement. You'd ease up to me, lay a hand on my back, and it was like having the strongest person in the world next to me."

He looked at his hands but I saw the dimples on his cheeks that gave away his smile. "That was a different time." His eyes met mine. "There was a lot at stake."

"And there isn't now? Not with your business and reputation?"

He shrugged. "Those things are nice, but none of them fill the hole."

The hole.

I didn't ask him to explain it because I had the same one.

"So how do you think Hayden's really doing?"

We looked over at him, sitting at the table, leg propped on another chair. He and Ginger were involved in a conversation but it wasn't hard to miss the rings under his eyes. "It's been a hard adjustment. He probably should sleep more. The doctor said no screen time at all, but I've caught him a few times on his phone or watching TV. He's bored. I get it, but it's the best way to heal."

"I keep catching him rubbing his forehead. Headaches?" I asked.

"He won't really admit it, but yeah. It's obvious." Jackson leaned closer. "And his temper. God. He's almost unbearable."

"I'll come by soon if you think it will help."

"It will help Oliver, that's for sure."

Glancing over at the bar, I caught Anderson still watching us, lines tugging at his mouth. I sighed heavily and nudged Jackson's foot with my toe. He followed my eyes and looked over his shoulder. "Should we make him jealous, like the good ol' days?"

"That's not funny." Although it was, a little, and I laughed darkly. "Shit. Maybe I do need that drink." *To get through the night*, I didn't add.

Jackson nodded and stood, giving me a hand to help me out of my chair.

So, I had a drink and then two more. I was finally relaxed enough not to care about the dirty looks Anderson had been giving me all night. It was a relief when he and Oliver took Hayden home. I watched his tall, broad frame exit the front door and said, "What's Anderson's problem, anyway? He certainly isn't making this situation any easier for anyone."

Jackson snorted. "Nothing new. Just trying to control the world and all the variables in it."

"He doesn't like me talking to you."

He looked over my shoulder. "No, and I'm pretty sure I'll hear about it later, too."

"What's he afraid of?" My tongue felt loose and my arms limber.

"That I'll do something stupid."

Liquid courage compelled me and I took a step closer, outside appropriate boundaries. His eyebrows raised in response. "We're adults, Jax. We can do what we want without Anderson's judgment. Fuck him if he thinks we can't be left alone to have a simple conversation. We're moving on, right? Doing this for Amber. For Hayden. We're adulting." I frowned into my drink, realizing it was empty.

Jackson leaned against the wall and brushed my hair over my shoulder. Inside I froze. The move…it was intimate, sweet…familiar. Outside, where my limbs were loose, I didn't step away.

"I've really missed you," he said, quietly.

"I've missed you, too."

I know all of Jackson's expressions, the way he looks when he's proud, or disappointed, or the way his forehead creases right before he comes, but he looks at me now with a different sort of intensity. Like he's afraid I'll break...or run.

For the first time in a long while, I didn't feel like going anywhere.

"Heaven," I heard, and turned toward Amber's voice. She shrugged her jacket on over her shoulders. Ginger's arm slipped around her waist. "You need a ride home?"

I didn't look at Jackson, but I felt him behind me. Waiting for my response. Ginger was blissed out enough by the evening that I wasn't sure she'd even noticed my hesitation. Amber on the other hand; her eyes darted between me and Jackson, the question lingering in the air.

"I think I'm good," I finally said, walking over to give them each a hug.

"Don't do anything stupid," Amber whispered in my ear.

"Who? Me?" I mumbled back, but I didn't want to put anything into the atmosphere. All I was doing was hanging with a friend. An old, handsome friend with eyes burning into my back as we spoke. "I'm just...looking for closure, that's all."

She pulled back and gave me a look that I couldn't quite discern. It definitely wasn't disapproval.

"Congratulations," I said. "Love you both."

"Love you, too," Amber replied, gazing at me and then over my shoulder. A moment later they were gone, and Jackson and I were alone and I wondered if it'd been a mistake to stay.

I turned to face him and took one look at his face and his body language; the way his hands were tucked into his pockets, the slight way he rocked on his heels, like a man tethered to his spot so he wouldn't pounce.

It would be up to me, then...to make the decision about where this would go from here. I met his eyes and fought the wave of insecurities warring in my belly and asked him to take me home.

82

Jackson

She asked and I said yes.

And prayed, the smallest of prayers that this was a step in the right direction and not a terrible, awful, unforgiveable mistake.

I walked her up the steps to her studio apartment, hands stuffed in my pockets, saying little. Any words spoken could blow this entirely. Heaven was a notorious overthinker. She ruminated. She worried. She always had and it left her vulnerable. But we'd worked through that and promised not to treat her like she was fragile, but now...I didn't know how to play this game.

She turned at the top of the steps, the wind blowing strands of her dark hair away from her face, and she was so beautiful. She'd always been beautiful, even when her world was falling apart. My heart clenched when her eyes landed on me—waiting for my dismissal.

I opened my mouth to do it first, soften the inevitable blow, but words rushed off her tongue. "I know we made a deal and I know why, because this is freaking hard. Just being near you—any of you. It scrambles my brain and my heart and all I feel is butterflies mixed with dread and..." she bit down on her red, bottom lip and looked away.

"Hey," I said, touching her chin, forcing her to face me. "I get it. All of it. I shouldn't be here, but—"

"I think maybe I need something final between us."

I sucked in a breath and repeated, "Final."

"Closure or...I don't know. Something that signifies the end, not what we had before where we all just vanished from one another's lives."

I swallowed and looked over her shoulder, out at the view of Allendale from her building's doorstep. I should leave. I should just walk away now, because what I wanted to do wasn't about closure and it sure as hell wasn't just about me. It wasn't just about Heaven. It was about all of us, it always was, and if I do something I regretted it could affect everyone.

But then I remembered...I was the first to kiss her then and the first to make her come. If anyone was going to take the chance— "Fuck it," she muttered, before I completed my thought, reaching for me.

Fire sparked between us when our mouths met; her lips soft, familiar, perfect. Heaven's hands fisted in my shirt, pushing me against the wall. That move was new, aggressive.

I liked it.

Dammit, I loved it.

Our relationship had escalated during college—we lost the shy, Heaven's- fragile-mentality with a lot of practice and communication. But the feel of her lips against mine, the weight of her body—different, curvier, harder—brought out a hunger I'd buried deep inside.

I didn't just want the old Heaven. I wanted the new one—the adult one. The bold one leaning into me right now.

The street light flickered over our heads and a car door slammed down by the street. The movements jolted me back and I looked down at her, my heart racing, my cock hard. Heaven licked her lips and said, "Come inside?"

I nodded and let her lead me in.

83

HEAVEN

WHATAMIDOING? WhatamIdoing? WhatamIdoing?

The thought ran through my head as I led Jackson to the stairwell. It was the old high school stairway that led to the second floor, and at the top landing Jackson pushed me into the corner and said, "There were so many times I wished I could have taken you at Allendale High."

"On the stairs?"

"God yes," he said into my neck. A chill ran down my spine. "Or in the locker room, beneath the bleachers, baseball dugout, classroom... I would have fucked you any damn place if I could have gotten away with it."

"You do realize we didn't have sex until almost the end of the year."

He smiled a deadly, seductive grin. "I said I wished. You know I was thinking about it long before we did it."

The fact that he wanted me so much then and that it hadn't changed one bit ignited a spark of lust. Pure lust, which wasn't the same as commitment, and that was what I could give. The glint in his eye told me the same of him.

My hands moved to the buttons of his pants, all shyness gone. "My neighbors have a pretty strict noise policy, it's probably better if we take it out of the stairwell."

"You ruin all my fun."

"I'll make up for it, I promise."

I didn't know where my sudden bravado came from. Maybe just knowing we were on borrowed time. One last chance to shut the door between us, once and for all. I fumbled with the keys while opening my door, my knees wobbly with desire. Jackson stood behind me, pushed my hair away and planted slow, seductive kisses along my neck.

I finally got the key in the slot and turned, exhaling in relief. His hands were on me before we crossed the threshold and I'd already unbuttoned the top button of his pants, fingers grazing at his zipper.

The door slammed too loudly, followed by the thud of my back against the wood. His movements weren't quite frantic, but there was an intensity, like he knew, like he felt as I did; that wouldn't get another opportunity and he didn't want to waste a moment. I caught my breath as he eased the hem of my skirt higher, watching him take in the new, older me.

Did he care that I was no longer that girl?

His fingers skimmed my thighs, traveling to my hips. I watched his Adam's apple bob and there was no doubt about the desire lurking underneath. I was struck in this moment of how much I wanted to *feel* the energy coursing between us. How much I missed it. And when his hands grazed my belly and his lips crashed against mine, I threw caution to the wind and chased it.

It didn't take long before our clothing hit the floor and my eyes were glued, *glued,* to his rippling six-pack. His body was thicker than before, more muscular, the deep-set V defining the space of his hips. The trail of his hair was coarser, less spare. I ran my fingers through it, reveling at the difference. We were still standing by the door of my apartment, intent and focused on one another.

"Jesus," he muttered, fingering the black lace edge of my panties.

Ones I thought I wore on a whim but now I wondered…did I have this planned? Did I make this happen? Lea had planted that idea in my head and more mature or not, bringing one of these men to my bed tonight was not unpredictable.

Our eyes met and a tiny line formed over the bridge of his nose. "I can stop anytime—"

"No," I said quickly. Firmly. "Don't stop. Do you hear me? Don't you fucking dare."

The line vanished and his lips curved and in an instant, I was lifted off the ground, wrapped in his strong arms. He took me to the bed, easing me down so our bodies never stopped touching. The hard tip of his erection pressed into my stomach.

My skin felt overheated and that only intensified as he moved down my body, fingers tugging my panties over my hips. I was hot, wet, and not even embarrassed. Those days were over. Jackson had fucked me a dozen different ways. He'd seen me begging for more, but with the way his fingers dipped between my legs, the way his tongue flicked out and licked his lips, he wasn't here to play games. He lowered his shorts, cock springing with release and stood over me. I saw the foil square in his fingers, watched him rip the corner with his teeth. I writhed, seeking friction as he rolled it down his hard erection and when he was finished, and he climbed back over my body, I sighed in relief. I sighed into his mouth, tongue hot and slippery. I gasped when he entered, swift and confident. I shuddered at the feeling—something I'd thought I'd lost—and when he rolled us over, allowing me to be on top, allowing me to set the pace, allowing me to have him one more time, like I hadn't had the chance before when it all ended too quickly. Abruptly. I kept my eyes open, watching him, me, the two of us. Watching every moment, knowing it would be the last.

～

THE BED SHIFTED beneath me and my eyes flew open, trying to make sense of the motion. That was when I felt the slight soreness between my legs and the hollow ache below my belly.

That was when I remembered the night before and my eyes flicked to Jackson's half-naked body as he rummaged for his clothes. He noticed me noticing him and he crawled toward me.

"I feel like shit for doing this because obviously we need to talk, but I have an early meeting at the gym." He kissed my forehead. "Last night was unexpected. Great. Amazing, but unexpected and you know me, I'm not one to bolt out of bed the morning after." He checked his watch and grimaced before continuing in a rush, "I don't want things to get weird after this. I want us to talk it over. I do not want this to fall into one of those awkward moments, okay?"

I hadn't moved an inch since I woke but I watched as he tugged his jeans over his hips, then his shirt over his head. I lamented the ladder of abs disappearing from view and fought off every mental thought flickering in my mind; every pounding, panicked heartbeat.

What. The. Fuck. Had. I. Done?

Him.

I'd done him and I enjoyed every, single, moment. But I had to tell him before he left what this was about.

I sat up, holding the sheet to my chest. "Jackson."

"Yeah?" he shoved his foot in a boot.

"We don't need to talk. I just want to thank you now for last night. I needed closure. Something final, you know?"

"Final. There's that word again." His second boot hung off his fingertips.

"We left everything so abruptly. I just needed a chance to...I don't know, say goodbye to that part of our relationship."

He nodded, eyes blinking, and crammed his foot in his remaining boot. He leaned over the bed and kissed me gently on the forehead and in a blink, was out of the apartment. Once I was alone I rolled on my back and stared at the ceiling, replaying the events of the night. We'd celebrated, we drank, but not so much I didn't know what I was doing. Oh, I'd known, and I wanted it. I wanted him one last time and damn, he didn't disappoint. He was bigger—stronger—unbelievably more confident in his body and skill. Which for Jackson...none of those things had been a challenge, even when he was younger. When he lured me to the edge, I came hard, biting down on his shoulder to muffle the sound and when he came, he kept his eyes open, watching me every second.

It was great, but...there was no such thing as a clean hook up, or booty call or whatever the hell that was in a situation like ours. There were three other guys to consider. Three other people that were tied into this relationship, and Jackson and I broke a major agreement with what we did. Not just between us but between *all* of us, and even if he and I maybe found that closure I'd been seeking, we possibly destroyed something larger.

I didn't just need closure with him. I needed it with all of them. Shit. I wasn't sure I'd thought this through.

My phone vibrated across the dresser, skipping across the surface. I grabbed it and checked the screen.

Oliver: Could use a little help with Hayden later today. You around?

I stared at the question for a moment almost wanting to say no, to hide beneath these blankets for the rest of the day and pretend I hadn't fucked up so badly.

But I'd made a promise to Hayden and the others I'd be there to help, and like every other time in my life, I couldn't say no to the guys. Not then and not now.

I sent my reply and got out of bed, planning to wash the sins of the night off my body before I faced two of the three other men in my life.

84

———

THE CLANK of metal weights slamming against one another ricocheted in my ears. The gym was packed with clients, more so than
during my last visit. Maybe because it was the weekend. Either way,
Peyton ushered me through the maze of machines until we arrived at
a small, private training room. The floors and walls were covered with
mats. Hayden sat in the middle of the room on the floor. His legs
stretched out, including the one with an ankle still wrapped in tape. I
saw the ridge of bandages under his cotton tank—the wrappings that
covering his bruised ribs. His shirt was soaked in sweat. Oliver sat
across from him, giving him some kind of direction. Wild fury rose in
my chest when I entered the room.

"What the hell is going on here?" I asked, eyeing him and Oliver.
"Why are you down here working out? You should be in bed. Resting.
You are not supposed to be down here!"

"Calm down," Oliver said, rolling his eyes. "This is part of his
treatment. Just a few stretches to get his muscles moving."

I moved to face Hayden. Sweat poured down his forehead. "Why
are you sweating so much, then?"

He touched his side. "Because it hurts like a mother-fucker, babe."

Babe. I rolled my own eyes and said. "This is ridiculous."

"It's part of the process, Heaven."

I knelt before Hayden and touched his forehead. "How's your head? Any headaches? I read the paperwork and the best thing for that concussion is full rest."

"I'm fine. Bored out of my mind. I can feel my muscles atrophying. I had approval to come down here—Oliver had approval to help me."

"Approval from who?"

They exchanged looks. "Sabine."

"Good grief," I muttered, wondering how we'd gotten into such a fix. "Well it looks like you guys are all under control. Why did you need me to come over?"

Oliver grimaced. "Because Jackson and I have a meeting with a new client this afternoon."

"I told him I didn't need a babysitter. Don't blame this on me," Hayden said, struggling to get off the floor. Oliver reached down and carefully helped him up. I handed him the crutches that were leaning against the wall.

"Where's Jackson?" I asked, hopefully in a nonchalant voice.

"We had a meeting this morning and he took Anderson to the airport. He came back and crashed up in the office. I think he drank too much last night or something." He watched me closely. "Did you stay with him at the bar last night after we left?"

"For a little while. He was okay when we parted." Not a lie. *Not a lie.* We just didn't part last night but this morning instead. "Wait, did you say Anderson left?"

Hayden focused on his crutches and Oliver frowned. "Yeah he said it looked like everything was under control here so he needed to head back."

I understood. His swimming had always come first, but it hurt a little that he didn't even said goodbye.

"So look, Hayden's been here for a while. Can you could drive him back to the apartment? His meds are on the kitchen table, with instructions."

"Sure," I said, glancing at Hayden. "You ready?"

"Yep."

I stepped ahead of him, moving to leave the room, but stopped short when I saw a figure in the doorway. I had a flash of the night before—a flash of kissing that handsome face in a similar spot. For the first time in ages, I felt a sense of peace at the sight of him.

"Uh," Jackson said, eyes lingering on me before shifting to Oliver. "Our appointment is here."

Oliver's eyes flicked between us. I glanced at Hayden. He was watching closely, too. "In the meeting room?"

"Yes. I'll tell them you're on the way." Jackson turned and walked away without so much as another glance my direction.

"This shouldn't take long, Heaven, and I'll be back to take over."

"Not a baby," Hayden reminded him.

Oliver rolled his eyes. "See you in a little while."

He left, going in the same direction as Jackson, leaving Hayden and I alone for the first time in a long time.

"My car is out front," I said. "Can you make it?"

"I swear to god, Heaven, if you guys don't stop treating me like a fucking invalid, I'm going to lose my mind."

I spun on my heel and faced him. "Hayden Pierce, you don't get to speak to me like that. I'm just here to help. And no one is treating you like a baby. We're trying to help you recover so you can get back on your feet—back to what you love." I tried to level my voice. "But if anyone is acting like a child, it's you. And if you don't want to be treated as such, man up and stop whining about everything."

His gray eyes had narrowed while I spoke and a strand of his long, dark hair fell against his cheek. His strong jaw tensed, absorbing my words and god, being caught in his gaze again left me completely unnerved, just like it had all those years before. I held my breath until his jaw loosened and a sly grin tipped his lips. "I've missed the hell out of you, Heaven Reeves, do you know that?"

"Really?" I said, wryly.

"I'm surrounded by these people that are always trying to make me do what's best for my career or my image. You just want what's best for me." He studied me for a moment. "I appreciate that more than I ever realized."

I didn't know how to respond to that, to the conflicted look in his eye. I just turned and walked out of the room. After a moment I heard the clack of his crutches following. I couldn't. He was right, I did want what was best for him which meant any kind of closure, like I had with Jackson, was off the table. He'd moved on with a new girlfriend and life. Any kind of action on my part would be a betrayal. I wouldn't be *that* girl and I knew Hayden wasn't that guy. I'd help him because I owed him, but the line stopped there.

At least that was what I told myself. Told my heart and the ache that longed for repair.

85

———

I sat through the meeting with the head of stunts for a major studio feeling the weight of Oliver's eyes on me. Both of us act professional. Both of us get the job done. Balancing work, teams, friendship, and Heaven ran through our systems like blood in a vein. Because of that closeness, that symmetry, I knew what was coming the instant our clients left and the door shut behind them.

I waited for him to speak first. To ask.

"What happened?"

I wouldn't lie to him. Not with so much on the line. "Heaven and I had sex last night."

"I'm sorry, what?" Oliver leaned against the conference table, jaw gaping. "You had sex. With Heaven."

"Yes."

"You're kidding."

"Nope." I shook my head, trying not to take his astonishment and possible anger personally.

"How the hell did that happen?"

I ran my hand over my face. "It was spontaneous. Fueled a little bit by drinking—but she wasn't drunk. Neither was I. It was…it was incredible," I admitted. "But this morning she said something I didn't expect. Not really."

"What did she say?"

"That she was looking for closure on that side of our relationship."

"Ouch."

"Right?"

He leaned back. "Holy shit, Jackson. This is a fucking mess."

"Yes. Apparently, what I thought was maybe a chance to, I don't know, get things going again, wasn't at all. That was it. The end." My stomach ached thinking about it.

"So, what? You think she'll hit us up one at a time for a farewell fuck and that'll be that?" His voice sounded angry—no, hurt.

"I don't know, Oliver. I really don't. All these years I've been able to read Heaven, but this? I didn't see it coming." Especially not in the middle of it. God, it was so good. Having her under me again. Being *inside* her. It felt like home for the first time in too long. I glanced up at Oliver and the sympathetic expression on his face. I looked away and walked toward the door.

"Where are you going?" he asked. "How are you going to deal with this? Because it's huge, Jax, and it has implications for all of us."

I sighed and gripped the door knob. "Right now, I'm going to change and beat the shit out of a punching bag. How am I going to deal with this? Fuck if I know. Let me know if you have any brilliant ideas. Obviously, my judgment is a little cloudy."

I left him there, knowing there was no good outcome for this one. Once Heaven made up her mind, there was little hope changing it. Also, who was I to push something she didn't want? She was healthy and happy. If all she needed was a little closure, then who was I to mess that up?

86

"Is there any way we can possibly not go back to Oliver's yet?"

Hayden sat in my car, passenger seat pushed as far back as possible. His legs were still cramped.

"Where do you want to go?"

"Anywhere." He focused out the window. "I've been cooped up for weeks and I just need some air."

I took a left at the stop light, going the opposite direction from Oliver's house. We passed the high school and area of town that housed the coffee shop and diner, where we spent countless hours in school hanging out. Hayden eyed them all silently. I understood the look. It was weird living in the town I grew up in, seeing these places, all of them filled with a mixture of good and bad memories. I'd had time to adjust. He hadn't. I didn't pause when we passed the street I grew up on and veered off the main road toward Allendale Park.

"Your mom sent me a card," he said suddenly. "When I was in the hospital."

I smiled. "She loves sending cards. It's one of her things. I think a holdover from being a preacher's wife."

"Have you heard anything from your dad?"

I shook my head. "No. Thank goodness. He's probably in jail—although if he was, we'd probably hear more from him. God knows what he's up to or who he's ripping off right now."

I drove down the long road, past the picnic tables toward the small pond where a mom walked with her small children by the edge, feeding the ducks. Hayden's focused on me now. I felt his eyes studying me. His hand reached out and tugged at my sleeve, revealing my forearms and the pale, smooth skin beneath.

I jerked my arm away and said, "Looking for something?"

"Just checking." He didn't look the least bit ashamed. Hayden rarely did.

"For cuts? Scars?"

"Yeah. Is that wrong?"

I parked the car and got out, needing some fresh air myself. Hayden struggled with his crutches and I helped him stand and stabilize. Once we were situated on a bench facing the pond, I turned to him and said, "You could've asked if you were worried."

"You could keep in touch—let me know how you're doing."

I crossed my arms defensively. "It's a two-way street. You don't make much of an effort."

"I tried," he said. "At the beginning, you know that."

He did. Texts and emails. I had no social media so that was out. He'd call but I didn't answer. I didn't respond. A clean break was what we agreed on. Eventually he joined the AU team, gaining fame and celebrity with the position. After that he didn't try anymore.

"Don't turn this on me and I won't turn it on you." I pushed my sleeves up, revealing faint scars, but nothing new. "I'm fine. Better than fine. I'm doing pretty good."

"So no cutting."

"I don't do that anymore."

"No...attempts?"

Suicide. It was a fair question, although it hurt that he didn't trust me. "No. Never again. I'm better, Hayden. Truly. I take my meds. I see a therapist twice a month. I have a great job. I have friends."

"Good. I'm glad to hear it. It was difficult not knowing—being so far away and so busy. Seeing you now makes me realize how well you've done since we broke up, or whatever the hell you want to call it."

"I didn't really have a choice but to move on. Did you?"

He shook his head and then surprised me by asking, "Dating anyone?"

My jaw set and I realized I didn't have an obligation to tell him everything about myself. Our eyes met and held for a moment but I didn't relent.

"Tell me about Sabine," I suggested even though I didn't want to know.

He shrugged and looked out at the water. "She was assigned to me by the coach to work through my last few injuries. I keep fucking up my ankle and then the concussions."

"Bad?"

"I know I should have rested longer, but I hate not being out there on the field."

"I know, but you've got to take care of yourself. I've watched you play your entire life. You take a lot of risks on the field. Dangerous ones." I touched the back of his head. "It's your brain, Hayden. You can't screw with that."

"I know, and Sabine has helped me with that. Making me slow down and do the training. Learn how to protect myself. That last game...things just got out of hand. That asshole striker was way over aggressive."

"You're a target on the field. You know that." I sighed and laid my hands in my lap. "I'm glad you've had someone to stick by your side. She's pretty and even though she was a little...uh, defensive, at the hospital, it was obvious she cares about you. From what I hear, the tabloids love her. And you. They love both of you."

"God, I hate those guys. They're everywhere. Like ants." He laughed darkly. "The love of soccer is growing in the US and everyone wants a piece of it. They're looking for the next David Beckham or Ronaldo. Someone to put on a pedestal—to be the face. Apparently, I'm the chosen one."

I smiled. "I'm not really surprised. You do have the face of a god."

"Shut it." He shoved his hands in his hoodie pocket. "It's been nice to have someone to go through it with me. I've never been one for the spotlight—well, at least off the field."

That was a jab. A small one but a jab all the same. Did I deserve it? Maybe. I sucked up whatever emotions I had and said, "I'm glad you've had some support during all of this. I know it's been a big change."

He gave me a sideways look. "It can be lonely. I miss you guys."

"I missed you all, too." I checked the time. "We should probably go. Oliver will send out a search team if he gets back and you aren't there."

He inhaled, like a man dying for air and then stood, wobbling on one foot while he got his balance. We were almost at the car when I asked, "How's the art going?"

His lips formed a thin line and he held onto the top of the car. "I'm not drawing much anymore."

"No? Not enough time?" Hayden always had his sketch book in his bag or back pocket. Always.

His eyes darted back to the water, the mom and her kid. Just before he ducked into the car he said, "I just haven't been inspired."

I took the crutches from him, shaken by his statement. Hayden's a man doing what he loves, with a beautiful woman at his side. How could he not be inspired?

87

At some point, Oliver's father retired and he and his wife moved south, seeking golf courses and warm weather. Oliver moved into the main house and offered Jackson a room, which left the back apartment empty and ready for my return.

The stairs were a bit of a hassle with my crutches, but I quickly worked out a system that allowed me a bit of exercise and stability so I didn't fall and crack open my head.

The irony was that due to my injuries, the guys came to me and soon we were all hanging out in that little apartment, like it was high school all over again. There were only two things—people—missing. Anderson and Heaven.

Currently, Jackson and Oliver played their nine-millionth round of Fortnite while I laid on the couch, leg propped up and iced to reduce the swelling. I had a battered sketch book in my lap, pencil on top, unopened. I carried it with me everywhere…out of habit mostly, but Heaven's question earlier in the day prodded me to get it out for the first time in ages. Her question, and as much as I didn't want to admit it, her presence.

"Dude, are you fucking kidding me?" Jackson muttered as a round of explosions went off on the screen. I glanced up and saw that his man was surrounded by aliens and Oliver's was far ahead, leaving him behind. "What the hell are you doing?"

"Playing how I want to," he replied through gritted teeth. There was something definitely off about the move, and Oliver made no attempt to correct, leaving Jackson behind. A string of curses flew from Jax's mouth, all directed at Oliver. I watched in silence as rage built between the two. It wasn't until Oliver stood up and threw his controller across the room, shattering it into a pile of plastic and wires, and Jackson rushed across the room that I realized this had reached a new level.

"I knew you were a selfish asshole," Oliver shouted as his friend raced toward him, "but this is a new low, even for you."

"Hey!" I shouted, unable to move to my feet with any sort of speed. Oliver caught Jackson in his arms and body-slammed him on the ground.

"You would have done the same fucking thing," Jackson replied. Oliver was bigger but Jackson faster and just as I was getting off the couch he landed a punch to the underside of Oliver's jaw.

"Shit! Stop! What the fuck!" I yelled, taking two steps around the coffee table and then dropping to my knees. I winced at the pain in my ribs and crawled over to them. I looked and felt ridiculous, but my best friends were pummeling the crap out of one another. Someone had to stop it.

Another fist landed, this time against Jackson's check. I managed to grab Oliver by the crook of the elbow. He looked back at me, fire and rage in his eyes, and I thought for a minute he was going to attack me, but recognition set in and he paused.

"Stop it," I said again and thankfully they both relented. Fist fights between us were rare but not unheard of. Only one thing caused them.

Heaven.

I shifted my attention to Jackson, who was on his back, breathing heavy, his cheek red from the strike. His eyes darted between us. "I had to take a chance. I had to. Someone had to before we lose her for good."

"Take a chance with what?" I asked slowly.

Oliver pushed off the ground and stood up, turning his back to us. "Tell him."

A touch of fear clouded Jackson's eyes, and he sat up on his elbows. "Heaven and I had sex last night. I thought it was about us reconnecting—turns out, she's looking for closure."

A dozen thoughts ran through my head, one being a strong understanding of the beatdown Oliver just gave him. I swallowed back that anger and replied, "She had sex with you for closure."

"Yes. That's what she told me this morning. We haven't spoken since. I don't know what to say to her when we do."

I sat on the ground next to Jackson, gripping my ribs. After a moment of cooling off, Oliver did the same. We were in a circle like five-year-olds. "Do you think she wants the same from the rest of us?"

Oliver's jaw was red from the punch. "I don't know if I can do it if she does." He looked at me. "You certainly can't. Not with Sabine. That will just fuck everyone and everything up more."

"True," Jackson said. "What if you and Heaven did it one last time and then you married Sabine? That shit would hang over all of us forever."

I simply nodded because they were right. I'd made my choice and I'd have to deal with it. I knew it when Bryant laid out my future and forced me away from my past. I knew it when I entered the relationship with Sabine.

"What about Anderson?" I asked. "What would he do if she asked him?"

Oliver shook his head. "I don't want to be there if she does."

Anderson had always made things more complicated than necessary, especially when it came to Heaven. Probably because he loved her so much. "Should we tell him?" I asked, looking at Jackson. "Are you going to tell him what happened?"

Both Jackson and Oliver averted their eyes. Nope. No one wanted to be the one to tell him. He and Heaven would have to figure this out on their own.

As for the rest of us, we were in uncharted territory, dealing with Heaven as individuals instead of as a group. I didn't like it but what could I do? If she wanted some kind of closure, she's entitled to it.

I just hoped it didn't tear us further apart.

88

Today was the last day of production for Creature Feature as we entered a break for the end of spring. The final show exceeded all the others with the number of cast, crazy storylines, terrifying costumes, and of course, extreme makeup. Lea and I spent three days working fifteen-hour shifts, showing up at 3 a.m. to start prep, and taking turns crashing on the couch in the back of the trailer. The whole process was exhilarating. So much fun, but by the end, I felt like a zombie myself and didn't even need the makeup to terrify anyone.

Making things more interesting was the Lea/RJ situation. The boy was smitten, I had no doubt. Sending her flowers, little notes, and an ample amount of coffee via his assistant all day long. After the final scene was over and we'd cleaned up our trailer, I commented, "Things seem to be going well with you two."

Her tired eyes lit up. "I don't want to jinx it but...yeah. Really good. I mean, we've been busy and not a lot of time to see each other, but I feel good about it."

"Is he going to stay around here for hiatus?"

Most of the cast didn't live here during breaks. Why would they?

Especially being young, famous, and having the world at your feet in Hollywood or New York.

"I don't know, we haven't had a chance to talk about it."

"I mean, you could go visit him, right? You don't have any obligations here."

"Just my dog."

"If you get invited somewhere exotic, I'll gladly take care of your dog," I told her.

"Maybe," she said, then raised an eyebrow. "How about you? Any progress on that closure thing?"

I fumbled with the brushes in my hand, scattering them across the counter. Quickly I resorted them into the containers. "A little."

"What does that mean?" she took a sip of her coffee.

I sighed. "It means I had sex with Jackson after my friend's engagement party."

Lea, coughed, choking on her drink and spitting it across the room. "You did what? When was this? Are you kidding me?"

"I had sex with Jackson. A week ago. And no, I'm not kidding, although I'm starting to wish I was."

"Girl, what happened?"

"We were alone and things just felt...right. I decided to go for it and the next day I told him why—about the need for resolution—and I don't know. He seemed okay with it but he hasn't spoken to me since and I can tell there's a vibe with the guys. I'm sure he told Oliver. He tells him everything."

"Why haven't you spoken to him about it?"

I shrugged. "I guess I'm afraid to. I've just been spending my time with Hayden, taking him to the park and stuff for fresh air. He's the least complicated of them all."

"Why's that?"

"Because he has a girlfriend and he's off limits and that means we just have to move on. Forced closure."

Lea rubbed her forehead. "Wow. What a mess."

"You're telling me."

"So did you get it with Jackson? Closure?"

I wanted to say yes, that we had sex and everything fit together like a puzzle and we were done, but that would be a lie. Having sex with Jackson only stoked some still-burning embers and I didn't know how to handle it. Hence the avoidance.

"Like I've said," I answered, "it's really complicated."

I picked up the party invitation taped to the mirror. It was for the season premiere, which was going to be held at a local theater next week. "You're going to the premiere, right?"

"Yeah, probably solo. I don't think either RJ or I are ready to go public with the whole crew."

I laughed. "You think they don't know?"

She looked horrified. "Do they?"

"You guys have been flirting non-stop for two weeks. I think everyone knows."

"Shit. I guess he and I need to have a talk about this, then."

"Well, if you want, we can go together."

"You don't want to find your own date? Maybe get the ball rolling for another night of 'closure' with one of your guys?"

I started to laugh her off, but Lea may have been on to something.

"Maybe. I'll think it over." I gave her a pointed look. "And you better get ready for the realities of being RJ Malone's girlfriend."

She groaned but there was a smile on her lips, giving me the feeling she was willing to make some sacrifices for him—which meant she really did like him.

I tucked the invitation in my pocket, thinking of the sacrifices I needed to make to finally find my footing as an adult with the Allendale Four.

I FOUND the perfect dress at a vintage shop down the street from my apartment. The shop had been there forever and carried the faint scent of dust and mothballs, but the selection was outstanding and the owner, having known me since my high school days of dramatic fashion statements, knew what I liked.

"Stefan," I'd said when I picked it up. "It's perfect for the premiere."

The older man had smiled with pleasure. "I'm thrilled you'll be wearing something from the store to the event. So exciting."

We'd agreed the dress needed cleaning, so I took it to the specialty shop the costumers suggested at work. The fabric was old and needed careful handling. They called for me to pick it up while dropping Hayden as his apartment, and I almost ran over Jackson backing out of the drive.

"What's the rush?" he asked, leaning into the open window. We hadn't spoken since he left my house that morning. "Trying to run me over?"

"Ha ha, funny. I didn't see you back there. Why are you loitering around the driveway anyway?"

"Hoping some hot chick with questionable driving skills will notice me."

I rolled my eyes and he gave me a sexy, lopsided grin. It was impossible to not fall prey to his charms.

"I'm about to run an errand. Want to come along?" I asked.

"Yeah, I'd like that."

A minute later I was trapped in the car with Jackson, overwhelmed by his scent, his voice, his presence. Maybe this wasn't a great idea after all.

"So is this where we finally have that awkward talk?" he asked when we were a few blocks away and he'd touched every button on the dashboard.

"We probably should...right?"

"It depends." He took a deep, steading breath. "Did you get what you wanted? Did you find closure?"

I stared out the front window and not into his piercing blue eyes.

"I don't know. I'm not exactly sure it's possible, not with the complexities of our relationship."

"You mean everyone else?"

"Yes."

"Do you want the same from them? Are you going to try?"

"I could," I said, turning at the light. "But what I realized with you is that there's this little part of me that doesn't want to let go. So what if that part exists with everyone else? What if it just gets bigger and with everyone still spread out, with Hayden...unavailable...what happens then?"

He ran his hand through his hair. "I don't have an answer to that."

"What about you?" I asked. "What was the other night to you?" I pulled into the parking lot of the dry cleaners and noticed I had five minutes before it closed. I held up my hand and said, "Shit. Hold on to that answer."

I scrambled out of the car and ran into the building. I saw a figure in the back and called out, "I'm here for a pickup."

"What's your name?" a voice called out.

"Heaven Reeves."

The figure paused before rummaging through the rack of cellophane-covered clothing. When the worker finally emerged, it took me a moment to catch my bearings, to recognize the person in front of me.

"The one and only Heaven Reeves." Spencer Harrison eyed the dress he was carrying. "I should have known."

I swallowed, ignoring the jab. I'd heard rumors about Spencer since high school; that he got arrested a few times. That he never graduated. That he worked construction. I'd never seen him. Not until this moment. "How much do I owe you?"

"Hmmm...well, that's a loaded question. How much do you owe me?" He rubbed his scraggly beard with a hand covered in tattoos. "What's the financial equivalent of a senior year of high school, a diploma, and a clean criminal record?"

I pulled a twenty out of my wallet and said, "I'm not here to rehash ancient history, Spencer. Just give me the dress."

"What? You don't want a little reunion?" He eyed me, looking me over for the first time. "You've only gotten hotter, Heaven. I always thought you were a little skinny, but now?" He made a gross motion, mimicking the outline of my body. "There's a little meat on you to hold onto, if you know what I mean."

There were moments in my life where I felt like I was walking in quicksand. When I was around my father, around Noah in college, around the closed-minded people in the town. Occasionally I ran into someone that knew me back then, that'd heard and believed the rumors, and all I felt was a wave of hopelessness that I would never be enough.

Spencer, despite his greasy hair and pathetic life, knew how to rattle me. He'd always had, and I turned to walk away, leaving my dress and getting the hell out of there.

I bolted through the door, listening to the cackle of his laughter. "You're like this dress, Heaven, old and damaged. You can try to clean it up but you'll always carry a few unremovable stains."

My eyes were blinded with tears so I didn't notice the man coming through the door. "Babe, you okay?" Jackson asked, hands on my shoulders, eyes focused behind me.

"It's no big deal, Jax. I don't want to do this today."

"Jackson Pierce! I had no idea you'd still be slumming after all these years."

"Shut up, Spencer." He threw an arm around me. "I do not have time to kick your ass today."

I tugged him toward the door.

"I guess Heaven's like a case of herpes. Impossible to get rid of."

And that was the final straw. Not just for Jackson, but for me. I pushed Jackson's arm off my shoulder and rushed toward the counter, flinging myself over it in a quick move.

"Heaven!" Jackson called, scrambling after me. But it was too late. Spencer backed away, shocked at my resolve, and I hauled out and punched him in the face. He stumbled backwards, dark evil glinting in his eye.

"Fuck you, Spencer. Don't you dare blame me for your shitty, fucked-up life. For the fact you work in this dead-end job and live a miserable life. You're the one with hate in your heart. Not me. I'm not that girl I used to be. I own my mistakes, my regrets, and my choices. You're just pathetic."

"If I'm that pathetic, then you'll know I've got no qualms about hitting a girl. Especially one as trashy as you."

He lunged at me and I held my ground, fists balled and ready, but Spencer never made it to me. Jackson lunged between us, crashing into him with a two-hundred-pound weight made of muscle and rage.

He grappled with his arms for a minute before using his considerable size and strength to flip him on his stomach, pinning his body and face against the dirty floor. I rushed over and stood behind him, smirking at Spencer's position.

"What do you want me to do with him?" Jackson asked, jamming a knee in his back.

"Nothing," I said, meaning it. "He's not worth it."

Jackson nodded but leaned down and said, "You're lucky she's here or I would tear you apart. Got it?"

"Fuck you."

I shook my head. Spencer would never learn, but that was why his life sucked so much.

"Come on," I said, tugging on Jax's shoulder. He was breathing heavy, furious and boiling with rage. We weren't kids anymore. If Jackson really hurt him, then there could be trouble. Real trouble none of us needed.

He stood and brushed off his hands before taking mine in his. At the counter, he opened the door to the side and grabbed my dress. I tossed the money on the counter. I stopped before I walked out the door, watching Spencer slowly get off the ground. There was a bruise forming on his cheek.

"Maybe it's time for you to figure out what's wrong with you, Spencer," I said. "Why you're so angry all the time and why you're obsessed with the things you can't have."

I didn't wait for a response. He didn't deserve my attention—not anymore.

Jackson sat in the driver's seat, hands squeezing the wheel.

He peeled out of the parking lot the second I shut the door and drove silently before pulling over into a gas station parking lot. He got out of the car and went inside, coming back a few minutes later with a plastic bag full of ice.

Back in the car he took my hand, the swollen one, and inspected my fingers before pressing the ice against it.

"Are you okay?"

"Yes," I said in a shaky voice. The adrenaline evaporated somewhere in the last five miles. "I don't know why he rattles me so much.

It's like he knows the truth about me instinctively. He always has. It's like he knows I'm a fraud—weak. That beneath the surface I'm still that girl from back then."

Jackson touched my chin. "You're not a fraud and you're certainly not weak. Not physically or emotionally. You've earned your success and if there's one thing I know for sure, it's that you're not the same girl as back then. You're a woman now; smart, strong, and breathtakingly beautiful."

I looked away from his eyes, they were too intense, too meaningful, and I knew the answer to my question I'd asked before I got out of the car. What did Jackson want?

Me.

I knew that and after that scene in the cleaners' and the words he just spoke, that if it were just about me and him--just the two of us--I would be hard-pressed to answer any differently.

89

Heaven

A few days later I fidgeted with the skirt of my dress, smoothing the slick surface, catching glimpses of myself in the theater windows. I was waiting for my date, who'd promised to meet me here, and now I stood, dressed like a wannabe Hollywood starlet, feeling wave after wave of anxiety roll over me.

I tried to accept that I deserved to be here, on this side of the cameras and bright lights. As a participant, strolling down the red carpet that'd been rolled from the street to the front door. That I was part of the reason for the excitement that tinged in the air, but it was hard. I'd spent so long trying to stay out of the public eye, to keep a low profile and just work, never realizing days like this would be part of it.

My phone buzzed.

Five minutes. Sorry. Traffic sucks!

If Hayden was surprised that I asked him here tonight, he didn't express it verbally. Probably because I told him that he was the only one that knew how to handle an event like this. That his fans would be happy to get a glimpse of his healed face and steadier walk.

Jackson watched me closely when I invited him, blue eyes curious. Did he question my motives? Jackson may be pretty, but he wasn't stupid. I guess the big question was, did he tell the guys what had happened between us?

I didn't ask.

Because in the end, I'd decided not to use this night as part of my wish for closure. This night was about me and my present. My future. My work. And I needed someone savvy on my side to help me get through it.

The premiere was being held at the Fox, a historic theater with a huge entry and elaborately detailed architecture. Photographers, fans, and guests all mingled in the large hallway. Even with our newfound fame as a tiny piece of Hollywood, an event like this was rare for Allendale. The producers of Creature Feature felt like they wanted to give back to the town that'd supported them so thoroughly. The result was that they went all out, turning this into a major event.

Me and big events never went over well, so I tried to blend in while not looking too awkward, something I surely didn't accomplish. Again, I fussed with my skirt, relieved when a commotion by the street caught everyone's attention. I craned my neck and saw a long black limousine idling at the curb. Security pushed back the photographers and press, and through a small gap I caught a glimpse of familiar black and purple hair followed by a breathtakingly handsome man with a freshly shorn cut.

RJ and Lea.

Together.

Making an entrance.

This was big. Really big.

I pushed up on my toes hoping to get a better glimpse, my heart beating for them with every click of the camera. I knew that feeling— the oppressive sense of being watched. Observed. Security swept them down the aisle and Lea caught my eye, stopping RJ in his tracks.

"Heaven!" she shouted. RJ turned and spoke with a fan, taking the photograph out of her hands and signing it.

I waved just as RJ looked my way. His smile widened, genuine. He waved me forward. I shook my head, throat clogged with panic. I should have taken a pill. Something to quell my nerves. RJ spoke with his assistant and the roped-off area was opened and suddenly I was ushered forward. I stopped short, toes on the edge.

"What are you doing over there?" Lea asked. "We're supposed to come down the carpet."

"I'm waiting on…" I searched for the term. Definitely not boyfriend. Friend? Ex-lover? But I didn't need it. Hayden appeared down the carpet, looking every bit as handsome as RJ and his fellow actors. No one stopped him, because in that tuxedo, with his hair slicked back and the flirty smile on his lips, he looked like he belonged on that red carpet as much as anyone else.

A ripple of recognition rolled through the crowd. Hayden Pierce. Atlanta United's star player was here. Healthy-looking despite a small limp. He didn't bring his crutches. RJ smiled broadly, proud.

"You invited Hayden?" Lea asked. She'd still never met him and she took in his every movement, every feature.

Hayden's eyes were focused on me, sweeping over my dress, my hair, settling on my face. "I did."

"Hey, man," RJ said, shaking his hand and introducing himself. Security used the distraction as a chance to shuffle me on the carpet, pushing me into the spotlight. Fans and the press started shouting, wanting Lea's name. Wanting RJ's attention. Asking Hayden a million questions. Cameras flashed and I blinked, feeling the panic rise. It wasn't the same. It wasn't, but…

A warm hand clenched against my waist. I looked up and noticed him squint into the flashing lights.

"Sorry I was late," he said, applying the slightest bit of pressure. "I haven't worn nice shoes in a month and with my ankle still swollen, I had to borrow Oliver's."

"It's fine. You look great."

"Looks like I got here just in time for the big appearance."

"I figured we could skip out on all this," I said, wondering if he could hear me over the roar of fans, particularly the high-pitched squeal of teenaged girls. RJ was immensely popular. Lea shined next to him. Comfortable, like they were meant to be like this next to one another.

Hayden grinned, wide and breathtaking, although I noticed the small line between his eyes. "You don't get to skip out on things like this, Heaven, but don't worry, this isn't my first time."

"Are you okay?"

"Just a headache—they come and go." He nudged me. "Smile and wave."

I followed his lead and all the nerves, the worry, it evaporated the instant Hayden was at my side. In an instant we were back as a force, handling the obstacles ahead of us. But these weren't the same, awful ones as before. No, these were promising and bright and I soaked them in like the sun.

90

Heaven

The afterparty was held on the rooftop of a local hotel. Twinkly lights and lanterns were strung in the air while a DJ played loud music—most from the soundtrack of the show, which spotlighted rising artists. Hayden stuck by my side all night, allowing me a chance to let him enter my world for a moment. He met my co-workers, the actors on the show, my bosses. They were all instantly intrigued by my relationship with Hayden Pierce. Why shouldn't they be? He was famous, more so than some of the actors on the show. How did this costume and makeup director meet him?

I'd started the night off in the corner, pushing panic attacks aside. I finished it in the middle of the action; suddenly a person of interest.

Now, with the clock approaching midnight and enough time passed for me to enjoy myself, I leaned against the edge of the rooftop, sipping my drink. Hayden sat next to me, taking the weight off his foot.

"You okay?" I asked, knowing it'd been a long night.

"Fine," he said. "What about you? I've never seen you like this."

"Like what?"

He shrugged. "Carefree. Happy."

I frowned. "I've definitely been happy before, H."

He crossed his arms over his chest and gave me a sly look. "Not like this. It's different."

"Care to explain?"

"You seem content...the anxiety and cloud that hovered over you for so long has lifted. You're confident. Secure." His eyes skimmed over me, head-to-toe. "You've grown up, Heaven Reeves, and it suits you."

My cheeks heated and I averted my eyes, watching my co-workers and friends still celebrating. "I don't always feel grown up. I almost had a panic attack before you showed up tonight."

"But you didn't." His eyebrow raised and god, he was so handsome.

"No," I acknowledged, "I didn't."

"Do you think this would have happened for you if we'd stayed together?"

"I don't know," I answered truthfully. "Not being in a relationship allowed me to focus on my career. While my personal life was falling apart, the timing was perfect for my job. The governor instituted the tax breaks and show after show started picking Allendale for their shoots. Makeup artists specializing in FX wasn't a common skill." I glanced at him. "What about you? Do you think you would have made it to Atlanta United?"

He leaned back on his hands. "I may have made it to the team but everything else? I don't think I would have had the endorsements or sponsor deals."

"Why not?"

"Exposure and celebrity is a game of politics. It's competitive and ruthless at times."

I frowned. "That doesn't sound like you."

"It's not but I wanted the position, I worked hard for it and the rest was a sacrifice I was willing to make."

"What kind of sacrifices?"

"The tabloids, being seen out with Sabine. Showing up at events like this—" I opened my mouth to speak but he held up his hand. "Not this one. I wanted to be here, but there were a million others I didn't."

I believed him.

"We all learned the lesson a long time age about what it was like to be in the public eye. This position with Atlanta United is a million times that. People say a ton of nasty things about me on Twitter and the sports blogs. They discuss me on the radio, on TV at night, and if Sabine and I go somewhere public, the cameras follow."

He looked over the edge of the building where a crowd of paparazzi waited below.

Something ebbed between us; a feeling, maybe a memory. It felt nice to be here with him just as a friend. He had a girlfriend and sure, that hurt, but it also took anything else off the table. Hayden was incredibly loyal and even though I knew this was nothing more than two friends together, he would feel the consequences from the night.

"How's Sabine going to feel when these pictures splash all over the internet."

He smiled but it wasn't happily. "I'm sure they're already up and I'm sure that's why I haven't checked my phone."

"Will she be angry?"

"Honestly, I'm not sure. This is a bit of uncharted territory for us." He exhaled, hands gripping the ledge. "What Sabine and I have..."

"You don't have to explain. I'm just glad you have someone."

I thought the words came out genuine. I hoped and he simply gave me a thankful nod, but his gray eyes lingered on my face and I felt that raw, masculine intensity Hayden had always possessed.

"Heaven!" Lea cried from across the rooftop, waving her camera. RJ hung by her side. "Come get in this photo!"

I glanced at Hayden. He lifted his chin. "Go. Celebrate. You deserve it."

I pushed away from the ledge and started over, but stopped before I got too far. I held out my hand. "Come with me?"

His eyebrow raised and I nodded. I wanted him to enjoy this with me. Share it with me. Hayden hobbled over, wincing at the pain in his side, but he slipped his arm around my waist and offered to hold the camera with his long arm.

"Thank you," I said, between shots. "For opening up like that and sharing a little bit of your life with me."

He smiled, a genuine one I hadn't seen in a long time. "For you? Anything."

91

———

The answer to Heaven's question about Sabine came in fast, furious texts the next morning. The photos of me walking the red carpet were one thing. I'd told her and Bryant about the event, and although she didn't like the fact I went with Heaven, she accepted that the world needed to see I was healing and healthy. Bryant, on the other hand, was thrilled that I would be seen at such a spectacle and immediately put out a press release that washed over my invitation as Heaven's guest.

No, the premiere was considered a success for my image. It was the after party photos that caused a problem. The press wasn't allowed on the rooftop but guests had cameras and posted on their individual accounts. A few of the actors, like RJ, have rabid followings on social media, scouring the internet for any sighting, which meant photos of me on that rooftop with Heaven went viral pretty quickly, particularly the ones of me and Heaven taking quietly. The selfies where everyone looked at the camera except me. No. I wasn't looking at the camera. I was looking at her.

Always her.

I'd just finished showering at the gym when my phone buzzed for the tenth time and I knew there was no way to avoid it any longer. The locker room was empty.

"Hey, Sabine."

"Finally, you answer."

"Sorry, I had my morning workout and PT. I just got a break." I didn't even try to say that too convincingly. She knew better. She'd set up the schedule. "I'm guessing you've seen the photos."

"I did see them. All of them. You guys made quite the splash last night."

"I think it was more about the success of the premiere than anything else." I put the phone on speaker while I tugged my shorts on and pulled a shirt over my head. In the mirror my exhaustion was evident. I hadn't been able to shake the headache from the camera flashes the night before.

"You're right. People love that show, which makes the fans even more rabid and any little piece of dirt travels like an STD at a Hollywood party." I heard the annoyance in her voice. "Don't disregard how eager your fans have been for any little piece of news about you."

"I know." I sat on the bench. "I'm sorry if anything looked inappropriate. I assure you that we were just there as friends. Nothing happened."

Sabine sighed. "Hayden, I told you in the beginning I wouldn't play second to anyone else. You're not the first athlete I've dated and I won't allow it to look like I'm being used in any way."

Sabine dated an outfielder for the Braves and a second-string quarterback for the Falcons before I moved to the city. I ran my hand through my hair. "It doesn't look like that. Anyone at that party can tell you we were completely platonic the whole time."

"It doesn't matter what people say, Hayden. It matters what they see." Frustration built in her tone. "We made agreements up front about this and it was a two-way street. I've held up to my part of this deal. You better hold up to yours."

"I will."

"Don't make me look stupid."

I stared at my phone. "I won't. I promise."

"Now that you're injured, your reputation and endorsements rely on more than your athletic ability. If people start digging around in your past and find out about the relationship you had with Heaven, the one you all had with her? It's career suicide."

"No one will know. You're blowing this out of proportion," I said, feeling sick to my stomach.

"I hope you're right," she said. "Because I'm not going to be collateral damage when it blows up."

Sabine hung up and I tossed the phone on the bench next to me. I ran my hands through my hair while a million thoughts ran through my mind. Would people dig into my past with Heaven? Would they find out and expose our unconventional relationship to the world? Did I care? I thought maybe I did but after last night, I wasn't sure. I also knew I could handle the scrutiny, but Heaven? She didn't deserve it. She'd been so nervous just taking her place on the red carpet. A place she earned. Once she relaxed, she'd been so fucking happy the night before. So confident. She'd found her place in the world and the last thing I needed to do was screw it up.

92

Heaven

Since the show was on hiatus, I had more time to be helpful with Hayden's recovery. Two days after the party I drove over to the gym in search of Oliver or Jackson to figure out what needed to be done. Chauffer? Gym partner? The premiere had gone so well that I wanted to spend more time with him.

Preferably without cameras.

I made my way up the staircase toward the guys' office when Jackson stepped into view. I stopped short, thrown off at seeing him even though I'd expected to run into him. I never got used to his handsome face. Never.

"Hi," he said, cramming his hands into his pockets. He looked good of course, V-neck sweater that clung to his muscular arms and tapered around his hips. That lock of curly blond hair hung in his eyes, desperate for me to push it aside. I kept my distance and nodded in greeting.

"Sounds like you had fun with Hayden the other night."

"Yeah, we did."

"He said your work is fantastic and that you should be proud."

The compliment from Hayden and hearing it from Jackson meant more to me than I expected. "I'm not used to saying so, but yeah, I am proud. The series is good. I've got a great team."

He clutched the metal railing. The clank of weights hitting one another echoed up the stairwell. The stairwell seemed to shrink around us. I couldn't escape the scent of his detergent. The heat from his body.

"Did you tell Oliver or Hayden about Spencer?" I asked. We hadn't spoken since that day.

He shook his head. "I decided you punching him in the face was enough of a beatdown for the time being."

"Good idea."

"I thought so."

"Have you thought any more about my question from the other day?" I asked. "About what you want?"

My question surprised him and this time he was knocked off guard. It felt good to have the upper hand for once.

When he recovered he smiled slowly, revealing the dimple in his cheek, and I knew a smirk was only a breath away. He still hadn't replied, and I knew very well what his hesitation meant.

"I don't think I've ever wavered on what I wanted," he finally admitted.

"So maybe we're not finished."

We'd been tiptoeing around the truth for so long, but it was time to clear the air. "No, I don't think so."

He took a step down and I took one up and his hand reached for me, brushing strands of hair over my ear.

"This is dangerous," I declared.

"For who?" His lips were red. Wet.

"For me. You. All of us."

"Have you broached this with the others? Did something happen with Hayden the other night?"

"No!" I said too harshly. "No. He has Sabine. Which," I admit, "makes it easier in some ways."

"Oliver?"

I shook my head. There hadn't been an opportunity.

"Anderson?"

I gave him a look. He smiled. Anderson was a case of his own.

"So just us."

"Just us," I responded. My heart raced in my chest. I thought about him naked. I thought about his mouth. His eyes flicked from my chest to my lips, over and over, and I knew he couldn't stop himself either.

A crash followed by a shout bounced up the hallway. Jackson's eyes shifted, looking past me, listening to the voices.

"Go," I told him. "Take care of business."

"And us?"

I swallowed. "We'll finish this later."

"Finish."

I nodded, feeling muddled by hormones and lust. We were using the word 'finish', but we both knew that most likely this was nothing more than the start of something new, something different.

93

Lea had the bright idea to host a game night. Already she and RJ were into "coupley" ideas, but what with still wanting their privacy intact, most were on the down-low, out of the public eye. Which was great, she told me, because who didn't want alone time with their new boyfriend? So anyway, would I come to her game night? And bring the guys.

"You want me to bring the guys?" I asked, suspiciously.

"Well the three that are here. RJ really likes them. He thinks Jackson and Oliver are incredibly smart with their gym. I think he's bummed he can't be an investor."

"And Hayden?"

"Oh," she replied with a laugh. "RJ is completely star-struck by Hayden. He wants him to come so he can bask in his athletic prowess."

I sighed. "Fine. I'll invite them but be forewarned, they're all extremely competitive. Like obnoxiously so."

She smiled happily and gave me a thumbs up. "Gotcha."

That was how we ended up sitting around a large leather ottoman in RJ Malone's studio apartment playing a crazy card game three days later.

RJ and Lea did invite a few other people. Carter, one of the co-stars from work, and his girlfriend-of-the-week Lacy. Lacy wasn't very into the game and thankfully seemed more into Carter than any of the boys.

Not that I had a claim over anyone. Officially. Anymore.

Yeesh.

After a few rounds, everyone was out of the game except RJ, Oliver, Lea, and Hayden. Neither Lacy or Carter seemed to care, they were more into snuggling up on the couch and watching videos on a single phone. Jackson was a little put out that he hadn't made it to the next round, mostly because he's notoriously competitive, especially against Oliver. As the game continued and the remaining players fought bitterly over whose fictional character or situation trumped the other, I decided to take a break.

"Anyone want a drink?" I asked, scrambling from the ground.

"Can you bring me one of those raspberry waters?" Lea asked. She'd been on a fruity water kick lately. I was trying unsuccessfully to ditch soda and coffee. I walked across the room, entering the spacious, wide-open kitchen. RJ's studio was in one of the newer buildings built in Allendale, mostly to support the thriving industry. I suspected a month's rent was the same as my yearly salary. I rummaged through the refrigerator, past the protein drinks and containers of pre-made meals. RJ had a nutritionist and followed a strict diet. It wasn't a surprise. I'd seen him barely clothed at work. His physique was amazing. He definitely put in the time and effort.

The drinks were in a drawer at the bottom and I bent over to get one. Fingers trailed over the skin of my lower back and I jumped, surprised, and came face to face with Jackson.

"When did you get the tattoo?" he asked.

"Oh," I tugged my shirt down, "a few years ago."

"Can I see it?"

I raised an eyebrow. "I'm not sure that's a good idea."

"Why not?" He wore an expression of pure innocence.

I narrowed my eyes. Did he really think he had the right to still touch me like that? Sure, we'd moved to casual flirting but touching? The chill skipping up my spine told me that even if he didn't, I liked the way it felt.

I handed Jackson a drink and took a can to Lea, resting it on the table. The conversation I'd had with Jackson about closure and finality lingered in my mind. He stood near the wide, granite kitchen counter, leaning on his elbows.

"Thor's hammer beats a basket of kittens beats a talking dragon," declared Oliver, speaking gibberish that only made sense in the context of the game.

"Bullshit," Hayden said, tossing down his own cards. "That's a radio-active squirrel—it can take out everything."

"Not the hammer," RJ said, siding with Oliver. Oliver grinned like a maniac and Lea clapped like it was the best match of wits ever, and without another word I slipped out of the room.

Designed with an open and spacious floorplan, it's hard to find privacy, but on the way to the bathroom I'd noticed a long hall behind the kitchen that separated the living area from the bedrooms.

I'd just stepped into the unlit area when I felt those fingers on my back again and a second hand wrapped around my waist. "Five inked stars," Jackson whispered in my ear, "I think we both know what that represents."

From behind, he pressed his body against mine. He was taunting me, I knew it, and it was leading us both down a slippery slope. When I didn't respond he kissed me gently on the neck and said, "That's not the kind of behavior of a woman that wants closure, Heaven."

My heart beat so hard that I was sure he could hear it, but he released me and I spun, craving the contact. I opened my mouth to speak, possibly to beg, but a shadow crossed the end of the hall. Oliver stood in the empty space, watching us.

Guilt flashed over me, but Jackson just walked by him and said, "Did you know Heaven got a tattoo?"

Oliver swallowed and shook his head.

"On her lower back. Five stars in a cluster." He clapped Oliver on the back and left the two of us in the hallway. Alone.

I took a deep breath and walked down the hall. Oliver didn't budge.

"It's not a big deal. Just a whim, you know?"

"Sure. You've always been the kind of girl that does permanent things on a whim."

"Did you forget how we met? I permanently wrecked my reputation on a dare. I don't always make the best decisions."

"True."

"Who won the game?" I asked when finally up close. He doesn't seem angry. Just curious; his eyes searching.

"I did."

"I bet Hayden's pissed."

"He'll get over it."

There was a beat. A pause and tension ebbed between us.

"Well, congratulations," I said, kissing him on the cheek. I moved to pass him but he blocked me with an arm. I looked up, eyebrow raised in question, but I only saw heat reflected back at me and in a swift move, Oliver bent down and pressed his lips to mine, kissing me slow and strong. It was the first time I'd felt his lips in two years, and Jackson already had my engine revved. Like a woman desperate for water I dove right in, kissing him in return.

I was breathless when we pulled apart and his chest heaved similarly.

"I've been wanting to do that for weeks," he confessed, rubbing his lips. "Sorry if that was inappropriate."

"It wasn't."

"No?"

A small curve lifted his lips and I ducked under the arm he used to keep me in the hall. Over my shoulder I replied with a final, "No," and rejoined the others for another round of games.

~

"WE SET A DATE!" Amber's voice conveyed her excitement. I sat on the couch in my apartment. "May 26th."

"That's in a couple weeks!"

"I know. Short notice, but when we started talking about it there wasn't any real reason to wait."

"Putting it on the calendar now." Who was I kidding. There was nothing pressing on my social calendar for the rest of the year. "Have you picked a location?"

"Well, that's what I wanted to talk to you about."

I pulled my knees up. "Oh yeah?"

"When Ginger came to Allendale this last time we did a little sightseeing—more than we had before. I took her down to Oceanside —to the beach."

"Okay." I knew where she was headed. "You want to have the wedding there?"

"Ginger just fell in love with it and, well, you know how beautiful it is." Incredibly beautiful. Especially in late spring like that. "But we both wanted to make sure you were okay with it."

I'd been back to the beach since that night. Many times. With the boys, with Amber. Oceanside held a lot of memories for me, not all of them good. It was near my father's church and the judgmental town I'd been happy to flee. But it was also where I'd survived and where love had truly, fully entered my life.

"I think it's a great idea," I said. "The ocean is a place of rebirth. Perfect for a wedding."

"Are you sure?" she asked, but I heard the relieved hope in her voice. "I want you to be honest."

"I'm sure. I've made peace with that time in my life. Oceanside is beautiful. I'm glad Ginger wants a part of your home to be in the wedding." I picked at the edge of the sofa. "And as long as we're being honest, I have a few things to tell you."

"What kind of things?"

"Things like I slept with Jackson and I kissed Oliver."

"Heaven! When? What? Tell me everything."

So I told her. I explained how I left her party and slept with Jackson, looking for closure, but instead seemed to have tugged on a thread. And that Oliver kissed me suddenly the night before, and that I was both jealous and thankful for Sabine if it kept Hayden happy.

"Does Anderson know any of this?" she asked.

"I hope not, but I haven't heard from him in weeks, so who knows. I'm sure the guys are as scared to broach this with him as I am. He's training hard right now. His qualifiers are coming up, now isn't the time to bother him with any of this."

"Well what does this mean?" she asked. "Are you getting back together? Or is this just a

hook up? Or like you wanted, closure?"

"I don't know."

"Well you have a month to figure it out before the wedding. I don't want any drama. Got it?"

No. Amber and Ginger didn't deserve that. Not on their special day. "No drama. I promise."

"Good. I have no doubt you guys can figure this out. Communicate. That's always been big between you all. Talk to them. All of them," she said, the implication heavy that Anderson needed to be told.

"You're right."

"And one more thing..."

"What's that?"

"Don't be afraid to have a little fun while you're figuring this out. Those boys are worth it."

94

———————

I'd thought long and hard about that kiss two nights ago.

Long and hard.

I'd barely slept either night, tossing and turning, reliving the moment, overanalyzing the way she responded before, during and after. I'd lied when I said I'd been wanting to do that for weeks. I'd wanted to do it for *years*. I wanted to do it again.

I hadn't been jealous when Jackson revealed they'd had sex. I was glad. Relieved that the embargo of the past two years had maybe finally been broken. Of all of us, Jackson was the easiest to let down your guard; I understood the appeal. Low pressure. Fun. Re-entering relationships with any of us required a different approach and at first, I was willing to bide my time. Until he said it was about closure and that stopped me cold. Closure?

That created a mass of dread in my stomach that'd I'd been carrying ever since, which was why when I had my chance with her at the game night, I didn't waste it. She liked it. I liked it, and it was time for us to move forward, except now it'd been two days since I'd heard from her—seen her—and once again my life was left to her discretion.

Fuck this, I thought, as the first light of the day sliced through my windows. I pushed back the twisted covers and reached for my gym shorts lying on the nearby chair. I caught a glimpse of myself in the mirror hanging over my dresser. I was no longer the skinny boy that dried Heaven's tears all those years ago. I wasn't the kid that waited for the girl of his dreams to call all the shots—make the decisions.

Hell no. The person reflected back was a man; a business man. Successful. Strong. I took in the muscles I'd developed and honed. In the two years we'd been apart one thing was for certain, I had control over my life and I didn't want to wait for her any longer.

I wanted to know what she thought.

I needed to know how she felt.

I tugged on a shirt and sneakers, then reached for my keys.

I needed to know and I didn't want to wait a minute longer.

95

SINCE BEING ON HIATUS, I'd taken to a morning run. Exercise became part of my life over the past few years, mostly due to my therapist demanding it as part of my long-term treatment for anxiety and depression. At first, I'd resisted it, refusing to believe that physical activity really made a difference. It didn't help that I was a spaz and had zero background with athletics other than mandatory P.E. classes. In college, I'd dragged the guys and Amber to a series of classes and sports, but nothing stuck until Hayden dragged me to the soccer fields one afternoon during his practice and told me to start running laps around the track. At first it was awful, like I was dragging my whole body through sand, but over time it got a little easier and now? I kind of liked it. I wasn't particularly good, but over the years, running switched from a chore to a habit and slowly became part of my daily schedule; vacation or not.

I rolled out of bed and reached for my tank and running tights. I pulled my hair into a ponytail and splashed some water on my face. After wedging my feet into my shoes, I slipped my key into my pocket, walking out the door and instantly tripping over a large, formidable object in the hallway.

"What tha—" I cried, falling forward, but regaining my balance before face-planting. I glanced over my shoulder. "Oliver?"

"Hey," he said, scrambling to his feet. "You okay? I didn't mean for that to happen."

"Yeah, I'm fine. What are you doing here?"

"I thought maybe we could go on a run together," he said. "And then maybe talk."

Oliver wanted to run. And talk. And he'd come over here at the ass-crack of dawn to do so.

"I can't run as fast as you," I said, eyeing his long, muscular legs.

"That's okay. You can probably run farther."

I snorted. "Doubtful."

I turned to head down the stairs, the same ones Jackson and I had flirted on weeks before. I didn't tell Oliver to follow, but he did, stepping past me quickly to hold the door for me.

"How'd you get past security?" I asked.

"I waited around until someone came in this morning. I'm not going to judge but I think I busted your neighbor on the third floor on the last leg of her walk of shame."

I laughed. "Well, we've all been there, right?"

"I don't recall anything we ever did as shameful."

I shook my head. "Then you must have a selective memory." I pointed to the right. "I usually head down this way and enter the park. There's a good five-mile loop."

"Five?" His eyebrows raised up his forehead. "Okay."

Oliver let me set the pace but his presence was undeniable, and it gave me the slightest challenge that was often missing in my runs. We wound through the running trail, a smooth flat surface that divided the old homes and newer construction and tiny coffee houses and eclectic bars. It was early and not many people were out, so over the quiet and chirping birds we fell into a rhythm, breath mingling, sweat pouring. Around mile four, Oliver slowed until he fell off completely and I turned to find him, bent over. I jogged back slowly.

"Dude," he said, between heavy pants, "you're killing me."

I rolled my eyes. "Stop. I've never seen you in such good shape."

He'd stripped off his drenched shirt when we entered mile two, tucking it into the back of his shorts. I made an effort not to ogle him, although it wasn't easy. His broad chest and tapered waist looked like something off movie sets I'd been hired to work on. Like the superheroes he trained. I understood why they trusted his expertise. He had the receipts to prove his worth.

"Weight lifting and body strength, yeah, but cardio? I've cut way back on my carbs and it leaves me a little winded."

I stopped before him, shaking out my legs that also felt the strain of the run. His chest heaved with exertion and a small part of me loved seeing him like this—trying to keep up with me.

"What are you smiling about?" he asked.

"I've never been the healthier one."

His eyes skimmed down my bare arms; free from fresh wounds, scars faded. "I'm proud of you," he said.

That was the second time one of my guys had paid that compliment lately. I blushed and looked to the ground before saying, "I'm proud of you, too. Your business. It's amazing." My eyes flicked to his chest. "And I can tell you work hard to get in this kind of shape. I'm impressed."

"I had to give up pancakes," he said, woefully.

"Aw. I know that hurt."

"So bad." His eyes lit with humor. "Hey," he said suddenly, "I know you have a strict no-social media policy, but we do have accounts for the gym. Can I take a photo of us to use on there? I try to put up healthy, active things."

I wrinkled my nose. "I don't know. Me and the internet don't mix."

"You can have final approval." He gave me a pleading look. "Everyone's been wanting to know who the fifth in A5 Gym is, anyway. Now's your chance for a big reveal."

"No one has been asking that," I said, shaking my head. But he gave me a pouty face that he knew I couldn't resist, and I finally relented.

"Thank you!" He smiled wide, the pout vanishing and his phone appearing in his hand. "Selfie?"

"Oh, I'm not going to be in this photo alone."

"Gotcha." We bunched together and his left arm slipped around my waist. He held the camera out and snapped a few photos. He looked at them and grinned. "Thank you. Again."

"You're welcome. But if this goes viral or something, please let me know, okay?"

"It's not going viral. It's basically an ad for A5. 'Hot girl running' is how I should tag it."

"Stop." I reached for the camera but he slid it into his pocket.

"I never thought we'd be like this, all grown up and functional." I rubbed my neck. "I've been thinking about it lately. Do you think we could have done that together? You know, like the five of us, together-together?"

If the question bothered him, he doesn't show it. He just said, "We'll never know, right?"

"No, I guess not."

"I need to head back but before we go, I need you to do two things for me."

"What's that?"

"Hayden is ready to get out like this—take a few easy runs. Can you do that with him?"

"Yep." I brushed my hair out of my eyes. "And the other thing?"

He closed the distance between us and swiftly pulled me to him. Our bodies were sweaty, gross, but my heart hammered being so close to him. He stared at my lips and I watched him stare at my lips, licking the bottom one in anticipation. "You and me? As far as I'm concerned, we're not finished. I need you to understand that. I'm not playing games, I'm telling you how it is for me."

I struggled to speak. "Okay."

"So if you want this to be over, tell me. Tell me now and I'll walk away. But if there's a chance, the slightest chance, I'm in."

His eyes pinned me with such an intensity, such a strength—I'd never seen Oliver like this. He'd grown stronger, not just in body but conviction. I wanted to know more. I needed to. He wasn't the same person I'd walked away from two years ago. Neither was I. Maybe I needed to give these people a chance.

"Okay."

"Okay, what?"

"There's a slight chance that I'm not done with you either."

His smile was slow and wide, like the sun climbing in the eastern sky. I thought maybe I'd burn from the intensity, but he moved his hands to my face and brought me in for a kiss. A sweaty, smelly, incredible kiss.

96

THE TEXT TOOK me by surprise. Not because it was 6 a.m. and I was already up and waiting for Hayden at the head of the trail, but because it was from Anderson.

Oliver got you to break your social media ban?

Good morning to you, too, Anderson.

Good morning, Heaven. So...

Yeah, I let him take and post a photo. He said it would be good for business

He's not wrong about that. It got hundreds of likes. And a lot of questions, too.

I hadn't looked. Just because Oliver took and posted the photo didn't mean I had to engage in it. Anderson was being weird. Not just because he was contacting me at the crack of dawn but the simple fact he was engaging me at all. We'd always communicated better this way. Through writing; notes slid across desks. Texts or letters.

People had questions or you have questions?

Busted.

Is this how I get you to contact me? Posting on social media?

499

Well, I did consider maybe the apocalypse was looming...

So what's your issue? The photo, or me in the photo with Oliver?

Confession: It's weird seeing you together like that.

Confession: It's weird for me too, but we've decided to work through some things. Jackson too.

Confession: I'm not sure how I feel about that.

Feel about that or feel about me?

I waited a beat. Then another. He finally replied.

Be careful. With yourself and with them.

A lump formed in my throat.

I will. I promise.

I waited for one more exchange—something else, but it never came. He was gone.

FOR THE SECOND TIME, it was hard for me to believe I was in better physical shape than one of the Allendale Four. Athletics had always been their thing and I'd done nothing more than stand on the sidelines. But with Hayden in recovery and taking tentative steps back into action, I felt like an Olympic gold medalist next to him.

"How's the ankle?" I asked as we took a break from the jog and walked slowly down the path.

"Fine." He flexed and stretched it out.

"Does it hurt?"

"No."

"Swelling?"

"I don't think so."

I looked up at him. "Then why the hesitation? I know you can keep up with me."

"I guess I'm worried I'm going to roll it again. Do something to set back my recovery time."

"When are you supposed to head back to the team?"

"June first."

Right after Amber's wedding.

"So you have another month. That's plenty of time to get your, uh, footing back."

My stupid joke made him smile, even though it wasn't the mega-watt one that made my knees shake. I was okay with that, though, Hayden had become my safe place. He was taken and that meant I didn't have to figure out how to navigate my relationship with him the way I had to with Oliver and Jackson.

"It'll be fine," he said, wiping his forehead with the hem of his shirt, giving me a peek at his spectacular stomach. He raised his eyebrows and we started to jog down the path again.

"What does Sabine think?" I asked.

"She thinks I need to go back to Atlanta and train there."

"Is she right?"

He shrugged, pumping his arms as he ran. "Like everything else, I'm not sure what's best anymore. Being back here has been nice, but I still have my passion for the game and I can't waste my opportuni-ties—well, as long as I have them."

We entered a tunnel and I stopped him by grabbing his arm. It was shady under there. Cool but also dark enough I felt like I could talk to him. "What's going on with you? You've always been confident and sure. I know this injury spooked you but you're doing great. Stop second guessing yourself."

"Things are complicated, Heaven. I've got so much riding on the next few weeks. Even if I walk back on the field my position may be gone. Sabine..."

I frowned. "Are things bad with her?"

"She didn't like the photos of me and you at the premiere."

"I can understand that."

"I can, too, but..."

"But what?"

His eyes blazed even in the dark. "All of this was easier when I was across the country. Travelling. Busy. But sitting around with too much time on my hands. Being back here—it's hard." He rested his hands on his hips. "I didn't know how hard it would be."

I laughed darkly. "Trust me, I know. Allendale is small and stifling at times. I mean, I'm happy here, but sometimes I want to pull my hair out."

"Allendale isn't the problem, Heaven." His voice was husky. I'd heard it before.

"Oh."

"I know about you and Jackson," he said. I wasn't exactly surprised. The guys never kept secrets and I didn't expect them to. "I also saw you and Oliver coming out of the back hall at RJ's alone, then a few days later the picture of you two on the A5 Instagram page."

"So? What's the big deal? We're working through some stuff. Is that wrong?"

"I just…I--we made a decision, and it feels like the three of you are going back on it."

"There were some unresolved feelings, Hayden. I think it's fair for us to explore them.

He exhaled, jaw tight, and rubbed his hands in his hair. "Look, I can do this on my own. Jogging isn't going to kill me and I don't really need a babysitter."

"I'm not babysitting you."

"We don't need to do this anymore, okay?" His gray eyes turned cold, distant.

"Fine. If that's how you want it."

"It is."

"Great." I couldn't pretend his words didn't hurt. But I understood. Too much. But before I walked off I had something else to say. "Relationships take work, Hayden. All of them. Ours. Yours. The Allendale Five. If we don't nurture them they'll die and that almost happened to us. But then you got hurt and it brought us back together and god, we're a total fucking mess. But I've come to realize I'm not ready to let this relationship wither, not completely, and if that means I have to let you go to save just a little piece of this, I will."

I spun on my heel and took off, actually running away this time. I didn't care because I wasn't just running from someone, I was running to someone. Someone that had made it clear what he wanted. Someone I knew was waiting for me.

97

HEAVEN

I DIDN'T HESITATE when I got to his house, knocking loudly on the door. The place was massive—his parents' dream home—and Oliver rambled around in it, basically alone.

It was still early and I knew Jackson often took the morning shift at the gym, training a few of the guys before work. Oliver opened the door in his pajama bottoms and a baseball shirt from Allendale High.

"Heaven?" He looked over my shoulder. "Is everything okay? Where's Hayden?"

Not answering, I took the step up. We weren't even because he was so much taller, but I closed the gap enough that when I clenched his shirt around my fingers and tugged him down, our faces met.

"I'm in," I told him before crashing my mouth to his. He didn't move at first, shocked at my forwardness. I'd be embarrassed, but I refused. Slowly he responded, hands moving to my waist, pushing me against the door frame. His mouth moved against mine. I felt the sweep of his tongue, the hum in the back of his throat, the bulge in his pants.

He pulled back an inch but I didn't allow the distance. No talking. No rationalizing. No thinking. He seemed to get it, pulling me away from the door and slamming it shut. He nudged me backwards and my back hit the granite countertop. I pushed at his shirt but he held down my hands.

"Not here."

"No?"

We'd never had the luxury of making out in a large empty house. My parents, his dorm room, crowded apartments.

He lifted me, carrying me in his strong arms while continuing to kiss my mouth, my chest, and neck.

"You taste like salt."

"Sorry."

"I like it," he said, licking my neck. "You were running?" His eyebrow cocked. He continued to walk, winding past a dining room table and down a long hall. "With Hayden?"

I nodded and pushed my fingers through his hair. I liked being the same height. "I yelled at him."

"You did?"

"He deserved it."

I nibbled under his chin. He hadn't shaved and the hair scraped against my jaw. Oliver dropped me in the hallway, kissing down my neck and shoulders. He pushed at my tank, moving it over my breasts, my shoulders and head.

I did the same to him, wanting to see him—feel him. His new body that was bigger, stronger. We grappled with one another—different for me and Oliver. We'd always been sweet and sex had been more lovemaking than raw.

This?

This was raw.

With his shirt removed, I ran a hand down his chest, feeling the swell of his muscles, the hard, lean mass, down to the thicker patch of hair under his belly button. Sharp indentions marked his hips and there was never any mistaking Oliver's cock. Big and thick; eager under the cotton of his pants.

"You've been working hard," I said, fingering the hair.

He inhaled sharply. "I needed something to do while missing you."

His words jarred me, hitting me straight in the heart. I didn't want to wait anymore. Why should we? Our hearts knew one another. Our souls merged. And the new differences? I wanted to try them out, too.

"Show me."

"Show you what?" he said, running a finger between my breasts.

"How much you missed me."

That command was all it took, his jaw clenched and his eyes grew dark—full of intent. He pulled me into the nearest room, a master bedroom complete with a massive bed piled high with luxurious blankets and pillows. He'd brought me here on purpose. I knew it. To claim me in his adult bed. We didn't need stolen kisses in the hallway or to be quiet behind dorm room doors.

Here we could be whoever we wanted to be. The people we are now, not then.

We finished undressing, his eyes glued to my body and mine to his. Before Jackson it'd been a long time since I had sex, and I couldn't help but feel the flutters in my belly every time I looked at the size of Oliver's cock. Lord.

He noticed and realization slowly fell over his features. He touched my cheek.

"I'll take it slow. Ease in."

"No," I said, reaching between his legs, feeling the hard length. "Don't."

His grin was wicked and he picked me up, laying me on the bed. His mouth traveled up my body, nipping at my skin, wetting it with his tongue. My stomach twisted—craved—hips rising off the mattress, seeking more. His fingers found me first, then his mouth. He kept moving, taking his time with my breasts, dragging his cock along my belly. Eye-to-eye he pushed my arms overhead, cinching my wrists with his hand. Butterflies sprang, nervous at his dominance.

"Open for me, babe," he told me, nudging at my knees. They fell open and I felt him between my legs; hard, ready, hot.

"Fuck me, Ollie."

In one swoop he did, pushing past my barriers, hands out of reach. He thrust inside, kissing my lips at the same time. He felt good, so good, and I cried breathy and reckless into his mouth with every push. My knees bent, wanting to take him all the way in. Our chests met, sparking desire.

It didn't take much, both of us already tiptoeing along the edge of it being too long, loving each other too much and the sheer want that flowed between us. Biting my lip, I shattered, brain fuzzy, body alive. When he followed, there was no holding back. Oliver gave up everything. His body. His heart.

I felt it. I knew it.

Sweaty and overheated, we curled up in one another, the fancy sheets wet underneath us.

"That," he said, pulling back an inch to give me a quick kiss, "was definitely unexpected. Fucking amazing, but truly unexpected."

"Something in me snapped. I didn't want to wait any longer."

He burrowed his face in my neck. "Thank god."

"Do you have to go to work?" I asked him, running my fingers through that alluring patch of hair on his lower belly. He flinched. Every time he flinched, and I loved it.

He waved a hand. "Jackson can take care of it."

"What do you think he'll say when he finds out about this?"

"He'll probably weep tears of relief. He's been waiting for us to figure it out and wanting you two to figure yourselves out."

I snuggled in close, feeling drowsy. Safe. "I want to do that, too."

He kissed my forehead. "You will. We will."

Yeah, I thought, drifting off to sleep, my body relaxed. We will.

OLIVER WAS sound asleep when I woke up. The clock said it was late morning and my stomach rumbled, confirming the time. Between my early morning run and my activities with Oliver, I'd exerted my share of calories. I needed food and he probably did too. I tugged on the baseball shirt and my panties and went to the kitchen to fix breakfast.

The sound of pots and pans along with the mouthwatering scent of bacon hit me before I made it halfway down the hall. My stomach growled right when I noticed the mop of blond curls and his body next. Shit, I thought, spinning on my heel.

"Heaven?"

Jackson's eyes zeroed in on what I was wearing, or maybe what I wasn't wearing. Pants in particular. Or a bra.

"Hey."

He placed the pan on the stove. "I, uh, I didn't know you were here."

"Yeah, I got here a while ago."

"I gather that." He cracked two eggs into the pan and glanced at me. "You want an omelet?"

I nodded. "Sure?"

I watched him cook, moving quickly around the kitchen, juggling the stove and ingredients he'd set on the counter. I spotted a container of cheese, an avocado, spinach.

"Is this weird?"

He shook sat in the pan. "To see you walk in here half dressed?"

I tugged at the hem of the shirt. "Yeah. I guess."

"A little weird, I guess, if seeing the woman of your dreams walk in the kitchen with no pants is weird."

"I'm sorry, Jax. It just kind of happened and I know we were working on our stuff but then Hayden pissed me off so I came over here and..." He turned to face me, a wicked curve on his lips. "What?"

"You got mad at Hayden and came over here and fucked Oliver?"

"Yeah, I guess so."

He broke into a wide, brilliant, gleeful grin. "God, I love it."

"You do?"

"Hayden will be furious—at himself, mind you—" he made this point with his spatula, "when he finds out he sent you straight into Oliver's arms. Classic."

I frowned. "Seriously, you're being competitive about this?"

"Hayden's being an idiot lately. He's feeling sorry for himself and don't get me started on this Sabine thing." Again, he pointed at me with the utensil. "Look what he missed out on. You, half naked, in the kitchen. His loss."

I sighed. "You guys are ridiculous."

He fussed with the omelet, turning down the heat on the stove, tossing in the cheese. I got lost in his movements, the way his fingers deftly used the knife, the confidence in everything he did. He cut the avocado into thin slices and said, "So how was it?"

I looked up from his hands. "How was what?"

"Sleeping with Oliver."

Warmth rushed up my body. "Good, actually."

"And this was for closure?" The question came out softly and that time he didn't sound quite so sure of himself.

"No, it wasn't."

His blue eyes met mine. "No?"

"No. Between you and him and," I looked at the counter top, "everything else. I don't think closure is really what I'm looking for."

I heard the scrape of the pan and felt his presence before I could blink.

"You're not looking for closure?"

I shook my head and his fingers grazed my hip.

"Thank fucking god," he said in a rush.

"You want more too?" I asked. I needed to know. I needed to clarify so we were on the same page. Me, him, and Oliver, at least.

"So much more." He kissed my forehead, my nose, and then lips. I linked my arms around his neck, tugging at the hair that curled at his nape. He tasted like coffee and smelled like soap. My desire, content a few moments ago, reared again, telling me I had room for more.

Jackson's fingers pushed at the hem of my T-shirt, slipping under the edge of my panties. He pushed me against the counter, my foot finding leverage on a drawer pull.

I lost myself in him; his touch, his mouth, his body. He moved his fingers so they rubbed between my legs, grazing over sensitive spots, igniting sparks of desire across my body.

Jackson used those fingers I'd just admired for their dexterity on me; stroking, swirling, caressing. My belly seized under the activity, my breath came out quick.

I was so lost that I didn't hear the footsteps in the hallway. Or sense Oliver's presence until he was all the way in the room.

Jackson looked up first, swallowed, and said, "Hey man."

I glanced over my shoulder, not knowing how he would respond. We'd always kept our physical relationships separate—discreet to an extent. It just seemed right. Sure, there had been mishaps, but the person that walked in generally walked back out. And there was an unspoken rule about hooking up right after one another. It wasn't a rule I made—it seemed more like an understanding between the guys. Something territorial.

But now Jackson held me, fingers touching my most intimate places, rubbing tiny circles. I didn't want him to stop and it sure as hell didn't seem like he wanted to stop. We both looked at Oliver although my jaw was slack, my brain and body warring for control.

My body was certainly going to win if Jackson didn't get his hands out of my pants.

Oliver's eyes drifted down my body, across the hard peaks of my nipples obvious through the thin, worn fabric of his shirt. Down to the where my ass hung out at the bottom. His eyes shifted to where Jackson fondled me, stroked me, and I held my breath, not wanting this moment to end but willing to stop it for the sake of our fragile, new co-existence.

Jackson still didn't stop and he focused his attention back on me fully. I gripped the counter, my elbows weak. I sensed Oliver move, I thought leaving us alone, but a moment later I felt him. He eased behind me, cradling my body against his chest, snaking an arm around my thigh, opening me for Jackson.

I sighed and relaxed into him, feeling stabilized and incredibly, overwhelmingly aroused.

Jackson continued his movements, continued his kisses. Oliver's mouth moved to my neck, sucking gently. His hands traveled to my breasts; cupping, kneading, twisting. I slid my hand over his shoulder and into his hair, linking our bodies together.

The moment was extreme, full-bodied, mind-melting. I writhed against Oliver. I bucked into Jackson's hand. I breathed into his mouth. When my second orgasm of the day came rushing over me I was surrounded by heat, by heartbeats, by warmth. I was surrounded by two men that'd stuck by me, that despite the rocky past two years, loved me, and I didn't hold back. I let Oliver support me. I rode Jackson's hand until I slowed, easing into blissfulness. And when I finished, finally finished, bleary-eyed and breathing heavy, they wrapped their arms around me and we hugged, the three of us, forging a different kind of bond.

98

Heaven

The dress had a dusty rose tint, the bodice shimmery with sequins and beads; the skirt made of netting that grazed my knees. I felt like a ballerina, but Amber looked like a queen. Her dress was ivory, straight and strapless. We'd both tried on our dresses and it was now my turn to stand on the pedestal, twisting to look at the back—it plunged in a deep v, revealing my slim back and the tattoo nestled at the bottom of my spine.

Five stars, inked like a constellation.

I'd gotten it just after the breakup, panicked and consumed with sadness. After years of not wanting to hurt myself I felt the need for something real—pain. Something to remind me I was still alive, even if they were gone. I didn't pick up the blade. I walked into the tattoo parlor and had the artist ink a star for each of us on my back. Even if they were no longer there, I still carried them with me.

Amber smiled when she looked at me, pleased at her choice. She wanted a fairytale-beach wedding and a dress like this for her maid of honor was just one step in that direction.

"God, it's gorgeous, you're gorgeous," she declared.

511

"It's an amazing dress. Are you sure it's not too much? I don't want to upstage you," I joked. I ran my hands down the netting, feeling the rough material. I liked this dress too. A lot.

I noticed a button needed fastening on Amber's dress and stepped down. "Turn around," I told her. As I slipped the button in the hole, I broached the question that had been circling in my brain all day. "Have you ever had a threesome?"

She glanced over her shoulder. "You're asking me that? You're the one that had four boyfriends at the same time."

My cheeks warmed. "I know, but I've told you before, we weren't really into that kind of thing."

I smoothed the back of her dress with my knuckles and she turned around. "Yeah, I have actually. With Ginger and Ben, back when he and I were trying out the open relationship thing. A few times, actually."

"Really?" I was a little shocked. "He was into that?"

"Oh yeah. Two girls at once? He was definitely into it."

"How was it? You know, overall?"

"It was sexy, but I may have been a little spoiled. Both of them were into me and I think I reaped the benefits." She lifted the hem of her dress and walked closer to the mirror. I made eye contact with her reflection. "Is there a reason you're asking?"

Amber wasn't stupid, and she'd expressed her confusion and surprise that we hadn't explored this side of our relationship before. I decided to just admit it. "The other day after Oliver and I had some amazing make-up sex, Jackson and I were kissing in the kitchen. Then Oliver came in and instead of leaving or us stopping or whatever we would have done before, he kind of, uh," I felt my cheeks burning hot, "he joined in."

Amber's jaw dropped. "Wait, wait, there is so much to unpack here. You and Oliver had make-up sex? Like you made up? And Jackson, too? And then right there in the kitchen?"

I nodded. "It was unbelievably hot. I mean, I'd fantasized about it some, but the guys seemed more comfortable keeping things separate."

"They baby you, you know."

"I know." Even though I'd tried desperately to get them to stop, they couldn't help it.

"Do you think you'll do it again? What's the next step? Do Hayden and Anderson know?" The questions came out in a rush.

"Yeah, I think it's likely we'll do it again. I hope so, you know? And I'm not sure on the next step, other than Jackson, Oliver, and I know we're not done with one another." She eyed me, waiting for the final answer. "Hayden knows a little but he's in a relationship with Sabine. Anderson? We've texted a few times, but he's isolated himself so badly now that no one even knows what's up with him."

"Wow," she said. "That is a lot. But you know what's crazy?"

"In my life? God knows, you tell me. What's crazy?"

"You look happier than I've seen you in a long time." She studied me. "You've been doing really well for a long time personally and professionally. Killing it, honestly, but there was something missing—a piece to your puzzle. I figured you'd fill it with someone else, something new, but I don't think that was what was wrong."

"I don't think it was either," I agreed. "I also think that after the other day I realized something else about me and the Allendale boys. We had to evolve and change in our relationship. Just like how we changed from high school to college, we had to evolve into adults. Open ourselves up more. Like you and Ginger getting married, sharing this new kind of bond. Me and the guys...well we needed to do that, too, with one another. The three of us together...it felt so right."

Amber gave me a weird look and then walked across the room, gathering me in her arms. Her hug was breathtakingly tight.

"What's this for?" I asked, when I could get the words out.

She leaned back and smiled. "My little girl is growing up and it's such a delight."

"Shut up," I said, pushing her away.

"Nope."

She did though, and I wrapped my arms around her too, thinking about how she was right; I did know what was wrong and two pieces of the puzzle were back in place.

Now I had to figure out what to do about the other two.

99

Hayden

Three weeks until I head back to training camp. Three weeks to get back in top condition. Three weeks before I can walk away from Allendale, the memories, and the past.

That was my mantra as I lifted weights, over and over I repeated it, willing myself to believe it. Bryant thought I could do it, he was counting on it. Calling me every day to check on my progress, talking about the future back in Atlanta, when I'd be done with Allendale for good.

I'd gone on a run that morning—alone—pushing myself faster than the day before. My ankle held. My ribs were still sore to the touch but I'd learned to work past it, adding reps to my weight training. Jackson was pissed I'd stopped using his program. Sabine was pissed I stopped returning her calls. Heaven...well, Heaven and I hadn't spoken since the day in the park.

The fight in the park felt strange. I'd been angry, but those feelings rolled over me more often lately. Deep down I knew I needed her mad at me, but I also may have gone too far, although distance would

514

be helpful so I could focus on recovery, on my career, and on moving forward. Coming back to Allendale had been a mistake. I blamed my agreement on the haze of drugs while I was in the hospital. The idea of being somewhere familiar—with the guys—seemed good while I was high, but I had no fucking clue it would be a catalyst for bringing Heaven crashing back into our lives.

I dropped the weights on the rack and stripped off the hand wraps, sweaty and wet. My shirt was drenched, sweat poured down my face and I wiped it away. When I looked up, RJ Malone stood in front of me.

"Hey man," I said, offering him a damp handshake.

"You're killing it over here," he said. "You'd never know you had an injury a month ago."

"Thanks," I said. "Doing it in here is one thing, but getting back on the field is another."

"How long do you have?"

"I report back to pre-season June first."

"Well, if I was a betting man I'd say you'll be just fine."

"Either way, I'll be ready to get out of here."

"You don't like Allendale? I kind of like it—way better than the traffic and insanity of LA or New York."

"Allendale is okay. I think I just outgrew it." I pointed to the bench press. "Spot me?"

"Sure."

I laid on my back and RJ took his position behind the bench. He watched as I lifted the weight off the rack and lifted the bar six times, each one getting progressively harder. On the last one I wobbled, arms exhausted, and he grabbed for the weight and helped me put it back in position. I exhaled and sat up.

"Any of this dislike of Allendale have to do with your ex, Heaven?"

I wiped my face again and glanced over. "Heaven told you about us?"

"I spent a minimum of two hours in her makeup chair a day. We talk about all kinds of things."

I laid back again, resting my head and back on the bench. Again, I lifted the bar, grunting under the weight. By the time I got to number six, my arms were wobbly like Jell-O and RJ grabbed the bar, guiding it back to the rack.

"Being around Heaven again has been a challenge. She's great—don't get me wrong, totally willing to help me out, but I've moved on for a variety of reasons, one being my career. I don't have the time to look back."

"Wow," he said with a small frown, "That sounds like agent talk."

I laughed. "How did you know?"

"My agent gives me the same talk at least twice a month. He's fucking obsessed with me and Lea dating—pissed that I went public."

"Why's that?"

"The fans like me single, available. I guess it helps fulfill the dream that I may be an option for them or some bullshit."

"But you took Lea to the premiere."

"I did, against my team's wishes. But I like her. Really like her, and I'm not letting this PR crap get between us." RJ stopped to do a set of reps with the twenty-five-pound weights. "So, what? Your agent is afraid you're going to cause a problem being away from your girl-friend for so long? The trainer?"

"Kind of. Sabine's not pleased about the press seeing me and Heaven together."

"Lea and I had to talk about my celebrity when we got together and how the gossip columns are and how they love to drag shit in the news. It's part of the life. She's gotta see that, right?"

Sabine knew good and well about the paparazzi. She toyed with them like cat with a mouse, but she didn't like being on the other side of things. "Sabine is savvy with the media. She's helped me out a lot with my career—getting endorsements and stuff."

"Building an image; a brand."

I nodded. RJ got it. He had to. It was his life, too.

"So being seen with Heaven messes with the image."

"And being injured and not seen at all the events."

"Is she why you got back on the field too soon last time?"

I shrugged. "Maybe. I had clearance but yeah, maybe. She and I both were afraid I'd lose my position if I didn't commit one hundred percent. That means working my ass off, cultivating social exposure, delivering for my endorsements."

"That's a big burden. Where does what you want come into play?"

"What I want?" I laughed. "I stopped thinking about what I wanted a long time ago."

RJ ran a hand through his hair. "That's no way to live, man. I get it. I really get it, but don't let the machine take over your life."

I raised my eyebrows. Easier said than done. RJ was young, powerful for his age. He didn't have injuries to contend with and a dozen athletes willing to kill for his spot on the team. I did have one question, though. "Did Heaven tell you everything about our relationship?"

RJ paused. "You mean how it involved you and the other guys?"

I nodded.

"Yeah, she did."

"Did she tell you about her past—some of the more private things?"

"A little. I don't pry."

I ran my hand through my hair. "If the press digs around on her background it would be bad for her. I'm doing everything I can to keep her out of it."

"What do you mean, everything?" he asked.

I shrugged, not wanting to be specific. "She's better off without me, that's all."

"Even if you still care for her?"

Instead of answering, I grabbed a towel and wiped my face.

RJ sighed. "I don't know if I could do it, but what you have; your friendships and your respect for one another. That's once in a lifetime shit, dude."

He offered me his hand again and I shook it, arms shaking from exertion. "Let me know if you need a workout partner. I'm around and willing."

"I will," I said. "And thanks. For the spot and the talk."

He grinned, one that was worth the salary they were paying him on the show, and I sat on the bench until he left the room. I felt better having spoken to someone—saying all of that out loud—I knew I was making the right decision. Keeping Heaven safe had always been my priority.

And it always would be.

100

I'D ADAPTED to coming and going from Oliver's house quicker than I expected. Probably because it was habit from back in high school, coming over to the property to visit him at his apartment. Or because the house was luxurious; with every possible need met, from kitchen appliance to electronic. When Anderson let us know his qualifiers would be live-streamed, Oliver set up the system and asked everyone to come over.

He invited Amber, who was still in town planning for the wedding that was now in three weeks. Her mother had taken charge, leaving her annoyed and frustrated. She'd hit Oliver's bar hard and fast, dulling the anxious energy she'd been holding after a full day of cake tastings and wine selection.

I'd also invited Lea and RJ, both happy to get out of their bubble and away from prying eyes. They were adorable, clearly falling in love, and their energy was infectious, especially now that I wasn't fighting my attraction to Oliver and Jackson.

Hayden had come reluctantly, irritable and exhausted. I kept my distance—tired of fighting against him. I wasn't going to waste my time trying to win him over. He had to figure it out on his own. In or out. As much as it hurt, I wasn't going to risk what I had with the others.

I was out on the patio with Lea and Amber before the game started, discussing wedding plans.

"My mom is okay with me marrying a woman. She swears she knew I was gay long before I did." She shrugs and sips her drink. "Maybe it's true. Did you think I was gay, Heaven?"

"No, but I wasn't surprised when you and Ginger started dating."

"It's amazing you found your soul mate so soon," Lea said. "I mean not as early as Heaven here, but college."

I rolled my eyes at the soul mate thing. The jury was still out on that one. We were making baby steps but I had a good feeling about at least Oliver and Jackson. They seemed committed in a way that felt more intense than before.

"Well, I know Allendale seems like a little Mayberry-ish, nice town but not everyone here is so open-minded. I don't think I would've had the guts to come out in high school. Look at what Heaven went through." She gave me a sympathetic grin. "To be honest, we've been quiet at all the vendors about details. A few are down in Oceanside and you know how they can be."

I definitely knew. Oceanside was where the rumors about me and Justin went wild. Close to my father's church with their antiquated ideas about women and sexuality. "I wouldn't push it either," I admitted. "Oh, did I tell you who we saw a few weeks ago?"

"No."

"Spencer." I said his name quietly.

Amber's jaw dropped. "No. Way."

I nodded. "Jackson was with me, but we didn't tell the other guys."

"Afraid they'd go down and kick his ass?"

"Who's Spencer?" Lea asked, looking between us.

"Spencer's the worst," Amber said. "A harasser and an abuser. He was the one that bullied Heaven so bad in high school. He tried to attack her." She glanced at me. "Did Jackson tear him apart?"

"No, actually," I said with a small smile, "I did. I punched him."

"Oh my God!"

"He was just as disgusting as before. He's learned nothing."

"Who knew being in a small town would be so exciting?" Lea asked. "I grew up in Portland. We just, you know, did normal stuff."

"Yeah but your normal stuff led you to that hottie in there," Amber said, raising her eyebrows at the guys in the other room.

RJ sat on the couch in front of the massive TV, talking to the guys about sports. He looked like he fit in. Definitely could have been one of the Allendale boys in high school.

Lea looked at Amber and asked, "Since Heaven will only give me the basic details, tell me, what were they really like in high school?"

"The Allendale Four?" Amber asks, eyeing the three at the party. "First of all, they were not my type."

"Obviously," I said, rolling my eyes.

"I'm just saying I wasn't one of their groupies, but," she said, pinching me on the arm, "they were a definitely a band of their own. Hot, athletic, smart, popular—and by popular, I mean, above popularity. They didn't have time for anyone other than themselves. Well, not until Heaven decided to break into their group and dismantle the school hierarchy in the process."

"I didn't break the school."

"She totally broke the school. Turned everyone on their head. She got the Allendale Four. She won their hearts. She called out the bullies like Spencer and made them pay."

"Damn, Heaven you were bad-ass."

I shook my head, feeling like Amber was recreating history. "Well, they helped me, too. I was in a pretty dark place."

"Well, I've been around these three enough to get why you were into them, but tell me about Anderson," Lea said. "He's an enigma."

"Oh, he's totally an enigma," Amber said, sucking on an ice cube. "Even when you get to know him."

"How so?"

"Well, he's ridiculously good-looking, but you know that. I mean, his body is a fucking work of art. Like God chiseled him out of some kind of genetically enhanced marble. Wing-span like you wouldn't believe. But he's also super smart and incredibly motivated and loyal. But don't forget stubborn. A complete pain in the ass."

"Amber—" I warned. "He's not that bad."

"He's definitely that bad." She grinned and then whispered, not so quietly, "He was Heaven's first."

"First what?" Lea asked, slow on the uptake.

"Love. Lover. Whatever you want to call it. They'd been lusting after one another since middle school. The boys...they fell for Heaven later, but Anderson, he always knew."

"Dude," I muttered. "Too much."

Amber took another sip of her drink, obviously not caring about revealing everything in my life. "He saved her life. Literally."

Lea's eyes widened. I'd told her I suffered from depression. About the cutting, but not about the boys and how they'd rescued me, time and time again. Those feelings were still a little raw, even after all this time.

I made eye contact with Jackson across the room and tilted my head at Amber. "Help," I mouthed. She was stressed. Tipsy. She'd regret this tomorrow.

Jackson, always there when I needed him, assessed the situation quickly and swooped in. "Amber, have you seen Oliver's wine cellar? His father spent decades collecting from all over the world. Come on, I bet he'll give you a bottle for the wedding. Oh! Or maybe champagne for the honeymoon." He doesn't wait for a response, just easing her away from me and refocusing her.

Lea gave me an apologetic smile. "Sorry if she went too far. I wasn't trying to be that intrusive."

"It's okay. She's just had a long week. Her mom can be a little intense, I can't even imagine what mine would be like planning a wedding." I took a sip of my own drink, thinking about it. That was the first time she'd mentioned any concern about having a same-sex wedding in the area. I wondered if something happened.

"So if all that's true about Anderson, then why haven't you repaired your relationship like you have with Oliver and Jackson?"

"Well," I said, weighing my words, "Amber may have a point about that stubbornness and pain in the ass thing."

"You think he won't want to take you back? Do you want him to?"

I glanced at Oliver, who saw me and gave me a slow, sexy grin.

"Things are different now, and that's not necessarily a good thing when it comes to Anderson. He doesn't like change and things have definitely evolved between me and the guys. This new situation with me, Oliver, and Jackson isn't the same as it was before. And I'm not sure where Anderson will fit in—if he ever will, or if he'll ever want to." I sighed. "I also think he's waiting for an apology."

"From who?"

"Me. He thinks I abandoned him—them. And I really don't know if that's true, but he thinks it is and well...stubborn pain in the ass."

"Heaven!" Oliver called my name from across my room. He held up his phone. "I'm calling Anderson before his race. You want to talk to him? I know you guys had some kind of pre-meet ritual. Maybe it's time to reinstate it."

"Here's your chance," Lea said with a smile. She and Oliver didn't know that pre-meet ritual was me giving Anderson an earth-shattering blow job, but still, the sentiment was nice. I squeezed Lea on the shoulder and walked across the room.

I let Oliver talk first, getting Anderson on the first ring. He used Face Time and ducked into the butler's pantry adjacent to the kitchen for some privacy. I heard laughter and some good-natured ribbing. Oliver only wanted the best for Anderson and he knew how to help him get psyched for the race. When he handed me the phone and I stepped into the quiet pantry, I only hoped I didn't ruin it.

"Hey," I said, feeling a rush at seeing him. I saw the collar of his swimmer's coat, lined to keep his muscles warm. His hair stuck up like always, wild despite his reserved nature. "How are you feeling?"

"Pretty good," he said. His green eyes softened when he saw me. "I feel prepared and my conditioning has been going well. I've been carb-loading for fuel. I think I may burst."

"I saw the photo of you eating that plate of spaghetti on Instagram."

His forehead creased. "You on social media now?"

"No, Amber showed me."

"Ah, of course."

"It was cute and made me a little sick looking at it. I wish we could be there." The qualifiers were in Toronto. "But you should see this set-up Oliver has. It'll be like we're in the aquatic center with you."

"I wish you were here, too," he said quietly. "I know the last few times we were together, things were tense. That was on me, Heaven. I needed to process some things, you know."

"Hey, do not stress about that now. You and I are good."

His lips quirked into a grin. "Yeah?"

"Definitely. We'll get together soon. For the wedding, and we can talk about everything then."

"I'd like that."

A dirty thought entered my mind and I couldn't help myself. "If I was there, I'd wish you luck like the old days."

His eyebrows raised. "That...that would be...wow."

"But I'm not there, so all I can say is good luck and I'll see you soon."

"Thanks, Heaven. That means almost as much as lucky head."

"Kick some ass, Anderson."

I stepped out of the room and handed the phone over to Jackson, who waited for me on the other side. He watched me carefully, knowing good and well that conversation could have imploded, but I kissed him on the cheek and walked back into the party.

Lea waited for me in the kitchen with a drink ready. "How did it go?"

"Pretty good."

"Maybe there's hope for that one after all."

Maybe there was.

101

HEAVEN

WITH ONLY A FEW days left before the wedding, Amber had her hands full with her mom, so I offered to head down to Oceanside to check on the chair rentals.

"I'll come too," Oliver said over breakfast.

"Don't you have to work? I thought Jackson said you had a meeting today with that new trainer."

He shrugged. "We do, but he can handle it."

The change was subtle and neither of us made a big deal about it, but it *was* a big deal. Oliver had chained himself to that gym for the past two years. Ever since we broke through our issues, there'd been a loosening of control. He went in a little later, took longer lunches, let the trainers and managers take on more responsibility. The result was that he seemed way less stressed and more relaxed.

He stood and grabbed his plate, kissing me on the cheek. "Let me go call him. I'll be ready in about thirty minutes."

I watched him go, feeling my heart pound as he walked down the hallway. The last few weeks had been pretty amazing. The three of us eased into our relationship with renewed passion and open minds while also a sense of comfort and rightness.

Two years of celibacy created a hunger in both of them that could not be satiated, but I tried, man I tried. But we all felt the burning, hot and intense.

My phone buzzed on the table and I picked it up.

Anderson.

"Hey," I said, answering his video call. He was bright-eyed already. His hair was held back with a pair of blue goggles and already wet.

"Hi."

"Done with your conditioning already?"

"Yep. Last one before I get on the plane." His eyes narrowed. "Are you at Oliver's?"

"Yeah I am. We just had breakfast and have a few errands to run for Amber."

"You got him to skip work today?" His eyebrows shot to his forehead in surprise.

"Right?" I laughed. "I'm trying to get him out of here before he figures it out and changes his mind."

"If his options are spending the day with you or going to work, I think the choice is pretty obvious."

I smiled at the compliment. "I really can't wait to see you. One of us will be at the airport at six, okay?"

He nodded. "Thanks. The weather looks good so I'm hoping for no delays. We've been having crazy thunderstorms lately."

"We'll keep an eye on it."

Someone shouted in the background and he looked over, telling them to give him a minute. "I need to run, but one thing…"

"What's that?"

"Any chance you can be the one to pick me up?"

I didn't fight the smile. "I'll try my best."

Oliver walked in as we hung up, wearing a clean T-shirt and hip-hugging jeans, and he noticed my grin. "What made you so happy?"

"Anderson. We've been talking a little lately. He seems…less hostile. A little more receptive, I think."

He leaned on the counter. "Have you told him about us?"

"He knew I was here."

"Does he know about, you know, the three of us?"

I shook my head. I hadn't told Anderson that Jackson, Oliver, and I were exploring new sides to our relationship. "I will, though. In person."

He crossed the room and slipped his arms around my waist. "You don't have to have that conversation alone, you know that, right?"

"I do, but thank you for saying it. We can play it by ear. The one thing I don't want is a bunch of drama for Amber's wedding. I'm happy to keep everything low-key until it's over."

He kissed my forehead. He smelled like shaving cream and detergent. "How'd you get so smart?"

"Juggling four temperamental men has taught me a lot about patience and timing."

"Hmm, speaking of, do you think we have time to head back to bed?"

I kissed his chin. "Nope. But maybe if we get done early, I can see if it'll fit in the schedule this afternoon."

He laughed and squeezed me in his muscular arms. "I love you, Heaven Reeves. I never stopped."

I rested my head on his chest. "I never did either."

PULLING onto the main road leading into Oceanside always gave me mixed emotions. I had fond memories of the beach as a kid. My friendship with Justin and even the early years of going to my father's church. Then everything shifted. My father was banished—sent to evangelize around the country. My mother and I were forced to move, humiliated and ostracized by the very church that had been the center of our universe. Years later, Justin and I made the deal that set me on a life-changing course. Two blocks away was the house we'd been in when we faked having sex during a party to hide his sexuality.

The main road continued past the church, through Jacob's neighborhood, up to the edge of the town by the water. I swallowed back years-old anxiety and Oliver didn't slow when we passed the small dirt road where I drove that night looking to end the pain, but he did squeeze my hand, letting me know he remembered.

Oceanside had its own small resurgence as Allendale's popularity grew in the movie industry. Small restaurants and shops started opening and tourists now visited the off-the-beaten track town for the beautiful views and gorgeous beaches. These new places were mingled in with the old, and from the outside Oceanside probably seemed like a quaint town. No one had a clue the devil ran through this place.

Following the GPS, Oliver drove down a small side road to the warehouse.

"Amber just wants verbal communication that everything is set for Saturday," I said, unbuckling and hopping out of the car. Hand in hand, we walked into the small office.

A woman worked at the desk, a phone held to her ear. She looked vaguely familiar and when she looked up at me, joint recognition took place.

"Heaven?" the woman said, eyes widening.

"Emily, right?" Discomfort settled in my belly seeing the girl from my past. My nerves only settled when Oliver rested a hand on my lower back.

"Yes, Emily McKeever."

"Of course! It's been forever. How are you?"

She shrugged, her curly black hair falling over her shoulders. "Not too bad. I've worked here since high school—took over the front office a few years ago. What about you?"

"I'm good. I'm back in Allendale, working as a makeup artist."

"And special-effects expert," Oliver added. "She works on TV shows."

Emily's jaw dropped. "Really? That's so exciting! Do you get to see the actors?"

"Sometimes," I said, realizing she has no understanding of my job and the people I worked with. I fought back a smile. Emily had been one of the ones involved in the spreading of the "Heaven is a whore" rumor in school. And now she worked at a warehouse desk and I worked with celebrities. Justice felt nice.

Emily must have known it, because she raised her eyebrows. "I remember how much trouble you and Justin got in back in the day. The rumors and gossip. All that nastiness with the police."

"Yeah," I said, not letting her jar me. "All of that seems like a long time ago."

"I remember hearing about you and all those boys and thinking there was no way it could be true. You had a hard enough time getting one date, not to mention four. I mean, if you'd had dates, why would you and Justin cook up that crazy scheme in the first place?"

Oliver tensed behind me, ready to come to my defense. I squeezed his hand and ignored Emily. "We came in to check on an order for this weekend."

"Let me see..." she thumbed through a stack of papers. "The Wasserman/Rollins wedding?" She looked up questioningly, eyes shifting over to Oliver and giving him a tiny smile.

In response, Oliver's fingers brushed over the tattoo on my back and dipped into the waist of my jeans. Emily watched us, taking in every bit of our intimate touches, before saying, "Everything is ready to go. Five p.m. wedding. A hundred guests. We'll have it set up an hour beforehand."

She handed me the paperwork. At the top, the bride and well, bride, were listed as A. Wasserman and G. Rollins.

"Is this your wedding? Are you guys getting married?"

"Oh, no."

"We're not getting married," Oliver said with a cheeky grin, "yet."

I rolled my eyes but I blushed anyway. "It's for my friend Amber and her fiancé, Ginger. They live in New York now but Amber grew up in Allendale. Justin knows her."

A small grin twisted her lips. "I bet."

I glanced at Oliver. *What was that about?*

"How is Justin?" I asked. "I haven't seen him in a long time."

"Oh, you know he moved after high school. People had a hard time with his, you know, personal life. Not that I have any problems with it, but Oceanside has never been very open-minded."

"No," I said, remembering how my mother and I were basically run out of town after my father left. "No, it's not. Well, I guess I don't blame him for leaving. Any of the old gang still around?"

"Oh yeah, Paul actually manages the company. His uncle owns it. He's back in the warehouse now."

Paul. I'd kissed him at a bonfire in high school, but he was one of Justin's biggest antagonists. He'd been friendly with Spencer back then, too.

"We really need to run," I said, clutching the paperwork. "Everything looks great. I think the wedding should go off without a hitch on Saturday."

Emily nodded. "I'm sure it will."

"It was good to see you again."

"You too, Heaven. I'll tell Paul you came by. He'll be very interested to hear about the details of the wedding."

There was something about the way she said it that sounded like a warning. For what?

"Ugh," I groaned when we were back in the car. "Running into people like Emily make me remember why I hate this place."

"She's got a lot of opinions, that's for sure," he said, shifting his car in gear.

"She always has."

Oliver backed out of the parking lot and two figures standing by the warehouse door caught my attention. Emily and Paul watched us drive away. The look on their faces made me uneasy—probably just leftover feelings from the past. There was a reason Justin and I used Emily and her group of friends to spread the rumor about the two of us having sex. They were gossips and shit-stirrers. One thing was for certain; I didn't trust these people then and I didn't trust them now.

WITH SUMMER ON THE HORIZON, the afternoon warmed up. To my surprise, Oliver took the rest of the day off, encouraging me to lounge with him by the pool.

"We have to pick up Anderson in three hours."

"We can do a lot of things in three hours. Lying by the pool is one of them."

"If I get burned, Amber will kill me," I said, after finally agreeing to stop by my apartment for my bathing suit.

"Don't worry, babe. I'll lather you up."

I snorted. "I bet."

Back at his house, I changed in the small bathing house adjacent to the pool. It wasn't my first time in the pool. The summer after graduation we spent hours here. Lounging, dreaming of college. But now that Oliver owned the house, it felt different. I felt less like a visitor and when I walked out of the small building adjusting the ties on my bikini, I had a sense of confidence I was unfamiliar with.

Oliver emerged from the house carrying a stack of striped towels, fumbling when he saw me.

"Fuck," he muttered under his breath, dropping the towels on a lounge chair. A similar sentiment clung to my tongue, seeing him walk across the pool deck in blue- and gray-striped board shorts. They clung to his narrow hips, the string tied under his navel. The golden scattering of hair caught my eye and I longed to run my fingers through it, knowing that my touch sent a powerful jolt through his body.

He'd crossed the deck in an instant, fingers blazing over the skin along my side. He fingered the ties at my hip, then the ones behind my neck. "I should have suggested this days ago."

"If I'd known you'd be game for playing hooky all the time, I would have."

He responded with a kiss, deep and toe-curling, and I wondered how in the world I'd let him out of my life. What had I been thinking? Clearly, I hadn't been.

To his credit, after a few well-placed kisses, he did lather me up, making sure to double up where the scars lingered after so many years. His hands skimmed over the tattoo and there was no doubt of his desire when he brushed against me, but he held off and let me stretch out on the lounge chair that was less chair and more couch.

"This is new?" I asked, resting my head on the pillow.

"I may have ordered it a few weeks ago when I saw it in a catalogue and thought of how useful a mattress would be by the pool."

I raised an eyebrow. "Really? Planning ahead?"

"I'm a very good businessman, Heaven. I'm prepared for most situations."

Our fingers linked in a lazy, unrushed way. I felt the build-up, the slow pace, and that too was different from our times before, when classes and friends and sports were always bearing down on us.

"Remember that time," I said after a while, rolling over on my side. Oliver's eyes glued to my chest, "when we came here late at night and skinny-dipped?"

"I do. You were wearing a white cotton bra and panties and I swear to God I almost came just seeing you emerging from the water, all wet and see-through."

My cheeks heated. It wasn't from the sun. "Stop. It's not like you hadn't seen me naked before!"

"I won't stop. I literally almost ejaculated, seeing you. Instant reaction. There's something about a thin layer of see-through clothing that makes a woman's body even more appealing. At least, I think so."

"You just like a challenge."

He laughed. "You've got me there."

We stared at one another for a minute, both of us thinking back to that time that seemed so long ago. We'd been so young. So horny all the time. He reached across the space between us and dragged his finger between my breasts, sending sparks across my skin.

I ran my hand down his chest, grazing his nipples with my nails, and tugging at the knot holding his shorts around his waist.

His stomach caved and his thumb circled the swell of my breast. I was so interested in Oliver, so interested in where his hands were moving, in how his body was reacting, I didn't see the shadow streak across the pool deck or notice Jackson cannonballing into the pool until he shouted and landed with a crash in the water.

Cold water rained from the sky, showering over me and Oliver. I jerked up, droplets running down my body.

"Dammit, Jackson!" Oliver shouted and we both scrambled off the chair, but he was already lifting himself out of the water. He smirked when he straightened and that was when I noticed he was only wearing tight, black boxer briefs.

"You two looked like you needed some cooling off," he said, sauntering over. Water rolled over his muscular physique and the little grin that tugged at his mouth made my stomach twist with desire. His eyes skimmed my body, leveled at my erect nipples. "Although Heaven may be a little too chilly."

Bold as ever, he reached for me, dragging me against his cold, wet body. His lips were warm but it did nothing to soothe the goosebumps across my skin. Instead my body reacted, sending a surging shiver down my spine. It wasn't until I felt the second set of hands grazing down my shoulders that my body warmed up—overheated actually, and once again I found myself blessed by the caresses of two men.

Jackson kissed me, then released me with a controlled spin so I faced Oliver. His eyes searched mine, making sure this was okay. I showed him how much with a kiss of my own, tiny ones atop his brown, round nipples. He sucked in a breath, his hands cupping my breasts. Jackson leaned into me, the hard length of his erection pressing into my behind.

This was good, so good. Why had we waited to do this?

My heart raced at the possibilities and I tasted them, both different, both familiar. How far would this go? I wondered. We hadn't done much more than this. Hot make-out sessions that tended to end with me spiraling. So far, neither of them had gone that far themselves. I was letting them set the pace—wanting them to be okay with what we were doing, but now that I was so overheated and everyone was half naked, it was hard to think clearly.

I latched a hand in both their shorts and opened my mouth to ask them to go to the mattress with me, to see how far they'd go, when the sound of the back gate opening scraped against the pavement and we all looked up.

Hayden and Anderson stood in the doorway, eyes widened and jaws slacked. Oliver and I dropped our hands, like children caught doing something naughty. Jackson on the other hand, let his fingers linger, kissing me once on the neck, letting his intentions be known.

"Anderson," I said in a shaky breath. "You're...here."

"I caught an early flight. I wanted to surprise everyone."

"Surprise..." Jackson joked, but Hayden's expression went from shock to full-out rage. He didn't react or respond verbally, he just walked away.

Anderson stood there silently, his jaw working in tight circles. This was not how I wanted him to find out. I stepped away from the boys and toward the fence.

"I think I'm going to go put my bags in the house," he said, walking in the direction of the back apartment. Hayden was surely already in there—thinking god knows what.

"Anderson," I said, running after him. The tie on my bikini slipped and I grabbed it just in time. "This isn't how I wanted to see you again. I wanted time to talk to you—we all did."

"We can talk later," he said, his voice less angry than I expected. Unfortunately, anger I could deal with. Whatever he was thinking—feeling--I didn't know, and honestly, it made it worse.

I let him go, knowing he needed a moment, and glanced back at Oliver and Jackson. They both looked worried as well, probably, realizing like I was that one stupid impulse, one dumb moment and this could be over before it even started.

102

ANDERSON

THE DOOR CLOSED with a click behind me and I dropped my bags on the floor. Hayden raced across the room, a flurry of motion. His hands were full of clothing and an open suitcase sat on the floor. He dropped the pile in and went back to the closet.

"What are you doing?" The question was dumb, but I felt dumb, or dumbstruck at least.

"Going home." He tossed in a pair of shoes and scooped up a row of medication bottles on the counter. "I can't deal with this any longer."

"How long has that been going on?"

"Those three?" He shook his head. "I have no fucking clue."

"But you're angry about it?"

"You're not?" He laughed darkly. "I figure if anyone would blow a gasket about the three of them not only getting together behind our backs but escalating, it would be you."

"Why me?" I asked, but I knew. The fact I wasn't more...something...about the situation confused me as well. Anger did flit by for the slightest moment when I first rounded that corner, but something about seeing my friends that way, Heaven that way, surrounded by love and positive energy...I didn't hate it. I kind of understood.

"You've never been one for change, Anderson. And what we just saw out there? That was a big fucking change."

I pushed the game controllers off the armchair and sat down. "I think you need to calm down and we need to go back down there and talk to them—figure it out."

"There's nothing to figure out, man. I'm leaving. Going back home to my job, to my career, to—"

"Your girlfriend?"

Hayden inhaled sharply. "Sabine has nothing to do with this."

"She doesn't? Why the hell not? Because if there was the slightest chance I could ever fall in love with anyone else, I'd be with that person right now." I laughed darkly. "You want to know why I'm not angry? Because I've been there. Everything bound and tied up in a twisted rage. And then that shifted into grief. Then depression and despair. I thought I was managing, but then you got hurt and Heaven came crashing back in our lives and I realized I needed to get over myself. So I spent the last few months dealing with my own issues about our relationship, about the break-up and realized anger wasn't part of the equation. Sadness? Yep. Loneliness? Absolutely. But anger? No."

Hayden gave me a dirty look and went into the bathroom to pack his travel bag.

"I decided to give her some space," I said, watching him run around. "And during that time, we've established a relationship again. A friendship. But I came here to win back her heart, hoping that you guys would be ahead of me, like you've always been." I rubbed my hair and glared at Hayden, who stood before me, jaw and shoulders tight. "I'm happy to see her with Oliver and Jackson. A little surprised, but happy. And I plan on doing whatever I can to get her to forgive me and see if she'll take me back. If they'll all take me back."

Hayden twisted the shirt he held in his hands, his mind absorbing everything I said. Maybe, just maybe, I'd get through and we could salvage this.

When Hayden finally spoke his voice was low, raw. "I can't live in both worlds, Anderson. I can't maintain the image I need to for my endorsements and be a participant in that relationship. If anyone found out about Heaven and her background and our," he waved his hand between us, "relationship, they'd massacre her in the press. They'd massacre me."

"That's no way to live, Hayden."

"You know why this isn't about Sabine?" I shook my head. "Because Sabine isn't my girlfriend. She's a fucking showmance set up by my agent when he did a little digging on my past. He's worked like a maniac getting my past cleared up online, but we both know the internet is forever and it's only a matter of time before someone connects me to all the shit that went down years ago. Bryant thought Sabine was the perfect solution to my image concerns. She was already my PT, beautiful and willing."

"Wait...what?"

"I've been in trouble with her and Bryant since I went to that premiere with Heaven and our photos were splashed all over. I've done everything I can to pull away from her because I'm terrified they'll dig into Heaven's past. What if they find her medical records or all the dirt on her father? I'm scared for her. Scared for me."

"Heaven can make her own decision about this. Talk to her and see what she thinks."

"No. I told you. Even if she's okay with it, I'm not. I've worked too fucking hard for everything to fall apart like a house of cards. I already don't know if I've got a spot on the team. If I'll pass the doctor's exam. But even if I do, and the world finds out that not only do we have this past with Heaven but things are even more intense, more convoluted now? I just can't do it. The whole thing is a fucking mess and the best thing I can do is walk before any of us gets hurt more."

He zipped up the suitcase and hauled it off the floor. "Dude, let's talk about this a little more. Enjoy the wedding. Give it a minute to breathe. You just dumped a lot of info on me and...well, I think I understand what you've been going through a lot more than before. Heaven needs to hear it."

Hayden grabbed his hoodie off the back of the chair and pulled it over his head. "You can tell her if you want, but I'm getting out of here before I do any more damage."

I didn't stop him. Physically I wasn't sure I could, but I could tell he'd made his mind up, even though his mind wasn't in the right place. Not for any of us.

I offered him my hand, he seemed surprised but grasped it with his own. "Good luck," I told him. "We'll be here if you need us, got it?"

"Thanks," he jerked his chin. "For everything, Anderson. You're a good friend."

I wanted to say more as he left the house, heaving his suitcase so it didn't drag on the stairs. A car waited for him at the curb, he must have called it before I even got up here—already determined to leave.

As he drove away I braced myself for the impending conversations, telling them about Hayden. Revealing my own heart. In truth, it was bound to be a complete shit-show, but then again, when did the Allendale Five do anything the easy way?

103

WAVING OFF THE BOYS, I retreated to the changing room off the pool deck, seeking a moment of privacy to recover from the shock of getting busted by Hayden and Anderson.

I needed to go up there, to find them both and clarify what was going on, but honestly, I was scared as hell that once we spoke about it, any chance for salvaging the five of us was gone. It might already be gone—I just didn't want to hear the words.

The changing room was exquisite, like everything else at Oliver's home. A small love seat, a wide ottoman, and a dressing table built into the wall. There was a shower with tiles made of dreamy blue-green glass and it was so pretty in there I felt guilty all over again for living this life while causing so much pain. Why did it have to be so hard?

I stepped in the shower and rinsed off the sunscreen. I didn't waste time, washing quickly. I'd just wrapped myself in a plush, white towel when I heard a rap at the door.

"Come in," I said, reaching for a comb on the dressing table. I expected Oliver or Jackson. Instead Anderson stood in the doorway, his face reflected in the mirror. I spun in my seat.

"Hi," I said, feeling a burst of butterflies at seeing him.

"Hey," he said, voice soft. "Can we talk?"

"Of course."

"Do you want to wait and get dressed? I can…"

"No, it's fine. Come in." I was afraid if I let him leave, something would happen and we'd never get the chance again.

He entered the small cottage, his body too big for the limited space, but having him so close made me feel better—complete. I searched his eyes for anger but there wasn't any, and that confused me more than anything else.

"I'm sorry about before," I said, cutting the silence. "I should have told you before you arrived that things had changed between the three of us and that I'm hoping—"

He cut me off with a kiss, arms wrapped around my back, tugging me closer. My brain had a million questions but my mouth, my body caved to his touch, something I'd missed so desperately.

When we pulled apart, he pressed his forehead to mine and said, "I don't know how I feel about what I saw earlier. I just know how I feel about you. I love you. I always have, and I always will, and if you'll take me back, I can work through anything else."

"Are you serious?" Anderson had never been easy to convince. I narrowed my eyes at him and he grinned, slow and sexy.

"As a heart attack, Heaven. The last two years have been a nightmare. Lonely and completely isolated. I've spent the last six weeks thinking about it. A lot. And the one thing I know is that I don't want to live that life anymore."

"Are you interested in…trying some new things?"

He swallowed. "Maybe. Hopefully. It just may take a while for me to get used to it. But I'm open minded and I promise not to judge."

"We can take it slow. Or not at all. Our relationships have always been unique, which is why it worked for so long." I brushed his hair out of his eyes. "But I've also realized that as we mature, so do other parts of our commitment to one another. We're different now and that's okay. Stagnating and trying to fit into the same mold as years before was what did us in. It's why the distance killed us. We needed to adapt but didn't know how."

He nodded in understanding and on a whim and rush of love, I jumped at him and he caught me in his long, strong arms. I didn't care that I was only in a towel and that it was slipping off my body inch by inch. I only cared about the way his lips felt, hungry and secure, the way his heart beat, hammering against my chest. I only cared that he was here, finally, and another piece of my life fell into place.

I eased myself out of his arms, using a hand to hold up the towel at my chest, although it was no longer wrapped around me, just hanging by my clenched fingers.

"How's Hayden?" I asked, well aware that his eyes were roaming. I linked my fingers with his.

"We need to talk about him, but probably with the others. I think I finally understand what's going on."

"Should we get Oliver and Jackson?"

"We should," he said, not all that convincingly. His tongue swiped at his bottom lip and I felt his hand graze my lower, bare back.

"Maybe in a minute?"

He took a deep, steadying breath, like he was wavering between tossing me on the couch and ravishing me right there and...well, not doing that at all. His mind was at war over something, probably all of this, and I knew it would be better if he had time to think it over.

"Let's go talk to them," I said, making the decision for both of us. "It's important, and maybe Hayden will come out of the apartment and stop sulking."

Anderson froze, his mouth in a grim line.

"What?" I asked, fearing the worst. It didn't take long for my concerns to come true.

"Hayden left right after I got here," Anderson said.

"Left? To go where?"

"Home," he clarified. "He flew back to Atlanta."

104

———

"Maybe I should go up there," I said, pacing the room. "Anderson and I have always been the closest. We've worked through Heaven issues before—maybe I can explain."

"Give him a chance to settle down," Oliver said. We'd both changed out of our wet clothes and were in the living room trying to decide how to handle the blow-up by the pool.

"God dammit, if we fucked this up..." I'd had a sick feeling in my stomach for an hour.

"Jax, we knew there was a chance they wouldn't approve. Sharing Heaven this way, it's different, and neither of them are big on change."

"I'm not sure I've ever seen Hayden that angry."

Oliver rubbed his face. "I don't know what to do about Hayden. He's been a mess since he got here. I thought coming home to recover would help, but he seems worse. He's restless, overworking himself, I don't think he's sleeping..."

"He's a fucking disaster," I agreed. "I have the feeling what he saw today may be the last straw. Maybe he's just too fucking proud to really commit to this relationship."

"Or he's just moved on."

We were both silent, mulling that over. Like any relationship, someone should be allowed to leave if they aren't happy, but something about Hayden's behavior didn't add up.

"So much for keeping the drama low for Amber's wedding. We're a bunch of assholes."

"That's the truth," Anderson said from the doorway. Oliver and I both looked his way. Heaven stood by his side, cheeks slightly flushed. They held hands.

My eyes lingered on the easy way their fingers wound around each other's and how he squeezed her hand before releasing it to walk in our direction. He stopped before me and his smile spread wide before pulling me into a massive, Olympian-sized hug. I peeked over his shoulder and saw Heaven smiling at the two of us, but there was still worry in her eyes.

"Good to see you, man," Anderson said.

"You too."

He released me and grabbed Oliver, hugging him tight. I raised an eyebrow at Heaven questioningly, but she just watched the three of us together and I knew in my heart everything would be okay.

"We good?" Oliver asked him.

"Yes, we're fine."

I eyed him skeptically. "It's not really like you to behave so rationally."

"I know, but while you guys have been working through things here, I've been working on myself." Heaven walked from the doorway next to Anderson, again slipping her fingers through his. "Hayden, on the other hand, isn't fine. In fact, he's—"

"Gone," Heaven said, her strong resolve cracking. "He's gone."

"What?" I asked. "Where?"

"Back to Atlanta. He unloaded on me when I got here," Anderson said.

"Sit," I told him. "Tell us everything."

He did, and when he finished we sat around the room, one person obviously missing from our circle.

"I had no idea he'd been carrying so much," Heaven said, wiping a tear from her cheek. "He'd been protecting me this whole time."

"He was protecting himself, too," Oliver said, eyes dark with disappointment. "He could have told us this was going on."

"I knew that Bryant guy was a creep," I said.

"Slimy," Heaven agreed. "I didn't like his teeth. Too white."

"He's just doing his job," Anderson said. "Hayden's not wrong about the branding and image stuff. He was also right to try to protect you. Somewhere along the way, things got really messed up and I think he not only lost us but he lost himself too."

"What should we do?" Heaven asked, looking at each of us. "We can't just let him go like this. We need to talk, even if…even if it's to let him go."

Anderson took her hand. "There's nothing we can do right now. Amber's wedding is in two days. You have obligations as her maid of honor that you have to fulfill. Hayden doesn't have the right to ruin her special day."

Heaven sighed and nodded. "You're right."

A phone vibrated, interrupting the discussion, and Heaven looked at her screen. We all waited, hoping it was Hayden changing his mind, but she shook her head and said, "It's Amber."

"Hey," she said, holding the phone to her ear. Amber's voice was audible, although unclear. Heaven's forehead creased, her lips turned down with worry. "Hold on, let me pull it up okay? Let me see for myself." She cut her eyes at Oliver. "Get me a laptop. Pull up the Oceanside Facebook page."

Oliver hopped up, going to the kitchen for his computer. Heaven spoke to Amber, "Are you sure? Who would do such a thing?" She waved Oliver back in the room and he typed as he walked, obviously pulling up the website.

"It's bad," he said, sitting next to Heaven on the couch.

Anderson peered at the screen. "Shit."

"What?" I asked, moving across the room to look for myself.

"We'll report it and get the messages down," Heaven said as I rounded the couch. "Don't stress. I'm sure no one has seen it."

There was a distinct lack of conviction in her statement. I finally

got a look at the screen and saw the Oceanside community page—
normally used for news and public announcements. Amber and
Ginger's engagement photo had been posted at the top of the page,
tagged with the headline, "Lesbians plan wedding in Oceanside! Is
this the type of event we want to host in our town?"

A hundred comments filled the box below. Most awful and hate-
filled. A few mentioned Heaven, including posting a few choice
photos from back in the day. Seriously? People kept those?

Someone tipped off the community about the wedding and
they'd decided to let the world know how they felt about it.

"Listen, babe," Heaven said over the phone. Oliver took a screen-
shot of the page and then reported the post. "We're going to get
through this. It's no fucking surprise those people are small-minded
idiots. I'll be over soon. Don't do anything drastic."

Heaven hung up and glanced at Oliver. "We did this, you know."

"I know."

"What?" Anderson asked. "How?"

"We went to check on the rentals. I knew the girl working in the
office and another guy in the back. Both were complete shit-stirrers in
high school." She looked between us, guiltily. "The ones that started
all the rumors about me and Justin. I had no idea they didn't know
the wedding was for two women."

"Uh, Heaven, there's something else." I'd followed the link that
showed the ancient photo of Heaven back in high school and it took
me to a different page. The profile picture explained a lot.

"Is that Spencer?" Anderson asked, leaning closer.

"Spencer?" Oliver repeated.

Heaven and I exchanged looks. I nodded and said, "We ran into
him a few weeks ago picking up Heaven's dress at the cleaners. He
was being a dick, like always."

"Tell me you kicked his ass," Oliver said through gritted teeth.

"Did he hurt you?" Anderson asked at the same time, his forehead furrowed.

I couldn't help but smile. "I didn't have to do anything; our girl
took care of herself."

Both Anderson and Oliver give Heaven impressed looks but she just said, "I did punch him, but Jackson kept him from retaliating. It was a joint effort and I'm not surprised he found a way to get back at me. He was friendly with Paul back then and if they still are, it probably didn't take much for them to start up their old tricks." She sighed. "It's like this shit just never goes away, you know?"

"It's not your fault," Anderson said, rubbing her arm.

"It is, and I need to fix it."

"How? What are you going to do? Find out who put up this page? It's best if they ignore it," I said.

"And what? Some of those comments were about protesting the wedding. That's not acceptable." She stood. "I'm heading to Amber's house to go check on her and see what we can do. I'll be back later."

"The wedding is in forty-eight hours, Heaven," Oliver pointed out.

"I'm not letting those bastards ruin it. We'll figure it out."

"One of us should go with you."

"No. I'm the maid of honor. I'll deal with it."

Oliver started to follow her, unwilling to let her take the heat alone, but I grabbed him by the arm. "Call us if you need anything, okay?"

She nodded and left, leaving the three of us together.

"I should go with her," Oliver said.

"No, I need both of you with me," I told them.

"For what?"

"We've never allowed our friends to be bullied. Not back then and not now." I pushed up my sleeves. "I think it's time we paid Oceanside a visit and kick their asses into the twenty-first century."

Anderson stood. "I'm in. I hate those pricks."

Oliver nodded and we let Heaven drive off before we piled in Oliver's Jeep and drove to Oceanside.

105

I arrived at Amber's house and went straight up to her room. I hadn't been there since college and it looked the same, a tiny snapshot in history. She sat on her bed, laptop in front of her, typing furiously.

"What are you doing?"

"They posted again, right after you reported it. Stupid bastards. Now I'm just going in and calling them out for being hateful assholes."

I slid on the bed next to her and slowly removed the laptop. She cried out but I took it, snapping the top shut and pushing it under the bed.

"You had no right to take that," she said.

"Arguing with assholes on the internet is a complete waste of time. You know that."

"I do, but I can't just sit around!. I haven't even told Ginger yet! She and my mom went out to run some errands. What if they bump into someone that saw it. My mom will be horrified. I mean, she's always been supportive but you know how this town is."

"Your mom has your back. Never doubt that." Amber's feisty spirit came directly from her mom.

"But what about Ginger? She'll be crushed. She doesn't deserve this."

"Ginger is a strong, capable woman, I have no doubt she can handle herself, but you're right, she doesn't deserve this. Neither do you."

Amber plopped back on her pillow. "I hate these people, Heaven. I knew having the wedding here was a terrible idea. Old mentalities die hard."

"Tell me about it," I said, lying next to her and taking her hand. "Why do you think I kept running from that place my whole life?" I took a deep breath. "I'm the one that let it out that the wedding was for two women. I thought they knew and the girl at the desk was someone I knew from way back. I had no idea she was still so awful."

"I don't blame you, Heaven. They would have figured it out when we got there. Two vaginas and no dick would have tipped them off."

"I'll do whatever I can to fix this."

"I don't think there is a solution and there's no time anyway. Maybe we just cancel."

"Hell no are we cancelling."

"Then what? Have it down there? People want to protest. You know I'm in for a fight, but..."

"Your wedding day isn't about giving these people a platform." I sighed. "We've fought against the closed-mindedness of this town before. And we won, but not without a lot of heartache and exposure." I took her hand. "Your wedding is about you and Ginger. It's not about making a stand to the idiots of this town. They'd love a fight. A big nasty brawl down on the beach. My father may even come out of the woodwork to preach the salvation if he heard about it."

"Oh god." She covered her face with a pillow. I lifted it up.

"I want this day to be about you. About love. About family. Not about the closed-minded simpletons down in Oceanside."

"How, Heaven? Where? It's too late to book anything. All the deposits and payments are in." She choked back a sob. "We should just head to the courthouse but they'd probably just follow us there."

"That's not what you want."

"Apparently it's not about what I want, anyway."

I wrapped my arms around her and held her tight. I knew what it was like to be judged, to be criticized and ostracized. I didn't want that for Amber and Ginger. I wanted them to have happiness and love—like they'd given me so many times before.

That desire planted a seed of an idea, one that I was determined to see to fruition.

106

———

It felt like old times, driving fast as hell down the highway toward Oceanside, boys in the car. We were only missing one person, but he'd opted out and I didn't know how I felt about that yet.

"So what's your plan?" Anderson asked Jackson. He'd told us to get in the car and drive.

"You know where the warehouse is?" he asked me. I nodded. "Go there. Hopefully we'll find Paul and teach him the lesson we should have a long time ago."

None of us had seen Justin in years, but he and Heaven made their peace years before. He packed up while we were in college, unable to live in the oppressive town any longer, and moved to a city more receptive to his lifestyle.

"Allendale's changed so much," Jackson said, his voice carrying in the wind. "I guess we forgot the rest of the area is still stuck in the past."

None of us wanted to see Amber or Ginger hurt and we certainly didn't need old wounds exposed. Not while things were finally back on track.

When we pulled down the street that led to the warehouse, Oliver slowed. There was a small crowd assembled out front, and a man with dark brown skin and wavy hair stood on the loading dock speaking to the group that included several photographers and journalists.

"We did not realize the wedding in question was for two women, and the instant we did we made a fast decision not continue business with the couple in question."

"Is that him?" I asked Oliver. He'd seen Paul the day before with Heaven.

"Yep."

"Oceanside isn't trying to be like Allendale, who has to bend to the whims of movie studios and celebrities. We don't want their money or their way of life. We've always been a close community. Moral. Ethical. And we're not changing."

"God, he's repulsive," Anderson said, leaning against the Jeep. The audience clapped and cheered at his statements and he continued to answer questions from the press.

"Are you going over there?" I asked.

"I think we should." He leveled his gaze at me. "You okay with that? Taking a public position?"

I nodded. "Hell yeah I am."

Paul noticed us before we got across the parking lot, his eyes trailing us with slight recognition. Emily stood next to him and nodded at Oliver. She recognized him from the day before. His smug expression faltered slightly, but he smiled down at the crowd and said, "Looks like we've got some heathens in our midst."

"Heathens," I muttered. "It really is like being back around Heaven's dad."

"Is there something I can do for you?" Paul called.

"Yep," Oliver said, pushing through the crowd. He wanted the press to get a good shot of him. "We just came by to get the deposit back for my friend's wedding tomorrow—which will no longer be held in Oceanside. Not because she's not welcome. The beach is public property, you can't run her off, but because like Paul said, you don't want outside money. You don't want tourists or visitors or people supporting your shops. That's fine. Come back to Allendale where the small-minded people don't venture."

"You're one of those boys Heaven Reeves hung around with, back in the day, aren't you?" Paul said. A sly smile twisted on his lips. He glanced to the back of the crowd where Anderson and I stood. "And you're the Olympian—one the members of her little harem."

"Did you say harem?" a photographer asked. Murmurs rolled through the crowd.

Anderson's fists clenched and I felt my heart race, anger welling up inside. Oliver seemed to have it under control though, he easily jumped up on the dock and stood in front of Paul.

"Let me tell you something; you can stay down here in your closed-minded, bigoted town, wallowing away in poverty and religious self-righteousness. My friends and I have faced your specific brand of hatred before and each and every time we win because our lives and relationships are built on love and respect, not hatred and pettiness."

"I know who you are," Paul said. "Do you really think your clients will support you once they find out you share her with four other men? What do you think the Olympic committee will say? Or the major league soccer association. Yeah, I know about Hayden Pierce, too."

The crowd shifted and a figure emerged, jumping up on the platform behind Paul. Spencer.

Fucking asshole.

"Oh, I see how it is," Oliver said, eyeing Spencer. "You're happy to have an attempted rapist and harasser in town rather than people in a committed relationship. Sure, that makes sense."

Paul crossed his arms over his chest, puffing it out. He wasn't small, but he looked ridiculous next to Oliver.

"Let me explain something to you, Paul. We're not afraid of you. We never have been, but the one thing that's unacceptable is hurting our friends. So, you have two options. One, you give me the money, or two..." Oliver nudged him aside and whispered in his ear, away from the crowd. Even I couldn't hear him. I didn't miss Paul's eyes widening as he spoke. Oliver straightened and said with a smile, "Your choice."

Paul shifted uneasily on his feet before he glancing at Emily. With a scowl, he said, "Give him the money back. We don't want it anyway."

Emily's jaw dropped and she blinked a few times, but walked into the office. A few moments later, she came back with an envelope. Oliver took it and immediately started for the car. The crowd, upset there wasn't more drama, started yelling. Shouting out, "perverts!" and "heathens!" as we walked across the parking lot.

"Mr. Anderson!" a voice shouted as we neared the Jeep. We all turned and found a reporter and photographer a few feet away. "Do you have any comments about the allegations made today? That you're part of a sex cult?"

Oliver snorted. I watched carefully, knowing Anderson needed to be careful. The Olympic committee was no joke.

"Yeah, I have a few comments." Anderson towered over the man. "I've been in love with the same woman since I was thirteen years old. I'm a lucky bastard that she has room in her heart for me and supports me as I pursue my dream of representing the United States in the Olympic games." He looked back at the crowd, now dispersing. "The real story is the bigots in Oceanside and the stand they're willing to take for hate and evil. If you're looking for a story about me, come see me in Tokyo."

The man looked a little flustered but nodded and said, "Good luck, son," and walked off.

"What did you say to Paul on the platform?" I asked Oliver when we were back in the car.

"I told him that if he came after Heaven or Amber again, personally or online, we'd use our celebrity connections to expose their bigotry to the world, file a lawsuit, and drag them through the courts."

"That was all it took?" Anderson asked, looking back at the warehouse as we drove away.

"Along with a few other well-placed threats of bodily harm." He smiled. "Turns out Paul's a little bit of a wimp, and we already know Spencer is worthless."

I laughed, unsurprised. Bullies usually are. "What are we going to do about the wedding? Even though the beach is public, I don't think coming back is a good idea."

"No," Oliver said, catching my eye in the rearview mirror. "But I have an idea and if Heaven will help us, I think we may be able to pull it off."

107

It took the whole night and the following day to get everything situated. Oliver used the money he got back from Emily and Paul for a company in Allendale that was happy to get involved at the last minute. How Oliver got the money hadn't been revealed, but I was doing my best to stay away from the news. I just hoped no one came to arrest him.

"What do you think?" I said Friday evening. The wedding was the following night. We'd made sure all the guests were notified of the change of venue.

"I think my step-mother had this backyard landscaped for parties. It's like she knew one day we'd have a last minute, taboo, lesbian wedding and would need a space to hold it," Oliver declared.

"Thank you for offering to do this," I said, slipping my arm around his waist and giving him a kiss on the cheek.

"Amber is my friend, too. It's the least I can do."

Jackson called him over to help with the sound system as Lea walked over, cheeks smudged with dust from working hard all day.

When I told her what had happened, she'd immediately come to the rescue to help me organize. We called in help from the people we knew from the industry that allowed us the opportunity to go through their storage units for the things we needed. Decorations, sounds system, podium. Even an arch for the bride and groom to stand under. We no longer had the beach but we did have a late spring garden and a lush, grassy lawn.

Brushing freshly dyed hot pink strands of hair behind her ears, Lea said, "I'll be back in the morning with the flowers."

"Thank you so much." I reached out and pulled her tiny body into a hug. "There's zero chance I could've done this without you. You've got a much better eye for decorations than I do."

"Eh," she shrugged. "It's a beautiful location. Better than the beach, in my opinion. Less windy, no sand, quieter."

"No bigots threatening to picket..."

"True. How's Amber?"

"Amber is a fighter, like, I know she wants to go down to Oceanside and take a stand, but it will also only make her miserable. I suspect they want us to go down there, stir the pot and get more attention for being back-assed." I thought of my father and his church. They would have loved an opportunity like this to grandstand.

"I saw they put some old pictures of you on the post. You okay?"

"I learned a long time ago I'd have to live with those decisions. I just don't feel like Amber should have to have my past tarnish her future." I looked around the backyard, feeling confident we made the right decision.

Lea took my hand and squeezed. "She's going to love it."

"I hope so. I just want her to be happy," I looked over my shoulder at the three boys working diligently to make everything perfect for our friend, "like I am."

∿

THE PRE-WEDDING DINNER, thank god, ran smoothly. After too much dessert and too many drinks, I gave Ginger the key to my apartment. She wanted to follow tradition, staying away from Amber for the

556

night. I was happy to give her some space and just settle in at Oliver's.

Back at his house, buzzed on drinks and the relief of pulling off a last-minute venue change, I kicked off my shoes and changed out of my dress. I pulled on an oversized Allendale baseball shirt and walked downstairs, where I could hear the boys on the patio. As much as we needed time to reconnect as a group, they were life-long friends and needed time to be together. It was sweet how much they loved one another. Sexy. Their commitment to one another was the foundation of our relationship.

It was why we worked then and why we may have a shot at the future.

Barefoot, I stepped out on the back patio, getting an eyeful of my men. I still called them boys but that was nothing but habit. They were men, in size, strength, and emotion. That fact gave me a little thrill, one that slowly inched up my spine. I watched them for a minute, relaxed and lounging on the comfortable furniture. They shared inside jokes, laughing off the stress of the day. They were sexy in their disheveled clothing; ties tossed aside, shirts casually unbuttoned and rolled at the sleeves. Jackson's blue button-down made his eyes bright even in the shaded room, and Anderson sat with his legs sprawled in front of him, hands supporting the back of his neck. Oliver looked more at ease than I'd seen him in months, the corners of his eyes crinkled with laugh lines. My stomach twisted at the sight of them, their camaraderie and closeness.

Things had shifted for us in the last twenty-four hours. Hayden's absence was noted, painful, but some of that subsided when I looked at how Anderson had easily joined back in the group.

He must have sensed my gaze, because his focus shifted across the patio.

"Hey," he said, and suddenly all of their eyes were on me, taking in my bare legs and the shirt that claimed them all.

"Hi." I walked across the stone floor, feeling Jackson's gaze sweep over my bare legs. "I think I'm headed to bed."

"Good idea, it's been a long day." Oliver was the closest and he laid a hand on the back of my thigh. "Tomorrow will be just as long."

He tugged me down on his lap and I succumbed, stretching my legs across the space where Jackson took them in his hands. I relaxed and said, "Amber's mom is going full mother-of-the-bride with hair, makeup, nails...the whole process."

"At least you get a day off the makeup, right? Lea's coming to help?"

"She is, although I'm probably going to do Amber's anyway."

Oliver's hand was on my hip, the baseball shirt bunched up. I felt his fingertips on my skin and Jackson rubbed my feet. I sighed, leaning back into Oliver, fitting perfectly into his chest. From the wicker armchair across from us, Anderson observed quietly.

Jackson's eyes flicked to his friend, a little smile on his lips. He leaned forward, bending my leg and kissing the cap of my knee. He made his way to my mouth, kissing me slowly while Oliver held me in his arms, stroking my legs with his fingertips. Jackson's lips tasted like chocolate icing, tinged with bourbon, and I licked his tongue seductively, intentionally, to catch Anderson's attention. Something we most certainly had.

"Good night, babe," Jackson said, not pushing it further. This was about giving Anderson a taste of what to expect. He stood and let his fingers drift across my leg, fist bumping both his friends on the way out.

Oliver placed his own goodnight kisses down my neck, including sucking slow along my collarbone.

"You want eggs or pancakes in the morning?" he asked.

"Eggs. Pancakes will make me bloated and I'll never fit in that dress."

"Not true, but whatever you want."

I snuggled into his chest and he ran a hand up and down my back, exposing my panties to Anderson, who I noticed shifted uneasily in his seat. Nerves? Arousal? I wasn't sure. His jaw was locked tight and his eyes carried a cool glint. Oliver lifted me off his lap, placing me on the seat next to him, making sure his hands touched as many parts of my body in the process. Staking his claim, no doubt, even while sharing.

"Love you," he whispered, just for me to hear. I said it back just as quietly.

And then Anderson and I were alone, sitting across from one another. My body hummed from the gentle touches of the other men, my heart raced out of fear for what Anderson would do or say.

His green eyes blazed in the shadowy patio, only lit by torches near the door. The smooth skin of his chest peeked out of his unbuttoned shirt. I'd missed him terribly—physically and emotionally—and the few feet separating us felt like miles.

"Was that—" I started, wanting to know if he was okay with the actions between me, Oliver and Jackson.

"That was fine," he replied gruffly.

"It was?" I straightened up; his eyes fell to my legs.

He didn't move, prolonging the odd tension ebbing between us, but I hated the distance and stood, taking the four steps to his chair.

"I don't want to rush you into anything," I said.

"You won't."

"I don't want you to feel uncomfortable." His long fingers reached for my hips, pulling me between his legs. From my vantage point, standing above him, I could see just how aroused he really was. Anderson tugged on my shirt, nudging me to sit in his lap. I climbed on top, straddling his hips. Oh yeah, he was definitely aroused.

He pushed his fingers into my hair and said, "I'm back, Heaven, don't worry about rushing me or making me feel uncomfortable. Don't worry about me leaving or blowing up. I've had a long time to think about how I want to live my life and one thing is for certain, what I want most of all is you."

"And the guys?"

He laughed. "They're a given."

He brought my face to his and we kissed, long and slow, both of us too exhausted to bring too much fervor into it. I felt the love in his touch, in the way his mouth worshipped mine.

"You know," he said, pulling away, "it's not like I hadn't thought of it before."

My breath caught. "You have?"

He nodded.

"Anything in..." a massive yawn over took me, but I spit out the final word, "particular?"

He shook his head and laughed. "I'm about to tell you my biggest fantasy and you're about to fall asleep!"

"No!" I cried, laughing with him. "Tell me, tell me your biggest fantasy!"

"Not a chance." He pushed his arms beneath me, lifting me with a mock groan.

"Where are you taking me?" I asked, legs dangling over his arm.

"To bed."

"Are you coming with me?" I raised an eyebrow.

"Not tonight. You're exhausted and I can promise you one thing..."

"What's that?"

"When you and I make love again, it's going to take all the energy you have."

I linked my arms around his neck and pulled him close, kissing him once more before he carried me off to bed.

108

HAYDEN

SPRING WAS a relative term if you lived in Atlanta. The calendar might declare the season but the weather jumped straight from cold to hot, adding a heavy dose of humidity to the mix.

The muggy air wasn't the only thing that welcomed me at the airport. Sabine along with two dozen fans dressed in my jersey, number 05, waving signs. A mixture of emotion crashed over me. It was an amazing feeling that the fans still wanted me back, that they hadn't abandoned me. But seeing Sabine waiting for me at the gate landed like a brick in my stomach. She wasn't happy, despite the fake smile plastered across her mouth, but she didn't show it. No, she was here to do a job and that meant I was back on the clock too.

I guess my recovery was officially over.

"Baby!" she squealed when she saw me. I scanned the area for the photographers I knew were waiting. Sure enough a flash, then five more, blinded me as Sabine pulled me into a tight hug. Dots swirled in front of my eyes from the camera and I felt a wave of dizziness crash over me.

"Smile, asshole. The cameras are watching," she whispered in my ear, followed by a wet kiss.

The fans went crazy when they saw that, well most of them, I noticed a few girls give Sabine scowls as she snuggled under my free arm. I fought back an amused laugh.

Ah, that explained the eye twitch. She wasn't just unhappy. She was pissed.

"There's a car waiting outside," she said, calmly, linking her fingers with mine. Under her breath she added, "You look good. Walking without a limp, no bruises. Everyone will be happy."

Everyone but me.

Security noticed our situation and came to help us out the airport door. The paparazzi wasn't done though. The cameras continued their assault and I held my hand up to black the flashes, each one compounding my growing headache. Along with the clicks, questions came fast and furious.

"Hayden are you all better?"

"Much better, thank you."

"How's your recuperation?"

"Painful. Slow. And hopefully over."

"Did you suffer a concussion?"

"I did, but thank goodness I have a thick skull."

"Will you be ready for the preseason conditioning Monday?"

"I plan on it."

"What was it like being back home? See any friends? Catch up with anyone?"

My eyes slid to the person that asked the last question, his eyes twinkling with mischief. I didn't change my expression, not once but replied, "I spent most of my time at the A5 gym getting my ass kicked —unfortunately there wasn't a lot of time for socializing."

The car idled by the curb and the driver held the door for us as we squeezed in the back. Sabine kept the smile on her lips as long as we were in sight of the cameras, but the minute we got enough distance, it vanished.

"Somebody hand me an Oscar," she muttered. "So listen, we've got a packed weekend. Once you told Bryant you were coming back, he wanted to get you visible before practice on Monday."

"What? No. I need a few days to acclimate."

Mope in my apartment was really what my plans entailed. Dwell on my anger. Stew about my friends. Try desperately not to think about how incredibly hot Heaven looked with my friends' hands all over her.

"You had eight weeks, Hayden, you don't get any more than that. Sure you'll get to ease into practice and they'll take it slow, but from here on you're back at work."

I groaned and reached into my bag for a bottle of medication. I took out three and swallowed them dry. Sabine watched me carefully, a flicker of empathy ran across her face.

"I'm glad you're home. My spring was boring as hell. Bryant didn't think it would look good for me to be seen without you and my schedule was packed anyway." She rested her hand on my thigh. "I know things have been strained lately. Your friends back home have a way of winding you up, but we can ease back into this again. Hanging out. Having a good time. You can prove to the world that you're better and ready to bring the championship home."

I stared at the window, watching the lights of the city get closer. The stadium just to the west. I made this decision, I told myself. I wanted this. I left, for god's sake. I could have had everything back, and I left.

Sabine's hand tightened against my leg unnecessarily, and I slowly removed it.

"Did you fuck her?" she asked, pushing her hair over her shoulder.

"What?"

"Heaven, that girl you're so obsessed with."

"I'm not obsessed with her, Sabine. We're just..." I swallowed. Saying the word cut me if I wanted to admit it or not. "Friends."

She snorted. "Well, whatever. I obviously can't get mad if you did. She's pretty. A little annoying, but as long as you were discreet, sleeping with an ex-girlfriend isn't the worst thing you could do.

Honestly, I wish you would have, then you could've knocked that chip off your shoulder."

I touched my temples, willing away the headache. "Shut up, Sabine. You have no fucking idea what you're talking about."

"I'm not stupid, Hayden. I saw how you looked at her." She rolled her eyes. "How you *all* looked at her. Is that the problem? Did you lose her to one of the other guys?"

I didn't say a word. Not one, because my mind was still a jumble from my melt-down with Anderson earlier in the day. Part of what threw me off was the fact that he didn't freak out. Why didn't he panic when he saw them together? Why didn't he get mad? He had a public career to handle. He hated change.

Why was I the only one still struggling?

The car pulled up to my apartment, a high rise downtown. The doorman opened my door but Sabine grabbed my hand before I could get out. "Get your shit together, Hayden. I'll give you tonight to sleep off the jet-lag, but starting tomorrow you're no longer the small-town nobody. You're Hayden Pierce, Star Goalie for Atlanta United. You have obligations."

I yanked my hand away and strode into the building, grabbing my suitcase on the way. I knew Sabine was right. I knew Bryant wanted the best for my career.

Unfortunately, neither of them would ever understand my heart.

109

"Everything's perfect," Amber whispered to me, taking a peek down the grassy aisle. Fairy lights twinkled in the tree limbs, creating a canopy of shining light. She clutched her bouquet. "Thank you for everything, Heaven."

"It was my turn to rescue you," I said. "I owed you."

"I also need to thank you for not letting me go down to Oceanside and burning that hell-hole to the ground."

"Bailing you out of jail for arson was not on my list of things to do today." I laughed. "Eating cake. Catching the bouquet, dancing...any and all of those things, but not jail."

"We'll get them. I already have a plan."

"Good. Count me in. Revenge is my favorite."

She smiled and pulled me in for a hug. "Oh my God, I'm so nervous."

Amber stood near the house, waiting for the signal. Ginger would enter from the other side.

"Don't be. She looks amazing. You look amazing. Two amazing people are coming together and I couldn't be happier."

"I don't think I'm the only reason you're happy." She looked across the yard at the three men wearing light gray suits, ushering guests to their seats. Jackson caught my eye and winked, sending a rush of heat across my skin. "You can thank me later for picking out those suits. Damn, they wear them well."

"Who knew coming back to Allendale would make everything better for all of us."

A small crease lined her forehead. "Well, not all of us. We are missing one of the four."

"Hayden made his choice."

"That's it?"

"For now. Yeah."

The Justice of the Peace nodded at Anderson, who then walked in our direction. His hair was casually swept back, an artfully arranged mess. I blushed as his green eyes swept over my dress. Jackson and Oliver both took positions on one side or the other of the Justice.

"I won the coin toss," Anderson said, offering me the crook of his arm. I slid mine into it, feeling the soft fabric of his jacket. There was something oddly intimate about walking like this. Bodies barely touching. "You look beautiful, Heaven."

"Thank you." His gaze held such warmth. How could I have ever let him go like that?

The violinist started the music for the procession and the guests stood, all eyes on the two of us. Especially four eyes in the front. I focused on them, on my footsteps and calming my racing heart. I felt Anderson's breath in my ear and a chill when he said, "One day, this will be us. I promise you that."

My step faltered at his statement, but he held me upright, so smoothly that no one noticed.

At the altar, I took my position and the music swelled, changing for the brides as they took center stage. But for that one moment it was me and the three of them up there alone, and I could envision what Anderson said, that one day we'd stand in front of our friends and family and declare our commitment.

I knew one thing for certain, now that I had them back in my life I would never let them go again, but something else nagged. Something that lingered despite the smile I wore as Amber and Ginger started down the aisle.

Once upon a time I was drowning, literally drowning, and four boys came and saved my life. I realized with startling clarity that one of us was gasping for air and it was my turn to come to the rescue.

110

I WOKE JUST BEFORE DAWN, bed sheets twisted around my torso, after my second long, restless night. My head throbbed, the dull ache that seemed to follow me around these days didn't make what I had to do any easier. I'd taken two days to acclimate being back in Atlanta. The first day nursing the mother of all headaches I could only assume came from dehydration and the paparazzi cameras. I'd also been sulking a little, knowing my friends were all celebrating Amber's wedding without me. A choice I'd made, but one that hurt all the same.

Today, though, I shed all aspects of the injured Hayden Pierce and ventured back into the world of fame, endorsements, and athleticism.

I was officially forsaking my past. Before there was one foot there, a strand of my soul still attached to the others, but Sabine was right. I needed to get my head into the game. There was nothing for me in Allendale anymore—there couldn't be.

My phone vibrated on the bedside table and I reached for it and the bottle of water.

"Hello?"

"Hayden! You're back!"

"I am," I said, trying to find my voice. "How are you, Bryant?"

"Amazing now that my star client is back and ready to prove to the world he's in tip-top condition. Tell me you're up for it?"

"Up for what, exactly?"

"I know the first day of practice is tomorrow, but since you came early and you've had time to rest, there's a small exhibition today for the Children's Hospital down at the stadium. It's the perfect chance to get your face back out there with a little meet-and-greet and autograph signings."

I sat on the edge of my bed and fumbled for two more pills, taking a huge gulp of water, pretty sure the flight left me majorly dehydrated. "Sure, okay, what time?"

"Starts at one p.m. I'll be there at noon to pick you up."

It was only nine now. That gave me time for a quick workout and shower before he came.

"Sounds good."

"Excellent!" Bryant sounded so happy—so pleased.

"I'll be ready," I said and hung up the phone. I stood, stepping over my sketch book and bag of pencils. I felt the ache of dehydration in my limbs, but there was no time to slack off now. I had to stick to my routine—focus—do everything I could to get back in the game. The charity event was the perfect opportunity to prove to everyone that Hayden Pierce, the athlete, the commodity, was back.

111

"Anything?" I asked as we walked through the airport.

Anderson checked his phone, scanning all the social media pages for updates about Hayden.

"Just that he arrived two days ago and met Sabine at the airport."

"I guess we go to his apartment then—hopefully we can catch him there."

I'd kept my mouth shut through the entire wedding, refusing to cause any sort of drama after the challenges of the prior days, but the instant Amber and Ginger drove off in the limo I gathered my boys to the side and told them my plan. There was no pushback about me going to Atlanta, only that Anderson come with me, since he still had an apartment here and knew his way around.

We caught the earliest flight, getting into the city mid-morning. I had a growing sense of urgency gnawing at my gut. Something vague, like we needed to hurry. I felt Hayden slipping through my fingers and the more I thought about him leaving without talking to me—talking to us, seemed wrong. Really wrong.

We'd already lost two years to poor communication, I wasn't willing to let him go so easily this time.

"When he stormed out the other day, did anything else seem off?"

Anderson ran his hand through his hair. "Just that he seemed lost —maybe even confused. I'm not even sure he was upset about seeing you with the other guys. It was more like an undercurrent of anger."

"He's been like that for weeks," I said. "We had a big argument on a run one day. He just stormed off and we'd barely spoken since."

"That really doesn't seem like him. None of this seems like him."

The city streets were clogged with traffic, despite the early hour. I wasn't used to so much traffic and the clock was ticking. Anderson's hand covered mine. A thought crossed my mind. "What if Sabine's there?"

"Sabine isn't his girlfriend," he reminded me, although that whole concept felt strange, but who was I to judge?

"What if he doesn't want to see us? Or won't see us? Or refuses?"

"Babe," Anderson said, as the driver cursed another car. "I'm not saying this is going to go the way we want it to, but it's Hayden; he'll listen to what you have to say."

I'd never been so nervous before and I felt selfish. Selfish because I wanted all them back—not just the three that I had. I wanted Hayden, too.

After what seemed like forever, the car came to a stop in front of a tall building with slick blue-glass windows. The entrance was sophisticated. Hayden really did live a different life now. Why would he want to give it up?

Anderson linked our fingers as we walked into the building. He showed the doorman a card he had, allowing us access to Hayden's apartment. He'd given it to him when they both first moved to the city, in case of an emergency. This counted, right?

My stomach dropped as the elevator soared to the top of the building, the floor numbers ticking off with a small chime. When they opened, Anderson led the way, walking down a wide hallway and turning past a large window that looked out and over the city.

I stopped and took in the view—a view that reeked of success, privilege. I felt Anderson next to me and said, "Maybe we shouldn't do this."

"What are you talking about?"

"Maybe he has what he needs here. What if that stuff about Sabine was a lie, just to give himself an excuse to leave. Maybe there's someone other than Sabine? Maybe there's a slew of other girls?" Oh god, I felt weak in the knees at the thought of that. I turned and looked around the tastefully decorated hallway. "Hayden has the success he's fought for his whole life. Who are we to challenge him on that?"

He sighed and rubbed his chin. "I don't think he's happy. He may be successful, but I don't think he's happy and I think that if our positions were reversed, he'd follow me across the country and kick my ass." He took my hand. "We need to talk to him, Heaven, because if we don't I'm not sure the rest of us can ever be whole."

I recognized the truth in that statement and followed him to the door. Anderson knocked against the solid wood, the sound echoing back in the empty hallway.

He held up the key. "Should I?"

"I don't know." But I knew I wanted to see his place. See where he'd been living all this time.

Anderson didn't ask me again, slipping the key in the slot. The bolt shifted and he opened the door. The apartment behind it came into view; everything was gray and white, expertly decorated. It was also sterile, void of anything personal. If I was looking for a piece of Hayden here, an insight to his life, I didn't think I would find it.

"Do you think he even came here?" I asked, walking into the sparse room. Anderson walked over to the kitchen counter where he picked up a ticket stub.

He held it up. "He at least came here after his flight."

"I'm calling him," I said, pulling out my phone. "We're here. He'll have to see us, right?"

Anderson nodded and started across the living room.

I hit the send button and heard the first ring. Another faint ring sounded back, but this one nearby. I frowned. "Do you hear that?"

"Yeah," he walked down the hallway toward the muffled sound of the ringing phone. It was coming from behind a closed door.

My heart pounded in my chest, wondering who or what we would find. Anderson stood before it and knocked, calling out his name. "Hayden, it's me, Anderson."

The phone switched to voicemail. I hung up and dialed again. The ringing continued. "Open the door," I whispered. "Open it."

He twisted the knob and pushed, but the door only opened a little. I rushed over as he peered in; an arm lay in the way, Hayden's body crumpled on the floor.

"Hayden!" I cried, squeezing in the small opening. The door edges scraped down my sides, but I was only focused on him. I tugged him out of the way, pulling his massive body so that Anderson could get in the room. "Hayden baby, wake up," I said touching his face. His hands were warm, but clammy. His eyes closed, but he was breathing. A bottle of pills was on the floor.

Anderson knelt down, phone already in his hands, calling 911. The look of panic on his face scared me more than anything else.

I barely heard Anderson on the phone as I wrapped my arms around Hayden's body. I'd known something was off. Wrong. I'd felt it in my bones. Why had we let him run off like this? How had I ever let him go in the first place?

I brushed his hair off his forehead and whispered in his ear, "Don't let go...do you hear me? Don't let go."

112

It was harder to wake this time, my head throbbing and nausea building in my stomach. I felt hands on my cheeks—bright lights in my eyes. "Mr. Pierce, can you hear me?" a voice asked. "Mr. Pierce?"

"Yeah," I rasped, my throat dry. "What's going on?"

I shoved the light away, it pulsed like a bomb in the back of my head. A man in a uniform crouched next to me. I frowned. "Who are you?"

"I'm Ryan," the man said. "I'm an EMT. Your friends called me when they found you on the ground and couldn't wake you up. Do you remember what happened?"

I struggled to sit, but he pushed me back down. I felt weak, confused. "No. I...well I was going to the gym but my head was killing me. And..." I shrugged. "I guess I passed out?"

"Can you tell me about this medication?" he asked, handing me the bottle.

"He suffered a concussion," another voice said, when I couldn't find the words to answer. "About eight weeks ago. It was severe. The medication was to help with the headaches."

I followed the voice and saw the familiar face behind it. "Anderson?"

"Hey, man."

I felt more confused than ever.

"Did you take more medication than prescribed?" Ryan asked.

I shook my head. "No. I don't think so. I just..." I touched my forehead. "I've just been feeling dizzy lately and thought maybe I was dehydrated."

Ryan pushed my head back and said, "I'm going to check your eyes, okay?" He flashed light in them once again and I grimaced. "It looks like you're still suffering from side effects of the concussion."

"I'll call his doctor," Anderson said. "Do you have his phone?"

I didn't know who he was talking to until I heard the reply, "Here. The number's at the top."

"Thanks, babe."

Babe. That voice. I made eye contact with her. "Heaven? What are you doing here?"

She moved closer and took my hand. Tears glistened in her eyes. "Don't worry about me. You rest, okay?"

"I'm fine." I struggled to sit, pushing the EMT's hands off of me. "Why are you here?"

She glanced at Ryan. "If you're done, can we have a minute alone?"

"It looks like you just had a dizzy spell from the concussion, so I'm not going to make you come in. But you need to see your doctor right away and don't overexert yourself. It looks like you haven't healed all the way yet."

His words were a jumble, filled with things I didn't want to hear while Heaven stood in front of me, possibly ready to say a million things I needed to know.

Ryan grabbed his things and Heaven walked him to the door. "Thank you," she said. "We'll make sure he gets follow-up care."

She shut the door behind him and came back over to the bed, sitting by my side. Impulsively, I touched her cheek. She smiled briefly and then said, "You scared the shit out of me, Hayden Pierce. First leaving without saying goodbye, and then finding you like that."

"I'm sorry," I said. "For both of those things."

She sighed. "I don't think I have the right to lecture anyone on unhealthy, risky behavior, but I should have seen how much you were struggling. The irritable behavior and irrational reactions. I knew you were pushing yourself too hard, but I also know that's your nature, except you've been so angry and that's not like you."

"I've been...lost, I guess. Confused." I looked up at the ceiling. "I thought I'd figured it all out, Heaven. I had a plan, and then I got injured and my whole life turned upside down. Suddenly you were back, except you weren't. And I had this whole carefully crafted life that I was afraid to mess up. Because if I fucked that up like I'd fucked everything up with you, what would I have left?" I felt her fingers touch mine and it was like a wave of relief washing over me.

"Despite our status, Hayden, we always have one another. Always."

"I thought maybe we could all just be friends again, baby steps, and I could figure out how to navigate both worlds, but then I saw you with Jackson and Oliver and I just lost it."

"That anger was valid. We should have told you."

"It wasn't anger," I said, "not really. It was mostly jealousy and fear."

"You could have talked to me."

"I should have."

Her fingers brushed over my forehead. "How long have the headaches been bad?"

"I mean, they never really stopped, but when I started working out harder they intensified."

"After you refused to run with me?"

I nodded. "That was a mistake."

"You're sick, Hayden. Your brain needs time to heal."

"But what if I lose my spot on the team?" All my work. The blood, sweat, and tears.

"If it means saving your life, I think it's a risk you have to take."

I glanced away, not sure if I could do it.

"You're more than Hayden Pierce, star goalie, to me. You're Hayden Pierce, artist, friend, lover." She nudged my chin so I was looking into her beautiful face. "You've taught me so much, but mainly you've taught me life is about living. Surviving. It's not about suffering and pain."

"When did you get so wise?"

She smiled. "It only took a few hundred trips to the therapist."

I snaked an arm around her waist and pulled her close. She leaned over, pressing her forehead against mine. It took a boat load of courage for me to admit, "I'm scared."

"I know, but you've got me to rely on and your three best friends, and if you stop fighting us maybe you can heal and get back to doing what you love."

I felt her breath on my face and we hadn't been this close in years. My body, even exhausted, still reacted to her the same. It took every ounce of self-control not to flip her over in the bed and claim her right then. She smiled down at me, knowing me well enough to sense my thoughts, and I brushed her hair out of her eyes. "I've spent too long not *doing* the one person I love."

Her eyes flared with desire and she bit down on her bottom lip.

I lifted my chin, willing to push past the pain to finally taste her once again, but loud voices interrupted us and the door flung open with a loud bang. Heaven sat up but I held onto her hands, and we both looked at Anderson and Bryant standing in the doorway.

"What the hell is going on?" Bryant shouted, looking frantic. "I get a call from the doorman about an ambulance showing up to your house and then there are EMTs all over the fucking place. And then this guy," he glared at Anderson, "had the fucking gall to tell me not to come back here."

"Bryant, now isn't the time."

"What do you mean it's not the time? You and I were supposed to be at a charity event in an hour. Sabine is waiting at the stadium. And you're what? Sick? Hungover? What?"

"I'm not better, Bryant. Not yet."

His eyes widened, but the set of his mouth confirmed he'd suspected. "Okay, we can handle that. It was a long shot and we knew it, but I can talk to your endorsers and we'll go over your contract with management to figure out the next steps."

"Thank you."

"Don't ever think your health isn't the most important thing, Hayden."

Heaven smiled at that, nodding in agreement. Bryant's eyes flicked over her and a different frown tugged at his mouth.

"Can we, uh, talk alone for a minute? About a few other things?"

About Heaven, no doubt.

"No." My answer was resolute.

"Later, then."

Heaven shifted to move and said, "It's okay, I can leave if you need a minute."

My brain worked slower than I'd like but I realized that this was my moment, the one where I finally made the decision about my health, my career, and my relationship.

Except it dawned on me. There was no choice.

There was only one path to take. One my brothers had already figured out. Maybe it was the brain injury, or my ego or just the fact I was a total dumbass that it took me so long to realize there was only one option.

"Bryant," I said, in a calm voice, "I need you to get the fuck out of here."

"Hayden, the press is already downstairs. I can explain your health, but," He glanced at Heaven and Anderson, "How am I supposed to explain them?"

"You tell them whatever you need to about my career," I said. "That's all. If they want to ask me about my relationship, you direct them to me. I'll handle it."

He snarled in Heaven's direction. "And Sabine?"

"I can handle that, too."

In the end, he didn't fight it or Anderson as he escorted him out the door. Having the air cleared with Bryant rid me of one more burden so I could focus on what was really important to me.

The Allendale Five.

113

Heaven

Once the press left and the team neurologist had done an examination with Hayden with instructions for an office visit in the morning, Anderson and I stood outside the guest bedroom door.

"Come get me if you need anything," he said, leaning against the wall.

"I will."

We'd decided that I would stay with Hayden overnight, making sure he was safe.

"I'm so glad you made us come out here. Good thing those spidey-senses were working," he said, cupping a hand around my neck and pulling me close.

"I should have noticed earlier that he was in such pain." Physical and emotional.

"Hayden's always been so strong and stubborn. I'm not surprised he got it past us. Do you know that in the third grade, he fell out of a tree at Jackson's house and walked around with a broken arm for four days before he told anyone?"

"No." I shook my head. "But that makes a lot of sense."

"We're here now," he said, kissing me on the lips. "Go take care of him."

"You go to sleep, you look exhausted."

"I am." He kissed me again. Long and lingering, enough to get my heart racing just before he left me. Freaking tease.

"Night, Heaven."

"Night, Anderson."

I moved down the hallway but felt fingers on my hip, and he pulled me back. "I love you."

"I love you, too. So much."

The following kiss was sweeter, shorter, and I finally dragged myself away. In Hayden's room, I found him lying on the bed, eyes closed. His chest moved up and down slowly.

Carefully, I eased my way into the bed, trying not to jostle him, but his arms wrapped around me instantly, pulling me close to his chest.

"Hey," I said, inhaling his distinct scent. God, it felt good to be so close to him. "I thought you were asleep."

"I was," he said, "kind of, but now that you're here it'll come easier."

"I'm so sorry about everything, Hayden. I didn't know you were struggling so badly."

"To be fair, I didn't know either."

"You told me weeks ago that you wanted to know about my health. Well, I want the same. Tell me, okay? About the pains and aches and if something feels off. Don't protect me."

He looked at me with soft, sweet, eyes. "I will. I promise."

"Thank you."

Exhaustion rolled down my limbs and I knew he was right, sleep would come easier with him by my side. I snuggled in and opened my eyes to find him staring at me. I pushed a lock of hair off his forehead and asked, "What?"

"I know I'm supposed to take it easy and I know this is...new again, but I really want to kiss you."

I exhaled. "Please. I'll be gentle."

That was the only permission he needed and I almost cried when his lips touched mine. It wasn't the seductive kind that he'd given me so many times before, but something different—full of love, not lust, full of promises, not demands, but mostly full of hope.

"For a while, I thought I'd never get to do that again and it almost killed me," he said with closed eyes, most likely from the headaches. "And I know we can't do it now, but very soon you and I are going to make up properly, got it?"

My heart rattled like it may explode at the thought. I rested my head on his chest, knowing he was already dozing off. "I can't wait."

In truth, I could and I would.

I'd do anything for this man, for all of my men. I needed him healed so he could come back to us whole, and then we would finally be complete.

114

———

Heaven

Days pass in Atlanta involving visits to the neurologist, a series of tests, and an official announcement by Hayden that he would not be able to return to Atlanta United for the next season. Bryant secured his endorsements, working out who still wanted him as the face of their product while he was injured. His frank transparency about his head injury brought him a lot of unexpected attention and most of the sponsors stuck by his side, willing to wait it out until he was better.

Oliver and Jackson were unable to travel to Atlanta with the entire cast of two superhero movies in town, but Anderson was able to balance his workouts with Hayden's needs and I was committed to staying by his side until we all returned together.

"I talked to my coach and he's willing to allow me to partner up with my old aquatics instructor at the University. They'd both noticed the strain I'd been under since moving here and think that being closer to home may help."

It was late afternoon and Hayden was taking a long, necessary nap. That was what the doctor prescribed more than anything else.

Long, intensive naps. Low movement—including sex. That made things awkward for all of us. We'd agreed if Hayden couldn't get any, neither could me or Anderson. The good news was that it gave the three of us hours to reconnect and heal our relationship as much as Hayden's body.

Anderson and I were intertwined on the sleek gray couch in the living room. I'd taken to wearing Hayden's jersey, the 05 embroidered on the back. It was much too big for me, but I'd always liked wearing their clothes. He may not be on the team, but I wanted him to know I belonged to him, to all of them.

"So you're really moving back to Allendale," I said to Anderson, playing with his long, slim, fingers.

"I am."

"And you'll move into the house with us?"

"I'll probably keep an apartment near the aquatic center but yes," he kissed my neck, "I've already talked about it to Oliver."

"Good thing that house is so big." We'd all have our own bedrooms. An arrangement like ours required a little space. "I doubt Oliver's step-mother had this in mind when she bought it."

It felt nice having a leisurely moment to spend with Anderson, but despite our no-sex agreement, the tension between us grew with every passing second, making it harder and harder to resist.

"What are you thinking about?" he asked me.

"You," I admitted. "And Hayden, and how I'll be happy when this sex embargo is over."

He groaned and ran his hands through his hair, making it stick up in a million directions. I loved him when he looked feral like that. It didn't help with the tension.

"It's killing me, babe. Like literally killing me. I think my balls are permanently blue."

"Don't be so dramatic."

Anderson grabbed me, shifting me until I was on his lap, straddling his long legs that are stretched down the length of the couch. "Feel that?"

Oh yeah.

"I've been like that for a week straight. And you prancing around here in that shirt with no pants isn't helping."

"I can put on pants," I said, starting to move. He held me tight and I swear he got even bigger.

He touched my cheek, my neck, and trailed his fingers down my arm. "Don't even think about it."

"I can't believe we let this go, you know?"

"I'm promising you now," he said, green eyes boring into mine. "It won't happen. The guys and I have spoken, we're in, one-hundred percent."

The way he said it sent a shiver up my spine. When the Allendale Four made a decision—a commitment—it would take an act of congress to change it.

He stared at me for a long minute, jaw tense.

"What are you thinking about?" I asked, flipping the tables.

"About how I want to bury myself inside of you. How I want to feel your mouth on me. How I want to taste you. How I know it's been too goddam long and a man only has so much self-control." His hand fisted next to his side, like he was barely holding back. I eyed him. All of him, his gorgeous face, his perfect lips and fantastic body down to his agile hands.

"What?" he asked with narrowed eyes.

"I think I'd very much like to see you slip, just once, losing that control." I bit my bottom lip. "Maybe break a rule or two."

It was a taunt, one that I knew would get under his skin. Anderson was a man of routine, strategy, and smarts. Very rarely did he lose control and most of those times had been with me. But never had he allowed his façade of control to truly slip during sex.

There was a beat between us, the absence of air, as the clock ticked the tension away. I spotted the smirk first and jumped, sensing something predatory and feral. I made it halfway off the couch before his long arms captured me, yanking me back against his chest. He didn't speak, he just tossed me on the couch.

A thrill ran through me as he exerted his power and I scrambled to get away from him, not because I didn't want him, I did, but I liked the chase. I wanted him to catch me. Claim me. I crawled over the arm of the couch, laughing as he prowled toward me. With the furniture between us, I hooked my thumbs in my shorts, teasing him with a peek of my skin. If I thought the obstacle would protect me, I was wrong. He smiled wickedly and used his long legs to climb over the cushions, cornering me in a small space against the wall.

"I think you're out of moves," he said, smiling wickedly.

I eyed the space to his right, just enough for me to get through to the hallway. If I could slip through...

Anderson was tall and lithe, his arms made to slice through water, but I was fast, small, and I feinted left, using his over-confidence to toss him off balance. I jumped over the coffee table, knocking a bowl of marbles to the floor, the sound of them hitting like pounding rain. I kept running, laughing as Anderson cursed at the hard balls under his feet, trying not to fall. I looked over my shoulder to make sure he wasn't following me and crashed into something hard.

"Oof," I said, the air knocking out of me. I looked up into Hayden's handsome face. "I was just..."

"Jesus, Heaven, it sounds like a herd of buffalo running through the house."

His eyes flicked over my shoulder, Anderson having made it across the landmine of marbles in the living room.

"We were just..." I tried again but trailed off when I saw the mischievous grin twist his lips. I looked back and forth at both men, weighting what was happening here, what was running through their minds when I saw them grin at one another and realized that I was absolutely, utterly screwed.

"Okay boys," I said, holding up my hands in surrender, "let's talk this over..."

Hayden wrapped his hands around my wrists, effectively taking me hostage while Anderson closed in from behind. The hallway was tight, there was no way out, but as their bodies moved closer to mine and my belly fluttered with excitement I knew one thing to be true; I didn't want out. I wanted this.

Hayden didn't wait for an invitation, kissing me hard on the mouth. Anderson's hands settled on my hips, pressing his hard length against me. I didn't want just foreplay this time or a hot make-out session, I wanted as much as I could get, as much as they could give, and before they could walk away *I* took control.

"We're not supposed to do this," I said to Anderson, my voice sounding different in the shadowy hallway.

"I feel like the exertion rule from the doctor was a little vague. I've been thinking about it. I think we have a few options."

I wait for Anderson to tell him he was full of shit, but a quick glance told me he was listening.

"Oh yeah?" I said, waiting to hear what he had in mind.

"I think we can get creative." It was so good to see that sexy, dirty smile on his face again.

I never wanted it to leave.

Anderson's hands cinched around my waist, encouraging me, so I did the safest thing. I tugged at the button on Hayden's pants, gently easing them over his hips. He stripped his shirt over his head and I kissed his chest, feeling the weight of his cock press into my belly.

"Now you," I said, suddenly, turning to face Anderson. His eyebrows lifted to his forehead but he didn't stop me when I loosened the tie on his shorts and pushed them to the floor. We'd already established how ready he was and there was no doubt when his cock sprang up. While I undressed him, Hayden moved behind me, kissing my neck and ear, whispering how hot it was that I was wearing his number, our number.

"And as much as I love seeing it on you, it's got to go," he said, lifting it over my head. Anderson made quick work of my shorts and Hayden's cotton pants fell easily to the ground. We were all naked, all fully aroused.

Their kisses blazed over my body, covering my front and back. Anderson, keeping his eyes off Hayden's naked body, lowered himself to his knees licking between my thighs, trailing his fingers down my overheated skin. I reared back, so very sensitive, hitting Hayden with my head, and he caught me, muttering, "Fuck," in my ear.

Anderson looked up at the curse and the three of us started laughing. "This, is sexy," he declared, "but a little awkward, right?"

"Totally," I said, hyperaware of Hayden's cock near my backside.

"But I like it. We've never been porn stars. We've never had an orgy and you two have never seen one another like this."

"So we just..." Anderson said, I saw the red in his cheeks.

"We take it slow," I said. "Or fast. Or however we want it." We're stripped down and bare, breathing heavy and completely, totally aroused. I reached out to both of them, dragging my nails down both their chests, traveling down their bellies and below. Hayden pressed his back against the wall and I made good on the promise to be creative.

Anderson did, too.

"This is new for me, for all of us," I told them, marveling at their exquisite bodies. "We'll learn together."

And that was exactly what we did.

EPILOGUE

"Do you have everything packed?" Oliver asked. He had a list on his phone and had been shouting out items all morning.

"Yes," I said, dragging my bag down the stairs. He walked over and took it from me, stacking it next to the others.

"Passport?"

"Yes."

"ID?"

"Yes."

"Money?"

"Yep."

"Chargers?"

"Yes, Ollie," I said, trying not to be annoyed. We'd gone over this already. A dozen times. "I've got everything."

"Me too," shouted Jackson, pulling his suitcase behind him. Oliver looked up when he saw his outfit and I covered my mouth to hide my laughter.

"You're not wearing that."

"Of course I am," he said, spinning so we could see his shirt. On the front was a photo of Anderson, standing beneath the A5 Gym logo. On the back was Hayden—same pose, same logo. "We have two clients representing us in Tokyo. It's a marketing dream."

"I can't believe we're going to Tokyo," I said for the millionth time. "I mean, it's one thing to have one boyfriend in the Olympics, but two?"

"I still have no idea how you're going to justify this to the press," Oliver said.

"I've managed okay so far." The Olympic promotional team was all over Hayden and Anderson being from the same small town and now representing the United States in the Olympics. We'd all be interviewed, saying nothing more than the fact we're a tight group of friends. We figured the world didn't need to know everything about our lives. Not yet, at least.

"Shit," Oliver cursed. "I think I forgot the tickets."

"Nope," I said, holding up the papers. "I've got them."

He gave me a smile. "You really do have everything under control."

"You say that like you're surprised."

"I'm not surprised," Jackson said, easing past me, giving me a kiss on the cheek. "I mean, you know that's why they want you there, right?"

"Who wants me where?"

"Anderson and Hayden...and well us, every day. Without you we have no map, no focus, no destination." He slid his arm around my waist. "With you? We're steady, and they need that steadiness in the stands during every match and event."

I fingered the ring on my left hand. They'd given it to me the night we found out they'd both made the Games. Not an engagement, not exactly, just a gift celebrating our dedication to one another. They gave me a ring and in return I'd given them a gift in return. I walked up to both of them and first pushed up Oliver's sleeve, kissing the tattoos on his bicep. Then did the same to Jackson, who had an identical constellation inked on his arm. Hayden's and Anderson's would be proudly displayed during the Games as well.

The boys grabbed the suitcases so we could get on the plane to meet up with our champions and I watched them go, thinking about those tattoos, the stars and what they meant.

There was one for each of the four; one for the boy that made me feel safe; that picked me up when I fell, when I cried, when I soared. One for the boy that made me laugh; with dimples and a lopsided grin. One was for the boy that made me feel sexy and adventurous, special and unique. And then one for the boy that had always owned my heart, keeper of my soul and my personal savior.

Together they connected, like markers along the way to the one star that linked them together.

It wasn't really a constellation, but a map, a map of our road to happiness.

115

"Look, I know it may be a little soon for something like this, but..."

"Well, think about it. The little eyes. The nose."

"I don't know. I'm not sure we're ready for the responsibility. I'm not sure *I'm* ready for the responsibility," I said. The guys were surrounding me, faces eager. They wanted this and wanted it bad. And I understood. Part of me wanted it too, but I was scared. Really scared. Nothing sounded more terrifying to me than being responsible for another living thing.

"The way I see it," Oliver said, leaning forward in his chair, "is there's no good time. It's something you just have to dive into. Make a decision and go with it."

I glanced at Anderson, sure he would feel the same way I do. He's not a fan of change or disruption at all, but oddly, his green eyes show interest. He shrugs. "A few months ago, I would have said no, but now?" He cast his handsome face in my direction, the face I'd never been able to resist. "We're all in the same place. There's usually someone home, so there would be no need for outside help. Everyone's matured a lot in the last year. It just seems like the next logical step."

Jackson punched him. "Dude. This isn't about logic."

"You know I can't help but think logically."

I glanced at Hayden. "What do you think?"

"I think we all have to be in agreement."

"But what do you think, personally."

He leaned forward and took my hand. "I'm ready. I'm ready when you are."

I exhaled and fell back against the cushion. With four deadly smiles aimed at me, I'd had little chance of changing their minds. And the truth was that I wasn't sure I wanted to. I was ready for the next step. The logical step. The big step.

"Fine," I said, embracing the excitement. "Let's get a dog."

Two weeks later, Sadie dragged me down the sidewalk, eager to get home. I found her desire to come home ironic, because she's always so excited to leave for the walk. I guess really, she's just excited all the time regardless. Thank god I kept up my running, because she needed a ton of exercise.

Once we decided to get the dog, things moved quickly. We all agreed on a rescue and we all agreed on a mutt. We went to the shelter and visited and finally settled on this adorable, stumpy-legged black dog that looked like a mix between a pit-bull and a corgi. It didn't take Sadie long to acclimate to our home and five loving owners, but soon it became clear that she had a fondness of me (and my runs) and followed me around all day.

Since we all moved in, we'd done our best to turn Oliver's house into a shared, cohesive space. We still had our own rooms and there was a bit of adjustment with both Anderson and Hayden moved back full time. Anderson was looking at one last Olympic games in two years, and Hayden shifted to a coaching position with our local team. Oliver and Jackson's gym, A5, had continued to thrive in Allendale's market and they were in the process of opening a new gym a few towns over.

"Good afternoon," our neighbor, Mrs. Richmond, said as she got her mail from her box.

"Hi, how are you today, Mrs. Richmond?"

Things with Mrs. Richmond and the other neighbors were always slightly tense. Oliver inherited the house from his parents and the people that lived nearby understood that. They'd also seen the boys come and go for years and even were familiar with my presence, but once we'd all moved in together there was no doubt a few had questions. Especially that lady down the street—Monique—who'd just moved in with her husband and two little kids. I saw her watching me and the guys when she strolled them up and down the street. Okay. I saw her watching the guys. I didn't blame her.

"Well my arthritis is acting up again, but that's what happens when the weather changes and it starts getting a little cold." She glanced down at Sadie, who was sniffing the ground like she was looking for a good place to pee. I gently jerked her leash. "I see you got a new dog."

"Yep, a few weeks ago."

"And this dog belongs to…"

"Oh, all of us, really, we take turns taking care of her."

"That seems like it will be complicated when one of you moves out."

I nodded. "I guess we'll have to play it by ear."

We'd all agreed not to make our relationship status known unless it was with people close to us. Mrs. Richmond didn't count, even though her house was right next door. I had a feeling she kept one eye out her kitchen window, where she had a good view of the pool.

Sadie, thankfully, lunged toward the house, eager to get home. "Guess that's my cue," I said, waving and letting the dog drag me down the driveway.

I opened the back gate and let Sadie off her leash. She darted across the patio, making a beeline for the pool. Anderson leaned over the edge, his broad shoulders and sculpted chest dripping with water.

He shook his hair and Sadie rushed for him, wagging her tail excitedly.

"Looks like someone is happy to see you," I said, dropping the leash and kicking off my shoes. I sat by the edge, dipping my legs in the cool water. Anderson's eyes skimmed my legs, and his fingers trailed water over my skin.

"I know I'm happy to see *you*. How was your run?"

"Well, we had to stop every few minutes to sniff and pee and check all the things out. Twice, we had to consider if Sadie could catch a squirrel, and then one of the neighbors down the street was at their mailbox, so obviously we had to visit."

Sadie loved attention, so if anyone else was around, she would make sure she got it from them, too.

"Mrs. Richmond or Monique?"

"Mrs. Richmond. She had a lot of questions about dog ownership and tossed in another hint about when we move out." I frowned. "Who's Monique?"

"The mom down the street—with the two kids? They always want to pet Sadie when we go out."

I snorted. "Sounds like an excuse to talk to you."

"The kids?"

I splashed him with water. "The mom. I've seen her watching you guys."

Truthfully, I didn't get jealous over other women checking out my men. They were handsome, sexy, and absolutely, totally mine. If I was going to have an issue over women, or men, finding them attractive, this relationship would have ended years ago.

"She's probably just curious, like Mrs. Richmond, wondering how we got such a smokin'-hot girl to move in with us."

My skin was hot from the exercise and Anderson's cool hands felt good. He ran them along my arms and I felt the buildup of anticipation in my belly. We were at the point in our relationship where there wasn't any question about where we stood or what we wanted. He wanted me and I wanted him, so when he rested his hands on my hips and pulled me into the water fully dressed, I let him.

The cold water hit my belly and I shrieked, pressing my body against his for warmth. My tank and shorts were quickly discarded, along with Anderson's trunks. The feel of his naked body in the water was electric and we floated together, fully intertwined. I loved kissing him and it took a force greater than the two of us together to get us to stop. The whining on the edge of the pool should have been a signal but I was too into Anderson's mouth and the way his hands cupped my breasts, the feel of his thumbs grazing my nipples, the nudge of his cock against my belly, to notice our agitated dog until it was too late. The splash of water rained down on us.

"Sadie!" The dog happily swam in our direction. Anderson shook his head. "So desperate for attention."

The sweet pup swam across the pool, bobbing up and down in the water. Anderson pushed her toward the step and climbed out after her, giving me a fantastic view of his body. He wrapped a towel around his waist and brought one over to the edge of the pool. Sadie licked the water off his legs and feet.

I exited the pool, covering myself with the towel, and pushed up on my toes, giving Anderson a kiss.

"Guess we have to consider the dog now when we make out in the pool," he said, brushing a wet strand of hair off my neck.

"That's okay." I link my fingers with his. "I had plans that require a bed anyway."

His eyebrow lifted in curiosity. "I'll dry off the dog. You get in the bed."

"Deal."

I'd taken a few steps when I felt my towel yank off my body. Cool air hit my skin and he grinned mischievously. "Sorry—I need it." He looked down at Sadie. "For the dog."

"Sure you do," I said, but I didn't mind one bit and walked off, knowing he had his eyes glued to my backside and that he'd be in my bedroom faster than he could swim the fifty free.

116

I was sitting in my car in the parking lot after work when my phone buzzed on the seat. I was still working on *Creature Feature*, which had turned into a bonafide hit, entering its third season. We'd been working non-stop for the last six weeks and hiatus was on the horizon. I couldn't wait to have a few weeks off, especially since I'd been fighting the same cold for weeks.

I picked up the phone and saw Amber's picture flashing across the screen in a video call.

"Hey girl," she said when I answered.

"Hey!" I replied, but my breath caught and I turned my head to cough.

"Holy shit. You're still sick?"

"Ugh, it's just this stupid, lingering cough."

"You sound awful. Have you been to a doctor?"

"Yeah, actually I have. The guys got tired of me hacking all the time and forced me to go. I'm on antibiotics—it's just a nasty case of bronchitis."

"Well good, I know you're busy and the last thing you need is to get sick."

"Yeah, none of the guys want to get sick either." I shifted in my seat. "How's everything? New York? Ginger?"

"Things are good. Just busy, you know. Ginger's about to finish up her master's program, which should give her a little more time to be at home."

"That sounds great. I know she's worked really hard in physical therapy school."

"Too hard," Amber said, with a sigh. "But it'll be worth it."

"Definitely."

"How are you and the guys?"

I looked out the window, watching the crew leave the set. "I'm good. They're good. Actually, we did something crazy a few weeks ago and—"

"I need to tell you something," she blurted.

I blinked. "What? What's wrong?"

"Nothing's wrong," she promised. "I just have some big news and I really want to share it with you. Like really, really, really want to share it with you. Actually, two big things."

"Well, tell me! Now I'm freaking out."

"Don't freak. It's a good thing. A really good thing." I could hear her nerves through the phone, but just looking at her I could tell she was about to burst. "First of all, once Ginger graduates, we're moving back to Allendale!"

"You're moving back? To Allendale? You're kidding!" That was a shock. I thought once Amber got out of here, she'd never look back. Despite my surprise, the biggest wave of relief washed over me. I'd missed having my best friend local. "That's the best news ever! Wait... what's the second thing?"

"Ginger and I have decided to have a baby."

"A baby?" I was floored, unable to even keep the astonishment off my face. "What? How?"

She laughed. "How? Good grief, Heaven. We'll find a donor."

"A donor, right, duh." I rolled my eyes at myself. "Who's going to carry the baby?"

"I am. Or that's the plan, at least. Ginger's eager to get in the work-force and use her degree and I'm ready to take a break. I've supported her while she's been in school and I think it'll be good."

"Wow. I'm just stunned. You're going to be a mom!"

"Hopefully!"

"I'm just...I'm really excited for you guys. Surprised, but excited."

"Thanks. You know you're my best friend. I just feel weird when I don't share big life things with you, you know?"

"Right. Yes, I know." Sharing with others had never been my strong suit. It was just my nature.

"Now, what were you going to say you and the guys did? Some-thing crazy?"

"Oh, right." The dog. Sadie. Something I thought was a major decision in our lives. Not that super-big-thing that people my age were doing. Nope. Once again, Heaven was out in left field doing her own, socially immature stuff. "Well, it's not quite as big as having a baby news, but we got a dog."

"You got a dog! What? When?" Her eyes were wide.

"Two weeks ago."

"Why didn't you tell me?"

"It's just been crazy. She's super sweet and fun and has brought a lot of joy to the house."

"I bet. Well, I need photos. Dozens of photos. And when I get down there, puppy kisses. Oh god, I bet she's cute."

"Super cute." I felt stupid for not telling her sooner, when she obviously wanted to know what was going on in our lives. That was what happened when you lived in a bubble. A bubble with four sexy men that kept me thoroughly occupied. I leaned back against my seat. "I really am excited for you. It's okay if I tell the guys?"

"Maybe hold off for a few weeks until I figure out the donor thing? Is that cool? I don't want you to feel like you're keeping secrets."

"No, it's totally understandable. It's a lot of pressure and excite-ment and new stuff."

"It's also a lot of girly-body part stuff and I don't know, you know how they get about all of that."

"Squeamish." We both laughed. The guys were the worst about girl stuff, although all of them have gotten used to buying me tampons and other things at the pharmacy. "Good luck, babe, and keep me posted, okay?"

"I will." She smiled into the phone. "Love you, Heaven Reeves."

"Love you, too."

We disconnected and I sat in my car for a few minutes, processing the information I'd just been given. Amber was going to have a baby. She was going to be a mom. Two things that absolutely terrified me. I was relieved she didn't want me to bring it up to the guys yet, because once I did the door would be open to us having "the conversation." The kid conversation, and I didn't think I was ready to do that yet. Not because they wouldn't want to—I knew how they felt. I wasn't the one being honest. I hadn't told them yet.

I'm really not sure if I ever want to have kids.

117

Oliver

"Can you remind me what time the meeting is on Friday?" Jackson asked, sticking his head in my office.

"Ten."

"In Oceanside?"

"Yep."

"Cool. I'll swing by here and pick you up. I'm sure you'll be here."

He had me there. Ever since word got out about our training programs for the celebrities that came through town for movies and TV shows, we we'd been busy as hell. So busy that we decided to expand to a second gym—closer to where a lot of the movies were filmed down near the beach. At first, we were opposed to creating a business in the racist, homophobic, backwater town, but then we decided to do it to spite them. Like the industry, we decided they could join us willingly or by force. We weren't going away.

The grand opening was a month away and my days were filled with contractors and designers and everything in between. That left Jackson managing the gym and me having to trust he was on top of everything. I possibly had a few control issues when it came to work.

My phone beeped—programmed in by Heaven—reminding me of our standing appointment.

Jackson's eyebrows rose, recognizing the chime. "Is it eleven? Fuck. I have a training session. Tell her I said I'll see her later, okay? We're taking Sadie to the pet store for treats."

I rolled my eyes. Jackson was majorly into this dog. "I will."

"You better get moving too, you know she doesn't like it when you're late."

I grabbed my phone and keys, following him out the office door and down the stairs to the gym floor. If I walked through the workout area I'd get stopped, so I ducked down the back hall and exited through the alley behind the gym. The phone rang before I left the parking lot.

"Hey, babe."

"I'm stalking you on the phone tracker. You should have left five minutes ago."

"I know. I'm sorry. Jackson came in and distracted me."

"You're really going to blame Jackson?" she asked, playfully. "Because if you want, I can call him and have him come distract me while I'm waiting for you."

"You wouldn't dare. This is our time together. You know that." I waited for a car to pass and turned on the main road. "Since we had to skip last week because you were sick, I'm definitely not missing out today. You still feeling better?"

"Yeah, a little bit every day, even though that pesky cough won't go away. At least we know I'm not contagious."

"I'd risk it." Going a week without our "date" had been hard enough. As long as she was truly feeling better, there was no chance she could keep me away.

I turned the car into our neighborhood, testing the speed limit. Since Heaven worked on a TV show she had every Friday off. And since it was hard for me to curtail my work habits, we arranged for some private time at home. Jackson was at the gym. Hayden at the training facility. Anderson in the pool. They gave us the time we needed.

"Two minutes," I promised and hung up.

The thought of my girl waiting for me, ready for me, gave me a thrill. One that never, ever lessened.

I screeched into the driveway, leaving the car halfway down, racing into the house. I was already hard, just thinking about her. My heart already hammering. I walked down the hall to the master bedroom, the one we'd given Heaven, and opened the door.

My eyes fell directly on her, waiting by the end of the bed. She wore a sheer black top with a lacy bra and panties. In all honesty, I'd expected her to be lying in the bed in her sweatpants and tank top reading a book, phone tracker on, ready to give me hell for making her wait.

She stood nervously, hand tugging at the bra. This wasn't her normal thing.

"Damn, you look beautiful."

"I thought I'd try something different."

I closed the distance between us and ran my hand down her arm. "You know I don't need any of this."

"I know, but you've been so sweet about me being sick I thought I'd surprise you. It was worth it to see that expression on your face." She ran her hand down my front, landing on the bulge between my legs. "And to make you excited."

"You think you don't always make me excited?" I bent and kissed her shoulder, working my way up her neck. I used my teeth to tug at her ear, my fingers to roam her back. I knew she liked to be touched all over, working her body into a frenzy before making love. "I think about you all day, babe, every day. I wake up hard and go to sleep hard, but I don't care if we have sex, or if you dress up like a goddess or just look like a regular, beautiful girl. All that matters is that I love you and you love me and that makes any time together with you special."

I dropped to my knees and kissed her belly, taking my time with her body. As much as I wanted to rip off that lace, I loved seeing her in it. Seeing the thin material hiding her best, most delicious parts.

She arched her back as I traveled lower, her hands skimming along my neck. Her hips moved, seeking friction, but I held off, kissing between her thighs. She pushed at the fabric and I chuckled at her impatience, blowing hot air across her skin before succumbing, lowering the thin, lacey straps down her hips. I sucked on her hipbones, below her belly button, and she reached for me, tugging me upward and pushing my shirt over my head. Every time Heaven and I had sex it was like a new experience. She explored my body with awe and appreciation. She touched my chest, my abs. She toyed with me, running her nails through the hair on my lower belly, scratching across my nipples.

When she had me panting, she moved to my pants, unbuttoning, removing, freeing my erection. I hissed when she stroked the length of my shaft, her fingertips soft and cool. I never, ever tired of her hands on me. Never tired of her body, her mind, her spirit.

I took my time peeling off her barely-there clothes, revealing her skin inch by inch. I reveled in her flesh, teased her nerves; licked, sucked, and caressed until she was hot, bothered, and begging for me to do what I'd wanted since I walked in that door.

I fell on my back, landing on the firm mattress with a thud, pulling her on top of me in one fluid motion. She landed on my hips, straddling me, wet and ready. Her dark hair hung over her shoulder, tickling my chest when she bent to kiss me, her mouth hot, her breath short. She hovered, guiding me inside, taking me in, eyes always expanding in surprise, like she doesn't expect my size after all this time.

We sunk into a rhythm, her hips rolling—pushing, pulling. I gripped her hips, touched her chest, pulled her down for a kiss. After all this time I knew what to expect, how to anticipate when she was close to the edge. Her breathing grew quick, her nipples tightened, her hips jerked with quick, fast motion. A thin line formed between her closed eyes and her lips parted, my name floating off her tongue.

Then she came, riding me through the waves, and I let her coast, holding back until I knew she was at the tail of her euphoria. I rolled her to her back and unleash the true desire I'd been reining in, teeth bared on her shoulder, cock buried in her body until my mind and my body separate, ecstasy claiming every fiber of my being.

I kissed her forehead, her cheeks, her mouth, and felt the warmth in her reddened cheeks. Heaven laid her head on a pillow, chest heaving, and turned to me. "I may have to get a new outfit all the time if that's going to be the reaction."

"Yeah?" I pushed my body closer to her, wanting to be in her space. "Whatever you want, babe, I'm in."

Her forehead creased quickly, then vanished, like she had a thought she wanted to rid herself of. I tilted my head, waiting to see if she would say it, but she didn't. Whatever it was vanished as fast as it came. I wrapped my arms around her and she rested her head on my chest.

That was why I took off from work. Why I made this standing appointment. Not for the sex or the orgasms or seeing her fantastic body—but this, the ending, the little period after where we laid close in a quiet house—just the two of us.

118

———

Heaven

A FEW WEEKS later I was standing in Amber's new house, in her new kitchen, drinking wine out of her new glasses. Cardboard boxes were stacked around the house, marked and labeled, most still unpacked. The move was quick—within days of graduation. Ginger found a job in town working at a physical therapy clinic near the university, and Amber started her full-time job of trying to be a mom.

On the counter in front of us was a list of compatible donors.

"You're so lucky," she said, glancing down at the list. "You don't have to worry about finding the right sperm donor for your kids. You've got four perfect guys in your life."

Her statement surprised me and I fumbled for an appropriate response, but none came, so I drank instead.

"I mean, not only are they all smart, ridiculously good-looking, loyal, kind, and generous, you've got two high-level athletes and two hard-working businessmen." She glanced up from her list where she had made a notation by one of the options. "Sure, on paper this guy is a good fit, but is he an Anderson Thompson? A Hayden Pierce?" She snorts. "Not a chance."

"Well," I started, trying to assure her. "It's not like they're not without flaws. Anderson hates change and is stubborn as hell. Hayden pushes himself too hard—obviously. Oliver works all the time—he's obsessed with making his business perfect."

"And Jackson?"

I laughed, thinking about the handsome, charming, sexy-as-hell Jackson. "Okay, you've got me there. I'm not sure he has a flaw."

"Can someone be too cute and charming?" she asked.

I picked up the list and read down the attributes. Each had a number and then a description, height, weight, education. I was overwhelmed just reading it. I couldn't imagine having to actually choose someone.

"I guess you have other problems, though."

I frowned. "Me? What kind of problems?"

Amber leaned her elbows on the counter. "Problems like, when you decide to have kids, which guy will be the dad? And will the others be upset? Or will you all have different parenting styles. I mean, it's not like you haven't struggled getting on the same page before." She shrugged and picked up the list. "I'm sure you've thought of all that."

I hadn't. Not really. My thoughts on not having kids were completely different—more Heaven-related, if anything.

"I guess it's a good thing it's not an issue."

She looked up at me. "Why not?"

I hesitate, as if knowing once I said the words I couldn't take them back. She noticed and frowned. "Hey, what's wrong?"

"It's just that...I'm not planning on having kids. Ever."

Her eyes grew big. "You don't want kids?"

Want was a tricky word—at least for me. It always had been.

"I like kids. I just don't think it's something I want to take on." Amber still looked concerned. "Look, I'm happy for you guys, really happy, and I can't wait to be the totally cool aunt for your kid one day, but personally, I'm not interested in bringing a kid into this world— well really, my world."

"Because of your relationship?"

"Because of a million things, our unconventional relationship being the least of my concerns."

Amber eyed me skeptically. She knew there was something I wasn't telling her. "Enlighten me. Really. I want to know."

I felt that familiar swell of anxiety in my chest when asked something personal. I'd never liked it, but I knew Amber was someone I could trust, so I pushed through. "I'm not sure someone with my history needs to have kids. I still take medication—would I have to stop? Change? Things are going well right now. I don't want to mess with that."

"Okay, but—"

I kept going. "The anxiety and depression is bad enough, but the suicide attempt? God, how would I explain that to a kid? And what if they're the same? What if I pass those issues on to them?"

Her expression turned sympathetic and she reached for my hand. "Heaven, you're a fantastic, smart, strong woman. Don't let those fears keep you from something like this."

"Why not? My fears have always dominated my decision-making. I try not to let it but it's just who I am." I felt the sting of tears in the corner of my eyes and stubbornly wiped them away.

"Have you told the guys how you feel?"

I shake my head. "No. I will. If it comes up."

She sighed and picked up her glass of wine and took a long drink. "It's your choice, obviously. Not everyone has to have kids any more than any other decision. I just want you to make the right one for you —based on want, not fear."

"That's the thing," I told her. "I'm happy the way things are. We all have amazing jobs, a beautiful home, a new dog—which is almost more responsibility than we can handle. She's a mess."

"Just because I'm making this decision right now doesn't mean you have to also. This baby is something Ginger and I really want. We're ready. You aren't there yet, if you ever will be. I respect that."

And that was why Amber and I were friends. We were different, we'd always been, but we also had each other's backs.

"I hope you're religiously taking your birth control pills."

I made a face. "Obviously. In fact, I just started a new one." She looked at me imploringly. I shrugged. "I was getting a lot of headaches. I thought they were from the bronchitis but the doctor thought maybe it was the pills. There was no reason not to switch it up."

"Good. You know that's one thing I don't have to stress about; accidental pregnancies. I mean, you can't get more organized than this." She pointed to the notebook. "Do you ever get worried?"

"I used to because I was worried about how my parents would handle it—or how it would derail my life, but it's been years now and it seems really unlikely."

She laughed. "You guys fuck like bunnies—there's no way you're not testing the chances."

She was right. We did have sex a lot and there were a few scares over the years, but none that lasted more than a day. I was pretty regular. I didn't say what I really thought. That maybe the gods and fate knew I shouldn't be a mother in the first place.

"I'm really glad you moved back," I said, ready to switch the subject.

"Me too, there's no way I could do this mom thing without you."

I took the list from her and start going over the names again, trying to look through an objective eye. It was hard, though. Like Amber said, when you have four perfect guys in your life, it was a challenge finding anyone better.

119

JACKSON

I AIMED the cue ball at the green- and white-striped ball on the left side of the table, lining it up with the stick. Hayden grumbled about how long it was taking, a method I'd perfected years before, knowing it made him nuts. When I was ready I knocked the white ball with just enough force to nail the green striped one into the corner pocket. Hayden groaned and I smiled. I loved playing pool against my friend. There were few games I could beat him at, and pool happened to be one of them.

"Any idea where everyone else is tonight?" he asked, watching me line up my next shot.

"Oliver's down in Oceanside checking on construction. Anderson's at some fundraiser his manager made him go to, and I think Heaven went for a run with Sadie."

"Another run? She went this morning, too." He followed that up with a laugh because I missed my shot. I waited for him to take his turn.

"The dog has a lot of energy."

"So does Heaven, but two runs in a day isn't like her, especially when she just got over bronchitis. I noticed she did it on Monday, too."

I leaned against my pool stick. "What are you saying? You think her anxiety is increasing?"

He aimed and shot, the balls clacking together. One sunk in. It was a miracle. He smiled at his success. He stopped to coat the tip of his cue with chalk. "Maybe. It's happened before. Maybe things are stressful at work or she's nervous about Amber moving back or something."

"She's also still on those steroids the doctor gave her. I think they make her jittery."

"I have noticed one other thing different lately."

"What's that?"

I wondered for a second if I should say it out loud. What if it wasn't the same for Hayden or the others? Was it just me? But we didn't keep secrets about things like this and if it had something to do with her mindset, I should tell him. "She's been a little more adventurous and definitely more horny, or something."

He nodded slowly. "Yeah same. With everything being so busy and our schedules we'd settled into once a week or so, but now it's every few days." He hit the ball again, this time missing. He swore and said, "Not that I'm complaining."

I chuckled. "No."

"But you're right," he said, "it's just another change in her recently. It could be her meds or just hormonal."

I frowned. "When did you get so good at psychology?"

"I had to after that incident in Atlanta to get back on the field." He shrugged. "And I wanted to know how to help her the best way—keep an eye out for things."

Hayden was quiet but thoughtful; I'm not surprised he'd taken a deeper interest in this. Heaven had been doing really well though, so we hadn't had a reason to worry.

"Let's just be aware, maybe tell the others."

He nodded. "Good idea."

I spun my stick like a baton. "Now stop distracting me so I can kick your ass."

"Not this time, brother."

But we both knew that threat was weak and I set up my next shot and blazed my way to a win.

120

Heaven

Sadie chased the ball into the water, leaping over the cold, frothy waves. Hayden and I paused, waiting for her to find the ball, and when she emerged dripping wet, worn yellow tennis ball in her mouth, we continued our walk.

"She really loves the ocean," Hayden said, grabbing the ball from her when she caught up. He tugged it from her teeth and threw it down the desolate beach.

"It was a good idea to come here," I said.

Hayden had cornered me that morning just before I left for my run, and suggested we go to Oceanside and introduce Sadie to the beach. Other than barking at the waves for a few minutes, she'd taken to it instantly.

We strolled down the beach together, fingers linked, shoulders grazing.

"It's so weird," I said, scanning the ocean.

"What's weird?"

"How calming I find the beach, even though it also conjures up some bad memories."

He released my hand and wrapped his arm around my shoulder, tucking me against his solid body. "That's the amazing thing about the ocean. It's in a constant state of renewal. Just like we are."

I glanced up at him. His hair was cut shorter than he used to wear it and his beard a little longer. His gray eyes still pierced into my soul every time he looked at me. We'd both gone through our struggles with loneliness and desperation, health issues, but now we were whole. At least, I thought so.

"Do you ever worry about your concussions affecting your future? Or like, the beatings your body took while playing goalie coming back to haunt you?"

"I do worry about my brain a little. Sometimes it's hard to remember things and I get headaches more often. It's better now that I'm not actively playing, but do I worry about the past coming back? No. Not really." He gave me a curious look. "Do you?"

"Sometimes."

"In what way?"

I didn't know how to say what I meant. "I don't know, like my crazy dad and my weird high-school days. The anxiety and depression. None of those things really go away. I just feel bad saddling someone else with my effed up genetics."

The wind blew up from the ocean, ruffling Hayden's dark hair, and he shot me an amused smile. "You trying to get rid of me? Because that's not going to happen. I know your dad and your sordid history—I'm part of it."

He came to a stop, dragging me into his arms. Being around Hayden made me feel safer and more protected than anyone else. Partially from his sheer size but also just his nature. He tilted my chin up and said, "What's running through your mind, Heaven?"

I shrugged. "I don't know. Changes, I guess. Amber moving home. Getting Sadie. The new gym expansion. Things at work are a little hectic. Our lives are progressing and I guess I find it a little scary."

"Progress is good, babe." He thumbed my bottom lip, opening it for him, and then bent down to give me a kiss. I allowed myself to sink into him the way I'd been doing since Amber got my mind reeling about the future and kids. Being with them physically kept me grounded, and I didn't know if it was hormones or fear or what, but I wanted them all the time. Certainly, none of them seemed to mind.

"You're right," I told him when we parted. "I'm good. Just being weird."

"That," he said, kissing my forehead, "I knew. But listen, if anything's bothering you, just tell me or the guys. We're here—always. You know that's how we do things; we get each other through."

I knew he meant it, but I couldn't help but wonder if he'd feel that way if he knew the truth about what I wanted or didn't want. If they'd still support me. Sadie ran up and shook cold drops of beach water over our feet.

I had a feeling we'd find out soon enough.

121

HEAVEN

SADIE and I were rounding the corner at the park when a wide stroller blocked our path. Monique, our neighbor, had her hands on the bar across the back—both kids were inside. The boy and girl, both looking like they were nearly the same age, squealed with delight when they saw Sadie. Sadie was also delighted and pulled me to a stop.

"Doggie, doggie," the girl said. She had on a pink hat with cat ears and shoes coated in glitter.

"Woof, woof," the boy added in. His hair was a shiny white-blonde and he had brilliant blue eyes.

Monique smiled down at her kids and then looked at me. "Heaven, right? I don't think we've formally been introduced. I'm Monique."

I shook her hand. "Sorry I'm sweaty."

"Ugh, I wish I could run again. They're just too heavy to lug all over the place."

"You were a runner?" I asked, discreetly checking her out. Monique had one of those bodies that was tight and fit and made you wonder how she'd had two kids already. Her cleavage was on point in her workout tank and her ponytail was messy but in that way that looked good—not like the disheveled mess of my own.

"Back in the day. Now I mostly go to the yoga studio. They have a child care center, which makes it easier for me to get to."

"Oh, well that make sense." Both kids leaned over and Sadie happily gave them kisses. "Sadie, stop, no one wants your slobber on them."

"Oh! They do. They love this dog! We see the guys walking them all the time."

"She needs a lot of exercise. Otherwise she starts chewing up things."

Monique laughed and looked down at her kids. "Sound familiar. Why do you think I have them out all the time? They make me nuts indoors."

I eyed the kids. I can't imagine Amber having one of these—and soon.

"I have to tell you, I was a little star-struck when I realized we were living down the street from Anderson Thompson. I'm a huge Olympics fan. Then my husband recognized Hayden. How in the world are you friends with both of them?"

"We went to high school together. We've all known each other forever."

"Oh wow, that's really cool." The kids started to squirm in their seats—bored with Sadie. "I can't imagine what it's like being around them, and not just because that level of athleticism has to be intense." She fake-fanned herself. "Not that the other two guys are bad looking."

"No, they're not." It came out more defensive than I intended but I didn't pull back. "But like all guys they're a handful; messy, distracted, obsessed with work."

"Tell me about it. My husband is commuting right now and he's only home on weekends."

"You've got the kids all by yourself all week?" That sounded like a nightmare. Score one more for the no-kids decision.

"Yeah, it's a lot, but he loves his job and we wanted a house in this neighborhood—in this school district." She shrugged, but I saw the strain on her face. "Not much I can do about it, though."

"They seem pretty close in age."

"Ashley's two and Davis is three and a half."

"Wow, that is close."

"Ashley was definitely a bit of a surprise." She looked at the girl and smiled. "A good one."

"Well, let us know if you need anything. One of us is usually around."

Her expression brightened. "That's really nice of you, but really I've got it under control." Just then the boy whined about being stuck in the stroller. She rolled her eyes. "Part of that is never stop moving! I guess we're off to the playground. It was nice to meet you, Heaven."

"Nice to meet you, too," I said, meaning it.

We went our separate directions, Sadie leading me back to our neighborhood, and in that very moment I was happy my only responsibility was my dog and the guys.

122

─────

HEAVEN SAT on the plush purple chair holding a glass of wine, nervously eating cheese off the plate on the coffee table. She'd been acting weird all afternoon, all the way up to us leaving for the house-warming party at Amber and Ginger's new house.

"What's going on with her?" I asked Hayden, who'd just come off the back deck with two cold beers. He glanced over at Heaven, taking her in.

"I don't know, man. I tried to talk to her about it on the beach and she told me some stuff about the changes in our lives stressing her out. I get it but, I don't know, we're really pretty stable right now, don't you think?"

I took a sip of my beer. "What kind of changes did she mention?"

"The dog. The new gym. Stuff at work." He looked around the house. "Amber and Ginger moving back."

"None of that is earthshattering."

"I didn't think so, either."

"Something's got her rattled. She's running all the time and I swear to god she's eaten twelve pieces of cheese in the last three minutes."

As though she sensed us talking about her, Heaven looks over with a questioning expression. Hayden raised his glass to her and I waved. Wow. We both watched her shove three pieces of cheese in her mouth.

"Maybe she's just hungry," I said.

"Maybe."

I drank the remainder of my beer and carried it over to the counter. Hayden wandered over to talk with Oliver and Ginger. I took the opportunity to head to the hallway bathroom.

I had my hands covered in soap when the door jiggled. "Hold up! Occupied."

I dried off and opened the door. Heaven stood on the other side.

"Hey—" she pushed me back into the room and followed me in, the door closing behind her with a click. Without hesitation, she fisted her hand in my shirt and pulled me down, pressing her soft, pink lips against mine.

"Remember back in high school how you found me in the hallway of that party, saving me from that asshole Spencer?" she asked suddenly.

I frowned. Why the hell was she talking about Spencer? "Yeah."

"I wanted you so bad that night. Not like this—not dirty and horny—but I had the biggest crush on you and god, you hated me."

"You know I didn't hate you." I brushed her hair over her shoulder. "I was being stubborn and jealous." I wrapped my hand around her hip. "And for the record, I was eighteen, so trust me, I was definitely thinking dirty and horny things about you."

She laughed, low and husky.

"Are you drunk?" I asked her, having tasted the wine on her tongue.

"Maybe a little." Her hips pressed into mine and suddenly her intent dawned on me.

"What did you come in here for, Heaven?"

Her blue eyes blazed. "What do you think I came in here for?"

Just her tone made me hard. The look she gave me and the thought of taking her right there. I glanced at the door, like I could see everyone else down the hall and in return they could see me, but the fog of lust overtook me and I muttered, "Dammit," and crashed my mouth to hers.

I lifted her on the counter, knocking off the box of tissue. "Thank god you wore a skirt," I said, pushing it up and dragging down her panties. I pulled her to the edge and spread her thighs, my height making the position perfectly doable. Her fingers twisted in my hair, mine lowered my zipper and then I touched her, making sure she was ready.

"Don't wait," she told me, reaching to pull me close. Her hand guided me inside and she exhaled, hot against my neck. It was awkward and hurried, sexy and exhilarating. It didn't take long for her breath to quicken, her body to shiver, her teeth pressed against my shoulder until she crumpled against my body with release. I loved the weight of her against me as I thrusted inside, loving her mouth, her hands, her everything.

"I love you," I told her, gasping—spilling—inside of her. "I love you so fucking much, do you know that?"

The words came out in a shudder of breath, honest and true. I was damn lucky to have this goddess in my life.

"I do," she said, kissing my neck, jaw, and mouth. "And I love you, too."

We stared at one another, content and happy in this awkward moment in our friend's home, until a knock rapped on the door.

"Time for dinner. You okay?" Hayden asked, obviously noticing our disappearance.

"Yep. Out in a minute," I replied in as normal a voice I could find.

We cleaned up and I left the small room first, bumping into Hayden at the end of the hall. His eyes skimmed my disheveled appearance. "Everything alright?"

"Uh, yes. Turns out Heaven was hungry for more than just cheese."

He laughed and shook his head, walking off toward the food.

When Heaven joined us a few moments later we all clicked into
place, her nervous energy from before dispelled. Maybe that was all
she needed, a quick fuck in the bathroom.

God knew it worked for me.

123

———

Heaven

The encounter with Anderson in the bathroom calmed my nerves—at least a little—for what I knew was coming. Amber had told me they'd found a donor and had the procedure. What she hadn't told me was whether she was pregnant or not. I had little doubt something was coming and it twisted my stomach into knots.

Dessert had been served, rich chocolate cake with pink and blue flowers on top. The boys were clueless, but I knew...I waited, and my two friends stood at the head of the table, hands intertwined. "We have some news," Ginger said, unable to fight the smile on her face. She glanced at Amber and together they said, "We're having a baby."

The guys reacted predictably, tossing out their congratulations, giving hugs all while I smiled, focusing all my attention on the two women as they explained the process they were going through, the miracle of science, and the decisions they had to make. Amber slipped to the kitchen and returned with a bottle of sparkling cider. Ginger gathered the crystal glasses they'd received at their wedding.

"We went through a long list of donors, but nothing felt right,"

Ginger said, filling each glass to the rim. "Finally, we decided to ask my brother. That way, a little piece of my DNA will be in the baby Amber's going to carry."

"That's really cool," Oliver said, smiling broadly. "I love that your brother is okay with this."

"It took a little convincing," she said, "but in the end, he understood. It's family—it binds us all together."

Jackson was sitting next to me and leaned over, arm slung over the back of my chair. "Did you know?"

"I knew they were trying." I took a bite of cake. A big bite.

"Well it's pretty exciting, right? A baby! I mean, I thought getting a dog was a big decision."

"It *was* a big decision, and it turns out, we're great dog owners."

He smiled that charming, dimpled grin at me. "Amazing dog owners."

I looked back at Amber and Ginger. "I think they'll make good parents, don't you?"

"Definitely." I felt his fingers twist in my hair. "Just like we will one day."

And there it was. The opening. The door. The question--or statement, rather. I knew this would happen once the topic was out there. I knew I'd have to deal with this.

This was the real change I wanted to tell Hayden about on the beach. This was the real reason my nerves were shot so badly I fucked Anderson in the bathroom (although, that one was definitely worth it), it was the reason behind my twice-a-day runs and everything else going on with me. I'd been looking for a diversion. A distraction. Anything not to have to face this day.

Thankfully, Jackson didn't expect a response. Unfortunately, I knew it was because he thought I agreed with him.

Glasses were deposited in front of each seat and I took mine in hand before standing. "I'd like to make a toast—to my friends—who are going to be amazing parents. I think I can speak for everyone here that we're so happy for you and excited about being part of this kid's future."

I raised my glass and everyone followed. I meant every word. I just hoped the boys would stick by me when I told them the truth about what I wanted. I hoped we'd all still be together to give the baby and our friends all the support they would need.

124

"Dammit," I muttered, rifling through my cosmetics counter, the drawers underneath and the cabinet on the wall. "Has anyone seen my rubbing alcohol?"

Lea popped her head around the corner of the small partition, separating the main area of the trailer from a small room in the back. "It was on the shelf yesterday."

"What shelf?" I snapped. Sadie looked up from her bed in the corner. Yep. The cool thing about working on sets like this was the ability to bring my dog with me.

"The shelf above the worktable."

I scanned the shelf in front of me. "It's not there."

Lea stopped whatever she was doing and walked over. She pushed up on her toes and reached for the shelf, plucking the container off with two fingers. She held it out. "You mean this alcohol?"

I sighed and took it. "Yes. Thank you. I swear, I couldn't see it."

"If it were a snake, it would have bitten you."

"I know." I rubbed my face. "I swear my brain is mush lately."

She sat in a makeup chair and spun around. "Do you want to talk about it?"

"No."

Her perfectly arched eyebrow rose up her forehead. "Seems like you're kind of all over the place."

"I'm just tired—I haven't been sleeping great and I've been running a lot." I glanced over at Sadie. "She needs a lot of exercise."

"So that's why you're looking thin these days."

I caught a glimpse of myself in the mirror. I didn't look particularly thin, but I did look tired. "Not with all the cake I've been eating. I made Oliver go to the store last night and get one from the bakery. I swear I ate half of it by myself."

She laughed. "You didn't."

"I did. You think those guys eat carbs? And look like that? If anything sweet comes in the house, it's up to me to eat or it gets trashed."

"No, I hear you. I'm pretty sure AJ doesn't eat anything but meat and eggs." She leaned back. "So, Oliver's getting you cakes...how are the other guys?"

"They're good. Oliver and Jackson are busy opening the new gym. The other two are training and at work. You know how it is." I sat in my own makeup chair. The actors wouldn't be back for another ten minutes. "What about you? How's AJ?"

She smiled when I mentioned him—even after all this time. I wasn't sure if they would stick, both of them so young and AJ being a rising star, but they were a good fit.

"Good. We're going to visit his family over the show break."

"Really? In Virginia?"

"Yep. They live on a farm. With animals."

"That'll be nice."

"Any plans for the break?" she asked.

"Just the grand opening of the gym. Maybe sleeping in." I hadn't told her about Amber and the baby. They were waiting a few months to announce publicly.

"Sleeping in sounds good."

There was a rap on the door and AJ stuck his head in. He was freshly scrubbed and his eyes went straight to Lea.

"Hey babe, can you get me in the chair early?"

Lea looked at me. I was in charge of AJ's makeup. "Yep. Let's get this started."

He stopped and kissed Lea on the lips before easing into my chair. I was glad for the interruption—glad to be busy. If there was one place of true solace in my life, it was in this trailer doing my job.

125

———

Jackson

The shift of the bed roused me awake and I reached out my hand, expecting Sadie's soft fur. She made the rounds at night, mostly sleeping with Heaven, but if she could find someone else to give her attention, she'd give it a shot.

Fur wasn't what I touched, instead it was the smooth warmth of skin. I pulled myself from the lull of sleep, my cock twitching on instinct.

"Heaven?" I asked, sitting up. Her palm moved to my bare chest, pushing me back down. I blinked into the dark, finally making out her form, her face in the pale light coming from the window. She straddled my legs and the twitching shifted to full hardening.

"I've been thinking about you all day," she confessed quietly. "While I was at work. When I was walking the dog. Later in the shower. I was in bed and I just kept thinking about you. About your mouth and your body and frankly, your dick."

She kissed me, bare breasts pressing against my chest. This...this was something different. Something unexpected.

"So you just walked down here naked?"

"Is that a problem?" I saw her head tilt in the dark.

"Nope. Definitely not."

My body and urges took over, not caring why she came in here late at night like this, only gleeful that she did. Her body ground down on me and my hands gripped her hips, our bodies warming up to one another.

Her mouth tasted like mint, her skin like lotion. I ran my teeth down her shoulder and kissed her breasts, licking her nipples until she shuddered and squirmed against me.

"I love how that feels," she said, more vocal than I'd ever heard her.

"Fuck, Heaven, you're killing me, is that your plan?"

She laughed in the dark. "I could think of worse ways to go."

I ran my hands up and down her body, cupping her ass and gripping her cheeks. She moaned into my mouth, lifting her hips and touching my raging cock. She guided me to the warmth between her legs, sighing with contentment.

"I love the way you feel inside of me."

Despite the late hour, the surprise, and lack of foreplay, it didn't take either of us long to fall into a quick, savage rhythm. Her moans were loud, fueling my need and want. I slipped my fingers between us, helping her along, and she leaned back, hair dangling down her back, giving me an exquisite view of her body.

"Just like that," she said, riding both my cock and hand. "Oh my god, Jax, just like that."

Her jaw slacked and her breasts bounced and I clenched my jaw, keeping my composure. I almost came twenty times just watching her on top of me, feeling the love and lust that intensified as she got closer and closer to slipping over the edge. Her body shifted gears, slowing, and I rubbed easy circles around her bundle of nerves until she sucked in a breath and cried out, shattering from the inside out.

"Beautiful," I said, watching her ride the wave. Her hips continued to roll, urging me on, and I grabbed the flesh of her thighs and pulled her to me. Her hands landed against my chest, rubbing my nipples beneath her palms.

"Does that feel good?"

"Yes," I grunted.

"Do you want me to go harder?"

"Jesus, Heaven." She leaned over me and slammed down. I wasn't sure what her intentions were when she came in here, but now I was starting to think she wanted to kill me. Death by orgasm.

Yeah, I'd take it.

I held on as long as I could, but with a goddess riding on top of me, her hair long and spilling over her breasts and the sheer sight of her I succumbed, thrusting hard with a deep guttural moan. I pulled her to me as I came, kissing her senseless, wanting to be connected, share the same air, touch in as many places as possible.

When I was spent I fell back on the pillow, looking up at the woman above me. She hadn't moved and I saw the small wisp of a smile toying on her lips.

"That was amazing," I said.

"It really was."

"I love you," I told her, meeting my eyes to her. I could never say it enough.

She fell forward and wrapped her arms around me, still connected at the hips. "I love you too, Jackson Hall."

I believed her and I was grateful as hell that she'd showed up in my room, but there was something off about this nighttime visit. Something that I'd follow up with in the morning, but for now I laid in the arms of my lover and held her tight, not wanting the moment to end.

126

―――――――

Thursday morning meant the four of us meet at six a.m. for a private session at the gym. The rest of the facility was open, but we had secure rooms for our high-profile clients. Really, we used the time to catch up, work out, and challenge one another like we always had.

Anderson was positioned under a large bench press, waiting as Jackson loaded the weights. Fifty pounds across both sides. I was on an identical one next to him and Hayden slid the same weight across the bar. We all moved into position. Me and Anderson lifting—the others spotting.

"You know the rules: first one to get to ten," Jackson said.

I focused on my own weight, trying not to get distracted by the grunting and movement next to me. I lifted the bar and pushed up— the goal was ten. The first six came easy, but the final four were a struggle. I grunted and clenched my jaw. I felt the burn down my arms and across my chest as my muscles strained.

"Two more, dude, two more," Hayden said watching closely, ready to grab the bar if I needed him. I heard Jackson encouraging Anderson. There was more on the line than pride. The loser had to buy drinks the next time we all went out—and the winner got to soak in Heaven's attention, while the rest of us backed off for the night. I didn't give a damn about the drinks, but I sure as hell wanted Heaven.

I pushed, struggling against the weight—moving forward with sheer determination. Hayden clapped behind me, a smile on his face, making me confident and giving me the boost I needed to get through to the last one.

"Ten!" Hayden shouted, at the same time as Jackson. I looked to the side and my elbows wobbled. "Fuck." Hayden grabbed the bar out of my hands and lifted it over the rack. Exhausted and drenched in sweat, I looked over at Anderson. He looked as beat as I did.

Jackson shrugged. "It was a tie."

"Are you serious?" Anderson asked skeptically. My boy didn't like to lose—even by a tie.

"He's right," Hayden agreed.

Anderson and I looked at one another. He sighed and swung his legs over the bench to a sitting position. I did the same.

"So how do we want to handle this? Rematch?" he asked.

"There's another option," Jackson said.

I glanced up at my partner. "What's that?"

"You could split the winnings. I doubt Heaven would mind."

Hayden leaned against the bars. "He's probably right."

I stood and walked over to Anderson, offering him a hand. He took it and lifted himself off the bench. "We'll give her the choice. She may tell us both to fuck off."

Jackson snorted before walking out of the room and down the hall. We always hit the sauna after our workout—a little time to decompress before the rest of the day.

Again, it was a private area—for our most exclusive clients. We quickly changed, wrapping clean, white towels around our waists, and took a seat inside, everyone finding a spot to sprawl out on the benches. The heat felt good against my sore, overworked, muscles.

"So, Jackson," Hayden said, cradling the back of his head with his hands against the wall, "I got up to let Sadie out last night and passed your room."

"Oh yeah?" Jackson's eyes were closed but he slowly opened them.

"Thing's sounded...rowdy."

"If that's what you want to call a surprise visit by Heaven, then okay." Sweat dripped down his face. "But seriously, she showed up in the dark and just...I don't know. She was ready."

Anderson nodded. "That was her in the bathroom the other night at the baby announcement. No complaints, but I didn't see that coming."

Their eyes swung to me. "Nothing unusual here other than her being pretty adamant about me taking time off to meet up with her."

I glanced at Hayden but he shrugged. "I haven't been on the receiving end of such treatment." He leaned over placing his elbows on his knees. "But we had a weird talk a few weeks ago—it seemed like something was bothering her. She was talking about 'saddling' people with her baggage. At the time I thought she was talking about us, but after the other night..."

"What?" I asked.

"She knew Amber and Ginger were trying to have a baby," Jackson said. "She mentioned it the other night." He looked at Hayden. "Is that what you think she was talking about? Passing her baggage onto a kid?"

"Maybe. She mentioned her mom and dad, her anxiety and depression—all things that would be hereditary. I just didn't get it at the time."

"Do you think that's what she wants? A baby?" Anderson asked.

"Or doesn't want, is more likely."

The four of us grew silent, taking in all that information. I had a strong, personal reaction that I kept to myself. I knew I wanted kids—with Heaven—with this family, but I also knew that was a decision I couldn't make on my own. From the looks on the others' faces there was no doubt they knew that, too.

"This is something we'll have to talk about, don't you think?" Jackson asked.

"Yeah," Anderson agreed. "I knew the day would come, I just didn't realize it would be so soon."

"It doesn't have to be," Hayden said. "We're not Amber and Ginger. We don't have to make a choice like this now."

"You don't think we need to at least know where everyone stands?" I asked. "Because this...this is the kind of shit that could be a deal-breaker. It could change everything." All three of them gave me a dirty look and I held up my hands. "I'm not trying to be a dick, but ultimately this is Heaven's choice, and then we have to decide if we want to go along with it."

Despite the heat of the sauna, every muscle in my body tensed with the realization of what this meant if Hayden was right. In one moment the trajectory of our lives shifted, one topic, one decision. We walked into that room one way and left feeling uncertain about the future. What did Heaven want? And would her desires line up with our own?

127

"Babe, it's my turn."

"In a minute."

"You've had the controller for an hour." Hayden reached for my hands. I jerked away. Sadie, asleep next to me on the couch, wagged her tail.

"I'm in the middle of something."

"You're being a hog."

"Shut up. You're just mad I'm on level eighteen."

He rolled his eyes but I kept my focus on the game in front of me. Two more levels. I could beat my score.

"It's your fault, you know," he said to Jackson, who was lounging on the chair near the sofa.

"How is her being a game hog my fault?"

"You're the one that taught her how to play. She used to just watch us but no, you thought it would be more fun if she joined in. Now she's a maniac."

I laughed. "I am not a maniac."

"You're obsessed."

I jabbed my thumb into the button and muttered a curse at the game. "I am *not* obsessed. You just suck and you can't handle it."

"Did you just say I sucked?"

"At the game, duh."

There was a beat of silence, which I took to mean he'd finally shut up about it, but my character was climbing the mountain, almost at the top near the treasure chest when—oof.

"What the hell?" I shouted, feeling the strong grip of arms around my chest. Jackson stood in front of me with a devilish grin on his handsome face. He plucked the controller out of my hands, while Hayden held me against his chest. Sadie jumped off the couch and barked at the two of us. "I wasn't finished!"

"Yeah, you are," Hayden said.

I watched in horror as Jackson reset the game. "What? Why did you do that?"

"Because there are rules, Heaven," Jackson said, shaking his head, "and you don't follow them. We take turns, no one hogs the game. You don't just get to come in here and mess with the system."

I squirmed out of Hayden's arms and turned to glare at him. Sadie circled our feet. "Well, your system sucks."

Anderson and Oliver walked out of the back room. The tall swimmer rubbed his hand through his hair, leaving it a rumpled mess. "What the hell are you guys arguing about?

"Video games—"

"Heaven's not playing fair—"

"Nothing."

They all glared at me. I shrugged. "*They* have a bad attitude."

Hayden's eyes narrowed and I placed my hands on my hips. A ripple of energy ran between us. I opened my mouth to say something snarky but he lunged, coming after me with those massive hands and ridiculously strong arms, and I yelped and bolted.

Somehow, I narrowly escaped his grasp, rushing around the kitchen table and through the narrow space. Jackson cackled with laughter, loving every moment. Hayden bent his knees and spread his arms, cornering me in. My heart hammered in my chest, not because I was really afraid of him, but because this was a game and I desperately wanted to beat him. I looked to my left and right, noting my only option was with one of the two guys watching the scene with interest.

I raised my eyebrows in Oliver's direction and he shook his head. "Don't involve me in this."

I shifted to Anderson, who held my gaze with his brilliant green eyes.

"Dude, don't interfere," Hayden warned.

"You guys are acting like children." Anderson crossed his arms over his chest. "I mean, is this what you're going to do one day when Amber and Ginger ask us to watch their kid?"

Jackson snorted, already involved in a new game. "Or when we have our own?"

It was like the air in the room evaporated. Hayden's entire body shifted, moving away from the playful stance so he could glare at Jackson. Anderson's hand thrust in his hair and Oliver's eyes narrowed. I glanced between them, the statement bouncing around my head. I'd known it was coming—there was no escaping it, but now? Like this? And the problem wasn't just that Jackson brought up having kids—it was the guilty, concerned expression on the guys' faces. They knew.

"Heaven," Oliver said, frowning a little.

I shook my head, not wanting to hear anything he had to say. The feeling of playfulness vanished in my gut and was replaced with unease. Not now. I turned and walked toward the door, Sadie nipping at my heels.

"Babe." I felt Hayden's hand, gentle on my shoulder. I shrugged him away.

"Not now."

"We're going to have to talk about this."

"There's nothing to talk about." Which was what you said when there was a shit-ton to talk about. I opened the door and let the dog pass through. "Have fun. I'll be back later."

"Heaven, wait—" Anderson called my name.

I shut the door—shut him out. There would be time for us to talk about this later, but not now. Not today.

128

———

"So you just left."

"Yeah, I left."

"And then what?"

"I came here." Sadie and I had shown up on Amber's front door twenty minutes before. She took one look at me and the dog and let us in. "I didn't know what else to do."

"Well, you could have stayed and talked to them."

"I'm not ready."

"I'm not sure you have that choice. All Jackson did was make an innocent comment and you flipped out. You owe them the truth."

"They already know. I saw it on their faces. They must have figured it out." I sighed and rested my elbows on the kitchen table. "You know they gossip like school girls."

She rolled her eyes. "They talk about you because they love you."

I looked at my friend. She wasn't showing much but there was a tiny bulge beneath her tight gray T-shirt. I was so happy for her, truly, but I was also jealous. Why did I have to make everything so difficult? Why couldn't just this one thing be easy?

"What am I going to do if they feel differently?" I asked. "What if they want kids? What if only two of them want kids and the other two don't?"

"There are a million what-ifs in this scenario and none of them will get answered until you sit down with them and talk it over."

A feeling of dread filled my stomach. "What if I lose them, Amber?"

She sighed and moved to my side of the table, bumping my hip with hers and wrapping her arm around me. "You guys have been through a lot—but avoiding stuff has never been the way to deal with it. Just talk to them, Heaven. Tell them what you want, what you're feeling. They'll understand."

"And if they don't?"

"Then it's better to deal with it now than five years down the road, don't you think?"

I knew she was right but the idea terrified me. They had stuck by me through a lot of rocky shit. I just didn't think it was fair to do it again, but like we all know, life wasn't fair. Not for me or the Allendale Four, at least.

I didn't know what to expect that night when I got home. Maybe the four of them waiting in the living room, ready to talk. Maybe they were still playing video games, the entire thing part of my paranoia and imagination. When I pushed through the back gate, Sadie got excited and raced ahead. Anderson was stretched out on the patio couch, feet dangling from the edge, book in hand.

Sadie rushed to him, giving him affection—too much, probably— by shoving her nose in his face.

"Hey, girl," he said, scratching under her chin. He sat up, eyes landing on me. "Hey, you."

"Hi."

He swung his legs around and placed his feet on the ground, still petting the dog. "You okay?"

"Yeah, I spent the afternoon with Amber."

He nodded. "Did you eat? Oliver made dinner."

"I had some food at her place."

Space stretched between us and I saw the tight clench of his jaw —the one that meant he was thinking hard. "About earlier…"

"That was me being weird."

"I don't think so, Heaven. I think it was about something you're not telling us." He leaned back against the cushion and Sadie took that as an invitation to jump in his lap. He grunted when her paws landed in his lap. "Come talk to me."

My first instinct was to run but that was stupid--pointless, really. I walked across the patio and sat in the chair adjacent to the couch. "I've been struggling a little since Amber told me she wanted a baby, and even more so since she announced she's pregnant."

"Why is it bothering you so much?"

"Because it made me think about myself—about us—and what I want and what you guys want for the future and how I'm not sure that's the same thing."

"I admit that we've never talked about it. I guess it just seemed far away and then there was that time we weren't together." He ran his hand through his hair. "But yeah, it's something we should discuss."

"I guess so."

"Well tell me, Heaven Reeves, do you want kids?"

I looked up at Anderson's face—the face I'd been in love with since I was thirteen years old. I wanted to tell that face yes, because part of me wanted that to be true. Did I want to carry his baby? Any of their babies? God, yes. I wanted that connection, that bond. But all of it fell away when I thought about what I was bringing to the table —I'm not a genetically superior athlete or confident business person. I'm a girl with a million problems and a shit-ton of baggage.

None of that came out.

"I don't know. I mean, I don't think so. I'm not sure."

"Okay." He nodded slowly. "You know we don't have to decide today, but it's still something to discuss."

"What about you," I asked. "Do you want kids?"

His eyes blazed and they held mine. "I'm not going to lie to you,

Heaven. I do want kids and I've always—I mean, *always*—assumed you would be the mother of my child."

My eyes filled with tears. That was the one reality with Anderson. He was always truthful and earnest. "I'm sorry."

"Hey," he said, standing and walking over to me. He pulled me off the chair and wrapped his arms around me. "Don't apologize. I made an assumption and that's on me. First and foremost, I want you in my life. Everything else is icing. Got it?"

I shook my head. "You deserve everything you want, icing included."

He wrapped his arms around me and I felt safe close to him. "Can we talk about this a little more? Figure out our feelings on it. It's not something we can just toss out there and run from."

I knew in my heart he was right. I also felt the insecurities in my mind, unraveling at the idea. I didn't argue it though, knowing there was no getting out of this one.

"You let me know how you want to handle this. We can talk about it together or separately. Whatever you want to do."

I sniffed and wiped my face. "Okay. Let me think on it."

"Take your time." He kissed my forehead.

Together we walked into the house, the dilemma still hovering over us like a dark cloud, but less urgent and panic-inducing all the same. The hard part was knowing I couldn't escape from this conversation. We would be having it and sooner rather than later, I would know exactly where my decisions would place me with the Allendale Four.

129

Oliver

It had been a long time since we'd had any sort of major argument or disagreement among the five of us. We'd been coasting on a honeymoon phase for quite a while, so I guess it was reasonable for a blip to come up between us. But damn, who knew that blip would be so big.

After Heaven bolted and ran to Amber's, she came back and spoke with Anderson. We all slept on our own that night, giving her space, and in the morning she looked a little better. Jackson forced me to stay home and did the same with the others. When she walked out of her room, he said, "Come on. We're going to the Diner," and for once, she didn't argue.

Now we sat in our regular spots in the circular booth in the back, mounds of food on the table. We'd long ago found the best way to order. Big stacks of pancakes, piles of scrambled eggs, a huge plate of bacon. We each took what we wanted, sharing from the middle of the table. We all ate less pancakes now than we did in our teens, but everyone still ate an impressive amount of food, while Heaven sat with her two pancakes, small scoop of eggs, and two slices of bacon.

Some things never changed.

"Sorry about my meltdown yesterday," she says after swallowing a mouthful of food. "I think I'd been stressing about this for a while and I just kind of blew up."

"Don't apologize, babe," Hayden replied, intentionally looking at Anderson. "We all have our moments."

"I know, but that was an epic moment, at least for me, and totally out of line." She glanced at Jackson. "You didn't say anything wrong. I've just been feeling sensitive."

I squeezed her thigh under the table, hoping she understood how much we supported her. Her hand lowered over mine and she squeezed back.

"Anderson said we could all talk separately or together. I'm fine with either—or both. But I want to be clear on my feelings with us all together so that nothing gets lost."

Hayden put down his fork and Anderson waited patiently.

"Amber announcing she wanted a baby totally threw me. It just hadn't been on my radar, other than just my own vague feelings I'd had for a long time. But she made me realize we're at that age where we have to think about things like this. It's no longer in the way-off future but around the corner, and that freaked me out." She inhaled and took a moment to sip her coffee. "The truth is that I don't think I can have kids—physically, yes—emotionally...I don't know. With my mental health background, my family drama, and my general distrust of people outside our circle, I just don't feel like it's the right thing to do." She looked at each of us. "Add in our unconventional relationship, I'm not even sure how it would work."

If one thing had been a constant in our lives, it was Heaven overthinking everything. This was clearly no different. Her feelings were valid, but also off-base. The hard part was telling her this without undermining her reasoning.

Each person at the table had on a game-face. Not one of the guys was revealing any emotion, although I knew they probably felt like I did, warring emotions between my love for Heaven, my desire to protect and make her happy, and then the absolute, primal need to make her a mother.

"I guess what I need you to think about, really think about, is will this be a deal-breaker for any of you?" she said in a quiet voice. "And don't tell me now. I don't want any fast answers. I just want you to be true to yourself and to what we have together."

"You got it, babe," Hayden said, throwing his arm around her shoulder. Jackson nodded and winked, not needing to say a word. I laced my fingers with hers under the table, holding on tight. She may have thought she's going to push us away—me away—but there was no chance in hell that was happening.

She looked at Anderson. "You okay with this?"

"Yeah, I'm okay if you are."

There was no doubt Heaven was struggling, but no more than in the past. We could get through this—she would get through it—but the bigger question was, would we get through it together?

130

Heaven

"I'm headed out for a run," I told the guys. They were focused on the TV screen and a baseball game. Hayden glanced up, eyeing the red leash in my hands and Sadie circling my feet. I reached down and scratched her head.

"This late?"

"Sadie's going crazy. We skipped our morning run because it was raining." I didn't normally run after dark, but it had been raining all day and the dog wasn't the only one restless.

"It's not raining now? You know you've had that cough. Are you sure you should be running?

"It's let up and I feel fine."

There was a play on the screen and everyone shouted. He looked over at the screen and then back at me. "Let me change and get my shoes. I'll come with you."

I didn't argue, because I'm not a fan of running at night alone—even with Sadie as company. I slipped out the back door and a few minutes later Hayden joined me, grabbing Sadie's leash and wrapping it around his fist. He wore a tight-fitting red Atlanta United T-shirt and black shorts. We started off at a slow jog and went down our regular route toward the park. It was fall, and wet leaves crunched under our feet. It's becoming my favorite time of the year—when things cool off and I saw a break coming in work. The TV show filmed late summer through early fall for the current season, then picked back up for the winter.

The trees blew over our heads, shaking raindrops down on our heads and shoulders. We weren't the only ones taking advantage of the break in the rain, and other dog walkers, joggers, and exercisers passed us occasionally. Hayden and I had worked out a compatible pace while he was in therapy for his twisted ankle. Obviously with his long legs he could out-run me, but he held back and together we jogged the lamp-lit park path.

Rain started to fall, big fat drops, and he reached for my arm, pulling me to a stop. The playground with a covered gazebo was just ahead. He tugged me and the dog in that direction and we ran over.

Two seconds after we got under the cover the sky let loose, dumping rain.

"Shit—we barely made it," he said, wiping his face with his shirt.

I did the same, feeling the cool rush of air now that I was wet and no longer running.

"Do you think we can talk?" he said, pointing to a picnic table. I followed him over.

"About what?"

He gestured for me to sit. I did, but instead of him sitting next to me, he stood in front of me. "About the having kids thing."

I looked down at my feet, my heart kicking into gear, stronger than my running speed. "Uh, sure."

"Just so you know, I never thought much about having kids. For the past decade my thoughts have been strictly soccer, food, and sex." He gave me a lazy smile. "Somewhere in there, you replaced the sex one with yourself and well, sex with you."

His words ignited a shiver up my spine. Hearing Hayden confess this wasn't a surprise but it certainly was affirming. He could have anyone—*anyone*. But he wanted me.

We hadn't spoken about the baby issue. Not since the diner a few mornings before. Everyone seemed to walk on eggshells—including myself. Hayden, historically, wasn't one to shy away from things. He was quiet. Thoughtful. When he was ready, he didn't hold back.

"But now that the topic is here and my life has slowed down a little more, I can see the bigger picture of the future—our future—and it's given me a lot to think about."

My stomach twisted nervously—so much I thought I may puke. Other than Anderson, none of the guys have told me what they really thought—or want.

"So," I said, bracing myself, "what do you want?"

He leaned forward, placing both hands on the table, on either side of my hips. "I love you. I love our family as it is. I love the way things are going. I love our dog and I love the time we spend together." He pressed his forehead to mine. "I'm with you to the end, babe."

His words rattled me, forcing me to ask, "Are you sure?"

"Once upon a time I deprived myself of you and this family. It was the dumbest fucking mistake of my life. I'll never do it again. I learned that sometimes we make sacrifices for the group as a whole—it's how we keep going. The idea of having a kid isn't a deal breaker for me. Not having you in my life is. Understand?"

I nodded, my heart feeling full. I grabbed his damp T-shirt and pulled him close. "Thank you for telling me all that."

"I've got nothing to hide from you, Heaven Reeves. You own my heart and my soul and have for a long damn time." He lifted a wet piece of hair off my neck. "I'd show you how much right now if we weren't in a public park and it wasn't cold as fuck."

He smiled cheekily.

"What about making out? Can we make out until the rain stops? It'll keep us warm and there's nothing indecent about that," I said, knowing that once Hayden was horny enough, he was anything but decent. The one thing I knew I could do was get him riled up enough to make it worth it when we got back home.

"Yeah, I can keep you warm." He moved to the table next to me and wrapped his arms around me at the same time his lips met my mouth.

A man of his word, I let him warm me up, and when the rain finally slowed we walked home, hand in hand, feeling on more stable ground. When we got back to the house the game was over, the guys all in their rooms, and I let Hayden lead me to mine so he could show me exactly how much he loved me.

131

HAYDEN

WE WERE DRENCHED by the time we got to Heaven's room—her skin puckered with goosebumps. I led her to the bathroom and turned the water on in the shower, pushing the heat all the way.

Even standing before me like a drowned rat; hair plastered to her cheeks, this woman owned me. I'd meant it when I told her so under the gazebo. She owned my heart, my body, my soul. There was nothing I wanted to do more now than show her, so as steam filled the room, I lifted her soggy shirt over her head and pulled my own off as her bra fall to the floor.

The shower was ridiculously large—built for Oliver's stepmother's delusions of grandeur. Two large showerheads arched overhead with a glass wall dividing the space. A small bench sat on the side, filled with Heaven's hair products. She stripped off her panties, giving me an exquisite view of her ass and I followed, dropping my rain soaked shorts. My hands were on her before she ever touched the steaming hot water.

Immediately I relished the warmth of the water and the closeness of her body. I was already aroused, had been since we walked through the door. My hunger only increased as she removed her clothes and entered the shower. My cock bobbed between us and she reached for me, stroking my length. I exhaled with relief and grabbed the bottle of soap off the shelf, squeezed a glob of purple goo in my hands and leisurely soaped up her body. The suds were slippery over her curves but I wasn't in a hurry. I pressed a hand against the wall and leaned into her, kissing her hard under the falling water.

I wasn't the only one enjoying myself—her nipples were peaked —her fingers traveled my body. I was cut—better than during my playing days when I was more about mass—needing the size for intimidation in the goal. These days I was leaner and Heaven's hands wandered the defined muscles of my abs, the sharp dip of the V I worked my ass off to get, and the hard expanse of my chest.

"This is my favorite part of your body," she said bending over, nipping her teeth at the soft flesh under my belly button. My cock sprung in reaction. She squeezed the soap into her own palm and coated my balls, shaft, and ass.

I ran a hand down her side, grazing her belly and inching below. My lips traveled from her mouth to her breasts and I heard her breath hitch—the signal that she was ready. I reached for her but she spun, backing herself against me. Ever since that first time we'd done it like this, Heaven made it clear it was her favorite position. I sure as hell agreed. She looked at me over her shoulder and I kissed her while lifting her leg on the bench. Her foot steadied on the flat surface.

With our bodies soapy and slick, overheated and wanting, I slid inside, taking my time so I could feel every inch of her. Her approval echoed against the tiles, music to my ears, and together we healed any rift between us, hoping to heal any worries she may still carry.

Our bodies moved in sync, our breathing combined, my balls ached, my heart twisted and I buried my head in her shoulder until she shuddered beneath me. I followed along; mended, bonded, whole.

132

———

Heaven

I woke up dreaming of swimming in a dark, heated pool, skin hot and sticky. I pushed back the covers, seeking cool air. It hit my skin, resulting in a chill. My head pounded and I groaned, falling back against the pillow.

The mattress shifted next to me and I felt the heavy weight of Hayden's hand on my arm. He stirred again, this time looking over the pile of pillows in the bed. I was greeted with tousled hair and perfect lips. Oh, and very concerned gray eyes.

"You're burning up," he said, touching my cheeks, then forehead.

"My head hurts."

"I bet it does. You definitely have a fever."

"And my whole body aches."

"Let me get you some medicine." He stopped in the bathroom door. "You're finished with those other antibiotics?"

"Yeah, a few days ago."

He left the room and I dozed, noticing him again sitting next to the side of the bed, water glass in hand. "Take these."

"Okay."

651

I swallowed the pills and water. Two seconds later, I had a coughing fit.

He sighed and smoothed the blanket under my neck. "I knew you were too sick to run last night."

"But not too sick for those shower shenanigans?" I closed my eyes when I said it, trying to block out the light.

"Were you feeling like shit last night?"

"No. Not really—I think maybe my bronchitis is back."

"Rest."

There was no argument from me. I curled on my side, already half asleep when I heard the door close with a click.

A COUGHING FIT woke me up, fluid thick in my chest. Once I got it under control, it was the voices from the kitchen that lured me from my room. I felt woozy, stopping occasionally to place a hand on the wall and rest.

"You were with her last night—how was she then?" Jackson asked.

"I asked her before we left if she felt okay and she said yes. And she seemed fine during our run and uh, after." There was an unmistakable hint of guilt in his voice. "I guess maybe the rain and exertion didn't help if she was already coming down with something."

"She needs to take it easy. I'm not surprised she got sick. She's been running herself ragged for weeks now." I heard the tap of metal on metal and the waft of something rich and warm. Soup. Despite feeling like shit, my stomach growled.

"We talked about everything last night—having kids. What I wanted."

"What did you say?" Jackson asked.

"The truth—that she was more important to me than growing our family. You guys are more important to me. I don't want that to change unless we all do."

"That's how you really feel?" Jackson sounded skeptical. "You really don't want kids?"

"It's not about what I want, Jax. It's about this family and how we move forward. Sacrifices aren't easy but we've all made them before."

There was movement in the kitchen; cabinets closing, the sink running. I took a deep breath and stepped through the doorway. Hayden saw me first, a deep line forming on his forehead.

"Hey," he said, crossing the kitchen. "You're up."

"I am." I leaned against the wall. "But still not feeling great."

Jackson looked me up and down. "I made you some soup. Want it in your room?"

The idea of soup made me equally starving and repulsed. I'd try to force some down. "Yes, please."

Then I had a massive coughing fit that brought Hayden to my side and he wrapped an arm around me. "Babe, you look like you need to get back in bed."

I nodded.

He touched my forehead. "You're hot."

"Thank you."

His eyebrow raised. "Like, you have a fever again."

I leaned against him. "Is that why everything hurts?"

"Probably."

His next move was swift, bending and picking me up bridal style. My head spun. "Woah. Give me some notice."

"Sorry." He kissed my cheek. "But you look like you're out of it and the last thing we need is for you to fall and crack your head."

I touched the back of his neck. "You would know."

He chuckled. "Damn straight. It's not fun."

Hayden carried me back to the bedroom and set me on the bed, pulling the covers up. Jackson followed with a tray of soup and a few crackers. Pain meds sat next to a bottle of something green.

"What's that?" I asked, picking up the pills.

"Gatorade." I made a face. "It'll help with your electrolytes."

I tossed the meds back and swallowed a mouthful. Yuck.

Anderson appeared in the door, his eyes searching and landing on me. "Everything okay here?"

"Yep," Jackson said. "She's just had her some medicine to reduce her fever and I made her some soup."

Hayden gave me a stern look. "She needs to stay in bed."

"Got it," Anderson said, walking into the room and over to a chair that was closer to the wall. He dragged it closer to the bed.

"What's going on?" I asked, looking between them.

Anderson spoke up. "These two are headed into work. I'm going to stay with you."

"I just have a cold and a little bit of a fever. I can be on my own."

"You could be on your own, but why should you when I'm here?" he asked.

"We'll be back later today. Message me if you need anything from the store," Jackson said, kissing the backside of my hand.

"You can take the other pills in about four hours. It'll help keep the fever down," Hayden said, bending over and pressing his lips to my forehead. It was a testimony of how sick I really was that I didn't drag both of them into the bed with me.

They left the room and I snuggled under the covers.

"You want this soup?"

"Maybe just the crackers."

He passed them over then brushed my hair off my face and stared at me with those deep, green eyes.

"What?" I asked, nibbling on the tasteless crackers. Oddly, they settled my stomach.

"Just thinking about how amazing it is that even though you're super sick, you're still the most beautiful woman I've ever seen."

"If you're trying to make me feel better—it's working."

"Good." He smiled, bringing light in the room like sunshine. "Anything else I can do for you?"

"Could you come lie next to me? I don't want to get you sick, but..."

He didn't wait for the rest, he was already circling the bed and lying on top of the covers. He scooted next to me and lifted his arm, giving me room to lay against his chest. God, he felt good. Warm and safe. Drowsiness overtook me and as I drifted to sleep I had the realization that although I knew my boys were great at taking care of me in moments of crisis, this was something different.

133

———

She slept for hours, sometimes fitfully, twisting up the linens. She had a few coughing spasms, never fully waking. I checked her temperature, smoothed the blankets and kept an eye on her all afternoon. I didn't like her sick—helpless. I wanted to do more to make her feel better.

The soup sat cold next to the bed, uneaten other than the few crackers I saw her consume. I kept a glass of ice next to the bed for when she woke. She needed fluids if she wanted them or not.

The doorbell rang and Sadie barked, racing out of the room. I paid for the delivery and came back in the room. She was awake, rubbing her eyes.

"Did the door wake you?" I asked. "Sorry."

"I feel like I've been asleep for days." She glanced out the window. It was still daylight.

"Just a few hours. Do you feel any better?"

"Maybe." She coughed again.

I held up the package delivered a few minutes before. "I got you some new meds."

655

"What? How?"

"Called in a favor from the team doctor. I looked to see what kind of antibiotics you were on before. He thinks maybe you need another round." I fished out a fat, white pill and placed it on her hand, then offered her the glass of water.

"Thank you."

I touched her cheek. It felt a little cooler. "You're welcome."

Sadie, hearing her mom's voice, jumped on the bed and snuggled in by her side. "She's been looking for you."

"Probably missing out on our daily run."

"About that..."

"Anderson, I'm not going to stop running with the dog."

"I think maybe you need to rest a little more. Until you're sure you're healthy."

She pouted. "Fine. I realize maybe I pushed it too hard too fast, but running makes me feel better."

I watched her for a minute, wanting to say something else, another concern I'd had on my mind. She noticed my quiet and said, "What? I can tell you have something to say."

"How do you know that?"

"Because you get this little line right here," she gestured between her eyes, "and it's like a red flag letting me know you have opinions."

"It's not so much an opinion as a worry."

She rubbed Sadie's ears. "Spit it out."

"I don't want you to think I'm undermining your thoughts or decisions, but this behavior has been going on ever since you found out about Amber having a baby." I leaned closer and took her hand. "None of us are going anywhere and I think you know that. I think you're the one still struggling with this decision and I think it's making you restless and extreme and ultimately sick."

She stared down at our intertwined hands.

"I've made this decision not because I want to, Anderson, but because I have to. I can't saddle a child with my baggage."

I exhaled, a million responses running through my head, but none of them were appropriate for the moment. She needed rest and healing.

"Fine. If you're comfortable with that decision, then so am I."

She looked up and eyed me skeptically. "What about wanting to have kids? With me?"

I shrugged. "Maybe that would have worked in another life—one where it was just the two of us, where there was no mental health issues, where everything was perfect. We'll never know, but what I do know is I'm not going anywhere."

"That's what Hayden said too."

"Then that's two of us."

"And the others?" Her eyes droop. She was tired and needed to stop talking about heavy topics, and rest.

"You think Jackson Hall is going anywhere? Or Oliver?" I shook my head. "Stop worrying about it and take care of yourself."

Her hand tightened in mine. "I want to. I do. I just can't..."

"Stop?" I stood and kissed her forehead. "I know. That brain of yours doesn't like to let things go. But you've got to. Once you're healthy, we can dig into this again."

She sighed but didn't argue, sleepiness rolling back over her like a comfortable wave. She was exhausted. God knew how much time she'd spent stressing about all of this. The late nights, the long runs, the excessive hours at work.

"I love you, Anderson Thompson," she said, turning her face to the pillow.

"I love you too, Heaven Reeves. Always and forever."

Those words were enough for me and I settled back in my chair to keep watch over her as she slept, hoping they were enough for her, too.

134

———

Jackson

After work we swapped places, with Anderson heading out for a late workout. I settled in the bed next to her, checking emails on my phone.

It wasn't long before she shifted in the bed restlessly, flinging an arm over my hip. I didn't move, not wanting to wake her, but she blinked. "Jackson?"

"Hey." I touched her cheek. God she was burning up. "How are you?"

"I don't feel good."

"No, I bet you don't."

"Anderson gave me medicine." Her words were a little slurred.

"He did, and it should totally kick in the next day or so." I started to move. "Let me go get you a cool cloth."

She flung her arms around my waist. "No. Stay."

"I'm coming back—right back."

I wiggled out of her arms and soaked a rag in cold water before coming back. I laid it gently over her forehead and got back into the bed next to her.

"You came back."

"I told you I would."

Her eyes closed and I held back a laugh. She was totally out of it.

"When have I lied to you?"

"Never," she whispered. Her hand moved to my chin, playing with my stubble. "Tell the truth; do you really want me if I can't give you a baby?"

I frowned. Anderson told me this came up earlier that day—that he sensed a possible wavering in her conviction. "I always want you, Heaven."

The truth was that I didn't know how I felt about the kid thing. It'd never crossed my mind. I'd been focused on work and building the business, living happily with my girl and best friends. Kids—they seemed like something far in the future. Something other people did. But that didn't mean I didn't want kids. I just wasn't there yet, and I certainly wasn't in the position to make a life-changing decision about it.

"Do you think I'm being dumb?"

I thought about it as she watched, through glazed eyes. I had no idea if she'd remember this in the morning and I decided to do as I'd said. Tell her the truth.

"I don't think you're being dumb. I think you're being rational—safe. But if you want to know what I really think, then I'll tell you." I inhaled and exhaled. "I think you'd make a fantastic mother. I think that all the struggles you've been through will make it so you know how to handle the worst kind of shit. You're strong and brave. I don't think you should let your fears—or the past—hold you back."

"You think I'd make a good mother?"

I nodded. "If you wanted, yes."

She ran a lazy hand down my chest. "You're sweet. And cute."

"And you're delirious." I kissed her knuckles. "Go back to sleep, okay?"

"Okay."

Her eyes fluttered closed—for good this time—and I stayed close in case she woke up again.

135

———

Heaven

Finally, I felt better.

When I got out of bed and my stomach rumbled, a real, hungry rumble, it propelled me to the kitchen for the first time in days. I saw familiar broad shoulders that tapered down to the curve of a muscular ass, just inside the refrigerator door. Oliver's head bobbed up and down.

"Are you fucking kidding me? I get sick and you turn into a barbarian?"

He jumped a mile, dropping the fork covered in cold spaghetti sauce on the floor. "Holy shit." He waited for his heart to catch up. "You're up."

"Yep. And you're eating straight out of the refrigerator."

He grabbed a napkin off the counter and wiped his mouth. "I was hungry."

"And too lazy to work the microwave?"

He grinned sheepishly, placing the bowl of leftover spaghetti on the counter and walking over. He pressed a warm hand against my forehead, then neck. "No fever."

"Nope. I think it's gone."

"Cough?"

"Just a little."

He looked relieved. "I was worried about you."

"I'm okay now."

"Do you want to talk about why you were working yourself so hard."

"No."

"Sure?"

I grabbed a bottle of Gatorade out of the fridge. There were three. Along with a huge container of soup, more crackers, pain meds, and anything else I needed. The doctor's number was taped to the fridge. These boys...the Allendale Four, never count them out when something needs to be done or someone needs taking care of. I owed Oliver more than what I was giving him.

"I don't know what happened to me. I just...I was freaking out about Amber and the baby. Me having a baby. What you guys wanted. What I wanted. It didn't help that I was hormonal and weird at the same time and like, really horny." He smiled at that. "So, I just made myself busy, working and running and well, spending time with you guys, because it seemed like it was making me feel better when it was really just making me into a mess."

"You're not a mess, Heaven. Your immune system just was low from the bronchitis and you relapsed."

"I feel like a mess. Like I'm all twisted up and confused about everything."

He walked over and gathered me in his arms. "It's okay to not be sure about things. We're young and we have time and it may just mean that we need to take our time on a few decisions."

"You mean like having kids."

He kissed my forehead. "Exactly like that."

"But what if...what if you stay with me and you want kids and I don't change my mind?"

"Then we'll deal with it."

"What about the others? They've already said they're okay with it."

"Then trust them. Accept their word. And stop stressing out about it so much. You're making yourself crazy for no reason, do you know that?"

I laid my cheek on his chest and felt the warm weight of his hands on my back. "It wouldn't be the first time."

"That's the truth." He squeezed me tight. "We love you, Heaven. Just exist in the now and stop stressing out about the future. Who knows what it will hold."

Oliver always had a way of calming me down, making me see things differently. He'd talked me off the ledge a million times and I should have just gone to him first. I didn't know why I tortured myself like this.

"Change is going to happen, you know that, right? One day I'm going to get gray hair and you're going to get wrinkles—"

"Hey!"

"And Anderson's going to have a potbelly."

I laughed. I tried to imagine it and the weird thing was that I could—not imagine him fat—god no—but a little older—like his dad. He'd definitely be handsome. They all would.

"Life isn't stagnant, Heaven, but I think one thing that's true is we're each other's constant. Good, bad, ugly, old. We'll figure it out, when life brings it our way." He pushed a hand under my hair, cupping my neck. "You're jumping the gun on this. Worrying about something that isn't even an issue."

I gazed up at him. "How did you get to be so wise?"

"Someone around here has to keep a level head."

I loved this man so much. Loved them all, and they'd shown me that all week by taking care of me. I felt a slight stirring below my belly, one that had been suppressed by my illness. It was too soon to act on it—I'd probably fall asleep—but soon we'd all be back to normal and he was right. I needed to let this go and move on. They'd made their intentions clear—they wanted me more than anything else.

136

Heaven

With my sickness finally gone and my fears put to rest, we settled back into a normal daily life. I was still on hiatus, but the opening of the new gym was fast approaching. A party was scheduled for the night before it opened to customers—mostly current members and ultra-high list celebrities that used A5 when they were in town.

I offered my assistance but Oliver and Jackson hired most of the party planning out to professionals. They wanted me to rest, but I was tired of being in the house. So, I called up Amber and asked if she wanted to go shopping with me. I needed something to wear to the party.

We hit our favorite shops, many still around from when we were in high school. This time, things were different. Amber's pregnant, her tiny belly just beginning to show. I wasn't there to buy the perfect dress of revenge. As our lives changed, they seemed to get less complicated. Thank goodness for that.

"What about this?" Amber asked, holding up a red, body-hugging gown.

"A little too formal," I said. "It is a gym, after all."

663

"A gym with celebrities."

"Some that I work with. I'm not quite that star-struck anymore."

"Well I am." She held up a black dress with gold edging. "You think the black will make me look skinnier?"

"You *are* skinny—you mean not pregnant? With all the effort that went into getting you knocked up, why would you hide it?"

"True. Ginger thinks my belly is sexy. She can't keep her hands off of it."

I flipped through the dresses and pulled out one that was tight-fitting. "Then try this one. You can walk around all night belly-cupping that tiny bump of yours."

She took it from me and hung it over her arm. "Ohhh, check out this one. It has Heaven written all over it."

I took the dress from her. It was a pale pink with a plunging V down the front—tiny jewels and sequins lined the bodice and it was fitted to the hem just above the knees. "I'm not sure I have the boobs to pull this off."

Amber cupped her own boobs obscured under her hoodie. "You know that's one of the odd perks of pregnancy—bigger boobs. Just go try it. I think you can pull it off."

We both headed into different dressing rooms and reemerge a few moments later. Amber was right, the dress did look good and my boobs held up the top better than I expected.

When I looked at her, I felt my eyes widen.

"What?" she asked, checking out her backside in the mirror.

"Holy shit, your tits are massive."

"I told you!" Again, she held them. I mean, I knew she said they were bigger, but under the hoodie I couldn't tell. They were big. Really big.

"I have a feeling it's not your tiny belly Ginger is into, just saying."

"It's the weirdest feeling. And I don't even want to know what happens later—when I'm nursing."

"Nope. Me either."

She looked me over. "Well you look smokin' in that dress. The guys will love it."

"Ginger will love that one, too. And well, probably everyone else that's into boobs, because holy shit." I couldn't help myself. They were perfect, round, and frankly a little magical.

"I'll take what I can get."

We spend the rest of the afternoon shopping and getting our nails done—girly things that help me feel a little more normal. In my panic over her pregnancy and my own decisions, I'd forgotten how much fun Amber and I had together. I determined that more than anything else, I was glad my friend was home.

"MOVIE OR TV SHOW?" Anderson asked, holding the remote to the television. I'd just turned off the light and settled back on the couch.

"Everyone at work is talking about this super cute movie that's kind of like Sixteen Candles but modernized."

He raised his eyebrows in question.

"Don't tell me you haven't seen Sixteen Candles."

"When did it come out?"

"I don't know, like 1984. My mom made me watch it with her. It's a classic."

"Yeah, no chance I've seen that."

"Well, then that's what we should watch for sure—*after* we watch the new one." I was in the mood for some sweet, uncomplicated, teen romance. I grabbed the remote from him and flipped through the options, while Anderson settled next to me on the couch. Tomorrow night we had the party and the other guys were at the gym going over final details. Anderson and I had decided on an evening of Netflix and chill, now that I was finally feeling human again.

We sat close on the couch, snuggled beneath a blanket, with a bowl of popcorn in my lap. The movie was adorable—the boy and girl both ridiculously cute. After their first kiss, a jumbled-up moment of desperation, I turned to Anderson and said, "That's almost like when I kissed you in the library that day."

"That was a good kiss. Too bad I acted like a dick afterwards."

"I wasn't playing fair. You didn't know the truth—just like that boy in the story didn't know everything going on with the girl." I gestured to the screen—frozen on pause. "Once I did, we were able to work past it."

"Are you seriously trying to equate our life to a teen movie?" There was an amused smile on his face.

"Our whole relationship has been like a crazy movie, don't you think?"

He slipped an arm around my shoulder. "Only if that movie went from PG to R to XXX."

"We are not triple X."

He snorted. "Who said our story is over?"

He reached for me, pulling me close enough to kiss. His lips tasted buttery, like popcorn. He'd just pushed a hand into my hair when there was a cough from the doorway and a small knock. We both looked up. Jackson waited with an apologetic expression and a tray of food in his hands.

Anderson pulled away and adjusted his jeans.

"Sorry to interrupt, but the caterer left some samples and I thought you may want some." He crossed the room and laid the food on the ottoman. It was quite the spread. Fruit and cheese. Strawberries with chocolate and a mound of whipped cream. "I'll leave you two alone."

I glanced at Anderson, who gave me a quick nod. "Jackson—stay. Watch the rest of the movie with us and share in the food."

He hesitated. "Are you sure?"

"Yep," Anderson said, shifting over and pulling me along with him. Jackson kicked off his shoes and sat next to me, dragging the blanket over his lap. I was snug between the two of them.

"So, what are we watching?" he asked.

I dipped a spoon in the cream.

"Heaven's enlightening me on the glory of teen movies and how our relationship, particularly in high school, was like one."

I took a lick of the cream and said, "Totally. Jackson was the handsome, popular jock that should have been a jerk but was really sweet."

He smiled at me, eyes darting down to my mouth, watching me clean off the spoon.

"Hey, what about me? I was a loveable jock," Anderson said. Jackson and I burst into laughter and Anderson grew defensive. "I was!"

"You were a sarcastic and stubborn jock. You made me crazy."

"He made us all crazy," Jackson added, plucking another strawberry off the plate and scooping up a dollop of cream on the tip. "But to be fair, babe, you made us the most crazy."

"Try this." He held the plump, bright-red strawberry up to my mouth. I took a bite, cream covering my lips. I was about to lick it off when Jax leaned over and did it for me. Anderson's hand that was on my leg under the blanket, tensed. "Delicious, right?"

"Very much so. Sweet." I leaned into Anderson's side, eyeing Jax. "What do you mean, I made you crazy?"

"Back then? God, it was those short skirts."

"Damn, those skirts," Anderson muttered.

"And tight blouses."

"That white one. The one she tied at the waist."

Jackson looked over my head. "Do you remember those boots?"

"The thigh highs?" He laughed and I felt it against my back as it rumbled in his chest. "I had dreams about those boots."

"Stop. You know I did all that to get a rise out of everyone."

"Oh, you got a rise out of everyone all right. Why do you think we got so protective?" Jackson replied, going for another strawberry and more cream. "I used to go home and think about what you wore, how sexy you were."

"I'd sit in my desk in class and try to will my boner away," Anderson admitted. I turned to face him. His cheeks were red but he shrugged. "I had to work twice as hard in the classes you had with me because I could barely pay attention with you sitting there. You smelled so good." He sniffed my hair. "And looked ridiculously hot. Sometimes you'd bend over, giving me a peek of your cleavage, and I'd have to recite the alphabet backwards to calm myself down."

"You did not."

"Oh, hell yeah I did."

Jackson nodded, popping the strawberry in his mouth. A tiny bit of cream remained on his lip and I had the unmistakable urge to lick it off like he'd done with me. His blue eyes watched me closely as I leaned over and gently sucked off the cream. His hands moved to my hips and he pulled me in for more. I sank into his kiss, fueled by their stories of high school boners and unwavering affection. Anderson ran a hand up and down my calf, creeping up my thigh. The twist of arousal churned in my belly.

I turned back to the tray and dipped my fingers in the cream. I brought them to my lips, smearing the sweetness across. Both boys leaned over and cleaned me up. It was, as Jax said, delicious and really, really hot. We normally spent our intimate times alone, but occasionally the stars aligned for something more spontaneous. Something more freeing.

The movie forgotten, each one of us thoroughly sunk into the moment. I felt their hands, their breath, tasted the sweetness between our lips. I felt the heat of Anderson on one side and Jackson on the other. My rocks. My loves.

Unlike the girl on screen, I didn't have to pick between the boys I loved. I chose them all, and they chose me, and as we bared our bodies and our souls to one another once again, that bond only solidified.

137

HEAVEN

IT WAS ALWAYS weird returning to my mother's house. I always felt caught in a limbo between the white clapboard structure being my home and now being a guest. I had a lot of firsts in this place. Good and bad. The good was really good; my first few dates with the guys. Dry-humping with Jackson on the front steps. Making love to Oliver on my single bed upstairs. The bad was the opposite side of the pendulum. My depression and anxiety. The cutting in the bathroom. The realization that I was being watched over my laptop. Reuniting with my father after his years away.

Then there was my mother.

We'd had our ups and downs over the years. In many ways she was supportive—sending me to therapists and doctors. Helping with my meds. But she also had an unhealthy relationship with my father that lasted for far too long. When she'd stuck by his side, through all his conniving and maliciousness, I had to let her go. Eventually she saw the truth behind his lies and slowly we've been rebuilding our relationship.

When it came to me and the Allendale Four, she was hesitantly supportive. She knew the guys cared for me but she also didn't think our alternative lifestyle was sustainable. There were times when I let her nagging thoughts get to me, but not recently, because things had been so good.

"So the grand opening of the new gym is tonight?" she asked, pouring milk into her tea. "Sorry I can't come—we're short-handed at work."

"I think it will be a lot of fun. It's super-VIP with a bunch of celebrities. Fingers crossed that the citizens of Oceanside manages to keep their bigotry on hold for a night."

My mother snorted, knowing fully well how awful they were. I continued, "I think the new city council person has shut down a lot of the hatred now that tourism is up. There's just no room in the economy for that kind of closed-mindedness."

"Who knew Oceanside would change their ways?" My mother was clearly thinking about how we'd had to pack up and move after my father left. "But I'm glad the boys are capitalizing on it."

"I was a little nervous at first but there were no problems." I pressed my fingers against my too-hot tea. "I guess people can change."

"So, speaking of change," I said, "this isn't wide spread yet but Amber said it was okay to tell you—she and Ginger are having a baby."

Mom's eyes opened wide. "A baby! Wait—who's carrying it?"

"Amber. It's really early, though. Like it's barely even a thing."

"A thing?" She shook her head and took a sip of her tea. "It's a baby, Heaven. Trust me, it's a thing right from the start. A big thing. Wow. Lesbians having babies. The modern world is interesting."

"Lesbians have been having babies for a long time, Mom." I rolled my eyes. "It's not a big deal."

"Sure it is. First of all, it's very intentional. It's not like one of them can claim it was an accident or a surprise. They had to put effort into that baby." She smiled. "That means they really want it. Good for them."

I was a little surprised by my mom's attitude. I kind of thought she'd be a little more judgey. I mean, that may have been why I came over here.

"So you're okay with it? You don't think they're too young or it's too soon since they got married?"

"It's a personal decision. No one can make it but them." She frowned. "Why? Do you?"

"I don't know. I mean, I'm happy for them, but I guess it's just a big change."

She smiled at me sympathetically. "It is, and I know it feels like you may be losing a friend, but you won't. She's going to need you and I suspect this baby will end up being good for you, too."

"Why would you say that?"

She dipped her teabag in and out of the water. "Well obviously you're not having kids any time soon—if ever—this way you can be an amazing aunt or godmother."

My mother had just said exactly what I felt. Exactly. Yet when I heard the words coming from her mouth, I felt a sharp twist of anger and offense in my chest. "What do you mean 'obviously'?"

"Heaven," she said, giving me an amused look, "you're not serious."

"Of course, I'm serious. What do you mean?"

She blinked at me, obviously trying to gauge my reaction. "I can get behind the mechanics and science of two women having a child together. Two married women in a stable, committed relationship. But, sweetheart, no matter how much you love those boys and no matter how devoted they are to you, that is not the kind of relationship you're in."

It was one thing to know something in your heart. It was another to hear them said out loud, especially from your mother. "You don't think we could build a family."

"For you and your dog, sure. With a child? That's insanity."

I felt the bile of anger rising in my throat. "Why? Exactly why would it be so crazy to have a child in a family with four loving fathers? Because I had a traditional one-dad kind of family and look how that turned out."

She turned, her face serious. "I don't know, Heaven, tell me how it would work? Would you pick one of the boys for a father? Which one? Do you want the swimmer or the soccer player? The businessman or the charmer? Do you think they won't care? That they'll willingly give up their right to have a biological child with you for one of the others? *That* is not how men work."

"Stop," I said.

"Or do you just throw caution and birth control to the wind and allow whichever one has the fastest, strongest swimmers take the role of bio dad? Is that how it works?"

"Mom. Stop." My hands clenched with rage. Fear.

She sighed and her expression softened. "I'm not trying to be a jerk. I'm trying to be honest. There is no way this is going to work for you. Even if you all think it will, it won't. There will be jealousy and territorialism. There will be confusion and hurt feelings. You're right, look at all the problems I had with one man in my life while raising you." She threw up her hands. "Do not go down this path. I'm begging you."

All the fears and mixed emotions welled up at once, knocking me off my feet. I fell back in my seat and cried, the stress and strain pouring out of me.

"Oh, honey," my mother said, walking over to put her arm around me. I let her. I knew she meant well and I knew her words held truth. I knew it in my heart. and that was one of the reasons I'd told them I didn't want kids yet, they'd made it clear they were okay with whatever decision I made. Maybe that was really why. Maybe they knew it was a bad idea, too.

Maybe we were all just sacrificing for one another, like we'd always had.

"I know this is hard for you," she said, with a look of empathy only a mother could give. "But it's better for you all to work it out now."

I wiped my tears away and reached for the warm mug of tea, hands still shaking. I didn't tell her that we'd already talked about it and that decisions had been made and that I was the one that initiated it. There was something in the moment that pushed me back to my younger self—how dare someone tell me *I* couldn't have a child if

I wanted. It was like those who said my relationship with the guys was wrong—twisted—perverted.

They didn't understand me and my family.

They didn't understand how we worked.

They didn't understand our love.

And for the first time, I realized that maybe I'd been wrong to let the fear dictate my decisions. At this point, though, it may be too late.

138

"You about ready?" Hayden called from the hallway. I was in the bathroom getting ready for the party.

"Yeah, five minutes." I was already running late because of last-minute panic over the fact that my dress felt too snug against my body—particularly my hips. I had to get Jackson to zip me up (which provided its own challenges.)

"I look like a cow," I'd said, overdramatically.

"You look gorgeous." His eyes were glued to my breasts, which were the only thing that looked better with a little bloat.

It was so fucking typical to get my period around a party like this. Not that I had it yet. I'd been waiting for days, dealing with the bull-shit symptoms of PMS. My boobs ached, my stomach was bloated and I'd had that irrational meltdown at my mom's earlier.

I dug around in my makeup drawer for mascara. Unlike my orga-nized work station, my stuff at home was a mess. My hands skimmed over a circular container and I blinked, looking across the counter at a similar one. I opened the birth control pack—it was my last one—

the one I'd been taking when I got sick, and to my surprise and sudden horror, there were four left.

"Fuck."

I'd been taking the placebo for a week now, waiting for my period to start. Things had gotten hazy while I was sick. I was on so many meds—the antibiotics and the fever reducers. I'd take all the pills in the morning but at least once I got confused and took my antibiotics twice in one day. Then forgot entirely on another.

Maybe my period was just confused—that happened, right?

No. It hadn't. Because I had one of those bodies that worked like clockwork—especially since I got on the pill. Every twenty-eight days. Five days of bleeding. The boys knew to clear out and leave me alone, with a box of chocolate and a heating pad.

I picked up my phone and checked the calendar. Thirty-three days.

Then I remembered how I'd changed pills this month—the new prescription--and that was probably it. It was stronger, and the doctor had said it may take a minute for my body to adjust. I assumed that meant different symptoms and maybe a different length period. I mean, that was why I changed, right? To help with my flow.

With shaking hands, I swiped on some mascara and ran a hand over my hair. I was being ridiculous. I'd been sick on those days—not having sex with the boys at all. And we'd only had sex a few times since.

I was definitely being overdramatic, and grabbed a stash of tampons because it'd be just my luck to start my period in the middle of the party in this tight, pale pink dress.

Hayden called my name—a bit more impatiently. "Heaven...I'm sure you look amazing, stop fussing."

"I'm coming," I said, taking one last glance in the mirror. I needed to get my shit together. I'd taken up so much head-space with these boys over the last month. This night was about them and their success. I rearranged my face and turned off the light and walked out of the room where Hayden waited for me. He leaned against the wall, hands in the pockets of his dark gray slacks. Between the heather gray of his shirt and the darker one of his jacket, his eyes looked like hammered steel. His dark hair flopped in his eyes and God, he looked...damn.

"I knew you'd look breathtaking." He smiled, eyes lingering over my body. All my insecurities vanished just having him look at me like that. How could they not?

139

———

WALKING into the party with Heaven, beautiful and sexy in her slinky pink dress, was enough to make me feel like a king. The party was fancy—catering to a high-end crowd that paid high rates for a level of training they couldn't find elsewhere. I was part owner—more silent than anything else—a face along with Anderson's to provide professional legitimacy, but in truth, A5 was all Oliver and Jackson. They'd done an amazing job and were on their way to building an empire.

"I'm going to go say hello to the boys," Heaven said, squeezing my hand and walking off.

I plucked a glass of champagne off a waiter's tray and watched her greet my best friends, hugging them in congratulations. At public events like this we kept our closeness on the down-low, a decision we'd all come to years before. Only we knew the truth behind the body language, the glint in one another's eyes. There was something intoxicating about events like this one where few knew the truth about our relationship. It was like the word's dirtiest secret and to be honest, it made me a little hard.

"Here," Amber said, walking up with Ginger. She held a full glass

677

of champagne in my face. "The waiter gave this to me. Drink it for me."

"My pleasure."

Amber had on a tight dress, one that clearly showed her pregnancy. Ginger beamed next to her, occasionally pointing out a celebrity or two. "How are things going—health-wise?"

"Good," Amber smiled. "Just the normal stuff. I'm tired all the time. None of my clothes fit. I only want red meat."

"Don't forget moody and irritable," Ginger added.

I looked between them. "Those are all normal?"

"Completely." Amber sighed and rested a hand on her belly. "Even the moodiness. There's a whole boat-load of hormone changes going on."

"Well you look fantastic. I think it suits you."

"Thank you." Her eyes followed a movement across the room. "I think those are the crab cakes. Will you get me a few," she asked Ginger. Her wife sighed, kissed her on the cheek, and walked off.

"How are you holding up," she asked me.

I tilted my head. "In what way?"

"I know you guys and Heaven have been dealing with some big issues."

"Right." I fought a grimace. Amber had always been up in our business, but Heaven needed someone to confide in—a female—and I didn't begrudge that. "I think we've worked through it."

"And you're okay with her decision of no kids."

It took me a moment to swallow the truth. "Yes—her fears are well-founded. There are a lot of obstacles that we'd have to navigate."

"I hate that our decision fell like a landmine in your house. You know how Heaven gets sometimes."

"She fixates, but we talked it over. She got sick too, which pushed it aside. Now that she's better she seems to have moved on."

"Good." She looked visibly relieved. Ginger reappeared with a plate piled with snacks. "Oh thank god, I thought I was going to die."

Ginger rolled her eyes and we shared a smile. Then she slipped an arm around Amber's waist, settling it on the baby growing inside.

A sweet moment between two expecting parents, and I felt a slight twinge in my chest.

"Hey guys," Heaven said, sidling up to us. "What's going on?"

"Just stuffing my cake-hole," Amber said, popping in another crab cake. "You want one?"

Heaven shook her head. "No way. I could barely get this dress zipped tonight. And ugh, the thought of seafood is not appealing. I swear I totally lost my appetite while I was sick and it hasn't come back yet."

I finished my drink and noticed Anderson coming our way. "They want to take some pictures with all of us," he said, once he reached us.

"Sounds good," I said, knowing publicity was part of my obligation.

Anderson looked at Heaven and she said, "What?"

"A5, babe. That means you, too."

"Oh, right, I can do that." She turned to Amber. "Do I have anything in my teeth?"

"Oh my god, you look fine. Go."

We walked off to meet the others, each watching Heaven closely. Following the photographer's directions, we huddled close, a circle of protection and love around our girl. I couldn't help but wonder if people could tell about us when we were all together like this. If they knew.

As the camera flashed and we smiled, celebrating success, I knew damn well that not one of us really cared.

140

HEAVEN

THREE DAYS LATER, I arrived home from shopping to the sound of shrieking children and splashing in the pool. Sadie raced around the pool's edge, trying to get to Anderson, who was holding a small child in his hands. Across the pool, Jackson urged a bigger child to jump to him.

It was like I'd entered the twilight zone.

I opened the gate and walked through. "Make sure you close it," Anderson said. "Davis is quite the runner."

I snapped the latch in place. "So, what's going on?"

Oliver walked out of the house with a tray of snacks. Crackers, cut-up fruit, cheese. "Monique stopped by and asked if we could watch the kids—she had an appointment and no babysitter."

"And you all just said yes—to watching a stranger's children?" Jackson's charm apparently worked on three-year-olds as well, because Davis jumped happily into his arms.

"She was in a bind," Hayden said. I turned and found him lounging on a chair in the shade. "We couldn't say no."

"Huh." I watched Ashley, in a bathing suit with built-in floaties, smile as Anderson cruised her around like a boat. It prompted me to ask, "How did you even know how to do that?"

"What?"

"Make her happy?"

He shrugged those broad shoulders and continued entertaining the little girl. "I taught swim lessons in high school. You know that."

"I guess."

That didn't explain whatever bromance Jackson and Davis had started up by the stairs or the little smile on Hayden's mouth as he laughed at Ashley's giggles.

"I guess you guys have it under control. I'll head inside for a bit." I'd been craving a nap the whole time I was running errands.

"Why?" Oliver asked. "You don't want to stay out here with us?"

"I'll come back out. I just need to put this stuff away and do a few things."

"Need any help?" Hayden asked.

"No, thank you." I smiled and slipped into the house just as Davis jumped in again, trying to splash Jackson.

I wasn't trying to be weird. I was trying to keep my emotions in check. I didn't care that Monique asked for a favor—god knew how she did it alone all the time. I should have offered before. But today something heavier lingered on my mind and I tightened my grip on the plastic bag in my hand and made a beeline for my bathroom.

I pulled the box out of the bag and laid it on the counter, trying to calm my nerves. It was just a test—a test that could change my life, rock my world.

Thirty minutes later I'd taken it out of the box and the stick sat on the counter while I sat on the closed toilet lid, studying the directions over and over.

This was dumb.

I wasn't pregnant.

I was just late.

I didn't even want kids.

But...

What if?

What if?

"Heaven?" Anderson called, startling me from my ruminations.

I steadied my voice. "Yes?"

"The kids just left. I was checking to see if you're okay."

I glanced away from the test—terrified. "I'm fine. I'll be out in a minute."

I needed a minute. I needed air, then I'd take the test. I just needed a few minutes to get ready. Maybe later when all the guys weren't home.

I flung open the bathroom door and yelped when I saw not just Anderson in the room but all four boys. "What are you doing here?" My heart raced in my chest.

"You seemed out of sorts—you've seemed that way for days," Oliver said. Jackson, changed into dry shorts, nodded. "Are you really okay?"

I glanced behind me, fully aware that the test was just out of sight but on the counter. "I was, uh…" Anderson looked at me with that line of worry on his face. Hayden's jaw clenched. I couldn't string them along like this. It wasn't fair. "I'm late."

No one spoke until Jackson replied, "For what?"

Oliver elbowed him. Hard.

"My period is late, which is unusual, but I was sick and on all those meds and then I changed birth control and it's possible that things got mixed up."

No one said anything. Not a word. I didn't blame them. What would they say? We agreed. We'd finally, totally agreed, and here I was, complicating things in the most complicated way.

"But you're not sure," Anderson finally said, hand running through his hair.

"No. I, um, I was going to take a test. I have one. It's in the bathroom."

Again no one spoke, like they were waiting for me to decide, and all the emotions of the past few weeks brought hot tears to my eyes. "I'm scared."

Jackson frowned. "Of what?"

"Losing you. Losing this. Us. All of it."

He got to me first but the others followed. It was one thing to be soothed by one person that loves you—but four? There was no comparison.

Anderson spoke first. "Heaven, we love you regardless of what happens when you take that test, and we'll deal with whatever the outcome."

"He's right," Hayden agreed.

Oliver nodded. "Absolutely."

"You're never getting rid of us, understand?" Jackson replied, kissing my cheek.

I nodded, believing them. I didn't really ever doubt it—I guess I doubted myself, but I'd been through worse—harder things, and it was time for me to step up and deal with reality.

Two minutes later we stood, huddled around the bathroom counter waiting for the test to confirm one way or the other.

Without looking, I grabbed it off the marble and I turned to face them. "No matter what happens, know that I love you so much." I exhaled. "Ready?"

Four handsome faces nodded in reply and I knew they meant it. We were ready. We'd always been, and that knowledge gave me the courage to face the truth.

I another deep breath, held up the test, and read the results.

EPILOGUE

Water dripped down my legs—not from the juice Miranda spilled all over the table. Or from the pool water Ruby just splashed all over the patio.

"Oliver?"

He looked up from the wrestling match with Christian in the shallow end of the pool. He'd let the six-year-old get him in a head-lock. "Yeah?"

"I think it's time." A sharp pain ran through my belly.

Jackson appeared in the doorway from the kitchen, concern on his face. "You think what?"

"It's time." I glanced down and grimaced. "My water broke."

"I'll call Dena," Jackson said, vanishing back the way he came. Dena was our mid-wife. Oliver was already out of the water, dripping wet and giving Christian a towel. He picked up his phone.

"Who are you calling?"

"Texting Amber, she said she'd watch the kids when the time came, remember."

I nodded. "And Hayden? Anderson?"

"They shouldn't be far—I told them not to go more than twenty miles until that baby comes. I'll contact them too, if Jackson hasn't already." Sadie came running through the room. "Shit, let me go put her in her crate."

"Okay," I said, feeling a flutter of familiar nerves. It never got old, the excitement and anticipation. This was my third pregnancy. Christian came first, followed by the twins Miranda and Ruby, and now this little one.

That first pregnancy scare was just that—a scare, but it also confirmed something for me. I did want kids. Just not then. It took a few years, but when we were ready we were all ready, and like my mother said that day about Amber: it was intentional.

We had to go over a lot of emotions—who would be the biological father—did we want to plan it, let it be spontaneous, would there be jealousies or hurt? In the end, their love for me and our love for one another prevailed, and we let nature take its course.

There was no doubt when Christian arrived whose gray eyes he inherited, and true to their word, my boys embraced him whole-heartedly as one of their own. Two years later I was pregnant again--Russian-roulette style with the other three (Hayden had to wear condoms for the first time in many years)—with twins. Girls who have never known such devotion from their daddies. As they aged and their features set, it was clear they weren't identical—dimples on Miranda, curly blonde locks on Ruby. It soon became obvious their fathers were not the same. Everyone was happy—completely and utterly exhausted.

Despite that happiness, there was one lingering desire. I wanted one last baby and for Anderson to be the father. He'd owned my soul for as long as I could remember. He wasn't petty or jealous. He was an amazing, outstanding father to our three kids. But it was something I wanted and something I knew he wanted, too. We tried hard. Often. For months. And it took a bit longer than it did with the others, but when I tested positive I saw the sheer joy and relief on his face.

He'd wanted this badly.

I placed a hand over my belly and watched as Dena rolled in with her supplies and set up the room. We'd opted from the beginning for home births—not wanting the questions or judgment from the hospital. Each had gone smoothly, thank goodness, and with baby

Thompson making an appearance within days of its due date, I felt confident this one would too.

"Is he here yet?" I asked Oliver after changing clothes.

"Yep. He's cleaning up. He'll be here soon."

Amber arrived in a flurry of her own two kids, Sadie barking at her arrival. I kissed them all and sent them on their way.

"You've got this girl," Amber said. "I'll call your mom."

"Call her in an hour. I don't need another person in here right now."

"You got it."

This was a moment for me and the guys, but I wanted a minute alone with Anderson first.

When he walked in the room, I was easing down on the bed that Dena prepped and sterilized. Handsome as ever, there were still traces of that thirteen-year-old boy I fell for in school. Now his stature was bigger, muscles lean and strong. His jaw sharper—all traces of youthful baby fat gone, even a bit of the sleek twenty-year old had vanished. I didn't care. I loved him at any age as much as I did at the beginning. A few gray hairs pulled at his temples but the mop on top was the same, wild and disheveled. His green eyes zeroed in on me and he came to the side of the bed.

A sharp pain hit just after and I grimaced.

"Do you need anything? Ice? Heating pad?"

"I'm better now that you're here." I gripped his hand. "I love you, you know that?"

He tilted his head. "Is there something I should worry about? Is that baby coming out with blue eyes or something?"

"No. I just know everything's about to get crazy and it will become a circus." A wonderful, amazing circus but a circus all the same. I touched his chin. "You've made me so happy, Anderson Thompson. I'm so grateful to have you in my life."

His hand landed on my belly. "You know I feel the same. Every day with you and this crazy, mixed-up family is a gift. Thank you for sharing your life, your body, and your love with us, Heaven."

He kissed me and another contraction rolled through me, causing me to break away and gasp. I tightened my grip on his hand.

"Time for Dena?"

I nodded. "Where are the others?"

"They're just outside."

The door swung open and there they were, waiting for me.

Soon the room was full, just like my heart, as the final piece of our family entered the world. As the baby squealed, wrapped tight in a cocoon of blankets, his shock of dark hair peeking out at the top, I leaned against the pillow, exhausted. Anderson's smile was a mile wide, the tiny baby tucked in his safe arms. Hayden peered over, kissing his tiny forehead. I'd learned the giant of a man was putty in the presence of a newborn.

"You did good, mama," Jackson said, kissing my cheek.

"The strongest of us all." Oliver picked up my hand. "We're lucky to have you."

But the luck went both ways, and we all knew it wasn't luck anyway. Nothing came easy in our lives, it never had, but we'd been blessed to find one another, and we'd fought for one another and cried for one another and lived for one another. In the end, we'd found our own little slice of heaven.

AFTERWORD

Thank you for reading final book in the Allendale Four series! If you'd like to follow my releases, news and receive updates please join my Facebook group, Monarchs. Come say hi. I do have cookies but they're gluten free.

www.ingramcontent.com/pod-product-compliance
Lightning Source LLC
Chambersburg PA
CBHW022007300726
48970CB00003B/780